The Trouble With Love

— A Kormèr Lezàl Story —

Maurice X. Alvarez
&
Ande Li

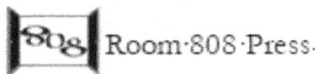
Room·808·Press·

Acknowledgements

As always, my first acknowledgement is to my wife, Ande Li. Without you, the sun doesn't shine, and the voices in my head wouldn't be as interesting to listen to.

AUTHOR'S NOTE

While Earth (Terran) English is the prevalent language of the Galactic Federation, the denizens of other planets often speak in their native tongues. For the sake of clarity, speech in Elmarian is represented in this text by the use of different quotation marks as in:

~~Jordinni C'grel dialect~~
<<Elmarian>>
||Averian||

1

PROLOGUE

ENSHROUDED in darkness by the moonless night sky, Castle Har'cairn stood boldly atop Cairn Hill. Deep within its stone walls, a door opened to a darkened room, and a short black-clad figure slipped out into the torch-lit corridor. Wide brown eyes peered out from an opaque mask, surveyed the corridor, left and right. Anxiety over the upcoming battle was thick in the air this evening, and the thief knew that many of the castle's inhabitants would not be able to sleep. Extra caution was necessary.

The lanky thief slinked swiftly along the curving stone corridor. It stepped silently past torches burning brightly in their wall sconces, past the few faded tapestries that graced the walls—

Voices!

The thief stopped, eyes scanning quickly for a place to hide. It ducked through a darkened archway and hugged the wall beside the archway's jamb, blending with the darkness. But the voices were coming closer! The conversants stepped through the archway... and passed, unaware of the shadow that watched them with wide, startled eyes. Once the corridor was clear, the thief let out a tense breath, then stepped back into the corridor and continued on its way.

The castle's corridors twisted and turned to thwart invaders, but the thief knew the passages well enough. The mask could not hide the eager smile that touched the thief's eyes as it spotted its objective. Just ahead, the corridor ended at a T-intersection, and there, on the far wall, were the two large wooden doors of the armory. The thief tiptoed closer—then skittered into the shadows. Just where the corridor turned, beside the double doors, stood a burly guard, quite alert, with an impressive broadsword at his side.

The thief fretted. How could it get past the armored guard without waking half the castle? Knocking him out was not the problem—sleeping powder was always at hand for such situations, and once in the eyes, mouth, or nasal lining, it worked quickly. But the guard's metal armor would clang deafeningly through the corridors. Eyes peered pensively through the slits in the thief's hood, calculating the bulky guard's weight plus the heft of the armor. Without a doubt, the combined load would be extraordinarily heavy, but the thief had no other options, and dawn was not long in coming. Soon the soldiers would be on their way, if they were not already, to gather their armor and weapons and head out on their three-day march to engage the enemy. The thief had to act now, regardless of the technicalities.

The thief dashed at the guard. The guard started, then hesitated, as if confused by what he saw. As the guard's hand finally flew to the hilt of his sword, the thief leaped and sprayed a cloud of powder into the startled guard's wide eyes.

~~Ey! What——~~ cried the guard in the local tongue. His eyes rolled up into his head, his knees buckled, and he crumbled into the arms of the thief. The thief sputtered, staggering under the weight and dropped to its knees, allowing the body to slide almost silently to the ground. Only a slight *pang* and some scrapes escaped the thief's care.

The thief fell back against the wall and, gritting its teeth against the pain, massaged its aching arms. But only for a moment.

The armory doors swung open, then closed behind the thief. Two torch racks with three torches in each lit the large room from the center. The strong odors of linseed oil and rancid fish oil formed a toxic mix in the sealed room. The thief pulled off its mask, and a boy's youthful face turned from left to right, his eager eyes scrutinizing the room. A variety of weapons hung from the walls or lay sharpened and oiled on pitted wooden tables. The boy knew the value of some of this fine craftsmanship, but he also knew that the prized pieces were not out in the open. At the room's rear were the locked closets containing the private armory of the royal family: the King, princes, and immediate male kin.

The boy moved along the walls, collecting the better valuables he came across, all the while edging toward the back. The closets stood at least twice his height, built of solid planks of a strong rich, dark wood, all embellished with gold-paint relief. He'd once glimpsed the valuables inside, and the memory drew him eagerly toward them until he stood only centimeters away. He immediately set about picking the bolt lock on a closet. The bolt slipped out easily, and the door yawned open. The royal men had two kits, one used in battle and a more extravagant set used for formal occasions. The jewels inset in the decorative legacy kit gleamed in reflected torch light.

The boy stared hungrily at the King's formal helm and gauntlets hanging on their hooks at the back of the closet. Below, lying on a red velvet cloth, were the King's weapons: a ceremonial long sword crafted of the finest metal on the planet beside its jewel-encrusted scabbard; an exquisitely forged battle sword matched with a scabbard etched in fine scrollwork; and a delicately carved black dagger, adorned with filigree along its blade. *That's adamantine!* the boy realized with a gasp, his fingers reaching yet hesitant to touch the exquisite blade, lest it vanish like a mirage. *Get it together,* he told himself. *There's no time to waste.* And he went to work grabbing everything of value.

After more time than he thought he'd get, the boy froze, his keen ears focused on the double doors. There was a whisper from the door. Then another.

<<Vronjl!>> the boy cursed quietly, in his own native tongue. <<I left the damn doors unlocked.>> He had little to worry about, his escape route near at hand in the form of a two-meter tall blue-glowing portal, a nearly magical doorway through which he had traveled to this planet from his own.

The doors blew open, and several men stormed into the room brandishing short swords and daggers, their personal, daily-use weapons. Their incredulous eyes fell on the nearly empty tables and almost bare walls. The boy knew them all well. They had taken him into their confidence when he had tossed his wineskin in the way of an arrow meant for the King.

~~What's happened here?~~ said one.

~~There's a light,~~ said another. ~~It's like a blue sky over by the garderobes.~~

Eyes turned and peered across the depth of the room to fall on the boy standing by the open closets, the King's adamantine dagger in his hand.

~~You there,~~ shouted the captain of the guard, advancing slowly with his sword ready. ~~Come out where we can see… YOU!~~

~~Aye.~~ The young man bowed mockingly.

~~You little thief! What do you think you're doing?~~ He advanced toward the boy. ~~I ought to give it to ya good! Wha—!~~ He stopped, jaw working and eyes wide as the boy turned the portal, casting its eerie light around the room and toward the man. ~~A sor-sorcerer! B-Back away from there!~~

~~My apologies, friend. Be well.~~ The boy stepped through the portal and left that planet behind.

CHAPTER 1

NUTMEG faux-wood covered nearly every surface of the large room, from the flooring to the wall-paneling to the dark ceiling with its dentil molding. Velvety burgundy drapes framed two tall windows, which themselves framed a brick fireplace on one wall of the room. The wall opposite the windows held floor-to-ceiling shelves full of books. It had been designed with nostalgia, a callback to a distant time on a distant planet, to an era of which the home's current occupants had no knowledge.

A semi-cluttered desk sat nestled at one end of the room with a small glass-topped snack table and two cozy black-fabric couches before it. Several chairs— some ornamental and one-of-a-kind—stood positioned randomly around the room, while sparkling glass cabinets displayed hundreds of knickknacks and memorabilia. The lamp on the desk was currently lit, but it was the warm glow of the fireplace that cast dancing shadows about the room.

And there was a single speck of dust.

The door opened, and a short, silvery robot whirred into the room, in its hand a mini dust-annihilator. The robot went methodically about the room, its meticulous optical sensors scanning for the slightest mote of impurity to destroy. It stopped now and then, zooming in with its high-resolution optics, then moving on. It found the single dust particle and annihilated it. A signal from its internal clock told it that the lunch hour had arrived, and it whirred out of the room, closing the door behind it.

Tiny pinpoints of light suddenly winked into existence in the air by the desk, as if a bottle of gold glitter had suddenly exploded. These coalesced into a single point of light that stretched in four directions, taking the shape of an almost flat, two-meter-tall rectangle that glowed a radiant blue.

Swords, halberds, maces, helms and pauldrons and dozens of other weapons and armor disgorged from this portal, clanging onto the floor in an increasingly large heap. This continued for nearly ten minutes before stopping completely as outraged voices cried out. More voices followed, only slightly distorted by their passage through the portal.

Then a boy's voice, much closer saying, ~~*My apologies, friend. Be well.*~~

A young man clad in black and brandishing a jewel-encrusted dagger in one hand stepped out from the portal.

His name was Kormèr Lezàl.

Kormèr turned to face the portal, his own private interdimensional doorway, and twisted an eight-buttoned tab that protruded from the top of the portal. The portal collapsed, reverting into the form of a crystal cube which Kormèr stuffed into his coat pocket. He stepped carefully around the pile of weapons and armor and launched himself backward onto a couch. He kicked off the soft leather pads from his feet and propped his feet up on the couch's arm. While his time on planet Jordinni had been educational—and profitable—Kormèr was happy to be back, not only in his own home but also on his home planet of Elmar.

Kormèr admired the dagger, tracing the filigree on the dagger's blade with his nail. ~~Poor HerrGo'rt,~~ he said, thinking of the guard captain. ~~You'll be held responsible for that, but next time you'll be more careful.~~

Kormèr's turned around at the slightest creak of floorboard just outside the room, wide eyes waiting for the one person that would never again walk through the door, his foster father, Yunzen Lezàl. Yunzen was gone for a year and a quarter now, but the sounds and smells of the house still evoked memories of the wonderful man who had raised Kormèr, still stirred Kormèr's heartstrings, more so because of the violence that had torn him from Kormèr's life.

The door opened, and another robot, also short and silvery but with a boxy body, whirred into the room and over to the couch where Kormèr lay. The young man smiled. ~~Trink—~~ He stopped and chuckled. <<Trinket!>> he said again, this time in his native language of Elmarian. <<It's nice to be home again. How have you been?>>

<<Fine, thank you, Kormèr,>> responded the robot. <<And yourself?>>

<<Excellent!>>

<<I see.>> Kormèr caught the bot eyeing the pile of metal on the floor. <<Is there anything you'd like to tell me?>>

<<Oh, yeah. Look what I found?>> He smiled sheepishly.

<<Smelt or sell?>>

Kormèr waved his hand dismissively. <<Sell what you can; smelt the rest and donate the metal. The proceeds of the sale can go to... um... I forget the address, but I wrote it in my calendar, so you can look it up. He needs it to pay for some kind of surgical procedure.>> He didn't have to tell Trinket that the donation was to be anonymous; the robot knew the correct protocol to follow.

He paused then, gazing at the adamantine dagger. <<How much would you value this at?>> He presented the dagger to the robot, who took it in its fingered hand and examined it in hundreds of ways no other creature could. After a moment, the bot handed the weapon back to the young man.

<<Elnreln thadzan gerhet,>> replied Trinket.

<<That much, huh?>> Kormèr was reminded of just how invaluable the little robot was. Without its trained eyes, Kormèr would have been 'robbed' of a good price many a time in the past. <<Well, that sounds too good to give away. We'll keep this one.>>

<<Lunch will be ready soon. Chef has prepared a sandwich of *hajadzèr* and *ynzo*, with *buor* on the side.>>

The young man smiled hungrily. Chef, the household robo-chef, made the best *hajaddèr* sandwiches on the planet. <<With *yuerg*?>>

<<With plenty of *yuerg*. Should I run you a bath first?>>

The young man looked himself over as if for the first time in a long time. But then, for him, it had been a long time. As far as this current planet, Elmar, was concerned, he'd left only moments before, but he had spent the equivalent of several months on planet Jordinni. This temporal discrepancy was because of his portal-cube, the clear crystal cube with a single blackened face, which accompanied him everywhere. Kormèr had appropriated the device from a traveling magician a short time back. He would never have done such a thing had the magician not also been a fraud, attracting crowds of common folks and keeping them enthralled while his assistant roamed among them, pilfering their meager valuables. That was something Kormèr could not abide: the poor of Vranja had enough hardship in their daily lives, without having to worry about such con men.

Kormèr had quickly discovered that the portal allowed him to travel to other planets and other times, spend as much time there as he wished, then return home to Elmar within moments of his original departure. He couldn't help but wonder what sort of temporal mischief that sort of thing could lead to. But the more he thought about it, the more confusing it got and the more of a headache he'd get. So he tried to think about it as little as possible.

<<Kormèr?>> Trinket prodded the daydreaming youth in the ribs until the latter chuckled, tickled.

<<Yes, yes! I really need a bath first.>>

<<Anything else?>>

Kormèr thought for a moment. <<Nope.>>

The robot turned, saying, <<Don't forget about your date with Menddilal.>>

Kormèr's eyes went wide. <<Tonight? Tonight! Of course! We set it up last night, didn't we?>>

<<Correct.>> And the robot was out the door.

Kormèr stood and removed his black ankle-length coat. The last gift he'd received from his late father, the coat was Kormèr's most treasured article of clothing. He had replaced the pockets with deeper ones, each with sewn-in smaller pockets in which he kept several tools of the trade, like the sleeping powder, lock picks, etc. *This is filthy. I'll have to get T to clean it well. Damn, it'll never dry by tonight.*

Kormèr left the study and hurried through the plush marbled corridors of his home and upstairs to his room. Outwardly, the Lezàl mansion was already the largest home in the city of Vranja, if not in the entire province of Vranja. But it otherwise seemed unexceptional, nothing more than a huge oval apartment building designed in an ultra-modern architectural style. The interior was another matter entirely. No one knew what Kormèr's foster grandfather, Seirojj Lezàl, had had in mind when he'd built the mansion, not even Kormèr's foster father,

Yunzen Lezàl. But with dead-end corridors, secret doors and twisting passages, the house was a standing testament to the complex man that had been Seirojj. Complex or troubled, Kormèr could never get a straight answer, not even from the bots.

Kormèr dashed into his room and quickly undressed, leaving a trail of his clothes from the receiving room into the bedroom. Then he meticulously extracted the contents of his coat's pockets into a drawer at his bedside, some eliciting a nostalgic smile as they reminded him of past adventures.

Trinket whirred into the room. <<What're you doing? You still haven't bathed?>> He prodded Kormèr toward the bathroom. <<Your food will get cold. Go on.>> Kormèr dropped the coat over the robot's head and, giggling, disappeared into the bathroom and eased into the steaming tub.

He activated the jets and the hot water pulsed around him, gently massaging his aches away. Over time, he had learned to time his portal travel so that he would arrive home at roughly the same time of day as the one he was leaving. Before he'd figured that out, he had occasionally experienced a full day on one planet, only to return home early in the morning and pass out before noon. Trinket had called it "travel-lag".

This time, he wasn't exhausted so much from travel-lag as from simply having been up most of the night. He'd caught a few winks after dinner, but then he'd donned his thief's garb and headed out to the armory. Catching ninety-plus kilograms of man and armor, followed by conveying kilograms of metal through the portal, also took its toll. He followed an exercise regimen his father had taught him; this kept him fit enough to do most of the acrobatics occasionally called for during his prowls.

But he was only three and a half years old, with 702 days left until his next birthday, at least on Elmar. He'd learned that the length of days, months and years varied on other planets. At one hundred-seventy centimeters and fifty-five kilograms, he was tall and lanky, but looked older than his age, due in part to his time spent away from Elmar.

As he relaxed, his thoughts turned to Menddilal, the beautiful Duchess of Vranja Province. Meeting her had been a thing of random chance, and yet inseparably tied to Kormèr's acquisition of the portal cube. He felt that fate had dropped both into his lap at just the right moment in his life.

The very night Kormèr had robbed the conniving magician, he had retired to his father's study to sift through the pilfered lot of "magical" artifacts. Standing out from the other flotsam, gleamed the near-perfect crystal, its only blemish being one blackened face. Roughly two and a half centimeters to a side, the cube had immediately piqued his curiosity. Kormèr had studied its one black face, finding that it wasn't painted or manually placed on the crystal. Rather, it was a natural tint in the unusual composition.

While trying to glean the purpose of the cube in a magic show, Kormèr had accidentally depressed the black face and triggered the hidden mechanism that caused it to expand into a portal. He had started and dropped the cube as it suddenly glowed bright blue. It had expanded directly beneath Kormèr's feet, sending him tumbling through into what he discovered was the provisional Duke's palace. Fortunately, the Duke hadn't been home that evening, but attending a gathering of the Vranjan Council, the provincial governing body. Home alone and asleep was the Duke's young wife, Menddilal. She'd woken and caught him rifling through the contents of her jewel cases. Rather than call for the guards, the mischievous vixen had had her way with her new toy. Kormèr later found out that she'd been fooling around with another lover by the name of Zolt. But cats never tire of novel playthings, and she was the embodiment of all things "cat".

Thrilled with this enigmatic girl, Kormèr had continued visiting her whenever the Duke was away. Their nights together were a random medley of teasing games, whimsical snobbery, sexual release and, Kormèr's favorite, thievery. For in his spare time, Kormèr browsed through the jewelry boxes and bureaus for tiny valuables that no one would miss right away—

<<Perhaps you would rather eat here?>>

Kormèr practically jumped from the tub at the voice that was suddenly beside him. <<Jees, Trinket!>> Kormèr put a hand to his chest, where his heart thumped away.

<<I'm sorry,>> said the robot. <<I didn't mean to startle you.>>

Kormèr shook his head. <<That's alright, Trink. I just didn't hear you, that's all.>>

The robot perked up.

<<Come to think of it, yes, I'll have my lunch here.>> He slid sideways in the oval tub, curling his legs so that his knees poked out of the water. Then he took the plate with his sandwich from Trinket and propped it between his knees and chest. Finally, he took a bite of the sandwich. <<Mmm,>> he groaned, closing his eyes and relishing the first familiar food he'd had in a while. Jordinnian cuisine hadn't been terrible, particularly at the castle as a guest of the king. The foods had been savory, if often overly rich and always salty. He'd enjoyed them while there, though he'd lived under constant worry that he'd catch some kind of stomach bug, considering the lack of refrigeration and food safety regulations. But nothing compared to the familiar tastes of home. When he could talk again, he said, <<Delicious, Trinket. Thanks.>>

Trinket grabbed a rolled towel from the towel rack and unrolled it onto the warmer. He drummed his small metal fingers lightly on his chest, an affectation that Kormèr was all too familiar with. The bot had something on its mind that it wanted to discuss.

<<Kormèr, the household is responsible for your well-being,>> said the bot, referring to the clause in Yunzen's will that had entrusted Kormèr's care to the exceptional household robots upon Yunzen's passing. Kormèr now understood

9

why Trinket had hesitated; an invader had murdered Yunzen in the mansion. It was still a delicate subject for Kormèr, but no less so for the robots, who blamed themselves for not stopping the invader and for having no evidence of his presence within the house at the time of the murder. The invader… the murderer had never been captured.

Trinket continued: <<Your relationship with the Duchess Menddilal is concerning.>>

Kormèr chewed, swallowed. <<In what way?>>

<<The Duke and Duchess are very public figures, as was Yunzen.>> Kormèr knew where this was going. Yunzen had been well known throughout Vranja Province because of his position as councilman in the Vranjan Council. Kormèr's biological parents had been aides to the Council and close friends with Yunzen. When they died in a fire shortly after Kormèr's birth, Yunzen had adopted Kormèr. <<So, I must know if you are involved in any activities that could jeopardize your reputation.>>

Yunzen had always let Kormèr know he was immensely proud of him, and had never hidden the fact that he was raising him. But he had been careful to keep his private life and his public life separate, and the former included Kormèr. So, while most Vranjan citizens knew that Yunzen had a son, few were familiar with what Kormèr actually looked like. Fewer still outside of Vranja City, and the Duke's mansion was located in another city, over two-hours travel from the capital.

But anonymity and lack of recognition could only protect a thief so much. Kormèr had grown up with the benefit of a caretaker who was himself a thief. And Yunzen had imparted his self-gained knowledge and skill onto Kormèr over the latter's short life.

<<Why do you do it?>> Kormèr had once asked, when the two were seated in the garden. He had been wondering why a man in Yunzen's position would risk losing everything by stealing. He knew already that Yunzen gave away everything he stole, keeping nothing for himself.

<<That is a very smart question,>> Yunzen had replied. <<There are… economic divisions in our society which you're too young to fully understand. But you'll learn in your schooling that there are times in history where such divisions have grown so out of hand that they've led to revolutions.>>

Kormèr had learned that word recently, and he wanted to show off how smart he was to his father. <<That's when people force the government to change.>>

Yunzen had smiled. <<That's exactly right. I don't want to see that happen here. I don't think there's anything wrong with our governing structure, just the corruption that manifests from time to time.>>

Encouraged by his father's smile, Kormèr blurted, <<The Charter of Elmar establishes the global governing and soci— socioeco—>> He paused. <<Socioeconomic framework,>> he finished.

Yunzen had ruffled his hair. <<You got it! That's a pretty big word that covers a very important and even bigger concept. Do you know what that is?>>

Kormèr had tried to remember the definition. <<Something about people and money, but not single people like you or me, people as in everyone and how they… um…>> He'd forgotten the rest.

<<You almost had it. It is the relationship between people and money and each other. When people have more money, they have access to more things, a bigger house, servants, groundskeepers—>>

<<Don't other people have household bots like we do?>>

<<Oh, no. Our bots were my father's.>> A distant look had come into his eyes. <<And he never explained why we're the only ones who have them as personal servants.>> He refocused on Kormèr. <<But that aside, do you understand what I mean about money and people?>>

Kormèr had nodded. <<I think so.>>

<<Well, the Charter establishes a working class and a ruling class. But over time, something has gone wrong. The income gap between the two classes has become increasingly wider, and from my… historical research, I fear we're at a point in time where, if things don't change, we'll head irreversibly toward revolution. I disagree with this interpretation of the Charter. I can't believe its authors ever meant it to create this kind of divide.>> His brow had furrowed and his eyes become unfocused again. <<And this interpretation is so entrenched in the ruling elite that even in my position on the Vranjan Council, I feel powerless to stem the tide of…>>

He had focused on Kormèr again, his grip on the arms of his chair loosening. <<Look, I want you to always understand that stealing is wrong. If we get caught, it's over. All of this,>> he'd swept his hand around to indicate the mansion, <<gone. You'd probably be sent to live with my sister.>> Kormèr must've looked stricken. Though he loved his auntie, who lavished him with sweets and money when Yunzen wasn't looking, he couldn't imagine not living with Yunzen in the mansion. <<I'm not trying to scare you, just to prepare you should the worst come to be. But also so that you understand why I teach you all the things I do. You must always be smart and careful in all you do.>>

Kormèr hadn't understood it all at the time, but that last lesson had etched itself into his young, impressionable mind.

Kormèr's drifting thoughts returned to the present, where he found a bite of sandwich sitting unchewed in his mouth. <<I am always careful,>> Kormèr told Trinket as he resumed chewing. <<She hasn't seen my face; I always wear the mask when I visit.>> He smiled wryly. <<She insists I keep it on, in fact. It thrills her.>>

Trinket tipped his head slightly to one side in a very human gesture. <<Really? Young people these days. What about names?>>

<<Eddrin Ciendd.>>

<<An old name. Good.>>

11

The poor often used older names with double consonants and tongue-twisting sound combinations that had been obviated by a language reform years ago. As far as Kormèr knew, only a few of the older affluent families steadfastly held onto the older style names, the Mernggos among them.

Still thinking of Yunzen, Kormèr wondered, *What made father think he'd make a difference?* Had Yunzen's efforts made a difference? Kormèr thought so. While Kormèr wasn't naïve enough to believe he'd ever see any grand-scale changes come of such meager efforts, he had seen people on the verge of true poverty recover because of his effort. And he'd witnessed older folk, unable to take advantage of their windfall, use it to make sure their children would never have to know poverty.

Trinket took the empty plate, and Kormèr started the water draining while he towel-dried himself. In the quiet, with thoughts of Yunzen fresh in Kormèr's mind, the painful memory of his death surfaced. The irony was that another thief had killed him, stabbed him and left him to die on the floor. Yunzen had never advocated the use of weapons, believing that their use carried too high a risk of serious injury. <<Stealth, deception and misdirection are our weapons,>> he'd instructed. And Kormèr had taken that to heart, swearing that he would never use a weapon to kill, even if cornered. If things got serious, a blunt object was acceptable, but only to incapacitate temporarily, never, absolutely never to kill.

Kormèr hopped out into his room while drying his left foot. His jaw dropped as his eyes fell on his long, *clean,* black coat hanging from a bedpost. <<Ha, ha! Trinket, you're the best.>>

<<Why, thank you,>> said the bot, sounding truly pleased.

Kormèr turned to see the short robot roll out of the closet with clean clothes for him to wear. <<How'd you dry it so quickly? You must tell me.>>

<<Household rules. We never reveal our secrets.>>

<<Bah.>> He relieved the robot of the light load and dressed while Trinket rolled off to the bathroom. <<Any messages?>>

Trinket answered from the bathroom, <<From Rasseur.>>

Kormèr perked up at hearing the name. Half-a-year his senior, Devron Rasseur was Kormèr's best friend and a talented thief in his own right, though Kormèr would never admit either of those things to Devron. The otherwise competitive nature of their relationship left no room to admit such things.

<<He said not to forget your cards tomorrow night for Mernggo's party,>> finished Trinket.

<<Blast! I had forgotten that as well.>>

Trinket hurried out of the bathroom then. He came to Kormèr's side and looked him over. <<Travel lag again?>> The bot didn't wait for Kormèr to respond. <<I wish you wouldn't go on these prolonged trips. I can't do my job if I can't monitor you.>>

Kormèr sat cross-legged on the floor, putting himself at eye level with Trinket. <<You don't have to worry about me, Trink. Father taught me well, and I know my limits.>>

Trinket bobbed its head. <<Kormèr, I trust *you*. It's other... beings that I don't trust. And I don't know if you have enough experience to judge the limits of others.>>

<<Hmm.>> Kormèr hated seeing the bot worried about him. <<Let me tell you about this last trip. Maybe you'll worry less if you hear how I handled things.>>

By the time Kormèr was done, Trinket wasn't any less worried.

Kormèr reassured him, saying, <<I promise that the next time I leave Elmar on some adventure, I'll keep it short.>>

<<Thank you,>> said the bot. <<You should head out.>>

Kormèr checked the time. <<Ack!>> He had just enough time to dab on some cologne and slip on his mask. He opened the portal and considered on his choice of entry point into the mansion. The Duke was supposed to be out on business, but one could never be too careful; some last-minute delay or change in the Duke's plans and the portal could appear right in front of him. Kormèr focused on a mental image of the mansion's roof. <<See you later,>> he said and stepped through the portal.

THE Duchess threw her arms around Kormèr's shoulders and kissed him deeply the moment he entered from the balcony into her bedchamber. <<Prompt as always,>> she breathed after stopping for air.

<<For you, of course.>> She smiled at his simple flattery. <<How are you this evening?>> he asked.

<<Sad.>> She turned away with sorrowful eyes.

Kormèr smiled, recognizing one of her games. She was a year and a quarter older than him and knew most of the coy games girls her age played. Kormèr had learned enough of them to play along. <<Oh?>>

She sighed.

<<Perhaps dinner will perk up your spirits.>>

She shook her head.

Kormèr stepped closer. <<Perhaps you'd like to talk about it?>>

She shook her head.

Kormèr stood only inches from her back. He whispered, <<Maybe I can do something—>>

She turned suddenly and strode past him. <<Actually, dinner sounds quite therapeutic.>>

Kormèr raised his eyes to heaven. *What a boring doll; always the same nonsense.* He sighed and followed her to a dining nook where a cart awaited with an assortment of food. *At least she feeds me well.* As he sat before the cart, he eyed the jewel box that was in its usual corner of the young lady's dresser. *I'll see* you *later,* he thought longingly.

MENTALLY and physically drained, Kormèr stared at the dark ceiling as the Duchess snored softly beside him. She had been at her most challenging this evening, and Kormèr had had to take extra care navigating the often frustrating twists and turns of her moods. After dinner she had wanted to talk, and she had talked incessantly about her family—her grandmother in particular, of whom she was very fond—and other government staff, often boasting of the audacity of overly flirtatious aides and council members, men and women alike. To hear her tell of it, one could easily assume that all desired her.

After more than an hour of talking, she decided she wanted to play an odd game in which, both blindfolded, they had to feed each other from the tray of desserts. They both ended up wearing more dessert than they ate, but apparently, that was also part of the game, the part that eventually landed them in her bed.

It was only now, hours after Kormèr's arrival, that the actual business began. He wondered briefly if he had time to go home and take another bath, to clean the sticky creams and juices off his skin, but he knew he only had a few minutes—the second rinse would have to wait.

Kormèr eased out from under the covers and tiptoed to the dresser. He checked his reflection in the mirror, naked except for the simple black silk mask that hid his face from the tip of his nose to the back of his head, leaving only the bottom half of his face exposed, along with his eyes and ears. Kormèr's eyes slid to the reflection of the unmoving, curved form in the bed behind him while his hands felt their way to the jewel box. They found the lock and pushed the slide… and nothing happened.

Kormèr cursed silently. She had always left it unlocked before. He slinked to where his clothes still rested on the floor beside the food cart that had toppled in the throes of their passion. He donned his coat and extracted a felt pouch from the coat's pocket. From this he removed a syringe-like device and then tip-toed back to the jewelry box.

Carefully inserting the needle into the lock, he played the object back and forth until experience told him it had done its job. He replaced the device in the pouch and tried the snap again. *Click.* He silently thanked the heavens as the box opened.

Even in the near-darkness, the glimmer of the jewels within was blinding to Kormèr's discerning eyes. *What beauty! What a trove! Eventually, I'll have every one of you little ladies. But for now…* He picked a string of gems set into a silver chain and placed it and the felt pouch into his coat pocket. He closed the box, then gathered his clothes. The Duke wouldn't be out for much longer; it was time to depart. The young Menddilal did not stir as Kormèr opened the portal and stepped through into his own bedroom.

He closed the portal and stuffed the cube into his coat pocket. He stared around his darkened room, getting his bearings in the dim moonlight that touched his gauzy drapes. The chrono at his bedside told him it was very early morning, confirming what his body and mind already knew. His eyes itched with exhaustion, and he could feel the adrenaline that had kept him going at the Duke's mansion now ebbing. His clothes and shoes slipped from his hand, and he trudged toward the bed. He crawled onto the bed, curled his knees to his chest, and hugged his coat around him. He fell asleep in seconds.

CHAPTER 2

KORMÈR tried to sleep in late that morning, ignoring the chrono alarm and burying his head under his pillow to avoid the morning's cheery brightness streaming through the windows.

<<Kormèr.>> Someone shook him. <<Honestly, Kormèr, I can't believe you've slept in your coat, after I had it cleaned and steamed only yesterday.>>

Kormèr peered out from under the pillow at his arms and realized he really had his coat on. <<Ugh.>> His tongue was thick and pasty. He rolled, sliding his arms out of the coat as he did, shedding it like a second skin. As Trinket took the coat away and examined its condition, Kormèr grabbed a corner of his bedcovers and rolled back into the warm spot he'd left, wrapping himself in the bed cover along the way.

<<Oh, no you don't,>> admonished Trinket. <<It's time for your lessons. Get dressed and go down to the study.>> Kormèr opened his mouth to protest. <<It's not any concern of mine how late you were out on your date. Come now.>> Trinket rolled out of the room.

Kormèr closed his mouth and slid groggily out of bed. A glass of juice awaited him on the bedside table. Kormèr smiled as he emptied the glass, quenching his thirst. <<Okay, fine,>> he said. Then he donned a robe, made a detour to the bathroom before heading out of his room to the study. On the way, he passed his coat hanging neatly on a hanger. It was wrinkle-free and spotless.

Schooling for Kormèr was a combination of virtual classrooms with both live and simulated instructors. These covered the fundamentals of reading, writing, arithmetic and the sciences, as well as the history and culture of the provinces of Elmar. After that, the bots provided supplemental home schooling. Their syllabus focused more on topics specific to government, economics, and debate. It was the latter two that Kormèr found most interesting, and the former the least. Regardless, as with most boys his age, he was most content when the school day ended. And that was particularly true this day, with Mernggo's party only hours away. The moment his schooling ended, he raced upstairs to get himself ready.

Vertiband Mernggo had made his vast wealth in real-estate, and remained the largest landowner in the duchy. His philanthropy was overshadowed only by his annual parties, which were famous throughout the Duchy of Vranja and its neighboring provinces. Known for the finest catering and entertainment—the latter including fine music, comedians, magicians and singers—the parties also hosted after-hours, high-stakes gambling. The latter consisted of guests playing their games of choice for as long as the last person could hold out—though usually no longer than the following daybreak.

Kormèr and Devron enjoyed mingling with the affluent of Vranja, but it was the games of chance that they most looked forward to. One particular card game had caught their attention some time ago, and when they heard it was practically a house game at Mernggo's parties, their desire to master the game had drawn them to the parties every year thereafter.

Kormèr checked his face in the mirror. Blast! No beard yet. He wanted so very badly to have a beard. Recently, he'd seen a man with an ideal beard that ran only along the perimeter of the man's face. Someday, he'd do the same.

He combed back a loose strand of hair and straightened his black formal jacket. Stepping back, he looked at himself in the full-length mirror and smiled. <<Hi, handsome,>> he winked, and laughed in self-deprecation.

Trinket rolled into the room. <<Will you be picking Devron up or he you?>>

Kormèr glanced at Trinket over his shoulder. <<Rass, pick me up? That'll be the day—>>

A buzzer interrupted him and signaled someone at the front gate. Trinket cocked his head, and Kormèr was sure that if the bot had had eyebrows, it would've raised them in surprise. Trinket quickly left the room with Kormèr staring after him. *It can't be. Could Rass be learning some manners? Who am I kidding?*

Trinket returned after several moments.

Kormèr dabbed cologne on his neck and asked, <<Who was it, T?>> But it wasn't the bot that answered.

<<Who else're you expecting?>>

Kormèr spun around, startled by the unexpected voice. Leaning against the doorframe, grinning smarmily, was Devron Rasseur. <<You *jjled*.>> Kormèr walked over to the young man, who met him halfway, and gave him a quick once over, from the caramel-hued vest over the white shirt with walnut neck-tie, down to the walnut baggy pants and leather boots. <<Don't tell me: that snazzy little clothing shop on Amalie Way.>>

<<How'd you guess?>> answered Devron, his mahogany eyes matching his long, pony-tailed hair. <<Actually,>> he continued, pushing away from the wall, <<I'm trying a new look for the new me. Allow me to introduce myself; I am Devron Rasseur.>> He bowed gracefully, extending a hand forward with a slight flourish.

Kormèr chuckled. <<Are you ill? Should I have Trink get your help?>>

<<Bah!>> Devron straightened quickly. <<You wouldn't know finesse if it ran you over. But the ladies'll love it.>>

<<It's fake!>>

Devron shrugged. <<Of course. But it makes *them* melt.>>

<<I think I'll just stick to being me. I'm not quite ready for that level of… finesse.>> Kormèr attempted to imitate the action.

<<No, no. You're putting your hand out too far. It's supposed to be here.>> Devron went through the motions with his hand ending up diagonal to his face. <<Then the lady places her hand in yours, and you kiss it.>>

<<Hmm. We'll see. So did you walk here or drive?>>

<<Walk, indeed!>> He walked to the door and held a hand out for Kormèr to pass. <<My brougham awaits.>>

<<Your father let you borrow the brougham?>> Kormèr asked as he passed Devron. <<I am impressed.>>

MERNGGO'S estate dated back to the classical era of Vranjan construction, when circular driveways and marble entry steps were all the rage. The two-story mansion, with its entryway sporting four elaborately grooved columns supporting a decorative triangular pediment, was no different. To each side of the entryway, the mansion sprawled out for several meters before bubbling out into rounded turrets, with the roofline of the entire structure topped by a balustrade.

Devron's automated brougham came to a stop at the foot of the steps. The boys exited, and the brougham followed some instruction transmitted by the estate's valet software as it rolled away to find a place to park. They followed other guests up the steps but stepped aside as they came to the open door and turned to face those now arriving.

Mernggo's parties drew an eclectic crowd of actual invitees and crashers. Invitees tended to be affluent members of society from all across Elmar—people traveled from far-flung provinces and stay in town overnight, making a holiday of the event. But they also included some who had successfully crashed in the past and made the right connections to get on the guest list. Yunzen had been on the invite list until his death, but Kormèr had been too young to attend with him. And Pauleo Rasseur, Devron's father, was still on the list, though he never attended.

Shortly after Yunzen's death, Devron had convinced a grieving Kormèr to crash the party, using Pauleo Rasseur's unused passes. Despite his initial misgivings, Kormèr had enjoyed himself, the revelry temporarily relieving his sadness and loss, and for that, Kormèr felt he would never fully repay Devron for that night.

One party soon followed another, and while Merngo's own children were young enough that no one had initially challenged the presence of two other unaccompanied young boys, Devron and Kormèr soon reached the age when they were expected to have their own invitations for entrance, not just as guests of an invitee who never attended. After a few unsuccessful attempts to talk or sneak their way past the incorruptible, eagle-eyed bouncers, Devron and Kormèr took to finagling invitations, either from Merngo's staff or from acquaintances.

Devron claimed it was more fun to attend illicitly, as "any party that would have me as a guest is probably not one I would want to attend, anyway." This year had been Devron's turn to wrangle the invitations, and he had cleverly come through with five passes.

Now they just needed to find two dates to enter with. As the minutes passed, Kormèr and Devron watched with growing disappointment as most women arrived, accompanied by male companions.

Kormèr checked his chrono. <<We might need to forego the other three--->>

Devron cut him off. <<Sh-sh. Look.>> Three unaccompanied young women stepped out of a lavish carriage, recognizable by the crest on its side as pertaining to an affluent family. Two sported auburn hair, and the third was blonde. One had her auburn hair up with her bangs swept to the side, accentuating her high cheek-bones. She wore a long-sleeved, navy blue, patchwork-lace mini-dress. The other redhead wore a form-fitting emerald-green dress that shimmered as she moved. The blonde wore a coral halter-dress, her hair hanging in loose curls over her shoulders.

Devron stole a glance at Kormèr. Kormèr raised a knowing eyebrow at Devron. <<There are three. What'll we do?>> asked Kormèr, already knowing what his friend would say.

<<We'll compete for her.>>

Something bothered Kormèr about thinking of the girls as prizes to be won, but there was no point in arguing that point now. <<I guess.>>

<<Excuse me,>> said Devron, approaching the trio of ladies as they reached the landing. <<Allow me to introduce myself; I am Devron Rasseur.>> Devron bowed as he had shown Kormèr earlier. He straightened up when his extended hand remained empty.

Kormèr sidestepped Devron and, with a smile—and an uncontrolled blush he wished he could hide—said, <<Hi. I'm Kormèr Lezàl.>> He wasn't shy about talking to girls, at least not one-on-one or even one-on-two. But he estimated that these girls were closer to Devron's age than his own, and three of them regarding him so directly made sweat break out on the nape of his neck.

<<We have relinquished our place in line to meet you,>> said Devron in a manner that Kormèr found both belabored and ineffectual, to his amusement.

<<Then you did so in vain,>> retorted the auburn-haired girl in the blue dress.

Kormèr cringed. The girls were turning to pass them by, and Devron looked stunned into silence. Thinking quickly, Kormèr said, <<Umm… Hi, again.>> He smiled, barely repressing the nervous laugh that threatened to fly out of his mouth. Sweat trickled down his back. <<We're without dates tonight, and we would be honored if you would allow us to accompany you this evening.>>

The women looked at each other and conferred in the silent way all women seem to be born knowing how to do. Smiling coyly, the blonde said to Kormèr, <<We would like that, yes.>> She placed her hand over Kormèr's extended hand. <<My name's Ildza.>> The redhead in the blue dress did the same on his right side, saying, <<I'm Jolie.>>

The other auburn-haired girl, wearing the emerald green dress, frowned, then gingerly placed her hand on Devron's. <<I'm Gredzen.>>

<<A pleasure,>> said Devron. And he kissed her hand.

Together, they passed through the double-doorway and into the grand foyer. Devron presented the invitations to the bouncer. Kormèr was sure the ladies had invites of their own, but they made no move to present them, and they seemed impressed that these two young men had five.

A greeting line followed, including the host, his wife and their three children: a boy, a girl and another boy, in descending age order. Beyond them stood several other "esteemed" greeters, none of whom Devron or Kormèr had any desire to greet.

<<Would you look at that!>> said Devron, stepping out of the greeting line and past a row of marble columns to a painting that hung on the wall beyond. <<I love the color of this piece, the way the artist cast the shadows from the light of the dawn sun.>>

Kormèr nodded, also feigning interest. <<True. But my favorite is this other one.>> He stepped to the right along the aisle, the greeting line now behind them on the opposite side of the columns. <<Even with so small a canvas, the artist managed to evoke such a sense of grand space. It takes my breath away.>> Kormèr looked at Ildza, the blonde. <<What do you think?>>

It was Jolie who answered. <<I think you're both a bit-->> She stopped, and Kormèr thought he almost caught a look being exchanged between her and Ildza. <<I mean... I think they're both fine pieces,>> she said.

<<I agree,>> said Devron. <<Let's head inside.>>

They followed the aisle to its end, safely past the greeting line, and entered the grand ballroom.

The live band played a slow, soft melody as the guests filed in and searched for acquaintances and for tables. Devron led them to a table off to the left and close to the dance floor. As the girls took their seats, Kormèr asked, <<Would you ladies like something to drink?>>

He took their requests, and Devron went with him to the bar. <<Good job with the invites,>> Kormèr told him.

<<Thank you,>> grinned Devron. <<They seemed impressed that we had five.>>

<<Yep. I was, too. That's more than we've ever gotten.>>

<<Well, you know, there was this fellow having relationship trouble with his *noggin*—>>

<<His what?>>

<<It's a new word I have for talking about women without them knowing it. But more specifically...>> He whispered into Kormèr's ear.

<<Uh... okay.>> *Oh, Rass,* Kormèr thought to himself, disappointed at his friend's crassness. <<So you fixed things up between them?>>

<<Of course not. She was much too good for him. I kept her for myself and convinced him he was better off without her. He was so happy he gave me two passes. She was then pleased enough to give me three.>>

Kormèr had to laugh. It was just like Devron to pull something like that and come out a winner.

When the dancing started, Kormèr faced a dilemma. He had two potential dance partners, but how could he ask one to dance without seeming to pick favorites? When Devron asked Gredzen to dance, Kormèr had to act. He stood and blurted out, <<Would either of you like to dance?>>

Ildza and Jolie exchanged some silent communique, then Ildza smiled and stood. *Whew!* he thought as they walked to the dance floor.

<<Your father wouldn't happen to be Yunzen Lezàl?>> asked Ildza while they danced.

<<That's right. Did you know him?>>

<<Not personally. But my father knew him. I'm sorry about his passing.>>

<<Thanks. Sometimes it feels like a long time ago, and other times it's like it just happened.>>

<<Oh, dear,>> she said, putting a hand to her chest. <<I didn't mean to make you feel bad——>>

Kormèr shook his head, smiling. <<No, no. I didn't mean to imply anything by that. You're father's Wenddel Nacav, right?>>

<<Yes. How'd you know?>>

<<The crest on your brougham.>> He grinned at her. <<And a slight resemblance to portraits I've seen of your mother. You're very pretty.>> He was sure there was a more eloquent and poetic way to compliment her, but all he could think was that he should be sincere.

She blushed at his simple flattery. <<Thank you. You're quite handsome yourself.>>

Kormèr knew he was grinning like an idiot, but he couldn't help himself. With a slight nod, <<Thank *you*.>>

When the dance ended, Kormèr walked Ildza back toward the table with every intention of asking Jolie to dance, but he found her already walking toward the dance floor to meet him. He noticed Devron had remained on the floor for the next dance, too. Gredzen seemed to be a good dancer and conversationalist, if Devron's smile was any indication.

<<How old are you?>> asked Jolie, as they danced.

Kormèr nearly choked. <<Umm… why?>> Had he done something wrong, committed some social gaffe that made him seem younger than he was?

<<You act like you're in your fours, but I think you're younger.>>

Damn, she's good! <<I'm three and a half.>>

<<Really?>> She looked sincerely surprised. <<I would've expected that from your friend.>>

Kormèr laughed. <<He's half a year older.>>

21

<<Well, I guess what they say is true: age isn't everything. Keep doing what you're doing, Kormèr.>>

Grinning like an idiot again, he said, <<Thanks.>> Though he wasn't sure exactly what she'd meant, her words encouraged him. He relaxed and enjoyed the dance. From Jolie's smile, he knew she enjoyed it as well.

When the next dance ended, as they returned from the dance floor, Devron said, <<You know, one day we must try a *Talambua*.>>

<<Here? I dunno. People don't react well to that dance.>> Kormèr could see them being tossed from the party and even blacklisted for performing the fast-paced, raucous dance at this fancy event.

<<Precisely,>> said Devron, wiggling his eyebrows.

Kormèr chuckled. <<Maybe another time. I'm not brave enough to try that here, yet.>>

<<Ah, 'yet'!>> said Devron, nodding sagely. Then he seemed to notice Jolie. <<Would you care to dance?>> he said to her.

<<No, thanks,>> said Jolie, taking her seat.

<<I'll dance,>> said Gredzen, stepping away from Devron and taking Kormèr's hand.

<<Ah, sure,>> said Kormèr and let himself be led out to dance, as Devron looked on with a raised eyebrow.

<<You dance well,>> said Gredzen.

<<Thanks. I was actually thinking the same about you while you were dancing with Rass.>>

<<Rass? Oh, I see.>> She laughed lightly. <<I'm glad you recovered for him earlier.>> Kormèr must've looked confused, as she explained: <<Outside, when we first met, we were ready to leave you standing there.>>

<<Oh. Well, I'm glad you didn't,>> he said. <<I like these parties, but it's much more fun enjoying them with good company.>>

Gredzen smiled. <<Yeah, there's what Jolie saw in you.>>

Kormèr had no idea what she was talking about, but it had to be related to what Jolie had said to him. <<What? What is it?>>

Gredzen laughed but never explained. Instead, she spun and danced until the song ended moments later. <<Thank you for the dance,>> she said, curtsying slightly.

Kormèr bowed slightly at the waist. <<The pleasure was mine.>>

She took his hand, and together they returned to the table. Kormèr saw Devron and Ildza taking their seats and realized they must've been dancing together behind him.

<<Old Mernggo must be trying something new,>> said Devron, tipping his head to point with his chin. In prior years, live staff had taken the food orders. So it surprised Kormèr to see an autonomous order-server robot roll up to the table, escorted by a live handler. The handler explained how to use the menu screen, and everyone at the table placed their orders. Kormèr had practically been raised by

bots since his father had died, so he was used to such service—and his bots were orders of magnitude more intelligent and autonomous than these. But the others found the experience so novel that they didn't stop chatting about it, for much longer than Kormèr felt it deserved.

More dancing followed. Both Ildza and Jolie chose to dance with Kormèr at the same time. Kormèr had seen young women do this sort of thing at other parties, and it worked quite well despite the fact that there was nothing personal about it. It was just fun. For the next song, Gredzen pulled Devron over, and they all danced in a circle.

The music slowed as the food service began, and everyone returned to their tables. In a new custom that bucked at tradition, everyone at the table shared their selections of appetizer and main course. The food was exquisite, as always, followed by absolutely sinful desserts.

When the meal ended, the floor lit up as entertainers performed for the crowd. While a magician performed his tricks, Kormèr and Devron tried to discern how he'd executed them. The girls' faces lit up with joy when a holographist came by and created a unique composition of sound-activated colors for each of them to take home. The rest of the entertainers were very good, though Devron remarked to Kormèr that it had been better the previous year.

Soon enough, the gaming hour was upon them. The dance floor emptied gradually as crowds gathered quietly around the scattered tables.

<<Do you play any games?>> asked Gredzen.

<<*Jgal* is our game,>> Devron proclaimed.

<<But we're still learning it,>> admitted Kormèr. <<Would you mind if we watched a game for a bit?>>

Jolie shrugged. <<My dad plays, but I'll admit I've never watched a full game. Sure.>>

They walked to another table to watch a game of *Jgal* that was already in progress. Kormèr and Devron looked on intently, taking mental notes and commenting to each other on certain points.

Jgal combined chance and tactics with the colorful, ornate cards symbolizing offensive and defensive units which two opposing players positioned strategically on the stylized table, in order to overtake each other's stronghold. The players' personal decks ultimately determined their fates: a fateful shuffle could either deal a player a devastating, irrecoverable loss, or a lucky final hand that delivered a decisive triumph.

Kormèr felt a tug on his formal jacket, but taken by the game, he disregarded it. After a second tug, he realized his pocket was being picked.

He whirled on a startled youngster who gasped, spun around and shoved through the crowd. Kormèr checked his pockets— <<My cube!>> he shouted, dashing after the boy.

The crowd parted before him, and Kormèr advanced quickly with his long legs.

The boy juked around tables, dodging hands that reached out to grab him. As he dashed out into the foyer, he must've realized that he had no chance of escape. The front doors were closed, and he'd never get them open in time. In one fluid motion, he spun around and tossed the only loot he'd grabbed back toward Kormèr.

Kormèr knew that if he acted quickly, he could both catch the cube and nab the boy. Kormèr could almost hear his father's voice: *A good rule in thievery is never to do what this boy has done. Just keep running.* With his mind set on giving the kid a good thrashing, Kormèr extended his hand to catch the cube… then noticed a blue glow overhead. Wide eyes flicked up. The open portal flopped down in front of him, and he tumbled right into it. His flailing hands caught the tab and turned it, sealing the portal.

CHAPTER 3

KORMÈR landed on his feet almost immediately, his fall no more than two meters. He thanked the gods that it hadn't been worse. He only had a fundamental grasp of how the portal worked, so virtually anything could have been waiting for him on the other side.

He ducked, instantly on alert at the rapid *whine-zap* of laser fire, a sound he had learned to recognize on another planet he'd visited earlier in the year. Looking about for cover, he scampered to a thick metal cylinder and pressed his back against it. With the laser fire safely behind him, he took a moment to scan his surroundings and orient himself.

The area where he stood was brightly lit by powerful white lamps that ran the perimeter of the strange metallic floor and arced away to either side. Beyond the lights, the floor ended in darkness. In the dark, white particulates like ice or snow fluttered past, driven by gusts that Kormèr neither heard nor felt. But the particulates never passed the lights; they appeared to be confined by some invisible barrier just beyond the lights. *I must be inside some kind of protective bubble,* he concluded.

He stood beneath a huge metallic bulk propped up and supported by four metal cylinders, one of which he now used for cover from the deadly bolts that zipped by. He peered around the cylinder and spotted a ramp six meters away that led up into the bulk above him. Another ten meters past the ramp sat several large metal crates. A few men were crouched behind them, on Kormèr's side, using them for cover. Beyond them, the large room enclosed by the protective bubble had a single entrance framed by a circular archway. The archway was open, revealing a metal tube that Kormèr could see snaking away into the void outside the bubble and adjoining the room to a silhouette half hidden by the dense gusts outside. It was from this archway that another group of men was shooting at the nearby group.

A bolt sizzled past, too close for Kormèr's comfort. He slid back around the cylinder and considered his next steps. Having just returned from months abroad on Jordinni, he had hoped to spend at least a few months at home before embarking on another adventure. While he rarely knew exactly where he'd end up when he stepped through the portal, he had a checklist of essential items that he preferred to have with him before embarking on a trip. Here he was, with no preparation whatsoever. Even his formal party clothes could draw unneeded attention during that crucial time he required to acclimate to his new surroundings.

On the other hand, people usually fought over things they considered valuable, such as land, wealth, loved ones… and this seemed to be quite the fight he had stumbled into. The promise of valuables and the unusual environment piqued his interest. *Maybe I'll just snoop around a bit before going back home,* he decided. *I just need to get away from these guys without getting fried. I need something that can act as a shield— I can use the portal as a shield! If I can make it to the ramp and upstairs, I can find another way out of here.*

There was no rush to get back, as Kormèr could return to the precise moment when he had left Mernggo's party whenever he wanted. He could take his time, tread carefully, and reap whatever rewards he found here.

He pressed the black face on the cube, and the portal immediately floated before him. Since the portal read its user's mind somehow to pick where it opened, Kormèr imagined it exiting into the Elmarian sun. It immediately beeped to warn that the exit was inhospitable, but this didn't worry Kormèr as the sound was too low to be heard over the near-constant whine of discharging energy weapons.

Kormèr grabbed the almost weightless portal by its sides, holding the opening away from him, and charged out from his hiding place toward the ramp.

Bolts fired at him passed through the portal and merged harmlessly into the violent energy of Elmar's sun. One bolt missed him entirely, ricocheted off the bubble-wall and struck a panel beside the archway, which exploded with a shower of sparks. The white lights along the room's perimeter suddenly pulsed yellow as a voice boomed through the room. Kormèr listened, but the language was totally unfamiliar to him. From the startled cries of those present, he decided it wasn't saying anything good.

Without a moment's pause, he ran faster and scrambled up the ramp into a narrow corridor. At least no one was shooting here. Kormèr sealed the portal and walked briskly, following the corridor in search of another way out. He passed several doorways, most of which were locked and others which led nowhere. He knew he was in trouble when he found himself back at the ramp.

Kormèr jumped as a bolt exploded at the base of the ramp. His heart racing, Kormèr looked down to see a man backing up onto it. With nowhere to go, Kormèr ran back to an open panel he'd passed. Dangling wires and conduits within left just enough space for him to squeeze into and hide. He lay horizontally on the floor and shimmied backwards into the cavity as footfalls *clonged* up the ramp.

JEREMY Tailor flinched as a bolt exploded on the opposite side of the crate he was using for cover. He prayed to the heavens that the delicate equipment inside didn't get damaged. The crates were sturdy, but their maker never intended them to provide cover against blaster fire. To Jeremy's right, Mack Houghton fired around the side of the crate he shared with Jeremy. Former military, his marksman's aim had so far taken out at least four of their enemy. Past Mack, the other four members of Jeremy's crew sheltered behind two other crates. They were all armed, but like Jeremy, they were engineers, mathematicians and doctors in varied fields and specialties—none were very skilled in armed combat or marksmanship.

Another shower of sparks flew over Jeremy's head, and he cursed silently, blaming himself for their predicament. If he hadn't crossed Harry G, his crew wouldn't be in this predicament. But his pride had made him carry his plans through, and now he and his crew of four had a galaxy-renowned warlord and an unknown number of bounty hunters on their tail.

"CLEAR THE PLATFORM. FIELD DEACTIVATION IN TEN SECONDS."

Just what I friggin' need. Someone had shot the control panel at the airlock, and the short circuit had activated the landing pad's launch sequence. In moments, the energy dome keeping out the elements would deactivate. *And these bastards're trying to keep us pinned down here until the containment field dissolves.*

"Mack! Jer!" Jeremy looked past Mack at his oldest friend and right-hand man, Roke. Roke crouched behind a crate, but he looked poised for action. "Cover me," he said. Jeremy didn't ask what Roke was up to; this was his crew, and he trusted them to know what to do as much as they trusted him and each other. Jeremy leaned out to the right of his crate and held the firing stud through three volleys before dropping back behind the crate. He hadn't hit a single combatant, but that wasn't the goal. Roke had made it to the ramp; if he could get the ship airborne, then he could provide the cover the rest of them needed to scramble aboard. *Crap! I lost count of how many seconds since ten.*

"CLEAR THE PLATFORM. FIELD DEACTIVATION IN FIVE SECONDS. SEALING ACCESSWAY."

Jeremy jerked his head around to exchange wide-eyed looks with the others. *What's that now?* "Did that just say what I think it said?" Without waiting for an answer, he peered around the crate to see the airlock door slam shut, sealing out all but two of Harry G's mercs. Mack signaled him, and Jeremy nodded. Jeremy provided cover fire while Mack popped up and lobbed a stunner. Then he dropped to the ground and covered his ears. Out of the corner of his eye, Jeremy saw the others do the same. Even with his palms clamped tightly over his ears, the shock from the grenade rattled his skull. A glance around the side of the crate revealed both mercs lying completely incapacitated on the deck. Jeremy got unsteadily to his feet and saw his men scurrying to the ramp.

"C'mon, Jer!" shouted Kit McQuinton from the ramp. Jeremy didn't need to be called twice.

"CONTAINMENT FIELD DEACTIVATING."

A howl erupted overhead, and the temperature instantly plunged below freezing as Jeremy raced up the ramp and slammed his hand on the retraction control. He felt the ship bob as it lifted off the platform, and he rushed up the narrow corridor shouting, "Get those crates! Don't leave without the crates!"

"Jer, dude, there's like no time," said Roke as Jeremy stepped onto the bridge.

"Make time! We didn't go through all that for— Know what? Retract the gear; I'll operate the winch myself." He sped out of the bridge and bounced along the corridor as the ship rocked in the heavy winds. He'd pay for the bruising tomorrow; the important thing was to get his pricey cargo aboard. The ship heaved just as Jeremy dropped into the gimbal chair that held the cargo tractor controls. Another second, and he would've been smashed against the bulkhead like a rag doll.

The comm crackled, and Roke's voice broke in. *"Jer, I'm having a hard time holding 'er steady in this storm."*

"Use the ship tractors to stabilize us," said Jeremy, his hands activating the winch and taking manual control. External cameras on the ship's hull provided him multiple views of the platform, and the transparent bulkhead afforded him a view of the inside of the hold. But with the rocking of the ship, it was almost impossible to keep it in view. He'd have to rely almost completely on the cameras. He swiveled two of the cameras until they focused on the crates, the latter now lightly dusted with sodium dioxide ice from the eruption plume streaming up from Io. He locked the cameras on auto-tracking to keep the focus on the crates through the ship's rocking. He then thrust the mag-winch arms out and latched onto the first crate. Quickly but carefully, he drew it into the ship's cargo area and into a slot. Once in place, the ship automatically secured it so it would not slip out as the ship moved. Jeremy moved on to the next one. Two to go, and they wouldn't all be as easy as the first.

As the second crate slipped into a slot in the hold, Morgan's voice broke in over comms. *"Jer, we've got company. Five bogies—correction, ten… check that. We got a lot of 'em. Kit and Jim are on weapons."*

"Gotcha," said Jeremy. "I'm just about done." He thrust the winch arms toward the final crate just as the ship juked. The arms slammed into the crate, and to Jeremy's horror, the crate sparked and skittered toward the platform's edge. Roke side-slipped the ship, bringing the mag-winch within reach of the crate just as it tipped over the side. Jeremy slammed the mags to high, and the crate teetered… then snapped up into the awaiting arms. The engines roared through the hull, and crushed Jeremy into his seat as the platform fell away into the cold dark of space.

Roke came back on the comm. *"Jer? Sorry man; they're comin' in hot. D'ja get them?"*

Struggling against the acceleration, Jeremy slipped the crate into a slot and punched the hatch controls. "I got 'em all," he said as the hold sealed. "That was a sharp maneuver there, to catch that last one."

"I did what now?"

Jeremy didn't answer. He let the acceleration press him into the seat as he thanked Lady Luck for saving him yet again. *First the airlock seals, and then the ship happens to move in just the right direction… I don't want to press my luck here, but if you're still listening, can you help us with Mr. G?*

"Jer?"

Distraction time was over. "I'm here," he said. "How're we doin'?" No, this wouldn't do. He needed to get to the bridge; not that he'd be able to do anything more than his crew was already doing, but he was blind down here and he needed to be in the midst of the activity. "Hold that. Can you give me thirty seconds?"

"Ten at best."

Jeremy loosened his seat restraints and locked the gimbal into position. "Do it!"

The moment acceleration cut out, Jeremy released the restraints and dropped to the deck. Ticking down the seconds, he ran to the bridge, past the occupied navigation and comms stations and jumped into the empty co-pilot's seat. He engaged the restraints just as Roke slammed the engines to full once again. He grunted against the sudden acceleration, wishing he'd splurged on the compensator package, but the *Stardust IV* was their experimental ship and not for investing in the creature comforts. After all, *Stardusts I* through *III* had ended up as scrap or as brilliant balls of fire, so any outlook for *Stardust IV* to escape their fate would be foolishly optimistic.

A trilling alert filled the bridge and nearly drowned the thrum of the engines. The sensor screens where Morgan Mifflin was currently seated, comms earpiece in his ear and his arms crossed defiantly against the acceleration, highlighted in glowing detail the small squadron of Cutter-class fighters that were on their tail. The small agile ships sat on the very edge of a line that demarcated their weapons' range, unmodified. But mercs often made modifications to weapons that gave them off-book abilities.

Jeremy turned his head. Behind the pilot's seat, Mack Houghton's hands crept over the nav console, fighting the pull of acceleration as he handpicked a jump destination for the navcom to lock onto.

"Dock control's throwing a fit," yelled Morgan over the din from behind Jeremy's seat.

"Screw 'em," said Roke, his eyes intent on his screens, his left hand hovering over a control entry grid while his right gripped the control yoke. Jupiter loomed large on the forward viewscreen and Roke used Jupiter's gravity to get them rapidly up to point one light speed, or cee in astro-navigation terminology. Even at 30,000 kilometers per hour, Jupiter barely seemed to get closer.

Space flashed with enemy fire. They were only at the theoretical border of effective weapon's range, but the experimental ship's shields and sinks were also not top quality. Even at this range, there was the possibility of significant damage. Roke triggered a programmed control, and an automated sequence juked and rolled the ship randomly to confuse targeting systems. "Wish we had some grapeshot cannons," Roke mumbled, just loud enough for Jeremy to hear. More loudly, he yelled, "Mack, any time now."

"Change course, down four-five degrees," called Mack. Jupiter rose until only a sliver was visible at the top of the forward screen. "Now! Punch it!"

Roke activated the FTL drive. The eodec-emitting coils whined up to full charge. Space distorted, enemy ships vanished and the trilling alert grew silent.

On the screen, Jupiter was gone, replaced by a new field of stars.

"Where are we?" asked Jeremy, experiencing a moment of panic at not seeing any planets, suns or other solar system objects.

Without turning from the navigation station, Mack said, "Short jump. Interstellar." He further mumbled as he worked, "Damn slow navi-comp. Just gimme the next damn breach-point." Roke turned in his seat to work with him.

Jeremy had never heard of an interstellar jump. As far as he knew, the breach-points which an FTL drive used to open wormholes only existed around stars. Astrophysics was more Mack's wheelhouse, but in Jeremy's basic understanding, it had to do with gravitational anomalies caused by solar masses.

"There," announced Mack. "Locked in."

"Got it," said Roke, spinning his seat back around. He confirmed the coordinates on his panel. "Prepare for maneuvers. Gonna slow burn us up to point-two-cee."

Gas jets fired to reposition the ship, then the main engines kicked in. Directional inertia increased slowly, but not enough to overwhelm the simple compensators like last time.

Morgan turned to face the direction of acceleration and to let his seat absorb the slight bit of pressure that slipped past the compensator. Before Jeremy could do the same, he saw Morgan's eyes slide right toward his panel. "What's this now?" Morgan asked rhetorically, tapping a blinking amber light on his panel. "Didn't notice it before in the rush." A window opened, showing the anomaly on-screen.

"Hmm." Jeremy stood and unclipped the blaster from his hip. "Mack, come with me. Seems we have a stowaway."

THE floor vibrated with a deep thrum that Kormèr felt deep in his chest. The structure lurched, reminding Kormèr of an earthquake that had struck the border of Vranja a year ago. He assumed the structure had toppled, since there had been a great deal of fighting going on. Then it swayed, and Kormèr was glad he was so well ensconced, or he would have slid across the floor and back. *What is happening here?*

Suddenly, Kormèr's stomach sank to his knees as a crushing force pressed on his head and shoulders. Only the wires and conduits kept him from sinking to his knees, but they were hardly a salvation as they cut into his underarms and stabbed into his thighs and back. No longer caring if anyone heard him, he cried out in pain.

He had no idea how long the force lasted, and he was just becoming aware that it had stopped when it started again. He'd managed to shift slightly, but nowhere near enough to eliminate the pain. When the spinning and lurching started, he lost all the food he'd eaten at Mernggo's party. Mercifully, his body was deeper inside the cavity than his head, so the vomit missed him completely, disappearing "down" past his feet. *Down?* Down had been to his right when he'd crawled in here.

Without warning, the spinning and lurching stopped. A deep whining followed, built to a crescendo, then crashed in a cascade that left Kormèr feeling utterly disoriented. If his stomach hadn't already been empty, he would've emptied it again. The crushing, the pain and the loud sounds had stopped. All replaced by a deep, gentle rumble.

Kormèr didn't dare to move. Besides not trusting his limbs to function properly after what he'd just been through, he reasoned that if the force returned and caught him standing in the corridor, he'd be hurled like a leaf in a gale. Part of him toyed with the idea that maybe he was in over his head on this one, and that he should open the portal and return home. He didn't like using that option, preferring to give a new location a chance. He'd had a few interesting adventures as a result. But this situation had too many factors that he didn't understand and that, frankly, seemed far outside his limited experience to even comprehend. Or maybe it was just the bruises and subsiding nausea talking.

The world lurched again, and Kormèr steeled himself for more pain. But the pressure came much more gently this time. *Thank the gods!* He breathed a sigh of relief. Whether or not he remained in this time and place, he couldn't stay in this crawlspace any longer. The corridor was clear in both directions, and the slight "downward" pressure wasn't enough to sweep him off his feet. He slipped his shoulder out from between the two conduits that had held him wedged in place—

Distant steps rang along the corridor, gradually growing louder. Kormèr cringed as four booted legs came to a stop just outside the opening. *Buomp! Now I'm really trapped!* The confined space left him no chance of opening the portal.

Two of the legs bent in a crouch, and something that resembled a weapon appeared, pointed at Kormèr. The rest of the figure loomed into view, followed by the man's bushy blonde hair and equally blonde mustache, then finally his brown eyes and small, rectangular, silver-framed glasses, onto which Kormèr locked his gaze.

The man's exclamation and wide eyes gave Kormèr the impression that they startled him to see him, but the man kept his weapon steady, thankfully. He quickly recovered, saying something else that Kormèr couldn't understand.

<<Hi,>> smiled Kormèr, displaying a calm that was barely skin deep. A friendly demeanor had gotten him out of a few scrapes in the past, so hopefully it would again.

The man appeared perplexed, his brown eyes peering curiously at Kormèr. <<Was that Elmarian?>>

Kormèr's eyes opened wide. The man had spoken Elmarian—badly accented, but Elmarian, nonetheless. <<It was. But you're not Elmarian.>>

<<No. Why don't you come out of there?>> He waved "out" with the weapon, then stood and backed up to give Kormèr room. <<It doesn't look very comfortable in there.>>

31

<<It's not,>> grunted Kormèr, gingerly detangling himself from the cables and squeezing past the pipes as he slid ungracefully back out onto the corridor floor. He stood slowly, slapping dust off his formerly white dress shirt and hoping that was all he'd gotten on it. He could still feel the places where things had jabbed into him. <<Thank you.>>

Now standing in the open, Kormèr saw both men before him, the bespectacled blonde one, and the second man, taller and burlier than the first, with a brown complexion and close-cropped black hair. Something about the way he stood, and that he was unarmed, made Kormèr think that this was someone he did not want to cross.

As he looked Kormèr over, the first man asked, <<Are you Elmarian?>> Kormèr eyed him skeptically. <<Can't you tell? Of course I am.>>

<<Alright, alright; take it easy,>> he said. <<Your accent's strange, and some of your words don't make sense.>>

<<Huh. I was just thinking the same about you.>>

The second man cleared his throat, as if to get the first man's attention.

The first man adjusted his glasses. <<Well, we'll figure all that out later. Right now, I wanna know what you're doing on my ship, and how you got in here.>>

Kormèr stared blankly. <<There, I just missed what you said. It sounded like you said 'ship'.>>

<<Yeah, shiii-pp,>> he repeated, slowly, accentuating the sounds of the word. <<You're standing in ours.>>

<<How is that...>> It didn't look or feel like any ship Kormèr knew; the walls were metal, and there was no rocking or drifting sensation to indicate movement around them. <<A ship? Really?>>

The blonde man glowered at him. <<Gimme a break, already. How'd you get in here?>>

<<The same way you did, I imagine.>> Kormèr couldn't tell them about the portal; that was his secret to keep and too dangerous to reveal. If they took it away from him, he'd be powerless to stop them, and he'd have no way to return home. He'd have to make it sound as if he'd already been there when the shooting started. <<I was trapped out there while you guys were all busy shooting at each other. So I escaped the only way I could. But when I went up the ramp, I was stuck in here with no way out.>> And now to deflect he added, <<What was the voice saying?>>

The man asked, <<What voice?>>

<<The loud one, outside.>>

The second man said something Kormèr didn't understand.

The first man frowned at Kormèr's puzzled expression. <<You don't know any *terr'n yng'lsh*?>>

<<*Terr'n* what?>>

The blonde one chuckled. <<C'mon, kid. You gotta know what *'terr'n'* is.>>

Kormèr shrugged. <<I'm afraid I don't.>>

The second man said something in the other language. The first man nodded and said something back.

Kormèr hated being in the dark. There had to be some way to get these men to talk and explain things to him. <<What are you called?>>

The first man answered. <<The name's Jeremy, Jeremy Tailor. And you?>>

<<Kormèr Lezàl.>> Kormèr didn't bother looking at the second man for a self-introduction, as he was sure there wouldn't be one forthcoming. The man just stood there, like a statue.

<<Lezàl, eh? Just like that Duke.>>

Kormèr shrugged again. *I guess?* History was never one of his passions, and he couldn't even be certain that Jeremy was speaking about Elmarian history.

<<There was a Duke on Elmar by that name, ages ago. But never mind that. Why were you on the platform? Are you with Jeez-men?>>

Platform? Jeez-men? Kormèr had no idea what Jeremy was asking of him. But he felt it was something they expected him to know, much like the enigmatic *ship*. <<No.>> There was only one way for Kormèr to get these people to trust him: lie. He sighed dramatically. <<Look, I ran away from home. I had no other place to go, so I was hiding out there, and when the fighting started, I got scared and hid in here.>> The lie sounded horrible to his own ears, but he added slumped shoulders and embarrassed averted eyes into the mix. He turned pleading eyes back on the men and asked, <<Throw me back out, or whatever. I didn't mean to cause any trouble.>>

Jeremy looked at the other man, and they conferred. He looked back at Kormèr. <<It was stupid of you to come in here, but you couldn't have known.>>

<<Known what?>> He didn't like the sound of this. The hair on his neck prickled uncomfortably.

<<We're on our way out of the Sol System and won't be returning for a long time. You won't see your parents for a while, unless you grab a ship at our next port of call.>>

<<I don't understand,>> Kormèr said honestly. <<What do you mean 'on our way out of the *sol system*'?>>

Jeremy looked at Kormèr over the edge of his glasses. <<How could you've been on Io without...?>> He grunted, then slipped his weapon into its holster as he mumbled something to the other man. To Kormèr he said, <<Follow me.>> Then he walked off.

The second man didn't move at first, waiting and watching Kormèr carefully. Kormèr looked away from that withering stare and focused on Jeremy instead. He followed Jeremy through the rest of the corridor, with the other man following him, past windowless walls and latched compartments. They stopped in a spacious area whose dominant feature was a rectangular table bracketed by bench seats. The wall to the right consisted of more storage compartments of varying sizes, all securely latched closed. In contrast, the far wall had items that vaguely reminded

Kormèr of food preparation, like serving implements and bowls, also contained behind clear walls. <<Just sit yourself down here and relax,>> said Jeremy.

Kormèr complied, dropping onto a bench, noting as he did that the seat and table were both bolted to the floor. Jeremy sat across the table from Kormèr, but the other man simply leaned, hip-shot, against the wall, as relaxed as a coiled spring.

Jeremy stared at the tabletop where one of his hands tapped a quiet beat, his brow knit. Finally, he looked up at Kormèr, and there was nothing but concern in his eyes. <<Kid, I don't know how to put this delicately… Was everything okay at home? With your folks?>>

Kormèr quickly replayed their conversation in his head, wondering at the intent behind the question. *Oh. Oh! He must think my parents are abusive or something. Oops.* <<No. It's nothing like that.>> Kormèr thought of Trinket. <<It's the opposite. You know: overprotective, always hovering about making sure I don't get involved in anything bad. I'm three and a half now! I need my space.>> Kormèr stopped himself before he could say anything that spoiled the narrative.

Jeremy was silent a moment, his fingers tapping a faster beat before stopping abruptly. <<We're having a little trouble communicating here; I'm still only catching two thirds of what you're saying. So what we're gonna do is teach you a language called *terr'n yng'lsh*. It's my favorite, and we'll be able to talk to each other easily. Okay?>>

Kormèr thought about that. He enjoyed learning alien languages. Besides, who knew when it would come in handy during his travels? And it would be a break in this conversation, which had the potential to spiral away from him. <<Won't that take a long time?>>

<<Not at all.>> Jeremy did something that caused a portion of the table top to light up like a computer screen, much like similar displays back on Elmar. <<With this little *gizmo* and your subconscious brain, we could have you speaking three additional languages within a week.>>

<<What's a *giz-mo*?>>

<<You know, a gizmo,>> he repeated, as if repeating the unknown word made its meaning clearer. <<It's an *urth* term meaning— Never mind. You'll find out. Now, just relax.>> He stood, opened one of the wall compartments, and extracted a black circlet. He adjusted it as he walked around to stand beside Kormèr. <<Okay, I'm going to put this on your head—>>

Kormèr cringed away suspiciously. <<Hold on! What's that going to do?>>

<<It just sits your head and makes it easier for the computer to work with you, to teach you the language. It won't hurt. I'd let you do it yourself, but it's got to be placed right, or it won't work.>>

Kormèr nodded but remained tense, as Jeremy moved to situate the circlet on his head. Kormèr looked over to the looming, sullen, brown-skinned man for some reassurance that his brain wouldn't liquefy, but there was no change in the man's expression. *Big help you are.*

Jeremy had to push aside some loose strands of Kormèr's hair, but finally seemed satisfied with the fit. <<And now we activate the learning program.>>

That was the last thing Kormèr heard, as everything closed in around him. Had he known that it would place him in a trance, he would have immediately torn the circlet off and tried every possible way to escape from this... this *ship*. But he never even had a chance to react, before he was insensate.

"HAND me the d-scan," said Jeremy, as Kormèr slumped forward. Jeremy caught the kid before he face-planted onto the galley table, and he eased him back upright.

Mack complied, disappearing momentarily, then returning with a palm-sized gadget. Jeremy flicked the scanner on and swept it over the boy's body twice, checking its high-resolution display. "He's clean. No bombs, bugs or tracers." He shook his head. "I don't get it."

Mack grunted. "I don't think he's one of G's men. Never known G to hire someone so young. The kid's tall, but I bet he's gotta be 'round fourteen."

Jeremy studied the boy's face and hands. "The years on Elmar are long; it's like four to one Earth. Might be he's three and a half, like he said. But you're probably right about him not being one of G's. Still, I'm not buying that runaway story, although it'd explain what he was doing on the pad."

"That was a good ploy, there, playing the child abuse angle."

Jeremy scratched his mustache where a stray hair was tickling his nose. "Not really a ploy, buddy. I take that kinda thing seriously, and he sounded too much like a kid in trouble. It's when he changed his story that I knew he was lying all around: the obviously fake name he stole from that duke, running away from drone-parents..." Jeremy shook his head. "What bugs me is: why bother playing dumb, like he's never heard 'Terran' or 'Earth' before?"

"It could be the language barrier," offered Mack. "Not knowing Elmarian, I couldn't read him outside of his body language."

"What'd that tell you?"

Mack shrugged. "He's a good liar. Without knowing what he was sayin', I'd guess he was lying maybe twenty percent of the time."

"That's all, huh?" Jeremy's gaze grew distant. *What a weird kid. If he's not G's, who the hell is he?* And then he thought, *And what the hell am I supposed to do with him now?* "Well, we're stuck with him for the time being. We gotta keep an eye on him. I especially don't want him near any comm panels. If he *is* with G, the last thing we need is word getting back about our heading."

Mack nodded. "We could put him on ice."

Jeremy frowned. "I'd rather not put him in stasis. I don't know what it does to Elmarian physiology." He peered over his glasses at Mack. "That is, if he's really Elmarian. What's your impression?"

"He talks and acts like an Elmarian," Mack said. "When you asked him, his indignation sounded pretty genuine."

"Yeah, he's got some attitude, doesn't he?" Jeremy muttered. "When he wakes up, we'll see if he's got the smarts to justify it. Until we know his story, get the word out to the crew: no one says a word about our destination."

"You got it," Mack nodded. "Our lips are sealed."

"I know yours are. Just make sure the others are aware. I think I can handle things from here," he said, looking at Kormèr's unconscious figure. "Oh, and I'll need everyone in here for a planning session in fifteen minutes." He noticed Mack's surreptitious glance at Kormèr. Jeremy picked up Kormèr's limp hand and dropped it, catching it with his free hand. "The kid's gonna be out for a while."

"Okay. See you in fifteen." Mack grabbed an apple from the food dispenser niche in the bulkhead, took a bite, and, munching, strode off to the bridge.

Jeremy looked the boy over. The tailored black jacket and slacks, the white dress shirt, the large platinum ring with what the d-scanner identified as a blue diamond. Jeremy didn't know what passed for fashion on Elmar these days, but on Earth, these kinds of styles cycled every few decades, and always among the wealthy, as few others cared or had enough money to spare for fancy clothes. Plus, the party clothes didn't fit the kid's narrative; Io station had been the customer-facing end of the Adelco-Zastra Mining Corporation, or A-to-Z, as it was more commonly known. When A-to-Z abandoned the extremely high-risk, low-profit operation, they leased the station's landing platforms and meeting rooms to anyone willing to pay. More often than not, their customers were freelancers, pirates and mobsters: not any place where you'd find a wealthy family. Not for long anyway, and certainly not a kid.

Jeremy shrugged and went through Kormèr's pockets. The jacket's breast pocket contained a deck of cards that Jeremy recognized as pertaining to an Elmarian game called *Jgal*. In the slacks pockets were an old Elmarian credit stick and a crystal cube with one blackened face. Jeremy analyzed the cube with the d-scanner, but if there was some hidden purpose to the crystal, the scanner didn't find it. As long as it wasn't a tracker, weapon, or communication device of any kind, it didn't matter to Jeremy.

He replaced everything as it had been, then returned to his side of the table and waited for the others to arrive. It would be another hour before the Terran English language lesson ended. Plenty of time to think about the next steps.

KORMÈR was sure he dreamed, though he couldn't remember of what once he awoke. Images and sounds flitted at the edges of his thoughts but eluded his clumsy, groggy attempts to focus on them. Eyes still closed, he focused instead on his breathing, a technique that calmed his mind. As his head cleared, the sounds became words, words he had heard but that had made no sense when he'd heard them: *Terran English, Earth, gizmo… Okay, that one's still weird, just like the word "okay".* The cacophonous warning alert on the landing pad on Io made sense now, and he envisioned Io as a splotchy orange, yellow, and black moon with an orbiting station.

"How do you feel?" asked Jeremy.

Kormèr's eyes snapped open. His head was on the galley table. He sat up, removed the circlet from his head, and rubbed the itchy spots where it had been wedged against his forehead. "You didn't say this thing would put me to sleep—" His jaw dropped, his annoyance replaced by amazement. He was speaking fluent Terran English! He could hardly believe it was true. It flowed so easily from his lips; he could even think in it! "This is incredible!"

"Isn't it?" asked Jeremy, grinning.

Kormèr's wide eyes were taking in his surroundings. "So *this* is what you meant by 'ship'. And we're flying through space?"

"Not flying, exactly. So, is this really your first time on a space-faring ship?"

"Yeah," Kormèr answered unthinkingly. "There aren't any on my planet."

Jeremy curled his lips. "Sure there are. It's not the most popular of places, but I've been there. Once."

Kormèr opened his mouth to protest, but the words died before he could even think them. A cascade of various clues fell into place, and Kormèr realized he must have traveled forward in time through his portal. In this time, his home world was probably on the galactic trade routes. *Galactic trade routes! So many new concepts! What must it be like on Elmar now?* he wondered. *Am I still alive there?* It was a pointless question, of course, since he didn't know how far forward he'd traveled. And there was no way he could trust Jeremy with the knowledge of the portal cube, so he'd have to wait until he could find an AI terminal. For now, he simply played along with his runaway story. "I haven't been there in a long time."

"Still, you… Ugh. Never mind. Are you hungry?"

Kormèr noticed the other man was no longer around. He relaxed and thought of his delicious dinner awaiting him somewhere within the walls of the ship. "A little." His stomach squelched hungrily at the thought of food, but his head hadn't fully settled from his earlier dizziness. Rather than eat, what he really wanted to do was to explore this amazing ship! "But can I see the bridge?"

"Later. Fill your tank up first."

Kormèr watched as Jeremy prepared some food, pulling ingredients and utensils from various wall compartments to assemble a dish that made Kormèr's mouth water in anticipation. Peering around Jeremy, he could now attach names to various things that he hadn't recognized before. *Amazing!* He turned the circlet with his index finger on the table. *If only I'd had this language machine before. It would've made my travels so much easier.*

The word "hamburger" came to mind as Jeremy set a plate down in front of him. He knew what bread and cheese were, but he'd never thought they would go so well with a browned piece of meat, but the savory aroma convinced him to try it. A contented "Mmm" escaped his manners as he munched on a big, warm, juicy bite.

Jeremy took a seat again. "Glad you like it. Ready to answer some questions?"

Kormèr nodded, swallowed. "I have some of my own."

"Good. I'll go first. You're not really a runaway, are you?"

Kormèr grinned sheepishly. "Well, not in the way I told you, no."

Jeremy stared at him a moment longer. "Care to elaborate?"

Kormèr watched Jeremy's face as he said, "Not at this time." Jeremy's stare grew intense for a moment, then his brow knit briefly. Kormèr had no basis on which to interpret these expressions; he'd learned that facial expressions could be cultural, and one thing could mean something entirely different somewhere else, even on the same planet.

Finally, Jeremy sighed. "That... that sorta puts me in a bind. I could get into a lot of trouble for taking you from Io."

"But you didn't know I was aboard until you left."

He shook his head. "But when I found out, I didn't take you back."

Kormèr was about to take another bite, but stopped. "Why don't you?"

"Because I can't go back."

"Because of *Jeez-men*?" Kormèr still had no idea what the word meant, but he'd gathered it wasn't something Jeremy was happy about.

Jeremy's frown deepened. "That's right. What do you know about them?"

Kormèr shrugged. "Only that you mentioned the word before. Ah, wait! The men who were shooting at you; are they *Jeez-men*?"

Jeremy stifled a chuckle. "It's 'G' as in the alphabetical letter. He's a Terran man," he said, a little begrudgingly, "and those were his mercs." *Mercenaries* filled in Kormèr's new language reference.

"Ah. Well, if it helps any, no one will be looking for me."

"What about your parents?"

Kormèr shook his head. "They're dead." He realized that was the first time he'd ever said that aloud, and it reignited a spark of pain to remember that he was essentially alone. While he had Yunzen's sister and her children as family, they were not *his* immediate family; they were not the ones he'd readily think of to go to for advice or consolation or protection. And yes, he had the bots for most of those along with his day-to-day needs, but it just wasn't the same. They were *like* family. After all, they'd been there all his life, and they'd been his guardians since Yunzen's death. But Kormèr regarded them as he did his aunt. They were all beings that cared for him, would be there for him if he needed them, just as he would be there for them. But in the end, they didn't *love* him, and he knew that he didn't love them either. His love was reserved for one person in his life, and that one person was gone. And here he was, floating in a metal bubble, a teeny grain in a universe that grew larger with each of his adventures. With not a single being in all that space that loved him.

Kormèr finished the burger, then realized it had gotten quiet. He looked up at Jeremy and found the man watching him quietly. Kormèr wiped his greasy mouth and fingertips with a napkin. He paid extra attention to his fingernails; he abhorred touching food with his hands and finding crumbs or stains lodged underneath his nails afterwards.

Finally Jeremy said, "That was either some actual truth, or you're one hell of an actor."

Kormèr looked at him uncertainly. "I didn't say anything, except that my parents are dead."

"It's not just the words, it's also how you said them," Jeremy said. "It's not something you talk about much, I guess."

Kormèr threw the napkin on the table, stood, and stomped to where he had seen Jeremy clean his hands. Kormèr looked for controls, but there weren't any. Then the instruction trickled into his mind to hold his hands under a sensor of some sort, and he watched in awe as gentle massaging waves seemed to vibrate the dirt from his hands. When he felt he could talk without yelling—or bawling—he said, "Believe me or not, I don't care." He turned to face Jeremy. "It's my turn now."

"What? Your turn for what?"

"To ask a question." Kormèr sat back down. "You're not Elmarian, but you could almost pass for one. What planet are you from?"

"Earth."

"That's the name?" Kormèr asked incredulously, and Jeremy nodded. "Doesn't that also mean 'soil'?"

Jeremy made a sour grin. "Depends on the context. That's why it's listed in the GF charter as 'Terra'."

"Ah. What's the 'GF'?" Kormèr waited a few seconds for his mind to parse through the knowledge that he had recently gained. "The Galactic Federation?"

"Yep, you got it," Jeremy smiled. "You're pretty quick. Okay, let's take this from the top: how'd you get here from Elmar?"

Buomp! This guy is persistent! "I can't tell you," he said, stressing each word.

"Can't or won't?"

"In this case, it's the same thing."

Jeremy's nostrils flared, his lips tight and his eyes boring into Kormèr's. But Kormèr didn't flinch. He'd faced off with an army of warriors on Jordinni. This was just some average guy, and while he had a blaster, Kormèr didn't believe he'd use it.

"You know what?" Jeremy threw up his hands. "Whatever. If you ever want to tell me the truth, you know where to find me. I just have two rules for you: don't walk around the ship unescorted; and don't cause trouble. You understand?" Kormèr nodded; it was a victory; there was no need to push the guy any further. "They're two simple rules to follow; you break 'em and I will toss you out an airlock. I've got enough to deal with right now."

He quickly switched topics, realizing that he really didn't know whether he was with the bad guys or the good guys of the conflict he had stumbled into. "Why were you fighting those men?"

Jeremy shook his head. "Trust is a two-way street, kid. You can't trust me with your entire story; I can't do the same for you with mine."

Kormèr tipped his head, acknowledging the impasse. "Fair enough."

Jeremy stared at him, and Kormèr filled the awkward silence by nodding again. Then Jeremy seemed to reach a decision. "Alright." He drummed his fingers on the tabletop. "Wanna see the bridge?"

Kormèr's eyes went wide. "Yeah!"

Now that he knew what a ship was, Kormèr wanted nothing more than to see it all, to understand how it worked. None of the planets he'd portaled to so far had exhibited the level of technology needed to travel through space. At best, one had had air-bound vehicles that ferried the inhabitants between their continents.

As Jeremy directed him along the corridor, Kormèr thought of Jeremy's telling him that ships would visit Elmar in the future. He felt a jealous pang at knowing that Jeremy had seen Elmar's future, and that it seemed to be more exciting than Kormèr had even considered possible. *But I was never curious about Elmar's future before,* he admitted to himself. Part of the reason was that he found Elmar fairly dull; he'd studied the history, the various cultures, even the planetary science. None of it held a flame to the things he'd seen and learned so far in his portal-travels. The other part of the reason was… he had been afraid to find out some catastrophic event loomed on the horizon. If he'd discovered such a thing, he would have felt compelled to intervene to prevent it. He didn't want that responsibility, didn't want to know where life would take him. He just wanted to enjoy living it.

Kormèr stopped in the bridge hatchway, his eyes wide as they swept over panel after panel of screens and controls. But what truly left him riveted in place was the star-speckled black of space that filled the main screen from border to border. "*Mràn hanjlal yren!*"

"Huh?… Oh, yeah. It is pretty extraordinary. Let's stick to English though. Not all the guys understand Elmarian."

"Sorry. But this is… I had never even imagined that I'd see space from within… uh, from…" He couldn't think of a verbal concept to describe what he wanted to say, even with his newly expanded vocabulary, so he simply ended with, "Wow."

Looking across the bridge at the intricate instrumentation, he wondered how one piloted a craft like this. He understood what navigation was, from the point of view of driving a land vehicle like a hovecar or a brougham, or a sailing vessel. But how one navigated in space was beyond him. As Jeremy stepped around from behind him and sat in the only unoccupied seat, Kormèr mumbled, "What I wouldn't give to learn to fly this."

A chuckle rolled through the cabin, alerting Kormèr that there were three other people present. "That so?" said the man, who appeared to be the current pilot. At first, all Kormèr could see were locks of blonde hair that reached a third of the way down the back of the seat in which the man sat. Then the seat spun around and revealed its burly occupant. Pale green eyes shifted into gray, as mirth colored his high, blonde-bearded cheeks. His smile was genuinely jovial, as he extended his right hand toward Kormèr and said, "So, our stowaway's finally up and about. The name's Roke."

Unsure what the man expected of him, Kormèr extended his own hand and said, "I'm Kormèr Lezàl."

Roke grasped his hand and gave it a firm up-and-down shake. "Whoa. Downright powerful name, dude. Hey, Jer', he belongs with us for sure."

Jeremy nodded, but said nothing.

"Kormèr. I'm Mack Houghton," said the man who had accompanied Jeremy and stood guard earlier. Kormèr still felt as if Mack's brown eyes were staring into his brain. Now that things were more relaxed, Kormèr noticed that Mack's face was bristly, as if he hadn't shaved for a couple of days.

"Hi, Mack," said Kormèr. He pointed at the panel behind Mack. "What's that do?"

Mack's eyes flicked to Jeremy so fast that Kormèr almost missed it. "Navigation," he said, without further elaboration.

"Umm. Okay."

Kormèr turned at a chuckle from his right. "You won't get much outta Mack if he doesn't trust you," said the last unfamiliar face. He had a device in his left ear. "I'm the comm officer," he explained, catching Kormèr staring at the device. "Morgan Mifflin, at your service." Morgan had jet-black hair just like Mack, but a lighter complexion. While Mack and Roke both had athletic builds, Morgan was slimmer, with long and agile-looking fingers that looked as if they were used to zipping over keyboards and controls.

"I'm pleased to meet you all," said Kormèr. "Weren't there more of you?" he asked tactlessly, remembering that there had been six men on his side of the crates during the firefight earlier. He realized belatedly that he was perhaps treading on a delicate subject. If two had died…

"The others are on sleep shift," said Jeremy. "You'll meet them later."

Kormèr was relieved. "Oh, good."

"So, what were you doing on our ship?" asked Roke, with a glance at Jeremy.

"Honestly, I was just trying to get away from the gunfight."

Morgan wrinkled his brow. "But that doesn't really—"

"Let it go, Mo," said Jeremy. "The kid's not ready to tell." Jeremy settled back in his seat and crossed his legs. "But we have an understanding. Isn't that right?"

Kormèr nodded. "Follow the two rules, or I'm out the airlock." He watched the men as he said this, trying to understand the various reactions—except for Mack, who was still just watching him. But he still had no context for their Terran expressions. On Elmar, Roke's would be a sign of disagreement with Jeremy while Morgan seemed to stifle a laugh; but that couldn't be right. Kormèr decided to change the subject.

"This is my first time…" He caught himself before he could say "on a ship", which would probably have gotten Jeremy started all over again with his annoying questioning. Instead, he finished with, "…on the bridge of a ship." He turned back

41

to the main screen. The stars were still there, seemingly unchanged. "Are we even moving?"

"Point two light speed," said Roke. Kormèr knew the speed of light, and he guessed that point two was probably two-tenths that, or sixty thousand kilometers per second. He couldn't believe that a ship could actually travel that fast, and he was inside it! "But space is real big, man. If you pick a star and watch it, you'll see we're moving."

As soon as Roke said that, Kormèr watched a pair of stars slide off the edge of the screen. "Whoa! Where are we going?"

Roke's eyes flashed to Jeremy. "Ahh…"

Jeremy said: "To your new quarters. We've got a long trip ahead of us, and these guys have to get back to work. Come on, I'll show you where you'll be staying."

Kormèr let his disappointment show with a grimace, but he obediently shuffled his feet back down the corridor. As he passed his earlier hiding spot, his body aches overwhelmed his dwindling adrenaline. He was tired. After all, he hadn't had any *proper* sleep—as opposed to the computer-induced sleep during the English lesson—since the morning of the party. He checked his chrono: it was near midnight, Elmar time. That wasn't actually very late for him on a normal day, but this day had been far from normal.

The party at Mernggo's would be in full swing now. Rass is probably having a great time, with the ladies all to himself. While he knew he was having a more… interesting time than Devron, Kormèr still felt as though he was missing out on something. He shrugged to himself, thinking, *I could just return to the party, like I was never gone.*

Along the way, Jeremy pointed out a hatch and called it a *head*, but his voice sounded dull and distant.

Kormèr's quarters turned out to be a section of the ship's cargo hold. They made an ad hoc bed for him amidst the crates he had first seen back on Io. Each bore scorch marks and scars on one side. "What's in these things that those men wanted so badly?" he asked, hazarding a guess at what G's men were after.

Jeremy didn't answer right away. "Something that many people are going to wish had never been invented."

Kormèr decided not to press the issue any further. More so since, the moment he lay down, he was fast asleep.

JEREMY watched Kormèr for a few minutes, his own mind working through all the data it had absorbed today. And as if he didn't have enough to worry about, now he had this mysterious boy to deal with. What did the kid's presence mean to the crew and their business?

Enemy or bystander? Would G stoop to using children if it suited him? But Jeremy had no answers. He didn't know Harry G very well— Well, everyone knew *of* Harry G. The man was one of the wealthiest entrepreneurs of the Sol system. His face was always in the media, always surrounded by a cadre of bodyguards. He was cunning, shrewd, and merciless. The rumor went that, if you fell into Harry G's cross-hairs, you either ended up wealthy or you ended up dead, presumably financially. His was a close-knit world of business contacts and partners. Only a very select few knew Harry G socially.

Jeremy and his group of engineers and scientists had fallen into Harry G's cross-hairs nearly a year ago. Things had started out peaceably, with requests for demonstrations, offers of backing... And the offers had been very tempting. But Jeremy and his team already had a buyer lined up on Mars, and so they'd politely declined Harry G's requests. That's when they found out that the rumored "death" for disappointing Harry G wasn't metaphorical: it was a very literal interpretation. Luck had intervened that day, and they had discovered in time a software hack that had been installed to cause the ship's power core to self-destruct upon engaging the FTL drive. Io had been nothing but a setup; G's goons had waited until the crates were unloaded, then tried to take the platform. Jeremy's gut told him someone had jumped the gun. Had Jeremy and the crew been split up between watching the cargo and attending a meeting, G's plot might have succeeded.

And now, here they were. It had taken only two attempts on their lives to make Jeremy and his crew get to where they couldn't even trust a teenager. He hated the feeling, but there was nothing he could do about it. Only time would tell. With three weeks of travel to go until they reached their destination, Jeremy wasn't taking any chances. He stepped quietly out of the hold, sealed the door, and locked it.

Chapter 4

KORMÈR awoke in complete darkness. He rolled onto his side and started, as lights immediately came on. Crates and metal walls surrounded him. *Hmm, it wasn't a dream.*

Kormèr sat up and stretched, his eyes roving around the spacious cargo hold. Six cargo crates had kept him company overnight: four occupying eight of the framed niches set into the hold's walls, and two on the floor. His bedding occupied an empty niche nestled between two stacked crates and an inner wall. He reached out to touch the crates; they were of an odd material that appeared to be a plastic alloy. They were cold and smooth and felt like ceramic, but the scoring from weapons fire revealed a tough, fibrous interior. It thrilled him to discover that, in addition to being able to speak Terran English, he could now also read it. Worn embossed lettering on the metal frames that formed the niches read: MAGNELOCK.

He had kicked off his blanket while he slept, and the cold dry air had penetrated his clothes and chilled him to the bone. He stood and stretched again, this time working his lateral muscles, then bending forward to touch his toes, jogging in place, anything to warm himself up. All the while, he casually scanned the hold, noticing the placement of hatches, compartments, and control surfaces. He tried to pick out audio-video devices, but the technology here was much more advanced than anything he was familiar with. Curious, he spent the next ten minutes browsing nearly every compartment he could reach; some were high up in the walls, and he wondered how anyone ever reached them. Most compartments contained tools or spare parts; others contained things he couldn't identify. Finding nothing of any real interest—or value—he walked to the hatch through which he'd entered. A glossy control surface beside the door remained dark and dormant, even at his touch. He tapped on the door, and the sound told him it was quite solid.

Bored and tired of wearing his formal attire, Kormèr sighed and opened the portal, holding a mental image of his bedroom as did so. He paused before stepping through and amended his mental command to the portal with: *Home, the same night I left.* It wouldn't do to show up days or even years later or earlier. Then he stepped through.

As the familiar sights and smells hit him, a tension that he hadn't noticed before melted away. While he enjoyed the adventure that traveling to different times and places provided, there was no greater feeling than being home.

He turned and stared at the portal. If he closed it now, there was a very high probability that he'd never get it to reopen to the exact place and moment in time. Kormèr had learned that getting the portal to open to very specific places and times often failed to work, regardless of the mental effort he put into the command. Experience told him that this would likely be one of those times. Leaving it open risked one of the crew members walking into the hold and finding it. This would lead to many questions that Kormèr did not want to answer. Despite the risk, however, he left it open and just rush through the tasks he wanted to accomplish.

The door opened, and Trinket whirred into his room.

<<Kormèr! I thought you were at the—>> He stopped spotting the open portal. <<Oh, I see. Did Devron leave you stranded?>>

<<No, nothing like that. There was this kid…>> Kormèr stopped and waved his hand. <<How long have I been out?>>

<<You and Devron left three hours ago. Where have you been, if not at the party?>>

<<I'll tell you about that later. First, I've learned a most incredible language.>>

<<Another?>>

<<Yes. English, Terran English.>>

Trinket was oddly silent for a moment. Then he said, <<Say something in it.>>

"Something in it. How's that?"

<<Curious,>> responded the bot. <<Where did you learn this?>>

Kormèr considered telling Trinket the story, but it would take time, and he didn't want to leave the portal linked to the ship for too long. <<Well, I don't have time to tell you right now, but I promise I'll tell you all about it soon. Right now, I'm eager for a quick hot shower.>>

<<Should I ready the water for you?>>

Kormèr walked to his dresser and grabbed some clean clothes. <<Actually, for the sake of time, sure. That would be very helpful, thanks.>>

Kormèr timed his shower by singing to himself a song that was exactly three minutes long. Three minutes and ten seconds later, Kormèr emerged from the bathroom, towel-drying his hair. He tossed the towel aside, which Trinket quickly picked up, and he slipped into a pair of wide-legged black trousers and a low-buttoned black shirt. Next, he reached for his coat, which was still hanging on his bed, and slipped it on, content to be wrapped in the warm familiar cloth.

<<I have to go,>> he said to Trinket, when he was ready. <<I'll be back soon.>>

<<Please be careful,>> said Trinket as Kormèr stepped back onto the ship.

<<I will,>> he said into the portal, knowing that Trinket could still hear him on the other side.

He almost closed the portal, but stopped himself. He recalled that Jeremy had mentioned something about the crew taking shifts. This gave him room to work, as long as he didn't run into anyone. He focused on the portal, thought of the lounge-kitchen area where he'd received his English lesson, and stepped through.

The galley was dark, save for a light over the sonic sink and some small status lights on various cabinets and gadgets. The corridor lights had also been dimmed. Kormèr sealed the portal and dropped the cube into his coat pocket. He then took the circlet—which he now knew was called an edu-comp headset—from its storage compartment and placed it on his head, trying to recall how Jeremy had fitted it on his skull. *Really, what's the worst that could happen?*

He sat at the table and tried to remember how Jeremy had operated the table-top computer. The screen lit up at his touch, and he was pleasantly surprised to find that the edu-comp program was still open. It took him a few tries to find the right menu, but the friendly user interface made it easy.

He was overjoyed to find that the machine taught not only languages, but various other subjects as well. He deciphered how to select a learning program of multiple lessons and prepared one comprising an expedited course in starship technology, starship piloting and another language called Spanish, just because it sounded like 'spinach', which he had just learned was a Terran word for a kind of leafy green vegetable. *What language would spinach speak, if not Spanish?* he thought with a chuckle.

Kormèr stared at the screen for a moment, trying to remember if he'd seen Jeremy do anything else, but he couldn't remember. He shrugged, rested his head on his arm on the tabletop, hit the activate key and—

SILENCE reigned on the bridge as Jim Blake monitored his navigation screen, waiting for the nav-com to notify him of any necessary course corrections. On the screen, a blue arc traced the path which Mack had set twelve hours earlier and which the *Stardust IV* had been following since. Only a touch of green remained to the arc, just ahead of the dot that represented the ship. At the end of the green sat their jump point.

Jim bristled at this ancient hunk of scrap yard tech; modern nav-coms were integrated into the piloting controls, making the adjustments instantly and with a precision that would have seemed like magic compared to the nav-com they currently had. But, considering that the *Stardust IV* had been assembled eighty years ago; they were lucky it even held air.

"One minute to jump," Jim announced, his dark eyes on the counter. To his right, Kit McQuinton turned around in the pilot's seat, his hazel eyes locked on the screen. Everyone was on edge since the micro-jump that had dumped them into interstellar space. While Mack had done so intentionally, it had been a risky maneuver; with nowhere near the training that Mack had, Jim knew he would never have tried it. They were very lucky that Mack had located a jump point only twelve hours away. It could easily have been days, months, or even years away.

And they only had enough resources aboard to sustain them for a couple of months, at best.

Once again, Mack's skill left Jim in awe. "No corrections required."

"Nice!" said Kit, turning back and waiting for the signal to engage the FTL drive.

"Jump in five... four... three... two... and... jump." Jim looked up at the screen and watched as space curved in on itself, formed a mind-bending sphere with a distorted view of their destination in the center and concentric rings of the same around the edges. With a flash of disorientation, they transited into the distortion.

Kit tipped his seat back and grabbed his metal-string guitar from where he'd left it, resting on the vacant co-pilot's seat. "Two hours in the tube," he said, then strummed a slow, wistful tune.

"Keep it lively," mumbled Morgan. He'd been napping in his seat, and Jim had almost forgotten he was there.

"Top o' the morning to ya, Mifflin," Kit grinned, switching to something a bit faster, his bright red curls bouncing in time with his picking.

"That's it," said Morgan, his legs stretched out, arms crossed and eyes still closed. Then he sang, familiar with the tune, an old sea shanty from centuries ago. Jim admired Morgan's voice. Even groggy, and not even really trying, he still crooned the best velvet sound Jim had ever heard, whether he was singing soaring arias or folk songs.

When he stopped, Jim said, "Now if I'd known we were going to ensemble, I wouldda brought my bass."

"We shouldn't get too loud, though," said Kit, a hint of old country brogue coloring his words. "Don't want to wake the others."

Morgan's eyes opened. "Speaking of that, that kid sure sleeps a lot. What'd he say his name was again? Corner... Lazar?"

Jim answered, "Jeremy said it was 'Kormèr' or something like that. He's Elmarian."

"With a name like that, I don't doubt it," Morgan said.

"D'ya honestly think he's still asleep?" asked Kit, switching back to low chord combinations. "I know teens can sleep, but nearly twelve hours?"

"You wouldn't ask that, if you've ever lived with one," grinned Morgan. "He's probably looking around the hold." Morgan could easily have checked the hold cameras, but he didn't seem motivated to do more than speculate.

"For what?" asked Jim.

"A way out, maybe," suggested Kit, playing a series of single notes followed by more chords. He seemed to be trying a new riff. "I'm sure he's already figured out the door's locked. What would you do in his position?"

"Look for a way out, too," shrugged Morgan. Kit aped his shrug and returned to his riff.

"He doesn't seem like a bad kid," said Morgan. "Definitely not one of G's men."

"You're thinking we should let him out?" asked Jim.

"We could. Accompanied, of course, but yeah. We have the time to watch over him," Morgan said, seeming to talk himself into the idea. "Hell, Averia's not for another few days. We can't just leave him locked up like a prisoner till we arrive."

"It's on your heads, boys," sighed Kit, not looking up.

Morgan stood and stretched. "You with me, Jim?"

Jim toyed with the idea momentarily. "Yeah, why not?" He stood and followed Morgan out of the bridge. "Be back soon, Kit."

Kit nodded. "Shout, if there's trouble."

"Right."

"Mackey thinks there's something off about this kid," explained Morgan, as the two rounded the corridor and past the darkened galley and communal lounge area.

"Oh, yeah?" Jim grinned. "Not really surprising, coming from him: Mack thinks there's something off about everybody."

"True, but it seems that this kid didn't know English, just some old form of Elmarian, according to Jeremy. And the way he was dressed, like he'd just come from a party. He didn't know what a ship was, either."

"Uh, huh," Jim said skeptically. "How'd he get on Io Station, then?"

"He won't say."

"Are you sure we should be lettin' him out?" asked Jim, but he didn't stop walking. The two neared the rear bulkhead where double-doors slid open at their approach, and beyond which was the cargo hold door.

"Yeah, it'll be fine. He's just a kid."

They stepped into the airlock and unlocked and opened the hold doors. The lights came on at their entrance, as the lights automatically deactivated after ten minutes of inactivity. But Morgan and Jim exchanged a puzzled glance, at seeing that the bed set out for the stowaway was empty. Unless the kid had wandered off and fallen asleep somewhere else...

"Kormèr," called Jim, unable to believe that the kid had somehow escaped. He even peeked under the makeshift bed, to be sure. It just wasn't possible! Besides, where would he go? The only other exit was the main hatch into space.

"Kormèr!" yelled Morgan, looking up and around at the crates and slots.

Jim did the same, half-expecting to find the kid hanging from a Magnelock frame above. Morgan tapped Jim's shoulder and gestured for him to circle around the crates on the floor to the right. Jim nodded, drew his weapon, and both men started off in opposite directions. But the kid wasn't hiding behind the crates. Next, they checked the larger of the storage compartments, and even some of the smaller ones.

Finally, Jim announced: "He's not here."

"Is it my imagination or were the doors locked?" Morgan creased his brow in worried confusion.

"They were locked. He's got to be here somewhere." Jim paused. "Let's scan the ship."

Kit looked up as the two men returned to the bridge. "Change your minds?"

"Not exactly," said Jim, and explained what they'd found, as Morgan sat at his station and initiated a life-signs scan. The scan revealed the six blips of the crew and a seventh in the ship's galley. Morgan looked at Jim, his lips curled in disbelief. "Are you kidding me? We passed by him at least twice."

"I'll be here," said Kit, as Morgan and Jim hurried back out into the corridor.

When the galley lights flickered on, the two men discovered the kid hooked up to the edu-comp, the display showing a list of tutorials currently running.

"Can you believe this?" Morgan paced behind the seated youth.

"It was dark," shrugged Jim, dropping into a seat across from the boy. "And look, he's changed his clothes; he's in black. We just didn't see him."

Morgan stopped pacing and looked the boy over. "Hey, he *did* change his clothes." Jim nodded. "Dude, he had nothing with him when we found him. Where the hell did he get a change of clothes?"

Jim shrugged. "The kid's full of surprises, Morg. I mean, how'd he even get out of the hold?"

The edu-comp tutorials couldn't be interrupted once begun, so Jim reported to Kit that all was okay, and then both men waited for the boy to awaken. With the last tutorial already two-thirds complete, the two didn't have to wait long before Kormèr woke up.

KORMÈR blinked several times at the surrounding brightness. He had anticipated being discovered, so the faces that came into focus once his eyes adjusted were not a surprise. "Hi," he said, stretching. He felt his mind cluttered with new information, and it occurred to him that there might be a limit to how much one mind could absorb. He wondered what happened, if someone exceeded that limit.

Morgan glanced at the other man, someone Kormèr hadn't met, then back at Kormèr. "How'd you get out of the hold?"

Kormèr appeared puzzled by the question. "I walked," he said, as he removed the circlet and set it on the tabletop. He was, of course, neither truly puzzled nor lying. He knew he was being a "smart aleck"—that was a new Terran phrase for him—but he really didn't see the point in their questioning. He'd done nothing to betray their trust.

Morgan pursed his lips. "Cut the crap, kid. Those doors were locked."

Kormèr shrugged. "Are you sure?" He looked around the small area as if seeing it for the first time. And in a way he was, as his mind now filled in the names and functions of the objects he was seeing.

"Hey!" yelled Morgan. "Look at me. This is serious. How do you expect to gain our trust if you—"

Kormèr did not anger easily. But he'd had it with having to defend himself for doing nothing more than sneaking onto their ship. "Trust?" he said, slapping his hand on the tabletop and interrupting Morgan. "So I broke out of your cargo hold; it was wrong of you to lock me in there in the first place. At least tell me; I'm not an animal."

"Now just a—"

"Second: I've done nothing wrong. Did I try to escape?" he said, ticking his points off on his fingers. "No. Did I break anything? No. I sat here where anyone passing by could find me and did a little learning. Where's the breach in trust?"

The men sat quietly for a moment. It was the man Kormèr didn't know who broke the silence. "You a politician, kid?"

Kormèr shuddered. "No way. Who're you, anyway?"

"Jim Blake." Jim was slim, lean and had light brown skin. His dark hair looked as if woven into long fuzzy strands and then pulled up into a dense bun behind his head. Kormèr imagined that when it was loose, the hair had to be long enough to reach the man's waist.

Kormèr extended a hand. "Pleasure. Kormèr Lezàl."

Jim looked surprised by the gesture, then he cracked a smile and took Kormèr's hand to shake it.

"Ah! Handshake. I get it now," said Kormèr. "On my planet it's like this." And he clapped his hand on Jim's shoulder, warmly.

"That's right," said Jim. "I remember from the time I was on Elmar, many years ago." He repeated the gesture.

"Okay, guys," said Morgan, "enough of that. The question still stands. Kid, you did nothing wrong, but you've got to admit that you're not trusting us either. What're you hiding?"

Kormèr deflected with, "How do I know you weren't the 'bad guys' on the platform back on Io Station?"

Morgan leveled his hooded brown eyes at him. "Oh, you'd know. You'd be out the airlock by now, if we were."

"So, you can tell me what's in the crates back there, then," Kormèr reasoned. "If you're not doing anything wrong, you would have nothing to hide."

Jim chuckled. "That's exactly our point, kid."

Before Kormèr could offer a rebuttal, Morgan shook his head. "Give it up, Jim. He doesn't want to tell us squat. Maybe he'll be willing to talk to Jeremy, and the two of them can reach some kind of compromise."

Kormèr thought it over in a matter of seconds. *What've I got to lose? Nothing. If these guys turn out to be criminals, I'll take what I can and portal out of here.* He extended a hand to Morgan for shaking. "Deal."

"WHAT'S up?" asked Jeremy, stepping out of the crew berth cabin. His drowsy eyes focused on Kormèr. "Hey, what's he—"

"He escaped from the hold," announced Jim.

"What?" Jeremy glanced at the men, then at Kormèr. "How?"

Kormèr almost said something smart-alecky—he really liked this phrase. But he held his tongue. Instead, he busied himself studying several conduits that ran along the fold where the wall met the ceiling, trying to figure out what they were for. Considering they were out in the corridor, they had to be an after-market installation.

"That's what we're about to find out," explained Morgan. "He agreed to talk, if we talked."

"Is that so?" Jeremy asked, watching Kormèr. He looked at Morgan and Jim. "Whose idea was this?"

Morgan and Jim pointed to each other.

"Fine," Jeremy said, running his fingers through his shock of blonde hair. "Let's head to the galley—"

"We've got trouble!" came an unfamiliar voice over the comm.

Kormèr was relieved for the interruption. His secrets would be safe for at least a little longer. But what was up?

Jeremy tapped the wall comm-panel. "This is Jeremy. What's up, Kit?"

"Jer, we're being tracked through lightspace. They're clever, riding in our wake. But I spotted 'em."

"What? How?" asked Morgan.

"The kid?" asked Jim, eying Kormèr.

Jeremy shook his head. "Nah. I d-scanned him; he's clean."

"Oh." Both Jim and Morgan took an obvious step away from Kormèr. Nothing Kormèr had learned clarified what a d-scan was, but by the reactions of the men, Kormèr didn't like that they had used it on him.

"How many bogies?" asked Jeremy.

"That I couldn't gander. At least one."

"Hmm," Jeremy said. "Do they know you know?"

"I doubt it."

"Good," Jeremy said, looking at the other men. "What's our status, otherwise?"

"We'll revert from FTL in five minutes."

"We can't outrun " Jeremy frowned.

"Not in this old bucket."

Kormèr saw the strain on the faces around him. Jeremy looked at Jim, and without a word spoken, the latter said, "The nav-com can't locate the next jump until we get to this one; and the one we need could be across the system."

"Make a stand?" asked Morgan.

"Not much of a choice," Jeremy nodded. "Wake the others, and tell them to man weapons. Then get yourself to the bridge." He turned back to the wall panel. "Kit, key in a rapid decel for the moment we exit."

"On it."

"I'll be right there." He turned from the panel. "I guess it's no use locking you back up—"

"I know the layout of this ship," interrupted Kormèr. "Maybe I can lend a hand with something."

Jeremy frowned at him. "I should probably slap binders on you so you don't—" He shook his head, "Just find a seat, and strap yourself in," Jeremy said. "This ride's about to get rough." He rushed off with Jim in his wake.

Kormèr turned to Morgan. "What's a rapid decel?"

"A maneuver… Just get yourself strapped down, fast." He rushed away to fulfill orders.

Kormèr paced for a moment. Things were getting out of hand here. Whatever these people were involved in, Kormèr was coming to the conclusion that he didn't want to stick around for it. Besides, while the edu-comp had provided him with excellent information, he didn't relish the idea of staying cooped up in this ship much longer.

Kit's voice came over the ship's comm,: *"Revert in five…"* Kormèr suddenly realized he was nowhere near anything to hold on to! *"four… three…"* He dashed for the galley, knowing he wasn't going to make it in time, but trying desperately nonetheless. *"two… one…"*

Kormèr's arms flailed as the ship slipped out from beneath his feet with a terrible groan. He pitched forward and slammed down onto a padded surface. Tremendous forces continued crushing him for several moments, his vision filled with crazy patterns as he struggled to breathe. He knew the engines were firing, but further thought eluded him. He couldn't even think clearly enough to wish the burn would end.

Sudden weightlessness. Insensate, he flopped down so that his feet were no longer over his head. His brain registered that the pressure was gone; the thrum of engine burn silenced. And he could breathe again.

Kormèr's head spun for countless seconds. Slowly, his crossed vision refocused, and he peered up a short, dimly lit shaft. Regularly spaced cutouts in the shaft wall climbed up to a hatch two meters over Kormèr's head. He got his elbows under him and eased himself up onto them. The upper half of his body had landed on the padded surface of a gimbal chair. It was this that had saved him from getting smeared to a pulp by the sudden maneuvers. His legs dangled over two footrests that protruded from below the chair. He realized he was sitting in an anomaly in the ship's structure, a small cabin located somewhere within the ship's hull. Much like the conduits in the corridor, this cabin had not been on the ship blueprints the edu-comp had shown him.

Using the footrests to push himself up, he shimmied into the chair and breathed a sigh of relief. *That could've gone a lot worse,* he knew. Which only reinforced what he had been thinking moments ago; he had to abandon this adventure. As he reached for the closest cutout to climb out of the cabin, he saw the hatch slide shut. Flickering lights drew his attention to two control surfaces that occupied fixed positions on either side of the chair. They winked to life, and a control yoke automatically sprang up from beneath the chair and positioned itself in front of him.

He jumped in his seat as the bulkhead beneath him dilated unexpectedly, and the cabin dropped out into space. Kormèr held his breath as he struggled to get up and out of the cabin, imagining the vacuum sucking the air out of his lungs and body. He grasped for the cutouts that would lead him up and back into the ship... then stopped struggling and took several deep breaths. He dropped back into the chair, panting, and looked around in dismay. *Why, the stupid cabin's made of glass! Or maybe it's just transparent.*

His racing heart slowing, Kormèr studied the readouts appearing on the tiny screen to his left. He looked out the glass-like dome around him as the purpose of the cabin trickled into his consciousness. *I'm in a belly-gun turret!* The multi-barreled LINX duo-phase repeating cannon, briefly mentioned by the edu-comp on a minor armament tangent, swiveled once, then again, then steadied. In glowing sky-blue letters, the holographic HUD displayed: **TARGET LOCKED**.

"HOW'D you spot them?" asked Jeremy, sliding into the seat beside Kit. Thankfully, Kit had stowed his guitar somewhere else, out of everybody's way. Behind him, Morgan took his comms station and activated several currently dormant systems.

Kit expanded a crawling text display window. "They're hiding in our wake, far enough behind so they don't get tossed, but close enough so they won't lose us. Right about here." He pointed to a change in the pattern of the numbers. "They're as blind there as we are to them. Fortunately, they're also impatient; they stuck their heads out for a peek. I did a quick scan and got back the contours of a Y-Tach."

Jeremy thought for a moment. "Y-Tach, hmm. So definitely not Gal-Pol. And weak shields to boot." His fingers suddenly glided over the controls. "You got the decel keyed?" Kit nodded. "I'm boosting the integrity stabilizers."

Mack raced onto the bridge and into his usual navigator's seat. Jeremy nodded at him, acknowledging his swapping places with Jim. They just might need Mack's particular skills before this was over.

Jeremy braced himself as Kit announced the countdown. Rapid decelerations at their velocity were not recommended at the best of times, and this was the second one they'd be pulling in the same ship... something much less recommended, especially with their junkyard special. But they didn't have much choice. At point-two light speed, it would take them a long time to loop around and engage their pursuer… or pursuers. Their pursuer wouldn't expect such a sudden stop and would overshoot them… and hopefully not crash into them.

They could then fire some disabling shots and hopefully make a run for the next jump point. That was the plan, anyway. Jeremy recognized there were a lot of holes in it, but he was a scientist and entrepreneur, not a tactician. And there hadn't been time to confer with Mack, who looked stone-faced but not openly critical.

Kit tapped the program initiator.

The ship exited FTL and immediately executed a nausea-inducing 180 degree spin along its central axis. The moment the ship was pointed in the direction from which it had come, the engines fired on full as maneuvering thrusters and dropped them fifty meters below their reversion trajectory. The *Stardust IV* shuddered and groaned, crushing the crew against their seat restraints. Jeremy's vision clouded over with distortion phosphenes. He grit his teeth, willing himself to stay conscious as his heart struggled to pump.

Jeremy was barely aware of when the thrusters stopped.

"We're at full stop," announced Mack, his voice distant. "Forward navigational shield is weak. I'm throwing up TAS to compensate." Jeremy focused on the acronym, reminding himself that it stood for "Trans-Atmospheric Shield", and the exercise helped to clear his mind.

"I just want to throw up," said Kit. "You're a machine, Mack."

Ditto. Jeremy wanted to say it aloud, but he swallowed bile and held his tongue. There would be time for banter later, he hoped. "Status?" he said, checking his own screen for any structural damage while Morgan checked the scanner results.

"Single craft," announced Morgan, a hint of relief in his voice. "Y-Tach model. Overshot us and coming about to brake now."

"Ready the gun pods." Jeremy wished he'd thought of that earlier. They could've fired a few shots as the ship passed them and maybe, if they were lucky, disabled it.

"Pods reading ready and locked on target," said Morgan.

"Transmissions?"

"None— *Shit!*"

"What?" asked Jeremy.

"There must've been more further behind. I've got five— no, fifteen more Y-Tachs dropping out of FTL. They're still moving too fast to get a solid fix on 'em. They must've transited into FTL at threshold speed."

That meant the other pursuing ships were traveling at point three light speed, since the FTL drive could only operate so far ahead of a ship. Too fast, and by the time the wormhole opened, a ship would have shot past it, like a car blowing through a traffic light. While this also meant they'd take longer to come about and engage, the new enemy arrivals were more agile, so *Stardust IV*'s lead time would not be very significant.

"Damn! Have we got enough room—"

The space visible through the cockpit flashed, and the ship shuddered slightly.

Morgan reported, "The Y-Tach ship fired from maximum range. TAS dispersed the energy."

"I've got our next jump point," said Mack, "but it ain't close."

"Grr! Can we jump back to Sol?" asked Jeremy.

"Not from this jump point. This would take us to Eps Eridani. Either way, we're at a standstill; at best, we'd crawl through the transit and they'd catch us on the revert. And this time, they're sure to leave some ships behind on this side to keep us from doubling back."

"So no options then."

Mack shook his head. "Sorry, Jer."

"Transmission," announced Morgan. "Putting it on overhead."

The bridge speakers came to life. *"Retract your turrets and prepare to be boarded."*

KORMÈR watched the engine flares of several ships arc across his line of sight and quickly take up positions in the space outside his turret. They were so close that, even with the barest of sunlight, he could make out their bristling weaponry, all neatly pointed at the Terrans' ship. "Looks like it's past the time for me to portal home," he mumbled. A movement across the HUD caught his eye. Absently, he read the glowing blue text that had appeared. But that changed as they sank into his consciousness. He read them again.

THERE IS A 64% POSSIBILITY OF ESCAPE.

Kormèr regarded the display curiously. Feeling slightly foolish at the possibility of his being wrong, he asked aloud: "Is this in response to what I said?"

YES. IS IT UNSATISFACTORY?

"Wow!" Kormèr stared at the display in wide-eyed amazement. The computer was responding to him. That shouldn't have surprised him, since his home on Elmar also had an AI. But he hadn't expected this ship to have one. He stammered, "N-no. It's satisfactory. I just… I didn't know you could hear me."

I CAN.

"Do you have a name?"

I AM STARDUST THE FOURTH.

"Nice to meet you, Stardust. I'm Kormèr Lezàl."

I KNOW.

A salvo flashed and raced across an invisible barrier outside the pod window. Kormèr gulped. "What was that?"

ONE OF THE SURROUNDING CRAFT HAS FIRED UPON US. A TRANSMISSION IS BEING ROUTED TO THE BRIDGE.

"Can I hear it here?"

YOU MAY.

"Retract your turrets and prepare to be boarded."

"Uh, oh. That's not good."

55

NO, IT IS NOT. STATISTICALLY, BOARDING BY HOSTILES DOES NOT END WELL FOR A SHIP'S CREW.

"I don't imagine it would," mumbled Kormèr, wondering how often such boardings occurred in this time. But a more relevant question came to mind. "Can you identify the ships? What type and who they belong to?" While Jeremy and the rest of the crew were tight-lipped about who was pursuing them, maybe the computer would reveal it. In particular, he wanted to know if these ships were property of the infamous "G".

I DO NOT HAVE SUFFICIENT DATA TO IDENTIFY ALL THE SHIP OWNERS. THE SHIP TYPES VARY, AND MANY HAVE BEEN HEAVILY MODIFIED. SHALL I LIST EACH UNIQUE TYPE WITH A COUNT AND WHATEVER OWNERSHIP INFORMATION I DO HAVE?

That had the sound of being more information than he needed, or even more than he could make sense of. But he feared that asking for less might cause the AI to omit something useful. Mimicking the AI's speech pattern, he said, "That'd be… satisfactory." Kormèr scanned the list that appeared. As he suspected, it told him little of value other than the count of ships. Jeremy was seriously outnumbered. But in the transmission, the speaker had referred to "turrets", plural.

"How many ships can we disable with the turrets we have, and how quickly?"

ASSUMING THE SHIPS DO NOT MOVE FROM THEIR PRESENT LOCATIONS, AT THEIR CURRENT SPREAD, IT WOULD TAKE 32.76 SECONDS TO DISABLE THE TEN THAT ARE CLOSEST TO OUR POSITION. The display altered to reveal a three-dimensional representation of the surrounding ships. **HOWEVER, THE OTHERS WOULD BE FREE TO FIRE, AND THE FIREPOWER OF A Y-TACH IS CONSIDERABLE.**

"It's hopeless then," Kormèr mumbled, sinking into the turret seat. He frowned, staring at the star-speckled span of space outside as the turret retracted and the iris sealed below him. He shifted his gaze back to the three-dimensional representation, and knit his brow defiantly. *Nothing is hopeless*, he told himself. *It's just more difficult to get out of.*

Wait! What am I thinking? Am I seriously considering sticking around? He weighed the idea of climbing out of this turret, opening the portal and going home, against sticking around to see how things turned out here. On the one hand, he was pretty well hidden here, so any boarders were unlikely to discover him. *But then what? And if they do discover me, there isn't enough room to open the portal in here.* He'd be trapped again, and he didn't think G's men would be as hospitable as Jeremy and the others had been.

And if they destroyed the ship outright… well, then he was out of luck. But considering they were planning to board, annihilation didn't currently seem to be their plan.

There is a third option, he thought, watching the display update to show a Y-Tach sliding into position alongside the *Stardust IV*. This would deliver the boarding party. *I know how to pilot a ship now. This ship might be doomed, but maybe, just maybe, I can get aboard that Y-Tach… if I could manage to commandeer it… how cool would that be!*

His mind flashed through various boarding scenarios in which Jeremy's crew overwhelmed the boarding party and used their ship to escape. But he was sure whoever boarded would be prepared for any escape attempt the six-man crew could pull. A single person, on the other hand… "How many crew members are there per craft?"

ALL HAVE FOUR-MAN CREWS.

"How many ships can attach to ours at one time?"

UNLESS THEY BREACH THE HULL AT MULTIPLE LOCATIONS, WE HAVE ONLY ONE BOARDING HATCH.

"Hmm. Four against six." *The question is: will they all leave their ship when they board? They probably would, considering the numbers, but there are multiple ships against one, in this case.* "Keep the turret hatch sealed and tell me when we've been boarded."

AS YOU WISH.

Kormèr divided his attention between watching the HUD and running through various scenarios of how he would get onto the Y-Tach. The display tracked the progress of the Y-Tach, as it came alongside the *Stardust IV*. What it did not show was the boarding itself. He had to keep watching it, waiting impatiently until the AI indicated that they'd been boarded. He could hear activity through the hull, stomping of feet, muffled voices, but these didn't provide him any information on what was actually happening.

As the minutes ticked away, Kormèr grew becoming increasingly impatient. Finally, he whispered, "Stardust, can you talk to me over comms instead of—" He stopped and stared at the message that had immediately appeared.

I CAN. WOULD YOU LIKE ME TO?

"Yes! Why didn't you do that before?"

"You did not ask," said a female voice through the comms, thankfully mimicking Kormèr's lowered volume.

Kormèr shrugged. "I can't argue with that. My plan is to sneak onto that Y-Tach; is there anything I should know now before I go?"

"Your plan has a high probability of failure, with a—"

"Stop," interrupted Kormèr. "Thanks, but you don't have to tell me the odds. Anything else?"

"Your chances would be better if we remained in communication."

"We can do that?" asked Kormèr. He wanted to find this AI's programmer and punch him in the nose. While the quality of the speech seemed very natural, the AI's delivery of content erratic. Used to dealing with his household bots and AI that better understood his needs and expectations, Kormèr grew frustrated with the ship's AI.

"That option is available if you have a p-comm implant," it offered.

"Um, I don't think I have one. What is it?"

A narrow compartment slid open in the bulkhead beside the chair. Inside were a pair of ear buds. "Take those and insert them into your ear canals. I will then be able to communicate with you. Though I will probably lose contact with you once you are aboard the Y-Tach."

Kormèr popped the buds into his ears. "Testing."

"I hear you," said the AI in his ear.

"Great. Please let me know as soon as the corridor's clear." Kormèr climbed out of the gimbal seat and up to the hatch. He didn't wait long before the AI gave him the all clear.

"Open the hatch and wish me luck."

The hatch opened. *"Luck,"* said Stardust.

Kormèr glanced at his chrono to track his time, then crawled out of the hatch and onto the floor of the corridor, where he took a second to orient himself. He'd tumbled into the hatch, so he hadn't seen where it was located relative to the corridor. He now saw that the turret sat ensconced in the port-side bulkhead, with the shaft perpendicular to the corridor. Ahead was the airlock hatch to the cargo hold. Past that and around the corner, the passage led to the starboard hatch and ramp. The corridor circled around to his left, past the port-side hatch to the crew berths and around the next corner to the bridge.

Scuffling noises reached Kormèr from around the bend ahead. Following the left corridor, he slipped off his shoes and stuffed one into each of his coat pockets. He stepped silently past the berth area hatch and to the next corner.

"You are clear, but there are two intruders on the bridge."

Kormèr nodded in response, though he figured Stardust probably couldn't see it. He stepped carefully to the entry of the bridge and peered cautiously through the hatch. Two mercs stood with their backs to Kormèr, blocking his view of all the bridge crew, except for Mack. One had scaly blue skin with spiny ridges on its bald head and a tan flight-suit, and the other looked human from behind. Mack's eyes flicked toward Kormèr, but stopped short of actually looking at him. As Kormèr slipped past the hatch, weapons discharged, and Kormèr watched Mack crumple in a heap.

Kormèr forced himself not to think about the fact that he might have just witnessed someone getting killed and instead focused on staying hidden. He was in no position to help Mack now, even if he wanted to. Kormèr rushed to the next corner and peered around it. Another scaly blue humanoid stood at the starboard-side hatch to the berth area. It looked down the corridor in Kormèr's direction, weapon held ready, then it triggered the hatch and immediately opened fire as it charged in.

This is really bad. Without hesitation, Kormèr scurried to the open airlock, even while his brain screamed at him to portal to the safety of home. *What are you trying to prove? You're probably the last one left alive on the ship,* he reasoned. *This is really dangerous, and no amount of treasure is worth this!*

He struggled to keep his emotions under control. *It's too late to turn back now.* He stepped through the airlock, and his feet left the ground. All sense of up and down vanished along with gravity. His body twisted uncontrollably as his momentum propelled him into the wall of the umbilical. He bounced off the wall and slowly spun, as his inertia continued to carry him forward, this time toward the other wall.

A klaxon sounded from somewhere ahead, and the airlock sealed behind him, cutting off any chance of retreat. He spotted a handhold on the wall and stretched, grabbing it just as he bumped into the wall. His body bounced again, twisting around, with the handhold now the pivot point of his motion. *This is crazy!* he thought. His foot bumped the opposite wall, retarding his momentum and bringing him to a near stop. Gripping the handhold as if his life depended on it, he righted himself, with his feet toward Jeremy's ship and his head aimed at the Y-Tach. With a firm push on the handhold, he propelled himself across the umbilical and toward the Y-Tach's airlock hatchway. He curled into a ball as he passed through the open hatch. Gravity snatched him from the air, and he crashed onto the deck. Wincing, he stood and glanced around. Over the klaxon's *oo-waah oo-waah,* footfalls boomed through the deck. He slipped into a niche just as another humanoid charged into view with weapon drawn. Kormèr had never seen anything like it before, its smooth, hairless body shifting from a light blue to white as it moved. It wore an almost transparent, chiffon-like robe, but no gender was detectable on its slender shape.

The creature slid warily to the open airlock, then whirled into the hatchway, its weapon aimed for a target that wasn't there. Kormèr launched himself from his hiding spot and rammed the alien from behind, his left shoulder jarring painfully from the impact. The creature tumbled into the umbilical and dropped its weapon, while Kormèr tumbled into the side of the hatchway. The alien spun in the zero-G with a grace that left Kormèr amazed. It stared at Kormèr, its face an eerie, expressionless mimicry of a human face. With another graceful spin, the alien sailed toward its weapon. Kormèr stepped back, away from the hatchway, ready to run and either hide or find something he could use to disable the alien. Then he spotted the control surface beside the hatch. He slapped the first button that looked like it would seal the hatch.

The alien snatched its weapon and fired, ineffectually striking the edge of the closing hatch. Through the hatch's round porthole, Kormèr watched the alien's skin flash pink, as a red light strobed just above the control surface. *Oh, no!* Kormèr recognized the warning light from his edu-comp training: *The airlock is cycling.* The alien must've realized it at the same moment; it turned and propelled itself across the umbilical toward the *Stardust IV*'s hatch. Kormèr jumped in surprise as a loud *whoosh* sounded through the hatch.

Kormèr checked the control pad, but there didn't seem to be a control for aborting the airlock cycle; the screen read: **REMOTE OPERATION IN PROGRESS.** He watched, in helpless, frozen horror, as the alien clawed frantically at the hatch control pad on Jeremy's ship, to no avail. It turned then, writhing as vacuum replaced the last of the air in the tube. Several agonizing moments later, the bloating alien silently burst, its innards splattering the porthole and blocking Kormèr's view.

Kormèr staggered backwards as a shiver raced down his back, and a heaviness weighed in his churning stomach. *I killed someone.*

But it was an accident, argued another part of his mind.

That's no excuse, he argued back, his eyes riveted on the syrupy purple blood and tissue that still coated the porthole. *It's my fault; it's because of my plan.*

It was you or him.

Kormèr shook his head, his eyes tearing. *Is that how the thief rationalized killing my father? 'You or him'? Is a life worth so little consideration?*

That last thought reminded him that there was still his own life to consider. Kormèr was still in danger, so this was not the time to ruminate on what he could no longer change. *I could still open the portal and go while I have the chance.*

A blinking amber light indicated that the umbilical had retracted.

"Kormèr, are you there?" came *Stardust's* voice in his ear.

Kormèr sniffled and wiped his eyes. "Yes. I thought we would lose contact." He wondered briefly why he should care; the *Stardust IV* was just a ship with an artificial intelligence, but he felt uncomfortable abandoning it to the mercy of the mercs. *Why should 'merc' and 'mercy' be spelled so similarly? This English is a strange language.*

Stardust continued: *"The intruders left their comms open, and I was able to establish a tight-beam channel to it. I am using their ship to boost the link to your p-comm, as they are still here aboard me."*

Kormèr barely heard the words, his every breath shaky from his shock and grief. Cradling his sore left arm, he started toward the bridge of the enemy Y-Tach. "What about your crew? Are they all dead?" he asked Stardust, looping in his head the scene of Mack being shot back on the bridge. *Another life gone—*

"I have only registered one death, in the umbilical."

"What? What about Jeremy and the others? I saw them get shot."

"They were stunned and are presently unconscious, but they are uninjured."

They're alive! Kormèr's heart jumped. *Thank the gods!*

"There is confusion among the intruders. I have isolated them from the crew and am attempting to incapacitate them."

"Keep at it," he said, running to the bridge. "We have to work fast, and we can't have them getting in the way." The lives of Jeremy's crew were now at stake, and he wasn't going to let anyone else die today if he could help it.

"What are 'we' doing?"

"That depends. Have the intruders said anything about why they're here?"

"I can only make an assumption, based on the comm transcript and situational context."

"It's more than I have. Whatcha got?"

"As I have not yet been destroyed, it would appear that they wish to seize me, my crew, or my cargo."

"Hmm." Kormèr thought but for a moment. "The best way, it seems, to get rid of these people is to get rid of their objective."

The connection was silent for a moment, then *Stardust* asked, a little tentatively: *"By 'get rid of', are you suggesting that my crew or I should be destroyed?"*

Kormèr's eyed widened. "No! That's not what I'm suggesting at all, but more like sleight of hand to let the mercs think that you're beyond their reach."

"My subroutines warn me of a high risk of danger involved in any escape attempt."

"There's always danger. There was danger in what I just pulled, but here I am." The words constricted his chest with a vice-grip of guilt, but he fought it back. "Danger's just part of the game," he mumbled, as he test the controls, nudging the ship fifty meters away from the *Stardust IV*.

"Please repeat."

"Never mind." The controls were newer than those he'd seen on the *Stardust IV*, but they actually matched those in the edu-comp curriculum. "What I have in mind is to make it look like the mercs from this ship have attacked you." He found the weapons screen. *By the gods, this ship has some impressive weaponry!* "Then we need a gigantic explosion, so they think you've been destroyed. But you really jump to FTL."

"I have not yet completed securing and incapacitating the intruders, and you are still on the other ship," the *Stardust* reminded Kormèr.

"I know," Kormèr said. "Can you mimic an explosion for cover?"

"I calculate that overloading and ejecting my backup core would produce the desired explosion."

"Great. But if you fire your engines, they'll detect the output."

"It is possible for me to slip into lightspace without lighting my engines. You would have to use the firepower of the Y-Tach to provide thrust. I am performing the calculations."

"Wait. Do you have certain areas of your hull that are… that can… well…"

"That can be destroyed without harming any of my vital functions?" finished Stardust. *"I do."*

The AI's flat tone gave away nothing of how it felt about the idea. Kormèr wondered if it would reject his plan.

"I have calculated the required weapons' output and points of impact. I need you to slave your ship to me; this will require timing and precision that you cannot achieve."

"Then, let's do it."

Following Stardust's instructions, Kormèr slaved the Y-Tach to her—perhaps because of the voice, he'd started thinking of the ship as female.

Immediately, a compartment popped open by his knees, and a vac-suit tumbled out. *"Please wear that."*

Without a word, Kormèr donned the suit, as the Y-Tach yawed to the left and positioned itself behind the *Stardust IV*. He was thankful that the adult humanoid sizing was generous enough to fit him and his coat, As Kormèr sealed the helmet, the ship opened fire on the *Stardust IV*.

Blam! The Y-Tach shook, nearly tossing Kormèr from the pilot's seat.

"The other merc ships are shooting at you, Kormèr."

"Ugh! I hadn't thought of that," he said, as another volley struck. Unfortunately, while Y-Tachs were fast little ships with potent weapons, they had weak defenses. A piercing whistle filled the bridge, and after a confused moment, he realized that a solid projectile had completely punctured the bridge. He jumped as a shower of sparks signaled another penetration only a meter from his seat.

<<Buomp!>> he shouted as the craft bucked under the barrage and a cacophony of alarms filled the bridge.

"I am evading as well as I can, while maintaining the required rate of fire. Just another thirty seconds. Then you will be engulfed in the flames after me. I have run 1,665,634 simulations. It should work."

Something exploded, and the bridge hatch slammed shut. "Should? Whoa!" The ship accelerated, crushing Kormèr into his seat. The image on the forward screen of the *Stardust IV* grew larger at an alarming rate.

Through pained eyes, he watched as shots impacted the hull of the *Stardust IV*, and bits of the hull exploded away. The screen popped and went dark, taking some of the warning klaxons with it.

Kormèr closed his eyes. *I should've portaled home,* he thought as a familiar whine crescendoed. *Sorry, Trinket. I really messed this one up.* He felt awful that the little bot would probably blame himself. A tremendous roar sounded through the hull, and Kormèr was thrown from his seat—

BROWN eyes watched the forward screen from a sharply angled face. The screen showed several merc ships surrounding Tailor's ship. The eyes flicked to statistical data that appeared at the borders of the screen: energy output, incoming and outgoing transmissions, among other things.

"They've powered down, Mister G," came a merc's voice over the open comm. The message was redundant, as Harry G already knew, but replying would be just as inefficient.

Harry G signaled his lead merc and commanded in a soft, resonant voice: "Royland, proceed with boarding. Subdue the crew; I want them alive when I board."

"Aye, aye. Starting boarding procedures."

Harry G sent another signal, and his ship maneuvered closer to the others. He had remained a safe distance from the potential conflict zone, though he knew the odds of any actual conflict would be negligible. But negligible didn't mean impossible, and could still be fatal.

62

He rarely involved himself personally in his business ventures; this was an inefficient use of his time. But he had waited a long time for this, and Tailor's motley crew had slipped the grasp of his employees twice already. This operation had warranted someone in the field to ensure a rapid success. He trusted only himself, and his trust had paid off. Once the mercs had botched the operation on Io Station, Harry G had quickly calculated the sequence of events that had led them to this moment, right down to the micro-jump using the old smuggler's route. Tailor's crew had acted predictably, once Royland had revealed his Y-Tach to them during FTL transit.

And now Tailor's revolutionary innovation was within his grasp.

Royland's Y-Tach moved alongside the trapped ship and extended an umbilical toward it, while Harry G's brain ran through a half-dozen simulations of the Y-Tach's crew boarding and subduing Tailor and his crew. As captain, Royland would remain on the bridge and provide logistical support over comms.

Within minutes, and matching the timing of two of Harry G's simulations, the umbilical retracted. A moment later, the Y-Tach pulled away, leaving the way open for Harry G to board. He stood, his large frame uncoiling to an imposing height. He signaled his ship to close with Tailor's and begin the boarding process.

A flash on the screen caught Harry G's eyes. Royland's ship had opened fire on the *Stardust IV*.

That was not in any of the simulations. Brow creased, Harry G dropped back into his seat. He had no time to contact Royland to find out what the hell he thought he was doing. It didn't matter, anyway. He only needed to stop the attack... immediately. "Fire at will on Royland," he ordered, without hesitation, his message instantly broadcast to all the other ships. "He is compromised." He watched as all but one craft concentrated their fire on Royland's Y-Tach; but Harry G had expected that one delayed response. Tailor's craft had had shields up, the only reason it hadn't been destroyed outright, but the shielding was designed to stop hypervelocity debris, not the focused firepower of a Y-Tach. The shields wore through almost instantly under Royland's continued, suicidal barrage, and bits of the *Stardust IV* joined those of Royland's ship floating through space.

Royland's Y-Tach rolled twice, then its engines flared brilliantly, and it shot toward Tailor's ravaged craft, as Harry G looked on. If the *Stardust IV* and its crew were destroyed because of Royland's insane suicidal maneuver, not only would Harry G lose his investment, but he would have wasted his time and effort, with not even scraps to show for it. He briefly wondered what had driven Royland to such extreme behavior, whether a competitor or something Harry G himself had done to wrong the man. But this, too, was irrelevant at the moment. Tailor's ship limped forward, as if it had finally decided that fleeing was its only hope. But it was too late. It burst spectacularly and silently: a core overload, according to the energy output. Royland's own craft vanished in the hailstorm of released energy. Nothing remained but glowing debris.

Harry G realized he had crushed the seat's armrest, and he loosened his grip. He breathed deeply several times. Then he signaled one of the other ships, and Hassera, its reptilian captain, appeared on the screen, her rigid posture betraying her angst. "I'm very sorry about Royland," Harry G told her. He knew they had been friends, and sometimes more. "Scan the debris and give me a full report. You have six hours." He opened the signal to the rest of the ships. "There's no need to linger here. Regroup at HOME," he said, using the moniker for the asteroid which contained the Head Offices of Mercantile Enterprises.

HASSERA watched impassively as, one by one, the other ships vanished into FTL space. She had already had her ship's scanners actively sweeping the debris field before Harry G gave her the order. She did not believe for one pico-second that Royland would have willingly participated in what had just occurred. He didn't think like everyone else, and no one understood him like she did. And even that was a stretch, at times. But this she knew for sure: Royland would never have fired on Tailor and his crew, and he most certainly would never have rammed their ship.

Before all the ships had departed, she had requested their sensor logs. She always trusted information and speed over firepower, and so she had equipped her ship—which she referred to simply as *Ship*—with some of the most powerful data processing she could beg, buy or steal. While everyone else let loose with their armaments, her ship performed an invasive analysis of the target and discovered its weaknesses. After that, targeted strikes almost always disabled or destroyed the target in half the time.

An hour later, the AI hissed that the scan of the debris and the analysis of the massive amount of sensor data had completed. She turned from the forward screen and studied the results. Something did not add up; the amount of debris did not match the mass of two ships, even accounting for vaporization. It almost matched the mass of one, but analysis of the composition of alloys and trace elements told a different story. Most of the debris belonged to Royland's ship.

Swiping quickly, Hassera fast-forwarded through the optical footage spliced from the sensors of all the ships. The AI had selected a two-minute sequence that it had deemed most relevant to her search parameters. Another hour passed before she cut the footage down enough to confirm her suspicions. The timing had been astoundingly precise; only an AI could have achieved anything like that. But the detailed high-speed optics of her ship had caught the moment she was looking for, the moment when Tailor's ship dumped a core and entered FTL. The detonation of the core obscured all else.

So, where did Tailor go? Jumping back to Sol would have been suicide. This jump point only provided access to one other system, Epsilon Eridani. Hassera considered heading straight there and then relaying a message to Harry G from the station, but she knew he wouldn't like that. He trusted evidence, not hunches—not even hers.

Annoyed to have to waste four hours transiting back and forth through the tube to Sol, she nudged her ship up to point one-five light speed and transited. She planned to send her message to Harry G when she got to Sol, then shoot right back to where she already was, just to go out to Epsilon Eridani. It was seven hours to Eps Eridani, plus the four hours to Sol and back… She hissed in frustration at the lost time.

Harry G had his reasons for wanting Tailor's crew. And now she had hers. She had the fastest ship in Harry G's fleet, so the race to catch up to Tailor was still hers to win. The sooner she made up for her wasted time, the sooner she would have her vengeance.

CHAPTER 5

SITTING on the floor of the bridge in near-darkness for longer than he could mentally keep track of, Kormèr had time to ponder the many mistakes that had led him to this predicament in which he found himself. Around him, wires and electronics dangled from scorched control panels, and spent canisters of fire-suppressant floated, suspended in zero-G. Had he not wedged himself between a console and the floor, he'd be floating around, too.

If the Y-Tach had made it to FTL, Kormèr couldn't tell; he couldn't hear the drive's whine, which was expected since the bridge was in a vacuum. But even with the suit pressurized, he couldn't even hear the whine through the hull. Peeking through the broken segments of the ship, he saw that space didn't look inky black as it usually did, so he took that to mean that he was still in transit.

He'd had to shut down most of the Y-Tach's systems to keep the ship from exploding outright. Even life support was gone. Not that it mattered, considering the various seven-centimeter holes that perforated the bridge. Twenty power feeds had fused after the massive explosion. If the power core was even still attached to the bridge, miraculously, it had not overloaded or otherwise detonated. If it was no longer attached, well, then Kormèr had a decision to make.

His cube was inside the vac-suit. While he didn't know a lot about space, he knew that extreme cold and lack of breathable air didn't make for a survivable environment. So if it came down to choosing between slow asphyxiation or a quick death in the vacuum of space with the possibility of escape through the cube... Well, he was hoping to not get to that desperate point.

He slept a few times, noting the passage of time from the diminishing oxygen levels in his vac-suit, as his chrono was inside the suit, too. In between naps, he peeked out one of the many holes in what remained of the ship to confirm that he hadn't missed the drop out of FTL. Sleeping was almost worse than being awake. His dreams were distressing, and he'd awaken crying or trembling in fear. He knew it had something to do with the alien's death in the umbilical. *Is this my penance?* he wondered.

CLONG!

He jumped, not realizing he'd fallen asleep again. But for how long? <<Buomp!>> he spat. He had less than ten minutes of oxygen remaining. *Better to try escaping than to sit here and die for sure. Here we go!*

He stood slowly, making sure not to set himself spinning, which would just complicate things. He had to remove his glove first, then undo the seal on his suit, get the cube from his coat pocket and activate it... all before his hand froze. At least the suit would seal the leaking arm to keep all his breathable air from venting. But that just meant he'd be alive long enough to suffocate slowly, the death he wanted to avoid.

He took two deep breaths, rapidly clenching and unclenching his fist to generate some last-minute heat. He twisted the glove to break the seal—

The bridge moved around him, and he bumped into the ceiling, nearly losing his glove in the impact. He twisted the seal back into the locked position.

His earbuds crackled with static.

The bridge yawed to the left and stopped, and Kormèr slid toward the ruined forward screen as the bridge moved backwards.

"Kormèr... thi... atus..."

The voice in his ears almost sounded like Stardust.

"Stardust, is that you?" He wasn't actually sure that the buds were two-way. The only time he'd talked to Stardust with them in place was while he was still in the turret. All the other times had been through her hack of the Y-Tach.

"If you can... move away... bridge hatch."

The words seemed distant. He heard them, but they didn't equate to anything he had to do. They just sounded disjointed.

The minutes ticked away, and nothing seemed to happen. Something was supposed to be happening, right? His suit showed that he had less than two minutes of oxygen remaining, and the air was feeling pretty thin already, so he tried to keep his breaths slow and steady.

"Whatever's happening, you'd better hurry," he said, hoping Stardust was listening.

Stars started blooming inside the bridge with him. He thought that was pretty cool. *Crap! I'm getting aoxic... anocix... what a stupid word.*

Brilliant light flared along the seam of the bridge hatch. Without thinking, Kormèr kicked his feet against the viewscreen and launched himself toward the light. Something snagged him, and he flailed blindly to get free. But whatever had him held him fast.

Something buzzed against his faceplate, then *thunked*, and cool air cascaded around his head. He gulped the fresh air in short, trembling breaths. His mind cleared quickly, and he focused on the emergency canister of compressed air that had been attached to his faceplate. Looking beyond the canister, he focused on Jim Blake's smiling face inside some kind of exoskeleton suit.

<<Jim!>> Kormèr shouted, excited. *They're alive!* he realized. *I saved them.* Mixed with that wonderful relief was still a measure of pain, as he recalled the panic-stricken face of the alien in the last seconds of its life. It felt as though that face would haunt him forever.

Jim gave him a nod, then steadied him against something solid with one arm while the other clipped a tether to Kormèr's suit. A tug from beyond started Kormèr floating away from Jim, past an array of dazzling work-lights and then on a slow tour of what remained of the Y-Tach. Kormèr's gut constricted at what he saw. The housing of the FTL drive and the core were practically the only remaining portions of the ship. The most critical of the systems, they had the strongest shielding and redundant backup controls. A few structural members connected those to the bridge.

The ruined craft passed out of view, and for a moment there was nothing but the black of space, endless, uncaring and unforgiving. Kormèr decided that maybe it was for the best that Elmar didn't look up to the stars for inspiration or with any sense of wonder, because honestly, he found space cold and daunting. If he no longer had the portal, he'd be perfectly happy living out his days on Elmar.

The hull of the *Stardust IV* slid into view, and Kormèr craned his neck to see that he was in the hold, the telescoping arms of the mag-winch extending out and gripping the ruined Y-Tach. Someone caught him from behind and held him steady as he watched Jim ride one of the arms back along with the light array and one of the larger tool crates Kormèr had spotted during his snooping of the hold.

"Stardust?" he said.

"I am here," she said in his ear. *"Welcome back aboard."*

"Thank you. If not for you, things would be very different right now."

"That is not entirely accurate, Kormèr. It was you who commandeered the intruders' ship. The escape was your plan, and it was you who slaved the ship to me so that I could carry it out. If not for you, too, things would be very different right now."

Stardust's words reminded Kormèr of how he'd set out to steal the Y-Tach and leave the crew of the *Stardust IV* to their fate. The AI didn't know this, of course, and so her perception of his actions was that he'd done something special. But Kormèr didn't feel that way. He'd only done what needed to be done, and a good part of what he *had* done was out of a need to mitigate his own guilt over the death of the alien intruder.

When everyone was safely aboard, the cargo hold door slid ponderously into place. As Jim stowed the equipment, someone removed the tether from Kormèr's suit and spun him toward the airlock. He didn't understand the urgency until he noticed that the flow of air from the canister had slowed significantly. They were supposed to hold between thirty minutes to an hour's worth of air. Had it actually been that long already?

As the airlock cycled, he turned to see Morgan flanking him. The man gave him a big lop-sided grin and patted his helmet.

Kormèr had never felt as much elation as he did when the airlock finally opened and Jeremy and the others swept in with howls of joy and praise at his having saved them and their ship. He was among friends again. Well, maybe not friends, but at least they're not trying to kill me.

THE first order of business, once Kormèr stripped out of the vac-suit, was a dash to use the head. According to his chrono, eight hours had elapsed since he'd left the turret to steal the Y-Tach. Combined with the time he'd been connected to the edu-comp, that amounted to an urgent need to use the facilities. He desperately wanted to portal home and soak in a steaming bath, but he settled for what the crew called a "naval shower", which consisted of a spray of water that only ran when Kormèr pushed a button. So he had to wet himself, lather, then rinse. Each time he activated the water, an airflow system kicked in and instantly whisked away the water. At the end, he ran the airflow system by itself so that, when he stepped out of the stall, he was nearly dry. The complete process took twenty minutes, but Kormèr spent most of that time fumbling with the controls.

When he stepped out of the shower, he frowned at the sad-looking pile that his clothes had turned into after all those hours crammed inside the vac-suit. He considered portaling home once again… but with a deep sigh, resisted the temptation and slipped back into the familiar threads.

Eating came next on Kormèr's agenda. Morgan escorted him to the mess and prepared some food for him.

"Where's everyone else?" asked Kormèr.

"They're scavenging the Y-Tach and assessing the damage to the *Stardust IV*," Morgan answered,

Kormèr cringed. "Sorry about that."

He turned and slid a plate of some brown, tangy-smelling meat with rice and vegetables toward Kormèr. "It's chicken teriyaki," he explained, as Kormèr took a tentative bite. "And don't worry. The damage wasn't bad. You hit all the right places to make it look bad without being bad."

Kormèr's mouth was full, or he would've told Morgan that he hadn't shot her up at all. *Didn't Stardust tell them what happened?* he wondered.

He heard footsteps in the corridor coming closer. An unfamiliar face appeared around the corner and grinned at Kormèr. The man had short, curly red hair atop a long gaunt face with high cheekbones. His deep-set hazel eyes sat beneath bushy eyebrows, bracketing a thin nose. By Kormèr's estimate, he seemed to be over a meter and a half tall. "Hey, it's our hero," he said, ruffling Kormèr's hair.

"You must be Kit," said Kormèr, recognizing the voice he'd heard over the comm just before he'd tumbled into the belly turret.

"How'd you know?"

"You're the only one I haven't met yet. I'm Kormèr Lezàl."

"So I've heard. But around here, most of us have nicknames. Right, Mo?"

Morgan had gone back to preparing another dish, and without turning, answered, "Sure, Chris."

Kit frowned. "Anyway… Kormèr Lezàl… D'ya have a nickname back home?" Kormèr shook his head. "Hmm. Kor sounds too… British. Maybe just your initials, KL." He pronounced it *Kayel*. "How about that, KL?"

Kormèr shrugged. It was still two syllables, so it didn't make sense as a shorter version of his name, but maybe he was missing the point.

Jeremy stepped into the room as Kit slipped onto the bench around the table. Jim came next with Mack and Roke on his heels, the latter shrugging off a vac-suit.

"It's amazing how that ship held together all the way through the wormhole," said Roke, who'd apparently been on the salvage team that had boarded the dead Y-Tach. "I mean, like, the ship was totally wrecked."

Kormèr struggled with getting the last of the meat off of the leg bone of the small, cooked animal he was eating.

"Kormèr," said Jeremy with a smirk, "chicken is finger-food. You don't have to eat it with a fork."

Kormèr stopped and looked down at the food on his plate. Kormèr had no idea what "terriarchi" was, since it hadn't been among the words the computer had taught him. But the thought of getting that stuff, however good it tasted, under his nails and all over his fingers was too disgusting. "That's okay. I'll just use the fork."

Jeremy shrugged, then grabbed some food for himself.

"By the way," said Kit, "he's got a nick now. It's KL."

"No way, dude!" said Roke. "Kormèr is such an awesome name! You can't shorten that." Roke punched Kormèr gently on the shoulder. "You'll always be Kormèr to me, man."

Jeremy scooped up a bit of mashed potato and sat back. "KL, we owe you *a lot* for what you did." Kormèr shrugged the praise aside. "Really. That was beyond bravery. It was damn crazy."

Kormèr shrugged. That was certainly true, and the crew didn't even know everything he had done.

"I'll admit: I had my doubts about you," Jeremy said. "But you risked your life for us and for our cause, not even knowing what it was or who we were."

Kormèr tried not to fidget in his seat, but it was uncomfortable having so many eyes on him. As though one of them would see through him and realize that his motives hadn't been so pure from the start, and his actions certainly weren't. "Forget about it," he mumbled.

"No way, dude," Roke repeated. "It's like you were meant to be there, on Io, so you could save the day."

Jeremy nodded. "Time for truth; we owe you that much. Those people back there were part of an organization led by a man called Harry G. He's one of the wealthiest people in the Sol System."

Kormèr recalled the name from earlier conversations, but the mention of wealth renewed his interest. He popped another chunk of chicken into his mouth and listened raptly. "How'd he get so rich?"

"Shrewd business practices… and as we've discovered, a lot of good old-fashioned racketeering. Among other businesses he runs, he monopolized the landing gear industry. It's illegal under Terran law, but he's got the leverage and muscle to do whatever he wants." Kormèr did not understand this very much; he grasped the concepts of monopoly, racketeering and paying from their definitions, but Jeremy's usage was unfamiliar.

Jeremy continued, "So when the guys here," he indicated the rest of the crew with a sweep of his hand, "and I came up with a new technology for landing gear, he tried to buy us out, threatened us… then he got his mercs after us. He knows our grav-repulse system will revolutionize travel, so if he can't have it, he wants to make sure that no one else does, either."

"I think I'm getting this," said Kormèr. "He owns all the… the rights to make and sell landing gear, right?" Jeremy nodded. "Since there are so many ships, and all ships need the ability to land, eventually, he makes money for every one of those ships." Jeremy nodded again. "When you try to sell something new and better, that will threaten his income."

"Hey, the kid's bright," said Kit. He sipped an amber liquid from his glass— whether it was juice or alcohol was hard to say.

"You got it," said Jeremy. "Io was a setup. We thought we'd found a buyer, but it was just his mercs."

Kormèr thought back to the chaos of gunfire back when he had stowed away with them on Io. "Hmm. Would he have really… killed us all?"

Mack shook his head. "We were only stunned, which tells me he had something else in mind."

"He probably needs what we know," said Jim, tapping his head. "Then maybe he'd consider other options."

Kormèr nodded as he finished cleaning his plate. Only bones remained sitting in a swirl of the brown sauce. He'd wiped up as much of that as he could with the last of the meat, and really wanted to lick the plate, but etiquette training from his father and the bots held him back. Instead, he sighed, satisfied enough for the moment.

"Now we just need to get to the next jump point before they come after us," said Morgan.

Kormèr frowned. "They're not coming after us." At the perplexed looks, he added, "That was the point; they think we're all dead."

"They think… Wait." Kit stared at Kormèr. "What?"

Kormèr looked at the faces staring back at him. "I figured Harry G wouldn't leave you alone unless he thought you were dead, so we worked out a scenario that would make it look like I had rammed your ship with the Y-Tach and destroyed us both."

"'We'?" asked Jeremy.

"Damn!" said Jim at the same moment. "That's devious! How'd you rig the explosion?"

Morgan slapped his forehead. "The secondary core! We've been frying our circuits trying to figure out what the devil happened to it."

"That's bat-shit crazy," said Mack, looking impressed, "even by my standards. Now I understand why the Y-Tach looks the way it does."

"You're one lucky dude," said Roke. "So now whatta we do with our live cargo?" Kormèr assumed he meant the three merc prisoners in the hold.

71

"We should space 'em," proposed Mack, eliciting protests from the others. "I'm just saying, if we leave 'em somewhere, word'll get back to G that we're not dead."

"Word will get back to him eventually anyway," said Jeremy. "I don't need three spacings on my conscience."

"Ægir station's got a Gal-Pol facility," suggested Morgan.

Mack groaned and rolled his eyes.

"What's Gal-Pol?" asked Kormèr.

"Galactic police," said Morgan.

Mack grunted, "More like…" He finished with something that Kormèr didn't understand.

The others chuckled, prompting Kormèr to ask, "Okay, and what's that?"

Roke coughed.

"I'm not going to translate that," sniffed Morgan.

Jeremy cleared his throat. "Mack doesn't think much of Gal-Pol, in case you haven't caught on," he said. "But I think that's our best bet. We'll take the chance that word will get back G sooner rather than later."

"I'll pay off whoever I can to make it later rather than sooner," offered Kit. "It might buy us some time to get the deal done."

Mack raised his hand to get Jeremy's attention. "Would it satisfy your conscience if we stuck 'em in an escape pod and launched them at Ægir station? It's almost en route to the next jump point, and there's no contact."

Jeremy considered Mack's proposal and nodded after a moment. "I'd be okay with that. We'd have to come up with a good message to explain the delivery, or there'll be a lot of questions the next time we come through. Will Ægir receive the message before we jump?"

Mack nodded. "I can work it so we get to the jump before they can reply."

"I'll draft the message and run it by you," said Morgan.

Kormèr really enjoyed how well the team worked together. They had clearly been at it for a while, so they each knew their strengths.

"Let's do it," said Jeremy.

"Great!" said Roke. "Then we're off to…" Something that sounded like "*frroo-wee-tsee*".

Kormèr laughed. "What was that?"

Jim chuckled. "The whistling? That's Averian. The planet's name is Averia… well, technically, its real name is Frrooweetsee, but most people just call it Averia. You'll love this place if you haven't been there before."

"Why'd you whistle the name?" he asked Roke.

"'Cause that's how they speak there. The natives are half-bird, half-human. That's why it's Averia… 'Ave' means 'bird' in one of the ancient Terran languages."

Kormèr didn't get it, but he didn't dwell on it, either, his mind busying itself with imagining what the natives might look like. *Which half is bird, and which half is human, I wonder?*

"That's why some don't really care for that name," said Jeremy.

Jim shrugged. "Those people should really just calm the heck down."

Oblivious to the exchange, Kormèr asked, "Wait, can they actually fly?" Kormèr sometimes dreamed that he could fly, and those were the dreams he loved the most. He'd sometimes try to hold on to thoughts of flying as he fell asleep, hoping it would trigger a flying dream. It never worked. The dreams came whenever they felt like it.

"They sure can," Roke chuckled. "They have bitchin' physiological traits that let 'em fly."

"Speaking of flying," said Jeremy, "I saw you took a piloting course on the edu-comp. Wanna pilot the ship to the next jump point?"

"You're joking," Kormèr said, but he couldn't hide the eagerness from his eyes.

"Oh, he never jokes," said Mack under his breath. "Not about the ship."

"Alright!"

THROUGH a quirk of physics, Epsilon Eridani could not be accessed directly from Sol despite the relative proximity of the two systems. Thus, it had remained a backwater system, with its only claim to fame being that it contained one of the first exoplanets ever identified, a factoid that, seventeen-hundred years later, no one cared about. But the datum existed in *Ship's* knowledge base, and it came up as Hassera read up on the system prior to FTL reversion.

Upon reverting from FTL space, *Ship* immediately alerted her of a nearby ship transponder, and identified it as Royland's Y-Tach. Before Hassera could get her hopes up, the sensor readings updated with the condition of the ship, coldly labeling it: **Debris**. An insignificant amount of other nearby debris displayed trajectories that tracked back to the Y-Tach, mostly bolts and bits of metal. The power core and FTL drive had been removed, hastily by the looks of it. The distance of the expanding debris from the remains of the ship revealed that the bits had probably started their journey around seven hours earlier.

Hassera channeled that information to the nav-com and had it calculate paths to the only two jump points in the system. One was starward and ten degrees above the elliptical, and the other was slightly to port, following the arc of the system's gigantic dust cloud. She requested a list of systems accessible from both jump points, hoping to divine which one Tailor might have taken from the downstream destinations. It seemed like an impossible task until *Ship* reported it had picked up an escape pod beacon. And it had originated from the direction of the second jump point.

With nothing more to glean from the ruined Y-Tach, Hassera accelerated toward the escape pod and activated comms.

"This is *SHP six six seven* hailing escape pod," she said. "Please identify your craft of origin." It took an hour for her message to reach the escape pod. Suspecting—and hoping—who might be in the pod, Hassera increased her speed to point-four light speed. So when the response came back, it took less than an hour.

"Hassera? It's Terl. Tailor's fricken AI got the jump on us. They dumped us out here." Hassera hissed in frustration. Why wasn't Terl telling her who else was with him? Also, sensors had picked up a ship leaving the local space station. It identified as Gal-Pol. If that light had just reached her now, that meant that the ship was a lot closer to the pod than she was. *"I hope Royland's with you, seein' as how your ship's kinda small for the three of us."*

Hassera's breath escaped in a low hiss. She turned to the nav-com board, dropped the escape pod as her nav-point, and replaced it with the jump point. *Ship* yawed to port five degrees and accelerated in the new direction. This created a graceful arc that would completely bypass the pod and the Gal-Pol ship. Hassera had no need for the merc trio, not if Royland was not with them. She knew now that Royland had probably been on the Y-Tach when it was destroyed, and that he was certainly dead.

"Hassera, are you—" She switched off the comm and once again brought up the list of downstream destinations available from this jump point. She would search them all if she had to, but she was counting on speed to pare down Tailor's lead. The ride down this tube would be ten hours. The next three jump points from the point of reversion there were ten hours, twelve hours and eight days distant. Tailor had a seven-hour lead, and Hassera had two and a half hours to go before reaching the jump point. Even if she didn't catch his light on the other end, if his ship was gone, she'd know which jump point he used.

She'd burn through cores pushing her ship through accelerations and decelerations to keep Tailor in her sights, but that hardly mattered. Royland would have done the same for her. One question would occupy her thoughts across the vast distances ahead: what would she do to Tailor and his crew once she caught up to them?

CHAPTER 6

THE night sky was its usual unmarred sapphire extravaganza. The day had been a hot one, and the warm evening air currents provided Cheert Reestee the lift he needed as he raced back to his store. He'd rushed out that afternoon, leaving his mother's birthday gift behind in his haste. Before his death four months ago, Cheert's father had always doted on his wife, giving her extraordinary gifts. Now that Cheert ran the family store, it was up to him to do the same for his mother.

He cursed his earlier haste. He'd been sitting comfortably at home, ready to eat dinner, when he'd remembered his oversight. He'd had to leave a wonderful oat salad and a hungry wife behind to complete his errand. Selfishly, a part of him hoped that his mother appreciated the trouble he was going through for her.

Cheert swooped down toward the storefront, deactivating the proximity detectors with a Terran-made beeper. *Crafty people, those Terrans*, he thought, absently, and not for the first time. He knew Averians were generally fond of Terrans, but he felt especially attracted to their culture and history, and he was proud to own a small collection of paper books from Terra. He frequently slipped this fact into conversation with his high-society friends.

He landed softly before the storefront, folding the ends of his silky wings behind him, and quickly deactivated the rest of the external security systems. He fumbled with the lock and entered, setting off the internal motion detectors as usual. He rushed to the comm unit, silenced the alarms, and put in the customary call to the Birshetland Police Department.

| | Hey, it's just me, | | he tweeted to the officer that answered. Then he trilled a code-song to confirm.

| | Good to hear from you Mister Reestee. This is off-schedule. | |

| | I forgot my mother's birthday gift, that's all. | | He reached for the light switch.

The officer on the other end chuckled. | | I've done that. Good thing you remembered. | | The lights came on. | | You'd never hear the end— | |

Cheert gasped. | | By all the gods! | |

| | EXCUSE ME. Excuse me, please! | |

The crowd reluctantly parted to allow Sylvestra Chrreel to pass. She understood that crime on Averia was a rarity, and a high-profile robbery like this one was even more so. But this was ridiculous. As soon as she was through the crowd, she turned to face them.

| | It's late, folks. Go home. | | No one moved. Maybe it was just her reading too much into their expressions and feeling her own self-doubt, but they even looked resentful of her. They had loved the city of Birshetland's previous Chief of Police, and they weren't ready to accept the young Averian woman that had replaced him after his retirement, even if she was his daughter.

Captain Phatheeo appeared at her right flank. | | You heard the Chief! | | he chirped. | | Move it! | | Murmuring quietly, the crowd slowly dispersed. Some stopped further away, but that was okay. As long as they weren't making a scene in front of the store. //*Make a celebrity of a criminal, and you'll only end up with others looking to make a name for themselves,*// her father used to tell her when he was training her—which was most of her life. It hadn't been easy being his daughter, but it had certainly prepared her for this position.

| | Thanks, | | she told Phatheeo, moving toward the shop entrance. The son of her father's captain, Phatheeo had been a close friend as she grew up, and he had accepted her fully as his superior. She had complete trust in him. | | Is it as bad as I heard? | |

| | Everything's gone. The owner had closed shop in a hurry yesterday evening and left his mother's birthday gift behind. He returned to get it and found the store empty, not a jewel left. | | His delivery, as always, was factual and to the point, without editorializing.

| | Everything? | | That was too incredible for her to believe. Chees was the largest jewelry store on Averia. For everything to have been stolen in a matter of hours... well, it was simply impossible.

They entered the store where Sylvestra paused and slowly took in the crime scene. She'd been in the store only once before, to review the installation of the upgraded security system. It looked almost exactly as she remembered it, only now the shelves and display cases were empty. It looked like a hastily vacated store, just waiting for a new owner to set up shop.

Sitting in a corner opposite the entrance, head hung and resting on his palms, was the proprietor.

| | They left the furnishings, | | answered the Captain. From anyone else, she would have assumed that to be sarcasm. But she knew he meant it as another fact. | | Reestee's in shock; he could barely tell us the story. | |

| | Was he harmed? Did he walk in on the robbers? | |

| |No, nothing like that. It was his father's business and, well, his father died only a few months ago, leaving the store to him. Well, you understand, the two losses are hitting him hard.| |

| |Of course.| | She continued toward Reestee, studying him along the way, automatically analyzing his body language. His snowy feathers reflected his high social rank. | |Did the robbers take the gift?| |

| |Ma'am?| |

| |You said he returned to get his mother's gift that he had left behind. Did the robbers take that, too?| |

| |No, the gift was a sentimental one, not particularly valuable or expensive.| |

| |Not everything has to be expensive to be valuable,| | she warbled. | |Anyway, what've you found so far?| |

Phatheeo checked his p-comm. | |The teams have been poring over the entire shop for hours. There's no sign of forced entry, no sign of the normal entrances or exits being used and no adjoining walls broken.| | He flipped dismissively through the rest of the list of reports from the various crime scene teams. | |Ah, here we go. This is the report you'll want to see first.| |

He passed her his p-comm, and Sylvestra reviewed the report. At the end, the report contained entire streams from each of the eight cameras that covered every square meter of the store, along with sensor data, all from the moment Reestee left the store until the moment he returned. The report summarized the findings from a preliminary analysis of the video and data. It said that the door was closed; evening darkened the interior; the door opened, and the lights came on; the store was empty. | |That's impossible.| |

| |I'm sure the events will reveal themselves once we make a thorough analysis. They always do.| |

Sylvestra handed him back his p-comm. | |That's true enough,| | she warbled, feeling somewhat rattled by the circumstances of this theft despite Phatheeo's reassurance.

She approached the proprietor. | |Mister Reestee.| | He did not respond. | |I am Sylvestra Chrreel, Chief of Police.| | Nothing. | |I assure you we will apprehend the thief.| | The man shuddered. Sylvestra frowned. She took Phatheeo aside and asked, | |Has his wife been informed?| |

| |Yes, but we've asked her not to come down yet. I wanted you to have a look first.| |

She nodded. | |Might as well call her, and have her pick him up. He's no good to us right now. We'll question him later… or tomorrow, once he's had a chance to relax with his family.| |

| |On it.| | Phatheeo walked off, and she heard him giving orders.

Sylvestra sighed and shook her head. Then she straightened, telling herself that the tough days made you appreciate the easy ones all the more. But her worries didn't go away that easily. This transition was not going well, and she knew it.

Her father had wanted a son to carry on for him once he retired, but things hadn't worked out that way. Her brother had died at birth from a congenital defect that affected any male child conceived by the couple. So her parents had stopped with her. Therefore, her father had been extremely overjoyed when Sylvestra had shown an interest in police work. He taught her all he knew and helped her get into the best academy on Averia. And when he retired, the Council of Constables gave her the job. She had the added distinction of being the first female Police Chief on Averia. Unfortunately, while the 'guys' in the department accepted her without outright complaint, the glares and subtle exhibits of passive-aggressive disobedience were telltale signs of their disapproval.

Her mind returned to the store, and she looked around at the bustle of the theft unit. Everyone was here; she'd spared no one. Sunrise was an hour away. This was going to be a long morning.

AVERIA had been nothing more than a bright dot against the background stars when they'd reverted from FTL. With Kormèr riding in the co-pilot's seat, Roke had shown him how to use the nearby gas giant to slingshot quickly up to point three light speed. After three weeks in transit from Epsilon Eridani, the crew were all eager to be planet-side. The extra speed would get them across the nearly one and a half billion kilometers from their reversion point to Averia in just around two hours, including acceleration and deceleration.

Sitting in the co-pilot's seat for the approach to Averia, Kormèr watched raptly, as the planet gradually grew to fill the forward screen. The immensity of planets fascinated him. Never had he imagined that a world could look like this, so round, so... so huge! And this one, unlike the others they had passed while in transit here, actually had life on it. They were close enough that he could see lights on the night-side. He was so enthralled that he missed when Jim tried to get his attention.

"Up and at 'em, dude," said Roke, punching him in the shoulder. He seemed to like to do that, but at least his punches felt lighter now. Either that, or Kormèr had gotten used to the good-natured pummeling.

"Huh?" Kormèr stirred. "Oh. It's just so incredible."

"Every time," said Jim. "Doesn't matter how many times you've seen it."

"I just cleared our landing with Freet-See Spaceport," announced Jeremy, who had filled in for Morgan at comms for this shift. "Landing vector incoming."

Kormèr had the nav-com screen up on the co-pilot's control board. The planetary stations allowed for operational flexibility for situations when ships carried less than a full crew. Kormèr watched as the scrolling display showed that the data had been received from planetary dock-control. He then grabbed the packet and shunted it over to the pilot's control widget. "Received and routed," he said, and glanced at Jim out of the corner of his eye.

Jim nodded, impressed. "You got it."

With a few deft keystrokes, Roke activated the landing sequence and let the ship take over. With a higher precision than any human could manage, the computer gradually maneuvered the craft about until it lined up with the designated landing platform.

"Does this ship have grav-repulsor gear?" Kormèr asked, the thought suddenly coming to him now that they were landing. If they had it, he wanted to be more aware of the landing.

"Of course," said Jim. "This is our showroom model."

"Oh," Kormèr said. "I guess it's a good thing only the upper hull took damage."

Jeremy snapped his fingers. "That reminds me… I should line up a repair crew now. They're probably booking up quickly."

Kormèr's eyes widened with interest. "By the way, if I can help with the repairs in any way, just let me know."

`Roke laughed. "Dude! You are ` *`too`* ` much!"`

Grinning, Kormèr turned his attention back to the boards. It was still night outside, so there was nothing much to see through the viewscreen but thousands of twinkling lights. He watched in rapt fascination as the ship slowly approached its landing platform, then positioned itself for the landing.

Kormèr closed his eyes as the ship set down…very smoothly. It was no wonder that the grav-repulsor technology was revolutionary. While Kormèr had no idea what other landing gear felt like, this one certainly felt comfortable and seamless.

"Outstanding job, dude," said Roke, slapping Kormèr on the back, almost knocking the wind from his chest.

Jim ruffled his hair. "Welcome to Averia."

"Thanks," said Kormèr, fixing his hair.

"That's great," said Jeremy, his attention presently focused elsewhere. "Thanks for squeezing us in on such short notice. Yeah. Got it. High sky." He pulled the ear-piece out and sat it on the charging receptacle, turning around to face the bridge crew. "We're in luck. They're expecting most holiday travelers to arrive starting tomorrow, so they're able to give us an open slot in one hour."

"Whoa!" said Roke. "That's awesome."

"Sure is. Can you guys take care of that while Kit 'n I head to Birshetland?"

"You got it, Jer," said Jim.

Kormèr asked, "What about me?"

"That's up to you," said Jeremy, turning back to his panel and tapping out a search. "It looks like there's still an open seat in the sky-hopper, if you wanna come with Kit and me."

Kormèr thought about staying behind and working on the ship, but while that might be interesting, it didn't sound very exciting. "I'll go along with you, if that's okay."

"I thought you might," grinned Jeremy. "I signaled ahead for an inoculation for you."

Kormèr frowned. "Inoculation against what?"

"It's a broad-spectrum vaccination; covers a bunch of maladies, from the common cold to some really nasty stuff. Trust me, you're better off with it than without it." At Kormèr's continued hesitation, he assured: "It's one needle, just a little jab. You'll barely feel it."

"I'm not worried about that." Kormèr didn't like the idea of having anything injected into him without knowing what it was and what effect it would have on him, but he relished the thought of getting ill even less.

Kit had been napping, so Kormèr and Jeremy waited at the foot of the boarding ramp. Kormèr glanced eagerly about for his first glimpse of an Averian. He spotted a few people in coveralls working on another ship in the distance, but it was still too dark, and he couldn't make out what they looked like. Freet-See Spaceport, on the other hand, took his breath away. The square landing platform connected via a short bridge to a low building that had to be ten times the size of Kormèr's home. It too curved away in the distance. Kormèr counted six other platforms to his right and three to the left.

Above and beyond the low main building, tiers of shadowy structures rose into the night sky and sparkled with the brilliance of thousands of lights, holo-ads and small-vehicle traffic that zipped about like fireflies.

A small robotic cart floated up to them. "Here we are," said Jeremy. "Roll up your sleeve, KL. It's either that, or you drop your pants."

Kormèr pulled his sleeve immediately and waited as Jeremy answered a few questions on the cart's touch display.

"No allergies or special medical conditions, right?" Jeremy asked.

"What?"

"Never mind." Jeremy shook his head. "We'll know if you turn blue, or if your tongue swells up." He laughed at Kormèr's frown of consternation. "I'm kidding. Hold out your arm."

A mechanical arm extended from the cart and rolled a chrome cylinder against Kormèr's arm. The cylinder hissed, and Kormèr felt a slight stinging and some pressure on his arm. Then the cart retracted its mechanical arm and floated away.

"That's it?" asked Kormèr, fixing his sleeve.

"That's it, kid; you're all set." He looked up and back at the ship. "And here's Kit. Right on time."

They crossed the bridge and entered the low building, with kiosks and maintenance bays lining the open-air "ground" level. The kiosks promised information, currency exchange, transit lodging bookings and ship repairs. The trio bypassed them all and passed through a doorway, into a corridor and onto a moving walkway that carried them past more shops and kiosks and deposited them by a sky-hopper stand. There, finally, Kormèr got his first look at Averians.

Aside from their wings and the coat of shining feathers that covered their bodies, Averians had an otherwise humanoid physique, bipedal and with long arms, part of which belonged to their wing structure. Their wings folded neatly against their backs, with the bend of the wings showing just behind their shoulders; Kormèr couldn't help but think of these as "wing tips", though he assumed they were more akin to wrists if they followed the same structure as birds. Their legs from the knees down bore very fine scales rather than feathers and ended in feet with three long toes in the front and two in the back, each with a curved talon sprouting from the tip. Their forearms were similar, only these ended in typical, unscaled, five-fingered hands.

The hopper pilot Jeremy was speaking to had dark brown feathers everywhere, with flecks of black along the edges of his arms and fluffy white down where feather met flesh along his ankles and wrists. The wing tips were folded back at the elbows, but even so, Kormèr estimated his wing span was easily over three meters. His face was mostly devoid of feathers, save for the downy brows and lashes that surrounded his coal-black eyes, which suddenly focused on Kormèr. The pilot twittered, ||This is your first time here, son?||

Kormèr flushed. He was glad he'd taken the time to learn the language from the edu-comp. ||Yes sir. I'm sorry for staring.||

||No offense taken. But watch yourself 'round here. Freet-See Spaceport's not a place for fledglings.||

||Thanks for the tip,|| sang Jeremy.

The sky-hopper ended up being nothing more than an open multi-seater skiff that hovered. It reminded Kormèr of his hovecar, only gray and… ugly. It was designed for utility, and every expense *was* spared in that department. Kormèr suspected that the yellow and green stripes on the side had to have some other function besides presentation. Hearing that this was Kormèr's first time there, the other passengers were nice enough to let Kormèr sit in the front, just behind the pilot. Jeremy sat to his left and Kit behind.

The wind tossing his hair, Kormèr looked back at the strangest city he had ever seen. The bright yellowish rising sun peeked through the Freet-See cityscape, a crazy mixture of tall buildings and odd structures resembling what Kormèr's English lesson told him were trees. They were supposedly some type of natural plant growth, but they didn't exist on Elmar, so there was no Elmarian term for them, except maybe "tall shrub". But these trees were of concrete and metal, not what real, natural and organic trees were supposed to be made of. Even the leaves were thin, inflexible sheets of metal that seemed to catch the sunlight. This confused him.

"Hey, guys, I thought trees were supposed to be made of wood."

Jeremy laughed. | |I'm sorry, KL,| | he sang in Averian, and Kormèr took the hint that he should speak Averian from now on. | |It's just strange to have someone bring up a question like that. There is no wood up here.| |

| |Up here?| |

| |You haven't noticed yet?| | Kormèr shook his head. | |Look over the side.| | Kormèr looked over the side of the sky-hopper. Immediately, he realized what Jeremy was talking about. Instead of a solid landmass, the ground whisking by below them consisted of large, island-like rock-masses that appeared to be floating in a sea of fleecy clouds. Kormèr thought of cereal flakes floating in milk. Behind them, the city of Freet-See rose atop one of these rock-masses, a colossally proportioned one.

Kormèr gaped.

| |Mm-hmm. Now you see. The Averians used to live down below the rock-clouds. But conditions became so bad that they migrated up here permanently. In fact,| | continued Jeremy, | |if time hasn't dulled my sense of navigation, the ruin of the first Averian city above the clouds is somewhere south of here, about that way.| |

| |Twenty more degrees west, sir,| | corrected the pilot.

| |Thanks.| |

Kit mumbled something about horseshoes, hand grenades and nuclear war, for which he received a nasty look from Jeremy. Kormèr didn't understand the reference, but he shrugged it off; there was bound to be plenty that he wasn't going to understand right away. These Terrans were odd enough, and Averians promised to be just as puzzling.

The sky-hopper traveled quickly, racing the coming daylight across the planet. Kormèr marveled at the sights, especially when they traveled over an area Kit called the Great Rift. It was a wide open area devoid of rocks or clouds, only hot, rapidly rising air. Most people believed that this had something to do with how the stone-sky had been created, but there weren't many running theories. Averia was an aerial paradise that everyone simply enjoyed; the science was left to others.

| |Where are we headed?| | asked Kormèr.

| |The capital of the planet. It's a city called Birshetland.| | When the sky-hopper sailed into the city an hour later, Kormèr found that, unlike Freet-See, it had no buildings. It was a vast city of metal and concrete trees—"pseudo-trees", Morgan had called them—built on another colossal rock-island. Kormèr watched, fascinated, as morning sunlight washed over the city, setting the millions of metallic leaves asparkle. Kormèr spotted a few Averians flying about, while sprawling promenade platforms connected the enormous trees for non-fliers. Several airborne vehicles flitted about, some dark and others brightly colored. Kormèr tuned in as the pilot sang something to Jeremy.

Jeremy seemed perplexed. | |He's ready to meet us *now*?| |

| |Yes,| | answered the pilot. Tapping his headset, | |I've just received the message. He specifically said you were to head there first thing after arriving.| |

| |Well, alright,| | Jeremy grumbled. | |But I hope he realizes I'm grouchy if I don't get my coffee.| |

| |He will provide coffee; he's dealt with humans before,| | chirped the pilot, and Kormèr caught the annoyed glance between Jeremy and Kit.

| |Hey, you're used to being up early,| | Jeremy twittered. | |We're not.| |

| |I understand. And you have come a long way. No offense meant.| |

| |None taken.| | He turned and winked at Kormèr and Kit, and Kit grinned wolfishly in reply.

Kormèr just smiled, unsure of exactly what he was supposed to do. He sighed, regretting that he hadn't taken a tutorial on Averian society and culture back on the ship when he had the chance. Perhaps that would have helped. He decided that, as soon as they landed, he would wander about to get a feel for the place. There was nothing like cultural immersion to gain a deeper understanding of an unfamiliar place.

The sky-hopper set down on a wide concrete platform which connected via a bridge to one of the enormous concrete trees. Kormèr gaped at two huge, gray-feathered birds that were tethered a short distance away. They were each easily three times Kormèr's height. *By the gods, they breed them big here!* He craned his neck to stare up at them but turned away when they seemed to look at him, just in case they took offense at his staring. Their shining black eyes were harder to read than human or even Averian eyes.

Kormèr approached Jeremy. | |I'm gonna go for a walk, if you don't mind.| |

| |Umm. Are you sure, kid? You know where you're going?| |

Kormèr nodded, amused at his concerned tone. | |I won't go far. Why?| |

Jeremy shrugged. | |I dunno. We brought you all this way, so I just feel kinda responsible for you, that's all.| |

Kormèr smiled. | |Thanks. But I'll be okay. This isn't my first time alone in a strange place.| |

Kit chuckled. | |I'd never've guessed. It's your first time here, though. Do we meet you somewhere later? Or, are you ditching us?| |

Kormèr hadn't thought about that. He really had no more reason to stay with Jeremy and his crew, but they didn't know that. As long as he held onto his portal cube, he always had the option of returning home, but hanging around Jeremy had its advantages, too. He couldn't decide now. He would think about it. For now, | |Yeah, I'll stay. You'll be here in the city?| |

| |For a while,| | sang Jeremy. | |At least until our sales pitch is over. Then we'll be staying at a classy little hotel in the center of town. Here's the address... Aw, crap. I forgot to get you a p-comm.| | He sang something to the pilot, and the latter handed him a digital flimsy. This was a tech that Kormèr knew well, since the thin, foldable sheets of plastic existed on Elmar as well. Jeremy swiped the address from his p-comm onto the flim and passed the latter to Kormèr. | |And... that's it, I guess.| |

| | I'll definitely try to catch up with you guys there. Later. In the meantime, good luck with your 'pitch'. | |

| | Thanks, KL, | | Jeremy nodded. | | For everything. | |

JEREMY watched Kormèr amble off through the morning rush and felt a twinge of wistfulness and parental concern. He usually felt that kind of anxiousness when he was testing out a new prototype or some other equipment in which he was heavily invested, not towards other people. Then again, it had been a while since he had interacted with children.

"Thinkin' twice about setting him loose?" asked Kit, noticing his pensiveness.

"Why should we care, right? He's not ours." Jeremy shrugged. "And hell, we've only known the kid for a few days."

"Yeah, but you'd miss him." Kit grinned. "Sure, he can be a smug little snot sometimes, but he's not a bad kid. He saved our hides, and once he got that chip off his shoulder, he wasn't as annoying."

Jeremy chuckled. "Sometimes, he acts like a kid who's forgotten how to be a kid." He thought back to the conversation that he had had with Kormèr, where the boy had told him that his parents were dead. "I wonder if he even has friends his own age."

Kit grunted. "It is kind of weird that no one seems to be looking for him. Mack's been scanning the missing persons bulletins as they come in, and there's nothing matching his description."

"'Not all those who wander are lost,'" Jeremy murmured.

"Come again?" Kit asked.

"It's a quote from old Terran literature. If you ask me, Kormèr's hanging out with us because he wants to, not because he needs to, or because he has nowhere else to go."

"That's a bit of a leap," Kit muttered. "He's just a kid."

Jeremy shook his head. "Maybe. Elmarians are an odd bunch, though. And this kid gives off a vibe…"

"Sure. Now he does, but before he met us, he didn't even know English. Maybe he acts that way because he doesn't know any better, or he's pretending to be more than he is."

"Bah, now you're sounding like Mack!" Jeremy shook his head. "We probably won't see him again, anyway. And right now, we have enough to worry about." He took a deep, fortifying breath and held out his fist. "You ready?"

Kit bumped Jeremy's fist with his own. "Aye-aye, Cap'n." He grinned, looking toward the café where they were meeting their prospective client. "If nothing else, I hope the coffee's good."

THE landing platform, and the tree to which it connected, turned out to belong to the Birshetland Port Authority. The bridge led directly into an arcade that tunneled through the tree. Kormèr followed the flow of the small crowd and absorbed the details, from the fresh whitewash on the concrete tree trunk to all the different signs. Kiosks lined the arcade, just like the ones at the port building in Freet-See. But unlike Freet-See's grittiness, the port here appeared well-maintained. Even the kiosk workers—some already seated behind their desks and others just arriving and opening up—took the time to smile and wish everyone walking past | |high sky| |, as the local greeting seemed to go.

Kormèr felt an idyllic vibe in the air that lightened his step. Maybe it was the perfect golden sunrise, or maybe it was just standing on a planet after weeks in space on a ship, and finally being able again to fill his lungs with crisp, cool fresh air. The light of the Averian sun—bright, yellow and clear—definitely enthralled him. It differed from the reddish tints that colored the Elmarian sky. Whatever it was, it had him smiling.

The arcade ended, and Kormèr stepped into a wide u-shaped platform onto which other arcades from four other trees emptied. Awaiting travelers, like him, stood in queues by openings in the railings. Flying vehicles swept in from the open end of the platform, stopped at the openings for the passengers to board, and then whisked them off to other destinations in the city. This intrigued Kormèr, as it reminded him of the hover-transports that carried farm workers from Vranja city out to the farms each morning. Was this the same thing? *Where would they take me if I queued up?*

And that's when he realized that he'd been shuffling forward slowly for the past few minutes, following the natural flow of pedestrian traffic. He peered around the person ahead of him and spotted one of the dark aircars he'd seen earlier hovering just ahead. He now noticed it had no visible windows and an emblem on the side panels, part of which read: *Birshetland Police Department. It's a robotic aircar,* he realized. Kormèr listened as, in a tinny voice, the car asked a family for identification. It ended the registration process with: | |Information recorded. Welcome to Birshetland. Enjoy your stay.| | Only then did Kormèr notice the sign suspended overhead that read, | |New arrival registration.| |

Kormèr stepped out of the queue and strode away, trying as much as possible to look like he belonged there, but also using the crowd to keep himself out of the aircar's line-of-sight. He had no intention of giving out any information about himself to the authorities. If the information were cross-referenced with Elmar, a lot of questions would come up that he wasn't prepared to answer.

He stopped short upon spotting another aircar at the next tree performing the same function. Looking ahead, he found aircars registering people at each of the arcade exits. He ducked into the next arcade just to bide his time while considering how he would get past the aircars. Now he wished he'd stayed with Kit and Jeremy. Having been here before, they were probably already registered. They might have been able to vouch for him, avoiding any awkward questions.

Midway through the arcade, a sign read, | |Returning residents| |. He only saw Averians using that corridor. Kormèr strolled past it, taking a good look as he did. But it was just another shorter arcade. He turned back, and this time casually took the exit, expecting someone to grab his shoulder or collar from behind and stop him. His surprise did not, however, come from behind. Instead, it came when the arcade ended at a two-meter square slab of granite-like stone jutting out from the tree. His stomach churned as his eyes wandered down, down and further down still to the ground far below. He wondered what insane reason would drive anyone to would build a walkway to nowhere. And with no safety railings either! *Of course, you dummy!* he chastised himself as the reason finally occurred to him. *It's made for returning residents. Averians! They don't need passenger aircars or safety railings.* His brow furrowed. *I wonder what they do with their luggage.* He turned on shaky legs and started walking back the way he'd come when a voice called from behind.

"Ey, Terran wan' a ride—"

Kormèr turned back. An orange aircar hovered at the platform's edge; a message board on its roof flipped between different languages, all displaying the same message: *Taxi.* A grinning, downy-faced birdman rested one forearm on the top of his door as he waited for Kormèr's answer.

||Hi. I'm not Terran.||

||Oh. My apologies. Elmarian?||

||That's right! How did you guess?||

The driver shrugged his wings. ||Just a slight accent; it's hardly noticeable.||

Kormèr nodded. ||My name is Kormèr.|| He had practiced sounding his name out in Averian during the voyage on the *Stardust IV*.

||Would you like a ride somewhere, Kormèr?||

I really don't know where to go. ||Uh…||

||New in town, eh?||

||You could say that.|| Kormèr's stomach growled again, and he realized he was smelling food. The taxi driver had something steaming in a cup that smelled delicious.

The driver must've noticed because he asked, ||Are you hungry?||

||Yes, I am.||

||A restaurant then?||

||That sounds great,|| Kormèr blurted, then absently stuck his hands into his pockets. *Idiot! I have no money! I should've asked Jeremy for some.* He had been so enthralled by the new sights and sounds that it just occurred to him now. ||Sorry, I don't have anything to pay with.||

The man laughed, the sound like bird chatter. ||I figured as much. Don't worry, I know a couple of cheap places that are close by. I hate to see someone go hungry, especially in Birshetland, and I'm on my break, anyway.|| He flipped a switch on his dashboard that changed the message board on top to read: *Off Duty.*

Kormèr was surprised by the man's generosity. ||Okay. Wow, thank you!||

He contemplated briefly that the man could have ill intentions, but there were too many witnesses watching their exchange, and he had already stated that he had no money, so Kormèr liked his odds.

As if the birdman sensed his hesitation, he whistled to a couple of other waiting taxi drivers. ||I'm taking my break, if anyone's looking. I'm going to take this Elmarian to—|| He whistled something that Kormèr presumed to be the name of an establishment, as the other drivers nodded approvingly and whistled back food orders.

Kormèr's driver fluffed his gray crest feathers with a snort. ||Ah! You snot-ceres still owe me from last time. Come on, Kormèr. Hop in.||

The rear door slid open, and Kormèr stepped in. The door shut, and they soared away from the port.

||You're young, no?|| asked the driver, looking at Kormèr in his rearview mirror.

||I am three and a half years old,|| replied Kormèr, not thinking of himself as being so young.

||That would be fourteen Terran years.||

Kormèr thought about that. ||Something like that, yes.||

||That's young for a Terran.||

What's this guy's obsession with Terrans? ||But I'm not Terran, I'm El—||

||Elmarian, I know. Please, do not take offense.||

Remembering Jeremy's response to this, ||None taken. Can we just stop talking about my age… and Terrans?||

||As you wish.||

A long moment of silence followed. Kormèr watched the scenery go by, first sparse trees that slowly grew denser until they entered the center of town. They glided above the white-granite promenades with their decorative gardens, fountains and even public baths in which Kormèr could see people swimming. The promenades connected to platforms that circled the tree trunks and granted access to various storefronts around the trees.

Kormèr spied a large crowd gathered at the edge of one promenade. ||What's going on there?|| he asked the driver.

The driver looked, too late, and turned the taxi about to get a look. ||Not sure. I heard a few passengers mention something about a robbery.||

||A robbery?|| Kormèr's stared fixedly at the scene, his curiosity piqued. ||Set me down here.||

||But the restaurant—||

||Oh, right. Is it far? Can I walk there from here?||

||Well, sure, but… Alright. I can see you've got your mind set.||

The driver set down some distance from the crowd while Kormèr rummaged through his pockets. He wanted to give the driver something for his efforts and his hospitality, but found nothing more valuable than a facetted gem he had acquired on some planet. It was a pretty stone, but too small for any practical purpose. Tentatively, he passed it to the driver. ||Sorry, I don't—||

||Wow! Thanks Kormèr,|| exclaimed the driver, who marveled over the stone. ||And you said you didn't have any money, you jaybird!||

| | High sky, | | chirped Kormèr bemusedly, and stepped out of the taxi.

Thanks to his slim build, he easily wove his way through the crowd until he reached a thin fabric film strung across the path directly ahead, around six meters from the storefront. No one stood guard at the path, but three official-looking Averians loitered outside the store, chatting. While most Averians wore nothing in the way of clothes, only personal adornments, these three each sported a belt with attached cross-shoulder strap. The belts supported utility pouches and short batons; the shoulder straps held a badge with a logo that matched the one on the side of the robotic police aircars.

The glass storefront must have had a special coating, as it had no glare or reflection, and Kormèr could see clearly through to the cases within. Though the cases were empty, he knew what they were, even before he noticed the sign above the storefront confirming his educated guess. This was a jewelry store! His heart leaped. His soul danced...

He stopped and moved slightly to the left as a flash of white inside caught his eye. Whatever it was had disappeared behind a tall case. He stood on his toes and leaned left to get a better look as the "something" turned out to be a someone, and that someone came back into view. The Averian was clearly female, but one of the most eye-catching Kormèr had seen thus far. Snowy-white plumage, laced with glints of silver, covered her slender form from forehead to calves. Her age was impossible to tell, but she appeared young to him—maybe not as young as him, but age was never a factor for him when pursuing his heart's desire. She moved with a dancer's fluid grace that, on anyone else, would have appeared practiced or contrived, but seemed perfectly normal for her. She met his eyes for a moment that seemed to linger forever, and her silvery-black eyes penetrated straight through into his heart and pinned him in place.

<<Wow! She is beautiful,>> he crooned, completely enthralled. *I must find out who she is.*

The crowd shifted, shoving Kormèr aside and breaking his eye-contact with the woman. Someone brushed past him, and Kormèr looked up as another woman rushed toward the store, snapping the flimsy tape in her haste. One of the trio of police officers jumped to her side immediately and escorted her inside. Kormèr watched jealously as the new woman conversed with the white-feathered beauty. He longed to be in there as well, in her presence, speaking with her. The new woman departed moments later, with a very forlorn man at her side—Kormèr overheard someone in the crowd say that it was the store owner and his wife. The remaining two officers escorted the couple through the crowd to a dark-gray hovecar that whisked them away.

Kormèr turned his attention back to the store and found the birdwoman looking at him again. She looked about ready to come outside, as if she was as curious about him as he was about her. He groaned as his stomach squelched. *I can't meet such a beautiful woman on an empty stomach; it'd be too distracting.* He took one last look at her—she had turned away—then stepped back through the crowd. He spotted his taxi waiting at the other end of the promenade.

||My break wasn't over, so I waited for you,|| the driver chirped with a big smile.

||That was very nice of you. Thank you, uh… What's your name?||

||Feestoo, at your service.||

||Well, thank you, Feestoo.|| Kormèr wondered if the gem had something to do with the man's sudden devotion. He entered the taxi and sat. ||I guess we can continue to the restaurant now.||

||I thought you might still be interested. But there is another more suited to your rank… that you might prefer.||

Rank? Rank. What could he possibly mean? ||I don't understand what you mean.||

||Forgive me if I offend you when I say that, when we first met, I misjudged your rank… your position in society. You are clearly of a much higher rank. I humbly beg your forgiveness.||

Kormèr waved his hand. ||Don't lose your feathers over it. But I would actually prefer to eat at the restaurant you originally mentioned.||

||No. Forget it even exists. It's not suitable for your tastes.||

||Now you offend me,|| tittered Kormèr, in jest.

||Oh!||

||You're saying that I can't adapt my tastes, that I am a snub-nosed aristocrat, or something.||

Feestoo made an odd choking sound, and the taxi juked erratically and pitched somewhat toward the ground. Kormèr had been purposefully laying the sarcasm on thick, but he realized that Averians might not understand Elmarian sarcasm as much as he didn't understand all their mannerisms. Based on the driver's reaction, the penalty for offending a high-ranking citizen might also be high. Kormèr decided to quickly pardon the birdman before they both plummeted to the ground.

||I'm only ruffling your feathers,|| he chirped, glancing nervously out the window as they barely missed hitting the top of a low tree. ||I'm not offended in the least.||

Feestoo regained control somewhat. But he still stuttered. ||Oh… I…||

||But please take me to the restaurant you first mentioned.||

Finally, ||Y..yes. As you wish. Forgiveness, please.||

||Think nothing of it.||

||Th… thank you.||

Kormèr sighed inside. He had to watch his wit on this planet. *I'm liable to send the wrong Averian into a molt.*

||DON'T look,|| Sylvestra told Phatheeo. ||I've looked twice, and he might get frightened away.||

Captain Phatheeo used the selfie camera on his p-comm to peer over his own shoulder. | |The young Terran man? Who is he?| |

Man? He barely looked old enough to shave, but Sylvestra didn't bother to voice her doubt. | |I don't know, but he has a unique curiosity. He's been staring intently at me for the last few minutes.| |

| |You think he knows something.| |

| |Not for certain, but I suspect so. Walk casually over to him and ask if he wants to come inside. If he says 'no' or runs,| | she tipped her head to her right, | |I guess just let him be.| |

| |On it.| |

Sylvestra waited a moment after Phatheeo walked away before turning to check on his progress. When she did, Phatheeo was on his way back, not having even reached the door. She looked to the window… The boy was gone. She turned to Phatheeo, and he shrugged. | |Maybe you weren't casual enough,| | she joked.

The Captain smiled. | |You should know that I'm not very good at casual.| |

He could look intimidating, but Sylvestra knew him to be a good and compassionate man. He just didn't know how or when to show it. | |Do I need to send you for training?| |

Phatheeo chuckled. | |Time away from the precinct? I'll take that.| |

The strange boy forgotten for the moment, Sylvestra frowned at the puzzling scene in front of them. | |Not today, old friend. Especially for this little mystery, we'll need all the eyes and ears we can get.| |

| |HERE we are,| | announced Feestoo as he settled the taxi down. There was nothing fancy about this restaurant's exterior, and from what Kormèr could see through the windows, it seemed cozy, or as cozy as it could be, for an establishment that catered to a clientele with an average three-meter wingspan. There certainly appeared to be adequate "elbow room" between tables. A sign above the door labeled it as the | |Cheery Diner| |, which made Kormèr smile. *Everything about this city is so... cheery!*

| |Thanks. What do I owe you?| |

Feestoo waved his open palm at Kormèr. | |No, no. You're covered.| |

| |I insist,| | chirped Kormèr, reaching into his pocket for another gem.

| |Please, Kormèr. It's okay. Go eat, and tell them to put it on my tab.| | He chuckled as Kormèr's stomach squelched audibly. | |I can hear how hungry you are.| |

Kormèr smiled. | |Alright. But why don't you come in and have a cup with me?| |

| |Oh, no. I can't. My break is nearly over. I'm grateful for the invitation, though.| |

Kormèr mulled over this. He didn't want to be overbearing and monopolize all of Feestoo's time, but the cabbie was personable and helpful, and Kormèr often found that he could learn a great deal about a place from speaking with the local transportation workers. | |Well, okay. I don't want to keep you. You've been more than generous with your time. I hope the gemstone I gave you was adequate compensation?| |

Feestoo's eyes brightened. | |Oh, more than enough. It's enough for a full day!| |

| |That sounds definitive,| | Kormèr laughed. | |It's as though you had it appraised.| |

| |When I dropped you off near Chees. The jewelry shop.| | Feestoo's feathers ruffled nervously. | |Can you blame me?| | he asked, defensively, but grinning. | |No one has ever paid me with a gem before. It's lovely, but I had to know for sure that you... I mean, that it was...| |

| |Authentic. I understand. Well, if you are covered for all the fares you'll miss in the next hour—and you don't mind sparing me a little more of your time—can I 'hire' you to have a drink with me?| | *And here I was thinking of trading these gems for local currency. Why bother when I can get this level of service with the real thing?*

||Well, Kormèr, I really should—|| Kormèr watched Feestoo's resolve leak away as Kormèr held up another small gem. The birdman sighed. ||Oh, why not? What's the harm in extending my break a while longer? I am a bit thirsty after my breakfast.||

Feestoo left the taxi parked off the edge of the promenade, and they both entered the Cheery Diner.

In Kormèr's experience, restaurants were almost universally the same, with technology being the biggest differing factor. They had eating surfaces—some long for big communal meals, some short for more intimate dining—and they had menus. Waiters varied from live people to robots. Birshetland had the former.

According to the menu, the diner served a variety of offworld foods, including Elmarian, but Kormèr was curious about the local fare. As Kormèr's eyes glazed over from the dizzying array of choices, Feestoo laughed at his conundrum.

||What would you recommend?|| Kormèr asked sheepishly.

Feestoo smiled wryly. ||Any allergies that you know of?||

||Not that I know of,|| Kormèr shrugged. ||I guess we'll find out together.||

Feestoo chirped a lengthy and elaborate-sounding order to the waiter, who listened and nodded intently without having to write anything down. Kormèr had never tried ingredients like "oat-flax" and "lumbricus", but he was too hungry to question Feestoo's selections.

Kormèr wasn't disappointed or left wanting. The feast included an assortment of crisp, hearty discs of a savory grain mixture, served alongside a generous helping of lightly browned sausage links. Feestoo picked up a small carafe of a nutty-flavored syrup from the table, which he explained was for dipping or drizzling over the oat-flax cakes. The flavorful sausages melted on Kormèr's tongue but had just a crunchy, satisfying snap to the bite. Two tall, cool glasses of nutria came with the meal, alongside plain water. The nutrient-fortified beverage provided the birdfolk with supplements that they didn't otherwise get from their diets, but the sweet, creamy flavor appealed to non-avians, too.

Kormèr devoured everything on his plate, but the sausages were his favorite by far. That they consisted of ground worms didn't even matter to him.

While Kormèr ate, Feestoo kept him entertained with stories of his family. He told of how his father had been a taxi driver before him, but how things had been different back when his dad had gotten started, since they hadn't had the excellently engineered hove-cabs of today, and so on.

Kormèr listened intently for a while, then slowly, less so, until he completely tuned out the rambling birdman and lost himself in his own thoughts. *I have to get a street map or something that shows where stores are. If there is one jewelry store, there have to be others. And if all Averians are as crazy over jewels as Feestoo is, they might even horde them at home. There's promise here.*

But this will take time and careful planning. I need to understand the culture here better, like this whole rank business. I wouldn't want to pick the wrong mark and end up hurting someone that doesn't deserve it. So if I'm staying a while, I'll need shelter once Jeremy and his crew leave. Someplace where I won't stand out; a little out of the way place, not too shabby but not too extravagant. Maybe Feestoo knows the right place.

| | And that's really what's wrong with Freet-See, if you ask me. | |

Kormèr nodded. | | I don't doubt it. Good thing we're here, in Birshetland. | |

Feestoo opened his mouth to speak, but Kormèr cut him off, | | Speaking of which, since I've just arrived, where would you recommend for a place to stay? | |

Feestoo sang, | | I know just the place. | | Kormèr paid for the meal with a small gem—with Feestoo's recommendation about the proper size and cut—and they returned to the waiting taxi.

A short ride later, Kormèr found himself in the lobby of an elegant hotel. *Wonderful,* he thought sourly, eyeing the rich furnishings and gold trim on the oval chamber entrances. This was not what he was looking for at all. Kormèr turned to ask Feestoo to take him some place else, but the birdman took his arm and pulled him toward the registration desk. Kormèr opened his mouth to protest, but Feestoo cut him short.

| | This young man would like a room, | | he chirped to the clerk.

The young birdman behind the desk eyed them both suspiciously, even curiously, as if he were not used to seeing an Averian man dragging an Elmarian youth around. Then it struck Kormèr that, based on the concept of rank that Averians followed, taxi drivers probably never entered the hotel outside of helping with luggage. *This is probably a high-rank hotel.*

| | Uh, how will you be paying for this? | | asked the clerk, his tone implying that there was no chance in hell a taxi driver could afford the rates.

| | Oh, I'm not paying. | | Feestoo pointed at Kormèr. | | He is. | |

Kormèr was stunned, wide eyes locked on Feestoo. *What's he trying to do? I don't have any money!*

Apparently, the clerk noticed Kormèr's shock. | | Please excuse me a moment. I… uh… have to check the master roster. | | He promptly disappeared through a door labeled *Manager,* in Averian.

| | What're you doing? | | asked Kormèr, tugging his arm out of Feestoo's grip.

| | Getting you one of the best rooms in Birshetland, | | answered Feestoo proudly.

| | I wanted a small place, nothing like this. | |

| | Your forgiveness, Kormèr, but you can eat wherever you want, shop wherever you want, and so on. But I will not let you rest in any trash-nest. Cheerees is the best hotel in town. | |

Kormèr saw that resistance was futile. Still, there was one major problem with this idea of Feestoo's. | | But I have no money. How am I supposed to pay for this place? | |

||But you *do* have money. When they ask for it, you just show them one of those shiny things in your pocket.||

Kormèr nearly slapped his forehead. Of course, he had money. Still, he wanted to be thrifty. It wouldn't do him any good if he ran out of gems paying for extravagances before he could get more.

The manager's door opened, then. An older birdman emerged, followed by the junior clerk. Over his mottled light-gray plumage, the birdman wore a short halter-style dark vest that didn't restrict his wings, with the hotel's logo embroidered over his breast pocket. He only glanced at Feestoo, but it was long enough for Kormèr to notice his skepticism. Even on the alien face, the expression was unmistakable. When the manager spoke, he looked at Kormèr. ||How may I help you?||

Before Feestoo could answer, Kormèr plucked one of his feathers and spoke up: ||I'd like a room, please.||

The manager smiled humorlessly, looking down his nose at Kormèr, though they were both the same height. ||Of course, young man. A deposit is required upon reservation, so how will you be paying today?||

Kormèr returned the rigid smile. ||Do you accept gemstones?||

The manager grew serious, but the condescending smile stayed. ||Look here, I have no time for games. Now why don't you…y..you….|| Kormèr watched the birdman lose his train of thought as the gem he held up refracted the light into a multitude of colors, at least three of which reflected in the birdman's reddish eyes.

The manager picked up a p-comm from behind the counter and said something into it that Kormèr couldn't hear. ||Please wait just a moment,|| sang the manager. ||Would you like some coffee or tea while you wait?|| He looked at Feestoo. ||Or nutria?||

||We're okay for now, thank you,|| sang Kormèr, again before Feestoo could say anything.

A flutter drew Kormèr's attention past a grand archway to the right, beyond which a birdwoman had just alighted from somewhere. Behind her, there seemed to be nothing but open space and a few balconies with doors and windows in the distance. She walked up to the registration desk, and Kormèr noticed she wore an embellished dark vest like the manager's. ||Where is it?||

||Ah, young sir,|| warbled the manager, ||please show Miss Sooreeo your gem?||

Kormèr took a step back and held out the gem at arm's length when he saw the woman produce a device similar to Jeremy's d-scanner, to examine it. After a moment, the woman nodded at the manager. Then she turned, crouched slightly and leaped upward, spreading her wings and gliding across the lobby and back out into the open space. Kormèr couldn't take his eyes off of her until she disappeared. *I can't imagine I'll ever get used to seeing that,* he thought.

||So do you have a room for me, or not?|| asked Kormèr, turning back to the manager and twiddling the gem between his fingers.

||Of course, sir,|| sang the manager with a smile. His junior assistant dashed off. ||Your name, please.||

||Kormèr Lezàl.||

||And how long will you be staying with us, Mister Lezàl?||

Kormèr grimaced, not liking the sound of that. "Mister Lezàl" was Yunzen, in his mind. He shrugged. ||I'm not sure. At least three or four weeks, but maybe more.||

||Very well. I will place you on our extended stay plan. Do you have any special needs we should know of to make your stay with us more comfortable?||

Kormèr had never been asked that question before. What would Averians consider special needs? He hoped the room had a bed, at least. ||Um... no.||

||Excellent. As you can imagine, we're nearly booked solid. But as you're here so early, the perfect room for you just opened up.||

A bellhop sporting a short burgundy vest brought complimentary nutria for both Kormèr and Feestoo, and Kormèr overheard Feestoo ordering food. Another staff member came and polished Kormèr's shoes to mirror perfection, then buffed Kormèr's two rings until they glistened. He then moved to brush the dust off his coat, at which point Kormèr declined with a conciliatory shake of the head.

The manager glanced down at his desk, possibly waiting for some status or signal, then up at Kormèr as he scooted around the desk. ||Your room is ready, sir. Please follow me.||

Kormèr took in all the details of the breathtaking hotel as he and Feestoo followed the manager. Like the pseudo-trees, the architectural details in the hotel's design imitated nature, with archways like thick branches that broke into fractals of smaller branches across the ceilings. Lights above the criss-crossing fractals made it seem to Kormèr as if he were looking up through a forest canopy.

They passed the grand archway and stepped out onto a walkway that circled the open space Kormèr had been so curious about. Kormèr's wide eyes followed the walkway as it spiraled up and around a hollow atrium in the center of the majestic tree. Ten flights up, an inverted glass dome capped the atrium and sparkled with sunlight that entered from above. From the lobby level where Kormèr stood, the walkway descended nearly twice the distance to the dome. Kormèr stopped counting at eleven, as any more would've required him to stray too close to the edge of the walkway, and since there was no railing, he wasn't about to take any chances. He kept a safe distance from the edge of the walkway as the manager led them up. Artificial lighting from lamps along the borders of the walkway augmented the natural light from the dome, such that no floor had any more or less light than any other, even those further down the spiral.

It was then that Kormèr noticed a shimmering around the rim of the atrium. He reached out to it and met a very solid resistance.

||To keep non-fliers from falling,|| whispered Feestoo, anticipating Kormèr's question.

Of course! Kormèr chided himself for not having expected it, as the Averians seemed to be so accommodating towards "non-fliers" in other respects.

The manager stopped and held open a room door. ||Here we are, sir.||

Kormèr peeked into a large room that reminded him too much of his own room back on Elmar, down to the elegant furnishings and ornate light fixtures. This would not do. ||Do you have anything smaller?||

The manager was aghast. ||Smaller? B... but, Mister Lezàl—||

Kormèr interrupted him with a raised palm. ||Please, call me Kormèr... or KL,|| he sang, trying out Kit's nickname. ||I mean it. This room is really too big.|| Within the room, a doorway led to another room that Kormèr realized was not an adjoining room but a bathroom that was larger than his own, back on Elmar! Why anyone would need a bathroom that large, he couldn't even guess. ||Something the size of the bathroom maybe,|| he sang, hearing his voice echo off the white marble walls.

||Are you sure, sir— Kormèr?||

||Very.||

A bellhop appeared from nowhere, exchanged a few whispered words with the manager, then vanished again, on her way to prepare another room. In the meantime, since Feestoo's food service order had been placed for this room, an automated cart arrived bearing trays from which wafted mouth-watering aromas.

The manager fidgeted, eyes wide.. ||Uh... Would you mind terribly eating here for now? I beg that you take no offense that your new room is not yet ready.||

Kormèr found it odd that the birdman would think him so unreasonable as to expect the room to be ready, considering he'd only just asked for it. *They must get some demanding clients in here sometimes.* ||No offense at all, uh... what's your name?||

The birdman opened his palms and held his arms slightly out to his sides. ||I am Theeseeo Whoorreea.||

Kormèr liked the greeting gesture that Theeseeo had made, and he repeated it, spreading his arms to the side, palms open. ||It's nice meeting you, Theeseeo. We'll gladly eat here.|| He glanced at Feestoo, who nodded eagerly.

||Yes, of course,|| twittered Feestoo.

Kormèr eyed the laden cart, then looked at Feestoo, astonished that his new friend had such an insatiable appetite. Kormèr wasn't hungry at all, having eaten less than twenty minutes ago. But he spied some items that looked sugary, and he always made room for dessert.

With the bellhops all having dashed off, Theeseeo pushed the cart into the room and set some of the dishes on the table. Then he stood to one side and pulled a chair out. ||After you,|| Kormèr warbled to Feestoo.

Theeseeo then pulled out the second chair for Kormèr, but Kormèr shook his head. ||It looks like we have enough food for three,|| he sang. ||Please sit with us.||

||Thank you, but I couldn't—||

Kormèr stopped him with a hand up. ||This is technically my room, right?||

||Yes,|| answered Theeseeo, tentatively, as if uncertain where Kormèr was headed with his question.

||Then forget that you're the manager, and that I'm a guest in your hotel. When you walked through that door, you became my guest... in my room. Please sit.|| He poured a glass of nutria and passed it to Theeseeo, who took it but looked as if he didn't know what he was going to do with it, as he hesitantly took the proffered chair. Remaining on his feet, Kormèr poured one for himself and raised his glass. ||A toast, to my first guests ever on Averia.||

||And to many more,|| sang Feestoo, also raising his glass.

Theeseeo looked at the two of them, as Kormèr took a bite of one confection, an oatmeal-like cookie with some bits of dried fruit throughout. ||Might I ask how you two know each other?||

Before Kormèr could respond, Feestoo sang, ||I'm his personal chauffeur this morning.||

Kormèr frowned at him. ||Feestoo! You're more than that; we've shared food.|| Kormèr looked at Theeseeo. ||He's my first friend here on Averia. And since you're my guest, I'd like to think of you as my second.||

||You honor me and my establishment,|| was all the manager could say.

Kormèr raised his glass again. ||I'm sure it was very honorable before I got here.|| He finished the cookie and immediately grabbed another. *These are delicious!*

||So this is your first time on Averia?|| Kormèr nodded as Theeseeo sipped the nutria.

||It's a very beautiful planet, from what I've seen so far.||

||Thank you,|| chirped both birdmen at once. They looked at each other uncertainly, then Feestoo continued eating.

Theeseeo looked back at Kormèr. ||Please avail yourself of our concierge desk. They'll help you find places and events that might be of interest to you.||

||Thanks, I will.|| Kormèr changed the subject in an effort to get the birdman to relax and stop being the manager. ||How has your morning been going so far?||

||What? Oh, well, quiet. Yes. But it's the calm before the gale, of course.||

||Why's that?||

||Most guests will start arriving today.||

Kormèr tipped his head. ||I'm missing something. Guests for what?||

||For Cheerretee.||

Kormèr frowned when the short set of whistles failed to translate or have any meaning. ||I don't know what that is.||

||It's our lunar festival,|| sang Feestoo. ||We celebrate the day our people came to live up here, among the clouds.||

Theeseeo shook his head. ||I'm sure that's just allegory, but that is the myth.||

| | Oh, it's no myth, my friend. When the sky went dark, and our natural tree-homes died, our ancestors flew up from below, following the light visible through the Great Rift. And when they got here, they found it'd been the light of the overlapping moons that had led them there. It's good fortune to be born during Cheerretee. | |

| | Real or not, | | sang Theeseeo, | | the festivities attract a very large crowd, both Averians and offworlders alike. | |

| | It sounds like I came at an auspicious time, then! | | Kormèr cheeped, delightedly.

| | Indeed. | |

| | You said to ask the concierge… but now that we've had a chance to talk a bit, what do other boys my age do around here for fun? What would you recommend? | |

Before he could answer, a bellhop appeared at the door. | | The room is ready, sir. | |

Theeseeo returned to his feet and waved a beckoning hand, and the boy entered. | | Kormèr, I'd like for you to meet my son. | |

The boy was just over Kormèr's height, his white plumage only the slightest bit tinged with gray. His eyes were his father's, large and bordering on crimson. Kormèr clasped a hand on the youngster's shoulder, before considering whether such a gesture would be taken as the warm greeting he intended, or misinterpreted as patronizing or aggression. After all, Jeremy and his crew had greeted him with offered handshakes.

To Kormèr's relief, the young man responded in kind, adding to his father's introduction: <<Good to meet you, sir. My name is Almp.>>

Kormèr was shocked and took a moment to realize that the boy had spoken to him in clear Elmarian. | | My name is Kormèr, but you can call me KL. Your Elmarian's very good! | |

| | Thank you, sir… KL. It's one of my favorite languages; I've been studying it in school for four years now. I'm trying to become fluent in it. | |

| | You're just about there, | | Kormèr nodded.

Almp nodded shyly at the compliment, his gray-tipped crest plumage fluffing briefly. | | Your Averian is excellent, too. You barely have an accent. | |

| | Computer taught, I'm afraid. | | Kormèr shrugged apologetically.

| | There's nothing wrong with that, | | sang Almp. | | It's more convenient to use a fast machine method than to struggle through it the hard way. The goal is to be fluent; how you get there isn't as important. | |

| | True enough. | |

Theeseeo cleared his throat. Almp looked past Kormèr to his father, then back at Kormèr. | | I have to get back to work, | | Almp warbled, then practiced a last line of Elmarian: <<It was nice meeting you.>>

<<Likewise. Maybe we can hang out sometime,>> suggested Kormèr, knowing that Theeseeo didn't understand. Theeseeo had introduced them, but that

didn't mean he would approve of Almp socializing with guests, especially with someone "upper-rank" like Kormèr.

Almp nodded. <<When we're away from these stuffy-heads, we'll talk.>> <<Great. See ya later.>>

Kormèr turned and found Feestoo leaning back, hand on his paunch, appearing distressed, as his eyes focused longingly on the remaining food, knowing that there was no way he was going to finish it. Kormèr chuckled to himself, amazed that Feestoo had finished as much as he had by himself.

He turned back to Theeseeo. ||Do you have others?||

||Others? Oh, you mean children.|| Kormèr nodded. ||No. My mate had only him.||

||He seems very nice.|| He wasn't sure what else to say: what did Averians consider a compliment?

Theeseeo seemed pleased and relieved at Kormèr's bland remark. ||Thank you. I'm honored that you think so.|| Theeseeo placed his glass on the table. ||If you're ready, I'll show you to your new room. Hopefully, it will be more to your liking.||

||I'm sure it will be,|| chirped Kormèr, glancing at Feestoo, who merely nodded. It appeared as though any slight effort on his part—even one quiver of his jaw—would cause him to disgorge everything he had eaten, so swollen was his paunch.

||I hate to waste the rest of the food, though,|| Feestoo bemoaned.

||I'll have it sent around to the new room,|| assured Theeseeo, as he stepped to the door.

||Thank you.|| Kormèr grinned at Feestoo's look of relief, as the birdman stood from his chair with an effort. ||Eyes bigger than your crop, maybe?||

||Just a bit,|| Feestoo warbled, slightly abashed. ||Everything is just so delicious!||

||You won't enjoy it, if it becomes an effort,|| Kormèr chided gently. ||How about this: I'll ask Theeseeo to have any leftovers packed to eat on-the-wing, and you can take it with you when you go.||

||Really?|| Feestoo looked on the verge of joyful tears at the thought of being able to feast like this another day.

||Yes. Just leave me some of the oat cookies. They look like they'd be good for dunking into nutria.||

||Since you're paying, I guess I could spare you those,|| Feestoo winked. ||Come, let's follow Theeseeo to your new room, before the food gets cold.||

||I'M coming to you live,|| chirped the reporter, ||from the scene of what's being labeled the greatest jewel heist in the history of Averia.||

Kormèr lay on the round squat bed in his room, with his head propped on pillows. When he had initially lain on it, the middle had yielded like a warm ball of rising bread dough, to accommodate his body. At first, he had found it extremely comfortable to have a bed that readily conformed to his shape, but after a couple of minutes, it had felt too soft and smothering, and too warm. The bed, like most of the furniture, was designed for Averian bodies, which were lighter, fluffier and more insulated, and therefore didn't sink or overheat as easily in a bed that looked and felt like a well-feathered nest.

Feestoo had chuckled at Kormèr's struggle with his bed, and showed him how to adjust the firmness and temperature settings until the bed felt cooler and more supportive of Kormèr's leaner, denser frame. With the addition of additional pillows from the closet, Kormèr finally made his ideal bed, and he lamented not being able to take it home to Elmar with him.

Feestoo had dragged a short perch out from behind the room's writing desk and planted himself in front of the food cart, but he didn't eat as ravenously as he had earlier, so perhaps there was a limit to his appetite, after all. The food cart now sat by the door, with the remaining food packed away in take-away cartons for Feestoo to enjoy another day.

Kormèr and Feestoo had lolled away the rest of the morning, eating and watching the news playing on the wall screen. While Kormèr was not accustomed to staying inside when the weather seemed so beautiful outside, he found the news program an informative and convenient means of learning about his new environment, as well as some of the local vernacular that had been lacking from his language lessons. Also, Feestoo had acquired a taste for the leisurely life of luxury, especially when someone else was paying, and was showing no signs of leaving soon.

| |Recapping our top story that we've been following since early this morning,| | continued the reporter, | |a heinous, audacious burglary in the heart of Birshetland! Late last night, a thief emptied the famous Chees jewelry store. Cheert Reestee, the owner of Chees, returned to his store after closing, only to find it robbed! In a caper that the authorities are still actively investigating, the thief—or thieves—stripped the cases of their priceless treasures in a matter of hours, leaving no traces of entry or exit. Earlier we interviewed a Sergeant Chreel Tseeo.| |

The image changed to that of a young police officer. | |We have nothing to report at this time,| | he was singing, | |but I assure you that the Birshetland Police Department is following up on every lead, as we speak.| |

From an anthropological perspective, Kormèr found the local obsession with the jewelry heist fascinating. The Averians were apparently such a peaceful, civil people that a bloodless, albeit expensive, crime like this was dominating the coverage on every broadcast program, to the exclusion of nearly every other news story. Feestoo seemed glued to his seat, raptly watching the news for any fresh developments.

| |Is it true you're bringing in sorcerers to help with the investigation?| | asked the disembodied voice of the off-camera reporter.

| |No, no. Don't believe all the rumors you hear. We're not bringing in any sorcerers.| |

This piqued Kormèr's attention. *They have sorcerers here, too? That's interesting.* Elmar also had sorcerers, though some centuries-past altercation had seen almost all of them exiled to an island. *Unlike here, it seems.*

||Is there any truth to the rumor that magic was used?|| asked the reporter.

||No, I don't believe magic was used.|| Feestoo spoke in unison with the on-screen police officer, even mimicking the young Averian man's dismissive scoff. ||The news is repeating, so I guess it's time for me to go.||

||Aww,|| mewled Kormèr.

||No, I've taken a long enough break and should get some fresh air.||. Feestoo groaned to his feet and waddled around a bit, stretching his legs. ||KL, it has been a pleasure, but I should pick up other fares while the day is young.||

||Do I owe you anything else for your time?|| Kormèr asked.

Feestoo slipped on his cap with a chuckle. ||Not a thing. Your gem will cover the fare, like I said, and the food is a welcome bonus. But the meter will tell a confusing story that I don't want to have to explain to my dispatcher.||

||I understand. Well, Feestoo, thanks for your help and your company.|| Kormèr hopped off the bed and checked his chrono. ||Ugh. I keep forgetting to set the local time on my chrono.||

||If that's like a p-comm, you should sync it to the data signal,|| suggested Feestoo.

||I don't think my chrono does that here.||

||Let me see. Oh! That's a really old— Here.|| He worked the small device he had strapped to his wrist, then removed it. ||Take this p-comm. No, no! No argument. It's an old model, if it makes you feel any better, but newer than the relic you're wearing. And you can keep contacts and notes on it too. I've just cleared mine, so it's all yours.||

||Thanks, Feestoo,|| sang Kormèr, taking the device. ||I don't know where I'd be right now, if you hadn't found me on the platform this morning.||

||No problem, KL. Glad I was there.|| He took the sack of food containers from the cart.

||Here, in case you do end up having to explain your meter.|| Kormèr dropped three clear little stones into the birdman's other long-nailed hand.

Feestoo gawped at the gems, then shook his head disbelievingly. ||My wife and mother will sing your praises when they see these! High sky.||

||High sky,|| chirped Kormèr, pushing the depleted food cart into the hallway for room service to retrieve, and closed the door behind Feestoo with a last wave.

Kormèr walked to the window, where the early afternoon sunlight set the gauzy drapes aglow. He had an almost unobstructed view of the intersection of two promenades below. He noticed the promenades had public baths, like ornate swimming pools, and couldn't help but notice how those using the baths left their belongings lying around before taking a dip. That led him to wonder if there were Averians who, like him on Elmar, robbed the greedy to aid the meek. Perhaps the thief that had cleaned out the jewelry store was one such person. He had to admire the thief's skill; from what Kormèr had heard, the thief hadn't triggered a single security system, though the store reportedly had the best security system on all Averia. Sure, Kormèr had pulled some fancy capers, but he'd give anything to shake that thief's hand... or wing.

Kormèr's thoughts drifted to the Averian police-woman he'd seen in the store that morning. His memory of her face had faded some, and he now remembered her with a sort of glow about her, and that made him even more eager to find out who she was. He had watched for her during the news coverage of the jewelry store robbery, to no avail. Perhaps Almp would know. He made a mental note to ask Almp the next time he saw him.

Watching bathers in the public baths below reminded him that it had been several days since he'd had a proper bath. Though the shower on the ship had left him clean, it just didn't satisfy the same way a bath did. Kormèr grabbed his coat from the chair where he'd tossed it earlier, took the cube from its pocket and, in moments, stepped into his home and, soon after, into a swirling, soothing bath. He decided that this would be his last return home for a while. He was visiting Averia now, and so far, he was having a good time. But to really know a place, he had to immerse himself and actually *live* there. Popping home whenever the mood hit him wasn't the right way to "live" a place.

He briefly considered why he wanted to return to Averia. It was certainly different from other worlds he had visited, in that he had no particular agenda in mind: no priceless artifact or jewel to pillage, no haughty, obscenely wealthy royal or noble to swindle or rob. *So, why?* Maybe *because* Averia had none of those things—that Kormèr had yet to see, anyway. It was a beautiful, idyllic, modern world, populated by quirky, friendly bird people; he could just take a break from his thievery and enjoy himself, somewhere far from Elmar.

When he finished bathing, Kormèr dressed and packed a valise with some clothes. Trinket looked on with disapproval. <<Kormèr, are you sure you don't want something to eat?>>

<<I'm sure. A quick bath is all I wanted. I'm heading back straightaway.>>

<<Well, alright. The food there is good?>>

Kormèr thought back on all he'd eaten. <<It's different. Not overly flavorful, but nutritious.>> Kormèr snapped the valise shut. <<That's that. Initiate away-protocol two,>> he told the bot, signaling that any callers would be told that he was on holiday. <<Oh, and send Rasseur a message that I caught the little slimeball who was trying to pick my pocket at the party. How long have I been away, anyway?>>

<<It has been a full day since the party.>>

That long! <<Tell him I'm sorry for not calling sooner, but that I... uh.. I was busy planning my vacation.>>

One of Trinket's lights pulsed as an affirmation. <<Understood. Make sure you're not forgetting anything.>>

<<I don't think I am. Let's see, clothes, messages…>>

<<Money?>>

<<Ah.>> Kormèr patted the bot on the head before heading to a walk-in closet from which he emerged with a velvet-like pouch. <<Once again, you're a lifesaver.>> He grabbed the valise. <<Don't work too hard,>> he joked, knowing that it was in Trinket's programming to be constantly in motion about the house, whenever he wasn't recharging or in maintenance mode.

<<Have a good time, Kormèr. And be safe.>>

Back in the hotel room, Kormèr opened the valise on the bed and sealed the portal. He then arranged his clothes in the closet and drawers, and stowed the valise. Just as he closed the closet door, a knock came at his room door. *Knocking,* he thought bemusedly. *That's quaint.*

Standing at the blank door, Kormèr wondered if it was safe to open it without knowing who was visiting. Then he spotted the small viewscreen next to the doorway, conveniently set at his shoulder height. *No buttons.* He touched his fingertip to the frame of the screen to feel for a hidden switch, and a clear color image appeared, showing what appeared to be the top of Almp's head.

||Hello?|| Kormèr greeted, not sure of whether to speak through the door or at the screen.

Almp's head jerked up, his eyes open wide in alarm, before he stepped out of the viewer's range. The automatic camera pivoted, trying to detect his new position, but Almp had tucked his head under his partially lifted wing. <<It's me. Almp,>> he called through the door in Elmarian.

Kormèr chuckled. ||Yes, I see that. Or, rather, I *saw* that. Why are you hiding from the screen?||

<<If you can open the door, please, I can explain.>>

Kormèr glanced around his room to ensure that he hadn't left anything valuable or inexplicable out in the open. Then he opened the door. <<Come in.>>

Almp darted inside as Kormèr shut the door. <<I'm not intruding, am I?>> At Kormèr's shake of the head, Almp's piqued crest settled. <<I apologize for the secrecy, but I'm still on the clock, so I'm not supposed to be visiting guests in their rooms unless called. If my father sees me on the room screens, he'll pluck my pin feathers for sure.>>

Kormèr nodded, wondering if Almp had been reprimanded before for socializing with guests. He was speaking Elmarian, so Kormèr followed his lead to be discreet. <<I understand. What can I do for you?>>

<<Do you like parties?>> asked Almp slyly.

<<Sure I do. Why?>>

<<There's one tonight at the Root.>>

<<The Root?>>

<<A local club. Good music, younger crowd… plenty of females.>> He winked.

Kormèr smiled. <<Sounds good. But you'll have to show me some Averian dance moves.>> He hoped that there wasn't a great deal of flapping or fluffing involved, or he was going to look like a fool.

<<Deal,>> he said, opening the door and glancing nervously up and down the empty corridor. <<I have to go. I'll leave you directions for where to meet me.>>

<<Okay. Go, before you get in trouble.>> As Almp walked off, Kormèr remembered to say, <<And thanks.>> Almp waved in response and disappeared around the corner.

What a strange kid. The way Almp stalked and snuck about reminded Kormèr of children playing spy games, but then again, working in a stodgy hotel under his father's supervision, Almp probably looked for excitement and fun whenever and however he could. Kormèr was most likely one of the few guests of similar age that Almp had met in a long while, and Elmarian, to boot.

Kormèr closed the door and drummed his fingers against it excitedly, his mind already imagining what an Averian dance club might look like. Not only would he be attending a cultural, social event, one with a possibility of meeting girls, but also one where he could practice his pick pocketing skills. Kormèr didn't really need the money, just enough to avoid depleting his gem supply. But Kormèr had detected a faint class structure among Averians, and it seemed to him that Almp belonged to an upper class. That meant there would most probably be money around. And, he had to admit to a modicum of curiosity regarding where Averians kept their valuables.

He considered not abusing Almp's hospitality by refraining from robbing his friends. After all, on the off chance that suspicion fell on Kormèr for any missing valuables, it wouldn't reflect well on Almp and might even jeopardize his job at the hotel. Tweaked by his conscience, Kormèr decided to wait until he'd scoped out the scene before making definitive plans: if he couldn't make a clean pinch, then he would save his efforts for another day; but if he found a mark who was too ripe to ignore… well, then it was just meant to be, wasn't it?

Kormèr walked to the closet, suddenly aware that he hadn't the slightest idea what to wear. Looking through his wardrobe, he decided that none of the clothes he had brought from home would do. He grabbed his gem pouch and called up the hotel directory on the wall-screen. There, he found that one corridor off the lobby led to a mini-mall of shops.

The attendants at the main clothing shop downstairs were most helpful in pointing out the latest styles and letting Kormèr know how he looked in them. Kormèr trusted the older attendants for his formal and evening selections and the younger ones for the club-appropriate styles. When he'd mentioned that he'd be going to the Root that evening, the attendant brought forth an entirely new selection for him to peruse.

When it came time to pay, Kormèr slipped a gem out of the pouch under cover of his pocket, still not entirely sure of the exchange rate for gems as currency. The gray-feathered attendant's eyes widened, as he asked: | |You're Kormèr Lezàl, aren't you?| |

Kormèr was taken aback. | |Yes,| | he answered, hesitantly. | |How did you know?| |

| |We'd heard that someone had checked into a room here and paid with gems. I hadn't expected you to be so… um…| | He stopped and fluffed nervously.

| |So young?| | Kormèr finished for him.

| |No offense.| |

Kormèr smiled. | |None taken.| |

The attendant looked at their check-out counter. | |Unfortunately, we don't have the ability to make change for your… payment, but if it's alright with you, we can charge your purchases to your room, instead?| |

Kormèr raised an eyebrow. *That's convenient.* He put away the gem as the attendant passed him his bag of new clothing. | |That's perfect. Thank you for your service.| |

The attendant and his assistants nodded their heads. | |Please, come again.| |

FROM only paces away, another shopper observed the exchange with interest. News of the robbery at Chees was everywhere, and the substantial reward for any information leading to the jewel thief's apprehension had everyone in Birshetland vigilant for suspicious activity. So the woman seized on the moment, before anyone else noticed.

The woman used her p-comm to snap a few surreptitious photos of the young offworlder that the shop attendant had identified as Kormèr Lezàl. Then she called the hotline to report what she had seen and heard. Young non-Averian male, brown hair and dark eyes, who paid with loose, unset gemstones.

She made sure they took her name and address correctly, to ensure that she received the proper recognition for performing her civic duty. And for the reward, of course, which would keep her family stocked with oat-flax and nutria for the rest of the year. That didn't hurt, either.

WHEN Kormèr returned to his room, he found a slip of flim stuck under the door. Almp had scrawled directions on it in Averian. Kormèr dressed quickly in one of his new outfits and hurried out to the lobby. The people he passed in the corridor weren't laughing or glowering at his clothes, so Kormèr took it as a good sign that he wasn't either overdressed or underdressed for a day out; not that there was time to go back to his room to change, even if he had inadvertently dressed like a clown.

The directions said to get to the base of the hotel tree, but they didn't detail how Kormèr was supposed to do that. Kormèr looked down the atrium, dreading having to traverse the entire spiraling walkway and wishing he could fly down.

With a sigh, he set off, following the walkway all the way down the atrium to the ground floor. He passed several things on the way down that he'd have to return to when he had more time, like the entrances to two theaters, a gym and spa, a "fun zone" and on the ground floor itself, a café and two restaurants with outdoor seating. All those amenities left no doubt that this was a first-class hotel: practically a city unto itself, where guests could spend their entire holiday without stepping outside.

Not me, Kormèr grinned. *I want to see it all!*

He found a corridor that exited at the base of the tree. Illuminated paths led away to other trees and other places unknown to Kormèr. And when he looked up, the surrounding sights left him awestruck. Well-hidden lights illuminated the towering, stately trees in amber and white, making them appear even more majestic than Kormèr thought possible.

Feestoo's p-comm beeped, and Kormèr looked to find the data from Almp's flim on it. He realized that he'd transferred the data between the devices without realizing it, and that he was now officially late. He rushed around the tree to where Almp stood, waiting for him.

||What took you so long?|| asked the Averian, arms akimbo. He had changed out of his uniform, into garments that were made from finer cloth, with more of a shine.

||I was shopping.||

Almp looked him over and chuckled. ||I see.||

||What?||

||You bought those upstairs, didn't you?||

||Yeah, why?|| Kormèr looked himself over, worriedly. There seemed to be nothing wrong with the clothes, which looked to have a similar sheen and detailing as Almp's. Had the young women given him bad fashion advice or something?

||Nothing bad. You just have expensive tastes… and an open wallet.||

Kormèr sighed with relief. He didn't look like a buffoon or a tourist. Although he was curious about how Almp knew that Kormèr's clothes were pricier than his own. ||Yeah, well…|| They started walking along one path.

||Say, is there any faster way down here than on the walkway?||

||The walkway?|| Almp switched to Elmarian, <<Vlaja naya! You come down all the way on foot?>>

||Watch your verb tenses… and yes, I did.||

||There are lifts, KL. I'll show you later.||

They walked in silence for a moment. Then Kormèr sang, ||I saw a woman this morning, beautiful beyond belief.||

||Where?|| asked Almp, interested.

||In the store they robbed.||

||The jewelry store?||

||Yeah. She seemed to be part of the police.||

||You probably mean Chief Chrreel. All the other police females are overweight or too manly; hardly pretty.||

||All women are beautiful, in their own way,|| protested Kormèr, irked at his new friend's superficialness. ||What'd you say her name was?||

||Chrreel, Sylvestra Chrreel. Don't ask me where that first name came from. It's totally off-planet.||

||You said she's the Chief... as in the chief of police?|| asked Kormèr, surprised. ||She looks so young.|| He caught himself, hearing in his own voice the same dismissive incredulity that he detected in others when speaking about him. If he felt patronized, he could imagine that she encountered similar reactions, especially for her position of authority.

||She *is* young, only sixteen or seventeen standard.||

||And she's the Chief? Isn't that kinda young for that position?||

||Yep. The last youngest was twenty standard. That was a fiasco.||

Twenty? For a chief of police? Maybe ages are different here than at home. At sixteen and seventeen, Elmarians are still in secondary school.

||Her father ruffled a lot of feathers a while back,|| continued Feestoo, ||when he retired and convinced the council of mayors to give her a chance. She's done a fair job, too. And you're right about her looks; she's a breeze under the wings.||

||Any chance she'll be there tonight?|| joked Kormèr. Almp clucked mirthfully. ||Hey,|| continued Kormèr, ||you still have to show me how to dance.||

They stopped, and Almp pulled him off to one side of the path. He looked around, then began twittering some music. He then began a complex little dance. Kormèr watched the elaborate footwork intently, then tried it himself. He stopped when Almp laughed.

||What?||

||Nothing.|| Almp held back the laughs, but his eyes betrayed an amusement beyond funniness. ||I've just never seen a non-Averian do that.||

||Don't offworlders attend parties?|| Kormèr was wondering now if Almp had invited him along to have a bit of fun at his expense. ||I won't be the only one there, will I?||

||No, no!|| Almp twittered, sensing Kormèr's distrust. ||The Root's more of a local spot, but the savvier offworlders find their way there, too. Anyway, just remember to place your feet one in front of the other more. And keep your arms out more.||

||Got it. Thanks.|| He waited for more, but Almp did not seem about to begin anything new. ||Is that it?||

Almp nodded. ||That's it. From there, it's just changes to fit your mood.||

||Interesting.|| They resumed their walk, and Kormèr instinctively noted landmarks and signage, in case he needed to find his own way back. It was unlikely that Almp would leave him stranded, especially if he would have to answer to his

father for any mishaps that befell Kormèr, which got him to thinking… ||Did your dad tell you to show me around?||

Almp laughed. ||No, I asked you on my own, because you arrived alone—rather, with a cabbie—and stayed in your room. Would you rather not go out?||

||No, of course not. Thanks for including me and inviting me along.||

Kormèr hoped he hadn't offended Almp by questioning his motives, but his new friend just shrugged his tufted shoulders. ||But since you mentioned it, maybe don't say anything to my father if you see him. He would think I'm being unprofessional.||

||THOSE people seem to be waving at us,|| chirped Kormèr, spying some Averian boys waving from across the room as they entered the club.

||Those are my friends,|| Almp explained, waving back. He had to shout to be heard over the music.

Kormèr followed Almp across the as-yet-empty dance floor toward his friends. On the way, he focused on the music, a twittering melody over a humming background, combined into an eerie, elusively hypnotic song; Kormèr strained to decipher the instruments, if they were even instruments and not just voices. To his novice ears, the lyrics were difficult to understand, until he realized that, instead of singing individual words, the singer's chittering conveyed entire thoughts or feelings.

Almp exchanged greetings with his three friends before introducing Kormèr. As he greeted them, Kormèr picked up a condescending vibe from all three; their greetings were distant or even disinterested, as if they were unwilling to let a stranger—much less a non-Averian—into their circle. *What should I have expected, warm hugs? I'm the outsider. This is a different planet, with different norms.*

Then again… Maybe on Elmar he wasn't treated like this—nor did he recall being so rude to anyone else—but that didn't mean it didn't happen there, too. Most people had the tendency to be clannish, whatever planet he visited. He had hoped that Averia was an exception, but maybe that was too much to ask for. *So be it.*

||Want a drink?|| Almp asked him.

||Point the way,|| chirped Kormèr, not about to let someone else get him a drink of any kind. *Paranoid? Me? Nah.*

Almp pointed to the bar. ||There. Would you bring me back a *woopree* with ice?||

||That's a drink, I take it?|| Kormèr asked, slightly annoyed at Almp's manipulation. He got the feeling that Almp was showing off in front of his friends by having the newcomer fetch his drink.

||Yeah,|| twittered Almp, nodding.

As Kormèr walked toward the bar, he looked around the place. Since the lights were dim, he hadn't noticed before that perches protruded from the floor

108

and dangled from the ceiling, like playground swing seats. Both Averians and even a few non-avians seemed to use them as seating throughout the venue.

At the bar, he placed an order for two of the drinks Almp had mentioned. While he waited, a young Averian woman sidled up to him and placed an order. Something about her posture and slight movements reminded Kormèr very much of Menddilal whenever she was pretending to ignore him. *There are girls like this on every world, I guess.* Proficient in these silly courtship games, he ignored her in return. When his drinks came, he flipped the tender a small gem, and while the young woman stared after the jewel, Kormèr bumped into her, excused himself, grabbed the drinks and returned to his party.

He handed Almp his drink, then moved off to one side with his own drink in hand and rifled through the wallet he'd picked out of the young woman's handbag when he'd bumped her. Syrree Theesl was her name, and by the number of different credit chips she had, he guessed she had to be well-off. *She's likely to have more money than just this,* he thought, closing the wallet and slipping it into his pocket. He recalled her plumage had been quite white, and her lipstick very red.

Sipping his drink, which tasted like some kind of slightly fermented fruit, Kormèr formulated a plan in his head as he returned to Almp's side. ||Do they take requests here?|| he shouted into Almp's ear.

Almp nodded and pointed at a birdman dancing by himself behind a small control board. Kormèr walked toward the music jockey when a burly Averian stepped in his path. The birdman wore a tight dark vest that highlighted his impressive pectoral and arm muscles.

||I've lost track of my sister,|| Kormèr chirped to the burly Averian. ||I'd like to have her paged.||

The light-gray plumed birdman looked him over, then made a motion with his head for Kormèr to pass.

Kormèr waved to get the music jockey's attention. The birdman pulled an earbud from one ear, and Kormèr asked, ||Could you page Syrree Theesl for me, please?||

He looked at Kormèr with a skeptical grin. ||Sure. No problem.||

||Thanks.|| Kormèr had seen Feestoo use his credit chip earlier, so he sent a small gratuity amount from one of Syrree's chips to the jockey and waited. The music jockey's warble came over the music, asking Syrree Theesl to please come to the jockey's station. In less than a minute, Kormèr spotted her gliding over. ||I thought your picture looked familiar,|| he told her.

||I'm sorry?|| she chirped, confused. ||Who are you?||

||I paged you. You must've dropped your wallet near the bar.|| He held it out to her, and she quickly took it and checked its contents. ||I saw someone pick it up,|| he sang, ||and start searching through it, so I knew it wasn't theirs. I claimed it from them and remembered your face from the bar.||

She seemed satisfied with what it contained. ||You're a lifesaver,|| she chirped. ||Daddy would've killed me if I'd lost my chips again.|| And she walked away without so much as a thanks. He'd expected her to thank him, and that would lead to a conversation, then a dance and maybe a shared drink… so it took Kormèr a minute to realize his plans had been foiled. *Ah well. You win some; you lose some.*

||Your sister, eh?|| grumbled the bouncer, flexing his arms as if preparing to show Kormèr to the door.

||Did I say sister? I meant acquaintance,|| Kormèr twittered quickly, holding out a small blue gem in his outstretched palm. ||Just a misunderstanding. Still getting the hang of Averian vocabulary, you know.||

The bouncer took the gem and turned his back to Kormèr without further comment or acknowledgment. The burly, hawkish bouncer seemed used to dealing with troublemakers, so Kormèr was glad for the quick, discreet and nonviolent resolution. Still, it was probably best not to try that again.

Kormèr returned to Almp's group. They had obviously seen the exchange, for as soon as he arrived, they huddled about him and reprimanded him.

||You don't want to associate with her,|| chirped one of the boys. ||Her white feathers are gray underneath.||

||I don't understand,|| chirped Kormèr.

||The Theesl family built their wealth on the wings of common birdfolk,|| explained Almp. ||They're on the City Planning Council, and her father heads the Advisory Committee for Environmental Concerns, which just introduces projects to drain money from the Birshetland coffers.||

||With nothing to show for any of them,|| added another of the group, whose name Kormèr didn't remember. ||The family could just as easily use their own money or crowd-fund the project, but they insist on cheating the commoners.||

The injustice offended Kormèr's sense of fairness. *This is what class differentiation leads to: harassment and blatant, unrestricted pilfering of the lower classes.* On the other hand, Almp's friends seemed more savvy and conscientious than he had originally thought; not only were they aware of the corruption in their society, they spared a moment to warn Kormèr of the danger posed by Syrree and her family.

||Thanks for the heads-up,|| he sang. ||The same exists on my planet.||

||It exists everywhere, I think,|| chirped Almp. ||Best thing to do is ignore her and her family.||

||No,|| chirped Kormèr. ||Ignoring the problem won't fix it, so I'll deal with it differently: infiltrate, and hit them where it hurts.||

||Just a minute,|| chirped the third boy, backing away. ||We never said anything about hitting anyone.||

||Relax, I don't mean literally,|| warbled Kormèr. ||Not physical violence, just something… different.||

||'Infiltrate'? With her? Impossible,|| chirped Almp. ||She won't let you in her circle.||

110

| |Hmm,| | chirped Kormèr. | |She's a challenge, that's for sure.| | He noticed that the music was finally up-tempo and rhythmic enough for a few people to dance. | |Maybe it's time for a little dancing.| | He stood and walked purposefully toward Syrree, who had her back to them.

| |Dance?| | he heard Almp chirp behind him, almost a screech. | |No, wait. You mustn't—| |

| |Don't worry,| | Kormèr called back. | |I know what I'm doing.| |

| |But, you don't understand—| | Almp's voice was drowned out by the music, as Kormèr approached his mark.

CHAPTER 8

THE Averian boy's talons click-clacked on the stone floor and echoed up the corridor ahead of him as he ran. A message had arrived for his master from outside the Hovel, the tree-home of the Hawk Sorcerers, to which the boy was apprenticed. This was wonderful news, for it meant they would probably both be called out to one of the other cities of Averia. While he was sure his master had been called outside before, it would be the boy's first time in many months that he would set foot outside the Hovel, just as many since he'd been outside of the city of Berdia. Perhaps he could even visit his betrothed in her own home, instead of her always coming to him.

He stopped outside his master's door and caught his breath. Then he knocked.

||Come in, Srrcheel.||

The young Averian pushed open the steel door and stepped into a candlelit room. His master was gathering some belongings in a sack. Srrcheel closed the door behind him and waited silently. Only one rank lower and three years younger than his master, Srrcheel still looked up to him with the same deference and respect as he showed the older Master sorcerers. Someday, he or his master would rise to their next ranks; then they'd go their separate ways, he with a new master and his master with a new apprentice. They might become friends then, free from the formalities of their current relationship. But for now, this *was* their relationship.

||You've heard,|| chirped his master without turning.

||Yes. It's true then; we're going outside.|| It was more of a question than a statement.

His master turned. The yellow light shimmered eerily in his multicolored plumage and cast his impressive stature in dramatic shadows. Srrcheel hoped to one day be like this man.

||It's true.|| He folded his hands. ||Since this is your first visit as my apprentice, I need you to get things ready for me.|| And he rattled off a list of magical components and objects for Srrcheel to fetch. As an apprentice, Srrcheel was expected to know the appearance and function of each one. Fortunately, he often spent many hours organizing and restocking his master's apothecary cabinet.

He grabbed a satchel from a pile by the cabinet. ||What are we being called for?|| he asked while collecting the artifacts from the various drawers and shelves and carefully adding them to the satchel.

| | There was a robbery in Birshetland; an impossible one, or so they say. The authorities there would like us to rule out that the thief used sorcery. A menial job, really. | |

Srrcheel considered their task and the possible *menial* actions they could undertake to rule out sorcery. | | I think I have an idea of how to do it. | |

| | Oh, you do, do you? | | sang his master indulgently.

His master expected Srrcheel to come up with his own suggestions on how to go about solving problems, but as he was still only an apprentice, he knew no real magic yet. And obviously, this situation demanded some spellcasting, if his master, a Novice-rank sorcerer, had been selected for the task. Srrcheel felt slightly embarrassed, but went on anyway and voiced his thoughts.

His master considered his suggestion while Srrcheel continued his task. When Srrcheel had filled the satchel, he placed the satchel by the chamber door.

| | You're low on a few things, master. I'll request them today, so they'll be ready for you when we return. | |

| | Thank you. Your idea is a fresh approach. I had something else in mind, but yours is unique. Of course, you forgot to consider that you might encounter radio signals using that method. | |

Srrcheel worked his mistake out in his head, then frowned.

| | However, | | chirped his master, encouragingly, | | we need only a minor modification to fix that. | | He smiled. | | Maybe I'll use it. Good job, Srrcheel. | |

The young birdman beamed. | | When do we leave? | | he asked eagerly.

| | First thing in the morning. You can spend the night here, in case I need anything urgently. Use the bed if you like. I'll be up most of the night making preparations. It's our first outing as master and apprentice; we were chosen out of twenty pairs, and it is a high-visibility task. We must not disappoint our elders. | |

Srrcheel nodded his understanding. This would not simply be a fun-filled excursion. Cheerretee was three nights away, but so was the raising ceremony—the Hawk Sorcerers' promotion ritual. If he and his master were being sent out now, that meant that Srrcheel was likely under consideration for a raising. This trip was his chance to prove himself, and Srrcheel was determined not to waste it.

| | WAS everything there? | | asked Kormèr, as he stepped up to Syrree. Her two female friends looked down their petite, slender noses at him with obvious disdain.

| | Huh? | | she chirped, startled by his sudden appearance. Then, | | Oh, you. Yeah, everything was there. | | She turned back to her friends, and they resumed talking.

Kormèr thought quickly. What had she chirped earlier... something about losing her chips? | | Good, 'cause when I saw the guy pocket one of those chips, I thought it might have been yours— | |

She turned on him. | | What did you say? | | Her hand was already lost in her bag, searching for the wallet.

||Well, he put something in his pocket. I don't know, maybe it was his, but I just thought you might want to know.|| Kormèr waited while she frantically took inventory of her wallet. He caught her friends looking at him again and smiled a mocking smile. ||Hi,|| he chirped to them.

They looked about to laugh. Then one asked, ||Are you with Almp's group?||

Kormèr considered his answer. They either thought Almp and his group were a bunch of losers, or they were honestly interested. He took a gamble that it was the latter. ||Yeah. Almp and I are friends. I met the others tonight.||

They nodded, and Kormèr realized he'd guessed right; one of them liked Almp. The other maybe liked one of the other boys.

||I think they want to dance with you,|| he lied to the girls.

They giggled, ||You're kidding.|| Syrree looked at him curiously and asked, ||Why would you tell us?||

||I don't care, if you know,|| Kormèr shrugged. ||So, is everything there?||

||Yeah. Whatever he took must've been his after all.||

||Guess so. Bye.|| He had used the chip to tip the music jockey, but he had returned it to the wallet before Syrree had reclaimed it; maybe she would notice a peculiar charge when the bill arrived, but Kormèr doubted Syrree was the type to pay attention to such details. He started walking back, wondering if he had overacted his indifference.

||Wait,|| called Syrree.

Kormèr smiled inside. He was in. He turned.

||I, uh… I never thanked you… for the wallet, I mean.||

||Don't worry about it. Just be more careful.|| He turned again, then turned back. ||You wanna dance?||

She glanced at the other two, as if silently asking for permission. They nodded for her to go. So she slipped her wallet away and joined Kormèr on the dance floor. ||But what about my two friends?||

||Look,|| Kormèr chirped, pointing. Syrree found they had moved toward Almp and his friends and were now engaged in a little coquettish teasing.

She smiled. Then, ||It just occurred to me but, do you know how to dance?||

Kormèr smiled and began the steps Almp had taught him. Feeling quite good with himself for scoring this dance with Syrree, he made some changes, as Almp had suggested, where the dance felt too rigid. He felt he was doing a great job when he noticed a perceptible change in the room's noise level. He stopped and looked around; all around him, people had stopped to stare at him, their expressions ranging from shock to mirth. When he spotted Almp laughing, Kormèr realized he'd been had.

Syrree looked sternly at him, then past him toward the laughter. | |Your dance is a courting ritual, you silly human, | | she chirped, looking him in the eye for perhaps the first time since they'd met.

Kormèr was too embarrassed to read anything from the expression. He simply chirped, | |It was my first time. | |

| |So I gather. No one would do that in public twice. | | She took his arm. | |Come on. Let's go for a walk. | |

THE sounds of the club faded behind them as they strolled along a path between the trees. The night was warm and bright, with the planet's two moons high above, almost overlapping. Kormèr inhaled deeply, savoring the clean, refreshing air. He noticed Syrree staring at him.

| |It's my first night here, and already I love this place, | | he told her. As it was late, there was almost no one around, and the sharp tones of his whistles seemed to carry everywhere.

| |Your first night? And you thought you could dance? | |

| |I thought Almp had shown me how. | | Kormèr flushed for a moment, but his anger at Almp made him forget his embarrassment.

| |Well, he certainly showed you how! | | she twittered. | |But you performed those moves very well, for a human. | |

Kormèr glanced at her, but her expression was unreadable. | |You think so? | |

She stopped walking and gazed at him. | |I know so. I want you to do that dance again for me | |—Kormèr raised an eyebrow, as her tones grew sultry—| |in private. | |

CHAPTER 9

BLEARY-EYED, Captain Phatheeo stared at his office wall, which displayed images from the crime scene at varying levels of magnification. One was a highly detailed 360-degree view, one of several taken from different points inside the store. He had been looking at these, on and off, for most of the day, but that's how it went sometimes. Experience had taught him that he might look at evidence multiple times and see nothing useful, until he did.

But considering that it was nearly dawn, he called it a day, a very long day. He could feel his brain just spinning sluggishly and no longer processing what he was seeing. He'd made discoveries in this condition in the past, but that was a rarity, and becoming rarer still, as his feathers thinned and lost their luster with age. *You've been in this game a long time, old bird.* He would be better off getting rest and tackling the images again later with a fresh mind.

With a quick hand gesture, he sealed the files and turned off his wall. Then he reconsidered and turned the wall back on, bringing up a chess game that he and Sylvestra had been playing for the past few weeks. Phatheeo had played the game with Sylvestra's father when he'd been Phatheeo's boss, and he'd continued the practice with her when she'd ascended to the position. He found the games cathartic, helping him deal with tough days or transition from work to personal time. He moved a piece, then deactivated the wall again. As he stood to go, his p-comm chimed.

||We had a call on the tips line, sir,|| chirped the caller.

Something about his phrasing made Phatheeo ask, ||When was this?||

||Um… last night.||

||Why am I hearing about this now?||

||Sorry, sir. It got missed during the shift change. Sergeant Tseeo's handed us our tail-feathers over it, of course.||

Phatheeo didn't need to reprimand the officer again, so he let the matter drop. ||What was the message?||

||A woman called and sent photos of a young human boy who was apparently—and I quote: 'flaunting a sizeable collection of gems' at a department store at the Hotel Cheerees. I've sent the photos to you.||

Phatheeo reactivated his wall and displayed the photos. There were only three, and they all appeared to have been taken hastily. Two were of the young man's back, but the last revealed his face, a face that Phatheeo recognized immediately. This could be the break they'd been waiting for.

116

||Thank you. Out.||

Phatheeo closed the connection and forwarded the data to Sylvestra. Then he rushed to her office.

His elation dropped a few notches when he discovered the chief was not in her office; it was only nearing dawn, but Sylvestra kept irregular hours, sometimes working in the middle of the night when she was less likely to be disturbed. Phatheeo considered calling her p-comm, but decided against it. It was a lead, but not enough to trouble her. He would follow up on it, and then have more to show her later, when she returned to the office. In the meantime, he trudged back to his desk to update the case file.

THE first hints of dawn chased the deep dark away from the night sky. The two moons had long since crossed the sky, leaving the twinkling stars in their wakes, and now they too faded slowly as the sky lightened. A gentle breeze shook the higher branches, filling the air with the tinkle of the metallic leaves.

Sylvestra enjoyed nights like these, especially when an urgent case had her working overtime. She would leave the office to take a break and stroll the quiet pre-dawn streets with only the tinkling leaves accompanying her. Occasionally, as she did now, she would sit on the edge of a public bath and dangle her feet in the caressing waters. And she would let her mind wander…

Relaxation didn't always come easily, especially when tough cases commanded her time and focus. And this jewel heist epitomized difficult: there were no clues, no leads, nothing. An impossible crime, a freak accident of nature. Normally, she enjoyed an intellectual challenge that tested her investigative skills and talents, but this one was just frustrating and annoying. This time, she wanted to close her eyes and forget about it, then wake up and find that it was all a dream. Nothing more, just an irritating, unsettling, bothersome dream.

The breeze picked up again and cooled her wet feet, sobering her. *Just disregard it,* she told herself, opening her eyes to the reality that she actually had more relevant things in her life than her career. *If that's possible,* she joked to herself. But it was true.

Her estrus cycle would start soon, and while that was usually a welcome and natural event, this time she wasn't ready for it. She was already beginning to get antsy when males were around, which was often, given her profession. She had worked too hard to get this far in her career, to get her life just so, that such a diversion only complicated matters. *Well, okay, so reproduction isn't merely a diversion. But it's just… This timing is awful!*

Sylvestra sighed at the warmth of the heated water, soothing her legs and relaxing her body and tense muscles. It would be so nice to find a partner, to settle down and raise a family. *Someday.* She knew it was impossible, given her current situation; if she paired off with someone now, her superiors and colleagues would assume that to be her priority, rather than her career. *Still, wouldn't it be nice?* Feeling

117

her troubles melt away in the balmy waters, she briefly closed her eyes and imagined strong wings around her, for just a moment. *Someday, but not yet.*

After a moment, she pulled her feet out of the water and continued her walk, circling around toward her home. That's when she heard the splashing of water. Up ahead, someone was using a bath! *At this time of night?* Well, she had been in the bath, so why not someone else? As she drew closer, she found it was a young human male frolicking in the bath. He didn't notice her approach and dove under the water as she came to stand at the side of the large pool. He moved like an aquatic, a graceful silhouette against the blue bottom of the lighted pool, advancing quickly below the water's surface. He stayed under for quite some time, and she wondered if he was human after all, or some reptilian species. But he soon surfaced and removed her doubts. He was clearly human.

||I haven't done that in a while,|| he chirped, startling her. He'd known she was there the whole time. He looked up at her, and she realized that this was the boy she'd seen outside the jewelry store. ||You're Sylvestra Chrreel, aren't you?||

||I am,|| she replied, surprised at how well he spoke Averian. ||It's illegal for humans to use the public baths—and there's an additional fine for doing so in the nude.||

He looked down at himself, as if noticing for the first time that he was wearing no clothes, then back up at her. ||I'm sorry. This is my first night here; I didn't know.|| He looked around. ||I didn't see a sign?||

||It's planetary law, and just common sense,|| she sang, eyeing him curiously. ||Come out of there.|| She waved him out with a wing.

He blushed. ||I... uh... don't have anything to dry myself with.||

She frowned. ||Dress yourself wet, then. You should've thought of that before you went in.||

He frowned back, then shook his head. ||Fine. Can you, please...|| And he made a turning motion with his finger.

She complied, giving him some space and turning only slightly to keep him in her peripheral vision, as he climbed out of the bath, his pale, featherless form illuminated by the soft yellow streetlight. She'd never seen a naked human before, only studied their anatomy in school. Rumor had it that, beneath their clothes, most were as naked as newborns, with only scant patches of hair adorning their bodies, but she refrained from verifying for herself and focused instead on the bath's water.

||What's your name?|| she asked.

||*Kormèr Lezàl,*|| came his tweets, distorted as if by distance. She spun, but he was gone. She visually scanned the vicinity, but she was alone.

||Impossible!|| Sylvestra spun again in case he'd gotten behind her. Unable to believe her own eyes, she fluttered up into the air for an overhead view. But there was nothing to see. The young human had simply disappeared, without a trace. *Just like the stolen jewels!*

118

KORMÈR stepped into his hotel room, sealed the portal, and hurled his clothes at the wall. <<Buomp!>> he shouted to himself. <<Dammit! She just had to come at that moment.>> He paced, angry with how the encounter had played out: how she had seen him at the bath, how she had caught there in the first place. How was he supposed to know that it was illegal for him to use the baths? Ugh! That was *not* the way he'd wanted to meet her. If only... if only...

Kormèr flopped backwards onto the bed and stared at the ceiling. He could hardly believe that, less than an hour ago, he'd reluctantly slipped silently out of Syrree's bed and ample bedchamber and snuck out of her parents' cavernous house after an unforgettable night. She was his first Averian, and he her first non-Averian: playful interspecies curiosity mixed with the potent cocktail of youthful hormones... and nature had taken its course. Kormèr had found the tactile feeling of feathers against his bare skin utterly thrilling, but the entire experience—even while working through some logistical, physical challenges—had been sublime.

Kormèr still hadn't quite had his wits about him, after departing Syrree's home, when he'd come across a public bath. Heart still racing and high on endorphins, he hadn't hesitated a moment before shedding his clothes, jumping in and splashing around, as he'd seen the Averians doing.

Then he'd heard the click-click of talons on the walkway. He hadn't been concerned about it; after all, he wasn't doing anything wrong, as far as he knew. But his heart leaped when a curious glance revealed the newcomer to be the Birshetland police chief, Sylvestra Chrreel. *Surely the most beautiful woman on Averia.* Seeing her up close, she seemed older than him, but that didn't matter to him, just as it didn't matter that he had just come from Syrree's bed. Syrree was a mark; Sylvestra was... someone he hoped to impress.

He'd dived under the water to plan what he would say when he surfaced. It would all be perfect; he would say something witty and she'd laugh, and they'd talk until the sunrise... But, much to his chagrin, it hadn't worked out that way at all. Although, he had to admit that his exit through the portal had been a stroke of inspiration—he didn't see her face, but he knew that such a dramatic exit had to have made an impression.

Kormèr got up, towel-dried his hair and slipped under the covers, wondering what Sylvestra was thinking at that moment. Was she wondering where he had gone? Was she wondering if he had been there at all? She was the chief of police; no doubt she could easily find out his place of residence. He expected a visit from her, or the police, at any moment.

After a period of futile, anxious silence, reality asserted itself, and he second-guessed his assumption. *Maybe I didn't make that great an impression, after all.* Still, his thief's instincts remained on alert, sensing that someone could come to his door at any minute. Waiting for that arrival, he fell asleep.

Knock, knock.

Kormèr jumped out of bed at the noise, then took a second to remember where he was. *Averia, where hardly anyone knocks.* By the knock, he assumed he knew

119

who it was, so he didn't rush pulling on his clothes. The knock didn't automatically trigger the screen, so Kormèr had to activate it to confirm his suspicion: it was Almp, wearing a convincingly contrite frown. Kormèr brought up the response messages and selected "Do not disturb". This would display prominently on the outside of the room's door.

Knock, knock. Almp was undeterred, and now he knew for certain that Kormèr was in his room, and awake.

Kormèr sighed and opened the door a crack. | |What do you want?| | he chirped curtly.

| |To apologize—| |

| |You wouldn't have to, if you hadn't done what you did.| |

| |No offense, please,| | Almp twittered. | |It was a joke; you weren't supposed to… well, I never thought you'd actually…| |

| |Bah.| | Kormèr left the door open but walked away to pick up the clothes he'd thrown and left on the floor. Almp accepted the unvoiced invitation and entered as Kormèr attempted to straighten his wrinkled slacks.

| |It's something we do to the young kids,| | explained Almp, as if that would make it alright. | |Even to each other.| |

Kormèr ignored him, but heard the nervousness in Almp's voice. Kormèr was of a higher rank than the boy, so perhaps Almp feared his father would find out what he had done when he wasn't even supposed to be socializing…

| |I'm really sorry,| | pleaded Almp. | |It was stupid of me; I was stupid to do that to you.| |

| |Hmm,| | agreed Kormèr without turning to face Almp.

| |Look, I'll do anything to make it up to you.| |

Kormèr stopped and looked at him askance. | |Anything?| |

| |Anything.| | Almp looked trepidatious at his impulsive answer, but he sounded earnest.

Kormèr smiled. | |Then teach me how to dance. Really.| |

Almp grinned, then broke into a smile. | |That's it?| |

| |Apology accepted,| | chirped Kormèr. | |But don't ever try that again.| |

| |I won't, I promise.| | As Kormèr went back to cleaning, Almp watched him dart about the room. | |I can get someone from housekeeping to come pick up for you?| | He glanced at the rumpled sheets. | |Straighten the bed?| |

| |No, thanks,| | Kormèr sang. Outside of his own house, he didn't like anyone touching his things, even under the pretext of cleaning. | |I like everything the way it is.| |

| |Alright,| | Almp nodded, and Kormèr could see him fighting the urge to pick up a sock that was by his feet. | |Listen, today's a rest day; how about I show you around Birshetland?| | He paused. | |If you have no plans, that is.| |

Kormèr considered it. He had seen some of the city in Feestoo's company, but the perspective of someone closer to his own age was welcome. | |Sounds good, thanks. But let's eat first. After last night, I'm starved.| |

120

Almp looked at him curiously. | | I *have* to ask. What happened last night—with Syrree and her friends, I mean? | |

It had been such a long night that Kormèr had to really think about that part of the evening. Not sure what Almp was referring to, anyway, Kormèr answered: | | Nothing, why? | |

| | Nothing? Well, let's start with why they were suddenly interested in *us*, when we'd never gotten so much as a glare from them on other nights at the Root. What did you say to them? | |

Kormèr shrugged innocently. | | Maybe you were wearing a new cologne. | |

| | Uhh, no. | |. Almp frowned. | | But then, you disappeared after you... your... dance, without telling anyone. | |

Worried about me, or what his father would say. | | I think that part's personal. But let's just say, Syrree is not as bad as you all made her out to be. | |

| | You left *with* her? | | Almp sounded shocked.

| | Yeah. And I hope you did the same with her friends—treat them well, that is. | |

| | We didn't get a chance, | | Almp frowned. | | They knew we'd played that prank on you. | |

| | I think everyone knew, | | chirped Kormèr. | | Your laughing might have clued them in. | |

Almp shrugged. | | Anyway, they said we were too immature for them and wouldn't dance with us. | |

| | Serves you right. | | He softened at seeing the dejection on Almp's face. | | Still, if they really like you, they'll forgive you. You can try again next time, but take them a gift. | | Kormèr's eyes went wide with sudden inspiration. | | Like flowers! | | This last was more to himself than Almp. That would be one way to approach Sylvestra the next time; what woman or girl didn't like flowers? But what kind...

| | They would probably like hwiite, | | mused Almp, unaware of Kormèr's internal dialog.

I guess that's a flower. | | Sure, why not? When's the next dance? | |

| | Tomorrow night. I'll tell the guys. We'll try then, | | Almp sang, brightening. | | I should be able to teach you to dance by then, | | he added teasingly.

Kormèr laughed. | | I may have other plans tomorrow night, so I might have to skip the dance. | | Almp looked a little disappointed at not having him there as the group's "wing-man". | | You teach me how to dance, and I'll try to teach you how to approach girls. In the meantime, I need to eat. Then, you can show me around Birshetland. | |

HASSERA had nearly lost Tailor. Speed alone had kept his ship in her sights for almost three weeks, relaying her position to Harry G via comm networks whenever the local system had one—Harry G could afford the high courier rates. But then she reverted into a rare system containing three jump points within four hours of the reversion point. Based on Tailor's crew size and estimating potential onboard resources, Hassera had dismissed one of the jump points, since there would be no stations or planets available for another two to three weeks. But one of the two remaining jump points led to the Iscande system, which had two inhabited planets and two asteroidal stations. The other led to the Aderuhy system with its single inhabited world, Averia.

She'd picked the Iscande jump and lost a day tubing back and forth.

She arrived at Averia and found that Freet-See had no room for her ship. Her only option would have been to park in orbit and ferry down to the planet, but Harry G's name carried some weight even this far from HOME, one of the few real perks of working for the man. The Spaceport Authority cleared a spot for her and provided two complementary power cores as a welcoming gift. Buy even Harry G's influence had its limits; the port refused to provide her security footage showing Tailor's arrival or the current whereabouts of his crew. Hassera had easily identified Tailor's ship berthed three platforms away, but as it was past midnight, she knew no one was aboard. Ports rarely allowed visitors to overnight in their ships unless they required specific environmental conditions that local establishments could not provide. So the crew had to be staying somewhere local.

||You'll have to work with the Constabulary for that kind of information,|| they told her. She had half a mind to let her ship's systems loose, but Freet-See had a reputation for security that belied it's laid back appearance. Having never dealt with the planet before, Hassera opted to leave forced intrusions off the table for now.

She slipped on her favorite lenses, a gift from Royland years ago. The lenses linked to *Ship's* AI and reacted to eye and hand movements. Public records and logs were often inconsistent and not the most efficient means of finding information, but her ship's AI handled such situations easily. It wasn't long before it had identified the transportation company and specific sky-hopper that had taken Tailor to Birshetland. Within a few hours, she found herself in the lobby of a hotel and conference center where a taxi driver had dropped Tailor off almost a day ago. The conference rooms were all reserved, but neither the reservation names nor the descriptions revealed anything useful. But the schedules had some potential. Someone had booked two rooms at around noon the day before.

While Harry G preferred to keep his mercs in the dark as to why he was after Tailor, Hassera had gleaned the information and shared it with Royland. So she knew that Tailor and his crew were most likely here to meet with a potential buyer. She drew a lot of stares as she made her way to the conference rooms, but no one questioned her. Unfortunately, all the doors were closed, and the walls prevented scanning.

Hassera returned to the lobby and purchased a drink at the restaurant. She carried her own live food in a pouch on her belt; the Averian menu had nothing for her species. She took a seat at the restaurant with a clear view of the lobby, and ate.

Four hours later, her patience was rewarded. She didn't need her lenses to identify Jeremy Tailor and Kit McQuinton as they crossed the lobby toward the exit. When Harry G had tasked her and Royland with finding them, Hassera had memorized the faces of the entire crew. She followed them to a taxi-platform where they waited for transport.

Through a comm linked to her ship in Freet-See, she relayed a simple message to Harry G: "Averia confirmed." During the weeks in transit, she had decided to hand the crew over to Harry G. She'd request to be the one to kill them, after the boss was done with them, to give Royland the justice he deserved. Harry G often obliged his people that way.

Now it was time for business. She pulled a stunner and stepped toward the men. She couldn't carry them both all the way back to her ship, but she could get them in a room and keep them there until Harry G arrived.

A taxi pulled up, and she stopped, keeping the stunner hidden at her side. The men greeted someone who was inside, as if they already knew him. Using her lenses, she scanned the two faces in the taxi; the data appeared almost instantly. One was a local boy, Almp Whoorreea… She'd read the rest later. The other youth came up as unknown: while that wasn't impossible, it was highly irregular. She herself kept a very low profile, as *Ship* actively scanned for any data that popped up on her and zapped it before the errant information could spread further. Unless this—*Terran? Elmarian?*—unless this boy had the same deterrent system in place, such anonymity wasn't feasible or tenable. But if he *did* have such a program in place… could he be another mercenary working for some other agency? Or even for Tailor himself? She submitted his likeness to *Ship*'s active monitoring subroutine as Jeremy and Kit entered the taxi.

Hassera slipped the blaster away. There would be other opportunities, but she couldn't lose sight of them now that she'd finally found them. As the taxi door closed, she spotted the mystery boy looking at her. Then the taxi pulled away.

Hassera stepped up to the platform's edge and signaled for another taxi.

||Follow that taxi,|| she told the driver.

||HIGH sky, gentlemen,|| called the taxi driver from the platform below as Almp and Kormèr stepped out of the hotel.

||Feestoo!|| Kormèr greeted the Averian contently. Kormèr sprang down the ladder rungs to the platform with an abandon that made Almp cringe. *Does he think he has wings now? One missed step and he could tumble over the side.*

||This is a surprise,|| sang Kormèr, clasping the driver's shoulder as Almp followed him down the rungs.

||KL, your generosity has given me a joyful mother, a happy wife and a happy boss. I'm at your disposal for the rest of your stay here.||

Kormèr laughed. ||You don't even know how long I'm planning to stay! Still, I'm honored to use your services, for however long you're offering them,|| chirped Kormèr. Then he pointed to Almp. ||You remember Almp?||

||Yes, hello. You, too, are welcome.|| Feestoo grinned. ||As for how long, it doesn't matter if you're here for a week, or even longer. Thanks to you, I am set for a while.||

Almp was too incredulous to respond. He simply climbed into the back seat after Kormèr, impressed at Kormèr's influence. What most astonished him was that the driver was acting as Kormèr's private transporter, given how much drivers could make on their fares, especially during the holidays. For someone who claimed to be a first-time visitor to Averia, Kormèr had certainly wasted no time making his mark on Birshetland.

As they soared around the city, Almp pointed out areas of interest and told historical stories about them. Feestoo added his own commentary from time to time, but mostly nodded his agreement and kept to driving, to let Almp provide the narrative.

||Why can't non-Averians use the baths?|| asked Kormèr, after a short tale about the baths from Almp.

Feestoo answered. ||That rule goes back to my great-great-grandfather's day. Birshetland had been closed to non-Averians from the start. The inhabitants at the time had decided they wanted to keep the city's culture pure, or something like that. Anyway, great-great-grandpa was in his teens when they opened the city to outsiders. The very first night, they found several offworld males fu— Err...|| He caught Kormèr's eye in the rear-view mirror. ||Well, they were using the baths for things that shouldn't be done in public. And that was the end of that.||

||I see,|| twittered Kormèr.

||I never knew that,|| chirped Almp.

||It's not something that's talked about much,|| added Feestoo. ||Don't want to offend anyone, you know.||

Almp furrowed his brow. ||How did you know about that rule, anyway?|| he asked, but Kormèr's attention was outside.

||Feestoo, slow down.|| The taxi driver obeyed. Then Kormèr chirped happily, ||Hey, it's them. Pull over there.|| He pointed to a platform where two tired-looking human men stood awaiting a taxi. As the taxi pulled to a stop, one wearing glasses opened the door.

||I'm sorry,|| began Kormèr, ||but this taxi's taken.||

Glasses-man poked his head in. ||KL!||

||Hey, guys! Come on in. The ride's on me.||

The man squeezed into the back seat next to Almp. His companion sat up front with Feestoo. ||Jeremy, Kit, this is my friend, Almp,|| introduced Kormèr. ||He's the manager's son at the hotel where I'm staying. And the diver is Feestoo. Almp, Feestoo, these guys own the ship that brought me to Averia.||

Everyone exchanged greetings. The human named Jeremy continued: | |Can you believe we just got out of the first round of negotiations? | |

| |You're joking! | | Kormèr seemed astonished. | |It's been almost a day! | |

| |Someone kept you working into a day of rest? | | asked Almp. | |That's not proper. | |

| |That's business, Almp, | | twittered Jeremy. | |Sometimes you have to make compromises for the things you feel passionate about. | |

| |You must be starved, | | sang Kormèr.

| |Actually, | | chirped Kit, | |we're more tired than hungry. But a little food would be great, especially if we can get some coffee with it. | | He yawned. | |Thank the gods it's a rest day. | | He shook his head to keep himself awake.

| |Feestoo, | | chirped Kormèr to the driver, | |you know my favorite place. | |

| |On our way, KL. | |

KORMÈR watched, amused, as Jeremy and Kit ate heartily from the dishes they ordered. They hardly seemed in the mood for conversation, but he tried anyway.

| |How'd the meeting go? After a day of negotiations, you must have made some progress, | |

Jeremy swallowed, then chortled. | |We ran through our marketing presentation in the first hour and a half. We spent the rest of the day answering questions from different people, and eating. | | He looked at Feestoo. | |Averians sure like to eat a lot during business meetings. | |

Feestoo shrugged. | |Many of us eat six meals a day, plus snacks. | |

Jeremy nodded. | |And you're all so svelte. Flying must be an excellent exercise. | |

| |And dancing, | | sang Almp, nudging Kormèr with his elbow.

Kormèr couldn't help but grin. | |Yeah, right. Dancing. | |

Jeremy raised an eyebrow, but didn't ask for Kormèr to elaborate. | |Anyway, there's still a lot to do. | |

| |For one thing, | | chirped Kit, wiping his mouth, | |the ship's not ready yet. Roke says it'll be another few days. | |

Jeremy nodded. | |And the client still has to test the... merchandise. | | He warbled the last, and Kormèr caught Jeremy's sideways glance at Almp and Feestoo.

| |Excuse me, friends, | | chirped Kormèr to Almp and Feestoo, | |but I have to talk with Jeremy and Kit in Terran English for just a moment. | | The Averians nodded their understanding and chittered quietly to each other to give the others some privacy. "You can trust them, Jer," said Kormèr.

"Pardon?" Jeremy pretended not to understand.

"The way you just looked at them, like you'd almost given something away."

Jeremy made a sour face, then glanced at Kit, who nodded his agreement with Kormèr's assessment. "Look, I don't know them. We barely knew you before you went off on your own yesterday, and now you suddenly have 'friends'?"

"Well, my aunt tells me I'm an excellent judge of character. I trusted you guys, didn't I?" He waited for Jeremy's begrudging acknowledgment. "They're not with G, if that's what you're worried about. The driver ferried me around yesterday; I paid and fed him well for his time, so I've won his loyalty. The young one can't be completely trusted, but he's more about playing childish pranks and figuring out girls than anything serious."

Kit looked unconvinced. "Listen to you: 'the young one.' That kid looks about the same age as you."

He had a point. Outwardly, Kormèr looked like any other callow youth, despite how he felt. "What's that Terran saying: 'it's not the years, it's the mileage'? Let's just say that I have more mileage than him," Kormèr said, looking at Jeremy again. "If you don't want to discuss business in front of them, I understand."

Kit snickered at Kormèr's wide, sad-looking eyes, as Jeremy pushed up the bridge of his glasses. "You're right, I don't. Even if *you* trust them, *we* can't afford to have either of them talk to the wrong person, or have someone eavesdropping on them."

"Okay, we won't talk business," Kormèr shrugged. | |Now let's stop being rude.| | To Almp and Feestoo, | |No offense.| |

It was clear from Feestoo and Almp's expression that neither of them felt insulted by their caution. In fact, they seemed entirely lacking in curiosity about what he and the other non-Averians had been discussing, so maybe Jeremy had a point that someone would let some details slip out in casual conversation.

| |So what've you been up to?| | asked Jeremy. | |You seem to've been busy.| |

While he had directed the question at Kormèr, his asking in Averian inadvertently invited Almp and Feestoo to add their own running commentary. Kormèr felt almost like a spectator by the end; his new Averian friends were more than happy to fill in the details about the people Kormèr had met, the nightclub he'd visited and some of the sights he'd seen. Kormèr met Jeremy and Kit's eyes with a pained, apologetic expression; he had to admit that they were right: Averians did like to talk, a lot.

| |You *were* busy!| | chirped Jeremy, accepting Kormèr's contrition with a subtle nod.

| |Did you say you were staying at the Cheerees?| | asked Kit.

| |That's right,| | Kormèr sang. | |It's very nice, and it seems to cater to non-Averian clientele, too.| |

| |Oh, we know,| | Jeremy sang. | |That's one reason we're staying there, too. That place is pricey, though.| | He narrowed his eyes, no doubt wondering how Kormèr could afford it.

Kormèr's brows went up, as he answered innocently, | | Really? Feestoo absolutely insisted that I stay there.| | Feestoo nodded sagely. | | What a coincidence!| |

Before Jeremy could probe Kormèr's finances further, their server returned to their table. | | Will there be anything else?| |

Jeremy stuffed the last bit of food on his dish into his mouth and sat back. | | I'm done.| |

| | Same here,| | chirped Kit, taking a swig from his stein of Averian ale.

Kormèr glanced at Almp and Feestoo and got nods from them. | | Just the bill then,| | Kormèr chirped to the server.

| | Just a receipt for your review, then? Very good, sir,| | sang the server.| | Kormèr frowned. | | I don't understand.| |

| | Your credit balance, carried over from your last visit, sir. It's more than enough to cover this meal, as well.| | He paused. | | I'm sorry, perhaps I misunderstood. Did you wish to pay a different way this time?| |

Kormèr thought back to the prior morning. | | Oh! The gem. That's fine, thank you. I just wanted to be sure it was enough to cover.| |

| | More than enough, sir,| | the server beamed. | | Hope you enjoyed your meals. Enjoy the rest of your day!| | The server grabbed up an arm-length of dishes and walked off.

Kit and Jeremy were staring at Kormèr. | | What?| | he asked, feeling the weight of their stares.

Jeremy shook his head. | | Nothing. Never mind. Let's go.| |

When they were all seated in the taxi and on their way, Kit shook his head. | | No, I gotta ask. Gem?| |

Kormèr nodded. | | Hmm? Oh. When I left you guys yesterday, I forgot to ask for money. So I had to make do with what I had on me.| |

Kit chuckled dubiously. | | And you carry around gems? Just like that, in your pockets? Where'd you get them?| |

| | Here and there,| | replied Kormèr, halfheartedly. His attention was on the jewelry store they had just passed, the same one that had been robbed. Was Sylvestra there? He decided he'd return after dropping Jeremy and Kit off at the hotel.

| | Oh, really,| | was Kit's sardonic response.

Kormèr frowned at Kit. | | Hmm? Oh, yeah. I've been to some places where these are as common as rocks.| |

| | Huh,| | tittered Jeremy, sharing Kit's skepticism. | | One of these days, maybe you can tell us where that is, exactly.| |

| | Sure. I'd be happy to,| | Kormèr grinned. | | One of these days.| |

| | Here we are, gentlemen,| | announced Feestoo, bringing the taxi to a stop outside the hotel.

As Jeremy climbed out, he sang: | | KL, we're in Room 28. There's plenty of space; if you'd like, you can stay with us, instead of paying for your own.| |

Kormèr wondered how to decline graciously. ||Thanks for the offer—||

||Mister Tailor,|| chirped Almp, ||he's practically paid for permanent residence.||

||I don't understand,|| Jeremy scowled, then relaxed his brow. ||Let me guess: paid with another gem?||

||Don't worry about it, guys. I'll be fine,|| chirped Kormèr dismissively, shutting the door. ||And good luck with the negotiations,|| he chirped to them through the window. ||I'll see you later.||

Kormèr watched the men step back from the platform and waved to them. As they pulled away from the stand, he asked Almp, ||Do you mind if we stop by Chees?||

||The jewelry store?|| Almp asked, looking confused. ||It looks like it's still closed for the investigation. If you want to stop somewhere to shop...||

Kormèr shook his head. ||No, I just want to take a peek. See how the investigation is going.||

||I suppose, just for a bit,|| Almp warbled begrudgingly, as Feestoo nodded his confirmation of their next stop. ||But, really, there are more exciting places to visit.||

Kormèr smiled to himself as he sat back. Not for him, not if Sylvestra was there.

AS the taxi pulled away, Jeremy and Kit entered the hotel together. Given their situation, it was best for them not to linger out in the open for too long. Jeremy had mentioned to Kormèr that one of the reasons that they were staying at the Cheerees was because the establishment accommodated offworlders; the other reason was that the hotel had excellent security: nobody loitered or lurked on the premises, unless they were guests.

In the spacious lobby, Jeremy shot a last look over his shoulder. "What do you suppose Almp meant by that: 'he's paid for permanent residence'?"

Kit shrugged. "Got me. But I'll be damned if you weren't right on the mark yesterday; that the kid seems to have the galaxy in his pocket. Considering the kid's never been here before, he's certainly making himself at home, and even developing a local's palate. Did you see the way he was guzzling nutria?" Kit shimmied with a grimace of distaste.

Jeremy laughed. "You've never even tasted nutria!"

"Nope, I can't even get past the name," Kit said plainly. "I keep thinking of those weird, orange-toothed, beaver-looking critters back on Earth."

"It's not so bad—the drink, I mean. It tastes like fruity, malty oat milk."

Kit feigned a gagging noise, which startled some of the nearby Averians into giving them a wider berth. "Anyway, the kid seems to have made some fast friends."

"Hopefully, they're good ones, for his sake," Jeremy said. "He could've ended up with a cabbie who took him for a ride or took him to a flophouse instead of the

128

Cheerees." He knew tourists who had been scammed by unscrupulous—and usually unlicensed—cabbies and the seedy hotels that paid them kickbacks for every "customer" delivered to their doors. That had been years ago, and at Freet-See. Birshetland was one of the safer cities on Averia, but Kormèr was still a kid.

"Yeah, this place is no flophouse, that's for sure," Kit murmured, staring up the central trunk at the sleek, modern and gilded furnishings and fixtures. "I hope this deal pans out, Jer. Unlike KL, we've got a budget, and a time constraint."

"I know," Jeremy said. "It's only a matter of time before Harry G realizes we're still breathing, and then he'll send someone to remedy that, p. d. q."

"You're assuming we're not already being watched," Kit said, casting a furtive glance around.

"I'm not assuming anything," Jeremy said. "Same reason I didn't want to say too much in front of the Averians before: we can't be certain of anyone around here."

"So, do we just leave the kid to wander around on his own?" Kit asked.

Jeremy shrugged. "He seems like he's staying out of trouble for now." At Kit's uncertain frown, he said, "Look, let's get our own business taken care of, first, and then we can see what we can do for him. Otherwise, if we still have Harry G on our tail, Kormèr's going to be better off without us."

CHAPTER 10

HARRY G read the third courier message that Hassera had sent, and it disappointed him. For a Suslixan, especially one that he considered nearly his equal in cold, logical reasoning, her running off after Tailor was nothing short of… emotional. In his experience, emotional responses invariably led to mistakes being made.

The three Y-Tach crew that Tailor had dumped at Eps Eri had had much to say. They revealed that Royland had not been involved in the shooting of Tailor's ship, but rather an unknown member of Tailor's crew had secreted aboard Royland's ship, trapped Royland in the umbilical and somehow perpetuated their escape. That was their theory, at least. They hadn't seen the other crewman, but Terl had effected Royland's demise before the AI on Tailor's ship had rendered them all unconscious. That outcome satisfied Harry G; Royland had been a thorn in his side for some time, ever since the man had dug into Harry G's business dealings one too many times. He would compensate Terl well for his work.

Harry G had no doubt that the freighter's AI had orchestrated the escape; only a computer could have acted with such precision. At one time, many of those old freighters had been equipped with an AI module, but several of the modules had become too sentient and gone "rogue", wresting control away from their owners after only a few months. The manufacturer had distributed a patch to dumb-down the AI, but after that, it had washed its hands of the matter. No record existed on how many of the ships received the patch. Tailor's clearly had not.

Terl and company had also revealed that Hassera had only asked them one simple question and then left them in the escape pod for Gal-Pol to recover. Another bad sign.

Hassera's fourth and fifth courier transmissions contained only location updates. From these, Harry G extrapolated possible destinations. But only one made sense: the Aderuhy system with its quiet, unassuming planet Frrooweetsee or, as everyone else knew it, Averia. Tailor and his crew had been smart to pick that planet; the laws and customs there limited Harry G's influence. But that didn't mean that he could do nothing.

Harry G prepared two couriers, one with a message for Hassera, and the other for some local help.

But he clearly could no longer rely only on outside help, particularly at these distances. He needed to be in the thick of the action once again, ready to make the decisions and take the steps that needed to be taken.

His ship chimed as it neared the jump point, then automatically transited.

SRRCHEEL turned his attention away from the two boys—one Averian, and the other not—peering in through the store window, and focused it back on his master. The latter moved with practiced ease through various *srootees*, the patterns that formed the foundation of spellcasting. Srrcheel recited the basics he'd learned in his head as he watched his master. *Filaments are the energy-rich fibers that a sorcerer weaves into* srootees *and which provide power to spells when you execute the* tep. *The* tep *is the action a sorcerer performs at the completion of a* srootee *to activate the spell and release its power.* He had the theory etched in his memory; that was the easy part. The difficulty came in putting the theory into practice.

Simply seeing the filaments had taken him months to learn. Now he could bring them into focus so effortlessly that he sometimes couldn't recall why it had been so difficult before. Spellcasting, on the other hand, did not yet come so easily to him. It involved controlling these filaments, weaving them into patterns through gestures. The patterns were sometimes called "power configurations" since, as a caster wove them, the spell's energy would build. A caster had to concentrate on his patterns until they developed into what the caster wanted: *that* was the hard part. The gestures were simple memorization, but the ability to tap the filaments had to come from within the caster; it couldn't be taught or learned in the same way. Having it, one could develop the skill through training, and that was what the Hovel was all about.

Srrcheel understood all this. | | But understanding and doing are two different things, | | his master had told him. | | One can understand the theory behind flying, the physics of moving through the air, and yet, when jumping from a tree, not be able to do it. | |

But Srrcheel was learning. He was almost ready to cast his first spell. He had studied its *srootee* and had spent the better part of the last month honing the mental discipline necessary to form the power configuration required. If his raising took place during this year's Cheerretee, he would have to cast it as part of the ceremony. Anxiety knotted his gizzard, and his attention returned to the store.

His master asked him for a few artifacts, then appeared to slip into a trance. His winged arms rose slowly and swirled with a hypnotic gracefulness. They swept in wide arcs from side to side, weaving and molding the filaments into the desired pattern. His master's smooth, relaxed method enthralled Srrcheel. *I hope I will be that patient, that artful when my turn comes,* he thought to himself. The spell Srrcheel had selected to learn was simple, almost a joke next to the intricacy of the spells his master cast. Its pattern would take only a moment to complete. Not so with the long and complex spell his master now cast. To rush this one risked reputation and status. Srrcheel couldn't imagine the concentration a Master or Grand Master level spell required.

The feathers on the back of his neck stood on end, and he turned to see the two boys still staring in at the window. When he turned back, his master was watching him. | | I'm sorry, | | he chirped quickly. | | They distract me. | |

| | It's okay, Srrcheel. This is a very long cast. You can go outside if you like. | |

Srrcheel hesitated. He'd never been on his own in the city yet. He feared getting lost or getting hurt by someone. He had heard stories of criminals… He shuddered. | | There's nothing I can help you with? | |

| | Not now. Later. Go now. I'll call for you. | |

Srrcheel nodded, turned and shuffled to the door.

| | SHE'S not here, | | mewled Kormèr, disappointed. He and Almp peered through the storefront window at the Averians inside the empty jewelry store. Some wore the police medallion, but two were clearly not police. One seemed to be a boy roughly Almp's age, the other a young man that Kormèr estimated to be around five or five and a half Elmarian years. Of course, he couldn't really be sure, and wondered briefly if Averians aged differently than Elmarians.

| | Well, you can't summon an updraft on a still day, | | retorted Almp. | | But look at that guy. I think he's a sorcerer. | |

| | Which one? | |

| | The one with the boy. Look what he's doing. | |

Kormèr watched as the young birdman moved in a series of manual gestures. | | What's wrong with him? Is he having a seizure or something? | |

Almp guffawed. | | No, dummy. I think he's casting a spell. | |

Kormèr looked at Almp, trying to judge the youth's expression. | | You're not kidding, are you? | |

| | No. I've heard stories of how they do it. They make funny movements with their arms and create wonders. | |

Kormèr marveled and turned back to watch. Real magic! Not the fake stuff the street magicians practiced on Elmar. While Elmar had a population of real magicians, they kept to themselves on various islands. This was Kormèr's first time seeing true magic at work.

| | Your planet gets more and more amazing by the minute, Almp, | | twittered Kormèr. | | Are there a lot of these spell casters? | |

| | There's an entire city of them. It's called Berdia. Thankfully, they keep to themselves. That there's one here is a big deal. | |

After a moment, the young man stopped his gesturing and spoke to the boy. Kormèr noted the boy's pale brown plumage, wondering where he fit in the social structure. After a moment, the boy turned and walked toward them.

| | Let's get outta here, | | warned Almp, moving away from the window and toward the taxi.

Kormèr grabbed his wing. | |Wait.| | There was an opportunity here. His mind raced with the possibilities.

| |Wait for what?| | Almp struggled free of Kormèr's hold. | |These people are dangerous. They can turn you into droppings if you make them angry. Come on.| |

But Kormèr held his ground until the boy stepped out of the store and gingerly closed the door behind him. The boy stayed there, at the door, staring straight ahead, at nothing in particular, almost as if he'd been ordered to stand guard. He didn't want to disturb him, but curiosity was killing him.

| |Excuse me,| | he chirped, coming to stand beside the boy. He heard Almp gasp behind him. | |I'm from Elmar. My name's Kormèr.| | He refrained from clasping the boy's shoulder, however.

The boy seemed to shiver, as he faltered, | |I... hi. I, uh, I'm Srrcheel.| |

| |Pleased to meet you, Srrcheel. My friend Almp here tells me you're a sorcerer.| | Again, a startled noise from Almp.

| |We, uh... he is a sorcerer.| | Srrcheel jerked a thumb over his shoulder at the young man inside.

| |And you?| |

| |I am his apprentice.| |

| |Oh. But you *do* know magic.| | It was more of a question than a statement.

| |Yes... well, I know *about* it.| |

Kormèr nodded. | |Can I learn it?| |

The boy visibly stifled a laugh. Kormèr's hopes shriveled.

| |I don't think so,| | the boy finally answered.

| |Because I'm not Averian?| |

| |For starters. There have never been offworlder sorcerers, as far as I know.| |

| |Hmm,| | tweeted Kormèr, not wanting to get into the fact that Elmar had sorcerers. | |Maybe you can help me then.| |

| |I don't see how I can, but what would you like?| |

| |This may sound silly; in fact, you probably get these kinds of requests all the time, but... well, could you cast a love spell for me?| | Kormèr braced himself for a laugh, but got none. The boy appeared to be pondering the idea as if it had never before occurred to him. | |I can pay you if you accept payment for services,| | added Kormèr, in case that was the reason for the boy's hesitation.

| |No, I don't. Accept payment, I mean. I was just thinking about what such a spell would involve.| |

| |You can do it then?| | Kormèr's eyes were wide with expectation.

| |Oh, sorry. I didn't mean to mislead you. I can't actually cast spells yet. Not until I'm raised on Cheerretee.| |

| |I thought that was the lunar celebration.| |

| |It is. But it's also the night some sorcerers go through their raising ceremony.| |

||Oh. Okay. What's it mean to be 'raised'? Like a promotion?||

||Not quite, but you have the right idea. It's more symbolic than a promotion.||

An idea hit Kormèr. ||You're from Berdia, right?||

||I'm from Freet-See. The tree in which I live is on Berdia.||

||I see. But your raising will take place there, on Berdia?||

||Yes.||

||I'd like to attend, if that's possible.||

||No offense, but no one except the sorcerers of my order may attend the raising ceremony.||

||Oh, I didn't realize that. No offense taken at all.||

So much for infiltrating Berdia. Apparently, the Berdians were as isolated as the sorcerers of Elmar. Kormèr could always use the portal to get to Berdia, once he knew a little more about the place, but Almp's words of warning had taken root in his mind. If the sorcerers caught him, would he have time to escape a magical capture? He didn't very much fancy the idea of being turned into droppings.

||As for spellcasting,|| continued Srrcheel, ||I wouldn't bother asking my master for help, if that's what you're thinking. We were summoned here for this, and this alone. Once this assignment is over, we will be returning to the Hovel.||

||The Hovel?||

||Our tree-home in Berdia.||

Kormèr nodded. ||I see. Thank you for your time, then.||

||I'm sorry I couldn't be of more help.||

||Thanks for listening to my silly questions . See you at the rai—|| he started, then stopped himself. ||See you around,|| he amended.

Kormèr followed Almp into the taxi.

||You've got your feathers growing inside your skull, you know,|| scolded Almp. ||They're making your brain stupid.||

Kormèr shrugged. ||Maybe, but I don't look like droppings, do I?||

||Luck.||

||Bah! He's a nice guy; didn't you see? He was friendly, like you or me. He's not a monster, just another Averian, who happens to have extraordinary abilities.||

||Tell it to all those people that've gotten turned to droppings. Oh wait, you can't; because they're droppings!||

But Kormèr wasn't listening anymore. His mind was on the raising ceremony and how he would get there. *That should really be interesting. I can't wait.*

PERPLEXED by the boy's last words, Srrcheel stared after the departing taxi. It appeared he was going to say he'd see me at the raising. He shook his head. Delusional Elmarian. He chuckled. Of course, that's the only Elmarian I've ever met. Maybe they're all that way.

A mental signal from his master had him trotting back into the store.

| |What did the boys want?| | asked his master.

| |One was an Averian who seemed to be more afraid of me than curious,| | chirped Srrcheel, assuming his master had seen it all. His master nodded. | |The other was an Elmarian who wanted to know if he could learn magic. I explained to him why it could not be.| |

| |Very good. Be mindful not to give away anything you should not say.| |

Srrcheel reviewed the conversation in his head. | |I was, I think. I was a little nervous.| |

| |You handled the situation well,| | his master chirped, and Srrcheel realized it had been a test.

| |Thank you, master.| |

| |You deserve a reward. How would you feel about a brief side trip to visit a good friend?| | He winked.

SYRREE heard the doorbell ring and waited for the telltale sounds of the maid answering. A moment later, the maid waddled into the airy room in which Syrree lounged and announced a young man to see her. Syrree smiled. She knew the Elmarian would return. They always did for her. Some part of her had been contemplating finding out where he was staying, to see if he was worth visiting; since he appeared to be friends with Almp, he was most likely a guest at the hotel where Almp worked. He had certainly dressed the part.

The Elmarian had been charming, open and very considerate of her; the perfect diversion. She had found him gone before sunrise, and his sneaking off early had irked her. But in the hours since, her ire had waned, replaced by a longing to see him again, and to bask in his attention. Now he was back. He must have missed her, too.

Her cockiness dissolved into surprise and disappointment when she passed into the foyer. Waiting for her was not the young Elmarian, but her betrothed. She remembered herself and smiled happily, rushing to embrace him.

| |Srrcheel!| |

He returned the embrace warmly. | |Syrree. How are you?| |

She stepped away a little. | |Surprised. What are you doing here?| |

| |Master's on assignment. I wanted to surprise you.| | He held out his hands, and she took them. But inside, she cringed. She despised when he spoke about his 'master'. It made him sound so basic, or subservient.

| |Wait till Mother hears. She'll be ecstatic.| | She was suddenly worried. What if Kormèr showed up? | |How long are you staying?| |

| |Here with you? Well, my master said I could stay until you tossed me out on my rump. But we're only in Birshetland until tomorrow.| |

Syrree felt torn between worry and disappointment. On the one hand, she feared Kormèr would decide to show up inopportunely, but she also wished Srrcheel could stay longer. While her relationship with Srrcheel was much more formal—they had certainly never gone beyond passionate kissing—he still satisfied her need for attention. And she so dreaded visiting the Hovel, that dreary reminder of past Frrooweetsee primitiveness. Of course, she would never tell Srrcheel this for fear of hurting his feelings.

Eagerly, she dragged him into the house for her parents to see who had unexpectedly shown up at their door, although the maid would have already informed them. It overjoyed both her parents to see him, and her mother immediately invited him to stay for dinner. It was difficult to tell if Srrcheel actually enjoyed her mother's cooking or just accepted to be polite, as he was always agreeable and sweet. He was the perfect suitor.

Syrree's father dominated the dinner conversation, boring everyone as he waxed on about good business practices and the importance of preparing for a good financial future. After dinner, Syrree's father pulled Srrcheel aside for some "male-to-male" talk in the den. Her mother joked that her father was probably trying to get Srrcheel to teach him sorcery, which was ridiculous since sorcerers were sworn to secrecy, and Srrcheel would never betray such a solemn vow.

Once finally alone, Syrree and Srrcheel stepped out onto the private veranda. The sky had darkened into early evening, the vestiges of daylight fading to the east. Srrcheel walked to the edge and looked out over the city and at the sunset.

He breathed deeply and sighed. ||This is nice,|| he warbled, as she came to stand beside him. He turned sideways to face her and leaned his elbow on the railing. ||Your father is too much.||

||And you tolerate him more than most people,|| she sang. ||What'd he want to talk with you about?||

Srrcheel grinned. ||'Male-to-male things',|| he twittered sharply, mimicking her father's stuffy manner. ||'Not to be discussed outside of this room, you understand.'||

Syrree laughed. Srrcheel had his moments of awkwardness, a result of his being cooped up in the Hovel from a young age, but sometimes he did make her laugh. ||That's Father.|| She waited, but when he didn't say more, she asked, ||So, are you going to tell me what else he said?||

||Oh... ah... Well, I... I don't want to go against his wishes.||

Syrree expected as much. She knew Srrcheel well enough to know that he stuck to the rules, no matter the situation, but she hated not having her way. ||Oh, stuff him! If we're to be married, you can't be keeping things from me.||

||Or you from me.||

Her heart skipped a beat. ||What do you mean by that?|| she blurted.

||I just mean that, if I'm not keeping secrets from you, it's only fair that you do the same. Right?||

||Oh, yes. That... that's fair.|| She relaxed her grip on the railing, glad that she hadn't been holding his hands instead.

||What did you think I meant?||

Syrree shook her head. ||Nothing. I... I thought you were accusing me of keeping some secret from you.||

||You've always been one to speak your mind.|| He put his hand over hers on the railing, his touch tentative. ||Your father just wanted to talk about my progress at the Hovel, and future... dates. You know, about us.||

Syrree's crest feathers prickled with agitation. ||He has it all planned out, doesn't he?|| Srrcheel looked like he'd been caught with his head in his preengland, but his silence spoke volumes. ||I knew it!|| Syrree didn't know whether to be angry or pleased. On the one hand, she wanted it to be the most magical experience of her life, and the only way that was going to happen was through proper and timely planning. On the other hand, she bristled at the idea of her father making all these plans without her input. She loved him with all her heart, but she hated how he controlled all aspects of her life, including this betrothal!

She nearly gasped at the thought. *But it's true*, she thought. *I do like Srrcheel; he's short and a little soft, but he's very sweet, and funny. And he'll be a sorcerer one day, and that's a lot of power.* He smiled at her, as she looked into his eyes, and she was conscious of her effort to return his smile. *But am I ready to get married to him? To anyone?*

Srrcheel's chest plumage puffed slightly. ||What I didn't tell him is that... I think I will go through my raising on Cheerretee.||

So soon! ||That's wonderful news! Why didn't you tell him?|| Syrree chittered excitedly.

||Shh,|| he hushed. ||It might not happen; I didn't want to say anything and then not have it happen.||

||I'm sure it will,|| she sang. ||If they can't see what a wonderful sorcerer you'd be, then I'll have to go there myself and tell them.||

||Wouldn't that be a sight!|| Srrcheel laughed, lifting his hand from hers. ||Oh, I'm going to miss this so much!||

||Don't tell me you have to go already. I thought you were staying until I tossed you out on your rump.||

||It's getting late,|| he warbled apologetically. ||Master and I have an early start tomorrow, then it's back to Berdia.||

||When can you come out again?|| she asked, moving closer and preening his colorful chin tufts.

||I can't be sure.|| He didn't ask her to visit him, as he was well aware of how inconvenient and unpleasant she found the austere dwellings in Berdia. He was very thoughtful in that way. ||If I am raised, I may get a little time to come out and celebrate. If I do, I'll come and see you.||

||I'd like that,|| she warbled. Then he leaned in and kissed her. It was lingering but still chaste, compared to what she had recently enjoyed with... She pushed any notion of betrayal from her mind, as though Srrcheel could read her thoughts. It was just her imagination, of course, as Srrcheel stepped back with his loving gaze intact.

As she walked him to the door, Srrcheel told her, ||A funny thing happened today; someone asked me about casting a love spell.||

||Is there such a thing?|| Syrree asked, intrigued.

||I don't know. But imagine if there is?|| he mused.

||That would be terrible!|| she exclaimed. ||No one would ever know for sure if their love was real.||

||That's true. I wonder, though, if they're happy, does it matter?|| He seemed to consider the idea of such a spell more seriously. ||And one can be in love and still be miserable, so what exactly was he asking for?||

Syrree shook her head at Srrcheel's train of thought. ||It does matter. Love shouldn't be tampered with—it should always be real. What horrible person asked you such a thing?||

||It was this Elmar—||

||Heading out already?|| interrupted Syrree's father.

||Yes, sir,|| Srrcheel chirped. ||Reluctantly, but I have to go.||

||Well, it was good to see you,|| her father sang, nodding at Srrcheel. Srrcheel bowed in return. ||And you too, sir. High sky, Syrree.||

||High sky.|| Standing beside her father, Syrree watched as Srrcheel unfurled his wings and, with a few bounding steps, soared away. Despite his stocky figure, he was a strong and graceful flyer, and she smiled at watching him glide away, warmed and cheered by her betrothed's companionable company.

She left her father to close the door, bounded up the stairs to her room and jumped into bed without turning on the lights. Just as she had drifted off to sleep, a scraping at the window roused her. She looked up and yelped! The window stood wide open and, silhouetted against the brightness of the double moons, his dark coat billowing like tail plumes in the draft, crouched the young Elmarian, Kormèr. The drapes swirled as he hopped into the room and turned to close the window.

He turned to face her and chirped, ||Hi.||

||You can't just show up unannounced, you know,|| she chastised. Her heart was pounding, and she wasn't sure if it was all from the surprise of his entrance, or something deeper. Love spells suddenly popped into her mind. *Did Kormèr cast a love spell on me?* She knew it was ridiculous, of course. Only Frrooweetsee natives could be sorcerers, as far as she knew.

And she knew that what she felt wasn't love, not the way that she had always imagined. Kormèr was a curiosity, and once that novelty wore off, they would go their separate ways. She would miss his company, but there would be others. And sweet, dutiful Srrcheel would be there, always; he may not have been her choice, but her parents had picked him for her, so she supposed he would eventually have to do.

||I'm sorry,|| Kormèr sang, in his limited offworlder way that was so endearing. ||I'll leave then, and call ahead next time.|| He turned to the window and reached for the latch.

||Wait. How did you even get up here?|| There was nothing outside her window, no purchase for a non-flier.

||I've been taking flying lessons.|| He stepped away from the window and walked slowly around her room, looking at everything as if memorizing it.

||Hilarious. What are you doing?||

||Trying to figure out what you have, so I know what to get you the next time I visit.||

He walked with such fluid motions, and when he turned toward her, she felt vulnerable kneeling on her bed. ||So you show up empty-handed?|| she managed to warble, trying to regain her composure.

||I have nothing but myself and my conversation,|| he sang. Spreading his arms, he twirled once.

She shook her head, delaying as she found her voice. ||No conversation tonight. The dance. Do it for me.||

Tossing his coat aside, Kormèr performed the courting dance, adding new colors to the already flowery set of movements. Before he could finish, Syrree crawled to the edge of the bed, grabbed his shirt, and pulled him onto the bed with her.

HAVING two targets to follow, and not wanting to lose track of either, Hassera had tagged both Tailor and the boy with trackers while they had been eating together. She had followed them back to the hotel: Tailor and McQuinton remained behind, while the boy and his Averian friend, Almp, continued on. Hassera had stayed with the boy, listening in on his conversations via the short-range transmitter on the tracker. She had to be within thirty meters of him, which was risky, especially if he was already aware of her. But nothing in his manner or conversation revealed that he suspected anything.

She had learned a lot about the boy in just a few hours. She'd learned that his name was Kormèr, that he came from Elmar, and that this was his first time on Averia. He'd only been here a few days, and he'd established the beginnings of an information and support network in that short time by paying Averians off with gems. Most importantly, he seemed to have his own agenda and target, a young local woman. His request for a love spell had confused Hassera… in fact, his entire conversation with the Averian apprentice at the jewelry store had left Hassera bewildered. Without more information to go on, she had to assume that Srrcheel had been a contact and their conversation some form of code. Both had played their parts convincingly, and the conversation had been awkward and superficially uninformative. Had she not already suspected this Kormèr of being more than he appeared, she would never have assumed their banter to be anything but a true first meeting.

The Elmarian and his local friend had continued touring the city, stopping here and there to stroll through a park, visit a museum or splash water at each other at a fountain. All very natural activities for someone trying to establish a precedent of normal behavior, except that the Elmarian boy was canny enough to stay out of the baths.

Late in the afternoon, the boys had returned to the hotel and parted ways, with Almp continuing on in the taxi while Kormèr had gone inside. Hassera had followed Kormèr as far as his room, but the hotel's security screens prevented her from further eavesdropping.

As she returned to the lobby, her p-comm chimed, the tone revealing *Ship* as the caller. The AI had continued poring over the vast amount of sensor data from three weeks earlier, and it had found something new. Two data points in two different bandwidths revealed that someone had been in the umbilical moments before Royland's Y-Tach had taken its erratic actions. She viewed the first data point, a thirty-second recording taken in the visual spectrum showing Tailor's ship and the Y-Tach joined by the umbilical. As they had been far from that system's sun, only the ships' dim albedos and running lights stood out against the starry backdrop. Hassera viewed the recording three times before she noticed anything amiss. For just the briefest moment, a faint glow had crossed a porthole in the umbilical. The camera's focus had been elsewhere at the time, catching this moment only by chance; there was no chance of enhancing the image further. But Hassera already had her suspicions.

Hassera hissed angrily as the second footage, taken in a different spectrum, confirmed her suspicions. Not only had someone been in the umbilical at the time the ships separated, but that someone had been Royland. At the same moment, two other beings had stood at opposite ends of the umbilical, one on board each of the ships. Royland had been intentionally murdered.

Hassera now knew that someone from Tailor's crew had indeed commandeered Royland's ship, spaced him, and coordinated their escape. They had probably perished in the process, based on the condition of the Y-Tach. But that hardly mattered to Hassera. This information changed everything for her. They hadn't been there to kill Tailor and his crew, but that crew had killed Royland in one of the worst ways possible.

Now that she knew the truth, Hassera couldn't help but act. The nature of her relationship with Royland demanded that she avenge him. To hell with what Harry G wanted.

CHAPTER 11

SYLVESTRA alighted onto the precinct's main platform just before dawn. With Phatheeo on the jewelry heist, she had looked forward to taking full advantage of the day of rest. Instead, she'd spent the day cleaning her neglected home and running errands. Her muscle aches now reminded her that she'd been neglecting her exercise routine as well.

She sang her hellos and ignored the few withering looks as she made her way to the break room, where she rinsed her mug and filled it with nutria-enriched coffee. Her office wall pulsed softly when she walked in, indicating she had an urgent message waiting. ||Show message,|| she twittered, and the wall lit up with the Chees case file. She spotted the fresh addition immediately and opened it. It held five photos, three hotline recordings and a handful of notes and observations from the hotline monitors and from Phatheeo.

The photos caught her attention first, since she recognized the boy in each one. Then she listened to a couple of recordings while she skimmed the notes. While nothing could be discounted, she couldn't quite reconcile the young man she'd met with the person being described. *Is it possible? Could that boy have pulled off this caper? How else would he be paying in gems? But why is he being so obvious? Is he an idiot?* She recalled his boldness when speaking to her and bathing in the public pool, so he certainly seemed to have a reckless disregard for authority.

She called Phatheeo into her office. ||How credible are these witness reports?||

||Very,|| he answered. ||I followed up on the one from the bartender at the Root myself. I can't believe we were that close to him.|| He held two fingers close together.

What had the boy said his name was? Ker... no, Kor-something. Kormèr! Kormèr Lezàl. She shuffled the digital files around, looking for any data from AvoNet on the young man, but there was nothing on the global law enforcement network. ||What do we have on him? I don't see anything here.||

||There's no record of his arrival in Birshetland or on the planet.||

||I know we're a little lax here, but Freet-See doesn't have anything?||

||Nothing. I have someone working with Freet-See port authority to review footage and other records for the past month. If there's anything there, and if Freet-See allows it, they'll find it. The only thing we know for sure is he's staying at the Cheerees.||

She furrowed her brow. | |Seriously? More wanton flaunting of his wealth; it's like he wants to be caught.| |

| |Sometimes they do. It's an extreme cry for help.| |

Sylvestra considered this sage nugget of criminal psychology. It certainly seemed to fit much of Lezàl's behavior, from the gems to the use of the public bath, even knowing that she was there.

Another thing that had struck her as odd about him was his fluency with Averian. He hadn't said much to her that night, but what he *had* said had not been mauled by any accent. It was common for offworlders to use learning mods and software to learn Averian all the time, but he seemed to have mastered enough of the complex chirps and whistles of the Averian language to actually be conversational. He could be considered a handsome boy, for a non-Averian, but she had known plenty of cold and calculating criminals who hid their treachery behind pleasant and unassuming facades.

| |What should we do?| | asked Phatheeo at the chief's pause.

| |I'm reasoning it out. I want to be sure these reports are real. First things first: try to recover the gems this boy's been using. At least one. I'd like Mister Reestee to check them out and verify that they're his.| |

Phatheeo frowned. | |You're not convinced that this is our man?| |

| |'Man'? I think you're being too generous with that descriptor,| | she twittered wryly. | |So, no, I'm thinking that Mister Lezàl is too young to have pulled off something like this.| |

| |You know his name?| |

| |Oh, yeah. I forgot to tell you, but I caught him before sunup yesterday morning using a public bath,| | she sang with slight chagrin. | |Sorry.| |

Phatheeo seemed unfazed by her oversight. | |Hah! What are the odds? Sometimes, I love my job.| |

Sylvestra smiled. | |It does get bizarre sometimes, doesn't it? Anyway, I won't let my doubts get in the way. Tag the guy. Pick someone you trust and have him watched. At the first sign of another gem, bring him in.| |

| |Gotcha. I know just who to put on him.| | The birdman turned to go.

| |Phatheeo,| | she called after him, | |don't hustle him too much. He's an offworlder; if he's innocent, we'll get hell.| |

Phatheeo smiled. | |Don't worry.| | And he was gone.

Sylvestra rotated the photos, looking at them from different angles. Three were from the same person, taken in a clothing store somewhere. Two were from the side and one from the back; all pretty useless. The other two actually captured his face, and in one, he was even looking into the camera. Sylvestra studied those eyes and wondered what thought processes were taking place just behind them at that moment. The way he looked at the camera… as if his eyes were saying: *Hi, I'm Kormèr Lezàl.*

She caught herself smiling at the image. She motioned, and the file sealed as her wall winked off.

Coffee, she thought, taking a long draw from the warm brew. *That's what I need. That, and for this crazy estrus to be over and done. I'm acting distracted and irrational when there's work to do.*

KORMÈR'S eyes snapped open. How long had he been asleep? Looking at the darkness outside told him only that it was still evening, but nothing about how late or how early. And his p-comm lay somewhere on Syrree's bedroom floor with his clothes. He hoped that Syrree's eagerness to shorten foreplay that evening had spared him the time he would need.

Syrree's molding-bed was even more comfortable than his hotel bed, and Kormèr almost discarded his plans just to rest in it a while longer, as Syrree's form draped over him felt like a cozy down blanket. He carefully slid off the bed and silently dressed, and Syrree didn't so much as stir. He checked his p-comm and frowned: he didn't have a lot of time.

He unlocked her room door and peered out into the hall. The house lights illuminated the hall in a dim reddish glow, their evening-mode designed to ease navigation without full, jarring illumination. Opening the door wider, he looked back over his shoulder to be sure that Syrree was still asleep, then moved out into the corridor and set a timer on his p-comm.

It had taken Kormèr only moments to memorize the floor layout on his last visit. Syrree's room sat at one end of a wide hallway on the second floor of the home. At the opposite end of the corridor was her parent's bed chamber. In between, a few guest rooms, two closets and a restroom lined the left wall, while the landing and side-hall stairs sat to the right.

Kormèr rummaged through the closets cursorily, but found nothing of interest. His p-comm vibrated; time to head back.

Safely back in her room, Kormèr walked to the balcony doors and peered out. The sky had lightened to gray during his prowling. It would be sunrise in just about an hour. He sat on the edge of the bed, debating whether or not to doff his clothes once again and climb back into its warm comfort, and back into Syree's embrace, even for just one more hour. He looked around for a tag on the mattress, wondering if he could ask Theeseeo to swap the bed in his suite for one like this.

Syrree stirred. Then her eyes opened a crack.

||Good morning,|| he whispered.

||You're still here.|| She smiled. He didn't answer, just continued watching her, the smooth lines of her face, the cottony fluff of her hair, the intoxicating curves of her body. He could almost fall in love with such a person. Just not *this* person.

She enjoyed his visual caress; he could tell by how her body trembled slightly under his scrutiny. But she would never let him know it; it wasn't in her character to be honest with him, even if he asked her. He presumed that if he dared to ask, she would have belittled and mocked him for his sentiment. She was just like

Menddilal in this way, and for this reason, this relationship would never last: he couldn't love someone whom he couldn't trust with his emotions, even a little.

Nonetheless, he chirped, ||I couldn't leave you a second time without one last look into your eyes.|| He leaned forward and kissed her.

There was a knock at the door.

As Syree sat up quickly and ran to the door, Kormèr opened the portal and stepped through to his hotel room. ||*Just a minute, daddy,*|| he heard her sing, just as he snapped it closed. She would turn to find herself alone in the room, but she would probably be relieved that he was conveniently gone, whether he snuck out or fell off her balcony.

Kormèr didn't even have a moment to relax, as someone was knocking at his door. *A knock means it's Almp.* Swapping his coat for a robe to throw on, Kormèr answered the door.

||Good morning,|| greeted Kormèr.

Almp shoved the door open and stepped in, closing the door behind him. <<I think there's someone watching you.>>

Kormèr grew serious at Almp's sudden switch to Elmarian. <<Why?>>

<<Just now, I was delivering luggage to a room, when I noticed a man at your door. He was taking some notes, then saw me and went back to his room—it's just down the corridor.>>

Kormèr thought quickly. <<It wasn't one of Jeremy's men? There are four you haven't met.>>

<<Humans?>>

<<Yes.>>

Almp shook his head. <<This guy is Averian. I checked the register after that.>> He shared his p-comm screen with Kormèr. <<Look. He checked in only thirty minutes ago, under the name Cheebeetoo.>>

Kormèr ran through all the Averian names he'd heard since arriving. <<Never heard of him. You?>>

<<No. I'll have to ask Father if he asked about you.>>

<<You can ask him, but he probably didn't. If he's being secretive about trying to find me, he wouldn't want to warn me ahead of time by asking around.>>

Almp nodded. <<I'll ask, to be sure.>>

<<Thanks for warning me.>>

Almp clasped Kormèr's shoulder. <<I owed you one.>>

Kormèr smiled, feeling a sense of relief. <<Well, this makes us even, okay?>> Kormèr didn't like having people indebted to him, almost as much as he didn't like being indebted to others. Almp nodded. <<In any case, I'll be away for a day or two, so maybe he'll think I left, or he'll just give up.>>

Almp seemed doubtful, but he held his tongue. <<Where are you going?>>

<<Under the circumstances, I'd rather not say. Just in case this man asks *you* about me.>>

<<Ah, right. Point taken,>> nodded Almp. <<I have to get back to work before father hears that I've been visiting you.>>

<<Not from me; you were never here.>> Kormèr held the door open for him. <<See you when I get back.>>

<<Have fun, and be careful.>>

<<Of course.>> Kormèr closed the door, then leaned against it and wondered who could be tailing him. *Could the authorities have finally caught on that I avoided the new arrival registration? Either that, or one of Harry G's men… but an Averian? From Jeremy's description, he's a very well-connected man, so it's possible. G's never seen me, nor have any of his people, but I was out in public here with Jeremy and Kit, so maybe I've been associated with them? It might not be G at all, but then, what would I have that someone else—*

It hit him then. *Another thief! Of course. Word's gotten around that I'm carrying gems, so I'm being cased.* Kormèr chuckled at the irony of that, but then he sobered up; it had been a thief robbing a thief that had led to his father's death. Kormèr followed his father's code and eschewed weapons, but not everyone was so honorable. If he was being targeted, then it was best to heed Almp's advice and be careful.

Maybe so, but I'm not waiting. He changed his clothes, left and locked his room, and walked to the end of the corridor, noting that a door had opened and closed behind him. *Is it the right one, though? What a great cover. It could just be coincidence that someone left their room at the same time I did.* He turned the corner and stopped short, intending to peer back around, when he heard quick footfalls coming closer. Whoever it was had passed his room and was coming toward him. He lengthened his stride, trying to appear casual while his heart raced.

If I look like I'm going for a stroll, maybe the thief will double back and try to break into my room. Or if they follow me, I might be able to identify them. He followed the spiral ramp down to the ground floor and left the tree, strolling along the footpath with the rush-hour crowd. His stomach rumbled before he even realized he was smelling food. He headed for a ground-level café a short distance away—it was a perfect stop to check if he was being followed.

Kormèr sat in the last booth against the front window, affording him a clear view of the pedestrian traffic and those entering and leaving the café. Someone had left an offworld newsflim on the table. He pushed the flim aside, scanned the menu and punched in his order. Then he scanned the newsflim with mild interest, trying, impossibly, to decipher the scribble-like language that was neither Averian, Elmarian, nor any of the two Terran languages he had learned.

His order soon arrived. He tasted the pastry first, finding it most acceptable, followed by some refreshingly cold nutria. Once finished with the pastry, he started on the main course.

While he ate, he considered his idea of giving Sylvestra flowers. It still seemed like a reasonable idea; on most worlds he had visited, girls and women generally liked flowers. The challenge was locating her and then getting close enough to give her the flowers. And it had to be private; he wanted her reaction to be genuine, not anything that she would feel the need to say or do in the presence of her colleagues or peers, or others in public. This would be the aim of his day: locate Sylvestra, buy flowers and then wait for—or arrange—the ideal setting to give them to her. He knew his best chance of finding her was at the precinct, but he didn't like the idea of surrounding himself with police. That would *not* be an ideal setting.

Kormèr checked the bill on the table-top display, and when the server stopped by, he asked, ||I'd like to open a tab.||

||Of course, sir. I can help you with that. How would you like to— Oh! I see,|| he sang as Kormèr took a small gem from his pocket and slid it across the table toward him. Immediately, there was someone at his side holding his arm.

||Excuse me, sir.|| The young man flashed a medallion. ||Sergeant Chreel Tseeo, Birshetland Police. Would you come with me, please?|| He plucked the gem from the tabletop.

||Is something wrong?|| asked Kormèr, his eyes wide. Inside, he feared this to be some kind of ploy to get him away from crowds, as he hadn't gotten a close enough look at the badge to see if it looked genuine. He had every intention of losing himself in the crowd once they got outside.

||We just have some questions to ask you.||

Kormèr had a sudden thought. ||Who's your superior?||

||Captain Phatheeo,|| he answered readily.

||And he reports to…?||

The Sergeant frowned at him. ||Chief Sylvestra—||

Kormèr grabbed the man's arm and pulled him toward the door. ||Can we stop for flowers on the way?||

||No.||

<<Buomp!>>

EVERYONE stared at Kormèr where he sat outside of the police chief's office, not only because he was a non-Averian boy, but because everyone knew he was the reason for all the arguing that was taking place in the office behind him. Kormèr caught parts of it, though the wall and closed door muffled most of it. Piecing together what he heard, he gathered that Sergeant Tseeo had moved on him too quickly. Apparently, as an offworlder, he had certain rights. And if… something he didn't catch… turned out wrong, something else he didn't catch could be considered having been violated. He stored that information away for future use and grinned impishly at the curious passersby.

The door opened, and the sergeant trudged away, glaring briefly at Kormèr. The heat that followed him out the doorway was almost palpable.

Kormèr heard her light footfalls coming towards the open door before he saw her. But he didn't have to see Sylvestra to recognize her graceful gait, and his heart raced. *Are my palms sweaty? If so, I hope she doesn't offer me a handshake.*

She stepped out and looked down at him. ||I'm sorry to keep you waiting. Please come in.||

Kormèr entered her office and looked around. The room was small and spartan, with two desktops, a large file cabinet and a movable desktop screen. Kormèr recognized the electronic walls that doubled as screens from his hotel room. The desktop closest to the door was also electronic. His coat lay draped across it alongside the objects from his pockets. Something had set off the precinct alarms when he'd arrived, so they had searched him and taken his coat.

A set of shelves toward the rear of the office held awards and trophies and other memorabilia, but no personal effects or decorative details. Still, Kormèr got the sense of a female touch, though he could not pinpoint what made him think so. | |Nice office,| | he sang, feeling stupid after saying it.

She looked at him unsmilingly, as if unsure of how to take his comment. | |Please, sit down.| | Kormèr did so on the taller of two perches in front of her desk. | |Mister Lezàl—| |

| |Kormèr, please.| |

| |Mister Lezàl,| | she repeated, taking up a flimsy and stylus, | |I have some questions I would like you to answer.| |

Kormèr nodded. | |I'll be happy to answer all of your questions. But before you start, I just want to apologize for running off the other night. I was… You caught me off guard, doing something I didn't know was wrong, and… well, I panicked, I guess.| |

She made a note on the flimsy. | |How did you run off so fast?| |

Kormèr's right eyebrow went up. | |I'm a sprinter back home,| | he told her, shrugging.

| |I see.| | She made another note, her face inscrutable. | |Exactly *where* is your home?| |

| |Elmar.| |

She ticked the flim. | |And you are… four years old?| | she twittered, wiggling her right hand in a *more-or-less* gesture.

Closer to three and a half, but he wanted to seem older. Besides, he didn't think it was wise to correct her. | |Just about, yes.| |

| |You're currently staying at the Hotel Cheerees where you checked in two days ago.| |

Kormèr nodded. | |Yes, that's right,| | he chirped when she didn't continue.

| |And how did you pay for your stay?| |

It dawned on Kormèr then, what this was all about. He hadn't even considered that he had made himself a suspect by using gems right after a jewelry store robbery. *You careless moron!* | |I didn't have any local currency, so I just paid using what I had on me.| |

| |Please elaborate.| |

Kormèr swallowed. | |I paid with a gemstone.| |

She leveled her gaze at him. | |Are you aware of the recent jewel heist at Chees?| |

147

||I am,|| he told her. ||I saw you there that morning, afterwards.|| *You looked beautiful that day.*

Her gaze was unflinching. ||Why were you there?||

||I saw the commotion and was curious.||

Another tick on the flim. ||Where were you before that?||

||I'd just come from Freet-See and was on my way to have breakfast.||

She nodded. ||Can anyone account for your whereabouts that night, before your arrival in Birshetland?||

||Sure,|| he chirped. Then he wondered if he should get Jeremy involved in this mess. Surely, the man had enough things to worry about. He opted to hold that card as a last resort. He simply sang, ||The people I came to Averia with.||

||And who might they be?|| she followed up.

Kormèr sighed. ||I'd prefer not to say, if I don't have to.||

She tapped her stylus on the desk and looked at him sternly. ||Mister Lezàl, you are within your rights to not say anything at all, but that will only make your behavior seem more suspicious, not less. Several witnesses and an officer in my precinct observed you using gems as money.||

||I see the connection.|| He frowned. ||I assure you, in all honesty, that I'm not the person you're looking for. I had only arrived on Averia for the first time that morning.||

She seemed unmoved and made another note on the flimsy. ||For the first time?||

||Yes.||

||Where did you learn to speak Averian so fluently?||

He admitted, with some chagrin, ||I learned it through an edu-comp.||

Sylvestra nodded and made another note on the flim. ||How did you come to be on Averia?||

Kormèr considered the question; it was an odd turn of phrase, and he tried to think of some equally ambiguous response. In the end, he opted to just tell the straight truth. ||I came by spaceship from the Terran Sol system.||

||You said you're Elmarian. What were you doing in the Sol system?||

||Impromptu vacation.|| *Not a lie.*

||Hmm.|| She stared off into the space just over his shoulder for a moment before focusing back on him. ||So you came on the *Stardust IV*.|| Kormèr was impressed, and he didn't hide the surprise from his face. *So much for protecting Jeremy.* ||I have the registration roster for all the members of that crew here. But there's no record of your arrival at Freet-See or in Birshetland.||

||Hmm? Really?|| *Why didn't Jer register me? He might get in trouble for that.* ||I'm sorry. It must've been an oversight. It was late, and we were all tired from the long voyage. If you check, there should be a record of a vaccination. That was me.||

She made some quick checks on the flimsy. ||We'll confirm that.|| She peered at him. ||Any details that you'd like to add or change to your story?||

148

Kormèr frowned at the dubious tone of her question. ||Why would I want to do that?||

She stared at him—almost through him—for a moment before making another note. ||Where'd you get your gems?||

||I've acquired them on some of the other planets I've traveled to.||

||You stole them.||

||Whoa! I acquired them. I bought or bartered for some. Some I received as gifts. Some I just found lying around.|| His heart was pounding fiercely, his mind on overdrive. He didn't consciously know what he was saying; instinct had taken over.

||And the other contents of your pockets, Mister Lezàl?|| Kormèr glanced at his coat. ||This dagger, for instance.|| She pointed to the item on her desk.

||It was a gift from a planet called Jordinni. They gave it to me for saving the king. I don't like to leave it lying around; it's very valuable.||

She didn't seem impressed by any part of what he had just said. She simply sang: ||Mister Lezàl, please do not leave the city for the next few days.||

||I'm not going anywhere.|| *Not anymore anyway*, he thought to himself. *I've blown it. Way to go, KL.*

She handed him back his coat—Kormèr almost hugged it.

||You can take your belongings, but I am confiscating your gems.||

||But I have no other money.||

She thought about that, then took a credit chip from a drawer and set it on her desk. She did something on the movable screen that Kormèr could not see, then swiped and the chip blinked green. ||You can use this as compensation money. It will only allow you to pay for the strictest necessities, including food and *basic* shelter, nothing more. You'll have to leave the Cheerees, I'm afraid. And do not attempt to make any cash advances with it.|| She slid the small cylindrical chip across the desk but didn't let go of it right away. ||If it runs out, come back here. But make it last, Mister Lezàl. Come back too soon, and you will spend the next few days in a cell.||

||Understood,|| Kormèr warbled. She withdrew her hand from the chip as he reached for it.

Kormèr stood and gathered the items from the desktop back into his coat's pockets; he'd sort and reorganize it all later. ||Thank you, for this and for everything else.||

As he opened the door, Sylvestra chirped, ||Mister Lezàl, have you contacted your parents to let them know you're safe?||

Kormèr shook his head. ||I'm an orphan.||

||Is there anyone you can contact?||

||No. Not anymore. High sky, Chief Chrreel.|| And he was out the door before she could say any more.

149

AS soon as Lezàl was gone, Sylvestra called in Phatheeo. | |What do you think?| | she asked. Phatheeo had been listening to the interrogation and speaking into her ear with relevant information, such as the arrival of the *Stardust IV* from the Sol system.

| |My honest opinion?| | he asked. She nodded. | |You could've been tougher on him. AvoNet records corroborate that a vaccination request was made from the *Stardust IV* upon its arrival at five thirty in the morning two days ago. No name was given for the recipient.| |

Certain planetary laws made information from Freet-See challenging to obtain. Sylvestra was glad that vaccinations and city registries were not on that list. | |So he probably wasn't lying about that, at least. Anything on his background?| |

| |Nothing on AvoNet. We've requested records from Elmar, but a courier round trip could take months.| |

Sylvestra tapped a finger on her desktop. | |But isn't that odd? Considering his age, the last census records should have included him.| |

Phatheeo shrugged. | |It includes a Kormèr Lezàl, listed as deceased three hundred and fifteen years ago.| | Anticipating her next question, Phatheeo swiped his flim, and an image appeared on her wall. | |This is one of a few surviving photos of him, all taken in the months before his death.| |

Sylvestra peered at the photo. The eyes usually revealed so much, while age and circumstance eroded the rest of the face and body. And she could almost see that wide-eyed, defiant mischief in them, though she knew it was absurd to even try.

| |Send the courier, anyway. This case had better be long solved by the time we get a response, but if anything we'll have either updated our records or confirmed that data was missing.| |

Phatheeo tapped his flim. | |Done.| |

She smiled at him. | |You're the best.| | She hefted the small, gem-filled velvet pouch in her hand; it felt like the weight of the world sat in her palm. | |This can't go into evidence; it's too much temptation,| | she sang, setting it back down.

| |Even for you?| | he asked jokingly.

| |For anyone.| | She avoided looking at the pouch and instead focused on Phatheeo. | |What's the word on Reestee? Where is he, while Chees is still closed?| |

| |Out of town until after Cheerretee, on a recovery vacation.| |

| |Let me guess, in To-Weetsa-Woo?| | It was the vacation resort destination city for the well-to-do. Phatheeo nodded. | |Alright, two things: let's image the gems and send him the photos for verification. Hopefully, he's monitoring his messages. Otherwise, we'll have to wait till he gets back so he can ID them, so find out when he's planning on coming back.| |

| |And if he can't confirm them as part of his merchandise?| | Phatheeo asked.

150

Sylvestra looked at him stonily. | | We shouldn't be relying on this one lead; we're still looking for more clues or suspects, I hope? Lezàl may be our prime suspect, but we would need more evidence than the gems to tie him to this case, if we're going to charge him. | | She tapped her stylus on her desk thoughtfully. | | And we have to be absolutely sure, before we accuse any offworlder of a crime on Frrooweetsee. | |

| | Understood, | | warbled Phatheeo solemnly. | | And the second thing? | |

Sylvestra retraced her thoughts. | | What? Oh, let's not wait until Cheerretee to track down the whereabouts of the crew of the *Stardust IV*. For all we know, they're not even planning to stay that long. Let's invite their captain in to account for non-registration of a passenger on his ship's manifest and further upon arrival here. We'll see what he has to say about Kormèr Lezàl. | |

| | On it. What about Tseeo? | |

Sylvestra curled her lips. | | He could've caused us a lot of trouble with the way he mishandled his assignment. We're lucky things turned out the way they did. I think I gave him enough of a chewing out, so let's leave it at that and see how he manages his next assignment. | |

| | Noted. Anything else? | |

She shook her head. | | We have enough to keep us busy the rest of the week, and Cheerretee's already got us spread thin for the next few days. | |

| | True enough, | | sang Phatheeo, turning to leave.

| | Hold up. Forgetting something? | |

He turned back. | | Hmm? | |

Sylvestra held up the gem pouch sitting on her desk. | | Get this to imaging, and send the output to Reestee, today. | |

With a terse nod, he took the pouch in hand. | | Yes, Chief. | |

She watched him leave, feeling a twinge of unsatisfied curiosity that she hadn't peeked into the pouch to see exactly what gems Kormèr Lezàl used as currency. Well, she'd see them eventually, once the imaging team finished their cataloguing for Reestee. Until then, she would have to wait.

Nothing but waiting, she thought. *I hate waiting.*

KORMÈR walked the length of a promenade before he had to sit down. His legs trembled and his brain rehashed his conversation with Sylvestra in a futile attempt to determine where he could have done things better. If he continued trying to walk home in this condition, he was likely to walk off the edge of a promenade. He hadn't been that close to trouble in a long time, and never before with a woman as beautiful as Sylvestra. Those moments alone with her in her office had been heaven and hell. He could still feel where her fingers had almost brushed his, when she'd handed him the credit chip. Her skin looked so soft, and the warmth of her hand so close to his had sent *krigold* bumps along his skin.

| | Looks like you're in love, | | chirped Feestoo.

Kormèr looked up and found he was in the taxi. He didn't even remember using the pager Feestoo had given him, much less remember getting in the taxi. ||I sure am!|| he answered. ||But I've really messed things up.||

||Well, don't let that ruin your hopes. Sometimes women like to see that you're fallible—the ones worth chasing, anyway. Can't be one-up on them all the time, you know.||

Kormèr took Feestoo's words to heart. He would never forget them, so important did they seem to him at that moment. Since losing his father, Kormèr had so rarely received useful advice about dealing with women that Feestoo's nugget of wisdom resounded with him, engraving itself into the foundation of his understanding of interpersonal relationships. The words, as simple as they were, afforded him the only glimmer of hope of ever having a chance with Sylvestra. Averian nature aside, she differed from every woman he had ever known before, so that meant his usual charms and manners wouldn't necessarily work on her the way he expected. He needed to put in a little more effort this time.

Kormèr looked around, feeling as if he'd just opened his eyes for the first time since leaving Sylvestra's office. ||Where are we going?|| he asked.

||You didn't say. So I'm just taking the scenic route back to the Cheerees.||

Kormèr glanced down at his hand, where he still held the chip. At least he now had some local money, meager though the amount was. He could use that for incidental purchases, to stop attracting attention to himself with gems.

But there was no way he was giving up his room at the Cheerees. In any case, according to Theeseeo, Kormèr had paid for nearly three years of lodging at the most favorable extended stay rate. Thankfully, the hotel accountant and gemologist had already appraised and cleared the jewel that Kormèr had used to pay for his room, so the police would not be confiscating the gem, as they had the rest of Kormèr's "pocket money".

He never carried all his valuables on him, so he still had a few gems stashed at the hotel, unless the police had managed to get a warrant to search his room and seize any potential evidence. Did they even need warrants here? *Ugh, that would be annoying.* Still, not an insurmountable hurdle: if he ran out of gems, he'd still have the option of popping back home. When he had reclaimed his coat and belongings, the portal cube had been the first item he grabbed, relieved that the police hadn't considered it an odd outlier gemstone and kept it with the others.

Kormèr checked his p-comm; it was just after noon.

||A stop at the hotel first, please,|| Kormèr sang. He had to tell Jeremy and Kit what had happened and warn them that the police might want to ask them some questions. ||And then I'll treat you to lunch?|| He smiled at Feestoo's enthusiastic nod: the man would never turn down a good meal.

||Any place in particular?|| Feestoo asked.

||Your choice.|| Kormèr's stomach was still in knots after his botched encounter with Sylvestra, but he knew he needed to eat something. Anything.

At the hotel, Kormèr left his coat in the taxi—the temperature had gotten too warm for it—and made his way to Jeremy's room. He reached out to activate the screen, but Almp's habit of knocking to keep his visits off the hotel records made him stop. Would it look more suspicious for him to visit the guys straight from the interrogation? Maybe Almp had the right idea. In the minute it took him to deliberate, a housekeeping cart hovered up and stopped a meter away, and an Averian male stepped around from behind it wearing the Cheerees staff vest.

||Are you going in?|| he asked.

||Ah… I don't know if anyone is in.||

The birdman produced a square metallic peg that hung from his vest. As he moved it toward the screen, he sang, ||I can't let you in, but I can tell you if anyone's in—|| Electricity arced from the screen to the peg with a *zznap*. The birdman shrieked and jumped back, holding his singed hand, some of his feathers charred along the edges. He staggered back, bumped into the wall behind and slid down, eyes staring blankly, as though he were in shock.

Kormèr stared at the birdman's unresponsiveness. *If I'd touched that screen… If the guys are in there and they touch the inner screen…*

Kormèr grabbed the end of the cart and tried to pull it, but it wouldn't budge. ||May I borrow this? Thanks,|| he twittered, not bothering to wait for an answer, and grabbed a dust-zapper from the cart. He threw the zapper at the screen, and the little duster exploded in a brilliant electrical flash and a deafening crackle that Kormèr knew he'd never forget, even after his ears stopped ringing.

Ignoring the pain from minor burns along his left arm and leg from hot flying zapper fragments, he rammed the door. Unlocked by the catastrophic failure of the screen system, the door swung partway open before slamming into something hard but yielding. The impact spun Kormèr around. When he got his footing, he looked across the room. The open door swung slowly on its hinges, and a scaled, forest green face stared back at him from behind it. It held one slender hand pressed to its face while the other gripped a tool—a tool that Kormèr recognized from his edu-comp lessons as one used for electrical work.

"You," the creature hissed in Terran English. "Who are you?"

"I'm Kormèr Lezàl. Who the hell are you?" Smoke billowed from the wall by the door where the inner screen had been removed. But Kormèr couldn't be distracted by that. He noticed the reptilian slowly inching toward the door… and a tool pouch.

Kormèr leaped to his right, placing himself within a meter of the pouch. The being would have to get past him to grab it now. It hissed again and hurled the tool at Kormèr, who dropped to a crouch and raised his arm to protect his head. Seeing him momentarily distracted, the being ran. As it passed him, Kormèr lunged with his free hand and caught its leg, but he was off balance. The being staggered, kicked free and dashed out into the hall, as Kormèr fell on his side.

He coughed and tasted the acrid flavor of burned electronics in his mouth. He coughed again as he scrambled to the pouch and found the weapon that he had

153

expected would be there. Kormèr jumped to his feet and dashed out into the hall. He looked both ways, but the reptilian intruder was gone.

He jumped at a hiss that erupted behind him in the room. But when he saw the smoke being drawn away and less billowing from the ruined screen receptacles, he realized it had to be the fire suppression at work.

||What happened?|| asked the housekeeping staff member, who still looked dazed, as he wobbled to his feet.

||It looks like a system malfunction,|| sang Kormèr, as he grabbed a towel from the cart to wrap around the weapon before the housekeeping attendee saw it. ||You should report it.|| He coughed again, his lungs spasming at what he'd already inhaled and his various minor injuries stinging like crazy. ||I'm going to...|| He coughed, pointed down the hall and walked away, passing other hotel guests and staff drawn by the spectacle; he didn't want to be around when the crowd formed. He had enough trouble to worry about without having to explain what had just happened, and with a weapon in his possession.

Checking behind him to make sure the reptilian intruder wasn't following, he made his way to the door of his room. There, he removed a shoe and gingerly held it to the door screen, gritting his teeth in anticipation of a repeat episode. But nothing happened. He opened the door and entered.

In the washroom, Kormèr stripped and examined his injuries, thankful that they were few and minor. His pants and shirt had taken the brunt of the damage, both sporting burns and holes. He plucked out two small pieces of shrapnel from his arm and three from his leg, then showered quickly to wash off the smoky smell. As he applied disinfecting liquid skin to all the small wounds, his door chimed, and Feestoo's face appeared on the screen.

Ah! I kept him waiting downstairs! Kormèr slipped on the complimentary bathrobe and called, ||Open.||

Feestoo entered, carrying Kormèr's coat. ||Something's happened in another room,|| he sang, setting the coat down on the table.

Kormèr winced as the liquid skin stung the larger cuts maddeningly. ||Yes, Jeremy and Kit's room. I think someone was trying to kill them.||

||Kill them? Where'd you get that idea?||

||I caught the... person in the room sabotaging the screens.|| Picturing the reptilian face suddenly jarred his memory. *And I've seen the creature before! Yesterday morning when we picked the guys up on the way to lunch. That creature was there. That's why it recognized me, too.*

Feestoo stared at Kormèr, wide-eyed.

||Excuse me while I get changed,|| Kormèr sang, indicating his robe. He found a clean pair of trousers and shirt, then walked to the mirror and brushed his hair.

Feestoo finally found his voice. ||I... I can't believe... Murder? In Birshetland?||

||I take it that doesn't happen here much,|| sang Kormèr, watching Feestoo in the mirror. He opened a compartment in the brush handle and pulled out the four gems hidden therein before slipping the brush into a drawer. He cleared his throat and still tasted smoke. *Damn.*

||In Freet-See, it's happened a few times, but here? Never.||

Kormèr sat on the bed while Feestoo sank onto a perch. ||That must be nice. So I can't tell you everything, but Jeremy's got a bunch of mercenaries following him. He managed to elude them, but now it seems they've found him again. Fortunately, the guys weren't in their room.||

||Where *are* your friends then?||

||I don't know. Like Jeremy said in the diner, he's busy negotiating a contract. So my guess is they're there now.|| He thought for a moment. ||I have to warn them. Maybe I can get through to Freet-See,|| he warbled to himself. Louder he asked, ||Can I call Freet-See from here?||

Feestoo stared. ||Your friends are in Freet-See?||

||No, but their crew is, so I just have to get word to them,|| Kormèr answered, then noticed Feestoo's look of consternation. ||It'll be quick. Then, we'll stop somewhere for lunch.||

SITTING in the bridge of the *Stardust IV*, Roke listened in on his headset as Mack finished up the welding and sealed the maintenance panel. *"Okay, Roke. Give it a shot."*

"Right." He performed the movements that had long become habit and heard the side thrusters fire on time. The readouts that appeared on the display noted the accuracy of their angle, firing time, and thrust ratio. All seemed satisfactory. "Looks good, dude."

"Awright," drawled Mack. *"How's it goin' with you, Morg?"*

Morgan reported: *"No problems here, either. I'm going in. Let's test 'er out."*

As Roke waited for his crewmates, a voice came over the external comm: //*This is Freet-See Port Control. Please respond.*//

Roke opened the connection. ||This is *Stardust IV,* receiving.||

//*There's an incoming call from Birshetland from a Kormèr Lezàl. He's been asking around for you.*//

Roke's eyebrows went up, as he exchanged a glance with Jim. ||Patch him through,|| Roke chirped, as Mack and Morgan entered the bridge. "Hey, it's Kormèr on the comm," announced Roke.

Mack frowned. "By himself?"

"Hi, guys," came Kormèr's voice. Roke thought the kid sounded tired. *"I've got bad news: someone knows you're here. This morning, someone tried rigging the door screens to Jeremy and Kit's room, I'm guessing to electrocute them."*

"What?" asked Mack, his brow furrowing deeper. "Why are you calling us? Where are Jeremy and Kit?"

"I don't know," Kormèr replied. *"Jer and Kit weren't in the room when I went by. I accidentally caught the merc still working, so there was no real harm done."*

"Awesome," beamed Morgan. "Nice work!"

"Are you okay?" Roke asked. "You didn't get hurt, did ya?"

"No, I'm okay," Kormèr said. *"But the merc got away."*

"You were lucky," Mack scowled. "You could've been in serious danger, even killed. What if the merc had a weapon…"

Jim lifted a hand to interrupt Mack's scolding, as well-meaning as it was. "We're glad you're okay, but Mack's right: it could've gone really badly, if someone had shot you, or if there had been more than one intruder in the room."

"But there wasn't," Morgan said. "So, let's give the kid some credit for saving our hides. Again."

"On behalf of the team: thanks, KL," Roke said, in part to avoid having a back-and-forth about Kormèr while the boy was still on the line. "We'll let Jer and Kit know what happened, if they haven't already been contacted by the hotel. In the meantime, did the merc see your face?"

"Yeah, we saw each other pretty clearly," Kormèr said begrudgingly.

"In that case, dude, try to lie low, and watch your back," Roke said. "If there's one, there may be more."

"I understand," Kormèr said. *"I just wanted to let you guys know to be careful."*

Mack gave the others a wilting glance, mouthing: "He wants *us* to be careful."

Jim grinned. "We'll try. Thanks for the warning."

"Oh, and one other thing," Kormèr said. *"The police might ask about me. It seems there was a robbery here, and I may be a suspect."*

"Why?" exclaimed Morgan.

"Dude! How'd you manage that?" asked Roke.

Kormèr's sigh came through as quiet static. *"It's a long story. The police know I came with you guys, but it seems I didn't get registered or something? I hope that doesn't cause you any trouble. I'd feel terrible if it did."*

Roke exchanged looks with the others. "Whoops."

"I assumed Jer did it," Morgan grimaced. "Guess it's true what they say about what happens when you 'assume': it makes an ass out of you—"

"We'll deal with it," said Jim. "Thanks for letting us know. What about you? You need some help?"

"No, no. I'm fine. It was just a misunderstanding. The police will clear it all up soon, I'm sure."

"Alright," said Jim, not sounding so certain to Roke. "But you holler if you need anything at all, okay?"

"I will. Thanks. Kormèr out."

Roke closed the channel. "What do you guys think?"

Morgan grinned. "That kid's quite a character."

"Not what I meant," Roke smiled, shaking his head. "What do you think about our situation?"

"I wish I knew what these guys wanted," said Jim, eyes distant and pensive. "I don't get it. First, Harry G tries to take us out on Io, then his mercs board the ship but only stun us. Now, he's trying to kill us again? I wish he'd make up his mind."

"Could be retribution for that guy that got pasted in the umbilical," said Roke.

"Could be," said Mack, "but this attempt strikes me as... different. I doubt G sanctioned this hit; he's colder and less emotional than this. If someone's out for revenge, working for themselves, then we've got big problems."

"Maybe G's not trying to kill us," Morgan proposed, "just trying to scare us into staying hidden, to keep Jeremy from getting the goods to market. Either way," he said, rubbing his hands eagerly in anticipation, "it's time we tested the ship out."

Jim nodded his agreement. "Yeah. Let's do that now. We're just speculating here, and we can't talk to Jer now anyway, if he's in a meeting." Jim's face lost its tension. "Morg, send Jer a text. He'll at least read it when he gets a chance; then we can chat with them later and hopefully give him the good news that the gear's working."

Morgan took his station. "On it. Then I'll work with the port to swap to another pad for our return landing. Maybe something a little more private."

"I'll run the preflight, in the meantime," said Roke.

Mack nodded. "We should have passive sensors on at all times, sending alerts whenever someone comes near the ship. And I don't think I have to mention: keep a well-charged pistol with you."

HASSERA exited the lift on the ground floor. Her enhanced p-comm showed that no other lifts were headed this far down; it seemed no one was chasing her. Fortunately, she'd managed to get a lift to herself for the entire ride down. She peered out the lift doorway, made sure there was no one around to see her, then exited the lift and took the nearest passage out of the hotel, her hand covering where the electrical arc had discharged across her face and neck and melted some of her clothes to her chest.

She walked for thirty meters before nearly collapsing. Adrenaline had kept her moving until now, but the shock of getting caught and nearly electrocuted overcame her at last. She stumbled off the footpath and fell heavily onto a bench in a secluded nook.

She'd thought she could do it. She'd seen so many of the others pull off a sabotage job that she imagined she'd pull it off with the same amount of finesse. But she'd botched it. Information was her trade, not direct confrontation. She wasn't even prepared to deal with her current situation. Hassera had no pain killers—and she desperately wanted those—no change of clothes or anything to hide her burned face. She could smell the burned flesh, and it repulsed her, reminding her of her failure.

She forced herself to sit up and thanked the fates that her species did not scream. On the one hand, it seemed like it could be very cathartic. But it would have attracted a lot of attention that she did not want. Her head felt heavy and light all at once, and she focused on controlling her breath to help keep from passing out. That's when the idea struck her.

When she felt capable of making the effort, she drew a utility knife from her belt and cut away her sleeve, fashioning it into a headscarf. It stung maddeningly when she slipped it gingerly over her head, but it fit perfectly, hiding most of her wound.

She timed herself to ensure that she didn't waste any more time than absolutely necessary and rested for forty more minutes before trying to walk again. When she felt comfortable that she would not pass out or collapse, she hailed a taxi. She had to recover, and her ship was the best place for her to do that.

CHAPTER 12

KORMÈR kept his visit to Elmar short and focused, limiting himself to only the essentials. He stepped out of the portal into his hotel room carrying a smaller gem pouch, which he secured in the room safe. This time, he planned to exchange a few gems for a chip of local currency, thereby attracting less attention to himself. But all that would have to wait until he returned from his trip.

His plan was to spend at least one night and one day in Berdia. Attending Srrcheel's raising ceremony would be a bonus, but the place sounded fascinating enough to visit on its own merits. Kormèr wasn't sure when the ceremony was due to take place, or how the security was around the venue, but it had never occurred to him to not even try. After his conversation with Srrcheel, Kormèr doubted the veracity of the "turn-into-droppings" threat, but he knew he could still get into serious trouble, either for trespassing... or just for leaving Birshetland.

Kormèr felt a little guilty about leaving, after Sylvestra had directed him to stay in the city. He justified his wanderlust by recalling that she didn't *order* him to stay put. And even if she had, she had no real authority over him; from what he had heard and seen, offworlders were entitled to a certain level of diplomatic privilege. So, no, she wouldn't be happy with him, but that would likely be that. And maybe he'd find a way to make it up to her.

Still, to ensure that his friends wouldn't get into trouble on his behalf, Kormèr had said nothing to Feestoo or Theeseeo about his trip, knowing that both were likely to disapprove and that both might be approached by the police inquiring into Kormèr's whereabouts.

Hmm. I know I'm forgetting something. But a glance around the room told him nothing. Finally, he shrugged. *I'll probably remember when I get there; no point in fretting over it now.*

Opening the portal, he thought of Srrcheel. This method of using the portal came with the risk of not ending up where he wanted to be. He therefore had to be very careful in focusing on not just the birdman, but also a point in time and a place. Otherwise he could end up in the past, visiting Srrcheel as a child, or in the distant future as an old birdman. Even so, the greatest risk would be finding Srrcheel in a public location, exposing himself and the portal for all to see.

He focused on envisioning Srrcheel, as he had seen him, in a private room. Kormèr realized with some trepidation that appearing in a quiet room increased the odds that he'd be revealing his secret to Srrcheel, but his instinct told him Srrcheel was someone that he could trust with knowledge of the portal. It felt odd to think that way, almost as if he were trusting someone with the combination to a safe containing his valuables. Almost.

Bracing himself for the unknown, but hoping for the best, Kormèr stepped through.

He emerged in a small windowless room, suited to hold one person comfortably, but not much more. Kormèr quickly scanned the room, starting with the desk on the right, which was currently cluttered with several tomes, vials and bottles of liquids and plants and other odds and ends Kormèr had never seen before. To the left stood a short bureau with an ornate lamp perched on its top. The lamp glowed, filling the room with its bright amber light. Directly ahead and pushed into the right corner of the room sat a typical round squat Averian bed.

The startled Averian youth sat cross-legged on the floor beside the bed, with his wide, reflective silver eyes staring directly at him. Srrcheel's voice was a little slower to respond, but it came in a rush: | |You! How did— But... how? | |

Kormèr grinned. *By the gods, it worked! I'm actually on Berdia, at the right time and place!*

He was just as relieved that Srrcheel just stared in awe at him and at the glowing blue portal swallowing up the already-cramped accommodations, instead of screaming in fear or raising the alarm to the other apprentices and sorcerers on the premises. He had made a good call in trusting Srrcheel. Of course, explaining the portal could be a challenge. Convincing Srrcheel to let him stay would be a bigger challenge.

| |High sky, Srrcheel! | | Kormèr tweeted cheerily. | |How are you? | |

As Kormèr took a second step out of the portal, Srrcheel lunged towards his feet in a panic. | |Watch it! I have those stacked in a very particular order. | | Kormèr took a half-step sideways instead, to avoid the precarious tower of small books, topped with a heavy-looking crystal orb. Srrcheel scrambled to move aside the stack and other items scattered on the floor, to give Kormèr enough space to stand comfortably. | |I don't know whether to scream, or ask the gods to take you back where you came from. | |

| |I doubt either would be very effective. Are you well? | |

| |I was, until now, | | Srrcheel answered curtly.

| |Okay, okay, before you get all airy on me, let me explain. | | He pointed to the open portal. | |This is a portal through which I travel from place to place. It's how I got to Averia... well, indirectly. | |

| |I see, | | chirped the young birdman, moving things away from the portal as he peeked behind it. Then he looked up at Kormèr. | |It's very interesting. You still can't stay here, you know. | |

| |I figured as much. | |

| |It's not my choice— | |

| |Then you don't mind if I stay? | |

Srrcheel scowled. | |Yes, I do mind. | |

| |Then you say I should go? | |

160

||No, but… Agh!|| His crest plumes peaked irritably, as if he realized that Kormèr would twist around anything he said.

||Do you, in all honesty, want me to go?|| asked Kormèr, pouting. ||I'll respect your decision. The last thing I want is to make an enemy.||

||Hmm,|| Srrcheel grunted in disbelief, flicking a fleck of down from his shoulder. ||I didn't invite you here—you invited yourself. As I recall, I told you that only the sorcerers of my order may attend the raising ceremony.||

Kormèr frowned. ||Did you say that?||

||Well, you seemed to comprehend that condition, in the moment,|| Srrcheel sang. ||You even said: 'no offense taken'. Which I now understand must be your way of saying: 'I hear your words, but I will do whatever I wish, regardless.' So, how do you plan to 'respect' my decision, exactly?||

Kormèr tried to figure out a way to talk himself clear. ||Suppose I take no interest in what you do, don't watch, so on. The rules are to prevent others from knowing about the rituals, but what would be the risk in my knowing anything about the ceremony?||

Srrcheel sighed deeply ||Look— Ahh… your name is Kormèr, right?||

||Yes, but you can call me KL.||

||Look, KL, your very presence here is a risk. My master saw us speaking, so if you're seen or caught here, the risk to you is minimal; you'll probably just be sent back to Birshetland. Me, I lose my position and everything I've worked for—I get cast out and shunned.||

Kormèr digested Srrcheel's words. ||I didn't realize. The last thing I want is to cause you trouble.||

Srrcheel nodded. ||Thank you.|| He looked up at the open portal. ||That really is a marvel, and I wish you and I could speak at length about it, but…|| He shrugged as a sign of helplessness.

||Not to worry. No offense taken,|| Kormèr sang, adding: ||And I do mean that, seriously. Can you do me one last favor?||

Srrcheel looked at him askance. ||Perhaps?||

||Think of a nice room here in the Hovel.||

||I don't understand.||

||Think of an empty room here that you're familiar with, just for a moment.||

Srrcheel looked at Kormèr with a "what are you up to" kind of wariness, but then he closed his eyes momentarily.

Kormèr directed a command-thought at the portal, hoping his trick would work. He was familiar enough with the device to know that it took mental commands, but he'd never asked it to read someone else's mind. He had no way to know if it had worked, as the portal gave no indication of its functioning, save for occasional warnings when it opened to hazardous environments. *No warnings this time. If this trick doesn't work, so be it.* He didn't want to overstay and get Srrcheel into trouble, after just assuring his new friend of his good will.

Srrcheel opened his eyes. | | I've done as you asked. Now please, go. I appreciate your visit, and I wish you well. | |

| | Thank you. Good luck with your raising. High sky. | | He ducked through the portal.

Darkness met him at the other end. Kormèr sealed the portal and waited for his eyes to adjust to the darkness.

His idea seemed to have worked. Kormèr had found that he couldn't instruct the portal to take him to places he had never been to. However, when Srrcheel had thought of a room, Kormèr had instructed the portal to read the location from Srrcheel instead of him, bypassing the limitation.

In moments, dark forms became visible here and there. After a few more minutes, Kormèr could tell that one dark shape was a bureau, another a desk and chair and a third a bed. On top of the bureau, he found the same kind of ornate lamp he had seen in Srrcheel's room. He searched through his pockets, but had nothing with which to light the lamp. But when he absently turned the knob on the side of the lamp, it glowed to life. Kormèr marveled at this and played with the various intensities of light until it was just right. He set the lamp atop the bureau, walked to the door, and made sure it was locked. Then we went to the bed and lay down.

A good ending to a rough day, he thought as he stared at the stone-gray ceiling. He fell asleep before he knew it.

JEREMY sat back in his seat as the heads of various corporate sectors of Averia got up to leave the conference room. He rubbed his tired eyes, then finished the water that remained in his cup. Night had descended over Birshetland as the negotiations had grown heated, and Jeremy hadn't even noticed, despite an entire wall of windows. *Great. Another day gone. I'd hoped to be done with this by Cheerretee.*

To his right, Kit spoke briefly with their lawyer, then closed the channel and sat tensely in his seat. "Relax, man," Jeremy told his partner.

Kit stared after the others. "Relax? Did you sit through a different meeting? Because in *this* one, things are not going well, mate."

Jeremy sighed. "They just have to see it. Once they get the product demo, they'll change their attitudes."

Kit shrugged. "If you say so. They're such a surly bunch."

"That they are," Jeremy laughed. He checked his p-comm, recalling that it had buzzed at some point. He had disregarded it, as the discussions had demanded his full attention, but now he watched Morgan's message scroll across the display. "Shit."

"Tell me about it."

"No, not that. A message from the guys. Someone tried to rig our room panel to electrocute us." Jeremy looked up into Kit's wide eyes. "KL stopped the guy, it seems."

"He what?" Kit was more than surprised.

"Beats me. That's what it says." He read, "'KL said he stopped the merc, but it got away.'"

"Merc? So one of G's men?"

Jeremy pushed his glasses up on his nose. "No idea. But wait; there's more. It seems Kormèr got questioned about the jewel robbery."

"That's ridiculous. I saw the media report on that; it happened the night we arrived, so he wasn't even on the planet."

"No, but they don't know that." Jeremy looked at Kit. "We didn't register him."

Kit grimaced. "Shite. But how'd he miss the registration check points here?"

"Dunno, but it seems he did. We should've escorted him through; he was our responsibility." Jeremy slapped a hand on the table. "Dammit! We don't need this crap now." He took a moment to compose himself. "Let's comm the guys. Or better yet, let's find KL. He seems to have a horseshoe up his ass."

As they got up to go, two police officers entered the room. One checked a hand scanner, then looked up at the two humans. ||Mister Tailor and Mister McQuinton?|| she chirped.

||I'm Jeremy Tailor. Is this about our room?|| he asked, hoping it wasn't about Kormèr.

She smiled mildly. ||We're not at liberty to say, but we'd like you to come down to the station and answer a few questions.||

Jeremy sighed. He and the crew had been to some worlds where such vague requests were often the precursor to brutal, unofficial "interrogations" or extortion bids. But thankfully, Averia was among the better, more civilized worlds.

||Sure,|| he sang, returning Kit's subtle nod. ||We've been in this meeting all day and night; what's another meeting?||

||We appreciate your understanding, sir. This way, please.||

SYLVESTRA stared up at the domed ceiling of her flat. How long had she been asleep? She couldn't remember when sleep had overtaken her. One moment she was looking over the Chees file, and the next—

She frowned. *I'm too young for this.* She sat up and looked at her work screen; it had locked at her inactivity and now sat patiently waiting for her to unlock it. She opted to ignore it for the rest of the evening. Her team wasn't getting anywhere with the Chees case anyway, and her staring at the data wouldn't do her any good.

She got up and stopped at the mirror on the way to the kitchen. This case was not doing her health any good at all. *Look at that, my tail's drooping! Ugh.* She hadn't been to the gym in months, and the loss of muscle tone was showing. She heard her mother's voice in her head, //Young lady, what you need is a vacation.// *Momma, I couldn't agree more. But I'm too much like dad; he wouldn't have let this case go, and neither can I.*

She continued on to the kitchen and made herself a strong mug of coffee. On top of everything, she had Cheerretee to worry about today. While historically an

Averian celebration, the pomp that had grown over the years around the holiday had attracted a large foreign audience. Thankfully, most stayed on Freet-See, since the planet's other cities contained little to attract tourists. But Birshetland was the closest to Freet-See, and so its service industry had grown to support an influx of visitors. And tonight promised to be a record-setting evening of revelers, based on the hotel totals.

Fortunately, Sylvestra had tasked a Major from another precinct as a task force coordinator for that effort. And so far, the Major had done a fine job. Her plan for the day's festivities had officers stationed at historical hot-spots and in key positions, ready to mobilize and respond quickly to the unexpected.

Sylvestra sipped the steaming brew and crinkled her nose at its bitterness. A better start to a long day hadn't yet been invented. And it would be a long day, between working on the investigation and continuing her inquiries on their sole suspect—the Elmarian, Kormèr Lezàl, that damned strange boy! She'd run his name multiple times, turning up nothing except the historic reference. An obvious lie, and no doubt the reason he hadn't registered on arrival.

She chided herself for not having been better prepared for Lezàl's questioning. But to be fair, she hadn't expected that Tseeo would bring him in. The bigger problem was that every time she saw him, she remembered their chance encounter at the public bath. After Lezàl had left her office, she had remembered how his wet footprints had ended abruptly, debunking his "sprinter" story completely. Where had he really gone? Without flight, without a place to hide on the open promenade, he had simply vanished! The pristine feathers at her crown stood on end, as they often did when she was irritated.

Could he have used tech? she wondered, sitting at her window and looking out at the dimly lit cityscape. There could be some tech that rendered someone invisible on many spectra; such a device would be capable of fooling the sensors in the store. *But he would have had to be inside already, at the time that Reestoo closed the store.*

She shook her head, dismissing the notion. The motion of the stolen property would have set off the alarms, as well. And the video footage showed no movement whatsoever. It was all there, then it was all gone.

Her body shuddered involuntarily, shedding her stress, and her feathers settled back into smoothness. *It's conjecture, not evidence.* She couldn't prove that Lezàl had advanced tech, even if it was the most logical reason for his miraculous disappearance. She couldn't devise any theory as to the kind of tech that might have been used at Chees, or how it had been used. Kormèr Lezàl was their best suspect—their *only* suspect. So why couldn't she shake the feeling that he was innocent?

Well, maybe not entirely innocent, but not guilty of the Chees heist. Something about him… There was definitely more to him than met the eye, as if he held some closely guarded secret, or was plotting some mischief. Even the way he stared so intently at her, with almost a flirtatious smile, like he was viewing her as a potential mate… *Oh! He has a crush on me!*

The realization hit her suddenly that, despite behaving like an older and more worldly adult, he was just a teenager, with raging hormones typical of young humans. Even with his big brown eyes, his knowing smile…

Stop it, Sylvee. She shuddered again. *Speaking of raging hormones.* Someone had to behave like a grownup in this situation, and it certainly wasn't going to be the infatuated boy, so Sylvestra was going to need to keep a tight rein on her estrus-driven instincts. *He's an Elmarian and a child, and you are neither. Well, not as much of a child as he is, anyway.*

Perhaps it really was time for Sylvestra to find a mate. She wasn't getting any younger…

She groaned, imagining her mother's voice in her head. | | It's bad enough to hear it from Momma, | | she muttered. | | Now I have to hear from myself? Great.| |

Her comm-buzzer sounded, and Sylvestra answered the call promptly, eager to distract herself from her train of thought.

/ / Good evening, Chief, / / came Phatheeo's voice over the speaker. */ / I didn't wake you, did I?/ /*

| | No, I was up, | | she returned, sipping her coffee.

/ / Ah. I messaged you first, but I guess you were offline, / / he sang.

She glanced guiltily at her dormant work screen. | | Yeah, taking a break. What have you got for me?| |

/ / Some interesting news, / / he sang mysteriously. */ / I sent you the report./ /*

| | Hold on, let me check my screen.| | Sylvestra sat back down at her screen and unlocked it, and it blinked to life with a detailed text report flashing into view. Phatheeo usually added a quick summary for anything that required her action or response, but he hadn't included one this time. | | Want to give me a rundown while I skim this?| |

/ / After we released Lezàl yesterday, he was involved in an incident at the hotel./ /

She saw a reference to an electrical fire. | | What was his involvement? Was he picked up?| |

/ / No, by the time we arrived on the scene, he had already gone. I only found out when I received the report myself./ /

The feathers on her crest prickled again, and she took a deep breath to settle herself. In her current state, the words on the screen in front of her seemed to jumble into an indecipherable mess. | | Okay, give me the essentials. Was anyone hurt?| | She closed her eyes and focused on her captain's voice.

/ / Tseeo followed Lezàl from the station to the hotel, and he was almost on Lezàl's floor when the power fluctuated. Following protocol, Tseeo headed back to the lobby to check with the manager and to make sure there wasn't a larger situation that required his attention./ /

Sylvestra nodded at this; power fluctuations at a hotel like the Cheerees were unheard of and definitely something that needed to be looked into from a public safety angle. */ / By the time Tseeo got back to the offworlders' wing, a small crowd had gathered outside a room, around a shocked housekeeping staff member. Tseeo called for a medical team,* then dispersed the crowd. *The staff member agreed to answer questions; he described meeting a Terran-looking male outside the room. He thinks he tried to open the door for the Terran, but something went wrong. When Tseeo showed him Lezàl's image, the staff member positively identified him as the male, and it's confirmed on the security footage. Unfortunately, Tseeo doesn't include many details after that. He called for a forensics team and cordoned the area off. They found a tool pouch and screens sabotaged to electrocute anyone that used them. Tseeo suspects that the housekeeper was struck by the sabotaged electronics.//*

Sylvestra smoothed her crown feathers tiredly. She imagined she already knew the answer, but asked the followup as a formality: ||Whose room was it?||

//The room is registered to Jeremy Tailor, and he is sharing it with Kit McQuinton.//

Not exactly who I was expecting, but directly connected, of course. Sylvestra felt her gizzard rumble queasily. Jewelry store robbery; attempted murder: These things had never happened in Birshetland during her father's tenure as chief, not that he'd ever shared with her, anyway. But now, they'd both happened over the span of a few nights. ||Have the two humans been brought in?||

//We have them here at the precinct; they're being questioned now. They're being very cooperative.//

||That's a spot of good news, at least.||

//Oh, yes. Maybe our luck is changing for the better, finally.//

||Hopefully. What are the Terrans saying?|| Some part of her dreaded hearing any corroboration of the possibility that Lezàl was trying to kill Tailor and McQuinton, but her duty was to find the truth, however unsavory.

//They've confirmed almost everything that Lezàl told us yesterday about their arrival, and that he contacted them after the incident to warn them that someone is after them. They claim that he actually saved their lives by apparently catching the intruder in the act.//

Sylvestra absorbed that. ||I see. Is there anything from the hotel security footage?||

//It's inconclusive. It shows what occurred, but there are anomalies. For example, the room door opens and closes by itself ten minutes before the events.//

||That's great,|| she warbled sarcastically. ||So we have a master thief and now also a mysterious saboteur on the loose in our city. During Cheerretee.||

//It gets better. Tseeo stayed on site until the team arrived, then went to check on Lezàl's room, but the boy was gone. Tseeo found the taxi driver that's been driving Lezàl around; his name's Feestoo. But the driver didn't know where the boy was. Feestoo says that the boy often wanders off by himself for hours at a time.// Sylvestra made a note of this. Hours were all that the thief had needed to clean out Chees. *//The hotel manager, Theeseeo, corroborated this. Tseeo also noted here that Theeseeo is apparently taking Elmarian lessons.//*

||For what?||

//So he can speak with the Elmarian boy who pays in gems. He seems to hold the boy in high esteem. In fact, so does the driver and everyone else who's met him.//

Not me. Sylvestra shook her head. *Some people are more impressionable.* ||Have the humans divulged anything new about Lezàl, so far?||

//Not much, but they confirmed that he appears to be Elmarian, three and a half years old. He arrived with them from Sol the morning of the robbery. They picked him up on Io, when he snuck aboard their ship for reasons that are not clear to them or which they're hiding—it's hard to tell. And he learned Averian from an edu-comp.//

Sylvestra scratched restlessly at the floor with her talons. Lezàl now appeared a less likely suspect in the Chees heist, unless he was fencing the gems or buying the humans' complicity. It annoyed her that Reestee hadn't yet responded, as if he didn't care that they were working around the clock to recover *his* livelihood.

||See if you can get an order to have Lezàl's room searched on probable cause. With this latest incident, the judiciary council must see that he's a key player in all our troubles right now, even if he's not the cause. If you get the warrant, make it count: search everything, inside and out.|| She hoped that an initial search would yield something useful, as they were unlikely to be granted a second chance.

//On it. We also have surveillance alerts set, so we'll bring Lezàl back in for questioning as soon as he shows up.//

||Good, keep me posted.|| While Sylvestra had told Lezàl not to leave the city for a couple of days, she was dubious about his ability or desire to abide by her wishes. She looked forward to another interview with him—she didn't know exactly what questions she intended to ask, but she had no shortage of topics. Including how he had vanished after their initial meeting at the public bath; that trick still flummoxed her.

//Gotcha, chief.//

||What about Freet-See? Anything on the port security video to confirm Tailor's account of Lezàl arriving on his ship?||

//Freet-See has footage, but they're throwing bureaucracy at us. However, going by the inoculation registration made by Tailor, we were able to find some record of Lezàl's arrival in Birshetland. The timestamp is hours after the robbery, so it doesn't prove anything. Until the Freet-See footage gets to us, we won't be sure.//

She silently cursed Freet-See for their strict adherence to privacy protocols. ||Got it. More waiting. Keep me updated.|| She clicked off, glad for the call from Phatheeo. The focus on work had interrupted her body's nonsense and gotten her thinking again.

Sylvestra turned back to her terminal and checked the case notes, reviewing and filling in details from the update she had received from her captain. There were new side notes on the section regarding Lezàl and his connection to the case, including the new unexplained event at the hotel room. A blinking gap was labeled "Tailor & McQuinton". It would fill with the interviewer's notes once the questioning ended. She grasped her neglected cup of coffee and sipped her warm bitter brew, intently watching the blinking space for updates.

CHAPTER 13

KORMÈR stretched to full alertness after a very relaxing sleep. The lamp still glowed obligingly from the bureau, though the morning light filtered warmly through the window screen. He checked his p-comm. *Must've been more relaxing than I thought,* realized Kormèr, having slept longer than he was used to. He stretched once more before getting out of bed.

Aside from the fact that he'd passed out unexpectedly, Kormèr had left his clothes on, in case he'd needed to make a quick getaway. Expecting to stay on Berdia only for the day, he hadn't brought a change of clothes. But even after sleeping in them, his clothes were only slightly wrinkled.

As he stood from the bed at the center of the chamber, he looked around, taking in his borrowed room in the daylight. There wasn't much more to see than what he'd already seen last night, only now in the daylight, the undecorated stone walls were white instead of amber. Peering out from the window, he saw that the room was fairly close to the ground, but the branches above angled out to the sides, affording an almost unobstructed view of the sky. *No wonder Srrcheel likes this room. The poor guy deserves a room with a window.*

Kormèr turned and stared, absently, at the conflicting shadows that formed where the lamplight and sunlight overlapped. What was he to do with his time? He hadn't really given much thought to what he'd do once he got here. He knew he wanted to see the raising ceremony, but he'd assumed he would have more freedom than this. Perhaps he should have listened more closely to Srrcheel's ambivalent tone when he was talking about the raising and the Hovel, but Kormèr had blanked on almost everything Srrcheel had said after the mention of sorcery.

Aside from his curiosity about all things Averian, it was the idea of magic that had really brought him here. He wanted to wander around the Hovel, explore the city of Berdia, experience its differences from Birshetland. He could easily pick a spot in view from his window and portal to it. But he wasn't about to do that in daylight, at least not without knowing what he'd be getting himself into. That threat—however hollow—of being turned into droppings by a sorcerer, still lingered in his head: best not to test that theory, no matter how outlandish.

What to do? He frowned, focusing on one of those areas where the lamplight and sunlight overlapped. There, beside the bed, the two sources of light created an almost-geometric shadow on the wall. Kormèr ran his hand over the spot and found that the lights fell across a nearly imperceptible groove. He traced the groove to the floor, then back up to a corner roughly a meter up from the floor.

What's this, what's this? He smiled, fantasizing about long forgotten stashes of gold and jewels. Kormèr pushed the groove, but nothing happened. He threw his bodyweight against it, again with no result.

He stepped back and eyed the area suspiciously. *Amazing; it's invisible from here. But I know there's something there. Hmm. A pressure plate, maybe.* Kormèr lightly probed the wall to either side of the groove until his hand sank into a hidden release high up the wall. Immediately, a meter-tall rectangular section of wall slid inward, and swung slightly open like a door. revealing darkness beyond. Kormèr took the lamp from the bureau top and peered through the doorway, across a meter and a half of dust, to another wall. The wall continued to the left and to the right, forming a corridor that extended beyond the reach of the lamp's meager light. The dust looked as if it had been undisturbed for decades. *I guess there's no danger of getting caught back here.*

Kormèr entered the passageway and held the lamp up to get a better view. It turned out that the corridor ended at the left wall, roughly where the room's doorway was located. Beside the doorway, an electronic interface hung on the wall. He activated it with a simple switch, tensing in case an alarm blared or the door slammed shut behind him to seal him in the passage. *A booby trap for sneak thieves.*

Instead, a glowing projection appeared on the wall immediately above the interface. The rectangular projection was further divided into quadrants which Kormèr quickly realized were views of his room on the other side of the wall. Kormèr frowned. *This is odd; I haven't seen any other technology like this anywhere here. Why would this be hidden in these corridors?* And of course that led him to another question: *Who designed this place?* He switched off the interface and moved on.

Picking his way through the corridor, he realized it followed the layout of the rooms, with side passages adjacent to nearly every room. Whether accessible by a side-passage or not, each room had a secret door and an electronic interface, like his. Kormèr tested a few of the doors, peeking randomly into an assortment of occupied and unoccupied rooms. The interface displayed an additional readout when the room was occupied, containing the vital signs of the occupant. It wasn't until the third occupied room that Kormèr realized that all the information was being displayed in Terran English. *What in the world? None of this makes any sense!* Again, it made him wonder why these corridors existed, and who had built them. After all, if Berdia was the first city the Averians had built, why would they have designed rooms to be observed in secret? And why did they use Terran technology and language for their displays?

Unsure if his lamplight would be visible around the edges of the secret doors, he turned down the lamp each time he passed one. Gradually, his eyes adjusted to the dimness so that he only needed enough light to illuminate his next steps, which now seemed to be never-ending. While the secret corridors initially provided some entertaining diversion, the novelty of wading through dust and pitch darkness was wearing thin, without some promise of reward or treasure at the end of the effort.

The corridor widened suddenly, the walls disappearing to either side of him. Unwilling to turn up the lamp just yet, he followed the walls with his fingers, his mind building an image of what the room looked like. A fairly wide crack ran horizontally along one wall, and a buckled metal bracket on the opposite wall had left a rivet protruding. He turned up the lamp to compare his mental image to the real thing and nodded approvingly to himself. The only thing he hadn't accounted for were his prints on the dusty floor.

He looked back the way he'd come and considered returning to his room. *But then what?* he thought. *Am I just going to sit in my room all day long? Damn. I should've brought food.*

Kormèr dimmed the lamp once again and continued on, eventually coming to a descending stairwell. *This is at least something different,* he told himself, as he followed it down. After forty steps, he came to a landing with a secret door but no interface. He put his ear against the door and listened for a moment before trying the release. The door popped toward him, and he pulled it open. He ducked and peered into the adjoining room, but without windows, it was just as dark as the corridor. He turned up the lamp, and its glow fell on dusty crates stacked high. With a smile and renewed vigor, he clambered over the smallest stack of crates and found that the room was somewhat large, his guess approximating six meters square by four meters tall. His interest lay not in the room, however, but on the crates themselves. Some crates had writing on them, but not in any of the languages he knew, though it appeared to be a combination of at least two of them. Still, the scrawling text made no sense to him.

Only one way to know... He tugged at the top of a crate, but the old canvas-like material was tougher than it looked. Putting his whole weight behind it, Kormèr yanked and fell back when the top finally came loose, taking with it the side of the crate. The crate's contents spilled onto the stone floor with such a clatter that Kormèr scrambled back to the door, expecting someone to come and investigate at any moment. He waited almost fifteen minutes for something to happen, but nothing did.

Feeling confident that no one would come, Kormèr returned to the mess he'd made and admired his handiwork. *No chance of getting that back to the way it was.* He pushed the items around with his foot, then turned the lamp up to max as his brain slowly realized what he had discovered: artifacts! Whether any of them were actually magical remained to be seen, but Kormèr doubted it; there were handfuls of wands, powders, carpet tiles, pendants, chains, gems, handless clocks, coins, swords, goblets in various metals... Why would anyone leave these things in a dusty, forgotten crate if they were valuable or useful, in any way?

He even found empty pouches. What could possibly be magical about a pouch? He held one up to the light, then examined its silky texture. *Ooh, nice material,* he thought, rubbing it against his cheek. *I think I'll keep this.* He tossed some of the finer-looking goblets, coins, and gems into the pouch.

The rest was junk to him. Since he knew nothing about magic, and it didn't seem likely that Srrcheel would teach him, he didn't really want to experiment. One large wand had a series of gems encrusted into it, however, and Kormèr tucked it thoughtlessly into the pouch. Then he frowned at the bag, noticing that the wand had vanished into it, despite the wand being slightly longer than the pouch was deep. As he lifted the pouch, he realized it felt no heavier or bulkier, despite all that he had dumped in it. The pouch remained as flat and as weightless as when he had found it. He peered into the pouch, but it was too dark to see anything, almost as if it were bottomless.

But where had all his loot gone?

He thrust his hand into the bag, and his fingers closed around a goblet. He pulled it out... and there it was. While nothing had appeared to be in the pouch moments before, here was a goblet. Kormèr dropped it back in and again stuck his hand in. He felt about inside the pouch, knocking into all the objects he had inserted and a few more that had apparently been in there to begin with. Elated by this discovery, he folded the pouch and dropped it in his pocket. He retraced his steps, found another pouch that looked the same as the first, and pocketed that one as well.

He looked about at the various artifacts, longing to explore further, and gazed at the towering crates all around, all promising treasures and wonders of their own. *This needs more looking into, but I don't want to hang around here that long.*

Vowing to himself that he would return later, he dimmed the lamp once again and left the room. If the Hovel had one room like that, maybe there were others. He re-entered the secret corridors with renewed interest.

At one point, his stomach grumbled loudly, and he realized savory scents had replaced the smell of dust. Following his nose, and glancing at the closest interface, he found he was behind the walls of an occupied communal dining hall. Kormèr hadn't had breakfast and had spent most of the morning wandering the secret corridors, so he assumed the gathered crowd was having lunch. *Where there's an eating place, there must be a kitchen. And I'm hungry.*

He moved to a nearby secret door and discovered that it had no interface. He listened and, hearing nothing, opened the door and stepped through. On the other side, he found himself in a small room with metal partitions boxing off four areas in which Kormèr discovered telltale holes in the ground beneath heated plank-seats. Beyond the stalls, the walls contained odd fixtures that Kormèr assumed to be some kind of hygienic apparatus, and finally, in the wall opposite the secret door was the only other door.

That door suddenly flew open!

Kormèr froze as a wizened Averian entered. Kormèr had nowhere to run, nowhere to hide. Besides, with magic at his disposal, the sorcerer could no doubt easily stop any attempt at escape. Kormèr braced himself, his mind already working to concoct an excuse as to why he was there.

The old birdman trudged partway into the room before he noticed Kormèr just standing there, slightly to his left. The birdman squinted through oval spectacles that appeared thick enough to be the vacuum-tight windows of the *Stardust IV*. With growing anxiety, Kormèr waited for a sudden cry of alarm, and for some magical punishment that was certain to follow.

||Thurrsee?|| warbled the old Averian. ||You look pale. What's wrong?||

Kormèr's jaw almost dropped. The old bird was blind! *Saved!* he cried in his head. Kormèr chirped, weakly, ||Just a little sick today. I think it's going away, but some food would help my recovery.||

||Well, now. I know just what to do about that; I'm not the cook for nothing, you know.||

Bonus! Kormèr wanted to jump and scream with delight, but he refrained. ||I was hoping you would say that.||

||One of my broths will help your gizzard straighten itself out.|| The old bird wriggled his nose in a toothless half smile as he waved one hand over another.

Kormèr watched, fascinated, as a bowl of liquid appeared in the old birdman's stationary hand, white tendrils of warmth rising from the bowl's surface. Now this was real magic! None of that up-the-sleeve stuff that the street performers pulled on Elmar. The old birdman had conjured the broth from nowhere, simply by waving his hand. He passed the bowl to Kormèr, saying: ||Go on, to the dining room with you.||

||No,|| chirped Kormèr, a bit too hastily. But the old cook didn't catch the urgency in Kormèr's tone. Kormèr quickly added, ||In case I'm ill with something contagious, I don't want to pass it onto anyone else. I'll just finish this up in here.||

||Suit yourself, but this isn't the ideal place to be eating, either.|| He pointed a grayed wing toward the booths, reminding Kormèr of where they were.

Kormèr shrugged and drank from the edge of the bowl. *Whatever this stuff is, it hits the spot. I'd ask, but I'm afraid it'll turn out to be something totally disgusting. Who am I kidding? I'm so hungry, I'm eating in a bathroom!*

The cook excused himself and entered a booth. Once the metal door closed, Kormèr slipped back through the secret door. He finished the broth in the dark, expecting to slip the empty bowl into the bathroom when he was done. But when the last drop had left the bowl, it vanished from Kormèr's hands. Startled, Kormèr turned up the lamp and looked along the dusty floor, but there was no bowl to be found. The magical bowl had vanished when its contents were gone. Kormèr smiled and shook his head. *What a wild place!*

JEREMY sat back in his seat dejectedly. Beside him, Kit sat quietly with his arms crossed. They'd had to spill their guts to the Birshetland police about their invention and Harry G, and even about bringing Kormèr, a stowaway, onto the planet. They'd apologized for forgetting to register Kormèr upon arrival, and then sat through the admonition and the threat of fines and jail time for impeding an ongoing investigation, as well as introducing dangerous elements into the city.

Now they waited anxiously while the officer made some final terse scratches on his flimsy.

||Well, gentlemen,|| sang the officer at last, ||thank you for your cooperation. In light of your willingness to cooperate and make amends with the hotel, we will refrain from pressing charges.||

||Thank you,|| sang Jeremy, feeling himself unclenching a little in his seat.

||This is, however, still an ongoing investigation,|| the officer reminded them, ||so we may need to ask you some followup questions. How much longer will you be on Averia?||

Jeremy exchanged a look with Kit. ||We're still in contract negotiations, so it could be a week or more.||

The officer cocked his head, as if listening to a distant voice. Then he looked back up. ||Very well. We may need you back here in nine or ten days. It may behoove you to stay at least that long.||

Jeremy frowned. While he might be around that long anyway, he didn't like the possibility of being forced to stay. ||I'll be happy to stay as long as you need me to, but my crew is free to leave on schedule, right?|| He didn't look at Kit, not wishing to speak on his behalf. The rest of the team, however, were better off leaving as soon as possible, if Harry G really was on their tail.

||Right now, their presence in Freet-See has no effect on the investigation,|| the officer sang. ||But something may come up later.||

||Understood.|| He fought the urge to apologize again, sensing that there was more than the typical xenophobic wariness at work here. If the Averians were struggling with their investigation, he and Kit didn't need to talk themselves into an even bigger hole.

||Good. That will be all, for now,|| the officer sang after a brief pause. ||We will see you out.||

Leaving the precinct, Jeremy appreciated the fresh air and cool, calming glow of the lightening morning sky, but all the time lost under questioning frustrated him. Taking a taxi back to the hotel, Kit fell asleep within minutes of sitting on the cushioned bench, leaving Jeremy plenty of quiet time to mull over their current situation. Unlike Kit, Jeremy couldn't compartmentalize so efficiently to sleep, regardless of how exhausted he was.

Jeremy had called Jim the evening before, on the way to the police station. But Jeremy had thought that they were only going to be there for a few hours, not the entire night. He now took a moment to send a quick message to the guys to let them know they were heading back to the hotel. The details could wait until later, and were better discussed in person, anyway.

They arrived at the hotel's taxi platform, and Kit managed to exit the taxi without help, but by the time Jeremy paid the cabbie and turned around, Kit had slumped again, propping himself up against the ladder rungs.

Kit's eyes opened and looked at him. "We really got our arses handed to us," he said groggily.

Jeremy nodded. "Did you know anything about that 'dangerous elements' law?"

"Nope. No idea. Could just be them taking the piss out of us, for all we know." Kit glared at the ladder. "What a stupid idea, to make people climb a ladder to get inside a building," he muttered. Jeremy stayed a couple of rungs below him, just in case Kit missed a rung, but he climbed the rungs easily to the entrance.

"What's the plan?" Kit asked, when they had both reached the top.

"I know we need rest, but can you smooth things over with the manager, find out about our belongings and stuff? I'll go see if I can find Kormèr. We still don't know if this was one of G's men, or someone new."

Kit nodded. "Right. On it."

As he watched Kit approach the hotel front desk, Jeremy tried to recall Kormèr's room number. *Wait a second—did he even tell us?* He wondered if the desk would tell him, if he asked, or if it would look suspicious for him to inquire, given the recent excitement.

||Hi.||

Jeremy jumped at the voice behind him. He turned to find a young bellhop behind him. The face then clicked in Jeremy's mind. ||Hi... Almp.||

The boy beamed. ||That's right. Are you looking for KL, by any chance?||

||I am,|| Jeremy sang. ||You wouldn't happen to know his room number, would you?||

||Sure, I do,|| Almp chirped. ||But you won't find him there.|| He fluffed his feathers. ||I thought he'd have mentioned to you that he was going to be away, but I guess he didn't.||

Jeremy schooled his expression. ||No, he didn't. Do you know where he's gone?||

||Nope. He wouldn't say. The event at your room had him a little spooked.||

Jeremy almost asked what Almp knew about that, but then decided against. He doubted the boy would have any more information than the manager or the police. Only Kormèr could answer his questions. ||Thanks for the info, Almp. Oh, do you know when he'll be back?||

||He said it was for a day or two.|| The boy shrugged.

That's a lot of time to get into trouble. ||Okay, thanks. If you hear from him, tell him to contact. Umm...|| Jeremy fished in his pocket.

Almp shook his head. ||You don't have to give me anything. Any friend of KL's is a friend of mine. High sky.|| And the boy walked off to help a family of new arrivals with their baggage.

Kit joined Jeremy as he finished with the manager. Something must've shown on Jeremy's face because Kit waited until they'd put some distance between them and any potential eavesdroppers before he asked: "What happened? Where's the kid?"

"Went off on his own and told his friend, the manager's son, that he may be gone for a day or so," Jeremy said. "Didn't say where he was going, of course."

"Of course," Kit echoed. "No surprise there. Oh, well. Theeseeo, the hotel manager, insists that the hotel is fully insured against mechanical and electrical failures, so he actually offered us compensation for our inconvenience and any damages; he's moving us to a new room, under a pseudonym, free of charge... pun intended. Our stuff is in storage right now, but they cordoned off the old room, if we want to check inside for anything... missing or otherwise."

Jeremy pushed up the bridge of his glasses. "Ah, that's very nice of him, but he knows that the damage wouldn't have even happened if not for us, right?"

Kit shrugged and leaned closer. "I'm sure they're well aware, but they don't want to draw attention to the fact, especially as the official cause is a malfunction. I get the feeling they'd rather us not make a fuss over it, that we should just smile and say 'thank you'."

Jeremy looked over Kit's shoulder to the concierge desk, where Theeseeo met his eyes worriedly. Jeremy smiled and nodded, and the manager's expression eased considerably. "I guess with their jewel thief still on the loose, the authorities wouldn't want word leaked that there's also a saboteur or assassin stalking guests at the poshest hotel in town."

"Can't blame them," Kit said. "The Cheerees has a stellar reputation to uphold. Come on," he said, nudging Jeremy in the ribs, "the manager gave us complimentary credits for the restaurant and bar. No way we can let *that* go to waste."

HAVING only slept four hours—not counting the catnap during the taxi ride back to the hotel—Kit could've used another three hours of sleep. But since Jeremy looked even more haggard and stressed than Kit felt, he did his best to be cheerful and positive. They had at least eaten a hearty buffet breakfast at the hotel restaurant before passing out in their new suite, so the morning wasn't a total loss.

"Ready to head back to Freet-See?" Jeremy asked, as they headed out of the hotel.

"I'm ready to leave Averia," Kit said, "but I'll settle for Freet-See, if it means seeing the lads again."

Jeremy clasped Kit's shoulder. "And we'll spend Cheerretee together, too. It'll be a hoot."

Kit cocked his eyebrow. "Is that an Averian joke, mate?"

Jeremy chuckled. "Glad you've still got your sense of humor. I don't know what I'd do without you at the table with me."

A taxi swooped down the moment the men stepped out onto the platform, and a familiar cabbie greeted them. | |Good afternoon, gentlemen,| | greeted Feestoo.

It was almost evening, but Kit wasn't about to quibble about that. | |You know Kormèr's out of town, yeah?| |

Feestoo nodded. | |I do. But since he's away, I'm happy to ferry you instead. Where to?| |

| |The city port, please,| | chirped Jeremy, and the taxi soared away.

| |Freet-See bound?| | asked Feestoo. Without waiting for an answer, he continued, | |I'd take you all the way there, but the aircars don't fly outside the city.| |

| |I never knew that,| | admitted Jeremy. Kit shrugged; that was new to him, too. | |So the sky-hoppers are special?| |

| |Indeed, they are.| | Feestoo seemed about to start on a dissertation on the various means of transport on Averia, but they quickly arrived at the port.

| |Take this,| | Feestoo chirped, handing Kit a small device. | |Use it when you get back, and I'll pick you up.| |

| |Thanks, mate,| | chirped Kit. | |High sky! Oh, and happy Cheerretee!| |

The dense crowd at the port had both men on alert as they kept their eyes and ears open for any sign of trouble, as they had no idea who or what was after them. Thankfully, their wait for a skyhopper was brief, but they sat tensely for several silent minutes, waiting for the rest of the passengers to board. It wasn't until they were well under way before they finally relaxed.

Jim and Morgan met them at Freet-See's hopper terminal, and Kit recognized their lean, dark silhouettes before they greeted them with wide smiles. Jim clapped Jeremy on the back and prefaced: "No questions about the ship till you see it, Jer."

Jeremy chuckled. "Okay. I'll resist the temptation."

"How about a colorful expletive or two?" Kit grinned. "We're entitled to that much."

"One apiece," negotiated Morgan. "Man, it's good to see you two. When Kormèr first told us the news, we all thought the worst."

"Yeah, well," Jeremy muttered. "We're mostly fine. We spent last night answering a lot of questions for the police. And spent a good chunk of the morning sifting through our stuff and moving into a new room."

Jim winced. "Ouch. About that: how big of a bill are we talking about, to pay for the damage to the room?"

"It won't eat into our profit margin, will it?" Morgan asked, not entirely in jest. "We've got a razor-thin overhead, as it is."

"Actually." Kit glanced at Jeremy. "Our room is getting comped, including some of the expenses. The hotel doesn't want any bad publicity, so they're chalking it up as a malfunction while the police are investigating behind the scenes." He held up a full shopping bag. "We bagged some take-away food and booze for you lads."

176

Jim snatched the bag from him first, but Morgan plucked a fresh seed roll from the bulging bag and took a hefty bite of the crisp, pillowy bread before Jim even peeked inside.

Kit shook his head, marveling at how slender Jim and Morgan stayed, despite their locust-like appetites. "Save the apples for Mack, ya ken?"

"I know better than to get between Mack and fresh produce," Jim said, pulling out an amber-tinted bottle of oat-flax lager, still cold from the hotel bar. "How much trouble are you in with the police?"

Jeremy sighed. "Could be worse, I suppose. We got raked over the coals more for not filing the registration for KL, than for anything going on at the hotel. I might get a fine for that, which I understand. The locals don't want unregistered offworlders sneaking onto their planet or through their ports. But, just the same, I'd like to avoid any more surprises, or this little venture of ours could get expensive."

"How much did KL tell you about what happened?" Kit walked behind with Jeremy, letting Jim and Morgan take the lead.

Morgan walked backwards to face them. "He said he'd gone looking for you guys and found the intruder inside, rigging the room screens."

"Reptilian," said Kit. "According to the police and surveillance footage."

"Oh?" said Jim. "Kormèr didn't mention that."

"What about Kormèr?" Jeremy asked. "When you talked to him, did he sound alright?"

Jim nodded. "He sounded fine; said he'd stumbled in on the guy. I didn't want to keep the channel open too long, so I didn't push him for details."

He's a lucky young bastard, that one. Aloud, Kit asked: "Any word on G?"

"No sign of him," Jim said, shaking his head. "Probably was one of his men, though."

"They called our bluff sooner than we expected," said Morgan. "Ridiculously sooner."

Jeremy shook his head. "It may seem too soon for him to have sent someone here, but no one else is after us. It must be G."

"We were talking about that last night," Jim said. "Why kill us now, when they were just trying to take us alive before? It really feels like it's someone new. Could it be local trouble?"

Jeremy and Kit exchanged glances. "I didn't pick up on anything at the meetings," said Jeremy. "You?"

Kit shook his head silently. He was usually pretty good at reading people, regardless of species, and their clients were tough negotiators, but they seemed legitimate.

They arrived at Hangar 14, where the ship sat berthed. It was closer to the spaceport entrance, but hadn't been updated like the others and was relegated to supporting the older classes of spacecraft. Dark, cramped, old and little used, the hangar didn't even appear on the public berth list, which made it a perfect hiding spot for the *Stardust IV*.

"Wow," muttered Kit. "This place is a real shite hole, lads… Ow!" He turned at the sharp snap of Jeremy's hand against his arm and followed his friend's gaze.

Jeremy and Kit stopped short and gaped when they saw the ship. The craft gleamed like never before—not since it was new—its repaired plating just as shiny as the rest of the exterior.

"Holy shite," mumbled Kit.

"Nice job, guys," murmured Jeremy in kind. "Very nice."

"She looks good, doesn't she?" Morgan smiled proudly.

Jim explained: "We used a new chemical wash developed on Umbikki II; works wonders on the hull. I'd say she's ready for show."

"Good," said Jeremy, leading the group onto the ship. "Because they're getting impatient." Catching the inquisitive glances from Jim and Morgan, he said, "Basically, things are in the air. I'll explain later, once we're all— Hey, Roke!"

The tall, long-haired blonde popped out of the cockpit at the sound of voices. Mack soon joined them from the crew quarters. Everyone gathered in the ship's mess.

"So, about the negotiations," said Kit. "Well, they could go more smoothly, you might say."

Jeremy was more plain-spoken: "The investors are leery, especially without seeing it for themselves. This is a big step for them, for the industry. You know, everything that we discussed when we started down this road."

"The good old days, eh?" said Mack. "Just before all our troubles began."

"Hey!" said Jeremy entreatingly. "Hold on a minute. We've come a long way, and things are turning around." Jeremy looked at the men's tired faces. "Look, I know it hasn't been easy, but we knew there'd be setbacks. We knew guys like Harry G would be after us. C'mon, we talked about this stuff, remember?"

"We're close, guys," said Kit, proselytizing. "Very close. Once they see the ship, ride in it and feel the tech doing its thing, we'll have them in our pockets."

"Don't worry," said Jim. "I can speak for all of us," he glanced around at the heads nodding in support, "when I say that we're with you all the way, man."

"We're not gonna bail, just because things get heavy," added Roke. At the blank looks around him, he clarified: "We've come all this way, as a team, and we're not gonna quit now."

Jeremy looked at the faces around him, old friends and co-workers. "Thanks, guys." He smiled at them, and they all clasped their arms over their shoulders in a circle.

"Go, Team Repulse!" cried Morgan.

Mack groaned and broke from the circle. "Nah-ah, we never agreed on that name."

"Yeah, I'm with Mack on that one," Roke drawled. "'Repulse' doesn't really charm the betties."

"How about Team Tailor?" Jim offered.

"You can stop kissing Jer's butt already," Morgan snickered.

"Okay, okay," Jeremy laughed at his team's fraternal bickering. "We'll figure out the name later. I'm just glad you guys are all still with me." He clapped and rubbed his hands together in anticipation. "Alright, everybody, the sooner we get this bird in the air, the sooner we get paid. Let's move!"

CHAPTER 14

THINKING he'd heard something, Srrcheel looked up from the history book he was reading. He looked curiously about his room, but hearing nothing more, returned his attention to the text.

He looked up again. That time, he had definitely heard something. He put the book down and looked around again. Was there an insect in the room? Or something else, squeaking in a pitch that sounded like far-off whistles.

Pop! | | I think that's it, | | squawked a loud voice. Then a bit more quietly: | | Do you hear me now? | |

Srrcheel frowned; someone had to be pranking him. | | This childish behavior does not suit you, novice, | | he chirped with all the gravitas he could muster. Srrcheel knew of a novice that was summarily expelled for picking on an apprentice. The rules became more flexible as one rose higher in rank. But it was also expected that one gained more wisdom with their higher rank, and would be above playing silly games.

| | Srrcheel, it's me, KL. | |

Srrcheel did not respond. *Is this a trick? Did someone find out about this crazy boy, and they're now playing tricks on me? Wait. the voice said 'KL', not 'Kormèr'.*

| | I see you standing there, looking around, so you must hear me. Say something. | |

The voice sounded close, but where could he be, to see him without being seen himself? | | What did you ask me outside the jewelry store? | | asked Srrcheel to test whether it really was the Terran... Elmarian. Whatever. No one else would know the details of their conversation.

| | Hmm, I asked you about a lot of things. Oh, a love spell! | |

So it is him! | | Where *are* you? | |

| | Don't worry about that. How're you doing? How's your studying going? | |

Srrcheel's crest rose with annoyance. | | It was fine until a moment ago. Why are you still here? Didn't you say you were going to leave me alone? | |

| | Not exactly. I said I was going to leave your room, so that you wouldn't get in trouble. | |

| | And yet here you are... somewhere. | |

| | No, | | Kormèr refuted | | I'm not in your room, so you can't get in trouble because of me. | |

Srrcheel thought about that for a moment, then clucked, | | If you get caught, I'll deny ever seeing you, you know. | | His master, of course, had witnessed their initial meeting at the jewelry store, but hopefully he would give Srrcheel the benefit of the doubt.

Kormèr sang agreeably: ||Of course. I wouldn't even mention your name. You realize that I'm making an effort to keep you from getting into trouble on my behalf. Why should I expect you to stick your neck out for me?||

Stick my neck out? Srrcheel wasn't sure if he had meant the last as an insult, but he didn't rise to the challenge. ||What do you want with me?||

||To be your friend.||

"Right," huffed Srrcheel doubtfully, switching to Terran English.

"You know Terran English?" Kormèr was stunned.

Srrcheel pursed his lips and mocked the boy with: "You can't?"

"Can't what?"

Srrcheel sighed, deflated that his joke was spoiled. "No, no. We sorcerers call Terran English 'cant', you know, like slang."

"Oh, I see. I've never heard it called that. And you slur or twist your words a bit."

"That's because I learned through conversation, not from an edu-comp," he said, realizing why Kormèr's diction was so smooth, for both cant and Averian. "Learning from one of those things is like using magic to cheat on an exam."

Silence. Then, "You can do that?"

Srrcheel matted down his crest with his hands. "Some try, I'm sure, but I'd rather follow the rules. Maybe that's why I'm still only an apprentice."

||But not for much longer, right?|| Kormèr asked cheerily, switching back to Averian.

Srrcheel cross his arms and leaned back against the wall. ||I should be studying. You're distracting me.||

||I could help you study.||

||No, because that would be cheating,|| Srrcheel returned. ||Don't you ever care about rules?||

||I care! About my own rules, I guess. Anyway, your rules have holes, but I'm still learning about your ways.||

Srrcheel considered this. ||What a strange, privileged life you must have.||

||That didn't sound like a compliment,|| Kormèr remarked.

||It isn't,|| Srrcheel replied. ||You say you want to learn about our ways, but you flout and sidestep our traditions and customs. Instead, you have your own 'rules', which sound like habits and preferences to suit yourself. It must be lonely, to have no accountability except to yourself.||

||What makes you think I'm lonely?|| Kormèr asked, sounding a little defensive.

||Because you refuse to leave,|| Srrcheel sang, now feeling a little sorry for the Elmarian boy. Srrcheel had spent the first few years of his life in an orphanage, so he was used to spending long stretches of time by himself, but he knew that

wasn't typical for Averians, especially one of his age. | |Isn't there anyone who misses you at home?| |

| |Not really,| | Kormèr warbled quietly after a moment. | |My father died recently.| |

Srrcheel bowed his head. | |I am sorry. I was an infant when my parents died, so I don't know exactly how it feels to lose a father—I can only imagine.| |

| |Who took care of you when you were growing up, then?| | Kormèr asked.

| |'Took care of me'? Everyone here, but no one in particular. A Master discovered me in the orphanage in Freet-See, where I was born, and brought me here to the Hovel. Once I arrived, I lived and grew up amongst other novices like me.| |

| |A Master brought you? Not the Master that you have now,| | Kormèr guessed.

| |No, an older Master, who is more attuned to the... 'spark' that sorcerers possess. Some travel all over Averia to find untapped potential.| | He stopped himself, sensing that he was talking too much. He could have gone on for hours, talking about the specialness of the spark, how only some were born with it, but they had to learn to shape, nurture and control it until they could direct it productively. *He's an outsider—you can't share these matters with him!*

Usually, on those rare occasions when he spoke to people outside the Hovel, their eyes invariably glazed over after a while, a visible signal that they'd tired of his rambling. But without seeing Kormèr's face during their conversation, he couldn't tell whether the boy was bored or laughing at his expense, or really listening.

| |From the Hovel to Freet-See. That certainly is far,| | Kormèr remarked.

| |What?| |

| |How far the Master went to find you, and bring you back here,| | Kormèr sang. | |He must have sensed something very special about you.| |

| |I don't know about that,| | Srrcheel twittered. | |There are apprentices who arrived after me, who've already gone through their first raising.| | He wasn't really in a rush; with the higher ranks came more responsibilities, more pressure to act and look a certain way... He looked down at his slightly doughy middle and knew his extra weight wasn't for lack of exercise or willpower at mealtimes: his body just wasn't ready to give up his "fledgling fluff" yet. *One of these days...*

| |Enough about me,| | Srrcheel sang, shaking his feathers with a shimmy. | |What about you? Apart from your father, who else is on Elmar, waiting for you?| |

| |Me? Hmm, well.| | Kormèr seemed to need a moment to really think. | |There are the robots, I suppose.| |

Srrcheel perked. | |Robots, in your actual home? Really? I've only ever seen them used commercially or in industry. Never within the borders of Berdia. What're they like?| |

| |Oh,| | Kormèr sang, sounding surprised at his interest. | |They're shaped and sized for their functions: some clean; others cook... stuff like that. They're funny sometimes, and they make brilliant companions.| |

||It sounds like you interact with them. To you, they're more than machines.||

||I suppose they are.||

Srrcheel waited for him to expand on the statement, but there was nothing else. ||Is that why you travel through your... magical blue doorway and... and this,|| he gestured at the air, ||communicating as a disembodied voice? To interact from time to time with other people, not just with your robot friends?||

||Aren't you going to ask me about the portal?|| Kormèr asked, almost deflecting.

Of course, Srrcheel was curious about the portal! But he was already losing focus, and he couldn't afford to. He shook his head. |No, you would tell me, if you wanted to. If you're caught, it's best that I know nothing about it. Just as I won't ask you about how you're speaking to me. I'm distracted enough, and I need to focus on my studies.||

||Ah, yes. That. I won't keep you, then.||

Srrcheel sighed. ||You're staying, though, aren't you? And probably availing yourself of one of the diplomatic guest rooms.||

||Actually, the chamber you were thinking of earlier, when I asked you to picture a nice room.||

||I had only looked inside it, but it seemed comfortable.|| Srrcheel tightened his lips into a tight line. ||Of course, you're staying in that one.||

||It was vacant,|| Kormèr sang innocently. ||I wouldn't have stayed there, if it had been occupied.||

Srrcheel imagined Kormèr popping through his blue portal to look at various rooms until he found a vacant one that he deemed suitable. ||Must be nice to have mastery over a device that allows you to come and go wherever and whenever you please.||

||Well... I wouldn't say I've *mastered* it, exactly.||

Srrcheel chirped with amusement. ||Well, it sounds like you're pretty familiar with how it works.||

||I don't know exactly how it works, but it does allow me to travel... just about anywhere, as far as I can tell. But it's tricky, so I have to be careful how to choose my destinations, or worlds.||

||I'm sorry, but I thought you used it only here,|| Srrcheel scowled. ||You're saying that you could return to Elmar right now, instantly, just by stepping through the portal?||

||Pretty much.||

Traveling between two points in space was no simple trick, even for the Masters, but traveling between planets was magic or technology of an entirely different level! ||That's phenomenal! If you don't completely understand its function, then you obviously didn't build it. How did you even get it?||

||Umm... I confiscated it from a wealthy, unscrupulous, self-proclaimed magician back on Elmar. He called himself that, but he was as much of a magician

183

as I am. He was taking advantage of his admirers and spectators, distracting them while his partner robbed them. So, I helped myself to his loot and returned what I could to the people he'd robbed. The portal was one of the items in his stash that I couldn't trace back to an original owner.||

||So you kept it.|| Srrcheel listened carefully to the precision of his words. ||When you say you confiscated… You stole another's property, just like your so-called magician stole from others.||

||Technically, yes,|| Kormèr sang, a little reluctantly. ||It's a little more complicated than that. My world has classes divided by economical means, much as your society is divided into social structures. We have a poor class and a rich class, and very few in between. Some of the poor revert to stealing from others to make ends meet. Some steal from the rich, and some from other poor.||

||What class are you in?||

||The rich,|| Kormèr warbled.

||You don't sound thrilled about that.||

||I won't deny that having money has its advantages, but many people in my class care only about amassing more money for themselves at the expense of others, even if it's more wealth than they can ever spend in their lifetimes.||

||There are some on Averia like that, as well,|| Srrcheel admitted. ||Money can often buy social status. There is ambition and greed everywhere.||

Kormèr nodded. ||Not you, though. You wouldn't jeopardize or cheat someone else to further your own goals, like your raising. You wouldn't hurt someone else to advance, would you?||

||No, of course not. I expect that kind of behavior would get you expelled from the Hovel.||

||Not from Berdia?||

Srrcheel's feathers fluffed with unease. ||Not necessarily,|| he warbled, unhappy with the answer and the reality behind it. ||There are other factions in the city, some more ruthless than others, but still within reason.||

||I see. Anyway, that's why Elmar's class structure is… flawed.||

||Ah. What does your class structure have to do with your portal?||

||Oh, right, the portal! Well, like I said, there are those in the upper class who steal, even from the poor.||

||That's terrible!|| Srrcheel shook his head. ||It's abhorrent, to cheat those who are already disadvantaged.||

||I agree. My father taught me that it's not enough to recognize the wrongdoing, to stand by and do nothing, so I even the playing field a little, whenever I see an opportunity.||

||By stealing?|| Srrcheel shuddered at the idea. ||I had always felt that theft was wrong, no matter the reasons.||

||I only take from those who deserve it, and only to give to the needy. I always have my hands open when it's my turn to give. If someone else keeps their hand closed, or opens it to pick from someone else's coffer, I help to ensure that

they give their fair share. The portal helps me in my line of work. Maybe it's wrong, but it's necessary.||

It made sense to hear Kormèr speak of it, like a social responsibility that the rich needed to exhibit. Yet if they had worked hard for what they had, why should they be forced to give away what was rightfully theirs? Of course, if the rich themselves had kept the poor downtrodden to achieve their status… Just like Kormèr was a member of the upper class but stole from others? *No, not exactly. Oh, this is not an easy topic!*

||Anyway, the portal,|| Kormèr continued. ||When I took it, it wasn't open, the way you saw it, otherwise taking it would've been much more difficult. When it's closed, it's in the shape of a crystal cube. I thought it was curious, like a strange gem, so I kept it. I found out the hard way what it really was.||

Srrcheel eyed his books, but Kormèr's tale had him sufficiently distracted. ||What happened?||

Srrcheel listened without interrupting, while Kormèr told him the whole story about triggering the portal device and falling through it for the first time—the first of many adventures on other planets and times. He felt as though Kormèr had needed to share his story with someone who could listen without criticism, so Srrcheel felt bad about even trying to rush him along, despite losing his precious little remaining study time.

||This duchess, Menddilal, sounds like a handful,|| Srrcheel twittered, when Kormèr finally took a pause. ||Is that who you want the love spell for?||

||Her? No way.|| The disdain was clear in Kormèr's voice. ||I'm interested in a particular Averian woman.||

||I see. So, then what's Menddilal about?||

||She and her husband—||

Srrcheel had taken to absently preening himself and now stopped, looking up into the distance. ||She's married?!||

||Yes, but she's constantly cheating on him. It's like a pastime for her. It's probably how she got to be his wife to begin with.||

Srrcheel stared into space, thinking that maybe he never wanted to visit Elmar. It didn't sound like a very nice place.

||Anyway, I'm after her wedding band.||

||Wow! You'll never get that. I'll bet it's closely guarded.||

||Not any more guarded than she is inside her mansion. But I admit it will probably take time.||

||You honestly think you can get it? You must be a very good thief.||

||I'm okay, I guess. I have stolen myself away here for a day without being discovered.||

||Yes, you have, haven't you,|| chirped Srrcheel, less than enthusiastically.

||I really want to be there for your raising tonight, you know.||

Srrcheel was quiet. The ceremony, as all else that dealt with sorcery, was very sacred, not to be witnessed by outsiders. But Kormèr had proven himself stubborn enough that he would probably find his own way, if Srrcheel didn't tell him. *I might as well save him the trouble and tell him where the grand hall is. He'll probably find it eventually, anyway.*

| |About that… there's a very large audience hall in the lower levels of the Hovel. That's where the ceremony will be.| | Srrcheel gave him the directions on how to get there, though he couldn't be sure how Kormèr was keeping track.

| |Do you have to go through a lot of preparations?| | asked Kormèr when Srrcheel was done.

| |Some.| | Srrcheel glanced at the book he'd put down and picked up several times during his conversation with Kormèr, no closer to finishing it than at the start of the visit. | |I was reading up on procedures just now when you stopped by.| |

| |Sorry. I'll let you finish up. We'll talk more later, after the ceremony. Good luck.| |

| |Thank you.| | He waited, but nothing changed. | |Are you still there?| | When Kormèr didn't answer, Srrcheel tried to continue reading. But after reading the same paragraph three times, he cursed silently. Finally, he stood, grabbed the book, and left his room. *At least in the library, I shouldn't be so easily distracted.*

BEHIND the secret door to Srrcheel's room, Kormèr stared at the interface, trying to remember how he'd enabled the two-way comm. Finally, he gave up and simply shut down the whole interface. As the corridor plunged into darkness, Kormèr ran through the twists and turns he'd need to take to get back to his room, and suddenly felt his energy waning. The soup had been tasty and filling, but that had been a few hours and many meters of walking ago. *This isn't good. I should've brought food, but I didn't expect to be doing all this sneaking around. What if the raising ceremony turns out to be really boring… I don't want to fall asleep.* He turned up the lamp and made his way back to his room where he lay on the bed, set his p-comm to wake him in an hour, and closed his eyes.

But he felt no better when the p-comm alarm woke him up. His head and neck ached, and he wanted nothing more than to stay in bed for more sleep. Except this had been happening to him more and more lately when he napped, and he had learned to recognize the signs of his body tricking him in its own stupid way. If he went back to sleep, he'd wake up feeling even worse.

Instead, he ran in place, forcing himself to alertness. Then he added a few stretches and bends to touch the floor until his p-comm chimed again, signaling it was time to go. The exercises had chased away the need for sleep, along with some aches. But the headache lingered. Trying his best to ignore the mild pain, he peered out the room's door. Since Srrcheel didn't know of the secret passages, his directions relied on the regular corridors. But after only a few minutes of watching the traffic in the corridor, light though it was, Kormèr felt it was too risky to go that way.

He returned to the secret passages with his trusty magic lamp and tried his best to approximate Srrcheel's directions. Anticipating he'd have trouble finding his way, he'd started out early, and his caution paid off. He took several wrong turns along the way and stopped frequently to check the interface screens. After nearly an hour and a half, he reached a small room with three long consoles and at least a dozen screens hanging on a wall. He examined the consoles, brushing the dust off the labels until he found what he was looking for. Most of the screens came to life at the touch of a switch, with only three completely dark and two showing only static. The rest displayed multiple views of a large cylindrical hall with rows of stadium-seating along the perimeter. Three Averians ambled busily about, apparently making last-minute preparations. This had to be the place. Now he had to find a spot where he could hide and yet still have an unobstructed view of the proceedings.

Hmm. Not many places to hide out there. I suppose I could just watch the ceremony from here. He frowned at the idea. One screen seemed to be angled upward, displaying a section of wall ending at a metallic mesh and struts on the ceiling. *That's promising.*

Fifteen minutes later, he found a stairwell that spiraled up and into the ceiling space above the hall. He brushed an area clean of dust and lay down on the metallic mesh, peering down through it into the room below. The room had nearly filled by now, and Kormèr found it interesting to see such a large gathering of only Averians. He grinned, prideful, knowing that he was the only non-Averian in witness of the proceedings. *Probably ever,* he assumed.

Far below, rows of filled perches swirled neatly around the center of the room, forming an octagon around the raised altar in the center of the room. On the altar, casting a magical yellow radiance throughout the room, blazed an impressive pillar of fire.

The air vibrated, as if every molecule oscillated with excitement, aware of the event that was about to take place. The robed ones hummed a haunting chant as their footfalls echoed in through the doorway from the corridor beyond.

Tongues of flame danced out from the pillar.

The chant intensified, permeated Kormèr's mind, entranced it with its rhythm. His pores expanded, and the chant filled each one. Kormèr marveled at the flexibility of his skin, and he laughed when the chant turned into musical notes along his nose, diving into the bowl of his mouth. They tasted a little bitter. His body vibrated in time with the chant. It was the most frightening and the most wonderful feeling he'd ever experienced. And he never wanted it to stop.

One with the metallic mesh, one with the room, Kormèr watched as a dream unfolded within him, on the raised altar of his heart, with its pillar of fire that pumped blood with huge balloon-like blood cells. Balls of feathers came to stand on the altar and perform strange acts that distorted the dream. He saw filaments, like brilliant golden strings, crisscrossing the room, humming with energy. The feather-balls warped the filaments, coalescing the power momentarily, then releasing it into brilliant flashes that made Kormèr's eyes turn inside out. But he couldn't look away. One feather ball was familiar, had a name, but the name didn't matter. Kormèr saw it bend the filaments until the light flashed. He tried to clap, but he had no arms, only doors, and they were closed.

The chant got louder, tore Kormèr into ragged strips that dried in the sudden arid heat. Kormèr gasped, the air flowing like a river across a dry, cracked river bed under a brilliant, cloudless blue sky.

The chant and ceremony went on for only a few hours, but Kormèr's transcendent experience continued long after they ended.

TWO hairless, smooth-skinned beings stepped out of the lift and crossed the lobby of the Cheerees Hotel. The duo ignored the stares of hotel patrons and Cheerretee revelers as they made their way to the room that had been Tailor's and McQuinton's. Activated by a courier message from Harry G, the Aggreyate mercenaries had quickly learned of the "incident at the Cheerees Hotel", as the media had reported it.

The door to the room was open, a fan blowing scented air into the vacant room. Stepping past the fan and into the room, the mercs analyzed everything as they moved. The damage to the room had been repaired, but the Aggreyates had other means of finding out what had happened. They willed their eyes to see in other spectra, and their skin to sense smells and textures beyond the capabilities of average humanoids. Using these native skills, they found things that others would have easily missed: fingerprints all around the sensor plates; singed scales crushed into the carpet and sitting on the edge of a dresser top; the faint smell of burned flesh.

They kept meticulous notes of their findings, and in moments, had a clear picture of what had occurred. It was exactly as Mister G had predicted: a reptilian being had tried to sabotage the room to kill Tailor, McQuinton, or both. A study of the organic material would confirm if the saboteur had been Hassera. It would then fall to the Aggreyates to subdue either Hassera or Tailor and his crew… or both. Once Harry G arrived, he would sort them out.

CHAPTER 15

JEREMY put down his fork and sat back, satisfied. He looked around the table at his friends and partners, and knew they'd made the right decision to celebrate Cheerretee at this quiet restaurant. It was their first time on the planet during this holiday, but no one felt much like being in a crowd that night. The restaurant afforded them all the food and drink they wanted, with an unobstructed view of anyone entering with nefarious intent.

"That was amazing," he said of his dish. He grabbed his glass. "Guys, I've been thinking…"

"Oh no," said Kit. "Here he goes."

Jeremy grinned and pointed at Kit. "I've been thinking," he repeated, a little louder, "that I couldn't imagine being here tonight, going through these negotiations, with anyone other than this team. The past ten years have been a lot of hard work, and we're here on the cusp of the fulfillment of that work. Here's to us." He raised his glass, and around the table, the others did the same with a "Hear! Hear!"

"I can't believe it's been ten years," said Morgan, after putting down his beer mug.

Mack finished his water, then nodded. "I count the blessings every day, so I'm keenly aware of exactly how long it's been."

Jeremy knew that after his stint in the service, Mack had struggled with odd jobs and ostracization for his involvement in the seizure of the asteroid Ida, a military operation that had had left twenty-four dead. Though Mack's function at the time had had nothing to do with the attempted infiltration of the asteroid, everyone involved in that mission had had their reputations tarnished. Mack's, perhaps more so, since his account had implicated several high-ranking people in the debacle. Jeremy alone knew the basic story, but even he didn't know the details of Mack's eventual honorable discharge. Jeremy had seen past all that to focus on the professionalism and attention-to-detail that Mack brought to the team.

"Amen, buddy," said Jim. "To counting blessings, I mean." He looked around the restaurant. "I gotta say, coming here was the best idea. I know there aren't any natives here tonight, but you all know I'm not a big-crowd lover. This is alright by me."

Wearing his favorite tweed flat cap, Kit nodded. "Fireworks every hour on the hour since sundown," he said, swinging his glass toward the large windows. "Ya can't beat the view."

Jeremy glanced out the windows. At the moment, the only illumination came from the myriad celebrations in the streets below, from laser lights that split the night in brilliant colors and from the fantastic projections on the facades of buildings and trees alike. The next set of fireworks would fire in minutes; each one lasted five minutes and represented some of the steps in the myth behind the celebration.

"Let's go watch," said Morgan, then downed the rest of his drink. The six men stood and made their way to the windows with a few of the other patrons. A minute later, the lights dimmed, and they watched the next set of fireworks fire off into the sky.

"After we get some clients under our belts," said Morgan, "I have got to get back here and really celebrate."

"For sure," said Roke. "We'll totally be able to afford front-row seats."

Jeremy looked across the city skyline, flashing in the spectacle of light from the fireworks and from the elaborate lighting schemes projected onto the buildings' surfaces. Tomorrow they'd be rehearsing their demo, and the day after that they'd be putting on the show of their careers. But for tonight, his eyes were only for Freet-See.

"I can definitely see myself coming back here," he murmured into the bright lights.

AFTER two days of accelerated healing, Hassera's face and neck still looked raw and discolored. She shut down the self-imager and tapped her claws on the console in frustration. She shouldn't have expected any different; the electrical arcing had caused serious tissue damage. Even with the derma-infuser and her natural regenerative ability, the wounds would take weeks to heal completely. She didn't care about appearances all that much, but in her line of work, standing out in a crowd drew fewer contracts and commanded lower pay. She knew she would heal, eventually, and that there wouldn't be much scarring once it was all done, but she hated the wait.

She was certain that the hotel did not have any footage of her transgressions. That, at least, she had done correctly, wearing her e-cloak to keep her hidden from electronic surveillance.

Her frustration mainly stemmed from the communique she'd just received from Harry G. A man of few words, Harry G hadn't said much beyond expressing his disappointment at the reckless way she'd delivered the message of Tailor's escape. She'd used the tightest encryption, so there wasn't a chance of the message being intercepted. But Harry G preferred his people delivering their messages in person, in his office. No one knew why; the only reason anyone could conceive of was security. He didn't trust what he didn't control, and transmissions, no matter how secure they seemed to be, couldn't be secure enough for him.

Hassera secretly imagined that Harry G simply enjoyed lording over everyone, in his large office, behind his desk, surrounded by wall screens and technology.

The first time she'd visited Harry G's office, he'd certainly impressed her. Royland had been with her, introducing her to Harry G for the first time. That had mitigated some of the intimidation factor, and she'd been less and less impressed with each subsequent visit. She saw him now for what he was, a man, highly influential, very corrupt, but just a man.

The communique had arrived via courier ship. These were small and unmanned, so their acceleration and transit ratios were extremely high. Thus, they were the preferred method of communications between systems. Hassera enjoyed tracking that sort of data, comparing the results between different classes of courier ships to see improvements in efficiency over time. It had therefore come as a surprise to her when Harry G's courier produced no origination tracking data. Someone had deleted this courier ship's point of origin and carefully made it appear as though it had become corrupted. Familiar with the ships, Hassera had searched the backup database for the clean data. This too had conveniently become "corrupted".

Hassera thrilled at the idea of a challenge, especially in her condition. If anything could bring her out of her funk, it would be diving into this mystery, especially since her search into the enigmatic Kormèr Lezàl had yielded nothing but more unanswerable questions.

Assuming someone had intentionally sabotaged the database, Hassera set her AI to examine other data that was less accessible. With the couriers, that was their travel logs and resource consumption. With both those data points, *Ship* could easily compute its point of origin.

While *Ship* worked on the data, Hassera picked off the third layer of skin she'd shed so far. Part of her healing process was for a temporary layer of skin to form over her wounds and then slough off after a time. This would continue until her natural green scales could grow back, though she doubted they'd ever grow back the same way they had before. The damage was simply too extensive. Thanks to the healing accelerants, the skin regeneration cycles took hours instead of days or weeks. The constant itching and hunger annoyed her to no end, but she endured it knowing that she had to get back out into the world soon, before her quarry could leave.

Ship chimed, and Hassera straightened to examine the results. She blinked, then rechecked the results. Sure enough, there was no mistake. The courier had originated from an intermediary star system between Eps Eri and Aderuhy. She ran a quick calculation and confirmed her finding. Hassera sat back to contemplate the new situation.

Harry G was on his way to Averia. And he was only five days out.

CHAPTER 16

SYLVESTRA stared out the bay window behind her desk. She didn't often take time to just look out her window; she had enough work to keep her busy, even if most of the time it was just reviewing schedules, policies and procedures, and staff rosters. And a lot of reports and presentations. The window wasn't large and opened to a narrow view of the city, but that suited Sylvestra just fine. She'd selected this office, rather than the one historically set aside for the Chief of Police, for the view and because it was next to Phatheeo's office, as well as closer to the rest of the department. She'd wanted everyone to see that she was accessible, not ensconced in some lofty office.

Though limited, the view offered a momentary escape when Sylvestra couldn't get away from work or when work just became overwhelming. Thankfully, Cheerretee had passed fairly quietly. Though the crowds had hit record numbers, only a handful were disorderly enough to require arrest. Numerous warnings and a few fines were issued, but that was very normal.

She turned at a knock and found Phatheeo standing in the doorway.

||Update,|| he chirped, and stepped into the office.

||What's up?||

||It's Lezàl; he hasn't returned to the hotel, and no one's seen him for two days. We pressed the hotel owner's son, who's been hanging around with Lezàl, and he admitted that Lezàl told him he'd be away, but not exactly where or for how long.||

Stupid boy; I told him to stay in the city. That alone is a misdemeanor, if nothing else. ||Freet-See?||

||He didn't know. Lezàl told him it was better he didn't know.||

||Damn!|| He'd disobeyed a lawful order to stay in the city. Offworlder or not, that gave her the authority to take the next steps. ||And the room search warrant?||

||The council rejected the request. The evidence we've gathered so far seems to clear him of suspicion.||

Sylvestra knew they were right. But her gut told her that Lezàl had some role in the sudden streak of events. Impossible robberies; attempted murder; non-Averians in the public baths; a strange young man paying people with gems and getting locals to learn his language. *It doesn't make any sense, but everything started with his arrival... more or less.* ||Put out an all points; if he's spotted, I want to know, and

I want him tracked. We don't have enough for an arrest, but we need to keep closer eyes on him.| |

| |Will do. There's more. We finally received some data from Freet-See.| | He swiped from a flim he carried, and the data appeared on the wall. | |They sent a report of a hopper pilot who shuttled Lezàl and two humans to Birshetland the morning after the heist.| |

Sylvestra sat on the edge of her desk, gripping the edge tightly. | |The morning *after*? And the 'two humans', of course…| |

| |Jeremy Tailor and Kit McQuinton.| | Sylvestra blinked and took a deep breath. Phatheeo nodded. | |We're still waiting for the visual confirmation, but now we have third party confirmation; their story checks. I think they're completely legit, though I can send a courier out to Earth for more verification, if you want.| |

Sylvestra waved it off. | |Not necessary.| |

With a nod, Phatheeo turned to go.

As Phatheeo turned to go, another officer stepped in. | |Excuse me, Chief. Cap, I got the info on the Terrans you asked for.| | He handed the flim to Phatheeo, who glanced through it cursorily and passed it to Sylvestra.

| |Tailor and McQuinton,| | sang Phatheeo. | |Their ship is berthed at Hangar Fourteen in Freet-See,| | he continued. | |They grabbed a hopper back there two days ago and are still there with their other four crewmates.| |

Dammit! Why didn't I think of this sooner? She met her captain's eyes, keeping her outward composure in the presence of her subordinates. | |Tailor and McQuinton returned to Freet-See, but what about Lezàl? Did he leave? He might be running, maybe not with them, but on some other ship. Notify Freet-See right away. Ask them to scan their outgoing off-planet flight lists for the last two days for Lezàl. He's got a long head start on us.| | Whether Freet-See cooperated was out of her control, but she had to go on record for trying. If anything, she might later use their lack of cooperation to force a policy change.

Phatheeo and the officer nodded and walked out as Sylvestra slumped onto a perch. *If I could get Lezàl and the others at the same time, I could probably clear this whole mess up in less than an hour.* She sighed. *Then I'd still have the entire case to work out without a single lead. Some days you just can't win.*

WEARING the head-sleeve she had fashioned, Hassera stared at the landing pad and cursed. Another ship sat berthed where the *Stardust IV* had been days ago. *My failure alerted them and they took off,* she realized. *Ship* had told her as much, that the *Stardust IV* had relocated—not departed, thank goodness—but *Ship* didn't know where. Still, Hassera had to confirm visually. Considering the circumstances, Tailor could have worked with the port to doctor the berthing data, hiding the ship from the port's public registry. But in this case, they had truly relocated.

Hassera considered her next steps as she returned to her ship. She was sure the new location had to be noted somewhere; ports were not in the habit of hiding ships from themselves. She decided the time had come to let *Ship* poke around a little and see what it could find. She had been willing to play with her prey, but that had backfired on her in multiple ways. That wasn't her strength; it was the strength of other mercs. Her strength was information, and that's what she needed now. With Harry G four days out, she had to move quickly.

Freet-See port would require a slow, methodical hack. They might eventually figure out that they'd been hacked. But Hassera expected to be long gone by then. She only allocated a fraction of *Ship's* processing to that task.

Another avenue existed that Freet-See had no power over, a ubiquitous source of public data that most citizens were barely aware of: p-comms. She allocated *Ship* to sifting—and hacking, if necessary—through every p-comm that came in range for any media that matched the crew of the *Stardust IV*. Using positional data for each hit, *Ship* would easily generate a cluster map which should reveal the location of the ship.

Within minutes, a short list appeared on her screen. Using voice recordings of the crew, *Ship* had found one voice match along with five physical recognition hits. Hassera created a new window for the map and watched the hit-locations appear as the list continued to grow. She reviewed and rejected some anomalies. After an hour, one recording caught her eye. *Ship's* comment for the recording noted, "Vocalization of 'Jeremy Tailor'." Someone had actually said Tailor's name aloud.

Hassera brought up that recording and played it.

HANGAR 14's blast doors were sealed. Jim had made sure of that before they'd taken off for their demo tests. If he'd learned nothing else from Kormèr, he'd learned to make sure no one could sneak onto their landing pad while they weren't paying attention. No one wanted another firefight now, not with the negotiations at stake.

With Cheerretee over, Jeremy and Kit were getting ready to head back to Birshetland to work out the schedule for the demo with the client's team. If all worked out as expected, they would escort the team back to Hangar 14 for the demo within a day or two.

Sitting on the ship's quiet bridge, Jim perused a tech journal, though his mind frequently drifted to thoughts of home. Almost everyone had someone waiting for them back on Earth. But no one knew that Jim had proposed to his girlfriend of two years, just three weeks before the Io fiasco. Her name was Wilhelmina Richardson, but she preferred Billie. The guys knew her, of course, but they had no idea he was engaged. And now he only yearned to be back home with her. But if this deal worked out, they would really have a celebration when he did.

A chime filled the bridge. Someone had come too close to the hangar doors. It had happened often enough that Jim ignored the chime. But when it happened again, he glanced at the scanner display and spotted the heat signatures of two figures standing outside the door. The scan labeled them as Averians. One reached out and hit the intercom just as Jeremy walked onto the bridge.

//*Freet-See police,*// sang the Averian face that appeared on the screen. The birdman held up a medallion. //*Officer Rroochee. I'm looking for Jeremy Tailor.*//

"How's that for timing?" said Jeremy. He moved into camera view and activated the comm. | |Speaking. What can I help you with, officer?| |

//*The Birshetland department is searching for Kormèr Lezàl. Would you happen to know his whereabouts?*//

Jeremy gave Jim an irked look. | |I haven't seen him in a few days. What's this about?| |

//*Would you mind if we came inside and looked about your ship?*//

| |As a matter of fact, I would mind. We've already answered questions for the Birshetland police, and we've paid our fines. My business partner and I are headed back to Birshetland, so I want you to understand this and report it back to your superiors: any further harassment of me or the crew of this ship, and I will get a lawyer.| |

//*Ah, yes, sir. We meant no offence, but we had to ask. High sky.*//

Jim closed the connection and watched Jeremy stare silently at the blank screen. "Whatcha thinkin'?"

Jeremy looked at him. "I'm just thinking about Kormèr. The kid's up to his eyeballs in something, but I can't tell if it's good or bad. He seems to think it's alright, but I'm..." He shook his head and took a deep breath. "I wish there was something we could do to help him, but we've got enough to worry about right now."

Kit appeared at the hatchway. "All set?" Then he must've noticed the dour mood, as he asked, "What's on, then?"

Jeremy briefly related his conversation with the police.

Kit nodded. "I like the kid, Jer, but it's not our problem. Our hopper's leaving in thirty minutes."

"Alright. Fine." Jeremy took a deep breath, held it and released it, along with his tension. "I'm ready. Let's go."

THE playback of the recording ended, leaving Hassera considering her next moves. *What an interesting and unexpected development; Tailor and McQuinton are returning to Birshetland. But also, the police are after Lezàl.* This was not good. Maybe they wanted him as a witness to the event in the hotel. He had seen her and could identify her. She hissed angrily. This was a definite kink in her plans. But this was her job, and she'd long learned to turn kinks into opportunities.

The police were looking for Lezàl here in Freet-See. But that didn't mean he was actually here. She instructed *Ship* to alter the search parameters to include the name Kormèr Lezàl and to search the planetary cloud network. She didn't have any images of Lezàl, so the search would either take longer or result in nothing. She would give the search two hours, then she'd leave for Birshetland as well.

THE first thing he noticed was the silence. His mind reeled. Where was the chant? He needed that chant! He thrashed around in search of the chant until he exhausted himself and passed out again.

The first thing he noticed when he again awoke was the darkness. But he dealt with this better, only tossing about until, exhausted, he stopped tossing about.

He lay still for some time, letting shock subside and logic take over.

Where was he?

Bad start. He couldn't even begin to guess that.

Who was he?

Yes, that was much better. Who, indeed? Lezàl. Kormèr Lezàl!

But what difference does it make? taunted his thoughts. *The chant and the light are all that matter.*

He breathed hard to control his thoughts, such tempting thoughts.

<<There is no light,>> he said aloud, in Elmarian, and the sound of his voice surprised him, but also reassured him. <<There is no chant. There is only me and the darkness.>>

His mind surrendered, and the memories flowed back in.

He had been watching the raising ceremony when… something had happened to him. Kormèr was intrigued, but distraught. He didn't like the idea of losing control, particularly to something he couldn't see and that hadn't even been directed at him. *By the gods, it was just a bunch of Averians chanting! Just chanting!*

He wondered if there was anything he could have done to prevent himself from succumbing so easily. He would just have to be more aware of things next time, be more prepared to fend off such an indirect mental attack. If doing so was even possible. *Srrcheel tried to warn me to stay away, didn't he?*

Kormèr's stomach growled as hunger suddenly and furtively asserted itself. And with it came a thirst unlike anything he'd ever experienced before. As the fog lifted from his mind, parts of his body were waking up to the current reality: he'd likely missed a few meals while entranced.

He rolled onto his belly and felt around for his lamp, but couldn't find it. Maybe, like the soup bowl, it vanished when its power source ran out. So he crawled through the dark, with no way of knowing if he was headed in the right direction. He didn't remember flipping onto his back; he barely remembered thrashing about. After a minute he came to the edge of the mesh on which he lay, and realized he'd gone the wrong way. He turned, cautiously, as the drop to the floor below had to be twenty meters, and crept back. A few minutes later, he felt the familiar edges of the walkway that opened onto the mesh. His leg cramped, and he flopped off the mesh. Then he stood and hobbled in circles until his leg stopped aching. Finally, he brushed himself off cursorily, assuming he was covered in dust; it was too dark to see. Then he made his way, slowly, back through the secret passages to his room. By the dim light of the magic lamp, he immediately noticed the note sitting on the bed. It could only be from Srrcheel, as it read:

||*Kormèr, where are you? When you get this, come to my room.*||

Kormèr frowned, worried. Just how long had he been entranced? He stuffed the note in his pocket and slipped back through the secret door.

Kormèr rushed through the secret corridors until he reached Srrcheel's room. He activated the interface, and a red flashing icon indicated that the two-way comm was open. The screen came to life, revealing the young Averian sitting at his desk, reading a book, and tapping his talons on the desktop.

||Hi, Srrcheel.||

||KL!|| Srrcheel's head snapped up, his silvery eyes darting about excitedly. ||You're alright?||

||Yes. How are you?||

Srrcheel ignored the question. ||Where have you been? I've been picking at my pinfeathers with worry. After the raising, I was sure you would come to congratulate me, or provide some commentary.||

||I'm sorry about that,|| Kormèr sang, touched by Srrcheel's genuine concern. ||I must have passed out or... or something during the ceremony; wild stuff happened there.||

||To an outsider, perhaps,|| Srrcheel sang. ||I warned you, of course. But when I didn't hear from you for two days—||

Kormèr coughed. "Two days!" he cried in Terran English.

Srrcheel must've heard the shouted words through the wall, for he stared directly in Kormèr's direction. "Are you... in the wall?" he asked, using Terran English, as Kormèr had.

"Two days," repeated Kormèr, his mind reeling. *Buomp! Sylvestra must be going crazy trying to find me by now. I hope no one's been arrested on my account. I hope Jeremy and the guys are okay.*

"Kormèr?"

"Hmm?" answered Kormèr, absently. "Oh. I've got to get back to— Congratulations, by the way."

"Thank you. I made these during the ceremony." He held up a pair of round-framed black glasses for Kormèr to see. "They're regular sunglasses during the day, but at night, they let you see as if it were daytime."

"Night-vision glasses! That's great!"

"You can have them, if you'd like. I'll slip them under the door to your room."

"Wow! Thanks. What do I owe you?"

Srrcheel's brow feathers rose speculatively. "Owe? You don't owe me anything. It's a gift."

Kormèr was a little stunned. While he sensed that Srrcheel wasn't rigidly parsimonious, Kormèr could tell from his new friend's austere room that Srrcheel lived ascetically, but that didn't mean that he didn't deserve some kind of repayment or compensation. "Really? But won't you get in trouble for giving them away? What about the rules?"

Srrcheel grinned and shrugged, his wings popping over his shoulders as he did. "What no one knows can't hurt me, right? Besides, the point of the creation ritual is to share the object, to symbolize that magic is a service to others."

Kormèr smiled, the gesture lost on Srrcheel. "Thanks," he said again. "Hopefully, no one will ask you what you did with your glasses."

Srrcheel smiled. "No one will ask, as the gifting is a private matter. You said that you had to get back?"

"Uh… Oh, yes. I've got to get back to Birshetland as soon as possible. I've stayed here far longer than I had intended."

"Than anyone expected, certainly," Srrcheel said bemusedly. "Will you return?" he asked with a tinge of trepidation.

"I wasn't sure you'd welcome me back."

"Well, that's an entirely different matter, isn't it? All I'm saying is, if you haven't tired of my company, it's easier for you to visit me, than for me to go to you. Most of us don't go out unless we are called for."

"I'll call for you then," said Kormèr.

Srrcheel laughed, the sound a light, happy mix of chittering chirps. "Okay. Sure."

"I'll see you soon, then."

"Yes, soon. Blue skies, friend."

"High skies to you, too."

Kormèr shut down the interface and wound his way back to his room. As Srrcheel had promised, the glasses sat on the floor just inside the door, the glossy black frames and lenses almost invisible in the shadows. He grabbed them and tried them on, but enough ambient light entered from the window that they operated just like regular sunglasses. Kormèr ducked back into the secret passage, and there the glasses made the corridor as clear as day! *By the gods! They really work! Srrcheel, you're a genius!*

He returned to his room and sealed the secret door. Then he slipped the glasses into his pocket, grabbed the cube, and opened the portal. He stared at it and wondered where to go first. He really needed to get in touch with Sylvestra; he had promised her he'd stay in town after all. Of course, he'd lied about that, but he hadn't intended on being away long enough for anyone to notice. But his clothes were a wreck. In his bespelled stupor, he'd sweated and picked up layers of dust and soot while creeping and crawling around the secret passages of the Hovel.

Bath first. He pictured his hotel room and stepped through the portal.

Kormèr stripped his clothes off too quickly, and a wave of nausea overcame him. He fell against the bathroom wall, just managing to catch himself with his hands before hitting his head. Then he closed his eyes and breathed deeply for a minute before the nausea subsided. He was still thirsty and starving… *Dammit! Too many things to do, and not enough time.*

He finished stripping off his clothes, more slowly this time, then slipped into the hot bath and submerged himself. The stinging water revitalized him, and he popped his head back out and drank a good amount of fresh water directly from the bath spigot.

After a few minutes, he felt stable enough to wash up.

As he dried and dressed himself, he considered his next move. Before leaving the Hovel, he had planned to portal directly to Sylvestra's home, much as he had done with Srrcheel. Since he'd never been to her home, it would require that same tricky focus with the portal to not show up in the wrong time or when she wasn't home.

In the end, he abandoned this terrible idea, not because of the difficulties with the portal, but because Yunzen had raised him to understand proper etiquette, especially around respecting personal boundaries. Kormèr knew he wouldn't want anyone portaling unexpectedly into his home; why would Sylvestra be any different? And thinking back, Srrcheel hadn't seemed thrilled about Kormèr showing up uninvited, either. *Scratch that idea, then.*

The difficulty was that he wanted to speak with her in private, without the entire precinct, but any attempt to arrange a meeting with her—or even approach her—would most likely end in disaster: certainly no chance of a personal conversation, and probably culminating with his arrest.

In the end, he had no choice. He grabbed a scrap of flim and wrote briefly: *Meet me where we first met, at 8pm. And please come alone; I just want to talk.* He recognized the uselessness of being cryptic; Sylvestra would bring backup she wanted, regardless of how he wrote his message. But he also didn't want to be obvious, in case someone intercepted the message; either she'd understand it or she wouldn't. *What've I got to lose? I've probably ruined my chances with her, anyway.*

Using his room screen, he ran a search for her contact info, not expecting to actually get a hit beyond the general precinct number. His jaw nearly dropped in surprise when her contact details appeared on the screen. Without wasting another moment, he sent his message to her.

SYLVESTRA switched off the connection with Phatheeo in the den. She walked languidly, her tail feathers swaying from side to side, as she made her way to the living room. Word had just arrived that Tailor and McQuinton were on their way from Freet-See. That was potentially good news; if Lezàl truly had close ties with them, that meant that he might still be on-planet.

Freet-See had come through with the request for departure records. The precinct's system was scanning the records at that very moment. So far, it hadn't found anything irregular. That was unfortunate, but not wholly unexpected; Lezàl had bypassed the scanners getting onto the planet, after all.

Also, Mister Reestee had finally returned and examined the gems she had collected from Lezàl. While he'd been greatly impressed with their quality, he'd admitted that they were not from his store. Reestee's validation essentially cleared

Lezàl of the robbery and landed the case back where she had started: with no clues, no evidence, and no suspects. Lezàl still had to account for leaving town when Sylvestra had asked him to stay, but his wandering off had no relevance to her case.

Sylvestra sighed. This would not look good on her record, and her lack of progress would only provide more ammunition to her detractors. *What if they're right, and I'm not ready?*

Her self-soothing urges intensified when she felt distressed or vulnerable, as she did now. Rather than pick at her feathers, she settled onto one of the padded perches and rocked on it gently, the easy sway calming her nerves. She let her mind drift and imagined strong arms embracing her now, a warm, broad chest to rest her head against, a companionship to support her in times of trouble—

A chime announced a new message arriving in her work inbox. It had originated at the Cheerees. | |Open new message,| | she sang, surprised at the warble in her voice, as well as the drumming of her heart, as she read the terse message.

She hailed Phatheeo on her p-comm, and sang before he could announce himself: | |He's back!| |

Within thirty minutes, Sylvestra stood perched on a branch high above the entrance to Chees. Hidden on other branches, forming a perimeter, sat several of her officers, all ready to swoop down the moment she gave the signal. Lezàl would not be getting away again.

WALKING along the promenade, his hands in his pockets, Kormèr felt anxious. He knew he was walking into a potential ambush. His imagination ran wild with ideal scenarios where Sylvestra would meet him alone or dismiss her officers once she realized his sincerity. One or two of those ended with their kissing. He couldn't help it—he was young, but still smart enough to know his abysmal odds of winning over Sylvestra. Still, he had to try, or he would regret his cowardice. Even if she didn't believe him, at least he would've given it his best effort. *Nothing ventured, nothing gained,* he had heard Jeremy say once or twice.

Why am I even doing this? he asked himself. *Why does it matter?* He pondered the question, thinking back to all that had happened over the past month, since he'd accidentally traveled to Io and fallen in with Jeremy and his crew. He had nothing to hide—at least nothing regarding the Chees robbery or the incident at Cheerees—and they couldn't have evidence against him, if he hadn't done anything wrong! They could try to charge him with something minor, though, hoping it would lead to something bigger, and Kormèr didn't like the idea of having any kind of criminal record, even one on another planet in his far distant future.

Besides, *she* would think he was guilty. *She already thinks you're guilty, you dope.* Maybe she did, but he couldn't compound that by running. He had to explain things to her… maybe even explain the portal. He shook his head, his instinct rejecting the idea immediately. Could he do it? *Should* he do it? Would it even help?

Help what?

Help her like me!

Why is that important?

It is important to me.

Why?

Because! He clenched his fists in his pockets.

Because what?

Because I really like her! A lot! And I want to know more about her, from her, without her looking at me like I'm a criminal.

He stopped, brow furrowed and breathing heavy. He'd never felt so impassioned before. It was reckless. But it was exactly where he wanted to be. And he knew he could pull this off. He'd pulled off robberies that were much more complex and higher risk than this. It made no sense that this should cause him to "freak out", as the Terran expression went. He took a deep breath and let it out slowly, feeling the stress flow out with it. He relaxed his hands and brow, straightened up, and walked on.

He had dined with Feestoo earlier and filled him in on most of what had been happening, minus the portal.

| | You know about her situation then, | | Feestoo had sung. When Kormèr had shrugged, Feestoo had explained Sylvestra's precarious position within the police force and how this case would likely determine her future.

Kormèr had been mulling over that nugget of knowledge for the past two hours. He still didn't know how that would work itself into his conversation with Sylvestra, or if he should mention it at all. He knew better than to admit to knowing of someone's vulnerabilities.

When he arrived at the meeting location, she wasn't there yet. He checked his p-comm and found that he had ten minutes until eight. Ten minutes to wait. And then, after that, as long as his hope held out.

THERE were few things Sylvestra hated more than a failed stakeout, and she knew she wasn't alone. She sensed the disappointment in her team. Not only had it wasted the team's time, it had also been boring. Adding 'fruitless' to the equation compounded the frustration. With the time being over thirty minutes past eight, they had all resigned to the likelihood that Lezàl would not show.

| | I don't understand, | | she murmured, looking across the promenade from left to right. She had come down to stand by the storefront just before eight, hoping to draw Lezàl out. She'd even had three officers go to the hotel to catch him there, but they hadn't seen him.

//*He must've gotten wind of us, ma'am,*// twittered an officer over the open comm.

201

She nodded. | | It sure seems that way, | | she mumbled to herself. She clicked on her hidden mike, which would carry her voice to the rest of the team. | | Ten more minutes. Then I'm calling it. | | When twelve minutes passed, she reluctantly keyed her mike again. | | Alright, that's it. We're done here. Sorry, folks; no action tonight. | | She waited for the whispered grumbles over mikes "accidentally" left open, and was surprised when none came. | | I'll take care of the report, | | she added, for the sake of the other senior officer on the scene.

/ / Are you sure? I have no problem—/ /

| | It's alright. This was my operation. I'm going to go straight home, so I'll just write it up there. | |

/ / Alright. Thanks, Chief. Have a good night./ /

| | You too; all of you. Thanks for coming out.

Knowing the positions of her small team, Sylvestra watched the six of them soar away. Then she sent Phatheeo a quick text: */ / It was a bust. Lezàl never showed./ /* She left it at that. They'd talk about it in the morning.

She took a last look around, hoping that if Lezàl truly had noticed her team, he might now come out of hiding. When another two minutes passed, she finally gave up. With a disgusted huff, she spread her wings, took a few running steps and took off toward home.

Thoughts of Lezàl occupied her mind. Why had he asked to meet if he hadn't intended on showing? Or, if he had intended to show, why hadn't he? What had spooked him off?

Better yet, she thought to herself, *why do you want him so badly for what's really just a minor infraction?*

Because… because I still think he's involved… somehow, dammit. I just can't figure out how.

Do you? Or do you just want him to be?

Hey! Whose side are you on?

She cut short her internal dialog as she swooped under a branch. Just below, she recognized the promenade where she'd run into Lezàl in the bath. And there, seated on the edge of the bath, was Lezàl. He tilted his head back, as some smaller children in the bath splashed water at him, and spotted her. He waved, then turned back to speak with the children and splash them with water.

'Meet me where we first met'! The public bath!

Sylvestra circled, chiding herself for thinking of the jewelry store first and also wondering if she should stop to call for backup. *He's a young man, alone and hopefully unarmed.* There were children present, too, so he wasn't likely to cause trouble in front of them—he wasn't the type.

She landed three meters from him, and immediately put her hand on the stunner on her belt. Lezàl's socks sat atop his shoes, which were neatly positioned beside him. His trousers were rolled up to his knees, and his legs dangled over the edge and into the bath water. The boy and girl in the bath—siblings by the look of them—giggled and peered around Lezàl to look her way. The boy, who seemed the older of the two, disappeared behind Lezàl again while the girl smiled at her and waved.

Sylvestra stepped to the side so she could get a clear view of the children. | |Okay, little ones, it's time to finish up and go home. I'm here on official police business with this young man.| |

| |Is he in trouble?| | asked the girl.

| |He is.| |

| |Go ahead,| | Lezàl sang to them. | |Thank you for keeping me company.| |

| |It was nice meeting you,| | sang the boy, stepped up out of the bath.

| |Nice meeting you!| | chirped the girl, following her brother. They shook off any excess water, then after a couple of false starts, the girl leaped away, followed by her brother.

Lezàl splashed his feet as he watched them go. | |You probably take that for granted, but that's just absolutely amazing to me.| |

What was he talking about? | |Flight?| | she asked.

He turned and looked up at her with his wide, brown eyes. | |You see! You do take it for granted. I've never encountered another species that can fly.| |

Sylvestra stared at him, her intentions momentarily derailed by his casual banter. Then she firmed up her posture and chirped, | |Mister Lezàl, you failed to comply with my order to remain in the city. For that infraction and for lying about your identity, you are under arrest.| |

He nodded. | |Alright, though I have not lied about my identity.| | But he made no other move.

| |Will you please step out of the bath?| | she suggested.

Lezàl looked down at his feet, then back up at her. | |Not yet.| |

| |So you're adding resisting arrest to your charges?| |

Kormèr watched her carefully. | |I'm surrendering to you… right here and now. You can see that, right?| |

She didn't answer immediately. Why had he arranged the meeting at all, if he knew she'd arrest him? | |Is that so?| |

| |Yes. I need to explain… I want to tell you the truth about myself. I need for you to listen to me. That's why I came here—| | He stopped and looked at her. | |I'm not under arrest for the robbery?| |

She sized him up. *I can jump him; I have the training and the arm strength to pin him easily to the floor. But then what? He's offering free information; I may not have any way to verify it right now, but he just might reveal something useful or incriminating.* Better to keep him talking, while he was willing. She kept her right hand over her stunner. The recorder in her badge was already capturing the audio and video of the proceedings, along with various other readings, such as heart rate and thermal. | |Tell me your story, Mister Lezàl, or whatever your name is. But be aware that anything you say can and will be used against you.| |

| |Thanks for letting me know that.| |

Sylvestra cringed inside. *Why does he have to be so damn pleasant?!*

| |I have to begin with one important thing,| | he continued, | |or nothing else will make any sense at all.| | Sylvestra tensed as he reached slowly toward his shoes, her fingers gripping the stunner, ready to draw. But then he merely plucked something that had been sitting atop his socks. | |I expected you'd be jumpy about me reaching for things in my pocket,| | he sang, | |so I left this here.| | She saw that he held a cube made of perfectly clear crystal, except for one black face. | |Watch.| | He looked around, then set the cube on the ground and let it go. The cube glowed and then appeared to vanish for a fraction of a second before it bloomed silently into a glowing sky-blue rectangle.

Sylvestra struggled not to get distracted by the strange device and lose sight of Lezàl. But she'd never seen anything like it before, and its alienness demanded attention. | |Some kind of trick or illusion?| | she asked.

| |I'm not that good,| | he smiled.

| |What, then? Magic?| | she scoffed.

She caught his shrug out of the corner of her eye and immediately focused on him again. | |Maybe,| | he sang. | |It's not anything I understand, that's for sure. I'm pretty sure it wasn't created on Elmar either. But what it is isn't as important as what it does.| | He lifted his legs out of the water. | |I'm going to stand now,| | he announced, and did so, all the while with his arms out to the sides. | |Now I'm going to get one of my shoes,| | he sang, and did so as well. | |Now this device you see is a portal… a doorway to other places. Right now, it isn't open anywhere. But let's say I wanted to go to the other side of the bath.| | He pointed at the bath with his shoe, then slowly raised the shoe to point across to the other side. | |All I have to do is picture it, and…| |

Sylvestra nearly screamed when another portal snapped open exactly where he pointed. Before she could react, Lezàl lobbed his shoe over the bath, and it sailed into the portal there.

Plunk.

She jumped back a meter, her stunner out and pointed roughly toward the noise. Her wide eyes assessed the scene: Lezàl hadn't moved; his first portal hadn't moved. But lying on the ground between her and that first portal was his thrown shoe.

| |Sorry; I didn't mean to startle you. Would you like to see that again?| | he asked.

She did want to see it again, because it didn't make any sense, and she knew there had to be a trick. But she was just as astonished when he repeated the stunt, and his second shoe landed on top of the first. *You can't just conjure doorways from nowhere… from glass cubes and… and… What in the heavens?!* As if to prove that it could function under stress, her brain suddenly made a connection. | |That's how you vanished the night we met here,| | she chirped, too loudly.

| |Now, *that* I am guilty of.| | His grin slipped. | |Hey, if you don't mind, I'm going to shut them down. I really don't want other people to see this. You can imagine how dangerous it could be in the wrong hands.| |

| |And your hands are the right ones?| | she sang, as he did something that closed the first portal and reverted it to the cube form. When it shut, the second portal vanished instantly.

| |I don't know about that,| | he sang. He picked up his shoes, dropped the cube inside one of them, and draped the socks back over them.. | |But I can imagine there are worse.| | Then he sat at the bath's edge again, but hugged his half-covered legs against his chest.

Sylvestra clipped the stunner back onto her belt. Seeing that he was in no rush to go, she walked around the bath and sat on its edge across from Lezàl. | |So, how does my knowing about the portal clear anything up? You realize that this implicates you in several potential infractions. Is that thing even legal?| |

| |I'll answer those in reverse. Umm… As far as I know, I have the only one, so its legality is suspect; yes; and knowing about it will help when I explain how I met Jeremy and how I am *the* Kormèr Lezàl.| |

She couldn't help but smile at the absurdity of the situation. | |Please, go right ahead.| | *Give it your best shot, kid.*

As he told her his story, the smile slipped from her face, and she realized why he'd wanted to show her the portal first. He had been right; if she hadn't seen it operate, she would have imagined him to be the craziest person she'd ever met. She hardly knew what to say when he was done. She blurted the first idiotic thing that came to mind. | |You're centuries old.| |

Lezàl tilted his head. | |I'm only three and a half. You get that I hopped here from the past, right?| |

She nodded. | |Yes, but…| | She pictured him at the end of an elastic rope, stretched across time and just hanging on with his talons before the elastic snapped him back to his own time. | |Never mind.| | But she had one glaring question that needed an answer. | |You could have gone back to Elmar at any time over the past three days and come back here after this case had been resolved.| | He nodded, confirming her statement. | |Why haven't you?| |

Emotions crossed his face too quickly for her to follow. | |I made a promise to a friend,| | he sang quickly, but she had the feeling there was more. Then, finally, he added, | |And because you— because I suspect you need help with this case.| | Something must've crossed her face, because he quickly defended with, | |Look, you're right: I am a thief. Not *this* thief, but at home where circumstances are… different. So consider me a subject matter expert.| |

That nagging feeling returned, the one that she always had when thinking about this case. She focused on it, and it told her: *He's right. You'll never solve this one alone.* She rebuked herself, *Shut up!* But after furrowing her brow in deep thought at him for an uncomfortable moment, she grudgingly accepted that he could be useful. *No alarms, no witnesses, no clues. His insight could prove valuable.*

When a few seconds passed without her reply, he sang: ||I'll make a deal with you, Sylvestra Chrreel. Don't arrest me now, and I'll catch the thief for you.||

||What keeps you from just disappearing on me, if things go wrong?||

||Trust. Like you said, I could've run off at any time these past few days.|| She nodded. ||Besides, I don't want... I mean... I can't have someone as beautiful as you thinking vile things of me.||

Her eyes widened and locked on his. *What did he mean by that?*

As if he could read her mind, he continued: ||Sorry. I didn't mean to say it like that. But there is this code that forbids one thief to turn on another.||

||My father used to say that, but... What code can there be among criminals?||

||We have our own form of honor; it prevents... let's say, misunderstandings,|| he sang. ||We are not of a low class with no dignity or social graces. There is law outside of *your* law, and that is one of ours.||

||Then you are breaking your own law?|| she chirped, half understanding his point.

||Yes,|| he replied solemnly.

||Why?||

Lezàl hesitated, then blurted, ||For you. Because since the day I first saw you at Chees, I haven't stopped thinking about you. Your eyes were then—and still are—like moons in my night, and your crest the stars. I would never, ever do this for any other. Only for you, Sylvestra.|| His eyes were alight, his voice firm and yet gentle, like a firm hand delicately handling a flower.

Sylvestra was speechless, torn between her duty that compelled her to arrest him while she still had her chance, and by the emotions stirred by the earnest, tender words of this young male. *He is young, isn't he? And yet...* Despite his physical age, he didn't seem that much younger than her; in fact, he behaved older than some males of her own age. She saw his eyes searching her face, waiting for a response.

But how could she respond? Sylvestra was unused to male flattery, especially from non-Averians, and from Kormèr Lezàl, it was a singular experience. She was thankful that he was just looking at her face, as on her neck and back, her shorter feathers were on edge with excitement. She calmed her breathing with an effort, but she recognized the hormonal responses within her body that were harder to suppress.

When she spoke again, her voice was lower, huskier than she wanted it to be. ||I think we should continue this discussion in the morning, in my office.|| In a more professional space, she would be more comfortable, more composed. She told herself that she could use his apparent infatuation to her advantage—but that would only work if she didn't let herself get swayed.

||I don't think so,|| he sang, as he slipped on his socks and shoes. ||Not your office or the precinct.||

Sylvestra stood and walked back around the bath. ||Where then?||

He stood with an effortless grace, his eyes level with hers. | | I'll find *you* tomorrow. | | He took a few steps toward her. | | Is there anything else you'd like? | | he asked in a near-whisper.

| | Yes, | | she answered as she looked into his richly brown eyes. She extended her hand. | | Shake, as a gesture of goodwill toward the deal. No promises, though. | |

Kormèr smiled wryly as he reached out and took her hand in his. The touch sent a shiver through her, though she had no conscious idea why.

| | Good night, | | he sang to her, as he let her hand go.

As he backed away, she inhaled deeply, as if for the first time in hours. | | Don't make me regret this, | | she heard herself say, and felt annoyed with herself for saying it. More softly she added, | | And good night to you, too. | |

He turned and walked away, fading into the shadows as he neared the edge of the promenade. She lifted her hand to scratch her delicate nose and smelled his faint cologne on it, and the way it mixed with her own subtle perfume. She shook her head to clear it of the mingled scents, as she spread her wings and continued her flight home. But the blend of colognes followed her to bed and even into her dreams that night.

MANY minutes passed before Kormèr's heart settled down into its normal rhythm. He had spilled his heart out for Sylvestra, and so far, she hadn't smashed it. She had shown up late, but it hadn't been so late that he'd worried... too much, anyway. And bonus, he'd gotten to hold her hand. He smiled at the memory.

The real trick was yet to come: actually solving the crime. That had been his eleventh-hour idea, to help Sylvestra with her tenuous circumstances. Kormèr's insides churned at this, the very concept going contrary to what Yunzen taught him: a thief must never betray another thief. Many thieves knew each other, Devron being a prime example. And thieves frequently had bounties on their heads. If thieves turned on each other for bounties, for spite, or simply for competitive reasons, the entire system would fall apart. Kormèr had enough common sense to acknowledge the flaws in this imperfect honor system: a thief would absolutely turn on another if under duress in some inescapable or dire way, like having a loved one or family being threatened.

But he knew his situation was hardly dire, yet he was prepared to labor night and day to prove his feelings for this woman by betraying a fellow thief. *Feelings? What are my feelings toward Sylvestra? I certainly like her a lot. She's clearly intelligent, and beautiful goes without saying.* He could envision taking her to all the wondrous places he had visited throughout the universe, showing her his home and seeing hers, and then deciding together where they wanted to live... Together. *Yes, I would happily live with her, wherever she wanted to be.* He paused there, questioning if he'd really give up on Elmar to come and live on Averia. It was certainly a beautiful and unusually peaceful planet. But could he honestly imagine leaving Elmar forever? *You'll always have the portal, silly. You can just pop back home whenever you're feeling homesick.* That was true enough. *Maybe I can make this work out!*

Once Kormèr got back to his hotel room, he set to work immediately.

Kormèr's first attempt at breaking into Chees was straightforward, simple, and detected instantly. Even before he stepped out of the portal into the empty jewelry store, he realized that the cube's opening had set off the motion detectors.

Kormèr's second attempt got him as far as the front door, but not without a surprise. Once he reached the door, light flooded the street from powerful flood lamps around the store. He'd never seen this kind of security system before. <<Buomp!>> he cursed, blinded by the intense light, and stepped back through the portal.

Safely in his hotel room, he dropped the cube in his coat pocket and paced, thinking about everything at once, but about nothing in particular. His thoughts moved through a morass of drowsy frustration for nearly twenty minutes, until the need for sleep finally bubbled up to the surface. He didn't even realize that the room's light was off and that, as he flopped onto the warm, giving bed, he was still wearing Srrcheel's night-vision glasses.

AFTER two hours with no new results, Hassera gave *Ship* another hour of search time, and her patience rewarded her. Someone on Freet-See had received a message from a Birshetland police officer stating that she would be on stakeout duty that evening and wouldn't make her dinner appointment. Though she wasn't supposed to say, she revealed that their target was an offworlder named Lezàl. This confirmed Hassera's suspicion that Lezàl was not on Freet-See.

Already set to leave for Birshetland, Hassera sealed *Ship* and headed for the sky-hopper port. She breathed deeply, savoring the cool evening air, especially after all the days she'd spent inside her ship. But mostly she enjoyed the anonymity of the night, particularly now as the darkness helped to obscure her healing scar. She knew of only one city on another planet whose inhabitants recreated full daylight during the night hours. Everywhere else, lights illuminated streets, but only just enough, as if there were something sacred about the night that it should not be banished completely.

Cheerretee was two nights gone now, but Hassera noted that few ships had actually left. Either the tourists had come for extended stays or had combined business and leisure, coming for the festivities but staying longer for business reasons. Considering Averia only had one resort city open to non-Averians, Hassera found it odd that anyone would want to come here for leisure. She had been to other planets that she had found more suitable for such activities.

She slowed her pace as she spotted someone exit their ship. Even at this time of night, a few beings still moved about the streets, but this one specifically caught her attention when it stopped at the bottom of the ramp, and the ship's lights revealed the creature's telltale smooth, blue skin. *An Aggreyate!*

Hassera cursed her obsession with Lezàl. It had distracted her. She should have been aware of Aggreyates on-planet, more so since she knew well how Harry G operated: never send in one merc when two or more will have a better chance. The real problem right now was that Aggreyates always worked in pairs, so where was the—

A noise behind her, and she realized too late that she'd been ambushed. Because of the damned hood, she'd been unaware of someone sneaking up behind her. She stopped, as the Aggreyate by the ship made no pretense of staring right at her.

"What do you want, Aggreyate?" she said to the one she knew was behind her.

"Just a friendly chat," came the silky male voice from behind her. "Professional to professional, yes?"

Hassera turned slowly until she met the yellowish eyes of the Aggreyate behind her. He had no visible weapon, but with an Aggreyate, that didn't matter. And she knew that partnering with them would provide her with the resource she desperately needed: muscle. And despite their naturally enhanced senses, she was certain that they could benefit from her particular expertise. They only needed to reach that mutual agreement. "Yes," she said. "Let's chat."

CHAPTER 17

SYLVESTRA'S cloud-white feathers glowed pearlescent in the shimmer of sunlight reflected off the thin, metal leaves of the surrounding trees. She stood on the edge of her balcony, ready to leap into the wind and glide off to work. She lifted her arms, extending her snow-white wings, catching the breezes and—

She checked herself to keep from smacking into the taxi that swooped down in front of her, glad that she hadn't already leaped from the edge. Her crest fluffed irritably, as she prepared to issue a citation or warning to the driver for the reckless maneuver, and it did not subside when the passenger door opened to reveal Kormèr Lezàl's boyish grin.

||Good morning,|| he chirruped happily, his eyes bright. ||Would you like a ride?||

||You don't know where I'm going,|| she returned, more reservedly.

||At this hour, I presume you're going to the precinct?||

She hesitated, unsure of whether to smile or frown, to follow instinct or logic. *Decide, one way or the other; you look like a fool just standing there.* She accepted the offer, but instead of taking the proffered seat next to him, she took the seat across from Lezàl and closed the door. ||You looked up where I live?||

||It's public information,|| he chirped, then frowned. ||Is that a problem?||

Her crest feathers settled smoothly back into place as the taxi pulled away. ||The information is not a problem—it's what you do with it. I don't know about where you come from, but here on Averia, people don't appreciate having visitors swoop by, unannounced.|| His expression showed surprise and a little chagrin. *He's used to going wherever he wants, especially using that magical doorway of his.* She had to ask: ||You haven't gone into my apartment, have you?||

His eyes went wide. ||No! Technically, I *could*, but I would never do that.||

She sighed, thinking of the security screens she would have to install in her apartment; it was a nuisance, but a necessary one. She didn't keep many valuables in her home, but her privacy was priceless. ||*Technically*, as a thief, don't you usually go where you're not welcome, by definition? With your doorway, I don't imagine that anyone could stop you.||

||If you'll accept my word, I promise I won't violate your trust.|| Her hesitation must've shown on her face because he chirped contritely: ||I'm sorry; I didn't intend to alarm you by telling you about the portal. If it helps, the portal

really only allows direct access to places I've visited before, or that I can picture clearly in my head.||

||It's fine,|| she chirped curtly, preferring to talk about something else. ||Forget it.||

He looked at her, uncertainly. ||Okay,|| he whistled finally. ||Then I hate to jump directly to business, but the ride to the precinct is short.|| She nodded. ||Have you decided?||

About what? Then she recalled their conversation the night before. ||About accepting your offer of help on the Chees case? I've been thinking about it, but I don't know if we can accept your offer, just like that.||

He seemed disappointed. ||Why is that?||

||Because it's just not done,|| she cheeped, exasperated. ||We don't ask for civilian assistance on cases.||

||There must be exceptions. What if you need an expert in the field? What about the Berdians? You called *them* in on this.||

She stared at him. ||How do you know about that?||

||I have a friend in the Hovel. That's actually where I was the last few days.|| Her crest feathers perked involuntarily at his reminder that he had defied her order to remain in Birshetland. ||I'm sorry about leaving town,|| he chirped hurriedly, ||but I had promised him I'd be there for his raising ceremony.||

Sylvestra was skeptical about his excuse. ||You were in the Hovel, for a raising.|| He nodded, seeming pleased with himself. ||Since they don't allow outsiders to attend their ceremonies, I assume you used the portal to sneak into the Hovel.||

||I wouldn't say 'sneak'...|| he started.

||Fine, so you used your portal to *steal* your way into the Hovel,|| she returned. ||Yes, that's much better.||

||There was no harm done,|| he defended himself, looking surprised by her reaction.

Is he trying to impress me? In fact, his accomplishment impressed her, but she didn't want to reward his selfish behavior or encourage more of the same. ||Had you ever visited the Hovel before?|| She knew the odds of that were slim, as the sorcerers of Berdia rarely allowed outsiders to visit, and almost never offworlders.

||Before the raising? Never,|| he admitted.

Sylvestra was torn between her personal distrust of Lezàl, and her determination to solve the case, even if she had to resort to unconventional means. ||I still don't trust you,|| she finally chirped.

||Why not?|| he asked, with an innocent confusion in his brown eyes.

Sylvestra had interrogated her share of charming and baby-faced criminals, but Kormèr didn't set off the usual warning bells in her head; he was a thief, but he was also still young, so maybe he could still turn his life around, with a little guidance. ||I'll tell you why: you said before, that you can only access places that you've visited before, or that you can picture clearly in your head. Yet, you reached the Hovel, despite never having been there before. So, if you can enter the Hovel uninvited, what's to stop you from going into my apartment?||

||A fair question,|| he replied without missing a beat. ||Because I wouldn't violate your trust like that,|| he chirped solemnly. ||I'm not sure what else I can say to convince you.||

She shook her head. ||You can't convince me with words, only actions. So, on behalf of my department, I'm going to accept your offer, conditionally: allowing for difficulties, you have seven days to solve the crime and find the thief.||

||Excellent!|| he warbled, relief in his voice. ||Seven days from now, you'll have your thief in cuffs.||

She smiled tightly. *Or perhaps you, if you're lying.*

The driver cleared his throat, interrupting her thoughts. ||Almost there,|| he warbled.

As the taxi slowed, Kormèr sang, ||By the way, when you step in there, you'll probably hear about two alarm incidents at Chees.||

||Last night?|| she asked, stopping herself from clenching her jaw. ||You acted before you got my consent?||

Kormèr swallowed. ||Yeah. Maybe that wasn't the wisest move, but I had to test the waters, to see what I was up against.||

The taxi stopped and Sylvestra got out. She turned back to face him squarely. ||Seven days as of last night then, Lezàl,|| she twittered, then closed the door and walked toward the precinct entrance. She heard the taxi pull away behind her, and her immediate instinct urged her to get a squad car after it immediately. But she had accepted his offer of help, so he deserved a chance to prove himself. *Not that he would wait for permission to forge ahead, anyway.*

The light clicked on automatically when she stepped into her office. She climbed onto her perch and opened both her email and the case file. As Lezàl had promised, a report of the two alarm incidents had been added to the case file. She noted with curiosity that one attempt had set off the internal alarms. *Probably used that magical doorway,* she decided.

Phatheeo knocked on the door frame. ||Bright skies, Chief.||

||I wouldn't know,|| she answered absently, ||I took a taxi today.||

||Huh?||

She looked up, startled. ||Oh… nothing. Just preoccupied. How're you?||

||Fine,|| he sang, but something in Phatheeo's posture made her pay closer attention. He looked like he was about to say more, but it was stuck in his throat.

||Come in a minute. And close the door.||

He did so, looking at her expectantly.

||Sit,|| she chittered, laughing. ||You look like a schoolboy outside the principal's office. Relax. What's on your mind?||

Phatheeo sat. ||Sylvee, I… I'm considering retiring.|| He sighed.

Her eyes went wide. ||I guess I should've expected this sooner or later. I was just hoping for later, I guess.||

||Believe me, it hasn't been an easy decision. But your dad was the last holdout from the old days besides me. I look around now and… I just feel… I dunno, old, I guess. I've got a few good years left, and I want to enjoy 'em with the grandkids and the old lady.||

Sylvestra smiled. ||I understand completely. You don't need to justify yourself to me.||

Phatheeo laughed nervously. ||I'm not just rambling for you. I have to convince myself, too. I've been doing police work all my life. Never thought much about this day, about not having to do the work anymore. It's as big a step in my life as when I chose to go into the business.||

Sylvestra nodded. ||Theeo, you've been invaluable to me since I got this position. You've been a confidant, an advisor, and a good friend. I don't suppose that you have anyone in mind to *try* and replace you?||

He smiled at her emphasis on 'try'. ||As a matter of fact, two candidates come to mind. May I?|| He used Sylvestra's desktop screen to bring up two files.

||Sergeants Tseeo and Freesewee,|| read Sylvestra.

||Freesewee's a new transfer from Freet-See. Very promising. He'd outgrown his position there, so they figured his talents would be more useful here. Tseeo… well, you know him. Headstrong, but bright and resourceful. Good tactician.|| Phatheeo's voice and expression gave nothing away regarding his leaning.

||You're not making this easy for me.||

||Hey, they're my shoes,|| he chirped, and they both laughed.

Sylvestra sat back, going over her thoughts in the momentary break in conversation. ||Lezàl is innocent.||

||Yes, he apparently is.|| He sighed. ||Which puts us back to square one.||

||Not entirely.|| Sylvestra fretted over what she was about to do. But if she couldn't tell Phatheeo, she shouldn't have made the deal to begin with. ||I made a deal with him: he promised to solve the robbery and deliver the thief within a week.||

Phatheeo's scowl caused his white brow feathers to pinch. ||A deal with a devil. The boy may not be the thief we're looking for, but he's still a thief. I can feel it in my pinfeathers.||

||I know, but that may be the skill set we're missing here. He might spot something that we're not seeing.|| She added, again with hesitation: ||He has a talent for getting into places where others can't.||

||That's what a thief does,|| Phatheeo replied.

||He managed to get in and out of the Hovel without getting caught,|| she chirped quietly. ||Name me anyone in our department that could do the same.||

Phatheeo grimaced, but his silence conceded to her point. ||You said you made a deal. What's your end of the bargain?||

Sylvestra recounted her conversations with Lezàl. She had to focus on remembering what she had said, as most of what she recalled were his words, his awkward attempts to flirt and impress... *My stupid hormones had me almost receptive, too.* | | He didn't ask for anything. Let's see if he's able to make any progress, first. | |

Phatheeo mulled over that and finally shrugged. | | What's done is done. We'll see if you were right in seven days. | |

| | Six, technically, | | she replied. | | Last night's alarms at Chees were his doing, from testing the alarm system, so we can write those off. | |

| | Last night. When did you make this deal with him? | |

| | I spoke to him last evening, after the stakeout ended, | | she admitted. | | I agreed to the bargain this morning. | |

| | You've spoken to him twice since last evening? | | Phatheeo looked at Sylvestra with paternal concern. | | Maybe I'm being too hasty in deciding to retire. | |

Sylvestra shot him a wry grin. | | Stop. I know what I'm doing. | |

She kept her confident smile in place, as she watched her captain leave her office, but Sylvestra felt less certain. She was potentially risking her career in agreeing to let Kormèr Lezàl consult for them, but there was something else weighing on her mind.

Phatheeo's question had reminded her that she hadn't offered anything in return for Kormèr's help. Kormèr's offer to solve her case for her had been so audacious... *Actions, not words.* She recalled the exchange more clearly now. *He's doing this to gain my trust?* If he succeeded, then what?

| | A deal with a devil, | | she crooned to herself, recalling Phatheeo's words, then shook her feathers to release the tension in her shoulders and neck. *If* Kormèr managed to do the near-impossible and uphold his end of the bargain, then she would have to give something in return. Until then, she had nothing to worry about. At least, not from Kormèr Lezàl.

FEESTOO sang a long *wheeoo* and followed it up with: | | I can't believe that just happened. I've seen you do a bunch of outrageous things, but that one... that's... | | He shook his head, at a loss for what else to say. During the ride to Sylvestra's, Kormèr had filled Feestoo in on the meeting he had had with her the night before.

Kormèr had been hoping that Sylvestra would accept his offer, but he had been preparing himself for the possibility of her rejection—on every level. Kormèr slumped in his seat, letting his pent-up tension drain out of him. | | I'll admit that I wasn't sure until just now, that she'd accept. | |

Feestoo grinned. | | It sounded like a serious interview. I wasn't sure you'd be able to answer to her satisfaction. | |

| | It felt like an interrogation, | | Kormèr replied. | | But that was important to her, maybe so she could start trusting me. | |

| | To be sure, | | Feestoo whistled. | | As long as you're not launching yourself from too high a branch. Do you really think you can solve the case? | |

A wave of icy dread washed over him. | | I hope so. | | He could only offer his hope, as he really did not know whether he could pull it off. The idea had come to him on the spur of the moment during his conversation with Sylvestra at the bath. He hadn't had time to think it through at all, and now he wondered if he hadn't over-promised.

He also wasn't used to anyone asking him about the portal in such detail. He was still learning his way around using the portal, what he could and couldn't do, and where he could and couldn't go, and Sylvestra's pointed questions had momentarily stumped him. All he could provide were his best guesses, informed by his own experience.

| | So do I. I'm rooting for you, KL. | |

Kormèr smiled. | | Thanks, friend. I appreciate that. Let's go back to the hotel for breakfast today. I'm not in the mood to eat out this morning. | |

STANDING just inside the door of their empty meeting room, Kit waited for Jeremy to finish his very pointed call with the meeting arbiter. No one had shown up to the meeting, nor had anyone let Jeremy or Kit know this in advance. Kit knew that would not be as politic as Jeremy, had he been the one on the line.

"I see," said Jeremy, leaning back against the conference table's edge. "Well, as I said, we would really appreciate a call if this happens again. Professional courtesy, you understand? Right. Thank you." He slapped the comm off and looked at Kit with eyes that looked ready to shoot lasers. "A 'town hall' meeting," he huffed. "I can't... I'm just..." He shook his head.

"It's like they're toying with us," offered Kit.

"I swear that it's like Harry G has reached across space and is messing with us."

Kit shrugged. "He just might be. So what now? Do we pick up again tomorrow?"

Jeremy walked over. "That's what they said. C'mon. Let's get out of here. I'm so sick of this room."

"Probably a good thing there was no one to order bagels," said Kit as they walked.

"Yeah; I feel like I've gained two kilos since we got here." He grinned and huffed with amusement. "Breakfast?"

"You buying?"

"Jeremy! Kit!" cried a familiar voice as they passed through the lobby on their way to the atrium restaurants. They turned and found Kormèr coming toward them with his taxi driver.

"KL! What a coincidence!" said Jeremy, and he clasped shoulders with the boy. "Hi, Feestoo."

| | Hello, sirs, | |

Turning back to Kormèr, Jeremy said, "You've got a lot of explaining to do, kid."

215

Kormèr grinned sheepishly. "I'll bet. Are you guys hungry? I was just ordering breakfast delivered to my room."

Jeremy looked at Kit, who shrugged. "Sure," he said for both of them.

"Alright," Kormèr smiled. "Place your orders, and we'll head up."

Jeremy gave Kormèr a cursory glance as they walked toward his room. Despite not having crossed paths in the past few days, Jeremy sensed that Kormèr hadn't really missed their company much. The boy seemed unaffected by the lack of non-Averian company and seemed at home among the birdfolk and their curious ways.

"How've you guys been?" asked Kormèr, after a moment of walking in silence.

"We've been better, kid," grumbled Kit.

Kormèr turned on his heel and walked backwards to keep them in view. "That doesn't sound good," he frowned. "The negotiations?"

"Among other things," Jeremy rejoined.

"C'mon in," offered Kormèr when they arrived at his room. ||Oh, Feestoo, are you okay with Terran English? I don't want to be rude.||

Feestoo shrugged his wings. "I is good to hear English. Speak not good." Switching to Averian, he sang, ||I could use the practice, but you may speak however you're comfortable.||

"How've you been?" asked Jeremy, entering the room and looking around. He immediately noticed the extra wardrobe closet that had definitely not been there before.

"Better question: what the hell've you been up to?" asked Kit, entering behind Jeremy.

"Uh…," Kormèr closed the door. "I've been busy on a project for the local police precinct."

"A project? The guys said something about you being a suspect."

Kormèr hopped onto a desktop. "Oh, that was just a misunderstanding."

More softly, Jeremy asked, "Kid, what's going on? What kind of trouble are you in?" Jeremy glanced inquiringly toward Feestoo, bobbing his head subtly in the birdman's direction.

Kormèr smiled at Jeremy's subtle cue of distrust. "Feestoo knows the whole story; I filled him in already. But I haven't seen you guys in days, so let me bring you up to date."

Kormèr explained all that had happened since he'd last seen them, with Feestoo reminding him of minor details along the way. He paused only when the breakfast carts came and then again when Jeremy stopped him, briefly, at his mention of the sabotage of their room screen. Jeremy asked for details on the saboteur, which Kormèr provided.

"G's got only a few reptilians working for him," said Kit between bites. "But from your description, that one sounded like a Suslixan. And there's only one of those we've ever seen."

216

"Hassera," said Jeremy. "Royland's partner."

At Kormèr's blank look, Jeremy added, "When Harry G first approached us, he had two people with him: his bodyguard, Royland, who was a species we'd never seen before; and Hassera, a Suslixan data specialist."

"Guess whose ship you commandeered," said Kit.

Kormèr's face took on the same haunted look he'd had when they first found him in the Y-Tach wreckage. His gaze unfocused, he echoed, "A species you'd never seen before." He looked up at Kit and murmured, "Royland was the guy that… in the umbilical."

Mouth full, Kit pointed at Kormèr with his fork and finished chewing. "That explains why Hassera's pissed off."

"Speaking of which," said Jeremy, "I remember how bad you felt about spacing Royland. Well, it turns out that you didn't do it." Kormèr stared blankly at Jeremy. Knowing the kid needed to hear this bit of good news, he continued: "While sprucing up the ship for the demo, Morgan discovered a log of a firewall breach from weeks ago. Turns out they only got away with some security logs, but those logs show that someone triggered the emergency disconnect from *our* ship."

Kormèr's jaw dropped slowly as the information sank in. "I didn't kill him?" His eyes went wide with stunned relief. "I didn't kill him!"

Jeremy nodded. "That's right, kid. Whether on purpose or by accident, his own crew did him in."

"Bloody mercs," mumbled Kit.

With renewed animus, Kormèr continued his recap.

||Wait… you've been to Berdia?|| asked Feestoo.

"Ah, yes." Something about the way the kid had answered piqued Jeremy's curiosity. Kormèr continued, saying, "That's why I didn't want to say where I was going; I know there's a lot of superstition around the sorcerers." He chuckled. "Almp thinks they can turn you into droppings, just for talking to them. But the one I met is actually quite nice." Suddenly he changed the topic, as if realizing he was on a topic he wanted to get away from. "Anyway, I just sealed the deal with the chief of police this morning."

"'Sealed the deal'?" Kit grinned wryly, with a wriggle of his brow.

Jeremy elbowed Kit sharply for his not-so-subtle innuendo and pushed up his glasses. "The guys said you were a suspect, but I had no idea. They actually blamed *you* for the crime, even though you weren't around?"

"They're desperate to find someone to blame." Kormèr sighed. "But like I said, that's all been cleared up now. I just have to figure out how it was actually done and by whom."

"How? It's supposed to be an impossible crime," commented Kit.

"Well, a lot about Kormèr seems pretty 'impossible', too," Jeremy said, shaking his head. "At your age, I was just getting into the nitty-gritty of computers at home, never even dreaming of doing the things you're doing."

Kit added, "Doesn't it ever seem to you like you're missing out on your childhood?" He quickly held out his hand, palm out, forestalling Kormèr's reaction. "I mean… well, take this as you will, but you don't act like a typical kid; more like an adult."

Kormèr thought about this for a moment. "You're the second one today to say something like that. If you're asking me whether I'm unhappy or wish I was just like every other kid, playing games with friends and all that, then I have to answer no. I've traveled to so many places and met so many people that I've never had time to think, 'gee, I'd really like to be doing something else, like sitting at home, alone.'"

Jeremy seized on Kormèr's remark, but let the boy continue: "Besides, to me life is sort of like a game: it has its rules and strategies, which you can follow to try to win, but there's always a chance you can still lose; if you try to break or finesse the rules, who knows what will happen?" He shrugged. "Maybe it's immature and irresponsible to think that way, but it's worked for me so far."

"I guess I just can't see it from your shoes, KL," said Kit, then sat back and sipped his coffee. "You've lived a charmed life, to have survived this long."

Kormèr beamed. "I suppose I have. I see and learn so much, make friends wherever I go, and I try to enjoy myself. I try to become a better person, and make life better for the people who befriend me. I honestly couldn't ask for more." He shrugged. "My choices aren't for everyone, but…what's that expression? Ah, yeah: 'be true to yourself.'"

Kormèr's words struck a chord with Jeremy and reminded him of his own cynicism, forged over years of hardship and disappointment. For all his experience, Kormèr was still just a kid, but his rosy view of life reminded Jeremy that his own worldview had skewed too far the other way. He had been so focused on getting his technology working, and keeping his friends alive, that he had lost sight of why he had worked so hard, and had become so exhausted and worn out by the struggle that he just wanted it all to be over: *I just want that damn contract signed.* That was the most important goal, right now. Jeremy owed his team that much.

Kit grinned, oblivious to Jeremy's inner monologue. "KL, you're the weirdest freaking kid I've ever met. And I'm glad to know ya."

Feestoo wiped his mouth and got up off his perch. ||Gentlemen, I have to go make a show of working,|| he sang with a grin. ||Thanks for breakfast, KL. High sky, everyone.||

When the hotel room door closed after Feestoo, Kormèr said, "I didn't think you'd want to talk about it in front of Feestoo, so I didn't ask. But what's got you guys looking so flustered?"

Jeremy glanced at Kit and found him glancing at him. Jeremy turned to Kormèr and explained the unexpected delays in the negotiations, just when they were ready to demo the ship.

"Sorry to hear about that," said Kormèr. "I wish I could help you with that."

"Kid, we can't be any more in your debt than we already are," said Kit.

Jeremy suddenly remembered the look Kormèr got when Feestoo mentioned Berdia. That reminded him that Kormèr had never explained a few details. "What is your secret, anyway? You never did tell us."

"My secret?"

"Yeah, you know, your story. Where you're from, and how you got to Io?"

"Oh yeah. I forgot all about that." Kormèr chuckled. "It's also a bit of a big deal, so I don't like telling people about it, but you've earned my trust, I guess." He paused to collect his thoughts. "Alright, so… I have this cube—"

Kit's p-comm chimed, and he tapped to check the message. "Now that's odd."

"What?" asked Jeremy. He glanced at Kormèr and saw the relief on the boy's face, so he didn't feel too bad about not hearing the kid's "big deal" secret just yet.

"It's Mack," said Kit, then read from his p-comm. "The guys have been split up, and he suspects something might be up."

Jeremy felt the hair on his neck prickle. "Split up, how? Where are they?"

"Jim and Mo got called away to settle a billing issue with the port. And Mack says the port notified them that all ships are being inspected and cleaned for a contaminant that's affecting the port, so he and Roke just evacuated." Kit stood and moved toward the door while speaking into his p-comm. "Mack, stay put and we'll be there as soon as we can."

"Good." Jeremy stood. "Hey, KL, I'm sorry but we—"

"Guys, wait," said Kormèr. "Let's go this way."

Jeremy turned to find Kormèr pointing at a floating blue rectangle that was suddenly beside him. "*This* is my secret," he said.

It looked like a door or a mirror. But it floated. And it was brilliant blue throughout, like an ocean or sky. "What am I looking at… exactly?"

"An interdimensional portal. Keep your mind focused on Mack or the hangar the *Stardust IV* is in as you step inside."

Kit shook his head, glancing at Jeremy. "We don't have time for games, kid."

"I don't play games, remember," said Kormèr, and vanished into the cerulean void.

"Holy shite!" cried Kit. He stepped up to the portal and poked the surface, his finger sinking through the blue and leaving a misty swirl in its wake. He turned to Jeremy and shrugged. "What have we got to lose?" he asked and then followed Kormèr through.

Jeremy closed his mouth. "I can't believe I'm doing this," he said to no one. Picturing Mack and Hangar 14, he stepped into the portal.

Jeremy's brain took a moment to adjust to what his eyes were seeing. A moment ago, he'd been standing in Kormèr's room in Birshetland. Now, the pungent odors of starship fuel, coolants and lubricants, as well as the massive orange blast doors of Hangar 14, assailed his senses and told him he was in Freet-See. *But I can't possibly be!* He turned to see where he'd come from, and he found

219

that impossible blue doorway staring back at him. An arm reached up from the right edge of his vision, did something, and the doorway vanished.

Jeremy's gaze slipped to the right, and Kormèr Lezàl smiled at him. "You okay?"

Jeremy nodded mutely and snapped out of his daze at the sound of approaching footsteps.

"Kit?" That sounded like Mack. But Mack hadn't been with them in Birshetland. How could he be... *You're in Freet-See, man. Catch the hell up.*

Jeremy turned and found Kit patting Mack on the arm, with Roke right alongside. "You just left me a message from Birshetland," said Mack. "How the hell did you get here so fast?"

"We've got the kid to thank," said Jeremy, hooking a thumb at Kormèr.

Kormèr waved at them sheepishly. "Hi, guys."

"But I'll explain later," Jeremy said, forestalling questions. "First things first: what's the status?"

Mack handed Jeremy a sheet of flim displaying an official-looking document. Jeremy skimmed the orders, which required crews to leave their ships so that scan teams could deploy their devices. "It looks official, but my gut tells me it's a fake," said Mack.

Jeremy couldn't tell either. "Damn that Morgan's away, too. Very convenient."

"Did you see the team?" asked Kit.

Roke shook his head, his loose hair swinging freely. "Naw, man. The police escorted us off the ship, and the scan team came in after us."

"The police didn't stay inside the hangar with you?" Jeremy asked. "Or say when you could go back aboard?"

Mack turned. "What? They didn't—" With a deep rumble, the hangar doors slid ponderously closed.

Jeremy's p-comm chimed, and everyone turned to look at him as he checked the display. "It's from the ship," he announced, with a deep frown. "Whoever's aboard just locked all the hatches." He felt both dejected and furious that the enemy was trying to take their ship—again—and might actually succeed this time. But what could the team do?

"Only three?" said Kormèr, not even looking in Jeremy's direction, clearly in his own world. "Where are they located?"

"Ah, what's Kormèr doin'?" asked Roke.

Jeremy absently looked at Roke, not really having heard his question, but merely because the man had spoken. But now he also saw Kit looking past him, at Kormèr, who had one hand covering his left ear and the other grasping a cube of clear crystal. *Damned if I know.*

"We'll be coming into the berths," Kormèr said to no one in the immediate area, "so warn me if they head that way." He focused on Roke, then slid his gaze to Mack, then the rest. "Guys, there are three mercs aboard. They've searched the ship, and one stayed in the hold while two are on the bridge. *Stardust* doesn't have any gas left, so she can't knock them out again."

"Who are you talking to, kid?" Jeremy blinked, then realized: "Are you talking to the ship?"

Kormèr tugged a comm pod from his ear. "Yeah, sorry. I guess I should've mentioned that." He tucked the comm pod back into his ear, then held a second one out to Mack. "Mack, I feel that you're just the man for this op."

"'Op'?" He looked uncertainly at Jeremy, his dark brow furrowed suspiciously, then back at Kormèr. "What are you talking about?"

"I'm going to open a doorway into the ship," Kormèr said, looking to Jeremy for validation. "Just like I got us here."

Using that crazy blue doorway?! Jeremy wanted to scream. He was still trying to figure out what had happened the first time, and now... What other option did they have? Jeremy felt himself nodding. "Mack, we have to trust him. This is the only chance we have to get our ship back."

"WE'RE coming in," Kormèr whispered to *Stardust*, as Mack stepped through the open portal. Jeremy and Kit followed, weapons drawn. Roke ruffled Kormèr's hair as he, too, stepped through.

Kormèr found the berthing cabin cramped when he stepped in. The space contained six berths, but was never intended to have everyone up and standing around at the same time. Just as Kormèr reached to close the portal, Mack tapped him on the forehead. Kormèr looked up at the imposing man, and Mack pointed at him, then at the portal, as if to send him back.

Kormèr shook his head.

Scowling, Mack brushed past everyone and back through the portal. Kormèr sighed and followed him.

Away from the others, Mack spoke freely. "You stay here. You're unarmed and have no business in there."

"Then give me a stunner."

"No. Stay. We've got this. In any op, someone's gotta guard the exfil path; that's you, kid."

Reluctantly, Kormèr nodded. He would've preferred to have a stunner. Mack gave him a half-grin, then stepped back through the portal. Kormèr listened, but Mack was too much of a pro to make any noise.

Not much foot traffic passed by Hangar 14, but Kormèr didn't want to take any chances that someone would spot the unusual glowing portal. He flipped it around so that the portal faced the blast doors. Then he leaned back against the doors and waited.

"How are things going?" Kormèr asked aloud.

Knowing that Kormèr couldn't be speaking to anyone else, *Stardust* responded: *The crew has incapacitated two intruders. One shot Roke. I am... I am fending off… The one on the bridge is skilled."* A moment of silence followed. *"She has sealed all my hatches. I can't override. She is slicing into the bridge systems…"*

Piercing static followed, and Kormèr yanked the pod from his ear. "Stardust?" he said, gingerly holding the pod near his ear, but screeching static was the only response.

The blast doors rumbled, and the *Stardust IV* roared overhead, arching gracefully into the sky.

<<Buomp!>> cried Kormèr, staring at the departing ship. With the hatches sealed, the crew would be locked out of the bridge. Without the AI to assist them, they didn't stand a chance. They'd be trapped in their own ship, no doubt headed for a rendezvous with Harry G.

Kormèr stared at the portal. *An exfil path isn't worth a damn if no one can get to it,* he thought, assuming that the hatch to the berthing area had also been locked. He could relocate the portal's exit to the ship's corridors, possibly giving the guys a chance to escape. But then what? He could relocate it again and have them charge the bridge. That would work.

He pictured the corridor where it turned toward the bridge, assuming that if the guys were anywhere, they'd be there trying to get onto the bridge.

This is adding up to a lot of assumptions. "Guys!" he yelled into the portal, knowing that sound passed through the portal just the same as matter. After a minute of no response, he grunted. "Sorry, Mack," he murmured, then he stuck his head through. Pressure immediately grabbed his head and twisted it painfully to the left.

Kormèr followed through with the motion until his head swing clear of the portal and back out into Freet-See. <<Vlaja naya!>> he cried, massaging his neck. He knew that feeling of pressure all too well, now that he understood ship functions. The ship acceleration ratio had overwhelmed the compensator, just like when he'd first boarded the ship at Io. *If the pilot is still at the controls, they'll be stuck in their seat. If I can get in there, and stay on my feet, I might be able to stop them. Or…*

No way. He looked up at the trail of the ship. *The pilot can't possibly be in control, right? Unless they can defy physics and can move effortlessly in that kind of inertia.* He clenched his fists, digging his nails into his palms. *Please, please, please, oh gods, let this work!*

Kormèr closed his eyes and pictured the bridge, specifically the space right behind the pilot's seat. He opened his eyes, turned the portal slightly, holding that image in his head. Then he thrust his arms through the portal. It was like punching into a thick mass. Jarring pain shot through the fingers of his left hand as they smashed into something. Wincing, Kormèr let his hand slide along the object. *Yes! That's it.* He found the edges with both hands, grabbed it, and yanked as hard as he could. Half of the pilot's seat teetered backwards through the portal, and the thrust from the ship pushed its occupant out of it and out of the portal right into Kormèr's stomach. Kormèr lost his grip on the seat and crashed to the ground with the merc on top of him. His breath knocked out of him, he still managed to wrench himself free and roll onto his knees. He stood, unsteadily, on the solid surface of Hangar 14, as the merc did the same.

"You must be Hassera," he groaned, finding the now-familiar reptilian staring back at him.

"Lezàl," she hissed, and drew a weapon on him.

Kormèr stared at the weapon. He'd had weapons pointed at him before, but never anything so potentially lethal. Was it set to stun or to kill? Would he even see the muzzle flash before it took his life? He took a few quick breaths to steady his voice. "I know why you're angry," he said to the weapon. He forced his eyes away from the weapon and up to the face of the woman holding it. And he felt sad and angry for her at the same time; he understood her pain and the absurd situation that had put her and... *What was his name? Ray? Boil? Roy... Royland!* "But we didn't do it," he told her. "I thought I had, by accident, and I regretted it, because it wasn't me. It wasn't any of us. It was his own men." *I really hope I'm making sense to her, because I'm just babbling the first thing that comes to mind.* "It was Harry G's men that retracted the umbilical while Royland was still in it."

Hassera tensed when Kormèr mentioned Royland, and Kormèr cringed. *This is it. I blew it.*

"Who are you?" she asked, her voice like fine-grit sandpaper rubbing against itself.

Crap. I assumed she understood Terran English. If she hasn't understood anything I've said... So he tried again. "My name is Kormèr Lezàl—"

"I know that!" she hissed, her voice a little clearer but odd, as if her mouth was not designed to form Terran English words. "But it's a lie. You don't exist. So who are you, *really?*" She didn't wait for him to answer. "You're no merc, and yet you have this tech." She flicked her free hand at the portal. "That can't have been cheap."

When she reminded him of the portal, he also remembered the ship, which was now pilotless.

"You heard what I said, right?" asked Kormèr, wondering if he could outrun her trigger finger and jump through the portal. But with the thrust pressure difference, he knew he would likely get flung back out.

"Lies from a liar."

Kormèr pointed skyward. "The ship has the evidence." Hassera blinked. "If it crashes—"

"It won't crash," she growled. "Now, shut up."

She hadn't shot him, and she appeared to be thinking things through rather than acting on emotion. So Kormèr kept quiet. After a moment, Hassera unsealed a pocket in her flight suit and pulled something out. "Take this," she said, and tossed a small black square at Kormèr. Kormèr caught it and found it to be a datachip. "Load your evidence onto it. But if you're lying, I will kill you the moment I see you again." She started backing away.

"Wait," said Kormèr, "how do I know where to send it?"

She pointed at the hand holding the chip, then when she reached the archway leading out of the hangar area, she turned and rushed off.

Kormèr exhaled, his shoulders slumping as the tension flowed out through his fingertips. *But the danger hasn't passed,* he thought, straightening up and looking at the seatback still protruding through the portal. He slipped Hassera's chip into his pocket and considered his next steps carefully.

He tried the earpod again, but it still screamed with static. He slid his hands along the sides of the pilot's seat and push them through the portal, again fighting the thrust pressure. Bracing himself, he gripped the bottom of the seat and used it to pull himself onto the seatback and into the bridge, head first. Even using the chair, it took all his arm strength to keep from sliding back out into Freet-See. His biceps screaming, he swung one leg out wide and catch the edge of the portal, sending it floating across the bridge, and leaving his body dangling off the back of the chair, now fully inside the bridge.

Finding a foothold on an open panel beneath the navigation station, he pushed himself onto the seat with one leg curled under him. When he pulled in the other leg, the seat rebalanced itself, leaving him upside down and facing the seatback. After another few minutes of gyrations, some of which felt as if he were dislocating several bones, he sat sweating and exhausted, but with his back firmly pressed into the back of the seat, and his butt in the right direction. In the center of the forward viewscreen sat Thencarree, the furthest of Averia's moons. Thrust vectors and other data indicated that the far side of the moon was the destination. In fact, the computer would execute a spin to decelerate in another three minutes.

"Stardust?" he groaned. No reply. "I'm guessing Hassera hacked you," he continued, hoping the AI might hear him, even if it couldn't respond. If he could barely move, he wondered how the rest of the crew was doing.

He racked his brain, trying to think of anything he'd learned from the edu-comp that might be useful in this scenario. While hacking had not been on the topic list, system failures had.

"The only thing I can think of is to restart you." *But the lessons didn't cover rebooting while in space and under thrust,* he thought, as his mind imagined any sealed hatch opening during the process, including exterior hatches. Had the system been programmed intelligently enough to cycle the airlocks as part of the process? It must have been; airlock hatches were designed not to open simultaneously. Why should a restart override that function?

The thrust he was less sure about. He tried to stop the engines, but the screens just buzzed at him, the pre-programmed course toward Thencarree locked in. Fortunately, kicking off the restart process comprised only two fairly simple steps: open the panel and hit the restart button. In this high-tech ship, none of the digital screens could be trusted during a system malfunction. Only the simple mechanical action of a button.

Forward thrust cut, and the lateral jets fired, spinning the ship clockwise. Taking advantage of the momentary lack of thrust, Kormèr reached for the panel release and bumped into something. *What is that?* Kormèr craned his neck and spotted a small device protruding from an input port. He grabbed it and yanked it out of the port. The ship completed its spin, and Kormèr sank into his seat as the thrusters kicked in again, now decelerating the ship.

"Stardust?"

Electronic static shot from the bridge speakers, but quickly settled into a low buzzing hum. A trebly voice squeaked in just above the hum. *"Restart. Now."*

With a renewed burst of energy, Kormèr fought the pressure, hit the panel release, and mashed the reset button. The engine burn ended instantly. The bridge went silent and nearly dark, illuminated only by the blue glow of the open portal. Kormèr swallowed his heart, remembering when the bridge of the Y-Tach had done the same. After a moment, he felt secure enough to stand and close the portal. Of course, that had the effect of immediately plunging the bridge into full darkness. Kormèr found the pilot's seat, sat and held his legs curled up to his chest. At least this time, he had the cube in hand, literally. Worst-case scenario, he could make an easy escape.

After what felt like hours to Kormèr, the forward viewscreen flashed once and remained glowing a dark gray. The low whir of the blowers followed as the environmental system came online. Kormèr inhaled deeply, the tension once again flowing from him as he exhaled. The bridge screens ran through their restart sequences, also flashing to dark gray, then displaying their startup parameters before settling into their normal displays and patterns. The forward viewscreen cleared, and once again showed the moon, along with a portion of the rear of the ship.

"Hello, Kormèr."

Kormèr smiled. "Stardust! You're alright!"

"I am, thank you. The slicer had invaded nearly my entire executing code. The restart wiped it out and reloaded my base code."

"Slicer." Kormèr held up the small device he had pulled from the data port. "Is that what this is?"

"Yes. If you hadn't removed it when you performed the restart, it would simply have taken over again."

"That would've been terrible," said Kormèr, trying to not imagine being in the same situation after the restart. "You're okay now, right?"

"Yes, thank you for asking," Stardust replied, then paused. *"The crew doesn't talk to me much."*

Kormèr felt sorry for *Stardust*, as the ship reminded him of his bots at home. Machines or not, if they were designed for self-intelligent learning, they thrived on interaction and conversation. "Aw. Maybe if we have a chat with them, we can figure something out."

"I would like that."

"Speaking of which, how are they—"

The bridge hatch whooshed open, and Kormèr spun in his seat to find Mack aiming a stunner at him before recognition lit his eyes. Mack lowered his hand slowly, muttering: "What the hell?"

Jeremy appeared from behind Mack. He had blood on his forehead that had run down the side of his face, and spots of blood speckled his shirt. When he spotted Kormèr, he shouted a bark-like laugh and shoved past Mack onto the bridge. He grabbed Kormèr around the shoulders and tousled his hair roughly.

Still sore and bruised from his fight with Hassera, Kormèr grimaced but didn't cry out. "Please stop that," he protested weakly, pushing Jeremy's hand away from his head. *Oww.*

"You did it again," Jeremy grinned. "You used your portal to get in here and save our ship."

Kormèr could only see the bright red streak of blood on Jeremy's head. "What happened to you?" He pointed. "Are you alright?"

"Yeah, yeah," Jeremy said, wiping his sleeve across his head. "It's just a bump from hitting the wall."

Mack stepped onto the bridge behind Jeremy, his eyes taking everything in, the stunner still in his hand, though aimed at the floor. "We got lucky that we made it to the mess when the ship took off."

Kormèr recalled the earlier status that he had received from *Stardust*. "How's Roke? I heard he was hit."

"How'd you know that?" asked Mack.

"Stardust told me." At Mack and Jeremy's blank stares, he said: "You knew the ship had an AI, I thought?"

"An AI, sure," Mack said. "I didn't think it was always on. I mean… Did the ship ever talk to *you*?" he asked Jeremy, who shrugged.

A cool female voice announced over the speakers: *"Kormèr enabled my voice routines."*

"She has a voice," Jeremy beamed wondrously, looking around as if seeing his ship for the first time. "The sales rep had mentioned an AI function when we bought her. But it wasn't a selling point for us, so we never really thought about it. Then we got busy with the project."

"Who did you think was talking to you on the screens?"

Jeremy shrugged. "I knew it was the ship's computer, but I'd assumed they were programmed responses. Sorry for assuming… Stardust. Do you mind the name?" He exchanged a bewildered look with Mack, as all this seemed new to him, to both of them.

The ship replied, almost coyly: *"I like my name. Thank you for asking."*

"It's nice to finally meet you," Jeremy nodded. "Anyway… Roke, he's recovering," he said, leaning over the pilot's seat to read the displayed data. "It wasn't anything major; just lost a few fingers on his right hand."

"That's not major?!" asked Kormèr, shocked at Jeremy's blasé explanation.

"Nah. Couple of weeks of regen, and he'll be good as new." He tapped the comm. "Hey, Kit, come to the bridge. Freet-See's not happy with the way we left port, and we need to get back asap." He turned to Kormèr. "Sorry, kid. No flying this time. Slide over. You can fill us in on what you did during the return flight."

Kormèr moved to the co-pilot's seat as Jeremy took comms and Mack took navigation. A moment later, Kit strolled in and sat in the pilot's seat. As Kormèr watched, the team quickly assessed the situation and decided on a plan of action. While Jeremy communicated with Freet-See, Mack and Kit planned to use their current velocity and trajectory to slingshot around the moon Thencarree, and back to Averia.

While they worked on that, Kormèr worked with *Stardust* from the co-pilot's screen to find the evidence of Royland's demise. He needed to see it for himself, to know with utter certainty that it hadn't been his mistake that had cost a life. First, he watched the surveillance footage, then he read the control audit logs. He felt the relief all the way to his core, as the evidence confirmed his lack of culpability. *Still, the poor guy,* he thought. *Betrayed by his own people. No honor among mercs there.* Then he slipped the earpod in his ear; he needed to converse with *Stardust*, but didn't want to distract the guys from their important tasks.

"Stardust?" he said under his breath.

"Yes, Kormèr?"

"I need to transfer the data I just viewed onto a data chip, but I can't guarantee the chip is free of malicious software. Is there any way to gather the data into a sandbox and isolate the transfer?"

"Yes. I have just done this. The flashing port on your right is safe for transfer. But I must inform you that the chip you are carrying is emitting a transmission beacon."

"What's that?"

"It is a brief traceable transmission, and based on the small power source in the chip, capable of achieving a range of only twenty to thirty kilometers."

Kormèr didn't like the sound of that. "I see. Keep an eye... err, monitor that and let me know right away if there is any change in the beacon, as I load the data on the chip." Kormèr touched the chip to the flashing port.

"The data has been transferred," announced Stardust. *"There is no change in the transmission."*

"Good. Destroy the sandbox and keep monitoring the beacon."

"Understood."

Three hours passed before the *Stardust IV* once again settled into her berth in Hangar 14. Kormèr had used the time to explain how he'd extracted Hassera from the bridge. Mack had been impressed by the portal, but visibly displeased at the substantial risk Kormèr had taken.

Jeremy likewise had chastised Kormèr for putting his life on the line. But Kit only ruffled his hair, saying, "You've got more guts than many I've known in my time, kid."

As Kit took the ship into the hangar, *Stardust* told Kormèr, *"The beacon has fully activated and sent a burst transmission. It is now inactive."*

"Was it my data?"

"The transmission was encrypted. I cannot tell."

Kormèr pursed his lips, assuming that Hassera had set the chip to transmit any data it contained once it came within range. His instinct was to destroy the chip, but without being certain that the data had been transmitted, he didn't want to risk it. "Can I prevent further transmissions?"

"The chip can be shielded to prevent all transmissions."

"Perfect. Is there anything aboard that can act as a shielding material?"

"Yes. Locker six in the cargo hold has a Faraday bag that will work well for such a small transmitter."

"Thanks."

Kormèr looked out the forward viewscreen and saw Jim and Morgan waiting at the blast doors with Freet-See police.

"Alright," said Jeremy. "It's show time. The police'll probably want to review logs, so I've got those ready."

"I'm initiating a refuel," said Kit. "Freak'n Hassera burned through a good amount of it."

Deciding he would only be in everyone's way, and keeping well in mind that his days as a free man were numbered, Kormèr said, "You guys are going to be busy here, so if you don't need me, I'm going to head back to Birshetland."

Jeremy chewed on his lower lip. "We came up with a story to cover your involvement already, so we should be good." He paused. "I guess we don't have to ask how you're getting back."

"Good luck solving the case, KL," said Mack.

Kormèr nodded. "Thanks."

As they filed off the bridge, Kormèr opened the portal and stepped through.

MUSCLE had one major flaw: it didn't think. As crafty as its owner could be, muscle could only succumb to that one intrinsic truth. Aggreyate muscle had a fair bit of craftiness behind it, and Hassera had worked into the late hours with the merc duo to convince them of her loyalty to Harry G, and then to plan their theft of Tailor's ship. It was a simple plan: use a few corruptible local resources to create some distractions; split up the crew; slip onto the ship. There shouldn't even have been a need for muscle, had the plan worked.

The plan did work! she told herself. They had boarded the ship without any confrontation. With the hangar's blast door closed, the ship's ramp raised, and the ship found to be empty, they should have had plenty of time for Hassera to slice into the ship's systems and take control. She would have only needed twenty or thirty minutes.

Then the impossible had happened; someone had been hiding on board or had somehow boarded and caught the Aggreyates by complete surprise. The moment that Hassera had heard the weapons discharge, she had known that the time for delicate slicing had passed. She had jammed her brute-force tool into a socket under the pilot's console and let it hack and slash its way into the system. It could damage the code, but hopefully nothing that was of vital importance to Harry G. Once she had sealed the hatches, she'd taken off under heavy thrust, hoping that anyone making their way to the bridge would get crushed by the acceleration. If she could get to the far side of Thencarree, she could wait out Harry G's arrival there.

Then, once again, fate had intervened to ruin her plan. Kormèr Lezàl, with his impossible tech, had yanked her off the ship and back to Freet-See! How? Hassera did not know what he had used; she'd never encountered technology like that before, in all her years.

But all of that paled to insignificance, considering what Lezàl had revealed to her. *If it's true,* she told herself, not for the first time. She couldn't let herself believe the enigmatic young man without proof. So, while waiting for the evidence Lezàl had promised her, she had set *Ship* to once again review the collection of data from the moment of Royland's death. It was true that there had been heat signatures on both sides of the umbilical at the moment the decompression cycle had begun. She had seen that before, but it hadn't registered. Now, she had Ship analyze the heat signatures to determine their species, and whether the one aboard Tailor's ship could be Terl or one of Royland's other two crewmates. Or Tailor's crew. That was also a possibility she had to consider.

Unfortunately, after a short while, *Ship* reported that it could not reach a conclusion based on the available data. The crude system that had registered the heat signatures was designed to find targets, not for this data mining.

Hassera spent some time searching through her library of banned technology, hoping to find something resembling Lezàl's localized wormhole device. When that yielded nothing, she switched to black markets. But after a while, she realized she wasn't getting anywhere and, to be honest, her mind wasn't into the search, anyway. Niggling at the back of all her thoughts was the question of what she would do if Lezàl turned out to be telling the truth.

Being a mercenary came with certain caveats: more often than not, your employer lacked a moral compass; you often had to perform tasks that compromised—or at least tested and impinged on—your own set of ethics; once you took a job, you always completed it. The last was where her penchant for data mining and information came in handy; she always found out as much as she could about a job before taking it on. Her ethics had their limits, and these limits had been like Royland's. That was one reason they'd been drawn to each other, and why they'd both done their research into Harry G when they considered working for him.

Thus. she knew who she was working for when it came to Harry G. And all he wanted was Tailor's crew and their ship; nothing that compromised her ethics. And even if Lezàl's evidence proved that Royland's crewmates had killed him, that didn't necessarily implicate Harry G. But it would be enough for Hassera to begin digging. So she could complete the job, get paid, and then follow the data trail.

She realized she had lost track of time when *Ship* alerted her it had locked onto a beacon. The data transferred in seconds and the connection dropped to prevent tracing. She reviewed the beacon signature; she had a few of these chips in circulation, and while it was doubtful that any of the others would end up here, on Averia, she checked anyway. The signature matched the chip she'd given Lezàl.

He wasn't bluffing, then? Without reviewing the data herself, she couldn't be certain. So, with renewed focus, she began her analysis.

CHAPTER 16

STANDING on the promenade across the entrance from Chees, Kormèr casually watched the storefront while munching on seed-nut clusters he'd purchased from a street vendor. Through the storefront window, he saw the owner approach a customer, a young, nervous-looking Averian man. Cheert Reestee's feathers had lost their ivory sheen, and now seemed limpid, thinned even, but he was cheerful and welcoming to his humble-looking customer.

Kormèr's eyes drifted around the store's façade, studying the exterior. Sensor technology had certainly advanced over the centuries; they'd been difficult enough to spot in his time, but now he supposed anything could be a security sensor. *What do the robbers know about this place that let them bypass that crazy security?* He wrinkled his brow. *There's no getting close to the place without setting something off. If I even look at it funny, the damned thing'll either blind or deafen me.* He sighed. *The police must already be investigating former employees and disgruntled customers. If it were that easy, I certainly wouldn't have made the suspect list. So, the thief has to be someone… unusual or without an easily discernable connection to the shop or the owner.*

What are you doing? rebelled Kormèr's instinct, again forcing him to briefly face the fact that he was looking to break a cardinal rule. Why was he trying to solve this case? Why was he putting himself in this position of betraying his own code, of revealing some of his deepest secrets to… to law enforcement agents!? He imagined his father looking down at him and shaking his head.

But then his eyes fell on Cheert again, and Kormèr felt bad for the birdman. Kormèr only stole from those who sought advancement at the expense of others less fortunate. While he knew nothing of Cheert as a person, Kormèr very much doubted that this humble-looking Averian could have done anyone any harm. In fact, the jeweler's eyes lit up merrily when his young customer settled on a modest piece. It didn't seem to matter to Cheert that the selection wasn't extravagant, as long as the customer chose it with care and sentiment.

He seems like a nice man. He doesn't deserve to be robbed. As Kormèr considered the situation more, he felt more justified in his decision to help: if he solved the case, he would right a wrong, and surely, his father would not fault him for that!

And of course, there was the "Sylvestra factor". Kormèr was still very much infatuated with her, and things had gone so wrong with her from the start, that he felt a grand gesture was necessary—like solving this case for her—to redeem himself. He couldn't leave her with such a warped impression of him, regardless of whether he had any chance of winning her love. *Ever?* Somewhere in the back of his mind, he knew the answer was probably "no". But she would at least think better of him than she thought of him now. And that was important to him—certainly more important than some thieves' code.

The customer that Cheert had been helping left the store, giving Kormèr a sidelong glance as he walked past. Kormèr smiled in return, and the young birdman rushed on his way.

Kormèr upended the carton of seed clusters into his mouth, catching the last of the delicious crumbs while trying not to choke on an errant seed, then tossed the carton into a trash receptacle. He inhaled deeply and strode into the store.

It took Cheert a moment to realize he was there. ||Can I help you?|| he tweeted, his voice thin.

Kormèr shook his head. ||Just looking, for now. Thanks.|| He noticed that only a few display cases had any jewels in them.

Cheert didn't look up, he just stared down into the half-empty case before him, but Kormèr's lack of interest wasn't lost on him. ||I'm sorry. My inventory isn't what it used to be,|| he answered, wispily. ||That's if you're shopping in earnest. Let me know if you need anything.||

I guess I'm not the first here to play detective. ||Thank you, I will,|| chirped Kormèr, making a note of the few visible detectors, camera-eyes, sensors and the security control panel behind Cheert. *This is impossible! There isn't a spot in this place that isn't covered by some kind of device or another.*

Cheert just sighed loudly, presumably dispirited by the barrenness of his store.

Kormèr made as if he had dropped something and glanced around under the cases when he bent over. *Sensors here, too! Amazing! Not an inch is missed.*

When he straightened, he peered at the ceiling. *Solid! No way in, through vent or shaft.*

||Are you alright?||

Cheert was staring at him through tired, concerned eyes.

||Just something in my eye,|| Kormèr replied, winking at Cheert. ||Do you have a mirror? I still feel something in there.||

At that moment, an Averian couple walked in and began looking at the jewelry. Somewhat cheered by this, Cheert looked from them to Kormèr, then sang to the couple: ||I'll be with you in a moment.|| As Cheert turned to fetch a mirror, Kormèr studied the control panel and scanned the store once again. *I've got to be missing something. Someone successfully broke in here, dammit!*

||Sir?|| sang Cheert, suddenly behind him.

Kormèr spun and knocked into the proffered mirror, sending it shattering on the floor. <<Damn!>> he blurted. ||I'm sorry. Here, for your trouble.|| He pulled a tiny gem from his pocket and handed it to Cheert, who just stared at it sitting in the palm of his hand.

Kormèr picked up the four pieces of broken mirror and set them on the counter as the couple whisked past him. When he looked back, Kormèr saw that Cheert had moved on and was now busy with his new customers. Feeling completely daunted by what little he'd found, Kormèr dejectedly shuffled out of the store.

He wandered aimlessly along the promenades, his mind working overtime on how he would've gone about breaking into Chees. He considered the very real possibility that someone knew the code for turning off the security system; it was the simplest and tidiest explanation. *An inside job? Insurance fraud? Do they even have that here?* It would certainly fit the situation. Kormèr hadn't seen anyone else working in the store. Now that he thought about it, he knew very little about the day-to-day activity around the store. He decided he'd have to spend more time observing the store in the coming days, if he was going to crack this.

He passed a group of young Averians sitting around a bath. Suddenly, one turned her head and Kormèr recognized her as one of Syrree's friends from his first night at the Root. *Oh, no! Syrree!* He checked quickly to make sure she wasn't among the teens, then rushed off before they recognized him. *It's been… four nights! If I visit her now, she will not be happy with me.*

He rushed back to his hotel room, thankful that Syrree did not know where he was staying. He could imagine that she might use her father's influence to get him evicted. As he changed into a fresh set of clothes, he considered getting her a small gift to make up for his time away. He could always give her a gem, though her family had plenty of wealth already. He didn't like the idea of fueling that fire, but he could just steal it back before leaving the planet.

No. That's much too complicated. If only I hadn't passed out at the Hovel! He stopped as a thought occurred to him. *I could backtrack in time through the portal and spend one of those four nights with her.*

<<Buomp!>> he cried out loud. <<I could do the same thing and witness the robbery!>> he said to himself. He sat on his bed. *But do I want to? What's the fun in that? Sure, it'll clear my reputation with Sylvestra. But… besides the danger that solving it too quickly could raise suspicions, it would be… dishonest?* He shook his head. *Disingenuous, that's it. I need to solve this myself, with my skills. If in*—he counted on his fingers—*four days I haven't made any progress, then I'll consider this again.*

He opened the portal, but just stared at it. He wasn't in the mood to pop onto Syrree's balcony. Maybe she'd be interested in going to a club tonight or eating out… anything for a change of pace. Not that he minded the sex; sex with an Averian was a unique experience, doubly so with Syrree's youthful exuberance. But having met Sylvestra, he felt… awkward continuing his relationship with Syrree. He knew he didn't owe Sylvestra anything, and that most likely nothing would ever happen between them. But a part of him felt that he'd have a better chance if he didn't tie himself down with someone else.

Besides, a few hours spent in carnal delights would not be enough to get his mind off the heist. But dancing or sharing a nice quiet dinner with a beautiful young woman would do the trick. And now that he'd scoped out the store, he needed to take his mind off it for a while.

He stepped through the portal and exited at the base of Syrree's home's tree. He'd cased the place one night and knew exactly where he could portal without being seen. As he closed the portal, he wondered what kind of side effects traveling through time like that could have. At this very moment, he was passed out in the ceiling at the Hovel. Theoretically, he could hop over to the Hovel and wake up his earlier self from the chant-trance and save himself all this trouble. But the possibilities got tangled up in paradoxes that simply gave him a headache.

Instead, he walked up to Syrree's front door and buzzed the scanner. He wondered what sort of reaction he'd get from her mother or father, if they answered. He'd state the truth, that he was just her friend coming over to see if she wanted to go out. He hadn't experienced any racism here so far, so he doubted they would take issue with his being there. It was Syrree who answered the door.

||Kormèr!|| She seemed genuinely pleased to see him. She moved in and surprised him with a warm hug.

||Oh! Hi, Syrree,|| he sang, melting into the hug with a smile. When they parted, he asked, ||Are you hungry? I was thinking we could go out to dinner tonight.||

Almost impossibly, her eyes brightened even more. ||That would be great. I know just the place too.|| She stopped. ||Unless you had some place in mind.||

Kormèr shook his head. He knew of a diner and restaurants near The Root, but Syrree seemed to have already made her choice. ||I was hoping you'd have a preference.||

The restaurant Syrree had in mind was within walking-distance from her home, along the footpaths. After they placed their orders, Syrree sang: ||This is the first time I've ever walked here.||

Kormèr didn't immediately understand what she meant, and it must've showed because she shimmied her wings and explained: ||We usually fly here.||

||Oh! Of course,|| he twittered with an embarrassed laugh.

||But it was nice to walk with you,|| she cooed, laying her hand invitingly between them on the table.

||Likewise, with you,|| he sang, taking her hand in his.

||You've never said anything about your homeworld. Tell me about Elmar.||

||There isn't much to tell. It's like any other world, though not as idyllic as Averia. We only have two class structures, the ultra-rich and the poor. We have robots... Do you have those here? I haven't seen any.||

||No. They're not allowed, except for server chores. Labor laws prohibit their use. In fact, only Frrooweetsee can hold jobs here.|| Kormèr had almost forgotten the planet's real name until he heard her sing it. ||Except for Free-See. But there they have strict ratios they must adhere to. What are they like?||

||The ratios?||

She chuckled. ||No, silly. Robots. I've never seen one.||

Kormèr blushed. ||Oh. Well, there are different kinds, some that are just single-minded task bots and then there are some with amazing personalities. I sometimes forget that they're bots. But if you think about it, we're just organic bots, following our own chemical base code.||

She wrinkled her brow. ||Wait, so you're saying that we're no different from robots?||

||Well, we created the robots, wrote their code. Our code...|| He shrugged. ||We don't know where it came from. It's really old and has probably become more efficient over time. But it's still a code, of sorts. Especially if you think in terms of DNA and the variability in that.||

||Huh.|| She seemed to give it some serious consideration. ||That makes some sense, I suppose. If you meet my parents, don't mention any of that, okay?||

Kormèr chuckled. ||Deal. What do they do?||

||They're both on the Birshetland city planning council. Daddy is the chair of the environmental committee. They make sure that Frrooweetsee stays as beautiful as you see it.||

||They are doing a fantastic job then.||

She flicked her wings. ||I don't pay much attention to their work. It's all very boring.||

||I can completely relate. My father was a politician, and I also found the line of work dull and uninteresting.||

The food came, slowing their conversation and eventually leaving them sated. Though not too stuffed to share a fruity dessert. Kormèr tried to use Sylvestra's chip to pay for the dinner, but Syrree wouldn't have it, insisting they split the bill. That ended up being for the best, as his half of the bill drained nearly all the money on the chip, anyway.

They strolled back to her home, in no rush and enjoying the night, the conversation, and each other's company.

||I won't be able to come by tomorrow,|| chirped Kormèr as he leaned against the doorframe of Syrree's home.

||Don't you disappear on me again,|| twittered Syrree, playfully twirling a nail against his exposed chest.

||I won't. I shouldn't be so busy again for a while.||

||Good.|| She pulled him close, and they kissed for some time before pulling apart, breathily.

||Gotta go,|| he whispered.

Eyes half-closed, she nodded. He gave her one last kiss, then strolled down the hall. Once around the corner, he opened the portal and stepped through into his hotel room, present time. With a broad grin, he sat on the bed. If things weren't going to work out with Sylvestra, Syrree had turned out to be a lovely girl. She was a little spoiled by her daddy's money, but she'd definitely grown beyond Kormèr's first impressions of her. She was nothing like Menddilal. While he couldn't see himself spending a lifetime with her, Kormèr reasoned that this could turn into a nice, long-term relationship. She wasn't Sylvestra, but if that was his standard, he risked being alone forever.

He rinsed his mouth to wash away the taste of dinner, doffed his shirt for another, then thought of Syrree's balcony and stepped through the portal. Their passionate kissing had left him breathless, and he looked forward to more of it.

STARING off into space, the book he had been reading momentarily forgotten, Srrcheel reflected on all the new things he had learned since his raising. He'd watched his master cast spells throughout his apprenticeship, all the while longing for his chance to do the same. And now here he was, reading through one of the Initiate Caster Level tomes that had been forbidden him before the raising. His night vision spell paled compared to the handful of spells he'd learned in just the past day. It had hardly required any manipulation of the filaments at all. The spell for creating food and water were more complex and used much more energy.

Yesterday, while practicing a new spell, Srrcheel had drawn on more energy than he was used to, and actually put himself to sleep. Such a possibility existed because the filaments primarily supplied life energy. The fact that the sorcerers could tap them for magic was a bonus. Fortunately, low-level spells weren't powerful enough to harm the caster, only exhaust those who hadn't yet built up a strong filament base. He imagined that high-level casting could be dangerous, as the energy draw of a single spell could thoroughly overwhelm the caster's energy reserves.

Srrcheel yawned and rubbed his eyes. Then he closed the book. He'd done enough for today. He needed to sleep and allow the filaments to recover their energy so he could begin anew in the morning.

But first, he wanted to try a communication spell that a few of the older boys had shown him. According to them, it was a Hawk Sorcerer tradition that this spell be passed down from the Fledged Caster Level sorcerers to the Initiate Caster Levels.

Srrcheel made himself comfortable, focused on the filaments, and weaved the pattern for the spell. The pattern wasn't very complex, but it contained two segments that reminded him of conjuration spell patterns. Conjuring anything other than food and water didn't usually get taught until the caster was further along in his studies. ||Oh!|| he cawed when a crystal ball appeared, floating before him. *It was a conjuration sequence!* he realized, pleased with himself for having recognized it.

A wave of exhaustion washed over him, no doubt a result of the weakened state of the surrounding filaments. But he marshaled his strength as the crystal ball clouded up and an image appeared in three-dimensions within.

||Hi, Syrree,|| he chirped. ||Hope I didn't wake you.||

||Srrcheel?|| Syrree's image in the ball was a little wavy, so Srrcheel couldn't be sure, but she looked disheveled. She glanced behind her and moved closer to

the pickup; Srrcheel knew from experience that on her end, the pickup appeared as a smaller glowing orb. In lowered registers, Syrree twittered, | |Where are you?| |

| |In my room,| | he chirped, grinning.

| |But how? I didn't know you could do this?| |

| |I'm an initiate caster now. So I cast a communication spell.| | She was quiet for too long. | |Are you okay? You seem a little… distracted.| |

| |I'm… fine,| | she tweeted. | |I wasn't feeling well earlier, so I went to bed early.| |

Srrcheel suddenly felt terrible for springing this on her without warning. *Heavens! What if she'd been in the bathroom?!* | |Oh, I'm really sorry. I thought I'd surprise you, but I clearly didn't think this through.| |

| |No, no. It's okay. Do you have any plans to come back here soon?| |

| |Not yet. And with my new training schedule… But things could change at a moment's notice.| |

| |Soon, hopefully.| | Her voice lowered even more. | |It'll be nice to see you again.| |

| |Same here.| | An awkward silence followed. | |Well, I won't keep you any longer. Get some sleep and feel better.| |

| |Thank you. Good night, Srrcheel.| |

| |Good night.| | Her face vanished as the crystal ball reverted to its clear state.

Pop! The crystal ball exploded. Srrcheel threw up his arms, expecting to be torn to shreds by shards of glass. But instead of glass flying everywhere, white cream splattered all over the room and Srrcheel. Srrcheel stared at himself in shock, the sweet-smelling cream oozing slowly down his body and dripping in globs onto the floor. He glanced at the mess around his room, then stopped. On one wall, the mess was in the shape of Averian writing. It read: *Initiate Sucker.*

KORMÈR'S eyes fluttered open in time to hear some whispers and see Syrree settle back into the bed. Her back was to him, obscuring whatever she'd been looking at, but he'd seen a soft glow around her and cast on the walls. | |What was that?| | he asked, and she jumped. | |Sorry,| | he added when she turned, wide-eyed.

| |Oh… ahh… I got a comm from an old friend from Freet-See.| | She turned under the covers to face him. Kormèr was keenly aware that she was keeping her distance from him and trying not to be obvious about it. Something was bothering her.

After their kissing—two nights ago for her—she'd been just as eager as he for an extended foreplay session. They'd chatted for barely twenty minutes before they were caressing and kissing again.

He moved closer to her now, draping an arm around her waist. | |Is something wrong?| | he asked, looking into her dark eyes.

She didn't look up at him. | |No. Yes.| | She sighed. | |This friend… my friend is in this situation. She's been betrothed to a man since they were born.| |

| |Hmm,| | hummed Kormèr. | |I've seen that before in other cultures. I didn't know it happened here too.| | Was Sylvestra also betrothed to someone? Kormèr had to find out before he made a complete fool of himself.

| |It does, unfortunately.| |

| |Unfortunately?| |

| |It's a burden, can't you see? She's lived all her life trapped by this betrothal contract, unable to be attracted to anyone else— No, I said that wrong. And that's the problem. She's attracted to others, but she can't do anything about it.| |

She spoke with such passion that Kormèr had to wonder if she wasn't talking about herself. That or a very close friend or relative. But he couldn't be sure, so he didn't mention it.

| |I see what you mean,| | he twittered instead. | |Is there any way she can get out of it?| |

Syrree was quiet for a moment. Then she shook her head. | |It's an old custom, from my grandmother's time. My parents were arranged too.| |

Before she could say anymore, he chirruped, | |If there's one thing I've learned, it's this: you're your own person. Parents try their best to guide you based on their experiences. But in the end, it's up to you to make of their guidance what you want. We have to choose our own path; if we let someone else choose for us, we'll never be happy with ourselves or with the people that pushed us in that direction.| | He shrugged. | |That's my opinion, anyway. For what it's worth.| |

Syrree was quiet again, and Kormèr thought he might have put her to sleep, but when he caressed her crest feathers, she looked up at him, then kissed him deeply and held him tightly. | |You're the best, Kormèr,| | she sang with a wide smile. Then she nestled her head against his chest.

Kormèr's eyes went wide. *Uh, oh. Could she be in love with me?*

CHAPTER 17

A flimsy slid across the desk, and Sergeant Chreel Tseeo looked up from his desktop screen in time to see the office messenger dash off. He snatched up the flimsy and read. He frowned, and he had to read it again to make sure he'd read it correctly. | | ...arrest order for Kormèr Lezàl in connection with the Chees jewel heist is rescinded... | | And Chief Sylvestra Chrreel had digitally signed it.

Tseeo was immediately concerned. His instinct told him something was wrong. While Mister Reestee had verified that Lezàl's gems were not from his collection, that hardly exonerated Lezàl of involvement in the crime. If anything, Lezàl could be part of a larger organization of jewel thieves. He had to be brought in for more questioning until he revealed the larger entity. Somehow, either by blackmail or threat of harm, Lezàl, or the organization, had gotten to the Chief, and being female, she was no doubt quite vulnerable to such things.

Tseeo once again read the order, checking the language for any clues, but it was just the standard form letter. He stared into the distance for a few moments, wondering what he could do to help the Chief. He wondered why Captain Phatheeo hadn't come to him with this; Tseeo knew the Captain favored him, having selected him for high-profile tasks on multiple occasions. But maybe the old man hadn't come to the same conclusions. *Which stands to reason,* Tseeo thought to himself. *As much as I respect his past accomplishments, Phatheeo can't possibly still have all his wits about him, at his age.*

The more he thought about it, the more Tseeo realized he had to take action. The first order of business had to be a fact-finding task: he needed to find out what influence Lezàl was exerting on the Chief. Ideally, he would have directly questioned Lezàl. But with the rescind officially logged, Tseeo's wings were clipped. He tailed Lezàl instead, which ran its own risk of a reprimand if Lezàl caught him. But Tseeo was sure the Captain would understand if it came to that.

He returned to the Hotel Cheerees and positioned himself at the end of the corridor with Lezàl's room. There he waited all afternoon and until late evening for someone to enter or emerge from Lezàl's room. But no one did. Tseeo strolled by the room several times, though he knew the doors were soundproof.

As dawn approached, Tseeo couldn't keep his eyes open any longer. Twice he'd nearly collapsed when he'd fallen asleep standing up. Reluctantly, he left the hotel and headed home for some rest. A few hours of sleep would be enough. Then he would renew his surveillance with a fresh head.

Soaring across the city, the cool night air woke him up some. Which was a good thing, as there were plenty of obstacles to avoid while flying. He wished the Council would outlaw taxis in Birshetland; there were limits to how many could operate at a time, but he still felt that they cluttered the sky ways. They were banned from most other cities, as were offworlders, a condition he felt very much in favor of. The crime statistics spoke for themselves in that regard: Freet-See ranked highest as the city with the most crime. Birshetland came in second, and Tseeo had no doubt that it resulted from being the second city with the highest population of offworlders.

A bluish glow caught his eye on the promenade below, but vanished as he approached to investigate. He circled around and spotted someone sitting on a bench across from Chees. He didn't know what specifically about this scene caught his attention, but his Sergeant's instinct nagged him to take a closer look. All thoughts of sleep vanished when he discovered it was Kormèr Lezàl sitting on the bench.

THE trees and streets of Birshetland were uniformly gray in the pre-dawn light when Kormèr stepped out of his portal. He closed the portal, pocketed the cube, and took a seat on a stone bench. Directly across the promenade from him was Chees.

The store was a unique structure in the Birshetland treescape. Because of its sophisticated security system, it couldn't sit directly on the promenade, or every passerby would trigger the proximity sensors. So it sat on a platform, separated from the promenade and connected by a short bridge. In front of the store, there was ample space for several people to browse the window displays without crowding, but only while the store was open during the day. Once the store closed, the three-meter gap from the promenade, plus the four meters of "browsing space", left an adequate buffer for "personal space" for the proximity sensor.

Though the platform supporting it was square, the store itself had a cylindrical shape with an arch just above the door. The arch displayed the store's name in Averian, and below it, smaller text read: *Makers of Fine Jewelry*. Kormèr wondered briefly if Chees had ever actually been a person. In his edu-comp vocabulary of Averian, the word didn't translate to anything.

The street brightened, and Kormèr looked up, his wide eyes falling on the metallic-leaf canopy above which glowed with the first rays of the morning sun. He was simply stunned by the beauty of this planet. He'd been to many fascinating worlds, but none paralleled the beauty and serenity of Averia. *I could live here*, he thought, and the idea shocked him. Never before had he even considered the possibility of staying on the worlds he'd visited. Elmar was his home, and that was that. But here… here, he could forget he had another life somewhere else.

Someone fluttered across Kormèr's upturned line of sight. He followed the intruder of his daydreams, watching it land on the platform side of the bridge and stride quickly to the door. Kormèr watched intently as Cheert ran through the routine of opening the store. But because of Cheert's haste and, no doubt, high paranoia, Kormèr could not see exactly what Cheert did. Kormèr frowned, realizing that from this vantage, he never would. It was just too far, and Cheert was very guarded.

I tried, so I get a medal for effort, he thought to himself. *But this was a waste of time.* He looked around to see if he could spy a better vantage point to watch from tomorrow morning. To the right were some good-sized branches, but unfortunately, they were too far back to afford a clear view of the store-front. To the left…

Kormèr frowned, squinting to get a better look at a branch where he thought he'd seen someone standing. There was no one there now. He stood and walked toward the tree, but closer inspection didn't confirm his suspicions. Kormèr wasn't sure why his curiosity should be so piqued; Averians frequently landed on branches to rest on their way from place to place. Already the air was filling with locals gliding to work or to the opening shops. Shrugging, Kormèr returned to his bench. He had a full day ahead of him of casing the store, and he didn't want to miss a thing.

SPENDING the day watching the store had seemed like a great idea when Kormèr had first thought of it, but when Feestoo dropped him off at the hotel that evening, Kormèr felt drained. He'd noted the activity around the store, including Cheert's movements, the entire day. While he'd learned quite a bit, like the fact that Cheert ordered lunch in, he'd gained no insight at all regarding the heist. Not that he'd expected any in just one sitting; he'd done this sort of thing before, and knew that "it takes as long as it takes", as his father would say.

But his patience this time around had its limits. He had a deadline hanging over him, and he had one less day remaining. And then there was the whole Sylvestra situation: he still felt had little to no chance with her, but that didn't prevent his mind from thinking about her.

He flopped backwards onto his bed and sighed heavily, rubbing his face with his hands. His body longed for a warm bath back on Elmar, but he fought back that urge. Part of his mind decided he should've gone straight back home from Io. He'd just returned from Jordinni, after all. What business did he have running off again on another adventure so soon?

But when he thought of all the new things he'd seen and learned, all the people he had met, he couldn't deny that it was worth enduring the tough moments to experience the good ones. *Especially Sylvestra.* That final thought was enough to silence his self-doubts.

There came a knock at the door, which Kormèr answered reluctantly.

At the door, Almp's smile faded before Kormèr could even say hello. ||You look terrible!||

Kormèr gave him a sour smile. ||Thanks.|| He returned to the bed, leaving Almp to close the door behind himself.

241

Almp took a perch. <<What's wrong with you? Sick?>>

Kormèr smiled at Almp's attempt to cheer him up by switching to Elmarian. ||Just a long day. I'm missing out on too much sleep at night.||

Almp's crest perked. ||Something to do with the police?||

Kormèr's right eyebrow shot up. ||How'd you know?||

||One of the guys you met at the club last week saw you get picked up at the diner a few days ago.||

Kormèr nodded. ||Ah.||

||So?||

||What?||

Almp jostled his wings in frustration. ||Are you gonna tell me what it's about?||

Kormèr considered not telling Almp, but the situation had him so stressed to the point of distraction that he decided it didn't really matter. If things got too crazy, he'd just portal home. *And to hell with this whole place.* ||It's nothing, really. I'm helping Sylvestra Chreel with the Chees robbery case.||

Almp was quiet for a moment. Then he laughed. ||Yeah, right. And I caught the Venusian Molt.||

Kormèr shrugged. ||Spent the whole day parked in front of Chees, hoping to find a clue.|| He rubbed his stomach. ||Had a worm-kebab from one of those street vendors—I don't think it went down very well.||

Almp blinked. ||You're not kidding, are you?|| Kormèr shook his head. ||Wow! You know something about police work?||

||Something like that.||

Almp seemed intrigued. ||What do you do back home, on Elmar?||

Hmm, best to keep it simple. ||Uh, my dad's a jeweler.||

||Ah! That explains...|| And he pointed at Kormèr's rings. ||And the gems.||

||I guess it does.|| Kormèr chuckled. He hadn't even thought about what he was saying, and it had fit in perfectly.

Almp sighed. ||Oh well, I guess you wouldn't be interested in going to the club tonight then.||

Kormèr furrowed his brow. While he was tired, he was still in the mood for some mindless fun, if only to lighten his mood. ||Well, now,|| he twittered, ||I wouldn't go that far.||

Almp beamed. ||So you're up for it?||

His body cried, *No!* He sang: ||Yeah!||

||Great! Coming alone?|| Almp asked, with a curious glint in his eyes.

Kormèr wished he could say that Sylvestra might be interested, but he knew that was unrealistic. However, there was another possibility... ||That all depends on whether a certain young lady is available on such short notice.||

Syrree was more than happy to accept Kormèr's invitation for an evening out. When Feestoo's cab swooped down toward the platform outside her home tree, she was already waiting outside.

||You sure have her wrapped around your talon,|| sang Almp, nudging Kormèr with his elbow.

Kormèr pushed Almp away. ||Bah. She's just being prompt.||

||I agree with Master Almp, KL,|| chirped Feestoo, coasting slowly toward the platform's edge. ||I've been driving for many years, and I've never seen a female waiting for her companion.||

Kormèr said nothing more, but he hopped out of the taxi once they'd stopped and held the door for Syree. She smiled and gave him a kiss before boarding the taxi.

The distraction of the night out with Almp and Syree worked pretty much as Kormèr had planned: between the music, dancing and socializing, he forgot all his problems for a few hours.

CHAPTER 18

CAPTAIN Phatheeo squinted from his office door across the open desks where his junior officers and detectives worked. One particular desk held his interest this morning, that of Sergeant Chreel Tseeo. This was the second day that he went looking for Tseeo and the Sergeant hadn't been at his desk.

| | Has anyone seen Tseeo? | | squawked Phatheeo in his most authoritative voice. He was met by blank stares and silence. Finally, Tseeo's neighbor spoke up. | | I thought he was on a case, sir. He left yesterday and hasn't been back. | |

| | In my office, | | chirped Phatheeo. He turned and leaned on his desk while the young officer rushed in. | | Close the door. | |

The young man did so, then turned to face his captain. | | Sir? | |

| | You're not in trouble, son. Relax. Now, just tell me why you think Tseeo's on a case. | |

| | I was on my way in the day before last, when I saw the Sergeant leaving the station. I said to him, 'Early day?' 'New assignment,' he mumbled. He seemed so serious and focused that I laughed, but he just flew off. | |

| | I see. Thank you for the info. | |

| | You're welcome, sir. | | The officer left.

Phatheeo scowled down at his desk. *What are you up to, Tseeo?* Phatheeo had always encouraged his officers to show initiative in their work. But he'd also drilled home the importance of adherence to protocol and procedure. It was unlike Tseeo to take off without letting anyone know what he was up to.

Phatheeo decided to give his man the benefit of the doubt. He gave him till early evening to report in. When the time came without a word from Tseeo, Phatheeo called his p-comm.

STRUGGLING to keep his eyes open and focused on Lezàl, Tseeo grumbled silently, *Damned Elmarian doesn't sleep!*

Not wanting to miss a moment of Lezàl's activities, Tseeo had kept up with the boy since spotting him outside of Chees, following him to the Theesl home tree. Tseeo had recognized Syrree Theesl almost immediately, stunned that she had been standing outside waiting to be picked up; why would the daughter of such a prominent man be socializing with this Elmarian? Perhaps it was just some rebellious immaturity on the girl's part, just as it was with Almp, the son of the

Cheerees Hotel's manager. Tseeo had even gone as far as paying the cover charge for club entry, to see who the boy was meeting there.

That had been hours ago, and there was nothing to show for his efforts. After accompanying Syrree Theesl home in the pre-dawn hours—the hotel manager's son had left the club much earlier—Lezàl had shuffled back to the bench across from Chees and once again parked himself there.

Tseeo had watched the boy fall briefly asleep at least twice. He'd been unable to keep count since he, too, had passed out once or twice before dashing off to buy a tall cup of coffee.

All day, Tseeo kept watch on the boy, choosing different locations to keep from being obvious, and to keep himself moving. For a little excitement, he'd even stood in line behind the boy to buy lunch from a passing vending cart.

Tseeo perked up when the boy suddenly stood and rushed to the railing. At the store doorway, the owner was just leaving and locking up for the night. When the owner turned, Lezàl cagily walked parallel to the storefront, no doubt monitoring it, while seeming to be just another passerby.

Boop-boop! Tseeo nearly jumped out of his feathers. He slapped a hand over his wrist-link to muffle the sound, then turned around and answered it.

||Sergeant,|| came his 's gruff voice along with his equally angered visage, ||where the hell've you been?||

Tseeo's eyes went wide. He'd known this moment would come, but he'd been putting off thinking about it, expecting to have found something by now to justify his efforts. Now his brain was so muddled with sleep-deprivation that he could hardly think of the right answer, never mind lying. ||Sir, I am following a lead on the Chees case.||

The Captain frowned. ||Your eyes are all dilated; how long has it been since you've slept?||

Tseeo had to focus to answer, his exhausted brain sluggish. ||Since yesterday morning.||

||What? Why didn't you clear this with me? Or at least check in?||

||I felt that time was of the essence, sir. Even now—|| Tseeo turned back to see what his charge was up to, only to find Lezàl was nowhere in sight. Frantically, he looked around, jumping from perch to perch to get a broader view of the street, but it was no use.

Lezàl had disappeared.

KORMÈR'S eyes burned, as if the fire of the sun itself had somehow trapped itself inside them. He cursed his stupidity at having stayed up all night. *What the hell was I thinking?!* he scolded himself. But he knew very well what he'd been thinking. He'd been having such a good time that he hadn't wanted it to end. He hadn't wanted to return to this daunting task so soon, and he'd continued partying, hoping—however unrealistically—that morning would never come.

But it had come, and bleary-eyed, he'd taken Syrree home—he thanked the gods that she'd been as tired as he was and hadn't wanted him to spend the night. He didn't fully remember returning to his vigil outside Chees. In his exhaustion, he'd sat on the bench again, instead of finding the better vantage he'd been hoping for. Then he'd passed out and slept through Cheert opening the shop altogether.

Somehow, he managed to watch the shop the whole day, falling asleep only three or four times during lulls in pedestrian traffic. He knew he wasn't being very effective, but he had at least gotten a better feeling of how traffic flowed in and around the store. This was just the sort of thing a good thief would—

His eyes snapped open. *Damn, fell asleep again.* The store door swung open and Cheert stepped out. Throwing caution to the wind, Kormèr stood and ran to the railing from where he had a slightly better view of Cheert's actions. He watched as Cheert passed a key over a sensor plate, turn and walk across the connecting bridge onto the promenade. Once here, Cheert pointed a small control box at the store. Something about this nagged at Kormèr, but he was too tired to think straight. Then when Cheert turned, Kormèr walked slowly along, hands in his pockets, as if he'd just been strolling past. Once Cheert had flown off, Kormèr made a note of what he'd seen on his flim-pad for reviewing once he'd gotten some sleep.

And did he need sleep! His vision had become totally blurred. Ahead of him there was something that he couldn't focus on no matter how hard he tried, like the shimmer of heat on a road surface, only this one had a vague oval shape and stood at nearly two meters in height. Then it moved! It snatched the flim-pad from his hands and appeared to look at it, if a large blur could "appear to look" at anything. But it held the pad as a humanoid might if they were reading it. *Kippin' ey! Now I'm hallucinating!* Kormèr rubbed his eyes, but the blur was still there, holding his pad.

||What do you think you're doing?|| twittered the blur in muffled tones.

||What... who're you?||

A weapon flashed up and pointed at Kormèr's head.

Kormèr was more awake now. ||Isn't it a little public to be doing that?|| he asked.

||No one can see or hear me,|| chirped the blur. ||If I kill you now, all they will see is you suddenly falling dead.||

||Harry G?|| Kormèr's brain seemed to be hard-wired to his mouth, and it had suddenly occurred to him that this might be the infamous "G Man". But he immediately realized that it couldn't be.

The blur ignored him. ||You will stop casing this store. Get it?||

||Casing?|| Kormèr's eyes went wide. ||By the gods! You're the thief! You're the one who robbed Chees!||

The blur shot forward, pressing the weapon to Kormèr's forehead. Kormèr tried backing up, but he was up against the railing. ||Listen to me closely,|| it chirruped, in a deep and menacing tone. ||Leave this place. Forget about it; forget about me.|| It dashed the pad against the ground and smashed it with a blurry pseudopod. ||I am the Unseen; I can go anywhere, unnoticed. You've been warned.||

The blur vanished, and the weapon went with it, leaving Kormèr shaking against the railing. He had already suspected that he was out of his element in this millennium. But this event had revealed to him, starkly and roughly, just how out of his element he truly was. And he didn't like that feeling one bit.

He ran off toward the hotel. It was time to call a friend.

||IF there are no objections,|| sang the arbiter, ||I believe we have reached an agreement.||

Jeremy couldn't suppress his relieved grin as he glanced around the table. *Finally!* After years of hard work, dodging Mister G and his mercs, exploding ships, death threats and failed negotiations, this was actually it! Even Kit's eyes were wide, with a mixture of incredulity and relief.

||Very well, then. If everyone would please e-sign—||

A throat-clearing interrupted the arbiter. All eyes turned to Tzee'oo Theesl, who was poking his flimsy with his stylus purposefully, almost theatrically. ||I'm sorry, ladies and gentlemen, but there is still the matter of the environmental concerns. I know it's something that is usually overlooked on other worlds, but not on Frrooweetsee.||

Jeremy sighed audibly and ignored any attention his rudeness attracted. ||How would you like us to address these concerns? We've already shown you the results of independently conducted tests.||

Theesl tapped his flimsy a few more times. ||Those tests were helpful, but rudimentary. I've just sent you all a file that outlines a small battery of tests that will be performed over the next few days to satisfy our requirements.||

Everyone reviewed the four-page outline. Jeremy glanced at Kit, who was visibly fuming. Even the arbiter kept his eyes on his flimsy longer than everyone else before looking up at Theesl. ||Is there any reason you waited this long to bring this up, Councilman Theesl?||

||With all due respect, Arbiter, these tests are a small but meaningful detail that hardly warranted mention if we did not complete the crux of the negotiation. Now that we are done with the latter, we can address the former.||

The arbiter looked skeptical but nodded. ||I suppose you have contractors ready to perform these tests?||

||I do. Their names, proposals and costs are all attached at the bottom of the outline.||

The arbiter's eyes remained locked on Theesl's. Then he addressed everyone assembled. ||Ladies and gentlemen, by law the contract cannot be signed until these tests are complete. This meeting is adjourned until then. Good day.||

Jeremy and Kit burned holes into Theesl with their eyes, as everyone grunted and grumbled out the doors of the meeting room. Theesl calmly shut down his desk station, then looked up at the two men. ||I'm very sorry for this extra

247

delay,|| he told them. ||But we Frrooweetsee value our delicate environment very highly. It would be remiss of me in my position to let such a matter slide.||

||Of course,|| sang Jeremy.

||Good day, gentlemen.||

Jeremy watched him go, then turned to Kit and cursed.

"You beat me to it," said Kit. "He did that on purpose."

Jeremy nodded. "Oh, I'm sure of that. The question is, why? What the hell does he have to gain by delaying us like this?"

Kit shook his head. "Who the hell knows? Let's get out of here. I can't stand this room anymore."

A police escort had been assigned to them after the incident on Freet-See. The two officers entered the room as Jeremy stood, perhaps concerned when their charges hadn't exited with everyone else.

||Sorry, fellas,|| twittered Jeremy to the birdmen. ||Looks like we're stuck together for a few more days.||

SRRCHEEL tugged nervously on his wing feathers as he stood waiting outside Grand Master Fitzbew's room. His eyes stared at the wall but looked only inward as his mind worked overtime trying to guess why he'd been summoned and what horrible punishment would befall him for... for what? There were so many things he'd done wrong since meeting Kormèr Lezàl. *This has to be about the Elmarian boy. Who else?* Srrcheel himself had done nothing else wrong that merited a summons by the Grand Master. This was either about Kormèr's visit to the Hovel or Srrcheel's giving him the glasses or—

The door opened, and his master stood in the doorway; his expression revealed nothing about whether this unexpected call would be pleasant or unpleasant. ||Come in, Srrcheel,|| his Master told him, stepping aside to let him enter.

The door closed behind him, and Srrcheel glanced once at the Grand Master before bowing his head to his superior. Grand Master Fitzbew wore a simple cowl instead of his formal cowl, the latter a masterpiece that Srrcheel loved to stare at. The Grand Cowl, as he'd heard others refer to it, had been designed ages ago using five colors which represented the five levels of discipline of Hawk Sorcerer magic. Each morning, the magic shifted the colors into patterns, sparking wild speculation whether they were random or had some significance, perhaps known only to the Grand Master himself.

His Master moved to stand between Srrcheel and the Grand Master. ||Grand Master, I present Srrcheel,|| he chirped.

Srrcheel did not look up, but he felt the Grand Master's gaze on him for some time. Then the Grand Master warbled: ||Initiate Caster Srrcheel, you have been summoned by an outsider who says that he knows you personally and now has need of your new talents.||

Srrcheel's eyes widened as he looked up at the Grand Master. *Me?* he thought, but sang nothing.

Grand Master Fitzbew shifted in his seat. ||If you choose to accept this summons, I have made a few provisions that should be to your liking. Your Master tells me you've been diligently studying since your raising.||

||Yes. Grand Master, I have,|| Srrcheel tweeted humbly. ||Thank you, Master,|| he chirped to his master, then turned back to Fitzbew. ||I accept the summons.||

Fitzbew nodded. ||Fine, fine. In that case, I am granting you privilege to the full set of initiate caster tomes in the library.||

Srrcheel's eyes nearly popped out of their sockets.

Fitzbew slid a data chip across his desktop. ||This holds digitized copies of the tomes, so you may reference them during your trip.|| As Srrcheel moved to take the chip, Fitzbew gave him a stern look and chirped, ||Don't lose it.|| He sat back, and Srrcheel took the chip. ||And don't be afraid to ask for help,|| he sang more softly, ||from any of us, if you need it. Most importantly, if you feel this is all over your head, speak up. Better that than to not be able to help someone in need. Seeking help would not reflect badly on you; it would show good judgment on your part, that you know your limits.||

||I understand, Grand Master. I can't express how grateful I am for this opportunity.||

||Sure you can,|| sang the Grand Master with a smile. ||Do the best you can, for us.|| Srrcheel nodded. ||Good luck. That is all; you may go.||

||Thank you.|| Srrcheel walked out, followed by his master.

||Congratulations. I would have given anything at your level to go out on my own.||

||Thank you. I'm a bit nervous, though.||

||A bit! I would have been shivering beneath my wings. But you'll have no problem. Just be sure of what you can do and what you can't. Grand Master's given you a wonderful opportunity, with your new access to the library tomes.||

Srrcheel couldn't help but smile, his heart racing anxiously. ||I'm going to the library now to see what I can pick up before tomorrow.||

As he raced ahead, his Master called after him, ||Don't wear yourself out; you'll need your strength!||

||I won't. Oh, wait!||. He stopped and turned back. ||In all my excitement, I forgot to ask: who summoned me?||

||An Elmarian. Kormèr Lezàl.||

CHAPTER 19

SYLVESTRA stared at the email from the mayor on her screen. Among other items, she was requesting an update on the Chees case, but Sylvestra had nothing to reply with. Her detectives had yet to produce any kind of evidence or suspect. Motive was easy, as there were only three options there: business rivalry, a private vendetta against Cheert, or just plain greed. They'd checked into his rivals, but none had the resources or motivation to pull a caper of this magnitude. The same applied to his few enemies... his known enemies, at least. Few precedents existed of Averians turning on Averians, however. Offworlders perpetuated most of the significant crimes.

That train of thought reminded Sylvestra that Lezàl hadn't contacted her in two days. This annoyed her, though she hadn't really expected to hear from him. She wasn't entirely convinced that he'd actually come up with anything, despite his boasts. As a thief, he might have an inside perspective into the criminal psyche and methods of operation, but he was too young, in her opinion, to have the means for a heist of that complexity. She frowned, realizing she'd never done the calculation, but three and a half Elmarian made him only three standard years younger than her. *Heavens! Is that the way everyone else here sees me?* She had known this, more than superficially, if she were being honest, but her categorization of Lezàl deepened her understanding of the behavior of many on her staff. This didn't excuse their behavior, but it gave her a frame of reference to work with. *Phatheeo must've understood this, too. That's why he's delayed his retirement for so long.*

Her eyes focused on her screen again, where the email waited for her response. She couldn't even admit to the mayor that she had Lezàl working on the case. At the moment, that hardly mattered, as Lezàl had done nothing so far. *But what if, by some stroke of luck, he does solve the case? I can't possibly give him credit; that would be the end of my career!*

She glanced at the clock and realized she'd lost track of time. She had wanted to go home thirty minutes ago. Frustrated, and looking for any excuse to put off answering the mayor, she locked her terminal and left her office.

As she walked out of the precinct, Sylvestra considered walking home. The evening was still warm, and she really needed to unwind with more than just a quick flight home. But she was quite tired after the long day, so she decided to forego the walk tonight. She walked to the edge of the platform, spread her wings— She jumped back as a taxi swept down before her. The passenger door opened, and Kormèr stepped out.

||Stop doing that!|| she protested, her heart pounding. But then she noticed the strained look on his face.

He turned and warbled something to the driver. As he turned back, the taxi pulled away and glided off.

||He calls himself the Unseen,|| he told her, as if she knew what he was talking about.

||Who does?||

||The thief.||

She stared at him in disbelief. ||You...|| She had so many questions, she couldn't decide what to lead with. ||You said, 'He calls himself.' You spoke with the thief?||

He looked past her at the precinct. ||Would you mind if we went this way?||

||What's wrong?|| she asked, catching up to him, as he shuffled quickly away. ||You seem... distressed?||

||I'm just exhausted,|| he sang. ||I've barely slept in the last two days.||

She frowned. This wasn't good. If he hurt himself because of their deal, she could end up in a lot of trouble, besides the guilt she would feel personally. ||Because of this case? Look, you shouldn't—||

||No, it's not just the case. Well, mostly, but... I've been casing Chees for the last two days, hoping to spot some exploitable weakness.||

||Oh. Be careful with that. I've had regular patrols watching the store in case the thief returned.||

||Hmm. Thanks for the warning.|| He yawned, unintentionally, almost involuntarily, and looked abashed. ||Oh. Sorry about that.||

If he lists, I'm not sure I'd be able to support his weight. ||Do you want to sit down?||

He laughed, too loud. ||No, no. I've had enough of that. If I sit, I'll just pass out.||

She remembered now to switch on the recorder on her badge. ||So, how... when did you meet the thief?||

||Today. Cheert had just closed shop.|| He told her what had happened.

||Backtrack a little,|| she sang, when he was done. ||I don't understand what you mean by 'a blur'.||

||Everything around me was absolutely clear, except for this blurry form in front of me. I thought I had something in my eye, but it wasn't that. When it pointed the weapon at me, the weapon was also clear, but the hand holding it was blurry.|| He shook his head. ||Maybe 'blurry' isn't the right word.|| He snapped his fingers. ||Distorted. That's it. Like I was seeing what was in front of me, but it was distorted.||

Sylvestra nodded. ||Very clever. So you don't know if the thief is Frrooweetsee or not.||

||He was fluent in Averian, but physically, I have no idea. Do you know of any tech that can do what I described?|| He didn't wait for her to answer, and

251

continued with, | |I was thinking it might have been magic, so I called out a sorcerer friend of mine.| |

| |Sorcerer friend? Oh! I almost forgot about your trip to the Hovel. Someday, when this is over, perhaps you can tell me how you managed that.| |

| |Someday?| | he smiled, his eyes brightening. | |I'd love to.| |

Something she'd said had made his demeanor improve, but she ignored that for now. | |As for the distortion effect, I've never heard of such a thing. And you say the thief even disappeared at the end.| |

| |That's right.| |

| |Like you with your portal.| |

Kormèr shook his head. | |The portal is very obvious. This was instantaneous.| | He shivered. | |He could be here now and we'd never know.| |

Caught up in his story, Sylvestra instinctively glanced around. But they were alone on the promenade. | |I'm glad you came to me with this.| |

| |I needed to talk to someone tonight. It couldn't wait until tomorrow.| | He stopped and slowly looked at her. | |I think I may have made a mistake. I think this might be beyond me. I'm not from this time; there are things in this time period that are beyond me, beyond my experience. I—| |

He stopped himself, as if afraid that he had said too much. He did almost seem scared and overwhelmed, and it pained her to see him this way. | |Kormèr, you've already succeeded where none of my detectives have.| | She cringed as the words left her mouth, knowing they were being recorded and could be played back in the future in front of those same detectives. | |I don't know exactly what you expected to accomplish, but you've already exceeded my expectations. You don't have to continue if you don't want to. I won't hold you to any more than you've already done.| |

| |Thank you for saying so. It means a lot to me.| | He glanced over at a bench, hesitated, then walked to it and slumped into it.

She smiled, shut off the recorder, and sat next to him. | |I do think you're crazy, you know. I can't believe you're putting yourself through this, even though it might be for nothing.| | *Just to impress me?*

| |That's the trouble with love,| | he mumbled.

She sighed. | |What do you—| | His head dropped onto her shoulder. Startled, she spun to rebuke him, when she noticed that, just as he'd predicted, he'd fallen asleep. Options flashed through her mind: shove him away, rouse him and let him wander off home… or just let him sleep.

Why did he have to be so infatuated with her, anyway? She squirmed a little, thrown by the accidental close contact; she had never been in contact with a non-Averian that she wasn't arresting or subduing, and never one so close to her own age. Curious about the golden glints of his fine-looking hair, she nuzzled her cheek against the top of his head; his hair was thicker than she had expected, but very soft. She picked up his slack hand: soft and smooth, as befitting his age, but also meticulously groomed. *The hand of someone who hasn't had to do a bit of hard labor in his life*. Reflexively, he slipped his fingers between hers and held her hand loosely, and she shot a glance at him to make sure that he was still asleep.

| | Insane young man, | | she twittered softly, closing her eyes. | | How can you think you love me, when you hardly know me? | | she asked him, knowing there would be no answer. | | What do you know about love, anyway? | | Maybe it was just attraction, and that she could understand; she was fond of him, despite what she knew—and how little she knew—about him. *And I call* him *insane! I should know better than to get involved with someone like him!*

How long should I let him sleep? She chuckled softly at the ridiculousness of it all. If anyone wandered by and saw them like this… Oh, the flurry of gossip she'd be fielding tomorrow! If her colleagues were questioning her competency already, what would they say about this?

A half hour later, she was still contemplating whether to wake him, when his head started sliding off her shoulder. She tried shifting her weight to keep him from slipping off too suddenly and hurting himself, but he instinctively caught himself, whipping his head back up as soon as it dropped. She slid her hand away discreetly, as he startled awake.

"Whoa!" he said. "What was that?"

"Terran English?" she noted. He traveled with Jeremy Tailor's crew, so that was no surprise.

"Yes." He rubbed his eyes. "I'm sorry for falling asleep on you."

| | It's okay, | | she chirped, switching back to Averian; English was not her best language. | | You needed the rest. | |

He smiled. | | And on such a comfortable shoulder. If only everyone could be so fortunate. | |

| | To fall sleep on a police officer, or on me? | | she asked, knowing very well what the answer was.

| | Yes, | | he twittered, not falling prey to the trick question. | | Thank you for your company, Sylvestra, and for not leaving me here to the denizens of the night. | |

| | Alright. Enough of the melodrama. | | She stood, and he followed suit. | | Now, I need to get home to sleep. | |

| | May I walk you? | |

She hesitated. *This is really getting awkward.* | | Not tonight, Kormèr. Thank you for the offer, but you need more sleep too; more than the thirty minutes you just had. | | He seemed slightly disappointed, but nodded his acceptance of her answer.

He nodded. | | Alright then. Good night, Sylvestra. | | He bowed slightly from the waist, turned, and opened his portal. Without turning to look back, he stepped through. The portal snapped shut, and he was gone.

And the first thought that crossed Sylvestra's mind was: *He didn't insist. He actually listens.*

AFTER losing Lezàl, Tseeo had returned to the precinct and told Phatheeo about his suspicions and his surveillance of Lezàl. Phatheeo paced slowly behind his desk while Tseeo stood, his tan plumage tight with tension, no doubt wondering how badly the Captain would chew him out. But Phatheeo had other things on his mind. His first instinct had been to deny that Sylvestra could be so easily coerced. But while he'd never seen it happen, he imagined that under the right circumstances, it could be possible. Surely she would have come to him, though.

He grew upset then, that despite their strong working relationship, she hadn't confided in him. And disappointed in himself for somehow failing her. Had he missed the clues? Tseeo was right that Reestee's lack of recognition of Lezàl's gems shouldn't have fully cleared the boy of suspicion.

And while the evidence of his arrival on Averia the morning after the theft was undeniable, it was not only a cosmic coincidence, but again, it did not eliminate the distinct possibility that Lezàl had connections to a larger group.

But without first confronting Sylvestra about these allegations, Phatheeo wouldn't undermine the Chief in the eyes of her underlings. He had to placate Tseeo, give him a task relevant to the situation without giving away his own concern for the Chief.

He stopped pacing and looked at Tseeo. ||Good thinking, Sergeant, though I guarantee the Chief knows what she's doing.|| He paused, then signaled for the door to close. Once the office door had shut, he sang, ||The rescind order was actually my idea.|| It was a lie, but a necessary one for now. ||But that's beside the point. You really should have come to me with this earlier.||

Tseeo nodded, clearly relieved as his plumage relaxed. ||I'm sorry, Captain. I had my suspicions about the boy, but I needed to make sure before involving you.||

Phatheeo grunted. ||You're a sergeant now, Tseeo, and that gives you some room to spread your wings. But you still need to check in with me when you're working a lead. You can't just disappear. Heck, even the Chief lets me know if she's going to be chasing a lead for any significant span of time. Understood?||

||Yessir.||

Phatheeo inhaled deeply, then exhaled. ||Right. I'm gonna let you follow your instinct on this one. But keep me apprised. And don't move on the boy without checking in with me first. I don't need to tell you that we need to circle carefully around this Elmarian.||

||Will do, sir. I'll start back at the hotel and see if he returned there. I *will* find out what he's up to.||

CHAPTER 20

CONSCIOUSNESS barreled its way over Kormèr, waking him but leaving him longing for more sleep. He looked at the clock and groaned. It was much too early. Didn't his brain realize he had two nights to catch up on?

He closed his eyes and buried his head under his pillow to block the brilliant sunlight that streamed into the room, easily bypassing the blackout drapes. But his brain wouldn't have it. It busied itself with thoughts of Sylvestra, Srrcheel's arrival, breakfast, taking a shower, and what might be good for lunch today... After minutes of listening to the thrum of his own metabolism, Kormèr sat up, yawned, slid off the bed and trudged to the bathroom. But the steamy shower that normally revitalized him had little effect this morning.

Kormèr dressed and dragged his feet out of his room toward the front desk. Ironically, as exhausted as he'd been the night before, he'd had trouble falling asleep once he'd gotten back to his room. He'd lain staring at the ceiling and thinking of how Sylvestra had let him sleep on her shoulder. Even now, his step lightened at the memory. Her allowance of his closeness, as well as the concern in her voice at his well-being... Maybe her opinion of him was changing for the better? That would have exceeded his wildest expectations, considering that he still hadn't delivered on his end of the bargain, but it was a glimmer of hope that sustained him, despite his tiredness.

<<Good morning, Kormèr Lezàl.>>

Kormèr was stunned that the familiar voice behind him sounded very much like Theeseeo's. Only Theeseeo didn't know a word of Elmarian. Kormèr turned. ||Theeseeo?||

<<Well you are?>> bubbled the smiling hotel manager.

Kormèr smiled. <<You are well?>> He switched to Averian. ||Just turn it around a bit.||

<<You... are well?>>

||Yes, that's it! That's great. Where did you pick that up?||

||My son. He loaned me one of his first-year study guides and pointed me to an app for my p-comm.|| He cleared his throat. <<I like red wine and cheese. My family has three people: me, my wife and my son.>>

Kormèr was impressed and flattered by Theeseeo's efforts. ||Excellent, Theeseeo!|| The birdman beamed. ||By the way, I'm expecting a guest today. A young Averian by the name of Srrcheel.||

||Very well. Would you like us to call you, or should I have your guest escorted to your room?||

||To my room, thanks.||

||Oh, and, Kormèr, please be careful how much you tip the bellhops. As much as I would love to see them all independently wealthy, someday, I still need them to work now, for the sake of the hotel and our guests.||

||Ah, I'm sorry. I didn't even think about that. I hope you haven't lost many.||

||Only one, here. But I've heard some other business owners grumbling. There is a diner you frequent?||

Kormèr cringed. ||Yes.||

Theeseeo nodded. ||Fortunately the owner is near retirement, and very well off since your patronage, but he's lost two servers.||

||Ouch. Thank you for letting me know. I'll be more mindful from now on.||

Kormèr returned to his room and tidied up, tossing his soiled clothes through the portal and into the washbasin on Elmar, where Trinket would take care of them. The rest of his mess he piled into drawers and closets. He dropped into a chair when he was done and had just starting to doze off when the door chimed.

"Hi, Srrcheel." He tipped the bellboy using the chip Sylvestra had given him.

"Hello, Kormèr. How're you?" Srrcheel entered as Kormèr stepped aside.

"A lot better than an hour ago, when I could barely keep my eyes open. And you?"

"Relieved, to say the least. I was nervous last night when the Grand Master called me."

"Thought it was about my visits or something?" asked Kormèr, grinning.

Srrcheel nodded. "Let's just say I'm glad we're meeting *here* today, and not at the Hovel. Thank you for calling for me through normal channels."

"Well, it was important to have you here, and I didn't want to get you into any trouble. How'd you travel here? Magic or sky-hopper?"

"No, no. More conventional than either of those. We prefer not to rely on the magic, if we don't have to. And we also don't allow sky-hoppers to Berdia. We either fly ourselves or ride the Argents."

"Oh? What's that?"

Srrcheel looked surprised, then his wings settled. "Of course, you found your own way onto Berdia; I can't believe I forgot that. Anyway, you must ride an Argent one of these days. They're the largest species of bird on the planet. We add harnesses and you ride strapped to their bellies. It's a thrilling ride."

"Sounds it," said Kormèr, imagining what it would be like to soar across the Averian landscape strapped to the belly of a giant bird.

Srrcheel frowned. "From the Argent station, I hailed a local taxi. The driver was an... odd fellow. When I asked him to bring me here, he asked me if I knew you."

Kormèr laughed. "Was his name Feestoo?"

Srrcheel thought about it. "I don't remember. I glanced at the driver's badge... no, I don't think it was Feestoo."

"Hmm. Maybe a friend of his. Feestoo's been driving me around in his taxi since I got here. Good guy."

Srrcheel rocked on his talons in silence, then said: "So... What is it you want me to do?"

"Relax. Grab a perch and I'll tell you all about it. Want something to drink? Nutria?"

"Umm, no. Thanks. Just some water, please."

"I haven't eaten yet, so I was going to order breakfast? You sure you don't want anything?"

Srrcheel nodded. "I'm fine. Thanks."

Kormèr brought up the room service menu and punched in an order. Then he pulled a chair to the side of the bed where Srrcheel had taken a seat. "Okay, now. Remember the jewelry store where we met, Chees?"

"Yes."

"Well, I've gotten... involved in the case—"

"I won't assist you in your stealing," said Srrcheel resolutely.

"No, no. It's nothing like that. Besides, I'm working on the side of the law this time. It all started the day I got here..." Kormèr told Srrcheel the complete story, up to and including his encounter with the thief.

Srrcheel just stared at him when he was done. Finally, he spoke. "You are the strangest person I have ever met."

And he's a sorcerer living amongst other sorcerers, so that's saying something. Kormèr frowned. "I've been getting that a lot lately."

"I meant no offense." Srrcheel smiled. "I actually feel more at ease when my friends are a little strange."

Kormèr's lips twitched in a smile. *He called me his friend.* "People are more interesting that way." Good or bad, Kormèr strived to learn from everyone he met, hoping he had something to share with them, too.

Srrcheel smiled and started to say something, but the door chime interrupted him. It was a bellhop with Kormèr's breakfast. Kormèr took the tray and again tipped with the chip.

As Kormèr started on his food, Srrcheel said, "I... uh... I don't want to ruin your appetite or anything but, you should know." Kormèr stopped eating and gave Srrcheel his full attention.

"I noticed the way you spoke about the Chief of Police. Are you aware that there is an Averian law that prohibits interspecies pairings?"

Kormèr felt his body go numb and forgot about the food. "Pairings? As in marriage or just relationships?"

"Definitely marriage," said Srrcheel. "Relationships are frowned upon, but not prohibited."

Though Kormèr was years away from contemplating a commitment as serious as marriage, and the odds of *any* kind of meaningful relationship with Sylvestra were miniscule at best, he still had difficulty processing what Srrcheel was telling him. "But... I'm sure she knows how I feel, but she... she didn't say anything."

Srrcheel sipped his water. "You said that the police are desperate to solve the case. Maybe she didn't think you'd help her, if she told you..."

"That I have no chance with her, ever?" *Have I misjudged this woman completely?* Kormèr was in shock for several moments, his mind trying to correlate his experiences, his conversations with Sylvestra and this new information. But the two wouldn't match up. *I couldn't have misread her so badly,* he thought.

Srrcheel's words came to him as if from a distance. "I just thought you should know, in case you were... you know, imagining what could be."

Kormèr looked up at him. "Yes, thank you. I might seem like a fool."

"It just means you're fallible, like everyone else," Srrcheel said. "Although, I am definitely glad that you didn't talk me into casting a love spell for you, like you wanted on the day we met—now that I know who you had in mind."

"Yes, that would've been awkward," Kormèr murmured.

Srrcheel shrugged his wings. "Let's get back to what you wanted me to do? About the robbery, I mean."

"Ah, right. Well, I have to admit that the way the thief appeared to me—that whole distortion thing—scared me. And it made me realize something very important: I'm really out of my depth here."

Srrcheel nodded sagely, then shook his head. "I'm not following."

"I told you that the portal allows me to travel to different places. What I didn't mention was that it also allows me to jump through time." Srrcheel's feathery brows went up in surprise, and Kormèr plowed on. "I am from Elmar, but the one from one hundred and twenty years ago." He paused. "No wait, those are Elmarian years. Here, it would be closer to four hundred and eighty years in the past. We have—*had*—technology on Elmar, to an extent, but nothing like what I've seen here. We don't—didn't—even have spaceships."

Srrcheel sat in silence for a moment, his eyes staring at nothing. "Ah. I understand now," he said, slowly. "You can't solve this heist based on your experience because this technology is beyond your experience."

"Exactly! I've thought about using Jeremy's edu-comp to bring myself up to date, but there's so much to learn and so little time. I wouldn't even know what fields of science to focus on."

Srrcheel wrung his hands. "I don't see how I fit into this picture yet. I can't bring you 'up to date', as I'm not familiar with technology at all, except from a usage standpoint."

"I know. That wasn't what I was expecting of you." Kormèr sighed. "I'm not sure *what* I expected, really. It was just such a sudden realization that I was kind of adrift, and you, with your magic, were the only thing I could think of that might make sense of what I saw. Maybe I overreacted. I'm sorry. I didn't mean to waste your time."

"No, no. It's alright. Besides, I'm here, and I can't go back without helping you somehow. Maybe if we go through all the details together, we can figure something out between the two of us."

Kormèr shrugged. "I'm willing to try anything at this point. Okay, here's what I know…"

Thirty minutes later, Feestoo's taxi slid into a taxi stop on the promenade close to Chees, and Kormèr and Srrcheel stepped out.

||Thanks, Feestoo,|| sang Kormèr. ||We'll walk back.||

Kormèr turned back and found Srrcheel staring in the jewelry store's direction. "Did you notice something?" he asked.

"Hmm? Oh, no. Just thinking back. It's hard to believe we met right there only a week ago."

"A lot can happen in a week."

"Maybe. But life wasn't as interesting before I met you, that's for sure."

Kormèr smiled as a Terran phrase came to him. "May you live in interesting times."

Srrcheel nodded, then frowned. "That almost sounds like a curse."

Kormèr laughed as the realization hit him. "Yeah, I suppose some could take it that way. Follow me. I was right over there when the thief revealed himself. He came at me from there…" He turned back when he noticed Srrcheel had not followed. Instead, the birdman peered through an elliptical sliver of glass as he scanned the promenade.

"What's that?" asked Kormèr.

As he continued slowly panning around, Srrcheel murmured, "A true-seeing eye. If the thief is using something to hide himself, spell or… some other trick, this should be able to reveal him. But I don't see anything out of the ordinary right now."

"That's good. At least we know I won't get a weapon pointed at me again. Twice in the past few days is enough."

Srrcheel lowered the glass eye. "Twice?"

"I'll tell you about the other time later." He waved for Srrcheel to follow as he continued toward the store. They crossed the bridge together and stopped at the window to the right of the doorway. Inside, they could see Cheert Reestee attending to a patron. Kormèr noticed that the display cases inside the store held more stock than they had the last time he'd been inside.

"What about inside the store?" asked Kormèr, suddenly connecting two data points. "What if the thief used that distortion tech to hide inside the store until closing time, then took everything, and waited again until the store reopened? He would've walked right out with all the loot, and no one would've seen him."

Srrcheel peered through the glass eye again, this time into the store. "That sounds possible, from what you described. But you also said that the sensors would have detected the movement of the jewelry itself as the thief moved it, no?"

"Yeah. That occurred to me as I was talking. But we don't know the limits of that tech. It's got to factor into this case somehow."

"Hmm."

"What?"

"You might be onto something. See for yourself." Srrcheel handed him the eye.

Kormèr fumbled the fragile object in his excitement. He managed to steady his hand enough to look through it. Remarkably, instead of the distorted view he had expected to see, a sharp image replaced his normal vision entirely. He swooned, momentarily dizzy. "By the gods!"

"Oh, sorry. Close your other eye before you look."

Now he tells me. "Thanks. That was not what I was expecting at all." Kormèr closed his left eye and raised the glass eye to his right, this time prepared for the enhanced vision. He found that as his own eye moved, the image shifted without his having to move the glass eye. "What am I looking for?"

"Up on the ceiling, almost over the counter on the left."

"Okay. I'm looking, but I still don't see anything special."

Srrcheel grunted and took the eye away from Kormèr. He peered through it once again, then handed it back. "It's not really anything 'special'. Look first without the eye, then with the eye. No, wait... ugh. Don't forget to close the other eye," he said, when Kormèr swooned again.

"Got it! Got it. This magic business isn't easy." Kormèr looked at the ceiling through his right eye, then, still looking at the same spot, slid the glass eye into his field of vision again.

"What you're looking for is right about where that smudge is on the ceiling."

Kormèr pulled the glass eye away, then back. He finally spotted it. "It's a shadow, not a smudge. When I don't use the eye, I see the shadow. When I use the eye, I can see a box or something."

"The box must be bending light to make itself invisible. It's probably the same tech the thief used. The eye unbends the light, focuses it."

"Amazing. So you mean to tell me that the shadow is an invisible box stuck to the "

"That's it."

"Buomp!" Kormèr cursed in Elmarian.

"Huh?"

"Nothing. What the hell is a light-bending box doing stuck on the ceiling? Could it be part of the security system?"

Srrcheel shrugged. "I've kind of heard of tech like this. And considering the thief seems to have been using something similar... If you ask me, they're connected."

"Can you get the box for me?"

"Perhaps. If it's not stuck there too tightly, I can think of a spell or two that might dislodge it."

"Awesome!"

"I'll have to find the spell, though. It's not anything I've studied so far, but it might be in the other Caster tomes."

Kormèr nodded. "How long will that take?"

"I should be done by evening, if I start right away."

"Ah. The store will be closed by then."

"Not to mention we have to get back to my room... Speaking of which, are you the one that arranged my stay at the Cheerees?"

Kormèr grinned. "Since I had no idea what you could do for me, or how long it would take..." He shrugged. "By the way, we'll be using the 'Kormèr Lezàl Express' to get back to the hotel."

Srrcheel quirked an eyebrow at him, then laughed. "Your portal! Of course. That would definitely make things faster." Then he stopped. "Hold on a minute. You can travel through time using your portal. Why can't you just go back to the night of the robbery and see it happen?"

Kormèr grinned, sheepishly. "I've considered that. But I want to try solving this case without... well, without cheating. It's kind of like what you said earlier about using magic: I prefer not to rely on it if I don't have to."

Srrcheel said nothing right away. Then he shrugged his wings. "I can respect that."

"In fact, forget the portal. It's a nice day. Let's walk back."

"Aren't you in a rush to solve this?" asked Srrcheel, keeping pace as Kormèr started off toward the hotel.

"Yeah. But I've been killing myself the past few days. I need to slow down, and this way we get to chat for a while. Like, I don't know what your favorite color is, or what music you like. I live with robots, and they have no preferences of their own."

Srrcheel smiled. "Robots? Now that's interesting. What do they do?"

SERGEANT Chreel Tseeo watched the two boys walk off and followed them at a distance. As he followed, he set his p-comm to run an identity match on Lezàl's companion. The boy seemed vaguely familiar, but Tseeo couldn't place him.

Within minutes, the p-comm buzzed. Tseeo read the data and could've smacked himself for not realizing it immediately. AvoNet had identified the boy as a Berdian sorcerer named Srrcheel, recently ascended to the rank of Initiate Caster. And now Tseeo recognized him as the assistant to the sorcerer that the Chief had called out days ago. But what was he doing here again? And why were he and Lezàl loitering around Chees? Could Lezàl have co-opted the sorcerers to help him? The sorcerers had always kept to themselves, using their arcane abilities outside of Berdia only when asked to do so, and only by other Averians. But Lezàl seemed to have a way with people; Tseeo could imagine him convincing them to do his bidding. But why would he be casing the same store? There was very little left to rob. *Unless he left some evidence behind and was trying to clean it.*

Sometimes Tseeo wished he could just bypass the law, grab Lezàl and "persuade" the answers out of him. He took a long, deep breath. *Relax,* he told himself. *That's not what you're here for. And who knows, if you catch Lezàl doing something wrong, you might still get your chance. But for now, it's just surveillance.*

The two boys arrived at Lezàl's hotel, entering through the ground floor entrances. They rode the lifts up to Lezàl's floor and stopped in front of the door across from Lezàl's room. They exchanged some words in Terran English, then the boy entered the room and Kormèr crossed the hall and disappeared into his own room. A few minutes later, Lezàl came out and descended to the hotel's shopping floor where he perused Averian women's jewelry and accessories shops. Tseeo bristled when Lezàl paid for his purchases with a gem. He reminded himself that he was only observing; he'd interfere only if he actually saw Lezàl breaking the law.

Lezàl stuffed his purchases into his coat pockets, then walked to a taxi stop where his usual driver swooped in to pick him up. Tseeo hadn't even seen where the taxi had come from. It was just suddenly there. He watched with a morbid glee as Lezàl nearly got into an argument with a Raelyan male who was waiting for a taxi. Lezàl asked the alien man if he wouldn't mind sharing the taxi, and the two got in.

Tseeo flew after them and landed nearby, as the taxi pulled over to unload the Raelyan.

||Here's my number,|| Lezàl was telling the man. ||Don't hesitate to call me if it doesn't work out. But I think if you consider the approach we discussed, she'll be more amenable to letting you fertilize her egg.||

||Thank you so much, Kormèr. I will let you know either way what happens.|| The man turned and walked into a nearby bank, leaving Tseeo wondering what that had been about. But before he could give it much thought, the taxi pulled away once again.

Lezàl stopped for lunch, spent most of the afternoon in the Museum of Natural History, then took the taxi to the Theesl residence. Tseeo frowned as they admitted Kormèr into the home. Once again, he wondered about Lezàl's relationship with the Theesls. *What business could he have with them?* His gizzard rumbled in sympathetic frustration. *I swear this boy will be the end of me!*

Lezàl exited a moment later, arm-in-arm with Tzee'oo Theesl's daughter again. They boarded Lezàl's taxi and went off to dine at one of Birshetland's more upscale restaurants. Tseeo's curiosity set his feathers on edge; he desperately wanted to know what business those two could possibly have together. But he had no way of getting close enough to hear their conversation, and he wished he had the authority to bug Lezàl.

His gizzard rumbled again, this time from hunger. Deciding he wasn't getting anywhere watching the couple eat, Tseeo dashed off to a fast-food joint and grabbed a savory larvae soup and jellied worm salad. He ate perched on a tree, in sight of the couple in the restaurant. They talked, laughed, ate... Lezàl paid the bill with another gem. Then it was back to the Theesl residence where both youngsters disappeared inside. A light came on in a room upstairs for about thirty minutes. Then it went out, and it dawned on Tseeo exactly the kind of business the two had together.

How disgusting! An Averian female cavorting with an offworlder! And the daughter of Tzee'oo Theesl, no less! He clucked disapprovingly, shaking his head. *Spoiled child; to do that to her parents. She deserves to have her flight feathers snipped.*

As his shock faded, Tseeo felt drained. He'd barely slept for nearly two days, and exhaustion did not make a good companion. He glanced up at the dark window and decided he wouldn't miss anything in the next half hour if he took a brief nap. He pinned his badge to his utility strap and settled on his haunches, talons automatically locking onto the branch. Quicker than he realized, he was asleep.

DESPITE a lovely evening with Syrree, Kormèr slept fitfully. Sure, the mystery box on the ceiling of Chees revealed itself to be nothing more than that, but it was the only anomaly so far, and one that connected with the thief's tech. And an anomaly meant a possibility, the outline of a door where before, there had just been a smooth, blank and very solid wall. When he did sleep, Kormèr dreamed of solving the case and holding Sylvestra in his arms.

Even Syrree, now in deep slumber at his side, had noticed his sparkling energy that night. He had even surprised himself, considering that his mind had been on solving the heist almost the whole time. Kormèr felt bad about that in retrospect, but nothing had ever meant so much to him as solving this case.

Bah! I can't sleep. He carefully lifted the covers and left the bed. He paced about the room for a while, hoping to tire himself enough to want to return to bed. But the exercise resulted in making him even more alert. With nothing better to do, he opened the door and stepped out into the corridor. He didn't have to worry much about being naked; Syrree's parents were at a function, so she had this floor of the house pretty much to herself. Besides, Averians viewed nudity differently than some other species. Syrree had told Kormèr over dinner that, as a species, they never wore clothes. Smooth-skinned species appeared to Averians as if they'd been plucked. She'd even admitted that the sensation of his smooth skin against her was one of the things that she enjoyed about sex with him. He'd laughed and admitted in return that he enjoyed the feeling of feathers against him.

Smiling at the memory, he walked purposefully to the furthest guest room. Days ago, on an earlier scout around the floor, Kormèr had discovered that this room was not a guest room at all, but Tzee'oo's work room. It was furnished and, Kormèr decided, served the same functional purpose as the study in his own home on Elmar. Kormèr found the desk stunning in design, with crystal accents on the otherwise blue and white mosaic. Two stacks of flimsies had sat on the desktop. Paintings decorated the left and right walls of the room, and valuable-looking curios sat awaiting Kormèr's closer inspection.

Kormèr cracked the door, making sure Syrree's father hadn't returned unexpectedly. He entered, and quickly rifled through the stacks of flimsies: two new policies, three proposals for upgrades to some air quality processors, grav-repulsor something-or-other, a few "Service Requests" and bills—

He stopped, then flipped back a few flimsies. *What's this? Grav-repulsor landing gear? Tzee'oo is involved in this, too?* Kormèr read through the file list. One contained the original proposal presented by Jeremy and Kit; it had editing marks all over it and block letters across the heading reading **REJECTED**. Two other files contained revised versions of the initial proposal, though they too had been rejected. A fourth revision had few markings other than a hand-scrawled note at the top which read: "Environmental tests pending". This had to be the current working revision. Kormèr read through it and liked what he found. If it passed, the proposal would permit the guys to establish a market for their product in Freet-See through a local vendor. Jeremy's team would retain all rights and patents to their product, and the product would sell under the name of their corporation. It didn't sound like much, but considering the hub of offworld activity that Freet-See seemed to be, not to mention Averia in general, the deal could end up being quite lucrative.

Kormèr looked up and out the large bay window behind the desk. The evening lights illuminating the trees had dimmed, and dawn had turned the world a deep gray. *Buomp! It's dawn already?*

Each of the six listed tests had links in addition to a message link enveloping them all. Bars colored green and amber appeared beneath five of the tests, and as Kormèr slid his finger over each one, a sidebar expanded, revealing that the bars represented completion status. Three of the tests had completed successfully, while the two with yellow bars neared completion. Curious, Kormèr opened the message; the lead tester had sent it. In it, he mentioned that, to the best of his judgment, the results of all the tests fell within acceptable parameters, and that it was unlikely the final test would be any different. He asked Tzee'oo to please review each of the tests and add any personal comments or adjustments as he saw fit. Kormèr considered adding a few favorable notes on some of the linked test requests; but he knew so little of the technology of this period that he decided against it. At best, any notes he made might get a few nods; at worst, it could cause the entire proposal to get rejected again or simply thrown out if illegal tampering were uncovered.

He replaced the flimsy in the stack, accidentally activating a flim tile that was attached to another flimsy. He would have ignored it had the tile not started blinking some very large numbers. Wide-eyed, Kormèr took a closer look and found it was a fund transfer receipt. He activated the attached flimsy, read it… and gasped. It was signed: "Harold G"! And it was dated from less than a week ago! The note had been carefully written, thanking Tzee'oo Theesl for his help but never mentioning names or details. Anyone reading this who wasn't aware of Mister G's involvement with Jeremy would never know what it was about.

Kormèr frowned, angered that Tzee'oo had taken a bribe from Harry G; this would not do. He put the note aside and returned to the flimsy containing the tests. He reviewed each test, but again concluded that he didn't understand enough about the tests themselves to make any legitimate-sounding comments. Instead, he replied directly to the lead tester with: "The results all look fine so far. If the last succeeds, pass them all and let's be done with this."

He sent the reply then slipped Jeremy's proposal back in its place. He grabbed the flimsy with the attached transfer slip and considered his next move carefully. He knew Tzee'oo would not forget about the transfer slip, but its absence could go unnoticed for a while. Kormèr made up his mind, slithered back out into the corridor and back into Syrree's room where he slipped the flimsy and transfer slip into his coat pocket.

As he eased back into the bed, Syrree stirred and turned, facing him with dream-filled eyes. ||Good morning, you sexy fiend.||

Kormèr smiled. ||Good morning, wild child.||

Syrree giggled. ||Daddy won't be coming in here this morning; he's probably still out.||

Kormèr raised an eyebrow. ||Indeed?||

||Yes,|| she chirped, moving closer. ||Indeed.||

HARRY G watched Seertsor, the closest of the Averian moons, drift past as his ship approached the bright planet ahead. He evaluated the untapped potential in Averia's two moons and considered whether he wanted to exploit them. As Seertsor passed beyond the viewscreen, he decided that the better approach would be to convince someone else to initiate that enterprise and then take over once it showed a profit.

Freet-See traffic control provided a landing vector and assigned him a berth. As his autopilot guided the ship along the landing vector, Harry G patched into the global public net and quickly found the report of his hirelings' botched attempt to seize Tailor's ship and crew. The hired mercs on Io he could understand causing such a ridiculous scene, but Aggreyates? Those Aggreyates would never find work again for their utter and very public failure. If Harry G couldn't count on Aggreyates anymore, who could he count on?

Hassera? He searched but could find nothing of her activities since her attempted sabotage of Tailor's hotel room. Had she come to understand her mistake? If anyone could figure out that Harry G was en route to Averia, it would have been her. Why hadn't she left a message for him or sent an update via courier? Too many unknown variables existed to understand what that Suslixan could be thinking. However, as he cleared the outer atmosphere, he received a message alert, and the routing identified it as having come from *Ship*.

"Mister G, I first want to apologize for not contacting you sooner. The news that Royland was killed by Tailor's crew unbalanced me. You've no doubt heard that I even made an attempt on Tailor's life." Harry G listened to the various nuances of her voice; whether over the wire or from a recording, his delicate senses often picked up on insincerities or half-truths. But as with most Suslixans, the voice carried only facts and little in the way of any emotion. *"I immediately realized that was a grave mistake. Now that I have recovered from the injuries I sustained, I would like to meet you to discuss my continued employment. I know you are en route, and so prepared this message to send when you arrive. Please consider that I would like nothing more than to personally hand Tailor and his crew over to you. Hassera, out."*

Along the interstellar journey, Harry G had dispatched another set of couriers, setting some wheels in motion, striking from the inside with a few bribes here and there. He had also decided that the time had come to ditch his all-mercenary hired guns. He knew he should have done so long ago, but they had always proven sufficiently effective that, for their cost, any small failures had not warranted drastic action. But his very mature business called for a more mature security team, and fortunately, he had discovered that a very good one happened to be in the neighborhood. Now, as his ship settled into its assigned berth, he considered Hassera's request. While she belonged to the old guard, she operated in ways that differed from their crude methods. And he'd never met a better information broker, at least not since himself in days long past. Her slip with the attempted sabotage revealed that she could lose control of herself, though she had clearly not followed through with a second attempt. Numerous other pros and cons iterated through his head before he finally responded to her, inviting her to his ship within the hour, and no later, or she'd be out. In person, he would get a better read from her. Then he would decide whether or not to welcome her back into the fold.

When the post-flight tasks were done, Harry G left his ship and found an alert but relaxed-looking man and woman standing a few paces from the ramp. The man had the height and leanness of a Jaltan, while the woman looked human, but Harry G could tell that the woman was actually Elmarian. Both sported slate-gray, tailored, loose-fitting uniforms with berets, a detail that amused Harry G for its call-back to ancient times. He found their neat appearance a refreshing change from the slovenly attire of the low-level mercenary types he'd hired until now.

The woman took a step forward. "Welcome to Averia," she said, her hands loosely at her sides; her brown eyes fixed on Harry G's eyes. "I'm Cial d'Eliz."

The Jaltan took a step forward. "I'm Kellan Toure," he said, his voice deep and rumbly.

"Nice to meet you both," said Harry G, with a nod. "Thank you for meeting me on such short notice."

Cial dipped her head slightly in acknowledgement. "You are familiar with our terms?"

"I am." He stepped to one side of the ramp, leaving the way up clear. "Shall we step inside and discuss the particulars?"

Cial strode confidently up the ramp. When Kellan didn't follow, Harry G looked over at him. "After you," said Kellan.

Harry G grinned. "Of course," he said, and followed Cial inside. So far, the interaction pleased him. If the pair lived up to their reputation, this would be a very profitable partnership that he could see lasting a long time. And they would also have a chance to meet Hassera and offer him their evaluation. Harry G felt confident that he would soon have everything under control.

CHAPTER 21

STANDING in front of a mirror, Kormèr considered his reflection. He had on a full-face mask that he rarely wore, mostly because its very appearance insinuated a nefarious purpose, and Kormèr didn't want to be caught with it. But this morning, with nothing better to do after breakfast with Syrree, Kormèr tried wearing the mask with Srrcheel's night-vision glasses. He had to wait for Srrcheel anyway, and the birdboy had not yet emerged from his room. While the mask and glasses combo didn't make Kormèr look any less sinister, he decided it wasn't a bad look. He frowned under the mask, knowing the outfit was quite impractical. He removed the face mask, and his rumpled reflection reminded him of the other reason he hated full-face-masks: they totally ruined his hair.

He tossed the mask on the bed and carefully folded the glasses into his coat's pocket, then ducked into the bathroom to fix his hair. He emerged minutes later, hair neatly coifed, and grunted when he saw how little time had passed on the bedside clock.

The door chimed, and Srrcheel's face appeared on the display.

"About time," protested Kormèr, opening the door.

Srrcheel stopped and held his arms akimbo. "Hey, this spell was not easy. I've been up all night."

Kormèr felt mortified. "Seriously? Wow! I'm sorry; I had no idea. You didn't have to do that."

"But you've only got two days left."

"Yeah, but... Well, I appreciate the effort."

Srrcheel's wings flicked. "I'm not entirely unselfish. If you don't succeed, I look bad, too."

Kormèr shrugged. "In that case, c'mon. Let's go get that box and see if we can close this case."

Kormèr opened the portal and waited for Srrcheel to step through.

"You first," said Srrcheel, grinning. "Stepping blindly into that thing... I don't know. I'm just not comfortable with it yet."

"I get it. Sometimes I wish it showed where it was opening to." Kormèr shrugged and stepped through. With a glance, he knew he stood exactly where he'd intended, a remote spot on the promenade behind a pseudo tree, but only a short walk from Chees.

Srrcheel stepped through a moment later, his plumage puffed slightly. He stopped and shuddered, and his feathers settled back into smoothness. "Yeah. That would take me a while to get used to."

Kormèr closed the portal, and the two boys crossed the promenade and entered the store.

||Hello, Mister Reestee,|| chirped Kormèr.

||Hello, young man,|| warbled the store owner, listlessly. ||Can I help—|| His eyes bulged as Kormèr came closer. ||You! Don't move.||

Kormèr stopped. *Uh, oh. What now?* His muscles tensed, prepared to dart out the door at the first sign of trouble. ||What?||

As Cheert Reestee rushed around the counter, Srrcheel whispered, "What'd you do?"

"I've no idea," Kormèr whispered back.

Cheert stood before Kormèr, holding him at arm's length. Srrcheel sidestepped them and circled around behind Cheert, where he began casting his spell out of the man's line of sight. Kormèr kept his eyes on Cheert so the birdman would not notice Srrcheel. Not that there appeared much danger of that, as Kormèr held Cheert's attention keenly.

||You gave me that gem the other day!||

I gave him a gem? Oh! For the broken mirror. ||Yes?|| warbled Kormèr, unsure if his admission would incur favor or rebuke.

||I made my biggest sale in a long... *long* time with that gem!|| crowed the birdman. ||Wherever did you get it?||

Kormèr sighed, his muscles relaxing.

Srrcheel continued his arm motions behind the man.

||Well, it's a long story—||

||Please, I must know!||

Kormèr glanced briefly at Srrcheel, who had stopped his casting. The birdboy stared at the ceiling, shaking his head. ||Oh, well. It's from another planet.||

||I know that!|| twittered Reestee, curtly. ||There isn't a mine on Averia that produces gems like that.||

Srrcheel rested his chin on his hand in thought.

||I suppose not,|| sang Kormèr. ||With your knowledge of gems, you'd be well aware of it, if one existed.||

Cheert nodded. ||I do pride myself on knowing my minerals, of course. But this other planet, what's its name? Do they export their gems?||

Srrcheel scowled, then swung his arms about in a tight, angry arc.

||They don't really know much about exporting offworld,|| sang Kormèr, stalling as much as he could.

Srrcheel snapped his arms toward the ceiling, and Cheert collapsed, following a metallic *clink* from the vicinity of his head. Another *clink* followed a *thunk* from the floor, as Kormèr caught Cheert's unconscious body before the birdman slumped to the floor.

Srrcheel's crest puffed in agitation as he rushed over. ||Oh no!|| He touched his hand to Cheert's head. ||Damn my clumsiness.||

"Don't worry. He'll be fine." Kormèr lowered his catch to the floor slowly, hoping that none of Sylvestra's team was watching the store at the moment. If they'd seen this, they'd be rushing in at any moment now. "I take it that was the box that fell on his head."

"Yes, the frustrating thing. I must have tried the same spell five or six times and done it wrong every time. Either that, or the box was really stuck on there."

"Well, that last try did the trick," said Kormèr, glancing around the floor. "Now, if we could just find it. You wouldn't happen to have an anti-invisibility spell."

"No. But I have the eye." He gestured with his hand and the glass eye appeared in it.

Kormèr grinned. "Yes!"

"There it is! By your foot… no, the other one. Yes, that's it— Careful, you're about to—"

Kormèr kicked the box. The showroom went completely dark.

"Kormèr?"

"Yes, Srrcheel." Kormèr felt about in the dark around his foot.

"What happened?"

"Not sure. Maybe I turned it on."

Rays of light speared out, and the store was bright once again. Only it wasn't exactly the store at the moment: the display cases brimmed with jewelry and brilliant gems; several customers milled about; a bright-eyed Cheert Reestee helped them gaily with their purchases. An Averian male stood over Kormèr, his eyes not on the jewelry, like the others, but on Kormèr… or rather, towards him. The birdman had dark silvery-gray plumage. He glanced around occasionally and moved his hands as if he were holding something in them.

Kormèr frowned up at the man. He waved a hand before the man's face. The man ignored him, continuing whatever he was doing.

"Srrcheel?!"

"You don't have to shout. I can hear you."

"Where are you?" Kormèr stood and looked around, but his feathered friend was nowhere in sight.

"I'm right where I was before the lights went out. Where're you?"

"I can hear you, but I can't see you."

"Same here, unless I use the eye. What's happening?"

"I don't know. But there's no question that the box is behind this somehow."

"Can you find it? The eye isn't as clear as it had been before. It looks like it's still by your feet."

Kormèr kicked around a bit until his foot struck something. "I think I have it." He reached down. "Oops. No, that's Mr. Reestee's head."

"Yes. Try to your right a bit…"

"To the right... Ahh... Yup. Got it." The box had to be roughly half a meter long and a third of that wide and tall. It felt dense as Kormèr slipped the tips of his fingers under one side and lifted it from the floor with a slight effort. He estimated it weighed around six or seven kilos.

"Turn it off. There's a set of switches on top. Wait, I'll just do it."

Kormèr balanced the bulky box on his thigh and felt for the buttons. "I'm tryi—" The scene vanished, replaced by an unconscious Cheert, and Srrcheel standing less than a meter away. "Trying," finished Kormèr. He looked down at his empty hands and knew only by weight and feel that he held anything at all. "Amazing!"

"What?" Srrcheel bent down to check on Cheert.

"Did you see the Averian man that was standing here doing what I just did, just looking at his empty hands?"

Srrcheel nodded. "He was hard to miss. I've never seen an Averian with such dark plumage outside of Berdia."

"Is that so? That's got to make him easier to identify. No wonder he hides behind that blur-tech."

"Aha! What you said just hit me, about how he was looking at his empty hands. He must've had the box in his hands."

"That's right. Ugh, this thing is annoyingly heavy."

"It's got handles on the sides. Oh, you already found those. There's a single handle on the side too."

Kormèr tried carrying it one-handed, but had to lean to the left as his right arm tired. "Nope. There's no good way to carry this."

Srrcheel stood. "I cast a very minor heal spell on Mister Reestee, but we should make sure he gets medical attention. That spell is meant for cuts and bruises, not concussions."

Kormèr stared at Srrcheel. "Okay. I don't know how to do that here."

"I just wanted to make sure that was alright with you," added Srrcheel, as he worked his p-comm.

"Of course it is. I don't want to see anyone get hurt."

"Good. The video footage is going to look inexplicably bizarre, though."

Kormèr closed his eyes. "Oh, of course. The security footage. It'll look like he simply passed out, but then all the other stuff..."

Kormèr broke off as Srrcheel's p-comm connected with another party. Srrcheel reported Cheert as having passed out unexpectedly. Kormèr rested the box on the countertop and kept a hand on it to make sure he didn't lose track of it. He considered what to do with it when the medical team arrived. It would look very odd if he were ambling about carrying it. He removed his coat and wrapped the box in it, but because of the dimensions of the box, that looked even stranger. He couldn't open the portal here or the security video would catch that. He had no choice but to call Feestoo, carry the box out, and leave it in Feestoo's taxi until the medics had the situation in hand.

"That's what it all reminds me of!" exclaimed Srrcheel once he closed the connection. "You know, the store changing and the customers and all. It's something I saw in a movie once: holography. I thought it was just movie magic and never realized the effect could be so… real."

"Is that what you think this does?" asked Kormèr, tapping the box. "You said something to that effect yesterday."

Srrcheel again peered through his magic eye. "The box has no markings; even on the buttons. But that has to be what it is." He passed the eye to Kormèr.

Kormèr peered at the device through the eye for several moments. "Hmm, a holographer… There are holographers on Elmar, but nothing that can do what this one does. Well, at least not in my time." He paused. "Let's talk to Jeremy. He might know more about these things."

"Jeremy?"

Kormèr nodded, absently dropping the magic eye into his coat pocket. "A Terran friend of mine. He and his team are pretty tech-savvy. You'll like them."

Feestoo's fob chimed, signaling that he was outside or on approach. "I'll be back," said Kormèr, grabbing the holographer. "I want to get this out of here before the medics arrive."

Srrcheel nodded.

||Hi, KL,|| greeted Feestoo from his open driver's window.

||You got here fast,|| sang Kormèr.

||I was dropping off a passenger nearby.|| He finally noticed Kormèr's awkward gait and asked, ||Is everything okay?||

||Yes,|| sang Kormèr, opening the rear passenger door. ||Very okay, in fact. You can't see it, but I've got a major piece of evidence in the Chees robbery here.||

Feestoo turned his head to look. ||Alright. But should you really be… um… taking it?||

||Yes, for now. I need to learn more about it before—||

Kormèr spun at the sound of sirens behind him. A pastel-green hover vehicle descended on the promenade across from Chees, its colorful lights flashing. Two police patrol cars accompanied it. The moment the cars landed, four officers dashed from them and into the jewelry store.

"Buomp!" spat Kormèr. "Sorry, Srrcheel," he mumbled, knowing that he couldn't go back in now without raising suspicion. The security footage would reveal him later, if and when someone reviewed it. But for now, Srrcheel would have to handle the situation on his own.

Kormèr sat in the back of the taxi and kept conversation with Feestoo light while he waited. While he wanted to mention the holographer and all that had happened moments ago in the store, he didn't want to burden Feestoo with too much information that might get the man into trouble with the police later.

Thirty minutes later, Kormèr spotted Srrcheel exiting the store and looking around. Kormèr climbed out of the taxi and waved until Srrcheel spotted him.

| | You didn't come back, | | protested Srrcheel, his switch to Averian a sign of his obvious annoyance.

"I'm sorry. When I saw the police… If I'd gone back in there, there would've been a lot more explaining to do."

Srrcheel frowned. "Yes, I suppose you're right about that. So, I did enough explaining for both of us."

"Thank you. What'd the police want?"

"Not much, actually. They just looked around and made sure nothing new had been stolen. Mister Reestee was confused, but was able to account for his property. Thanks to my spell, he didn't have any suspicious bruise on his head for the medics to find. So then they just let me go."

"Good. Nice going with the spell."

Srrcheel sighed. "So now what? Off to see these friends of yours?"

Kormèr nodded. "Yes. I'll let them know we're coming. Their ship was hijacked recently, so they might have tightened security."

"Hijacked?" He mused. "Well, they know *you*, so of course, that makes sense."

"Hey!"

"No offense," Srrcheel added with a smirk.

Kormèr smiled and shook his head as he opened a comm connection to Jeremy. "I'm bringing a guest," he told Jeremy after greetings and after asking for permission to stop by. "Alright, thanks. We'll be there in a few minutes. Out."

He closed the connection and grabbed the invisible holographer from the taxi before closing the door.

| | Thanks, Feestoo. Sorry for holding you up, but we're off to Freet-See for the afternoon. | |

| | No worries, KL, | | sang Feestoo. | | Enjoy the trip. | |

As the taxi pulled away, Srrcheel said, "Hold on. Your friends are on Freet-See?"

"Yep," said Kormèr.

"But you told them we'd be there in a few minute— Ugh. The portal again."

Kormèr nodded. "Yeah, sorry. I don't have the luxury of time."

Srrcheel shook his head. "No, I get it. Let's get it over with."

They returned to the remote location, and Kormèr opened the portal. He stepped through and into the corridor by the ship's mess on the *Stardust IV*. Roke was there, and the long-haired man beamed Kormèr a smile, as Srrcheel stepped out of the portal.

"Welcome aboard, dude!" greeted Roke, then nodded at Srrcheel. "And bird-dude!"

Kormèr returned the smile. "Thanks!" he said, naturally matching Roke's chipper effluence. "Roke, this is my good friend, Srrcheel."

Roke bobbed his head at Srrcheel. "High sky, man."

"High sky," said Srrcheel, a little surprised by the warm welcome.

Kormèr sealed the portal and dropped the cube into his coat pocket. He walked to the table and sat the cloaked holographer atop it. "So Jeremy and Kit are in Birshetland again?" he asked while sliding into a seat. Srrcheel followed his lead, sitting to his right.

"Yeah, man. Some necessary prereqs completed, so they went to, like hopefully, finish the negotiations."

"That would be awesome," said Kormèr.

Mack walked in from the crew compartment area. "Hey, KL! What's up?"

"Hiya, Mack."

Mack grabbed a seat across the table from Srrcheel. ||Hi, I'm Mack,|| he sang to Srrcheel.

"Nice to meet you, Mack. I am Srrcheel."

Mack's eyes went wide. "You speak Terran English!"

Srrcheel nodded humbly. "A little."

"Well enough to be understood, that's something," Mack gave him an approving nod. "You're the first Averian I've met who speaks English so fluently."

Srrcheel smiled shyly. "Thank you… Sir."

"I hate to jump to business," said Kormèr, "but I've got something here that I'm hoping you can help me with.." He paused as he gently pat the invisible box sitting on the table. "You know I've been working on that jewelry store robbery; well, we discovered this at the crime site." He pointed at the table where he had put the box. "We think it's a holographer, and I was wondering if any of you guys can show me how it works."

Mack watched Kormèr for a moment while Roke looked from the empty table to Kormèr and back. "Uh, Kormèr…"

Kormèr wrinkled his lips. "Really, guys?" He pushed the box toward Mack, and it scraped along the table. "It's hiding itself." To further illustrate, he pulled a dish towel from the counter and draped it over the invisible box. It looked to be floating in mid-air.

"Whoa!" said Roke.

Mack felt the box's dimensions beneath the towel, then slid his fingers along one side and, after a moment, switched off the invisibility screen and tugged off the dish cloth, revealing a silver device entirely enmeshed with shiny black optical-stripping.

"So, you recognize it?" Kormèr noticed that the buttons occupied the spaces between the mesh.

"Yeah," said Mack. "Enough to know that these things are contraband. Actually, that's putting it mildly: they're outlawed by the GF." It took Kormèr a moment to remember that 'GF' was the abbreviation for the Galactic Federation, which he still had little understanding of. "Where'd you get it?"

"It was on the ceiling of the jewelry store that was robbed. I imagine the personal version that the thief wears is just as prohibited?"

"Are you saying you saw the personal version of this?" asked Mack.

Kormèr had never seen Mack look shocked before. To see that look on his face now left Kormèr ill at ease. "I didn't so much see *it* as see its effect."

Jim and Morgan appeared from the crew quarters. "Hey," said Jim, rubbing sleep from his eyes. "I thought I heard voices."

Morgan clapped Kormèr on the back. "How's it going, kid?"

Kormèr took a moment to introduce Srrcheel, but Mack didn't lose his train of thought. "Kormèr, tell us what you saw."

"What's going on?" asked Morgan.

"And what's that thing on the "

Mack held up a finger, catching and holding Kormèr's attention with his intense gaze. Kormèr told them all about his encounter with the thief.

Jim's eyes were wide. "Damn, KL! Jer was worried about you, but if he heard about this… I don't know what he'd do."

Morgan nodded. "He'd sit you down for a serious heart-to-heart, that's for sure."

"Dude, they're right," added Roke. "You've gotta bail on this idea of yours of catching the thief."

Of all the eyes on him, Kormèr felt the weight of Mack's the most. Arms crossed, he watched Kormèr. "Here's my heart-to-heart," he uttered at last, "stay away from this guy." Kormèr opened his mouth to protest, but Mack cut him off. "I mean it, kid. This is military tech, old tech. But that personal version sounds new. You're dealing with someone who's got connections and tech; you *do not* want to be trifling with them."

"If he's got that kind of resourcing," murmured Jim, "I wonder why he's hanging around the jewelry store."

"How do you even know it's a he?" Morgan asked Kormèr, as Mack pulled the holographer closer and inspected it.

"I accidentally caused one of the recorded scenes to play," explained Kormèr. "We saw him using the device."

"He's a… unique individual," added Srrcheel, and then described the thief.

Mack sat back again. "Like I said, this is an old military-grade model. The last ones produced for the military came with a beacon because people used to switch them on and forget where they were."

After Mack's rebuke, Kormèr stifled a chuckle, but he couldn't keep from grinning. "I'll bet that's what happened to this one. It's the only reason we can think of for him to have been there."

Roke's eyes lit up. "Oh! Unless he also left some loot behind."

"It doesn't matter," rumbled Mack, not looking at anyone. Then he focused on Kormèr. "Look, kid, you wanted to solve this heist? Well, you did it. Be happy with that, take this evidence and give it to the police. We'll happily accompany you, just to be safe."

Various scenarios played out rapidly in Kormèr's head. In some he'd continue digging for motive and other factors in the robbery. In others he'd do as Mack said and simply hand over the evidence, and let the police take over. In all of them, he tried to guess what the outcome with Sylvestra would be, and realized that it didn't matter. Averian law forbade their relationship, and Sylvestra represented the enforcement of that law, among others. As Mack had said, with the holographer and the scenes it contained, the case was practically solved, and Kormèr would have kept his word. To Kormèr, his word mattered more to him than anything else.

Kormèr nodded. "Alright. Then just show me how to work the buttons. Once we get to the police station, I'll need to know how to replay the scene—"

A distant explosion resounded through the hull.

Startled glances shot around the small space.

"Stardust, what was that?" asked Jim.

"Checking," responded the ship's AI. "Early indications are that a ship's cannons malfunctioned "

"Is there any public camera or media drone footage?" asked Mack.

"Yes." The wall behind Kormèr lit up and displayed the scene from several vantage points as the disembodied voices of anchors reported on the event. Fast burning flames roiled from a section of Pad 20; text overlays on the screen mentioned that fuel lines or tanks may have been hit. A brilliant flash blanked the image, and a secondary explosion rumbled through the hull.

"Wow," murmured Srrcheel. Kormèr glanced at him and saw his wide eyes locked on the screen.

Jim watched Mack as Mack watched the screen. "What're you thinking?" asked Jim.

Mack shook his head. "Probably nothing..." His voice trailed off.

Jim waited a moment, then he added, "But...?"

Still watching the screen with eyes that seemed to read the image like text, Mack grumbled, "But it could be a distraction."

"Stardust, forward camera please." The image changed, and now displayed the four armed Averians standing by the pad's blast doors.

Kormèr tensed at the armed figures. "Who are they?"

"Sentries posted there by the local PD after the events the other day," answered Morgan. "Didn't you see them on the way in?"

Shaking his head, Kormèr replied, "I portaled in."

After a few more minutes of watching the media report, the tension in the room slowly evaporated.

"Blasted malfunction," grumbled Morgan, running his fingers through his hair with relief.

The tension broke as everyone chortled nervously at the unintentional pun. The screen remained on, but Jim muted the sound.

Mack studied the holographer with Roke watching over his shoulder and asking occasional questions. When he was ready, Mack showed Kormèr which buttons recorded and which buttons played back recordings. Even Jim and

Morgan watched as Mack set the machine to record for a minute. "Okay, now you two move over there," he instructed Jim and Morgan. "And KL, you go there." Kormèr slid out of the seat and stood by the end of the table as Jim and Morgan circled around. "Here goes." He enabled the playback.

With a flash, the room appeared to reset back to where everyone had been seated or standing a minute earlier. As they watched, Mack went through the same motions and uttered his earlier directive again, and Kormèr watched himself get up and come toward him until the image merged into himself. The same happened to Jim and Morgan. *Flash.* The playback ended.

"That was totally gnarly!" cried Roke.

Srrcheel nodded. "That was quite impressive. But it's optical, isn't it? Can it fool other types of sensors?" He looked at Kormèr and nodded slightly, his gray-feathered eyebrows high, as if seeking acknowledgement that it was a good question. Kormèr returned the nod. *It was a good question.*

Mack traced the mesh with his index finger. "This one probably can. This looks like infrared... and possibly other spectra. Like I said, this is military grade."

Kormèr wondered briefly how Mack knew so much about the device, considering it was illegal, but this did not seem the right moment to bring it up. Besides, Kormèr's mind was on a different track as he contemplated the holographer. He understood now how the thief had likely used the device to clean the store out with the slightest of ease.

The thief would have remained in the store, hidden, until closing time. Then, with the holographer active and masking his presence completely from the security sensors, he made his way around the store, pocketing every valuable. When Reestee returned to the store and opened the door, the thief walked right out with everything except the holographer itself. It now made sense that he hadn't yet hit another store and that he had returned to Chees on at least one occasion; he couldn't leave such a valuable piece of evidence behind.

And that's how we can trap him! realized Kormèr, a plan formulating in his head. But the plan dissolved as he looked up at Mack and found him watching him back. He knew Mack would never part with the device until it was in the hands of the police. Peering into those eyes, Kormèr felt as if a mote of understanding passed between them, as he suddenly knew that not even then would Mack part with the device. Mack would hand over the recoded evidence, but the device would disappear.

He thought about saying something, but he got no further than that.

A deep muffled *clang* filtered through the hull from outside. So soon after the malfunction, tension filled the room instantly.

"Incoming transmission," reported Stardust.

"Play it," said Jim, leaning forward with his arms against the table. | |This is *Stardust IV,*| | he sang.

//*This is Officer Psteeree again,*// tweeted the voice over the comm. //*I just wanted to let you know that we've sealed the pad doors as we've had to send two of our team off to assist with a problem at pad 20.*//

||Any concern with that problem?|| asked Jim.

//*Not at the moment. We will notify all ships in the vicinity if necessary.*//

||Got it. Thank you. *Stardust IV* out.||

"I don't like it," offered Mack. "Two're easier to bribe than four."

Roke's eyes widened. "Yo! The ramp's open."

Morgan yelled, "I got it!" and raced out the door, hand on his sidearm.

Jim switched the wall screen to display the views from the ship's external cameras, and the mess grew uncomfortably warm as everyone watched the tiled views for any sign of movement.

"We're missing something," muttered Jim.

Srrcheel leaned toward Kormèr and whispered, "What's going on?"

The whir of the boarding ramp motors cut through the tense silence as Kormèr briefly filled Srrcheel in on Harry G's moves to steal the crew's invention. Just as Kormèr finished the recap, Morgan appeared in the doorway. "Well, at least there was no one there."

"I still don't like it, man," said Roke. "I totally think that malfunction was anything but."

"A distraction?" suggested Srrcheel.

Everyone stared at Srrcheel as if noticing him for the first time. "Maybe," grumbled Mack. He'd gotten an apple from somewhere and now took a slow, deliberate bite. "You both need to go, now," he instructed Kormèr.

Kormèr pursed his lips and crinkled his brow at him. "You should really stop treating me like a child. If I had listened to you last time, you and your ship would be in G's hands." Even as he said this, he remembered standing on the wrong side of Hassera's weapon, and how vulnerable he'd felt.

Mack's gaze drilled into him. But briefly, his eyes flicked to Kormèr's left and back, and Kormèr realized it was more than his own life at stake this time.

Kormèr gave Mack the barest of nods. "But I guess I should get back to Sylvestra with the news," he muttered, as if thinking aloud. "And that," he added, pointing to the holographer.

Mack shook his head. "Maybe just the first part. You can let her know we're keeping it safe for you."

Kormèr frowned. "Yeah, that's what I figured." He looked at Srrcheel. "Come on. We're only in the way here." He eased out from behind the table, and Srrcheel followed.

"You have something?" Jim asked Mack as Roke gave Kormèr a nod in farewell, and Morgan flicked them a brief wave.

"Yeah," said Mack. "We've got a blind spot. Stardust, give us topside sensors."

Out of sight from the mess, Kormèr dug in his pocket for the portal cube. "The guys can handle this themselves," he told Srrcheel. "We've got to get back to Birshetland and close this case—"

Outraged cries came from the mess, then the ship's voice and a warning klaxon drowned them out.

"Intruder alert. Intruders have bypassed cargo hold door security."

Kormèr looked up. They were just paces from the cargo airlock. He pulled out the cube as Mack and Roke dashed around the corner toting blasters.

Mack grunted when he saw them. "You picked the wrong direction. Move!"

Kormèr turned to race out of the way when a shower of sparks rained from the airlock doors, and they whooshed open. Light flashed behind him, and his body went numb. Everything went black as he tumbled forward into Srrcheel.

JEREMY grinned as Theesl frowned at the results of the environmental tests, and his wings flicked a few times. The results had been sealed until only moments before, so that all the interested parties could see them at the same time. Jeremy and Kit exchanged a knowing glance; they'd passed.

| | I... uh. | | Theesl made a strangled noise in his throat. | | The... That is, the results are all... satisfactory. | | He looked up and around the table. Jeremy noticed his hands were trembling. | | I have... nothing further to add. | |

The Arbiter sighed, and Jeremy realized he'd also been holding his breath. He exhaled, and the tension flowed out with his breath.

| | In that case, gentlemen, | | sang the Arbiter, | | if no one has anything further to add... | | He looked around the table, almost daring someone to speak up. | | Your signatures on the contract, please. | |

Jeremy, Kit, and the representatives from the manufacturing conglomerate simultaneously inserted their signature sticks into their terminals. *"Contract approved,"* announced the automated recorder.

| | I pronounce these proceedings concluded, | | chirped the Arbiter. | | Congratulations, gentlemen— | |

He was about to continue when Jeremy's p-comm chimed.

Kit's eyes widened as Jeremy read Jim's unfinished message and gasped. He jumped from his chair. | | I'm sorry, gentlemen, but it seems my crew is being attacked by an armed group. I must run. No offense. | |

He darted out of the room with Kit on his heels. "It's G," he told Kit when they were out of earshot from the meeting room. "He's broken in."

"What? What about the guys?"

"No idea. But I really wish we had KL's portal right now." Without it, it would be a desperate rush to get to Freet-See as soon as possible. If it wasn't already too late.

CHAPTER 22

VOICES burbled as if under water, echoed through the buzzing return of consciousness. He'd never been hit by a stunner before, but he'd seen the effects and heard them described. The pervasive numbness, the difficulty focusing, all left him feeling as if he were swimming through a thick fog, wanting to stay in the warm numbness, but struggling to regain control of his limbs. Bright light filtered through his eyelids, but Kormèr kept his eyes closed, assessing the situation before broadcasting his wakefulness.

"Your message to Mister Tailor saved me the trouble," rumbled an unfamiliar voice. *Is that Harry G?* wondered Kormèr.

"You won't get away with this," growled another voice. *That was Jim,* Kormèr realized.

With indifference, maybe-Harry G muttered, "So you've said."

Kormèr risked a peek, opening his eyes just enough to get a sense of his surroundings. He immediately recognized the burgundy cloth pressed against his face as the seat cushion around the table in the ship's mess. Someone had lain him down there, just about where he had been seated earlier.

Something brushed the top of his head. He opened his eyes wider, rolled them up as far as he could, and found someone sitting there, their back to him. But without moving, he couldn't see enough to tell who it was. From his position, he had a fantastic view of the underside of the table, but not much else. Where were Srrcheel, Roke, Mack and Morgan? And what did Harry G look like, anyway? Kormèr had heard enough about him, but he had never gotten a description.

There are other things to think about, Kormèr, he told himself.

A breeze wafted across Kormèr's face as the environmental system kicked in to cool the warm room. He felt its coolness on his face... and neck! Kormèr tipped his chin down toward his chest, glad for the return of even this much movement. Just past his legs, he spotted a feathered lump. *Srrcheel!* The birdboy rocked, using his wings to sit up, his movements jerky, no doubt hindered by lingering numbness. His head rolled and then settled as he glanced around. He squinted at Kormèr, and Kormèr flicked his eyebrows at him in greeting.

"Hassera," said Harry G, "tell me where Mister Tailor is now."

Kormèr's eyes went wide. *Hassera is here? And she's working for him again? Even after the evidence I sent her! Was I totally mistaken about her?*

Sure enough, Hassera's raspy voice answered a moment later from the comm. *"Tailor and McQuinton have just boarded a sky-hopper for Freet-See."*

"Of course. They have no choice, and they know it."

Kormèr craned his neck back and confirmed that the back he'd seen earlier really did belong to Jim. Jim's arms were bound at the wrists behind his back with what appeared to be a constricting coil of some sort. Kormèr had used a similar device on Elmar to keep a door closed while he…well, while he went about his business. He had never considered this horrid use for it.

A *boop-boop* sounded. "Yes," said Harry G.

Kormèr strained to hear a very faint tinny Averian chirping. //…*contract's been signed.*//

"I see. And just how did this occur? I thought you had things under control."

//*I did. Several tests were supposed to fail. I had it all set up. But when the results came in, they were all clear. I don't understand how*—//

"I don't need your excuses. It's a simple business matter. You did not provide the results that I paid for. The money is now being withdrawn. Our business is concluded."

By the gods! thought Kormèr. *That's what Harry G's payoff to Syrree's father had been for!* He grinned, pleased with himself for unknowingly undoing G's efforts to stall the contract negotiation.

Kormèr moved his shoulders, and slowly, a tingling sensation trickled through his arms all the way to his fingertips. He realized then that he no longer had his coat on. Someone must've removed it while he was unconscious. This made sense, but also sent his heart racing. *The cube!* As the tingling flowed like a cool wave down his spine and into his legs, he kicked out, and his legs dropped off the seat. He used their momentum to jerk his torso upright, and almost made it, but he fell back onto his right elbow. Hands gripped Jim's upper arms and lifted him bodily from the seat. Holding him was one of the largest men Kormèr had ever seen, easily five times his mass. The man set Jim down on another seat and turned his gaze back to Kormèr.

"Hmm," he rumbled. "Hello there, young man." Kormèr just stared. The man wore his pitch black hair slicked back, a look that would've made his already broad face seem overly large if not for a pair of tinted glasses that completely obscured his eyes. That head sat on a neck as thick around as Kormèr's waist. The weight was not fat, however, as the trim-fitting navy-blue gabardine jacket revealed. The single line of polished silver buttons ran from just below the neckline, over a broad chest and down to a wide but trim waist.

The large man reached down, and powerful hands lifted Kormèr effortlessly onto the table. Not yet able to fully control his legs, Kormèr kicked awkwardly, knocking something across the table. Now with a clear view of the room, Kormèr found Morgan, Mack and Roke seated on the other side of the mess table; all had their arms behind them, so Kormèr guessed their hands were bound, just like Jim's. He couldn't completely feel his own hands yet, but he assumed they too were also bound.

In addition to Jeremy's crew, a tall, dark-skinned man stood just inside the mess doorway, his eyes alert. Beside him, a woman leaned casually against the doorframe. Both wore nondescript uniforms, their blasters dangling loosely at their sides. Kormèr squinted to focus on the woman, her features very familiar, but his mind refusing to accept what his eyes told him. Finally, the unmistakable truth pushed through. *She's Elmarian!*

Kormèr focused back on the big man whose proximity commanded Kormèr's attention. "You're the one who engineered that getaway into lightspace," he snarled. He did not wait for Kormèr to answer. "Very resourceful, for a boy so young." He peered over his shades, his large brown eyes piercing Kormèr's. "I see. You're Elmarian. That explains it some." He dropped a confused Kormèr back onto the couch.

How did he know? Kormèr met the Elmarian woman's eyes, and in her smirk, he saw that she'd betrayed him. *What's happened in her life to get her to the point of betraying her own?*

"And Hassera tells me you don't exist," continued the big man. "A complete blank in the galactic record." He chuckled deep in his chest. "Now *that's* an even greater feat. A few weeks ago, I would've offered you a job." He stopped there and shrugged, leaving any "But now…" implied. Watching Kormèr a moment more, he again chuckled that deep menacing chuckle.

Harry G's gaze shifted past Kormèr and regarded something behind him momentarily. "I have no disagreement with your kind," he said, obviously speaking to Srrcheel. "You're free to go once my business here is through."

With his back to Srrcheel, Kormèr couldn't see the birdboy's reaction. By the same token, no one could see his fingers working on the mechanism of the cinch-coil that bound his wrists. He had dismantled and rebuilt the one he had used on Elmar. *But dammit, I'd had that one in front of me. This won't be easy.*

Harry G focused on Kormèr once again. He smirked, rumbled deep in his chest again, then turned and walked toward the doorway, where he conversed quietly with his uniformed agents.

"So you're Harry G," blurted Kormèr before he could stop himself.

The big man turned slowly. "And you claim to be Kormèr Lezàl. Somehow I don't see you as a centuries-old duke."

"That's good, because neither do I. And not just the centuries-old part; I'm just not that into politics."

Harry G harrumphed, then turned away again.

"But you really do fit the profile of the entrepreneur I've heard you are."

Harry G spun around and regarded Kormèr. "You have a mouth on you after all." Kormèr shrugged. "What have Tailor's boys been telling you about me?"

Kormèr shrugged, hoping it hid his hard swallow. He imagined the fast beating of his heart could be heard throughout the ship. "Nothing our being here, now, hasn't proven to be true. You tend to get what you want."

Harry G cracked a smirk and rumbled in his chest again. "Huh." Kormèr couldn't be sure, but that could've been a chuckle. "Maybe... you just might be a fit for politics after all."

Kormèr considered saying something biting, but not only couldn't he think of anything, he doubted annoying Harry G would be of any use. "We're so far from Earth, and yet you had a local government official working for you. I'm surprised that this small operation would pose such a threat to you... to your... empire."

Harry G crossed his arms and peered at Kormèr. "Now you have piqued my curiosity. What do you think you know?"

This is a dangerous path, dude, Kormèr told himself, hearing Roke's voice in his head. *Don't play your Wizard card too soon.* "I heard you on the comm. You wanted the tests rigged, but they passed instead."

Morgan gasped. "Whoa! What?"

"Son of a bitch!" cried Jim.

Harry G nodded. "Hmm. That makes more sense now." He turned away.

"You never answered my question."

Harry G didn't bother turning back. "I know."

Kormèr chewed his lips, as he desperately tried to think of something, anything, to keep Harry G occupied in conversation. If he could keep Harry G engaged, that would be less time for the big man to think of other nasty things. But nothing came to Kormèr's mind that didn't seem ridiculous, even to him. So instead, he ignored his cramped wrists and fingers and continued fiddling with a bolt he had managed to loosen on the cinch-coil binding his hands. The bolt would either be the one that unwound the coil or one that had the potential to activate the constriction mechanism. He felt fairly confident he had the right one. *Sort of confident.*

JEREMY pushed his glasses back up his nose and stabbed a finger at the comm. ||No offense, but I don't care what report you get back. I received a distress message from my crew, and I want backup!||

Through the sky-hopper's transparent windscreen, the rocky landscape of Averia zipped past in a blur. Jeremy and Kit were the only passengers, as arranged and paid for by the manufacturing conglomerate: now that the conglomerate had signed the contract, they had a vested interest in their partners' welfare and product, so they expedited the men's passage to Freet-See to check on their investment... and the crew.

After a pause: //*Mister Tailor, a squad will be prepared for your arrival.*//

||A squad? How many is that?|| The concept of "squad" differed all around the galaxy; just what were they giving him?

//*Ten or twelve officers are all we can manage, Mister Tailor.*//

"Dammit!" Jeremy pounded his fist against a seat, drawing a glare from the pilot.

Kit patted Jeremy's shoulder reassuringly. "That may be all we need. How many men can G have with him? If they were able to get into the ship unnoticed, maybe there aren't that many of them."

"That's a big maybe." Into the comm he sang, ||Fine. That's fine for now.|| He glanced at Kit, who gave him an encouraging nod. ||Thank you,|| he chirped with an effort. ||We'd certainly appreciate any additional support you can provide, just in case. If worse comes to worst, like I think it will, you may not need more than a pillowcase to hold what's left of your squad.|| And he closed the channel.

Kit clicked his tongue. "Averians, feathers, pillow case... That's something *I'd* say," said Kit.

"I know. It was mean, but I'm frustrated." Jeremy squirmed in his seat and tugged nervously on his mustache. G would surely have his mercs waiting for their arrival. "If we're walking into a trap, I'd like to be sure of some kind of backup."

Kit nodded. "That'd be nice, for sure, but we've managed without, before."

"Yeah, but G's not likely to underestimate us again." Jeremy peered ahead, unwilling to broach the most probable outcome of their arrival: a standoff, with G inside the ship holding the rest of the crew hostage, while the port authorities locked down the ship from the outside. Would G threaten to execute the crew if Jeremy didn't give in to his demands? The enigmatic man had a public image to preserve, after all. Or, did he have Freet-See so under his thumb, the same way he had so many other things, that even an attack this audacious would just get ignored by the authorities, and eventually just be forgotten?

Not if we can help it. Freet-See looked small on the horizon, but Jeremy saw that the sky-hopper pilot had the throttle nearly at full. They would not have to wait long to find out just what awaited them.

SITTING at the far end of the mess table, Srrcheel kept quiet. He would have liked to imagine that he was keeping composed, but his frantic mind had no time to even think about that. At the forefront of his thoughts, he repeated to himself, *I'm not prepared for this.* The Hovel had higher-level sorcerers that could handle delicate situations such as this. And while Harry G had said that he would let Srrcheel go once his business with these people was complete, Srrcheel had no way to know if he could trust his word.

Kormèr had taken the full stun blast earlier, and he'd knocked Srrcheel down as he collapsed. As a result, Srrcheel had been dazed but awake when the largest man he'd ever seen walked in. The man had stepped into the doorway, as his partners had rushed ahead to incapacitate the rest of the crew. The towering, looming figure had stared at Kormèr and Srrcheel for a moment, as if deciding what to do with them. Srrcheel had stared back, wondering if those would be his last moments. But then the man had scooped up Kormèr with one arm and Srrcheel with the other and had deposited them in the mess, with surprising ease and care. One by one, the big man and his partners had collected the other crew members in the mess, less gently, and bound their hands. Only Srrcheel remained unbound. He suspected it had been so because, despite not being stunned, he'd remained quiet and still. Whether or not they knew it was fear that paralyzed him didn't seem to matter.

Srrcheel desperately wished he had access to Kormèr's portal. With that, he'd have been able to make a hasty escape. But the cube was in the pocket of Kormèr's coat, and Harry G's partners had confiscated the coat earlier. Escape was out of the question.

Srrcheel could do nothing but wait.

Sproing!

Srrcheel looked up. The noise hadn't been loud, but it had come from Kormèr's direction. Kormèr sat perfectly still, head hung forward, facing away from Srrcheel, as he had been for the last hour. At the base of his back, out of sight of anyone but Srrcheel, Kormèr's hands were active. Srrcheel watched in amazement as Kormèr jiggled the cinch-coil free of his red, irritated wrists, manipulated it in some way and then slid the loose cinch-coil up his sleeve.

Kormèr then looked up, and Srrcheel followed his gaze to Harry G's Jaltan partner. The tall, dark-skinned man watched Kormèr with professional interest, his hand resting on the grip of his weapon. The man's eyes flicked to Mack, then back to Kormèr. He then stepped toward Kormèr.

Oh, no! He'll be discovered! With barely a thought, Srrcheel cast the easiest spell he could think of.

Mack belched loudly, drawing looks from everyone. The Jaltan jumped, his weapon immediately in his hand and aimed at Mack, whose wide eyes belied his complete surprise and embarrassment. "Umm, excuse me?" Mack said.

The Jaltan took a moment to look around and ensure that no one had moved, then he holstered his weapon and returned to stand in the corner, his arms crossed, as if daring someone to do something.

Srrcheel sighed. He'd always thought the belch trick to be completely useless, except to prank other sorcerers during focused spellcasting or solemn ceremonies. Never could he have imagined he'd need to use it under such extreme circumstances. But another thing occurred to Srrcheel that he hadn't considered until that moment: none of Harry G's group knew that Srrcheel was a sorcerer. Srrcheel had assumed that when Harry G said "your kind" he'd meant Berdians. He realized now that the man had simply meant Averians. If they'd realized that Srrcheel could cast spells, they would likely have thrown him in the hold or worse, killed him immediately.

This gave Srrcheel an advantage, but one he would have to use very carefully. The wrong spell at the wrong moment would definitely get him killed. He ran through the spells he had memorized to get some idea of which would come in handy. Unfortunately, without access to the digitized catalog of spells, his personal repertoire contained very little that would be of any use.

CONTRARY to Jeremy's expectation, no one slowed their way as he, Kit and the squad of six Averian officers raced toward Hangar 14. Four of the officers had stationed themselves at several major intersections along the way to keep the path clear. The squad leader, Lieutenant Sylrroo, assured Jeremy that anyone unlucky enough to get in the way or act suspicious would undergo a thorough screening before being arrested or sent on their way. As the group passed the intersections, the officers stationed there joined the force's rear guard.

They slowed as they came to the archway that opened into the old section of the port. Sixty meters in stood the blast doors to Hangar 14.

||What is it?|| asked Jeremy, as Sylrroo called a stop.

||There's no one at the blast doors. There should be two officers posted here.||

Jeremy peered ahead. ||Haven't they been reporting all-clear for the past hour?||

||Someone has.|| Sylrroo shrugged his wings.

||Your language is not that difficult to learn,|| chirped Kit. ||Anyone could easily have faked those reports.||

||There were confidential codes that were included in the report, Mister McQuinton, that no one else would know.||

Kit scowled. ||I can't explain that, but you've must agree that something went wrong here.||

Sylrroo hesitated, but admitted: ||Yes. And someone's wings will be clipped for it once we're done here.||

Sylrroo tapped the side of the monocle he wore. ||All security cams here show the way as clear. Wait. I have a group of five approaching from the rear.|| He tagged three officers. ||You three, check it out—||

||Hold on,|| interrupted Kit. ||Splitting up's a bad idea this close. We all check it out together.||

Sylrroo hesitated, not pleased about his order countermanded by a civilian, but he seemed to appreciate that Kit and Jeremy were more familiar with the threat they were facing. ||Very well.||

The party of three Sammakkoens and two Terrans were not expecting to be surrounded by an armed squad of police officers. Half-drunk, the Sammakkoens burbled apologies through their translator implants. One of the Terrans brazenly complained of his right to be there, but when he took a few unsteady steps toward the officers, a stun shot sent him tumbling back to collapse into the arms of the other Terran. A quick screening revealed they carried only light defense weapons. Considering their inebriated state, Sylrroo radioed for a squad car to pick them up. He left Officer Theerl behind to watch the group until their escort arrived and directed the rest of the squad back to the hangars.

They crept to the large, thick steel doors of Hangar 14 unchallenged. The group stood back as one officer made his way to the controls. ||It's unlocked,|| he reported after a moment.

||Open it,|| ordered Sylrroo.

||Wait,|| cheeped Jeremy. ||Do you have eyes inside?||

||I do. The path to the ship is completely clear.||

The blast doors creaked open and brilliant light stabbed out through the slim opening. *Why are the ship's lights on in port?* Wondered Jeremy. Faster than his brain, his reflexes spun him around, and he launched himself at Kit. Both men tumbled into a side corridor as stun shots pulsed through the opening, reducing the ranks of the Averian squad to motionless bodies on the ground.

"Jees, Jer! You could've warned me," complained Kit.

"My glasses fell off. Do you see them?"

Crunch.

Jeremy looked up and didn't need his glasses to see the business end of a blaster pointed at his face.

OFFICER Theerl jumped at the five *thwoops* that rang out from the direction of the hangars. Ignoring the fleeing Sammakkoens, Theerl dropped to one knee, blaster aimed at the archway and one eye on the remaining unstunned human.

||Lieutenant?|| he called into his p-comm, using the team's channel.

||Anyone?|| No reply. Theerl was so tightly strung on adrenaline that when the squad car pulled up, he almost shot it.

||Yo, yo! Theerl!|| squawked the driver, seeing the barrel pointed at him. ||It's just me.||

Reasoning broke through, and Theerl lowered his weapon. ||Radio for backup,|| he ordered, wishing he'd thought of it earlier. ||And tell them to hurry.||

He raced to the archway and, back flat against the wall, chanced a glance toward the hangars. He could see the pad doors, and the last of his squad being dragged across the threshold just before the blast doors sealed.

Theerl returned to the squad car as the driver helped the second human into the back seat.

||Let me use your radio,|| he twittered to the driver. ||It looks like we need an army here.||

CHAPTER 23

"AH, crap!" spat Morgan, breaking the tense silence that had followed the announcement that Jeremy and Kit had arrived. Kormèr looked up as, hands manacled behind their backs, Kit and then Jeremy stepped into the mess, followed by the Elmarian woman and Harry G.

"Glad to see you boys are doin' well," said Kit, with false cheer, the look on his face belying his angst.

The woman took a position to the right of the doorway as Harry G stood victoriously at the head of the table.

Jim spat, "You son of a bitch!"

Harry G stared at him contemptuously. "Yes, well, I have nothing of any value to say to you either." He turned as Hassera appeared in the doorway. "Hassera, alert the port that we'll be leaving and prep for takeoff. I've set my ship to follow." He moved aside and opened a hatch that contained the holographer... and Kormèr's coat!

Kormèr had only caught a glimpse of the holographer, but he believed he knew its orientation and just where the buttons would be located. The question now was: could he slip past Harry G and turn it on? And if he did, what would his next move be? Harry G's dark-skinned henchman stood only less than a meter from the hatch. Kormèr had seen the man's reflexes and knew he'd be moving to stop Kormèr within seconds. The effects of the stunner had completely worn off, so Kormèr had regained full control of his limbs. But he knew he still wouldn't have much time to do anything particularly useful, even if he managed to turn on the holographer.

"You've succeeded," rasped Hassera, still standing in the doorway, now with her weapon drawn.

"I have," rumbled Harry G without turning. "That outcome was never in doubt." He picked up the holographer and studied it, as if assessing its monetary value and its purpose. Kormèr cringed: the holographer was the only piece of evidence that Kormèr had to capture the thief of Chees. If in his ignorance, G erased the recorded scenes or destroyed it...

G turned his head and peered at Hassera. "Why?"

Hassera replied in her cool and methodical way: "Because it is when you are most vainglorious, that you can comprehend true loss." She raised her weapon.

With a clear line of sight of the control surface on the holographer, and with Harry G momentarily distracted, Kormèr seized his chance. He dove low, anticipating that anyone shooting at him would expect him to stand up. He rolled on his shoulder behind Harry G, using the man's massive silhouette as a shield as stun beam flashes filled the room. Part of Kormèr's mind knew that all the shots had missed him, but he was too focused on his task to consider how amazingly lucky he'd been. Kormèr looked up; Harry G held the holographer just out of his reach. He stretched, reaching up to the activation control... Harry G's hand opened, and the holographer whisked by Kormèr's face and smashed onto his foot.

Kormèr gnashed his teeth against the pain, reached out and hit the control.

The room exploded into myriad rays of light that coalesced into a jewelry store. The *thwoops* of stun beams cut through the confused cries that filled the small space.

Steadying himself with one hand on the wall, Kormèr stood and felt blindly for the compartment that Harry G had opened. Finding it, he reached inside and felt the soft, familiar woolen fabric. *Yes!* Something shoved his chest and sent him sprawling to the floor, but Kormèr held onto his coat. He slipped into it as a grunt and a clatter sounded nearby. He instinctively looked up, but of course, there was nothing to see but the replay of Cheert Reestee tending to customers at his jewelry store. If only he could see...

Of course! He reached into the pocket and found Srrcheel's magic eye. At the moment, he couldn't recall pocketing it, but he never questioned such luck. He looked through the glass and found the dark-skinned man on the floor, seemingly unconscious. Walking away from him, Harry G headed directly for the Elmarian woman. He appeared to be having no trouble at all seeing where she stood, while she appeared as disoriented by the hologram as everyone else.

He can see! Kormèr realized. *But how? It must be the shades!*

Kormèr stood and watched in shock as Harry G smashed his massive fist into the side of her head. She dropped in a heap, her blaster clattering to the ground next to her. Kormèr glanced back at the dark-skinned man, then at Harry G. *What in the world is G doing? Those are his own people!*

Harry G then turned toward Hassera, and Kormèr saw his face. Hassera must've heard the blaster fall, and she fired a stun beam blindly in that general direction. The bluish flash coruscated over Harry G, but did not even slow him down. Kormèr silently mouthed, *What?!* The stun shot hadn't even slowed him, but aside from that... did Hassera know she was shooting at Harry G? She had said something a moment ago, and Kormèr now wished he'd paid attention. But whatever it had been, the murderous look on Harry G's face made it clear that Hassera would be his next victim. He stalked towards the doorway, ignoring Kormèr completely.

With one last look through the eye to fix his bearings, Kormèr dropped the eye into his pocket. *Time to even the odds,* he thought to himself. He charged and jumped on Harry G's back. He swiped for the shades, but Harry G swung around so fast that Kormèr nearly flew off, and he clasped his hands together to hang on.

Something grabbed his collar and yanked, lifting him so that only his hands remained clutched tightly to each other, his arms around Harry G's thick neck. As his grip slipped, he snatched the shades. Wrenched free from Harry G's neck, Kormèr experienced a moment of surreal disorientation, as he soared across the jewelry store—weightless for a second—then slammed against the wall of the mess. Blistering pain shot through his right knee, spreading throughout his leg.

The holographic scene suddenly changed: the jewelry store appeared upside down now, dark and empty, except for the owner, who set the alarm and locked up.

Cradling his leg, Kormèr heard a gasp to his right. Someone else cursed.

"Dammit!" spat Harry G.

Kormèr managed a smile despite the pain, as he slipped on the purloined shades... A message blinked against the dark background: *Searching for available spectra...*

The *thwoop* of a stun shot echoed in the mess, followed by a thump. *Another one down?*

"Hassera," snarled Harry G. "You could've had so much."

"There is only one thing I want now," said Hassera.

The scene changed again, abruptly: the store was open again—and still upside down—and a sturdy Averian female stood above Kormèr.

//*Excuse me, sir,*// chirped the holographic customer loudly. The sudden shuffle of real feet on the ship's decking sounded incongruous with the events in the holographic playback.

"Holy crap!" cried Kit.

Kormèr jumped as another *thwoop* and thump sounded elsewhere in the mess.

"*Spectrum acquired*" flashed on the shades, and the room reappeared, only not in the way Kormèr had expected. Instead, thin black lines and dots superimposed themselves, almost chaotically, over the holographic scene. It took Kormèr a moment to adjust to this new input, particularly since the lines and dots shifted with every slight movement he made. He quickly identified the table, then the walls and general shape of the room, and finally he made out its occupants.

Kormèr's stomach churned queasily. Things did not look good. Jim, Morgan, Kit and Roke lay sprawled on the floor, and Kormèr hoped they were only stunned. Jeremy and Mack crouched low on either side of the table. Srrcheel was standing, moving about in such a way that made Kormèr dizzy to watch him through the shades. *I hope he's casting,* Kormèr thought, turning away from that storm of lines and dots.

Kormèr was in the back corner of the mess, to Srrcheel's left. The holographer appeared as a mess of lines on the floor three meters ahead of him. And Harry G stood less than a meter from it.

Kormèr gawped helplessly, as Harry G shuffled forward until he kicked the holographer. *I've got to get that damned machine away from G.* Ignoring the pain in his knee, Kormèr stood, but as soon as he turned towards Harry G, his leg buckled under him. Kormèr was on the floor, tears of agony flooding his eyes uncontrollably.

He looked up, fists clenched in frustration, as G raised his foot to stomp the holographer. Harry G's foot stamped down, only to suddenly sweep up into the air. The big man tipped backward as if he were falling, but instead, he remained floating on his back, suspended in mid-air.

The ground slipped away from beneath Kormèr, and he, too, floated off from the ceiling of the jewelry store.

"Whoa!" cried Jeremy as he also drifted from where he'd been hiding.

Angry hissing from ahead revealed that Hassera, and even Harry G's two unconscious victims, hovered a meter off the floor.

"What the hell is this?" Harry G roared.

Someone walked past the edge of Kormèr's vision, and he felt something clamp onto his injured leg. Almost immediately, the worst of the pain subsided. He slowly settled back down onto the ceiling of the jewelry store, which, considering the scene was upside down, meant he was back on the floor of the ship's mess. He rolled and sat up to examine his leg. A glowing set of dots enveloped his knee, lines bending inward and disappearing into his leg. As he watched, the glow vanished, as if it had melted into his knee. Gingerly, he drew his knee toward his chest, anticipating the return of the intense pain. But he felt only a throbbing tightness.

The holographic scene suddenly collapsed into lances of light and vanished.

"*Optical spectrum detected*" reported the shades, and the confusing lines and dots vanished. Craning his neck, Kormèr took in the now-normal view around him. Everyone floated roughly a meter off the ground, except for Srrcheel, who stood by Harry G's floating body, the holographer in his hands. Beyond them, Hassera flailed her arms, trying to right herself, not knowing about the magic that held her up. She had dropped her weapon, and it now lay out of her reach.

Kormèr smiled, as Srrcheel came to him and gave him a hand standing. "You saved the day," said Kormèr.

"Thanks. I won't tell you how many tries I gave it before it worked."

"A sorcerer!" said Harry G. "You should've gone when I told you to. Now that offer is off the table." Kormèr recognized Harry's attempts to use zero-G maneuvers. But whatever Srrcheel's spell did, it wasn't the same as zero-G. "Let me *down*, birdboy."

"Hey, G," said Kormèr. When the man turned his head to him, Kormèr smirked and said, "Wait your turn."

Harry G furrowed his brow, seething at Kormèr. Kormèr spotted a cinch cord dangling from Harry G's neckline and fished up his sleeve, but the cinch cord he'd stashed there was gone.

Srrcheel released Jeremy and his crew from the float spell while Kormèr removed their cinch cords. Roke, Morgan and Jim were still stunned, and would be out for at least another five to ten minutes, but thankfully they had sustained no other injuries.

Mack produced a blaster—either from the crew's own stash or from one of the mercs, Kormèr wasn't sure—and fixed it on Harry G. "Hey, Srrcheel," said Mack, "can you push him into that corner there? Without touching him, I mean."

Srrcheel considered the request, then nodded. "Yes." He performed a quick cast, and Kormèr saw the pleased look on his face when the spell worked on the first try. Harry G glided through the air toward the corner, cursing and squirming the whole way, and he growled when his head bumped the wall.

"There are a lot of misconceptions about your kind… Sorcerers, I mean," Jeremy told Srrcheel, offering his hand to the young birdman. "I don't think I can thank you enough."

Srrcheel beamed, accepting the handshake. "You don't have to, sir."

"Call me Jer." He ruffled the feathers on Srrcheel's head and rejoined his crew to discuss their next steps.

Kormèr snickered at Srrcheel's annoyed pout as he smoothed down his crest feathers. "I think Jeremy does that to everyone. It means he likes you."

Srrcheel looked unconvinced. "Is that why Mack keeps his head bare?"

With Harry G out of the way, Kormèr gathered the weapons onto the table while Mack and Jeremy bound the waking, floating Elmarian woman and the dark-skinned man with some kind of tape. Then he stopped in front of Hassera, as she continued to dangle at his eye-level in mid-air. Kormèr looked up at Hassera. "Would you mind explaining what happened here?"

"The plan was to stun him," she said, swaying purposefully, as if testing the limits of her motion. "Let him think he'd won, then take it all away."

Jeremy walked up beside Kormèr, scowling at her. "You used us as bait?"

She turned her calm gaze towards him. "I knew he wouldn't harm you. He doesn't want you dead."

"That's a gamble I can't abide by." Jeremy looked at Kormèr. "Don't use the cords; I hate those things." He turned. "Srrcheel, how long will she stay suspended?"

Srrcheel shrugged his wings. "As long as I don't lose focus, I think."

"Alright. Just leave her there for now."

Hassera hissed irritably, glowering at Harry G. "He killed my… my good friend. I want him to suffer."

His eyes still on Hassera, Kormèr nodded. "I'm sorry for your loss. What about them?" He flicked a thumb toward the Elmarian woman.

"Cial and her partner are working for me. I thought G would have more mercs to deal with, so I wanted help on the inside."

"Uh, huh," said Jeremy. "Leave them all floating for now, too." Then he turned to Harry G, who was bound and unmoving, but intently watching and listening to the group's exchange. "So," began Jeremy, "it comes to this, you basta—"

The comm chimed.

"Yeah." Annoyed by the distraction, Jeremy kept his eyes fixed on Harry G.

//*This is Lieutenant Sylrroo of Freet-See police. We have the ship surrounded. To whom am I speaking?*//

||Ah, Lieutenant! This is Jeremy Tailor. The situation is under control.||

//*Please open your boarding ramp.*//

||Of course.|| Switching to English, he directed: "Stardust, please lower the boarding ramp."

"Yes, Captain," replied the ship's AI.

Kormèr rummaged through his coat's pockets, as he took a seat. He sighed when his fingers closed around the cube, thankful that it didn't look like anything special. Srrcheel set the holographer on the table and sat beside him. Kormèr stared at the holographer, wondering whether or not to hide it from the police. None of the Averian officers were likely to recognize it for what it was, but he still didn't want to risk it. He took it from the table and placed it on the floor at the back of the table, out of sight.

As he straightened, Kormèr heard footfalls in the corridor. He turned and watched four armed Averian police officers enter and fan out around the mess, eyeing the floating figures. He heard others moving through the corridors of the ship.

One officer approached Jeremy, but his eyes were on Srrcheel. ||What's this? Sorcery?|| he chirped derisively.

||Sometimes more efficacious than a blaster, and neater, too,|| retorted Srrcheel.

Kormèr grinned. *Hah! Nice snarky reply, Srrcheel. 'Snarky'—what a great Terran word!*

The officer grunted. ||Let them down, one by one.||

||My pleasure.|| Srrcheel stood and walked with the officer. ||That one first.|| He pointed, and the Elmarian woman descended slowly to the floor. Hassera had called her "Cial". Another officer scanned her for weapons, then cut away the tape binding and replaced it with real manacles. Her eyes opened during the process, but she remained quiet.

Kormèr desperately wanted to speak with her, as she had knowledge of modern-day Elmar; he could see it for himself by portaling there, but it was her viewpoint that he truly wanted to hear, to understand the future of his homeworld through the eyes of someone who had grown up in that environment. He met Cial's eyes as she was led away, but there was no curiosity or connection there in her gaze.

Jeremy nudged Kormèr's elbow, as they watched Srrcheel and the officers work. "You know, kid, I was actually worried about the company you were keeping."

Kormèr raised an eyebrow. "Worried? Why?"

Jeremy crossed his arms and shrugged. "No reason, apparently. You've done very well for yourself, and for us, I might add. I've lost track of how many times you've saved our asses—you're probably tired of hearing this, but we owe you. Thanks, kid."

Kormèr grinned. "I have one more surprise for you: I have proof that Tzee'oo Theesl was being paid off by Harry G to cause some tests to fail on your landing gear."

Srrcheel had just lowered the dark-skinned man to the floor and pivoted on his talon. ||What did you say?||

Kormèr noted Srrcheel's sudden interest and switch to Averian. "Um, just that I found evidence that someone was on Harry G's payroll to stop the contract from being signed."

Srrcheel closed his eyes and shook his head. ||The name, what was the name?||

To both Jeremy and Srrcheel, Kormèr said, "Tzee'oo Theesl."

Srrcheel frowned. ||No! You must be mistaken. I also overheard Harry G's comm-call; no names were mentioned.||

Kormèr fished in his coat pocket and withdrew the transfer slip. That Harry G hadn't found it surprised him, but maybe one of Harry's helpers had taken his coat, not Harry G himself. "That comm-call was what helped me put the pieces together. This is the *real* evidence." He gave the slip to Jeremy. "It's a fund transfer slip to Theesl's account. It doesn't have Harry's name on it, but it was attached to a letter—"

"Payton Agronomy and Agriculture," said Jeremy, reading the stamped signature. "That's one of Harry G's companies."

Srrcheel's wings flicked sharply. ||How did you get that?||

Kormèr's mind raced to craft a dissimulating response until he knew what had Srrcheel so agitated. "It was in Theesl's house." At Jeremy's focused stare, Kormèr felt his cheeks warming. *Stupid brain!* It completely blanked on him, leaving him nothing to explain his relationship with Syrree. "I've, umm... well, I've sort of been involved with his daughter, and one night—"

Srrcheel's eyes widened, and both Hassera and Harry G crashed to the floor.

Harry G rolled deftly onto his feet, body-slammed the closest police officer and snatched his blaster before anyone could react. He tottered precariously, countering his momentum, then brought the blaster to bear on Srrcheel.

The other officers aimed their weapons at him, shouting at him over each other. Distracted by the din, Harry G didn't notice Hassera until she was already on his back, digging her claws into his skin through his clothes. G's arms bent back at impossible angles and grasped for Hassera, but her nimble fingers snapped closed the loose cinch coil that dangled around Harry G's thick neck. She activated it with a twist and leaped away, as the coil bit into his flesh, faster than Kormèr had ever imagined it could. *By the gods, she's killed him!*

With a strangled, gasping yell, Harry G dropped the blaster and clawed at the coil frantically, causing it to constrict even faster.

Jeremy grabbed Kormèr's shoulders to turn him away from the scene, but Kormèr had already averted his eyes. Still, he heard the sudden, horrible *crunch* as the coil cinched to its smallest size, and something *whumped* heavily on the floor.

Afraid of what he'd see behind him, Kormèr instead focused his eyes forward on Jeremy's grim visage. "Don't look, kid. Don't turn around."

Kormèr shook his head, his gut in a tight knot, his feet affixed to the floor. He was grateful for Jeremy's firm grip on his shoulders, helping him stay upright.

"Holy crap!" came Mack's voice.

"Whoa!" cried Roke. "Did I wake up at a most auspicious moment!"

Slowly, Kormèr turned, as he felt Jeremy's hands fall from his shoulders. He almost turned away again, as he spotted the dark liquid that pooled around Harry G's body, then he realized that the semi-translucent mahogany fluid couldn't be blood. The torn halves of Harry G's neck exposed bits that gleamed like metal and wires… *What on all of Elmar?!*

"An android," gasped Jeremy. Then louder: "The freakin' bastard was an android!"

"That's why he couldn't be stunned," blurted Kormèr.

"Not with a stunner made for people," said Mack.

Kormèr looked for Srrcheel to share in this surprise with his friend, but he found the birdboy sitting at the far end of the table, shoulders slumped, eyes distant. *Poor guy. He must feel bad about his spell fizzling too early.* As everyone recovered from their shock, Kormèr sat across from him. "Don't be so hard on yourself. It was your first time—"

Srrcheel's neck feathers puffed as he looked up, and his eyes burned into Kormèr. | | Betrayer, | | he warbled.

"I…" Kormèr blinked. "What?"

| | How can you sit there acting so smug, after what you've done? | |

Kormèr closed his dropped jaw. "Srrcheel, what are you talking about?"

| | All this time you've been calling me friend… Was it all a big joke to you? Ha, ha! 'The stupid birdboy thinks I'm his friend.' | |

"Please, tell me what's wrong! I have no idea what you're talking about."

| | Don't you? | | Srrcheel looked wounded and furious. | | Syrree Theesl! That's who I'm talking about: my betrothed! | |

Kormèr felt the blood drain from his face. *Buomp!* "She's your… By the gods! Srrcheel, I swear I didn't know! I never would've…" *Would've what? What can you say that won't bury you deeper?* "I met her at a dance club my first night here. I didn't even know you then." He paused. "Srrcheel, I'm sorry. But I really had no idea."

| | Excuse me. | | Kormèr and Srrcheel looked up at the officer that had approached, with Jeremy at his side. | | I'm Lieutenant Sylrroo. Mister Tailor tells me you have evidence incriminating Harry G? | |

Kormèr looked at Srrcheel. The birdboy sighed and warbled: | |Yes, he has a transfer slip from one of Mister G's companies, to the head of the Advisory Committee for Environmental Concerns.| |

Sylrroo looked from Srrcheel to Kormèr. | |May I have that, please?| |

Kormèr passed the slip to the Lieutenant, who placed it in a stasis container. | |There was a letter attached to that related to test requests,| | sang Kormèr, switching to Averian. | |I don't have that.| |

| |I see. How did you come by this document?| |

| |I was visiting the family, when I made a wrong turn on the way to the bathroom.| | Better prepared for that question this time, the small lie came easily to him. | |I spotted Jeremy's contract on a desk, and that slip was just sitting on top.| | Kormèr couldn't exactly read Sylrroo's expression, but he had the feeling that the Lieutenant didn't buy his bathroom story. | |That doesn't invalidate the evidence, does it?| |

| |No,| | chirped the Lieutenant. | |Evidence is evidence, no matter how it is obtained.| |

Behind Sylrroo, a forensics team scrutinized the ship's mess, scanning the walls and floor. One collected the fluid that had leaked from Harry G's nearly severed head, while another imaged the fallen android from various angles. As officers secured Hassera and led her away, she cast a disdainful eye towards the figure of her former employer but went without struggle or comment with her police escort. She seemed to give Kormèr a parting nod, but it was so fleeting that Kormèr wondered if he imagined it.

Kormèr returned his attention to Harry G's body. | |Is he… it dead?| | asked Kormèr.

Sylrroo turned his head to look at the body. | |I've no idea. It looks like the body deactivated when the head was disconnected. But I've never seen one this sophisticated before, so it's hard to tell. Forensics'll figure it out.| | He turned back to Kormèr. | |For now, I need to ask each of you some questions.| | He glanced at Srrcheel, then back at Kormèr. | |Let's begin with you. I have a feeling yours is the more interesting story.| |

| |I think you should definitely have that checked out, | | Kormèr told the Lieutenant, as Jeremy stepped into the crew berth cabin-turned-interview room. | |With a little one on the way, you owe it to your family to take care of yourself. | |

Standing and leaning against the wall to the side of the entryway, Sylrroo nodded. | |You may be right, KL. Thanks for the advice. | |

Jeremy cleared his throat while absently pushing his new glasses up to the bridge of his nose. "Um, excuse me. Hello. Everyone's finished in the mess, and your men are done interviewing everyone else."

Sylrroo checked the time on his p-comm and let out a long whistle. | |Wow! Yes, well. I think we're done here. Thank you for your time, | | he sang to Kormèr.

Kormèr stood and clasped his shoulder. | |High skies, Lieutenant. | |

Turning to Jeremy, Sylrroo chirped: | |I ask that you remain docked while we process the investigation, in case anything else comes up. | |

"No problem."

| |Thank you. Have a nice day. | |

When he was gone, Jeremy said to Kormèr, "What was that about?"

Kormèr shrugged. "He has a lump…" He shook his head. "Never mind. It's not important. Let's just say that it's nice to know a member of the local police force that doesn't hate me."

"Okay," Jeremy said dubiously. "You didn't tell him about your portal, I assume."

"Nope." Kormèr smiled innocently. "Somehow it never came up."

Jeremy grinned and shook his head. "By the way, Srrcheel asked me to tell you that he hopes he's been of help, but that it was time for him to return to Berdia. If there's anything else you need, you can contact a 'Grand Master Fitzbew' again."

"Damn! He left?"

Jeremy nodded. "He also says that if you need help again, Master Fitzbew can recommend someone 'less gullible'? What did he mean by that?"

Kormèr dropped his head. "Before meeting him, I met his betrothed, Theesl's daughter."

Jeremy winced. "Ouch. Now, by 'met' you mean…"

"She didn't act like she was in a relationship, if you get my meaning. So, yeah," Kormèr sighed. "Big ouch."

"Oh."

Kormèr shook his head. "He's such a nice guy; if I'd known beforehand, I never would've gotten involved with her. I feel terrible."

"The way I see it," said Jeremy, pushing up his glasses, "it's not your fault. Sounds like she's the one that led you on…"

"Maybe." Kormèr shook his head. "One night, she told me of a 'friend' who was betrothed but didn't love her intended mate. I knew she was talking about herself, but since I didn't know who the guy was, I simply didn't care."

Jeremy simply said, "Hmm."

"I figured, hey, if she's not happy in this relationship, maybe I should encourage her to end it. And then, I discover that her father's in Harry G's pocket."

"For what it's worth, I'm glad you did," Jeremy said. "Find out the truth about Theesl, that is. G's done, but I'll make sure that bastard Theesl never stands in anyone's way again."

But Kormèr didn't care about that right now. Staring off into space and thinking of Srrcheel, he murmured, "I've got to find some way of making it up to him. And I think I have an idea how." He looked up at Jeremy. "How long're you going to be on Averia?"

Jeremy tipped his head toward the door. "Let's go sit in the mess," said Jeremy. As they walked, he continued, "The contract is signed, so there's a lot to do. We'll be here for at least another two months. Why?"

They entered the ship's mess where the rest of the crew sat around the table, atop which sat the holographer. The floor had been cleaned up, and everything seemed to be back to normal. But Kormèr felt an air of surrealism surrounding everyone, including himself. No one could deny that something had happened in this room, and it would take a while before it felt the same again.

"Well, now that I think about it, two reasons. First is that I could really use your help in catching the jewel thief. Mack knows more about the holographer than I do. His knowledge on that, plus his tactical experience, would be a huge help.

"Second thing is that, since Srrcheel was such a help, we owe it to him to let his superiors know."

Jeremy grunted. "I like your second reason much more than the first."

"Hey, Jer," said Mack as Jeremy and Kormèr sat, "the holographer has been actively recording since just before G boarded. We have the whole thing as evidence," he said, beaming.

Kormèr's heart lurched into his throat, suddenly worried that all *his* evidence from Chees was lost. "That didn't overwrite what was on there, did it?"

Mack waved his concern aside. "Nah. This thing's got plenty of storage."

"Can you make a backup of the recording?" asked Jeremy.

Mack rubbed his chin. "Probably, but we'd still need the holographer to play it back in three dimensions."

"Hmm," Jeremy said. "In that case, can you record the recording onto something else?"

Mack nodded. "That's easier. You just want a backup in case something happens to the device?"

"Yeah, that's right."

Good idea, Kormèr mused. *Just in case the holographer gets locked up in an evidence room.*

"I'll try to do both and see what happens," Mack said, looking the holographer over. "The copy might not be as easily admissible, though."

Jeremy considered this. "Yeah, maybe. But it doesn't hurt to try. In the meantime," Jeremy glanced at Kormèr, "KL's got it in his head that he wants to catch the thief."

"No," grumbled Mack. "I've already told you to forget that."

"That's not going to happen, Mack," said Kormèr. "I'll do it alone if I have to, or figure something out. But I need to do this."

Mack looked at Jeremy and the rest of the crew. "You're all considering helping him, I can tell."

Roke grinned disarmingly. "Let's hear him out, dude. Maybe we *can* do this safely."

Mack sat back and crossed his arms. The rest of the crew watched, waiting in silence. Kormèr considered what he'd do if Mack blocked him; somehow he'd have to steal the holographer back.

Mack inhaled deeply and held it. "Alright," he said at last. "But any plan has to be airtight, or I'll nix it."

Kormèr smiled. "I'll agree to that." Better to have Mack find any flaws in the plan than the thief.

"Okay. In that case, you might want to see this." Mack activated the box's menu and quickly found what he wanted. Beams of light shone out from the box, and the ship's mess became the jewelry store once again. Jewelry glittered in the display cases as Cheert Reestee activated the security systems, turned off the lights, and rushed out the door.

Kormèr frowned as something flickered. Then again, and very quickly again, and Kormèr finally realized that the jewelry was disappearing from the cases. As he had suspected, nothing moved; entire panels of jewels simply vanished.

"This guy's fast," observed Morgan, his disembodied voice jarring against the backdrop of the scene.

"Now, watch this," rumbled Mack's voice. Though the scene remained that of the store during the heist, the contrast flashed painfully. Kormèr shut his eyes, then peered carefully through slitted eyelids until the shift settled. When it did, his eyes went wide. Completely visible, encased by an eerie white aura, the thief moved with practiced motions from one panel to the next. "The machine can reveal cloaked objects on playback," said Mack.

The thief's hands worked some mechanism just before handling each panel, and the white aura extended over the panel. Then he scooped the jewelry into a sack and, leaving the empty panel behind, moved to the next. After he'd emptied a few cases, he hung the sack from his waist and proceeded to fill another. This went on until Reestee appeared at the door again. By then, the thief had emptied the cases. But Reestee's return had clearly caught him by surprise.

The light came on, and Reestee stood transfixed at the security console, only a meter from the door. He relocked the door as he sang into the comm, explaining that he'd been robbed and yet denying that it was possible at the same time.

"Here's where it gets interesting," said Mack.

Perhaps seeing that he couldn't leave the store, the thief attached something to each sack which lifted them up to the ceiling, where they remained suspended and cloaked. Kormèr watched as the police arrived moments later, his breath coming faster as Sylvestra entered, her beauty not the least diminished by the eerie contrast.

The thief sidled up to the door, careful not to collide with any officers, opened it, then he held up an arm, and the playback ended. The scene collapsed, returning the ship's mess to view.

"It looks like he used a remote to stop the recording," offered Mack as he shut off the holographer.

"But he left all the loot…" Kormèr's eyes went wide. "That's why he's been hanging around and why he warned me away, even though the store is practically empty!"

Mack nodded. "Best I can guess is he assumed he'd get caught and wanted to make sure he left the loot stashed safely until he could return to retrieve it. No one would think to check the ceiling, especially with no visible sign of anything being there."

"So why hasn't he returned?" asked Roke. "With all his tech, it should be totally easy!"

Mack shrugged. "Maybe he has? Maybe he got some, but not everything. Who knows?"

"Maybe he forgot where he left them all," mumbled Kormèr, deep in thought. He looked up, meeting Mack's eyes. "But this gives us a great in!"

"Hey, Mack," called Jim. When Mack looked over at him, Jim tossed him an apple.

Mack caught it easily. Still holding the apple where he'd caught it, Mack peered sideways at Kormèr. "Alright," he said with a smirk. "Let's plan this." Then he took a bite.

WHEN Srrcheel was much younger, before the Hawk Sorcerers discovered his latent magical talent, he would sometimes escape the aerie he shared with the other orphans and fly up to perch on the rooftop of the highest structure on Freet-See. Over the years, newer structures had dwarfed the older ones, and their builders had installed deterrents to such behavior, much to Srrcheel's disappointment. Still, he found no substitute for his old haunt, and nothing that provided the clarity of mind that the old familiar rooftop brought him. And this late afternoon, as he stared out over the city, he very much welcomed that clarity.

The altitude placed him far above the bustle of the very active city, making Freet-See appear like a peaceful work of modern art. It was his birth-home, and yet he found its architecture and culture alien, especially compared to other Averian cities like Berdia, or even Birshetland.

Thinking of Birshetland, his thoughts settled on Syrree. He had taken his anger out on Kormèr, and he was not ready to let that go because it provided another outlet than Syrree herself. But the truth niggled at the back of his mind: Syrree had broken the trust, just as much as Kormèr, if not more so. After all, she had knowingly betrayed their arrangement, while Kormèr knew nothing of Srrcheel's involvement. And truly, what could Srrcheel expect from this alien, whom he'd met only a week or so ago, and who was ignorant of Averian ways?

Srrcheel sighed, then heard a shuffling behind him. Assuming another Averian had had the same idea, he turned, ready to greet the newcomer. He nearly jumped off the edge of the rooftop in surprise when he found a non-Averian standing just a few meters away. The man looked Terran, sandy-haired and roughly the same height as Jeremy, though he looked lean, even in the gray, calf-length coat he wore.

"Oh, hey, there," he said in an easy drawl, with a greeting wave. "I didn't expect anyone to be here."

He didn't move any closer, so after a pause, Srrcheel folded his wings. "Um, I could say the same?"

The man smiled, his eyes crinkling at the corners when he did. "My name's Reilly. I think I startled you— I didn't mean to. No offense?"

Srrcheel shrugged. "None taken."

The man peered at him expectantly. "Do I..." He stopped himself. "No. Never mind."

"What is it?"

"You remind me of someone, but you're... Well, I'll ask him next time I see him."

Ask whom what? wondered Srrcheel. *What a strange man. I should probably leave.* But his curiosity had the better of him. "What are you doing up... How'd you get up here?"

"I'll answer the almost-question: I come up here sometimes to just think and put things in perspective."

Srrcheel fluttered his wings and gave the man a wry look. "Really?" *What a coincidence,* he thought facetiously.

Reilly walked to the edge of the roof and placed one foot on the parapet. He leaned forward with one elbow on his bent knee and stared out over the city. "Sure. Some friends of mine got into a bit of a pickle, and I'm here to lend them a hand. It seemed like a big problem, but now that I'm up here, it doesn't seem that big anymore."

Srrcheel couldn't argue with that, as he came here for exactly the same kind of reassurance and perspective. Even the new taller buildings seemed to emphasize that there could always be larger issues.

"Relationship troubles?"

Srrcheel's eyes snapped back to Reilly. The man hadn't moved, but he smiled at Srrcheel. "I recognize that look. I've been in your place, so take my word for it: it's not always as bad as it seems, and even if it is, it'll pass."

Reilly had an odd way of speaking, using some terms and phrases that didn't make sense to Srrcheel. *What did he mean by friends that 'got in a pickle'?* But Srrcheel's curiosity had had enough, and this distraction had certainly helped him figure out his next steps.

"You're probably right about that. Thank you, but I must be going."

Reilly put his leg down. "Okay. It was nice meeting you."

"It was nice meeting you, too." Srrcheel stepped up onto the parapet and flipped over the side. He glided for several blocks, alighting on a street near a comm booth.

He made one call to update Master Fitzbew on his progress and, on a whim, to ask permission to remain the night. He had already checked out of the luxurious room at the Cheerees that Kormèr had reserved for him, as Srrcheel no longer wanted his hospitality, but Srrcheel had some money of his own that he could use to pay his own way. Perhaps sensing Srrcheel's unsettled mood, Master Fitzbew had granted his request and even suggested a nice hotel for the night.

With that out of the way, and no other excuse to stop or delay the inevitable, Srrcheel sighed and punched in the Theesl home number.

| | Oh, hello, Srrcheel! | |

| | Hello, Missus Theesl. | | Srrcheel felt a pang of guilt talking to her now, knowing the things he knew. He wondered if she knew about her husband's illicit deal. Would she escape the coming storm, or would she go down with Mister Theesl? No, complicit or not, her life would never be the same. Inanely, he asked, | | How are you? | |

| | Fine, thank you. You're in Freet-See? How delightful. Will you be able to visit? | |

Srrcheel hesitated. | | I'm not certain yet. Is Syrree around? | |

| | Yes, dear. Just a minute. | | The screen dimmed, and Srrcheel tapped a talon nervously on the desktop. He briefly considered hanging up, but knew that realistically, that was no longer an option.

The screen brightened again to reveal Syrree's face. | | Hi, Srrcheel. | |

Srrcheel's mouth locked up. *Hello, Syrree,* seemed so inappropriate all of a sudden. He had so many things he wanted to say to her, to yell, to cry... Instead, he did none of them and just stared.

Syrree frowned. | |Srrcheel, what's wrong?| |

| |I... I understand our relationship is a difficult one, as I'm always stuck in Berdia and visit so infrequently. It would've been unrealistic and selfish of me to expect you not to go to nightclubs with your friends and dance... or perhaps even partake in a relationship with another male.| |

Syrree stiffened. | |Srrcheel, what—| |

Srrcheel's crest feathers flared. | |Kormèr Lezàl.| |

Syrree's hand flew to her mouth, as though she had been struck. | |How did you... I mean...| |

Srrcheel waited a moment for her to finish her response, and when she didn't, he closed his eyes and relaxed his crest. | |So, it's true,| | he twittered softly, opening his eyes again.

| |I'm so sorry,| | she whispered, tears welling in her eyes. | |I never meant to hurt you.| |

He wanted to believe her, but not at the cost of his own dignity. | |I think you're just sorry that I found out.| | He recognized her face and voice, but on a profound level, he realized he didn't know her anymore. Somehow, because of that realization, his pain didn't feel as sharp or deep anymore. | |I don't believe you're the same person I fell in love with.| |

Syrree's chin trembled. | |I'm... I'm not the same person. We're apart for such long stretches of time, I think we've both changed. I'd sensed something different for a while, but I didn't know what it was, until your last visit: I realized I wasn't in love with you anymore.| |

On that, we can agree. Srrcheel bit back his more caustic retorts at seeing the remorse on Syrree's face. She had hurt him, but he would not be cruel in turn. | |So, are you in love with Kormèr?| |

She frowned and sniffled. | |No. I don't think so. But being with him... it made me very aware of my feelings and of our situation. He's the only one this happened with, by the way.| | At his stony silence, she continued, | |I know it doesn't make it better, but I just wanted you to understand that it wasn't something I did lightly.| |

Nope, it doesn't make it better. | |Well, thank you for your honesty.| |

| |Can you really blame me?| | Syrree chirped shrilly. | |We've grown apart; you have your life there in the Hovel, and I have mine here in Birshetland. You can't deny that we barely know each other anymore.| |

You've sensed it for a long time, too, boy. Srrcheel frowned, not sure how to answer her, if at all.

She didn't wait long for his reply, as she continued: | |Our parents meant the best for us when they arranged our betrothal, but they aren't us. We shouldn't have to live by rules and decisions they made for us. We have to choose our own paths, ones that will make us happy, and live by our own rules, or find the loopholes in the ones we can't avoid.| |

Someone's been listening to Kormèr's advice. Srrcheel recognized Kormèr's voice and philosophy in Syrree's words and decided, once and for all, that their relationship was over. Her view of their betrothal and their future was irreconcilably different from his, and there would be no common ground; any marriage with her would be utter misery for both of them.

Syrree sounded genuinely contrite. | |I'm truly sorry. I never meant for you to find out about Kormèr, of course. I still care for you, Srrcheel, and I'd never do anything to hurt you on purpose.| |

Srrcheel sighed. | |It's clear that you would never be happy married to me, so there is nothing more to say.| |

| |What about you?| | Syrree asked. | |Would you actually be happy married to me?| |

Now, you're thinking of my happiness? | |I've always considered marriage to a bond between equal partners and friends, one that transcends the need for perfect alignment and endures after physical desire has waned.| | It was obvious that Syrree had a different view, perhaps a simpler one, judging by the blankness in her expression.

She blinked, as if she didn't entirely grasp his words or his mindset. | |Wait, does that mean you still want to be married?| | Her chirp held a panicked tremor.

Srrcheel replied, carefully, so that there was no confusion: | |I don't want to marry someone who doesn't want me, so we are done. You can break the news to your parents, however you wish.| | He realized the irony in his words; there could be worse news coming very soon, if Mister Theesl was charged based on Kormèr's evidence. | |I hope the path you choose leads you to joy,| | he chirped solemnly.

She nodded. | |Thank you. I wish the same for you, though I don't think my parents will be as kind.| |

Typical Syrree: she'll find a way to place the blame on me, somehow. He shrugged indifferently. | |I'll be fine, and so will you. Goodbye, Syrree.| |

She opened her mouth to say something, but stopped. Then she sighed.
| |Goodbye, Srrcheel.| |

After he closed the connection, it occurred to him that he hadn't told her about her father's corruption, and the impending inquiry into his dealings. Part of him wanted to let her know of what was coming, but he thought better of it: his warning would only embarrass and upset her, and possibly implicate her, if she told her parents. He would have also had to explain how *he* knew, and that would lead to questions about his acquaintance with Kormèr—none of which he wanted to discuss on a comm.

Then there's Jeremy Tailor and his crew, he mused sullenly. Outsiders or not, the Terrans deserved fair and honest treatment, and likewise, Mister Theesl deserved censure for his egregious behavior, but the fate of the rest of the Theesl family was yet uncertain. *I suppose I should thank Kormèr that I'm not involved with that family anymore.*

Srrcheel didn't feel grateful or relieved. He actually felt a little numb, with perhaps a touch of pity for Syrree, but he had nothing more to say to her. He turned his back on the console and fluttered off toward the setting sun and the hotel Master Fitzbew had recommended.

CHAPTER 25

THE sun had not yet risen when Sylvestra woke up. She'd gone to bed early, for a change, and her internal clock had awoken her after her usual six hours of sleep. Unfortunately, it was too late to go back to sleep; another hour of sleep wouldn't do her any good, anyway. She yawned , shimmied to fluff and smooth her feathers, and stretched, luxuriating in the warmth and comfort for just a moment longer, while she could.

Since she had the time to spare, she opted for a proper bath instead of the shower. While the offworld invention sped up the process, it only went so far in satisfying basic needs. The drawback to soaking was that she now had to spend a half-hour drying out her feathers. She could've used the air-dryer, but once again, she shied away from the offworld technology… for a change of pace. Plus, the dryer tended to over-fluff her vanes and leave her looking downy—not a good look if she wanted to be taken seriously.

As she patted herself down with a towel, thoughts of work invariably crept into her mind, which led to thoughts of the Chees investigation… which led to thoughts of Kormèr. For the past two days, since the night on the promenade, she hadn't heard from him or seen him and she… missed him? *I'm concerned,* she corrected herself automatically. *But yes, I miss him, too.*

Damn hormones, she chastised herself once again. *And it's getting worse by the day. Maybe it's a good thing he hasn't been around. I should probably take some vacation days until this nonsense passes. A week on To-Weetsa-Woo would do very nicely… Hasn't it been a week since I gave Kormèr his ultimatum?* She counted the days in her head, absently ticking them off on her fingers as well. *It has! Today is his last day!* She frowned. *Why hasn't he called?*

She tossed the towel onto the hook and puffed her feathers as she gave her body two quick final shakes before looking in the mirror. *You look miserable!* She had to find something to focus on, to distract her mind from Lezàl and from her hormones. And immersing herself in her work, at the office, was the only way that would happen. *Just not the Chees case.* She grabbed her sash and her badge and left her apartment in a rush.

It didn't help matters any that, over the last few days, her officers had made absolutely no progress on the case. Another similar robbery had taken place two nights ago. Though not as large as Chees, the jewelry store boasted the largest collection of full fire sphene gems. The brilliant gems drew Averians in large numbers, particularly those with the right color plumage. The store had been robbed overnight, much in the same way that Chees had. Sylvestra's team had spent nearly the entire day on the scene, and they'd returned with as much evidence as they had gathered at Chees… next to nothing.

Sylvestra rounded the corner toward the open-air lobby, which ended in a wide archway that opened onto a spacious landscaped plaza. She stopped abruptly, her gizzard doing a joyful jig in her belly: Kormèr Lezàl stood at the comm console, scanning the resident list.

He must have caught her movement out of the corner of his eye, as he stopped to glance her way. He smiled brightly upon seeing her. | |Good morning,| | he sang, turning to face her.

Where have you been? Why haven't you called? | |Uh, hi?| |

He looked more mature when he was serious, as his smile faded a little. | |Is everything okay?| |

She nodded. | |Yes. I just didn't…| | *Get a hold of yourself!* She tapped her badge, activating the recorder, and the touch focused her attention back on work. | |What're you doing here?| |

He grinned impishly. | |Are you prepared to make an arrest?| |

| |Who am I arresting?| | At the triumphant gleam in his eyes, she furrowed her brow. *No, he couldn't have solved it… could he?* | |Are you tugging my tail feathers?| |

He seemed ready with a quip, but he shook his head instead. | |I'm not. I gave my word that you would have your thief in seven days.| |

If this is some kind of trick, I swear… But his face was serious again; he wouldn't joke about something that he knew was so important to her. | |Yes, that you did. So, you know who the thief is and where to find him?| |

| |I have footage of the robbery itself and video of the thief. And I have a plan to catch him, but it might still take a while.| |

| |You have a *plan*? Kormèr, this is serious. Just give me the evidence, and let my people handle it from here.| |

Kormèr's smile evaporated altogether. | |I can do this with you or without you. I'd prefer the former, but I've read up on your citizen's arrest laws, and I know what needs to be done.| |

Sylvestra wanted to argue with him, to arrest him for withholding evidence and interfering with an active investigation. But she'd seen that determined look in his eyes before, when he'd first proposed solving the case, and she knew that there was no dissuading him. If she arrested him, she might never see the evidence, but if she didn't go with him and he got himself hurt or worse…she'd never forgive herself.

If I play along, maybe I can find an opportunity to get the evidence before he gets himself into trouble. | |You've got one chance at this, Kormèr. One. If it even remotely looks like the winds are turning, I'm calling in my team.| |

| |I'll accept that. Our ride awaits.| | He stepped aside to reveal his taxi sitting at the edge of the plaza.

||Where are we going?|| she asked, but she followed him toward the taxi, anyway. She suspected that either she or Kormèr, or maybe both, were under surveillance, so she didn't worry about following him into potential danger.

||To Chees,|| he sang. ||I'd like your help to enlist Mister Reestee's help.||

||Good morning, Chief,|| sang Feestoo as Sylvestra climbed into the taxi.

||Good morning… Feestoo, right?||

||That's right, ma'am.||

Kormèr climbed in and sat across from Sylvestra. As the taxi glided off, she anticipated a ride spent in awkward silence, but instead, Kormèr launched into a detailed summary of the past few days.

||A holographer?|| sang Sylvestra, when it seemed that he had stopped his narrative. She knew of the holographic technology, often used for children's games or as presentation tools. They were usually simple devices with very limited use, but Kormèr's description went far beyond that. ||A portable one, no less. Are you serious?||

||I am. I know it sounds implausible, but I promise everything will become clear soon.|| Kormèr visibly relaxed in his seat, as if a weight had lifted from his shoulders.

Sylvestra frowned. ||You're asking me to put a lot of faith in your word, and this story of yours is… extraordinary. If I'm to help you, I need some kind of proof.||

Kormèr nodded. ||I understand, and I agree. And that's why we're headed to Chees. The proof you want is there, and has been there since day one.||

She zipped through his story in her head until his words made sense. ||The loot?||

||Yes.||

That's ridiculous! She wanted to argue that it was impossible for the loot to have been right over their heads the entire time, since that first day, while they'd been gathering forensics. But arguing would be pointless; she would know the truth soon enough, and either Kormèr would be vindicated, or not.

The taxi approached the promenade where Chees was located.

||I can't go in there with you,|| Kormèr sang. ||If the thief sees us together, he'll definitely get suspicious.|| He drew a palm-sized, matte-black box from his pocket. ||My friend Mack figured this one out,|| he sang, as a red-holographic menu appeared over the box. With very careful motions of his fingers, Kormèr navigated the menu until he seemed to find what he wanted. ||Alright. I'm going to vanish, but I'll still be here.|| He ticked the menu with his finger and vanished, along with the box.

Sylvestra gasped. ||By the gods!|| She'd never seen anything like it—or seen *nothing* like it, so to speak—in all her life, but suddenly Kormèr's story and the unsolvable robberies made sense. Instinctively, she thought of the infinite possibilities for lawlessness, if something like this were to ever become more available. *Heavens! Crime would be rampant—we'd slip into anarchy!*

//*Crazy, isn't it?*// sang Kormèr's disembodied voice. //*I'll walk into the store with you, and here's what'll happen.*// He explained their immediate next steps as the taxi swooped down to the taxi stop across the promenade from the jewelry store.

Sylvestra looked through the window and across the promenade at the store, and she considered whether or not to follow along with Kormèr's suggestions. Going over them, he'd had a few holes, one that she'd corrected and one that she'd just improvise on… *if* she went through with it. She turned back to the space beside her, where the indents in the seat cushions betrayed Kormèr's presence. *It's a risk, but it's the best chance we have. I have no choice.*

//*All clear,*// announced Kormèr after a minute. She couldn't see what he'd done, but he'd told her he had some kind of magical device that allowed him to see cloaked objects. He had scanned the promenade for the thief and hadn't seen him.

Sylvestra breathed deeply, opened the door and waited until the indent in the seat puffed back into shape. Then she got out, closed the door and strode across the promenade to the jewelry store.

Cheert Reestee was just opening the store. He stopped and turned to face Sylvestra. ||Good morning, Chief Chrreel. Is this a social call or have you finally made progress in the case?|| His tone had a rough edge to it that dug into her skin. But considering the precinct's lack of progress in nearly a month, she could understand it.

||Good morning, Mister Reestee,|| chirped Sylvestra, evenly. ||May we step inside, please?||

||Of course.|| He turned back to the door, and with a few deft movements, had the door open. Once inside, he rushed to the comm, deactivated the alarm and put in the call to the police. As the lights came on, he faced Sylvestra once again. ||Now, what can I do for you?||

Sylvestra examined the thick storefront windows. ||Mister Reestee, can you darken the windows?|| He nodded tersely, and she asked: ||Can you do that, please?||

||Chees, windows opaque,|| he sang into the air, and immediately the morning sunlight vanished as the windows darkened. ||Now what's this all about?|| he asked.

||We're still clear?|| Sylvestra asked.

||Pardon me?|| sang Reestee.

//*Yes,*// warbled Kormèr after a few seconds, eliciting a wide-eyed look from Reestee, who was uncertain where to direct his gaze.

Kormèr appeared out of nowhere beside Sylvestra. ||Hello, Mister Reestee,|| he greeted, slipping the portable holographer into his pocket.

Reestee's wings nearly swung open. ||You, again!||

Kormèr extended a fist out toward Reestee. Slowly, he opened his hand, revealing five small gems that reflected brilliantly in Reestee's wide eyes. The man's wings rustled closed, as he tore his eyes away from the gems and looked at Kormèr, then at Sylvestra. ||This is… I just can't… I mean, I…||

||Please, I insist, for your troubles,|| chirped Kormèr. ||Do you have a ladder or something tall I can stand on?||

Reestee looked back at Kormèr. ||What? Oh, yes.||

Reestee turned toward the door to the back room, then spun back. ||Those aren't merely for the use of a ladder, are they?|| he asked, pointing at Kormèr's outstretched hand.

||Ah, your time is more valuable than these little stones, of course! I'm sorry,|| Kormèr sang sheepishly. ||I believe I'll be able to find something better to compensate you for your troubles, momentarily.||

||Oh. Well, thank you.|| Reestee cleaned his songbox. ||A ladder, you said.|| He disappeared into the back room.

||I thought we confiscated your gems when we brought you in the first time,|| Sylvestra warbled softly.

||You did. Those particular gems,|| Kormèr replied. ||I want them back, by the way, if you're not holding them for evidence.||

||Let's see how your plan goes,|| she chirped. ||At least you didn't steal them back from the evidence locker.||

||No, I wouldn't want to get you into more trouble, on my account.||

||I don't mind a little trouble, as long as I get what I want in the end.|| *Good heavens! What are you saying? He already likes you—no need to flirt with him!* That hadn't been her intention at all, but Kormèr's lack of response was telling.

He placed the gems onto a display case, then took a piece of glass from his pocket and held it to his eye. ||Amazing. Srrcheel and I both looked at this ceiling last time we were here, and we never noticed that those flattened panels were out of place.|| Sylvestra looked up but noticed nothing out of place on the ceiling. ||I just assumed they were part of some sophisticated security system.||

Reestee returned with a foldable ladder a moment later. Kormèr took the ladder with a murmur of thanks and opened it. He climbed up and, looking through the glass with one eye, touched something that caused a square gray panel to appear. The panel peeled away and floated down to the ground a meter from Sylvestra's feet. On the floor, it looked like nothing more than a gray sack, with a matte-black box atop it.

||What is this?|| asked Reestee, bending and reaching for the sack.

||Don't touch that!|| chirped Sylvestra, sharply. Reestee looked up at her and straightened. ||Please,|| she added more gently. ||It is evidence.||

Kormèr climbed down and picked up the box and sack heedlessly, and Sylvestra suppressed an exasperated cry. She'd yell at him later, but right now her curiosity needed satisfaction: would this really turn out to be the thief's sack of loot, as Kormèr had described?

Kormèr unhooked the sack from the box and pocketed the latter. He set the sack on the display case next to where he had placed his own personal gems. With practiced finesse, he teased the cinch cord open and tipped the sack slightly, spilling rings and necklaces and other jewelry onto the velvet-lined display tray.

Reestee gasped. | | My merchandise! | | he chirped brightly. He looked up at Kormèr, then turned to Sylvestra. | | That's my merchandise! | |

Kormèr looked thoroughly pleased and relieved, as he watched Reestee rejoice at his recovered goods. The smile on the Kormèr's was the widest Sylvestra had ever seen on him, but yet when he looked at her, she noticed a touch of sadness in those stunning nutmeg-colored eyes. | | There's more, just like that, | | sang Kormèr. | | Since you came back to the store, the thief must've been afraid to get caught. As far as I can tell, he left with little to nothing. | |

Reestee stared at the ceiling. | | How do you see them? Can you get them all down? | |

| | Yes, but no. I—| | Sylvestra caught Kormèr's eye as he replied, and she shook her head. | | That is, um… Sylv— Chief Chreel will explain from here. | |

Sylvestra gave Kormèr a quick smile as Reestee turned to face her. | | Mister Reestee, we can't get them down just yet. I don't want to lead you on, so I will be honest with you. This is a most unconventional thief, as you are well aware. | | Reestee nodded. | | So we will use an unconventional method of luring him into a trap. | |

Reestee nodded. | | Yes, yes. I'm happy to help however I can. | |

| | I'm glad to hear that, | | Sylvestra smiled. | | Because we will need to borrow your store. | |

| | 'Borrow'? You expect me to *close* the store? | |

| | I understand it is an inconvenience, but—| |

| | Chief Chrreel, you do not need to explain. | | He pointed to the gray sack and his jewelry. | | This is more than I ever expected you to recover after a month with no progress— Apologies. I meant with no *apparent* progress on the case. This must be a very devious thief indeed, for you to have kept your team looking as incompetent as you have been. | | Sylvestra's eyes went wide, as she took affront at his comment on behalf of her team, but she held her wings steady. | | The store is yours… ah, for the day? | |

| | That all depends, | | she sang slowly, testing that her voice didn't sound as wounded as she felt. | | We need the thief to take the bait. Mister Lezàl here can explain the details in that regard. | |

She listened while Kormèr explained some of his plan, interjecting where it strayed from what the law permitted. But while part of her brain occupied itself with that, the rest mulled over this situation and how her department would look to the public once they apprehended the thief. There had to be a way for her precinct to share in the glory of the capture. One question plagued her: if she was forced to choose between her team and Kormèr, which side would she take? Watching the glowing, eager look on his smooth featherless face, as he poured out his plan, she wasn't as certain about her decision as she would have been at the start.

SERGEANT Tseeo soared across Birshetland, enjoying the first light of dawn for the first time in days. He breathed deeply, in sync with the motion of his wings. He sliced through the crisp morning air, invigorated and ready to resume his surveillance of Lezàl. All due to twelve hours of sleep. Tseeo had tailed the boy back to the Hotel Cheerees after his overnight stay at the Theesl residence, but by then all his hours of surveillance had caught up to him and he'd been unable to keep his eyes open any longer. As much as he'd hated leaving a junior officer staking out Lezàl, Tseeo had recognized that he'd grown... inefficient from his lack of sleep. Officer Teersoo now waited for Tseeo's return to relieve him.

Tseeo had been disappointed to learn of the second jewelry store robbery. The theft had followed the same pattern as the Chees robbery, pointing to the same culprit. Not only did it look bad for the precinct, but according to Teersoo, Lezàl had been in his room at the time, meaning that he had not been involved in the crime. Not directly involved, in any case, and that reasoning had given Tseeo the green light to continue the surveillance.

A taxi caught his eye as it zipped by a hundred meters below. Tseeo focused and spotted the familiar number on the roof of the aircar: it was Lezàl's taxi. He tilted and turned gracefully, paralleling the path of the taxi while he activated his p-comm.

||Teersoo, come in.||

//*Good morning, sir,*// sang the young officer.

||Teersoo, are you with Lezàl?||

//*Yes, sir. He hasn't left his room all day. No room service; no visitors. Nothing.*//

||Is that so?|| He took a breath. ||Let me get back to you.|| He closed the connection and landed on a high branch as the taxi came to a stop at a tree Tseeo knew well: the plaza that led to Sylvestra's apartment complex. He glared pin feathers at Lezàl as the boy exited the cab and strolled casually into the lobby. *How in the world did he get past us?! I'll have Teersoo's wings clipped if he fell asleep.*

Minutes later, Lezàl reappeared with the Chief at his side. The two disappeared into the taxi, and the taxi pulled away.

What's the Chief doing with him? The memory of Lezàl's overnight visit to the Theesl's home came unbidden and unwelcome, though the thought that the Chief could... that she would... *No! I won't believe it.* He shuddered, then he flew off after the taxi.

Minutes later, he alighted on another branch and watched as the taxi stopped near Chees. The Chief got out alone and entered Chees. A moment later, the windows opaqued.

Tseeo mumbled some notes into his recorder, ensuring that the date and approximate times of the morning's events were captured. He snapped a few photos of the storefront with its blue opalescent windows. Then he snapped some photos of the taxi. From this vantage, he couldn't see Lezàl inside. He considered moving, but then decided against it. He'd gain nothing if he got spotted and

312

spooked Lezàl away. Something very odd was happening here, and Tseeo wanted to capture as much of it as he could.

Nearly an hour later, nothing had changed. With time to spare, he remembered that Teersoo was still at the hotel, wasting his time.

||Teersoo, come in,|| he chirped into his p-comm.

//Here, sir. Nothing to report.//

||Teersoo, did you fall asleep at all last night?||

//No, sir!// was the immediate reply.

||I won't be angry if you did. Just be honest.||

//Sir, I am being honest. I didn't fall asleep.//

||Did you step away?||

//No, sir. What's happened?//

||I saw Lezàl riding around in his taxi this morning,|| he chirped, leaving the Chief out of the story. The fledgling didn't need to know about these things. ||How is that possible if we've both been watching his room since the night before last?||

//I don't know, sir. I can only tell you that he didn't leave his room once during my shift.//

Tseeo glared at the p-comm. ||Alright. Go home and get some sleep.||

Teersoo hesitated, and Tseeo could almost imagine him worrying over having missed Lezàl leaving the room and the hotel. After all, Tseeo hadn't been the one to miss him. //Thank you, sir. Teersoo out.//

Tseeo closed the connection as the store windows suddenly cleared. The store lights turned off. The door opened, and the Chief exited, followed by Reestee, the latter carrying a secure-case in one hand. Tseeo positioned his p-comm for pickup and turned up the gain. The police model of the devices was designed for audio surveillance. At this distance, he would pick up more ambient noise that useful conversation, but he had to try. Cupping one ear, he listened.

Reestee hesitated at the door. //I can't believe this is it,// he warbled, his tones pained. He locked the door to the store, but did not enable the security system. Then he and the Chief walked across the promenade, and Reestee climbed into the waiting taxi. The Chief recited an address to the driver; the distance distorted a portion of it, but Tseeo recognized it from the robbery case file as Reestee's home. The Chief watched as the taxi pulled away, then she turned and looked at the dark store. Then she twittered something, unfurled her wings and flew off in the direction of the precinct.

Tseeo snapped another photo of the storefront while he contemplated what he'd seen. *Could Reestee have closed the store?* The best way to find out would be to check the store status on the city board. He pulled up the information on his p-comm and confirmed it. The store was listed as closed for business. Not only that, but a search turned up a multitude of media results, all reporting that the famous Chees, unable to recover financially from the robbery, had been forced to close permanently. Tseeo looked up in the direction the Chief had flown. She'd get to the precinct before him, but he would call this situation in first. | | Tseeo to Captain Phatheeo. | |

PHATHEEO stepped into his office and put his breakfast down on his desk. The morning had been cool—it seemed to him that the mornings became cooler and cooler as the years passed—and Phatheeo had opted to wear a parka. He removed the parka and hung it on the hook by the door. He sat and opened the packaging for his breakfast, the smell of the hot fresh food tantalizing.

The comm chimed. *//Tseeo to Captain Phatheeo.//*

Phatheeo sighed. Some mornings he wished he'd retired already. | | Phatheeo here. | |

//Captain, have you read about Chees this morning?//

Phatheeo glanced at his blank console. | | Not yet. Why? | |

//Are you aware that it's gone out of business?//

This piqued Phatheeo's interest. | | No. Aside from a security perspective, why should I be? | |

//The city board is overflowing with articles about it. The Chief herself apparently just oversaw the closing.//

That definitely ruffled Phatheeo's feathers. *Why didn't Sylvestra tell me about this? What the heck is going on?* | | I'm glad someone did, | | he told Tseeo casually, again burying his concern over Sylvestra. His next call would be to her p-comm if she didn't show up first. | | Is there anything else? | |

//Yes, sir. The Chief wasn't alone when she went to Chees. Lezàl was in the taxi with her. He stayed in the taxi while the Chief escorted Reestee from the store. Reestee rode away in the taxi with Lezàl. I believe the Chief is on her way back to the office now.//

Phatheeo wanted to find out how Tseeo had come about these very detailed first-hand observations. Before he could ask, he recalled Sylvestra's politically suicidal pact with Lezàl. In all that had happened over the last seven days, he'd all but forgotten all about it. Were Tseeo's observations all part of whatever plan she had in mind? There was only one way to find out. | | Thank you, Tseeo, | | he chirped curtly. | | Good work. Phatheeo out. | |

Phatheeo glanced forlornly at the breakfast he wouldn't be eating anytime soon, then got up and nearly barreled into Sylvestra outside his doorway.

| | Sorry, | | he sang. | | I was just coming to see you. | |

| | Oh, good. I need to speak with you, too. Come in. | | He followed her into her office and signaled the door closed, then took a perch in front of her desk. Sylvestra held a pair of dark glasses over her eyes and looked carefully around the room. Then she set them down on her desk and sat. Without waiting for him to say anything, she sang, | | I had a surprise visit from Kormèr Lezàl this morning. | |

He felt some of his tension ebb away at hearing her admit that so readily. He wanted his instinct to be right about her, that she did have some kind of plan brewing, one that would lead to the arrest of their elusive jewel thief. Or perhaps she'd finally learned that Lezàl really had nothing to bring to the table in this case. ||So I heard,|| he warbled.

She raised her brow at this. ||You heard?||

||I've had Tseeo tailing Lezàl for a few days now.|| Her wings flicked, and Phatheeo held up a hand. ||Hear me out.|| She nodded. ||Tseeo took it upon himself to follow Lezàl after your rescind order came out. I covered for you on that, by the way. Tseeo didn't like that you did that, so I told him it was my idea.||

||Why? What concern is that of his?||

||He thought Lezàl was coercing you somehow.||

Sylvestra peered at him. ||Honestly? Or, is this a sexist thing?||

Phatheeo shrugged his wings. ||I don't know. I want to believe his concern is professional and genuine.||

Sylvestra considered this. ||Alright. So by tagging him on Lezàl, you chose to err on the side of caution.||

Phatheeo sighed. ||Yes. I tried justifying it another way too: if nothing came of it, it would at least keep Tseeo from stumbling on the truth, which could be even more damaging to morale.||

||So he witnessed my meeting with Kormèr this morning.||

||He saw everything, *and* he found the news articles... I take it those are all part of some intricate plan to... what, draw out the thief?||

Sylvestra smiled. ||Did I mention how much I'm going to miss you, Theeo?||

||Not enough,|| joked Phatheeo. ||When were you going to tell me about this plan?||

||I only agreed to it this morning.||

Phatheeo didn't like the sound of that, and he hoped his immediate frown sent that message. ||But the news articles mention your involvement. At least, that's what Tseeo reported.||

Sylvestra shook her head. ||That's all Kormèr's doing. Well, he and his Terran friends.||

Phatheeo harrumphed. ||Did you read about what happened on Freet-See? The official report, I mean.||

||I did. I also got the first-hand account. They were all in the store today, hidden by a holographer.|| She explained Kormèr's theory on the thefts and how he'd discovered the stolen merchandise. She then told him what they had discussed at the meeting in the store with Reestee.

Phatheeo listened intently until the end. Then he shook his head. *By the gods, was Tseeo correct? Has she been taken in by this boy to where she can't see she's making a terrible mistake?* ||Sylvestra, you'll forgive me if I disagree completely with this. You were stretching things already by involving Lezàl in the case; now you've crossed the line beyond reason.|| She chewed on her lower lip, but said nothing. ||Think about what you're doing; you're ignoring your own officers and letting a civilian derail the investigation!|| Phatheeo knew that yelling would get them nowhere, but he wanted to yell at her, to reprimand her for this blatant, stupid misstep, which was uncharacteristic of her. Instead, he stood and paced. He ran his hand through his crest feathers. ||I thought you were smarter than this, and now I wish you hadn't told me about this scheme of yours. Which isn't even yours!||

||I'm sorry, Theeo. I… I understand your point. But this is exactly why I wanted to talk with you about it… why I *need* your support or advice, more than ever before. I'm stuck in this up to my crop already.||

Phatheeo stopped pacing and faced her. ||So, stop assisting him in this foolishness.||

||He'll go through with his plan without my help—||

||Then, arrest him!|| He knew he was yelling again, but he couldn't help it. How was she not seeing the simple path out of her situation?

||I've considered that.||

||You should've. It's your job.|| She withered under his stern reprimand. He counted to ten, then sighed. ||Look, we all want to catch the culprit,|| he warbled softly. ||But you must never sacrifice your team or your mandate under the law. Never. If you ever do, you may catch your criminal, but you'll lose everything that really matters.||

||Thanks, Theeo. That's exactly what I needed to hear.|| His paternal, patient voice restored her sanity and reminded her that her work was everything to her—being Chief was all she had ever wanted to be, ever since she was young. But her integrity was as important as the job: as tempting as it was to pick the easy way, if it didn't feel right, she couldn't allow herself to choose it.

Phatheeo nodded. ||Good. Now… it's not too late to undo the damage.||

||Without losing the opportunity to catch the thief?||

Phatheeo absently pinched some pin feathers on his chin. ||It'll be tricky, but if we start working on it now, we have a chance. That is, if you're with me.||

Sylvestra nodded. ||Of course, I'm with you. We need to do this right, or not at all.||

CHAPTER 268

WITH all the pieces in play, and with Mack coordinating the Terran crew, Kormèr had very little to do except wait and over think everything. What-ifs played out in his head as he paced the promenade near the jewelry store. But with so many variables and as many unknowns, he couldn't possibly know which scenario would come to pass. And so, he simply paced and worried over all of them.

Logically, it was unlikely that the thief would make his move during the day; though the alarms had been disabled; the door would still need to be opened, or a window broken. Attempting such activities in the day risked drawing unwanted attention, and the thief needed time to find and recover the twelve sacks of loot he'd stashed. No one, however, was likely to return to the store in the middle of the night, leaving him eight prime hours of darkness to work undisturbed.

What if...

Kormèr tensed. Out of the corner of his eye, he spotted deliberate movement coming toward him. Relief washed over him when he peered left and saw who it was. ||Hi, Almp.||

<<Hi, KL,>> Kormèr noted his use of Elmarian and knew this needed to be a discreet conversation. <<I came to warn you that you're being watched again, I think.>>

Kormèr instinctively looked around. <<Right now?>>

<<No.>> Almp also glanced around. <<I mean, it doesn't look like it. At the hotel, though. There've been police perched in the branches outside the hotel for a few days, according to the guests. They've even come inside a few times and walked the hall outside your room. One was there when I left just now.>>

<<Hmm.>> *I've been using the portal a lot lately. They probably don't even realize I'm not there.* Kormèr had seen Averians perched on the branches of the pseudo-trees since his arrival, and he'd grown complacent with the sight of them there. He hadn't even considered that any of them could be police. Now he looked up and around, but he couldn't see anyone clearly enough to tell whether they were police or civilians. Suddenly, he felt very exposed. <<Thanks for letting me know.>>

<<What've you been up to?>> asked Almp. <<I haven't seen you much these last few days.>>

<<Not much. Spent yesterday in Freet-See with Jeremy and his crew.>>

<<Were you there during that incident at the spaceport? I heard they arrested some famous businessman.>>

317

<<Yeah, I was there. Right in the middle of it, to be exact.>> Kormèr told Almp the story.

||By the gods!|| chirped Almp, slipping back into Averian in his incredulity. ||That's amazing! You sure get mixed up in some of the craziest stuff that has happened around here in… ever!||

Kormèr had nothing to say to that; it was accurate enough.

||Those others escaped, by the way.||

||What others?|| asked Kormèr.

||The lizard lady and the other two you mentioned, who were working with her.||

Kormèr stared at Almp, not believing what he'd heard. ||They escaped? From custody?||

Almp nodded. ||Yes. They disappeared right out of their cells. It's got FSPD stunned.||

What if…

Almp continued: ||They've been trying to hush the story, but word always manages to get out—|| He stopped, peering into the distance.

Kormèr noticed his sudden pause and asked, ||What is it?||

||That guy. He looks familiar.||

Kormèr turned to see an Averian male standing outside Chees. The man hesitated, then walked up to the window and peered inside. <<Buomp!>>

Almp laughed. ||What's that mean? I haven't learned that word.||

||They're not likely to teach that in school. But I know that guy too. That's Sergeant Chreel Tseeo, the guy that arrested me when I paid for lunch with a gem. You were right: they must still be tailing me, though I don't understand why.||

Has Sylvestra had them monitoring me all this time? Or is this more of Tseeo acting on his own?

||My dad called the precinct when I told him about the guest complaints. He's going to get them to at least move further away from the hotel. The tree canopy might be public space, but they can't affect business unless they have a writ of consent. At least that's what Dad told me.||

||Good luck to him. The police can be tough to reason with when they have their minds set on something.||

||Are things working out yet with Sylvestra?||

Kormèr shushed him. Almp was clueless as to what was going on here and could very well blow the entire operation accidentally. He had to get rid of him.

||I'll tell you about it later,|| Kormèr told him. ||I was actually working on that matter when you got here, if you know what I mean.||

||Ahh! Sorry. I didn't mean to interrupt.||

Kormèr smiled at him. ||Friend, this has been a very welcome interruption.||

Almp beamed. ||Alright! Club tonight?||

He shook his head. ||Sorry, I can't make it tonight. But soon, I promise.||

||Right. Good luck. High sky.||

Kormèr waved goodbye, then went back to watching Tseeo parade in front of the store. *That idiot! What the hell does he think he's doing? If he screws this up...*

The hairs on the back of Kormèr's neck stood up. He spun and once again faced the whirlwind blur towering over him. ||I warned you to stay away from this place,|| sang the distorted voice.

Kormèr took a step back. He hadn't expected the thief to appear this early. Whatever calm he could muster, he channeled into his voice, while the rest of him remained unnerved by the Unseen's eerie presence. ||Last I checked, the promenade is a public place.|| *Barely a warble, good job!*

The blur loomed closer. ||Maybe I wasn't clear,|| he hissed, then vanished completely. Pain smashed Kormèr on the left side of the face, nearly knocking him off his feet. Before he could react, something kicked into his legs, sweeping his feet out from under him. He fell onto his side, and the air went out of him as an invisible kick slammed his stomach. He was picked up roughly by the back of his coat and held, dangling head-first, over the side of the promenade. Kormèr was vaguely aware through the screaming pain of his body that the ground was over three hundred meters down. He waited for the inevitable plunge into the depths. But it never came.

Instead, gasps and cries filled the air, along with pleas for him not to jump. Something grasped his right arm and pulled him back from the edge. ||If I see you again,|| chirped the blur in his ear, ||you're dead.||

The thief released his grip on Kormèr, leaving him bent over the railing, a blood-red string of saliva jiggling toward the ground. Kormèr spit it out before allowing himself to be helped down off the railing by the helping hands of the bystanders. Still gasping for air through the pain in his diaphragm, he collapsed into a ball on the ground. His left ear rang like a constant whistle, and he could feel his face heating up. But on his swelling face was a smile, and in his mind, one word: *Hooked.*

PEERING through the storefront window into Chees, Tseeo almost couldn't believe what he was seeing. The store looked as empty as it had the day of the robbery, with the words ||Out of business... For rent...|| scrolling across the windows from the left to the right. His fists clenched, and his wings rustled with agitation at the thought that the blame fell primarily on his precinct for not having solved the case or recovered the stolen merchandise. Even worse, the same fate would likely befall other stores—until the culprit was found and captured.

Tseeo turned and stared blankly at the ground, his brain trying to make sense of all the disjointed bits of information he'd gathered. If he could only get them to fit together... He'd made notes on his p-comm and reviewed them numerous times after his earlier brusque conversation with the Captain. But he was missing the common thread that had to be there, the one critical piece that tied all those bits together.

Tseeo's head snapped up as many voices cried out. At the same moment, his p-comm trilled with an urgent message.

Tseeo tapped the p-comm to display the message, as he curiously eyed a crowd that formed across the promenade. He started walking toward the crowd as he read, but then stopped and focused on the message. Someone had made a breakthrough in the case. A sting operation was in progress to capture the thief. Officers were on their way now to take up positions around the jewelry store, the site of the sting. But since Tseeo was currently the closest officer to the jewelry store, his task was to ensure that Lezàl did not interfere with the operation. Lezàl and his Terran friends were to be detained on sight, even if not officially arrested.| |

Tseeo nodded, pleased with this news. The Captain had been right; the Chief had matters under her control.

Tseeo sent his acknowledgement with a single tap, then closed the message. He continued toward the small crowd. | |Birshettan police, coming through. Break it up, folks.| | He stopped and gaped as his eyes fell on Lezàl, lying balled up on the ground. *This is my lucky day*, he thought cheerily as Lezàl slowly rolled and sat up. Tseeo took in the bruised face and spattered blood. | |You there,| | he pointed at a young man, who suddenly looked like he wanted to be anywhere but there, | |what did you see?| |

| |I uh… He was bent over the railing when I first saw him. I thought he was going to jump. But then he fell and lay there until now.| |

| |I see. Did he hit his face as he fell or before?| |

| |As I fell,| | chirped Kormèr, though his swollen face slurred his tones. | |I'll be alright… Sergeant Tseeo, isn't it?| |

Tseeo frowned down at Lezàl. Then he turned to the young man. | |Thank you for your help.| | The young man dashed away, and Tseeo turned back to Lezàl. | |What's the story, Lezàl?| |

| |What that guy said.| | Kormèr waved a hand in the direction the young man had vanished.

| |You were trying to jump and fell back, hitting your face on the pavement?| |

Kormèr snorted. | |Yeah, whatever.| | He started to stand, but Tseeo put a firm hand on his shoulder.

| |Take it easy, son,| | chirped Tseeo, loud enough for everyone around to hear. | |You've had a rough day. Why don't we have a doctor check you—| |

Kormèr brushed his hand away. | |I don't need a doctor. I'm fine. I have to be going anyhow.| |

| |No, no. That bruise looks very serious. I'll call for the paramedics.| | As Lezàl opened his mouth to protest, Tseeo leaned in close and whispered, | |We can do this the easy way or the hard way. Either way, you're going to the hospital.| |

Kormèr glared at him, then sat still and crossed his arms defiantly.

Tseeo grinned as he called the paramedics. He knew a doctor who owed him a favor that was about to pay up.

ASSIGNED to a private room in the hospital, Kormèr behaved himself as a nurse took him through some basic tests: temperature, weight, eye reactions, and so on. She cleaned the blood from his face while she asked him questions about the date and whether he remembered what he'd been doing before his fall. Finally, she rested a thin glowing device over the swelling without explaining its function. It hummed and made his face itch as it conformed to the contours of his cheek, but more surprisingly, it remained in place without actually touching him.

As his injury was only on his head, the nurse allowed Kormèr to remain in his clothes, but he had to remove his coat, which the nurse hung behind the door for him. The nurse assured him the doctor would be by momentarily, then left the room.

When he tired of waiting for the doctor, Kormèr spent the next hour or so perusing the contents of the few cabinets and drawers in the room. They didn't contain anything overly interesting, but Kormèr was surprised by how little he recognized. Either Averian medicine required different equipment, or the centuries since his time had ushered in dramatic developments and advances. He knew the truth was closer to the latter, but it still surprised him and reminded him of that very distinct feeling that he was very much out of his familiar element.

Nearly an hour and a half after Kormèr's arrival, a doctor entered his room. Amidst idle chitchat and banal pleasantries, the doctor removed the device without fuss or warning and examined the bruise.

||You have a nasty contusion there, young man,|| the doctor chirped. He gestured at Kormèr's face, and the wall to Kormèr's left changed to show a gray-scale image. Kormèr peered at the doctor's hands and noticed a very fine webbing covering some of his fingers. ||There's a hairline fracture just above the tooth line that runs right up to just below your eye-socket,|| he sang, and pointed at the image on the wall with his right hand. Kormèr just barely made out the thin dark line that meandered drunkenly from the top of the image toward the bottom. The doctor placed the device back over Kormèr's face. ||This regenerator will help it heal quickly. In the meantime, I'd like to keep you overnight for observation.||

||Overnight?|| chirped Kormèr. ||I can't stay overnight. I have something important to do tonight.||

||Now what could a boy your age have to do that's so important?|| chirruped the doctor, grinning. ||No, no. There could be side effects; the face is a delicate structure. From this kind of injury, you could pass out or go into seizures; I can't release you in good conscience with those potential risks.|| *I'll just bet you couldn't,* thought Kormèr, detecting insincerity in the doctor's voice. ||It's better all around if you spend the night.|| Kormèr opened his mouth to protest, but the doctor silenced him with a finger and two quick clucks. ||Uh, uh. Now be a good

boy and lie back and relax. You can go back to playing with your friends tomorrow.||

Kormèr fumed: there was nothing he hated more than being treated like a common child. He controlled his temper, however, as any outburst or tantrum would only land him in more trouble, or worse: medically induced sedation. Perhaps the doctor, like so many other adults before him, just couldn't fathom that someone of Kormèr's age could have pertinent and significant ideas, feelings, and experiences.

Kormèr recalled his conversation days ago with Kit and Jeremy about not regretting having a normal home life like most children. He never would've seen and visited all the places in his travels, had he simply lived a "normal life". But there was a catch: people would always underestimate and disregard him, simply because of his youth.

He wanted to comm Jeremy and his crew to let them know he was being detained but otherwise fine, but his p-comm had been removed during his check-in. ||Can I at least get my comm back? I need to make a call.||

The doctor looked up from the notes he was making on Kormèr's chart and considered the request. ||Maybe later, after we run a few more tests. Just relax for now. Everything'll be alright. You'll see.|| The doctor seemed to notice Kormèr's coat hanging behind the door for the first time and reached for it. ||You don't need this here. I'll take it somewhere safe.||

The hell he will! Kormèr fumed. *He wants to deal with a child? I'll show him a child.*

||No, I won't relax!|| Kormèr cried. ||My family's probably looking for me, and you won't even let me contact them!|| He sniffled and let his lips slacken and quaver. ||I miss my dad,|| he wept, using the memory of Yunzen to muster genuine grief. ||Can I at least keep his coat with me?|| he beseeched.

The doctor looked taken aback by Kormèr's show of emotion. ||Your father? I thought you didn't have family?||

Kormèr sniffed. ||Why would you assume that?|| *Unless someone already told you?* Oddly enough, Kormèr hadn't been asked for personal information or for an emergency contact during his intake process. ||Of course, I have family.|| *Technically speaking, just not on Averia... or in this century.*

The doctor handed the coat to Kormèr and retreated from the room hastily, presumably to check the veracity of Kormèr's story. Alone once more, Kormèr slipped on his coat and opened the door a crack. He cursed silently upon finding a police officer posted just outside. He closed the door, trudged back to his bed, and sat heavily. He briefly considered using the cube to escape, but he assumed he was being watched over a concealed camera. He wasn't about to reveal his biggest secret to spying eyes. He'd just have to bide his time until he could find an opening in which to slip away.

Besides, he had enough to think about, to pass the time until he could get to a comm to talk to Jeremy's crew. Would his plan work? Or would the thief somehow manage to grab his stashed loot and escape, despite the careful setup in place?

Kormèr shook his head, trying in vain to push away the questions and worries. There were too many possibilities to consider, and worrying over them wasn't going to get him anywhere, especially with him stuck in a hospital room. Of course, wanting them to go away and actually making them go away were two different things. Worries had a way of digging in and not letting go.

He reached into his coat's pockets and pulled out the magic sacks he'd found at the Hovel. *These would make excellent pockets,* he realized. Fishing out a small fabric repair kit he always carried, he set to work replacing the coat's pockets with the magical ones. This, at last, distracted his mind for the time being.

CHAPTER 27

POSITIONED at a higher promenade that ran perpendicular to the one on which Chees was located, Jim gripped the railing, his knuckles white and his heart pounding, as he watched Kormèr being attacked. Jim could just make him out: the kid's feet on the railing, as the rest of him dangled over the edge of the promenade. Beside Jim, Mack mumbled curses as he watched the attack unfold through an augmented reality scope.

Mack had chosen this spot as a better location from which to surveil the storefront and the area in front of it. Unfortunately, the location left them ill-positioned to rush to Kormèr's aid.

"What do I do?" asked Roke over the comm. He was the only member of the team within range to assist Kormèr.

"There's no visible target," growled Mack. "At least not from this angle. Can you see anything?"

"No. Kormèr expected this," said Morgan. The truth of the statement didn't make watching the savage attack any easier. Mack had been against Kormèr putting himself in danger, but with Kormèr's annoying penchant for doing as he pleased, he had lost that debate.

"He can't have expected getting killed," said Jim through his teeth. He wanted to scream, if for no other reason than to feel like he was doing something.

"What?" asked Jeremy. *"What's happening? If the kid's in real danger, screw the op! Get the hell in there!"*

Jim watched in growing horror as passersby rushed toward Kormèr and seemed to be pushing him. But then he realized they had actually grabbed his arms. Mack sucked in his breath as Kormèr tumbled from the railing and onto the promenade, and Jim let loose a string of expletives in relief.

"What happened?!" cried Jeremy.

"Kormèr's on the ground," Jim reported, "but he's surrounded by a few locals, so I can't see him."

"They're too close," said Mack. "The attacker must not be there, or they'd bump into him."

"I wonder what they thought was happening," said Kit. *"Probably thought the kid was going to jump."*

"They saved his life without even realizing it," said Jeremy.

Unable to make out any detail with his bare eyes at this distance, Jim's focus wandered across the promenade. "There's someone at the storefront."

"Birshetland PD," announced Mack a moment later. "He's headed toward Kormèr."

Mack gave everyone the play-by-play as the events unfolded, until the ambulance flew off with Kormèr and the officer.

"Well, that's just gnarly," said Roke. *"What now?"*

"Now, we wait," said Jeremy. *"Let's give the kid some time, see if he contacts us once he gets the chance."*

"At least he's with the police now," said Jim.

Mack looked at him, his pupils flickering with the minute images displayed on the AR lenses he wore. "Doesn't mean he's any safer. The guy could've boarded the ambulance right along with everyone else."

That disturbing thought sank in and settled heavily in Jim's stomach. Then he shook his head. "Maybe, but he really wouldn't have any reason to do that, right? He wants Kormèr out of the way so he can get into the store, and now he's got that."

Mack nodded. "That would make sense. But if Kormèr doesn't comm in twenty minutes, we'll need to decide what to do."

Twenty minutes later, they commed him, but he didn't answer. They tried him again ten minutes after that, still with no answer.

As they considered whether to send someone to the hospital, Mack interrupted. "I have activity."

"The thief?" asked Jim.

"No." He adjusted the handheld scope that transmitted the view to the AR lenses. "Amateurs," he grunted. "Birshetland PD is on the scene. I count five. They're trying to blend in, but they're broadcasting their presence like their crazy mating dances."

"To everyone or just to you, you think?" asked Kit.

Mack bobbed his head. "Alright, maybe just to me. Hopefully just to me, anyway. If the thief gets wind of them…"

"The better question is, like, why are they here at all?" said Roke. *"I thought the Chief was gonna let us fly solo."*

"She must've changed her mind," said Mack. "They're sweeping the places we would've been if we'd stuck to the original plan."

"The kid's not gonna be happy about that," said Jeremy. *"But that's a break for us. Now we just have to make sure they don't spot us."*

"So, we proceed with the plan?" asked Morgan.

"It's a 'go'," replied Mack immediately. "We planned this so that no single person is pivotal to success, including Kormèr. We owe him enough to go ahead." He muttered to Jim under his breath, "Hell, we owe him more than that."

"Right on, man," said Roke. *"I'm with you."*

"I've got BPD on our level now," announced Mack. "It's now or never."

"Then let's do this," said Jeremy.

Jim glanced around to make sure no one was looking their way, then he activated his portable holographer. He watched as Mack reached for the small device hanging from his belt, tapped the activator, and vanished.

EVENING settled over Birshetland, as the sun dipped behind the pseudo-trees. The traffic on the promenade thinned as the sky turned a rich cobalt blue. When the trees lit up for the night, the jewelry store door opened and quickly shut, the lock clicking into place by unseen hands, the hands of the Unseen.

Finally, Jeremy said to himself, watching the movement around him, as he remained perfectly still, and cloaked, in position by the store wall. His joints had stiffened up from the long wait, but he forgot about his discomforts now that the end was in sight. *Well, technically invisible and cloaked, but whatever.*

Jeremy watched a tile appeared in midair, morphing into a sack bearing a mini-holographer, as it descended. The sack stopped its descent a meter from the floor, caught by unseen hands, then moved to the top of a display case. Another sack appeared two meters away, also descending. It, too, was caught and placed on the display case. In moments, eight sacks lay neatly on the display case. A pause followed, during which no other sacks appeared. The display case rattled, as if struck by something, but the strike itself produced no sound.

The cinch on one of the sacks loosened, and the opening pulled open. *POP!* The sack jumped as if startled, then slid off the side of the display case and onto the floor.

Gotcha, bastard! | |You've been tagged!| | sang Jeremy. | |We can see you and track you! Surrender or—| |

Blinding light flashed through the windows and filled the store with its brilliance. Police sirens blared as shadows flitted through the light. The windows shattered, and two objects clattered across the floor. Jeremy dove behind a display case as glass crunched underfoot.

Whoosh! Whoosh! The two stun grenades flared, lighting up the store like tiny suns in the already bright light flooding in from outside.

As the effect subsided, Jeremy stood and looked for Kit and Morgan, but both men were as cloaked as he was. "Kit? Morg?" he said into his p-comm. No response.

The door burst open and ten armored officers charged in. Undetected by them, Jeremy carefully stayed out of their way as they took up positions around the store. Two stood guard at each window while two others remained blocking the door. These parted as a single armored officer entered, waving a hand scanner slowly around the room, and Jeremy spotted his sergeant's badge. The sergeant lowered the scanner and stared at the sacks on the display case and the one on the floor.

Two other officers entered and took in the scene from the door. Jeremy recognized the female as Sylvestra. In the armor, she almost passed for Terran. She moved with a lithe grace, despite the bulk of the armor, and exuded an air of authority and calm amidst the chaos. *Okay, I get what Kormèr sees in her.*

Jeremy forced himself to focus, figuring that the stun grenade must've affected him, even through the counter. What the hell were the police doing here? Had Sylvestra betrayed Kormèr? That was the only explanation his muddled brain could think of.

He scanned the floor for the marker they had hidden in each of the sacks. When the thief opened the first sack, the marker had sprayed out over him; his tech would still cloak him, but the marker would be visible with the right eyewear. But Jeremy didn't see him in the store anymore. However, he spotted a streak of the marker on the wall by the left window. He activated his p-comm and updated: "The thief is tagged, but he's escaped out the storefront. Does anyone have eyes on him?" No one in the store could hear him, thanks to the cloak tech.

"Not yet," reported Jim. While that wasn't the answer he wanted to hear, Jeremy was glad that at least *someone* on the team had heard him.

||No one,|| chirped the sergeant. ||There's no one here.||

Sylvestra looked around, then stared at the windows. ||I told you the thief would be cloaked.|| She faced the sergeant.

||Yes, so I went with the proven tactic of shock and awe.|| The sergeant raked the floor with his talons. ||Maybe he's just here on the floor, still cloaked.||

"Kit? Morg?" Jeremy called again into his p-comm. Again, there was no response. *Dammit. Oh, well, might as well get this over with.*

Jeremy deactivated the cloak and placed his hands behind his head, bracing himself for what he knew would follow. ||The only ones you'll find—||

The shouts of half a dozen officers drowned his words, but a shrill whistle from Sylvestra silenced them all, as they kept their various weapons trained on him.

||Stand down,|| Sylvestra chirped, calming her officers. ||Mister Jeremy Tailor,|| she sang, stepping toward him.

||Chief Chrreel. I hope you're taking care of our mutual friend?||

She ignored his question. ||Are you aware that this is an active crime scene and that you are trespassing?||

He assumed she was putting on a show for her team, since they'd gone over the plan together earlier in the day. *I guess she has to save her own hide first. Never trust a cop unless you absolutely have to,* he thought glumly. ||I heard this store is for sale and was checking it out. Mister Reestee will corroborate my being here.||

||I'll just bet he will.||

Jeremy frowned. ||What now?||

Sylvestra ignored his question again. ||So, where's the thief?||

Jeremy gritted his teeth and stabbed a finger from one of his raised hands toward the smashed windows. ||Gone.|| He scowled at the sergeant. ||Your sergeant here allowed the thief to escape through the window.||

THEY'D found him. He'd been careful, but The Guard were crafty and had access to tech forbidden to the rest of the Galactic Federation. He'd wanted to be one of them, the protectors of Averia. He deserved to be in their ranks; he'd been born to it. Both of his parents had been members of 'The Unseen', the forward units of The Guard. However, The Guard had turned him down; said he was 'unstable'. But they were the unstable ones, complacent with their power and tech. He'd overheard them speaking about dismissing him, and he'd taken matters into his own hands. He had gotten his hands on some of their tech and fled. But they no doubt had other tools that they'd used to track him down.

He'd been just fast enough to dash to the window when the police arrived at the store, but he hadn't escaped the full effect of the stun grenades. His wings and right leg tingled excruciatingly with pins and needles. The Unseen had limped past the troop transport that had disgorged the troopers that now surrounded the jewelry store, past the squad cars behind the transport and clear of the small crowd that had gathered at the edge of this thrilling police spectacle. Such things were so rare in Birshetland that when they came, they were big events.

The Unseen walked a good distance away from the scene as his nerve endings settled back down. He massaged his leg as he looked back at the chaotic scene he'd left behind. This had been his intent upon leaving The Guard: to create chaos; to reveal The Guard's dwindling control, and maybe even to reveal them to the world. Averia needed to know the truth that he'd discovered there, the truth about their artificial lives on this artificial world. But to progress his plan, The Unseen needed resources, and to acquire those, he needed money.

The jewelry store had seemed like the perfect target, stocked with enough wealth to fund his ambitions, and the crime would be unsolvable, thanks to his tech. But then he'd nearly been caught, and he'd had to wait, to be sure that The Guard wouldn't perform their own investigation. He'd monitored the store for over a week, even robbed a second store to draw attention from this one, but no one had come, as far as he could tell.

The Unseen stood now, the tingling in his leg almost gone. He rustled his wings, testing them, and cringed at the pain. They had absorbed the brunt of the stun blast as he'd jumped through the broken store window. He wondered if the Guard sentries who tried to trap him got caught in the blast. That would make his pain and effort worthwhile.

The Unseen unfurled his wings. They prickled uncomfortably, but he felt he could tolerate it for the short flight back to his hideaway. He took a few steps and leaped into the air.

ABSOLUTELY no one had come to check on Kormèr since the doctor's departure. He completed the work on his coat and placed his belongings back into the new pockets. The pockets worked in a simple way: Kormèr thought of what he wanted, reached into the pocket and the object would be there, ready to be taken.

If he simply thought "anything", then all the pocket's contents would be there for him to feel about and take.

Not sure of how the magic in the sacks worked, Kormèr had sewn one pocket into place first and tested its capacity to ensure that he didn't accidentally "break" its magical nature by piercing it. The stitching wasn't the best, but it was the best for now. If this worked, Trinket would touch it up once Kormèr returned home. To Kormèr's relief, the bag seemed to function just fine, so he had proceeded with the second. Pleased with the results, he donned the coat, then checked the time.

He scowled at the door. This felt very much like a delay tactic. But by whom? And why? Sergeant Tseeo's involvement could not be denied. So, that begged the question: was he under orders? If he was, had Sylvestra changed her mind and decided to let the police handle the thief's capture? This disheartened Kormèr, for two reasons. One, despite knowing the plan, Sylvestra and her team would have a difficult time catching this teched-up thief. It could even be dangerous. Two, it meant she'd used him. This thought brought a crushing feeling to his chest, and that surprised him.

Until now, his feelings for Sylvestra had been tempered by the reality that any relationship with her was as unlikely as finding a crystal cube that turned into an interdimensional portal. He'd already been that lucky once; a second chance of a lifetime…? But then he'd spent that time with her in the taxi and at the store, and before that, sleeping on her shoulder… Something had changed inside him, something he hadn't realized, until now. He couldn't stop thinking about her: the softness of her feathers; the graceful features of her face; that smile that could light up a dark room like a small sun. *But she betrayed you!* some part of his brain cried out. Was it true? He didn't know. But he had to find out, and to do that, he had to get out of here. There would be no opportunity of escape from this room other than the opportunity he made for himself.

It was time to check out.

Kormèr opened the door to the room's bathroom, and the light turned on automatically. A shower stall stood mostly obscured by a curtain to the left, alongside a small sink and mirror. The waste facilities sat straight in. He scanned the walls and ceiling, but he knew he probably wouldn't recognize any surveillance device even if wasn't hidden. Would someone really monitor the restroom? Anything was possible.

He stepped into the shower and closed the curtain the rest of the way as the door swung closed automatically. He waited a few minutes, standing as still as possible. Five minutes later, the light winked out. Moving slowly and hoping the shower curtain blocked his movements, he drew the cube from his coat pocket and opened the portal. Remarkably, the light remained off. He thought of his usual out-of-the-way spot on the promenade, then stepped through.

He pocketed the cube as a hubbub of tweets and chittering filled his ears. He stepped out from around the tree trunk and found himself at the perimeter of a large crowd. *Damn! Something happened!* He picked a random bystander and sang, ||Hi. What happened?||

The young woman looked at him and shrugged. ||Dunno. The police have Chees surrounded. I heard someone say there's a human inside.|| She gave him a once-over.

He smiled at her. ||Thank you.||

||Clear the way!|| The shrill chirps sounded artificially amplified, and they had the desired effect. The crowd parted, and Kormèr stepped back as Averian officers wearing armored uniforms created a clear path through the crowd. Kormèr now saw the large police transport and other vehicles parked on or floating along the edges of the promenade. *By the gods, what's happened here?* The answer came to him immediately: desperation. The police had to catch the thief; it had taken them too long already. For a city with barely any crime, these two robberies would frighten the masses if it continued unsolved. Not to mention, there was a very good chance that these robberies were only the beginning, the thief stretching his wings and testing the air currents, as it were.

Kormèr sympathized with Sylvestra's determination in that regard. But he'd really wanted her to trust him, or at least trust the plan. The guys had really put a lot of effort into it, too. *Jeez, the guys!* He scoured the crowd, looking for familiar faces, and slipped deeper into the mob as several officers came quickly along the cleared path towards him. Kormèr recognized Sylvestra, resplendent even in the armor, and ducked his head to avoid her notice.

Kormèr jumped, as he felt a brief, passing shove against him. He panicked instinctively, wondering if anything had been stolen, but found to his surprise that someone had pressed something into his hand. By the time he looked down and saw that he had been handed a p-comm, whoever had done it was gone. Without hesitation, Kormèr strapped on the p-comm. "Guys?"

"KL!" replied Mack through the comm. *"Where've you been, kid?"*

"Forcibly detained at the hospital, as far as I can tell. They confiscated my p-comm, sorry."

"Don't sweat it," Jim chimed. *"We always keep a spare around; hope I didn't bump you too hard passing it to you. You had us worried for a while there."*

"Yeah, but I'm okay now," Kormèr said absently, watching the commotion and chaos. "What's happened here?"

"It's a mess," Mack grumbled. *"BPD crashed our party and let the thief escape. Kit and Morgan are stunned, I think."*

Kormèr sidled towards the area where he knew Mack and Jim would have been positioned, had things gone according to the plan. "Jeremy's with the police, I'm guessing?"

Mack's heavy sigh came across as static. *"Yeah, his p-comm is transmit— I'm painting the target!"* he yelled, clearly no longer speaking to Kormèr. *"Taxi stand!"*

Kormèr pushed through the crowd toward the closest taxi stand. He burst out of the throng and into the path of Sylvestra and her officers. Their eyes met.

"He's taking flight!" said Jim.

||Lezàl?|| The voice was Tseeo's. ||What the—||

Lances of stunner fire crisscrossed the air. People screamed and ducked, many fluttering away in a panic. The police tried to control the scene, but between the panicked crowd and the lack of targets, they were overwhelmed. Kormèr watched, wide-eyed, as Roke, Mack and Jim appeared only meters away. He rushed toward them as they advanced, converging on one spot.

Pistol trained on the ground, Mack squatted and reached down with a free hand. Their quarry, the Unseen, appeared, lying unconscious on the ground in full view of everyone.

"Hey, kid," drawled Roke, when Kormèr arrived. Then he noticed Kormèr's bruise. "Dude! Whoa, what happened to you?"

"Another run in with this guy," said Kormèr, pointing at the immobilized Averian on the ground. "Sorry I missed the fun, but an overeager sergeant confined me to the hospital."

"Hey, dudes," said Roke, "it's time to put the guns down." He did as he said, bending and dropping his gun on the ground before holding his arms out to either side. Mack and Jim did the same as Kormèr turned to find over a dozen officers charging them with weapons drawn. Sylvestra and Tseeo led the charge, but only Tseeo held his weapon ready. Sylvestra kept hers pointed at the ground.

||All of you, on the ground!|| yelled Tseeo.

But Sylvestra stepped closer and asked, ||What's going on here?|| She spotted the birdman on the ground. ||Oh!||

Kormèr turned to her and bowed slightly, also keeping his arms out to his sides. ||Chief Chrreel,|| he chirped loudly, for the benefit of the crowd watching. ||As promised: the thief of Chees… by citizen's arrest.||

||You have no authority here, Lezàl,|| squawked Tseeo.

Kormèr straightened. ||But I do, according to the very laws you uphold, *Sergeant*.|| Tseeo bristled, his jaw tight. ||Now, I turn the culprit over to your capable hands, Chief.|| He warbled more quietly, ||That's all you wanted anyway.||

Sylvestra stiffened at hearing his last words but didn't respond. ||Escort these men to the transport,|| she chirped sharply to her team. ||Everyone's coming to the station for statements.|| Officers immediately jumped into action, pairing off with the Terrans as they moved toward the transport. Others came forward to gather the weapons and other evidence.

Kormèr met her dark silvery eyes one last time, before he joined the others at the waiting transport.

CHAPTER 28

NOTHING in her training, or even in that of her predecessors, had prepared Chief of Police Sylvestra Chrreel for the situation in which she now found herself. She stood surrounded by a crowd of civilians and media reporters, with waves of questions and comments coming from every direction. The nervous glances of her officers at last put things into perspective: they were just as out of their element as she was, and they were looking to her to give them reassurance.

So who could she look to? Phatheeo had walked off with Kormèr and the Terrans, escorting them along with the incapacitated thief to the transport. She could just see the top of the transport over the heads of the crowd, but nothing of the people boarding.

She had no one but herself, and that's the way it would be from now on. The thought stirred uneasily in her gizzard, much as she imagined must've happened when she first fledged, though she remembered nothing of that time. However, just like that time, she also imagined that the subsequent feeling when she soared through the air must've been exhilarating. As she tapped her p-comm to amplify her voice, she hoped that the next few minutes would be the same, and that she wouldn't plummet to her doom... metaphorically or otherwise.

||Alright, alright!|| she chirped, then waited a moment as some of the hubbub settled. ||Quiet down!|| She charged ahead without waiting for complete silence; if they wanted to hear, they'd shut up. ||We have apprehended the thief, so there's nothing else to see. Please disperse.||

||Is it true that the Terrans helped?|| someone cried out to her right.

She ignored the question. ||There will be a formal press conference tomorrow once we've processed the thief and had a chance to interrogate him.|| The crowd's volume ramped up, and she increased the amplification a few steps. ||Go home, please. There's nothing more for you here tonight. Thank you for your cooperation.||

She turned and faced her officers. ||Good job today, everyone. Let's pack it up, now. Tseeo!||

||Chief,|| twittered the Sergeant tacitly, standing at attention as other officers filed past him. He knew he'd messed up, which was to his credit. At least he had the capacity to recognize his mistakes, but Sylvestra had her doubts about his ability to learn from them for the future.

No need to rebuke him here. She checked her mood and ordered: | | Assess damages to the store, and give me a repairs report by noon tomorrow. I need to know how much this will cost the department. | |

| | Yes, Chief. I'll leave an officer behind to watch the store until the windows are replaced. | |

She nodded, wondering how much additional *that* would cost. | | Get to it, Sergeant. | |

As Tseeo rushed off, Sylvestra returned to the store. The forensics team carefully bagged the loot sacks, which had been emptied of jewels by Reestee earlier in the day and apparently refilled with the homemade marker bombs by Jeremy's team, unbeknownst to her. Nano dust still marked the positions where the Terrans, Kit and Morgan, had fallen, stunned by Tseeo's ill-conceived stun grenades. *Medical bills for them, added to our tab.* Even the streak of marker by the window had been imaged and collected. She nodded, satisfied that everything was under control here. Reestee wouldn't be happy with the damage to his expensive windows—*she* wasn't happy about the cost to replace them, either—but nothing could be done about that now.

She exited the store and was glad to see that most of the crowd had dispersed. Some non-Averians remained, but these had at least moved away from the immediate area. They watched from a distance as the last of the officers loaded into the transport. Phatheeo glanced her way and nodded before he, too, boarded, and the door sealed behind him.

After one last look around to ensure the scene was under control, Sylvestra returned to her aircar. She sat staring at the controls and decided she was in no condition or mood to pilot herself. | | Return to the precinct, | | she instructed, and the car lifted off.

Though she watched the passing scenery, none of it registered as she focused inward to replay the events of the evening. The memories slowed to a crawl as they remembered the look in Kormèr's eyes as he was led away. She'd read his gaze as something more akin to disappointment than betrayal or hurt, but she didn't know any Elmarians, so she couldn't really be sure. *Am I projecting my own feelings onto him?* she wondered. *No, that can't be. I did the right thing.* And she knew it to be true.

She hadn't felt so comfortable in her role as Chief of Police until she'd taken control of this situation and organized the operation. While she didn't begrudge Birshetland for its relative tranquility, it provided little that truly tested her mettle as a Chief. Her father had said as much, once, but she hadn't really understood, until now. And now, it was as clear as day. Despite the training programs she had in place for her staff—who performed their duties admirably—a gap existed that had let Kormèr discover what her staff could not. Now that she saw the gap, she would address it.

The stress and adrenaline rush of the operation had also dampened her hormones enough for her to recognize the mistakes she'd made with Kormèr. Had it not been for Kormèr and his friends, the thief would still be at large, but she had clearly stepped over the line with him. For the sake of doing her job, she might have ended her career. *How crazy is that?* There would be some repercussions from Kormèr's broadcast of a citizen's arrest, but nothing she couldn't handle.

As her aircar slipped into the motor pool hangar, Sylvestra spotted the transport, already settled in its spot and disgorging personnel and cargo. Sylvestra climbed out of the aircar and let it park itself, as she spotted Phatheeo stepping out of the transport to direct the accompaniment of the Terrans for debriefing.

Kormèr stepped out next, wearing a regen unit on the side of his face. The sight of his bruise sent a pang through her. *It's not hormones this time,* she told herself. *Just empathetic decency.* Phatheeo assigned him an escort, but Sylvestra chirped, | | Hold on. | |

Phatheeo, Kormèr, and his escort turned to face her. She looked down at Kormèr, realizing for the first time that she was a few centimeters taller than him. Beneath the blue glow of the regen unit, the welt on his face looked purple. It had to be more than a superficial injury for it to still look that way after using a regenerator. | | What happened? | | she asked, pointing at her own cheek.

| | The thief, | | Kormèr twittered, curtly.

Sylvestra felt her crown feathers flutter in irritation. She'd wanted to keep him safe from harm, and he'd gotten hurt anyway. | | We'll have Doctor Pharree take a look at you once you're inside, | | she sang.

Kormèr raised his brow. | | As long as it's not the same doctor who confined me at the hospital, | | he chattered, annoyance in his tone.

Sylvestra glanced at Phatheeo, who shrugged his wings. | | Probably not, | | she told Kormèr. | | I'll escort him inside, Captain, | | she directed Phatheeo. | | You're in charge out here. | |

The precinct had a good history with Doctor Pharree. Married to the brother of one of the officers, she'd served as the Force Medical Examiner for as long as Sylvestra could remember. Sylvestra called the doctor on her p-comm, as she led Kormèr to an interrogation room. The precinct only had two, and with all the Terrans to process, there would be a queue outside. But she had no other place to take him other than a cell or her office. The first was out of the question, and the second was too intimate. She'd had him in there once before, and that had been the start of her mistakes.

Doctor Pharree surprised Sylvestra when she responded to the comm a moment later, to tell her that she was already on site.

| | *Two officers cut themselves pretty badly on glass,* | | she sang, and Sylvestra sighed tiredly at the needless injuries. | | *I'm almost done with them. I'll meet you at your office.* | | Before Sylvestra could protest, Pharree closed the connection.

| | Detour, | | she told Kormèr, taking the next turn to a bank of lifts, where an aide stood waiting with a push cart containing the evidence that had been collected. The aide smiled and greeted Sylvestra as they all boarded the lift together.

Sylvestra was grateful for the aide's presence, as it delayed her having to speak to Kormèr just yet; she would have to explain herself to him at some point, but the conversation seemed to sound worse each time it played out in her head. Kormèr also seemed to avoid speaking to her, and instead smiled at the aide. ||Take good care of those items. They're extremely rare and very important to the case.||

The junior aide nodded, glancing at Sylvestra, as his wings twitched nervously. ||Of course.|| He nodded his thanks to Kormèr, who held the lift door for him and the cart when they reached their floor.

Pharree stood waiting in the doorway of Sylvestra's office when they arrived.

||WHO told you there was a fracture?|| asked Pharree after checking Kormèr's bruise. Kormèr told her about his stint in the hospital, though he hadn't gotten the names of the people that had attended him. ||Well, rest assured that there's no fracture. It's just a nasty bruise, although even that's just about healed up.||

||Why hasn't it already healed?|| sang Sylvestra, taking her perch behind her desk, once she had removed her armored vest and helmet. ||He's been wearing the regen unit for at least an hour.||

Doctor Pharree nodded. ||The regenerator was set too low—it defaults to Averian physiology,|| she sang, still looking at Kormèr. ||The attending doctor should've known better. But there's no sense in turning it up now. You won't need it in another ten minutes or so.||

Kormèr looked over at Sylvestra, who met his eyes directly. Kormèr glanced down at his hand, as the medic passed him a plastic slip. ||Take that if you experience any pain in the first twenty-four hours.|| She nodded at Kormèr's murmur of thanks and turned to Sylvestra. ||Anyone else hurt?||

||Three stun victims.||

||Concussions?||

||Most likely, yes. Two are Terrans, one Averian. The Averian fell from a height, so he might have other injuries. They should be in interrogations; you can check with Phatheeo for where they are. That's it. Thanks, Pharree.||

The doctor walked out, leaving Kormèr and Sylvestra staring at each other across the desk. ||What now?|| he asked her, and realized as he sang it, how ridiculously vague the question was. But he didn't bother clarifying. He felt drained, and his face itched maddeningly under the regenerator.

She reached for her badge, hesitated, then touched it. Kormèr peered at it and, for the first time, noticed the small lens in one corner, now activated to record their conversation. ||You didn't mention the marker bombs this morning,|| she sang.

He looked up at her, and a very fitting Terran term popped into his head: "bury the lede". ||You told me I had one chance,|| he warbled, then added, ||this morning.||

||I did. And I'm sorry, but it was professionally wrong of me to make that deal… to lead you and the Terrans on. *We* needed to close this case.||

Kormèr sighed. ||I can understand that,|| he conceded. He had felt the pressure when he himself had made little progress on the case after five days. He could easily imagine the pressure she had felt as the one person responsible for actually solving the case. ||But you could've just told me. Instead, you sent 'Sergeant Loo-Loo' to confine me to the hospital.||

||It was Sergeant Tseeo,|| chirruped Sylvestra. ||Loo-Loo is just a detective.||

Kormèr stared at her, trying to decide if she was joking. But she was serious and apparently oblivious to his intended sarcasm. ||I stand corrected.||

||I'm sorry about the way that was handled,|| added Sylvestra. ||But you were so insistent, and I wanted you out of harm's way. Clearly, I was right to be concerned.|| She flicked a hand to indicate the regenerator.

Kormèr frowned. ||Just me? But it was okay to leave Jeremy and the guys in harm's way?||

The thin tufts of her brow knit irritably. ||Of course not! I had a few officers looking for them, but your friends weren't where they were supposed to be,|| she replied pointedly.

Kormèr nodded. ||The original plan had too many assumptions. We had to reduce the risks.||

||When I reviewed your plan with my captain, we also noticed those risks.||

||Phatheeo?|| Kormèr recalled the birdman from the trip over on the transport. ||He was coordinating our transfer back here to the precinct.||

Sylvestra nodded. ||Yes. He's a good man, and an old friend.||

They stared at each other in awkward silence for a moment, each waiting for the other to speak first, then they spoke at the same time, stopped mid-sentence and waited again. Before either of them could finish their sentences, Captain Phatheeo entered. He glanced at Kormèr, then dropped a flimsy on Sylvestra's desk.

Sylvestra looked over the flim sheet. ||Sreel?|| she sang. ||No last name?||

Phatheeo made a clucking sound and tipped his head toward Kormèr.

||I think he's earned it, Theeo,|| she warbled.

||There's sensitive information there,|| protested the Captain.

||He's *earned* it,|| she repeated.

Phatheeo shrugged his wings. ||Your call,|| he cheeped, taking a perch. ||That's it, no last name. Nothing much else on AvoNet, except that he might have been some kind of military. Highly classified.||

||Military?|| asked Sylvestra. ||What military? A rogue group?||

||I haven't the slightest idea. And he's not talking much. Just a lot of nonsense about an ancient guard that's supposed to be protecting Averia, and how they need to be exposed and shut down to protect our culture and way of life...|| He made a fluttering motion with his hand. ||It goes on like that. We might need to get Doc Scrree-woo to determine if he's insane, or if it's an act.||

Kormèr shook his head. ||He's not insane.|| Sylvestra and Phatheeo turned to him. ||He was very deliberate, and his tech impressed even my Terran friends. Maybe if we'd had some time to question him, we would've gotten some more reasonable answers.||

Phatheeo looked ready to deliver a blistering rebuke, but Sylvestra interceded calmly, ||You understand why we had to take over, don't you?||

Kormèr nodded, noting Phatheeo's reproachful, distrustful glower. He answered Sylvestra, ||I understand: you wanted to save face, as the Terran expression goes.|| Before he could curb his tongue, he continued: ||Only you underestimated what you were up against, while I did not. Which is why I succeeded—||

Kormèr shut his mouth, realizing he was letting his anger speak for him. He was annoyed at Phatheeo for arriving just as he and Sylvestra were about to have an earnest conversation, and the moment was now lost. Kormèr looked across the desk at Sylvestra's pained expression and realized that he was making it worse, all by himself.

||You interfered with a police investigation, young man,|| Phatheeo chirped sternly.

||I was sanctioned to do so.|| Kormèr stopped himself short of adding, *old man.*

||Theeo, leave him be,|| twittered Sylvestra, with a resigned sigh. ||He's right. For the official record, I asked him to help, so I'm ultimately responsible.|| She subtly gestured to her badge, specifically to the lens. ||Any repercussions and feedback should be addressed to me.||

Phatheeo clucked, his wings rustling for a moment behind his back, before he finally nodded at Kormèr. ||Fine. I'll admit that your insight into how the thief perpetrated the crimes was helpful. It might have taken us some time to come to that conclusion by ourselves.||

Kormèr realized Phatheeo was tempering his comments, out of loyalty and maybe even protectiveness towards Sylvestra. Whatever his personal feelings towards Kormèr, Phatheeo had Sylvestra's best interests in mind and would prefer not to go on record arguing with an underaged offworlder.

||Thank you for your acknowledgment,|| Kormèr sang, following the older man's example. ||I merely wanted to help.||

Phatheeo flashed Sylvestra a glance. ||Yes, you were emphatic on that point. Still, when we didn't see the Terrans where they were supposed to be, we assumed that with you out of the way, they wouldn't follow through with your plan.||

||We *Terrans* have a saying about the word 'assume',|| twittered a voice outside Sylvestra's office. Jeremy stepped into the doorway, and the rest of his crew appeared behind him, peering into the office over each other's shoulders. ||And we owed Kormèr too much to abandon the effort.||

||Ah, come in, gentlemen,|| chirped Sylvestra. They did as told, grabbing an empty perch, reclining on a desktop, or leaning against a wall. ||I'd like to begin

by thanking you for your efforts. I also apologize for how the events unfolded; as my Captain said, had we known that you were still proceeding, we would've amended our approach.||

Jeremy shrugged. ||No lasting harm done. Every plan's got its glitches, right? The important thing is the thief was captured.||

||Thank you for understanding,|| she sang.

||There's one thing I don't understand,|| began Phatheeo, looking at Kormèr as he spoke. ||How did *you* see all the objects hidden by the holographer?||

||Yes,|| twittered Sylvestra. ||You mentioned magic, but didn't provide details.||

||I hired a Berdian friend of mine,|| sang Kormèr with some reluctance. It had been Phatheeo's question, and Kormèr still felt enough animosity toward the man to want to ignore his questions. But since Sylvestra also wanted to know...

||You are friends with the Berdians?|| Phatheeo asked.

Kormèr took a deep breath, sighed, and rolled his eyes toward him. ||With one specific Hawk Sorcerer, yes.||

||The one whose raising you attended?|| asked Sylvestra. Phatheeo made a strangled noise that didn't translate, and she ignored it. ||We contracted a Berdian, too, but ours had no luck finding anything.||

||My friend was his apprentice at the time,|| Kormèr sang, the memory bringing a slight smile. ||Didn't you ask them to check whether magic was used to perpetrate the theft?||

||That's right,|| warbled Phatheeo. ||Even they confirmed that there was no magic involved.||

||Well, Srrcheel—my friend—he had a different perspective. He never told me whether he suspected holography or if it was just luck, but he had something that he called a magic eye, a special looking glass that completely bypasses the holographer's effect. He spotted the holographer before I did, and he even detached it from the ceiling where the thief had stuck it. The holographer tech may not be actual magic, but it fools the eye in a similar way.||

Phatheeo's crest feathers fluffed as he exchanged a look with Sylvestra. ||It sounds like we owe him some thanks as well.||

Kormèr finally gave Phatheeo a level look. ||I think he'd appreciate that very much. That was his first mission, and I still owe him my feedback... via his superiors, I guess.|| Kormèr hadn't thought that far ahead yet. He assumed he would have to provide his feedback to Srrcheel's master, or perhaps even Fitzbew.

||I'll make sure he gets a special mention from us, as well,|| sang Phatheeo, tapping out a note into his p-comm.

Sylvestra turned to Mack. ||Mister Houghton, in your deposition,|| she tweeted, staring at her screen, ||you mention that the large holographer unit contains actual footage of the thief robbing the store?||

| |That's right, ma'am,| | answered Mack, his broad frame dwarfing Kormèr, especially looming behind Kormèr's seat.

| |That will be useful as evidence,| | sang Phatheeo. | |I don't suppose you know where this kind of tech is sold. Our thief's not telling.| |

| |I'd love to know where he got it, too,| | warbled Mack.

| |Well, perhaps we'll find out as we check into his background more deeply,| | Phatheeo chirped hopefully.

Mack seemed less than convinced. | |Maybe.| |

Sylvestra looked at him. | |You seem to have some familiarity with the device.| | Mack said nothing. | |Would you be willing to give our tech staff an overview of the device?| |

| |With all due respect, I would rather not. That device doesn't belong in the public domain, not even in an evidence locker.| | Mack straightened. | |I'm going to be honest with you: I fully expect a higher authority to come looking for that thing, and for the smaller units, as well… and possibly for anyone that knows anything about them. I wouldn't want to be on that short list.| | He held out a hand, palm out. | |I will show you how to use the menu and run the scenes, but strictly off-record; I want nothing else to do with that thing.| |

Sylvestra nodded solemnly. | |I understand, Mister Houghton. That may be all we need, and I appreciate your perspective and offer.| | She looked at each of the Terrans. | |Gentlemen, while your depositions will probably suffice, can we call on you to testify if it becomes necessary during the trial?| |

Jeremy nodded. | |A recent business deal will keep us on Averia for several months, so we'll be available.| |

| |What will happen to Sreel?| | asked Kormèr.

Phatheeo sniffed. | |That will be up to the courts to decide, but a conviction is certain. For the biggest crime in Birshetland's history, our citizens will want to see justice.| |

Sylvestra stood and came around her desk to stand by the doorway. | |Well, I have nothing else at the moment,| | she sang, as Phatheeo joined her, glancing at him to verify that he had nothing to add. At the subtle shake of his head, she chirped, | |Gentlemen, thank you for your time.| | She shook each of their hands as they filed out into the hall.

Kormèr lingered in the office, hoping to finish his conversation with Sylvestra. | |See you later, guys,| | he twittered, pulling the regenerator off his face and scratching blissfully but gently at the healed wound.

Morgan smiled at him. | |Catch ya in Freet-See, KL.| |

| |Later, dude!| | called Roke, already in the hall.

As Jeremy passed through the door, Tseeo nearly crashed into him, as he barreled into the office waving a sheet of flim. | |What is the meaning of this?| | he cried.

Sylvestra took the flim and scanned it, her brow knit. Her silvery eyes flashed to Kormèr, then Jeremy, as she passed him the flim. | |Is this your doing? You, or one of your men?| |

Jeremy looked at the flim and shook his head. | |Not me.| |

Kit peered at the flim over Jeremy's shoulder and shook his head. | |Now who would've done a thing like that?| |

Tseeo was apoplectic, his feathers ruffling in agitation, as Jeremy passed back the flim and trailed his crew towards the lifts. | |Chief, you're just going to let them go? You can't let them get away with this!| | He looked at Phatheeo for some kind of support. | |Captain?| |

Frowning, Kormèr stood. | |Get away with what?| | Sylvestra passed him the flim.

His eyes went wide as he saw the cause of Tseeo's angst. The flim contained a collage of various media headlines, all reading the same: **Offworlder Kormèr Lezàl Solves Chees Heist, Catches Thief (full story below)** Each one had a small graphic beside it, which expanded at his touch into a close-up photo of him, lifted from one of the *Stardust IV*'s security cameras. Kormèr couldn't suppress the chortle that bubbled up from the surprise of seeing his image and the over-the-top headline. *I can't believe the guys did this! They're crazy!*

He looked up to see Sylvestra, Phatheeo and Tseeo all staring at him with varying levels of suspicion. | |Well, *I* didn't do it. When would I have had the chance?| |

| |I'll take that.| | Phatheeo plucked the flim from Kormèr's hands. | |Come with me, Sergeant.| | Shaking his head, he led a frantic Tseeo out of Sylvestra's office, toward his own.

Sylvestra closed the door and waved him to a seat, but he shook his head.

Before she could say anything, Kormèr started. | |Listen, about our first agreement... A lot's happened over the last week, and my motivation for catching this guy just... it's just not the same as it was at the start.| |

She returned to her side of the desk but didn't take her perch. | |I see. So, you're no longer interested in impressing me?| |

Kormèr shook his head. He'd been rehearsing this line in his head since Phatheeo's entrance earlier. | |I've just come to certain realizations about people that I need to sort through, and I don't think pursuing a fruitless relationship with you, based on my childish notions, is going to help anyone.| | *Ugh, that sounded even worse out loud.*

| |Fruitless?| |

He looked at her. *That's what she took away from that?* | |Yeah. Srrcheel told me about your law, the one forbidding relationships between Averians and non-Averians.| |

| |Oh, you mean *that* kind of relationship?| | Sylvestra nodded with understanding. | |I see. So, you knew about our law, but you broke your thieves' code anyway?| |

340

Kormèr wasn't sure how to answer. ||No… yes… Wait.|| He paused to collect his thoughts, and found it easier without looking directly at her. ||I wasn't looking for just a physical relationship; that's not what I meant by 'fruitless', not at all. Let me try again: I gave you my word that I'd solve the case in seven days, so regardless of the law, I had to honor our agreement. Otherwise, what good would my word be, ever again?||

She looked at him askance. ||Your word is that important to you.||

He held her gaze fixedly. ||My word is everything. I don't give it lightly, or often.||

Her face softened with a slight smile. ||That's good to know,|| she sang. ||Don't ever change that about yourself, Kormèr Lezàl.||

He tried to smile back, but he wasn't feeling it, so he didn't know if he succeeded. ||I suppose I'll be at the hotel if you need me, before the trial.||

||Oh.|| She seemed surprised that he wasn't staying. ||Yes, of course. Thank you for your help with all this.||

He extended a hand out to her. ||It's been a pleasure working with you, Sylvestra.||

Sylvestra hesitated a beat before reaching across the desk and clutching his shoulder, in the traditional Elmarian style. ||High sky, Kormèr… KL.||

He turned, opened Sylvestra's office door and left the precinct, thankfully without being accosted again by Tseeo or Phatheeo or anyone else. He was grateful, too, that Jeremy and his crew hadn't still been lingering around, either, as Kormèr was not in the mood for company, not even the well-meaning type.

From the precinct, Kormèr took the longest walk of his life back to the hotel. All the while, his mind churned through anger, frustration and despair. Though he'd played it cool in Sylvestra's office, and though he'd almost convinced even himself that he could get over his infatuation for her, he couldn't avoid the cold, hard truth: *I love her.*

He would give up anything, for the chance to spend the rest of his life with her: to share the highs and the lows, to see her smile and to be there for her—if and when she needed him—and for her to be there when he needed her, too. *Like now.* The aches in his body were nothing compared to the pain that gripped his heart.

Kormèr arrived at the Hotel Cheerees via a footpath and took a lift directly up to his floor. Already, Kormèr had noticed curious looks from passersby and from other hotel guests, as he realized that news of the Chees robbery arrest was likely spreading, along with his photo. While he was sure that Almp or his father, Theeseeo, would have some congratulatory and well-intentioned words for him, he wasn't in the mood for any of those, either.

He trudged the last meters to his room and entered the empty, darkened space with a sense of relief that he could finally be alone and drop the cheerful, positive façade he'd maintained for others. While he could have used the portal to find his solitude anywhere—even back home on Elmar, if he wished—he wasn't ready to leave Averia just yet.

Physically drained from the day's activities, and wracked with hopelessness over his feelings for Sylvestra, he stumbled with half-closed eyes to his bed and belly-flopped onto it. He curled into himself and cried into the pillow, releasing his pent-up emotions of grief and discouragement, until he felt raw and emptied of all his pain.

Finally exhausted and spent, he slept.

CHAPTER 29

FACE crushed into his sheets, Kormèr stared at the wall, his eyes unfocused despite the morning light filling his room. For the first time that he could remember, since he'd arrived on Averia, he had nothing pressing to do. His time was his own, to walk around town and truly enjoy the sights.

But doing so was the furthest thing from his mind. In fact, if not for one remaining task, he would've opened the portal and gone home already. But he needed to square things out with Srrcheel; he owed the birdboy that much for all the help he'd been. After all, if it hadn't been for Srrcheel, Kormèr would probably never have found the holographer, and Jeremy's landing gear would now be the property of Harry G.

Still, Kormèr lay unmotivated on the rumpled sheets of his bed. Even through the insistent knocking at his door.

<<Who is it?>> he asked absently, not realizing he was using his native tongue. And also not remembering that only one person ever bothered to knock on his door.

<<It's Almp, you fool. Open the door.>>

Kormèr's eyes focused, and his eyebrows twitched. He turned his head to squint angrily at the window, as if the day had no right to be so cheerily bright.

Kormèr flipped onto his back. <<Whadda you want?>>

<<C'mon. Let me in and I'll show you.>>

Kormèr grunted and sat up. He glanced at the time and saw that he'd slept through nearly the entire morning. <<Alright. Come in.>>

The door opened. Almp and Theeseeo scurried into the room and closed the door hurriedly behind them.

Almp grimaced at Kormèr's bedraggled state, but Theeseeo didn't even notice as he rushed over to Kormèr and embraced him in his powerful arms. ||Congratulations, KL!||

||What?|| Kormèr managed on his last breath.

Theeseeo released him, but kept him at arms' length. ||You're a celebrity! A hero!||

||Easy, Dad,|| chirped Almp, tugging his father's arms off Kormèr's shoulders. To Kormèr, he sang, ||We've been fending people away all morning who want to leave you messages and know where your room is.||

||What? Me?|| Kormèr's head felt sluggish. ||Why? I mean, why do they want to know?||

Almp frowned at him. | | Stop joking around. You know why! | | Kormèr shook his head. Almp laughed. | | You solved the greatest crime in Averia's history! Don't be so modest! | |

| | Oh, that. | | Kormèr shrugged, recalling the day before with disquietude. Yesterday's events already felt like a blur, and so emotionally taxing that he had no desire to be reminded of them. | | It's no big deal. | |

| | No big deal? | | Theeseeo's wings fluttered. | | Tell that to all the people lined up in the lobby. I'm nearly overbooked because so many people want to stay at the hotel where Kormèr Lezàl is staying. | | Theeseeo snuffled, shaking his head. | | No big deal, indeed. | |

| | But I didn't do it for attention, | | protested Kormèr.

Almp grinned. | | Does it matter? You have it anyway. Your face was on the front page of every news site. | |.

Kormèr rested his head in his hands. | | Yeah, I saw that. | | What had seemed yesterday like a huge blessing given by Jeremy's crew to exonerate Kormèr, was now feeling like a curse.

| | Well, now that you're awake, | | Theeseeo chirped brightly, | | don't hesitate to call down to the desk if you need anything sent up. The crowd downstairs doesn't look like it'll be thinning anytime soon. | |

| | Thank you for the warning, | | Kormèr replied, as Theeseeo let himself out.

Almp stayed behind, standing next to the bed. | | Things didn't work out with the Chief, did they? | |

| | No. | | He turned his head to look at Almp. | | Not that the odds were very good to start. I fulfilled my end of the bargain, so that was it, and we parted ways. | |

Almp's jaw fell. | | You went through all that trouble for nothing? | |

| | Not for nothing, | | Kormèr replied tersely. *I did it for her, for the sake of love.*

| | I mean: there's no reward or repayment, from her side or from Birshetland? | | Almp scowled.

| | Just my continued freedom; I didn't ask her for anything else. | |

Almp shook his head. | | You are one strange kid, KL. | |

Anger flared at hearing that again, but then the ridiculousness of hearing the remark from Almp hit him, and Kormèr cracked a smile, which turned into a chuckle. | | So I've been told, repeatedly, so I guess I am. Thanks for coming by. I needed a wake-up call. | |

Almp frowned with uncertainty, then relaxed his brow. | | Oh, you meant figuratively, not actually having my dad and me rudely waking you. | |

| | Both, I suppose, | | Kormèr smiled. | | See you later. | |

Once Almp left, Kormèr rushed off to take a much-needed shower. When he finished, he stopped to wipe the condensation from the mirror and saw his reflection for the first time in what felt like days. The bruise on his face was nearly gone, with just a slight yellowish patch where the ugly purple swelling had been the day before.

He dressed, cracked the door to peer out into the empty hallway, and stepped out. Heeding Theeseeo's warning about the state of the lobby, Kormèr walked to the staff doorway and knocked. When no one answered, he entered and found a small room painted in utilitarian gray, with supply shelves to the left and right and a lift door ahead. He called the lift and when it arrived, pressed the button for the ground floor, relaxing gradually as the floors ticked past without stopping for additional passengers.

Once the lift stopped on the ground level, both front and back doors opened. The front door opened into the same sort of small utility room, while the rear door opened into a much larger space, with a loading dock and other machinery, and a regular doorway next to two large bay doors in the distance.

Kormèr walked out onto the loading dock and jumped down to the ground. He walked to the regular door and cracked it open enough to peer outside. No one seemed to be about. He stepped out and triggered Feestoo's pager.

He had barely a moment to take a breath when the familiar taxi swooped down and landed a few meters away. The door opened, revealing Sylvestra sitting in the passenger area.

||I was thinking,|| she started, ||now that the case is behind us, maybe we could start over. As friends?||

Kormèr smiled and nodded. ||I'd like that.|| Maybe her superiors tasked her with smoothing things over with him, given his newfound fame and popularity, but she seemed sincere, and he welcomed another chance to become friends. *Even if nothing more comes of it, it's enough.*

She checked her watch. ||It's almost noon. Would you like to have lunch with me?||

||Sure,|| Kormèr replied, entering the taxi.

||Good morning and congratulations, KL!|| chirped Feestoo.

Kormèr patted Feestoo's shoulder. ||Thanks, Feestoo!|| To Sylvestra, ||I know a cozy little place—||

Sylvestra shook her head. ||No, no. The city's paying, so I've picked the place. Feestoo?||

||On the way, Chief.||

BIRSHETLAND'S business district resembled the rest of the city, in terms of the promenades and splendor of the pseudo-trees. But many more Averians than Kormèr had ever seen at once swooped around or bustled along its streets, and these promenades sported fountains instead of public baths.

With so much "pedestrian" air traffic, Feestoo had to adhere to stricter flight paths as he crossed the airspace and settled at the restaurant's private aircar stop. Someone opened the taxi door from the outside, and Sylvestra stepped out and thanked them. Kormèr followed and looked up at an elaborate white-marble entrance, with real flaming torches on either side, all of it speaking to the opulence of the establishment. The signage above the door read: *Soni-Ee*, which translated to "Brilliance". Kormèr thought it sounded presumptuous, but as their personal valet led them to their quiet table, he hoped the place lived up to the name.

||This is very nice,|| he told her, taking in the décor of faux-wood panels inset with local artwork.

||I don't come here often,|| she sang, also looking around, but with eyes that seemed to see memories rather than the décor. ||But my dad would bring us once a month to celebrate with the family. And once a year, he'd rent the place out for the precinct.||

||That sounds... expensive.||

Sylvestra chuckled. ||It was, and the mayor gave him hell, the first time. He visited the precinct to chew my dad out in person. But my dad,|| she paused and shook her head, ||he was crafty. He brought the mayor out onto the floor and announced that he was the man who had made their meal possible. The response so overwhelmed the mayor that he agreed to allow the event going forward, but only once a year.||

||Your dad sounds like my kind of guy.||

Sylvestra nodded. ||I thought he might.||

The Averian server brought them each a decorative flimsy that turned out to be the menu. *No simple digital menus for this upscale clientele*, Kormèr realized.

||Any recommendations?|| he asked, scanning the menu. The items were listed only by name but could be expanded to list the ingredients, cooking style and beverage pairings. Kormèr tried not to look at the prices, but he couldn't avoid the three-digit numbers. He glanced over the top of the menu at Sylvestra. ||We could split the bill.||

She fixed him with a raised brow. ||Birshetland's paying,|| she reminded. ||It's the least we can do for the 'offworld boy detective'. Sorry, I didn't coin that nickname,|| she simpered. ||You don't always get to choose how people perceive you.||

He smiled. ||Oh, yes, I'm painfully aware of that.|| He would endure being called anything, if it meant having the chance to gaze into Sylvestra's silvery eyes once more...

||Anyway, recommendations,|| she chirped suddenly, dropping her eyes to the menu flimsy. ||They harvest the lumbricus for the braised special fresh every morning, and it's my dad's favorite. The sprouted seed and mixed berry salad is excellent, but not very filling. The cricket-flour dumplings with citrus gastrique are my personal favorite.||

Sylvestra ordered the dumplings, while Kormèr ordered the lumbricus, only realizing when his plate was placed in front of him that his order amounted to a tangle of earthworms bathed in a casserole of rich brown gravy.

Sylvestra laughed at his look of consternation and nudged her elegantly garnished platter of tulip-shaped dumplings closer to him. ||If you want to switch with me, just say the word,|| she offered. ||I should've warned you about what it was.||

||No, it's okay,|| he chirped. ||I try to keep an open mind about new experiences and tastes.|| Feeling as though half the eyes in the dining room were focused on him—not to mention Sylvestra's—Kormèr twirled one worm like a noodle onto his fork and placed it in his mouth without looking at it too long.

The sauce was pleasantly savory, and the lumbricus itself was chewy but not distractingly so, and tasted curiously like… mushrooms?

||Worms take on the flavor of where they're harvested, and the chef here finishes his lumbricus on a proprietary blend of organic mulch and mushroom compost,|| Sylvestra remarked, taking a delicate bite of her first lemon-streaked dumpling. ||What do you think?||

Kormèr took a sip of his water. ||Delicious, but that was never in doubt. I trust your dad's taste.||

Sylvestra smiled warmly at his compliment of her father, as she took a sip of her wine. At the glimmer in her crinkling eyes, Kormèr forgot all about food and lost himself in daydreaming, but he snapped out of it when he noticed her lips moving. ||What?||

||I said that all of this must seem mundane to you,|| she repeated. ||What fantastic things you must have seen, with all the places you've visited.||

||Actually, of all the worlds I've visited, I think Averia may be the most exciting and unforgettable of all,|| he sang.

||Are you saying that to be polite?|| she asked.

||Hardly,|| he grinned. ||It's not on every planet that I get to meet such incredible people, or help the authorities in their work.||

||That's right,|| she smiled. ||In your line of work, you usually try to avoid the authorities, not help them.||

He chuckled. ||I guess there's a first time for everything.||

THEY rode back to the precinct in Feestoo's taxi, after their lunch stretched into two hours without their notice. Sylvestra had to return to work, and Kormèr was more than happy to ride with her, if only to spend as much time in her company as possible. Kormèr stepped out after Sylvestra when they arrived, both oblivious to the stares in their direction.

||Thank you for a wonderful lunch,|| he told her, bowing his head slightly. ||Well, thank you to Birshetland for the lunch, but thank *you* for the company.||

||It was my pleasure,|| she replied. ||Maybe we can go out again, sometime.||

||Umm...|| He wasn't certain whether she was being sincere, or just polite, and he feared rushing things, but he had to ask: ||Do you really mean that?||

She smiled, and he melted in her gaze. ||Just as friends.||

||Of course. In that case, Sylvestra—||

||You can call me 'Sylvee'.|| He raised an eyebrow at her slight change in tone. ||It's what my friends call me.||

He nodded, feeling his heart skip a beat. ||Sylvee, what are you doing tomorrow?||

||Working,|| she reminded with a patient smile, then she glanced at her p-comm. ||I should get back.||

||Yes, of course.|| He looked up at the imposing façade of the police precinct and suppressed his instinctive urge to flee.

||You can come by my office tomorrow after work,|| she suggested deliberately, noticing his disquiet. ||Six o'clock.||

||I'll be there,|| he pledged, backing into the taxi. ||Enjoy the rest of your day.||

||You, too.||

He watched her as Feestoo pulled away. She watched the taxi go, then turned and walked into the precinct.

||You two make a delightful couple,|| twittered Feestoo.

Kormèr realized he was grinning like an idiot, but he couldn't help himself. ||We're just friends, Feestoo,|| he chirped, despite a part of his mind still holding out hope for more.

||Ah, young love,|| Feestoo crooned.

Kormèr chuckled and slapped him on the shoulder. ||Feestoo!||

Feestoo laughed. ||I'm just ruffling your feathers, KL. It's good to see you smile again. Where to now?||

||Let's make a stop at Chees. I want to check in on Mister Reestee. Then... then I'd like you to take me some place of your choice: your favorite spot in all of Birshetland. I'm going to be staying here for a while, it seems, so I should get to know the city, as the locals do.||

SITTING with Feestoo, at the crater's edge of the rock that supported the grand city of Birshetland, Kormèr gaped at the site before him. He breathed a low, ||Wow,|| as the late afternoon sunlight set the towering white pseudo-trees ablaze, and lit the metallic leaves in reflected orange light. Kormèr knew he would never forget this truly spectacular sight for as long as he lived.

||I proposed to my wife here,|| twittered Feestoo.

||I imagine that was a guaranteed success,|| mumbled Kormèr, still in awe of the beauty of this city.

Feestoo grinned. ||Eventually. We had been together for three months when I asked her to marry me the first time. She turned me down, so I tried again after we had been together for a year. She turned me down again, but the third time...

This place, this view—everything came together perfectly, and she finally said 'yes'.||

||It's a good thing that you didn't give up,|| Kormèr remarked.

||True love is patient,|| Feestoo chirped. ||You can't force it or rush it.||

Kormèr considered Feestoo's advice. ||Thank you, my friend, for bringing me here. You've brought a wonderful finish to what had started as a terrible day.||

Feestoo smiled broadly, as the two quietly watched the sunset.

CHAPTER 30

FOLLOWING instructions given to them by Sylvestra, Kormèr and Jeremy walked past the busier part of Birshetland's port and through a low, airy passage lined with kiosk windows, most of which were closed. The few that stood open had signs that scrolled and flashed, promising: "The thrill ride of a lifetime for non-fliers"; "Fly Argent Airways and never fly sky-hoppers again". Apparently, this attraction might have once been quite popular. But the short lines at the few open registration windows told a different story now.

Kormèr and Jeremy had already registered, so they bypassed the windows and exited the passage onto a circular, open-air platform. Like the sky-hopper platforms, this platform looked out beyond the edge of the city, into the great expanse of Averia's late afternoon sky. The sun had dipped behind the treetops of Birshetland, casting long shadows across the platform. The view would have been stunning if not for the five, four-meter tall birds that stood tethered to the platform. Kormèr stopped and stared in awe at the majestic creatures that would soon transport him and Jeremy to Berdia. The Argents reminded Kormèr of pigeons, with mottled gray plumage and vacuous expressions. Each had an Averian handler standing nearby or conversing with the few non-Averian tourists present, perhaps trying to convince them that the Argents were safe.

"Good freaking god!" cried Jeremy, causing an alien standing near one of the enormous birds to turn and look at them. Kormèr waved, and then noticed that another alien of the same species had already been harnessed to the Argent. The alien raised an appendage that ended in a triple-pincer and clicked two together. Then it turned and let a handler harness it onto another Argent.

"I can't believe I let you talk me into this," protested Jeremy, as a handler beckoned him forward. "I know I owe Srrcheel, but this is crazy. Plus, I've heard things about Berdia that'd turn your stomach."

Kormèr stood by as the handler positioned Jeremy, then began fitting him into the harness. But his attention was focused on the alien couple. "Jer, I've been to Berdia. I even spent a few days passed out in the rafters of one of their grand meeting rooms. Trust me, they're not omniscient, and they're not evil."

Kormèr cringed as the handlers released the tethers of the two alien-toting Argents. The huge birds dashed for the edge of the platform and leaped, spread their wings and soared away.

Kormèr swallowed hard; he really would have preferred using the portal. His informal lunch "date" with Sylvestra had gone really well, and he didn't relish the

350

idea of dying by carrier bird when things were going so well. But this was an official trip, sanctioned by the Grand Master himself, so the portal was out of the question.

"I do trust you, kid," Jeremy said with a grin. "That's one of the reasons I'm here." Kormèr watched closely as the handler carefully secured Jeremy into the harness, the man's back against the bird's belly, and his legs hooked back into stirrups.

The handler noticed Kormèr's inquisitive stare at the stirrups. ||That's so your feet don't drag on the ground during takeoff and landing.||

Kormèr nodded. ||Makes sense.||

||Are you comfortable, sir?|| the handler asked Jeremy.

Jeremy held his arms out and made propeller motions with them. Then he nodded. ||Yes, I seem to be fine. Thank you.||

||Your Argent is ready for you, sir,|| sang the handler, and extended a wing to Kormèr's left. Kormèr looked to see the next handler hooking a feed bag to a post with a grunt. The young female Averian turned, clapped her hands and kicked a stepstool into place in front of her Argent.

Kormèr stepped up the stepstool and positioned himself as he'd seen the other handler do with Jeremy. "What other reasons do you have for being here?" Kormèr asked Jeremy, keeping the conversation going to keep his mind distracted from the eventuality of what was coming.

Jeremy shrugged in his harness. "A certain amount of curiosity; I can't imagine many Terrans have ever been to Berdia... if any! Berdia holds a lot of mystery and history."

Kormèr giggled, as his Argent's handler's talons inadvertently tickled his side. She looked at him and smirked, but kept her professional detachment as she continued working deftly on the clasps. "What kind of history?"

"It's the first city in the sky that the Averians built when they ascended from the sub-surface of the planet. Or so the legend goes. I really don't see how it's possible that they actually evolved down there in the near-darkness and then came up here, but who am I to question their beliefs?"

The idea fascinated Kormèr. "What's down there, on the sub-surface?"

Jeremy shrugged. "There are stories, but I've never bothered to look into it."

Kormèr imagined flocks of Averians popping up through the clouds between the rocks for the first time and finding this beautiful sunny terrain on which to begin a new life. "What must they have felt, coming up here and discovering this place for the first time?"

"Quite inspired and hopeful, no doubt," said Jeremy. "They celebrate the history of their ascension every year. It's called 'Cheerretee'. Just passed, in fact."

Kormèr nodded. "Yeah, I missed it. That's when I was on Berdia for Srrcheel's raising ceremony."

"Now, that sounds like it was worth it!"

Kormèr shrugged as best he could in the harness. "It might have been, but I kinda passed out or something. It was… weird."

||You're secure,|| chirped Kormèr's handler. ||Let us know when you're ready.||

Kormèr grinned at Jeremy and answered: ||I think you'd be better off just surprising us. We're never going to be ready.||

The handler chuckled. ||You have nothing to worry about. It's quite safe.|| She let loose a shrill whistle, and released the tethers that held the birds to the platform. Kormèr's breath caught in his throat, as the giant bird rushed forward and over the edge of the platform, carrying him with it. Its huge wings whooshed as it picked up speed and soared out over the edge of the rock-mass of Birshetland.

"Holy shit, kid!" shouted Jeremy over the rush of the wind. "This is amazing! Waaahoooo!"

Kormèr loosed a nervous laugh while his stomach heaved from the takeoff. The land rolled past far below, thrilling and horrifying at the same time. Though they crossed the same terrain as when riding the sky-hoppers to and from Freet-See, Kormèr found this experience much more visceral. He attributed this to the fact that he rode on the belly of a bird, with nothing between him and the ground. But also because, in this position, he practically faced the ground, figuratively facing almost-certain peril.

Rather than appearing as just a huge dark, featureless ocean spanning the floating rock surface of the planet, the Great Rift was now more like an endless chasm, deep and foreboding with a constant updraft of hot air. Seeing it brought to Kormèr's mind the possibilities of what might be living down there. What had driven the first Averians to venture up into the light? As curious and intrepid as he was, Kormèr also knew his limits, and exploring down there would never be on his to-do list.

The transit across the Rift took fifteen minutes by sky-hopper and thirty by Argent, but they were still hours away from Berdia, and Kormèr had already wearied of Argent travel. After the Rift, the view in every direction became an indistinct sea of floating rocks, so there was no longer even a view to distract him. After an hour, when Jeremy's Argent came a little closer, Kormèr saw the man's arms and head dangling loosely in carefree slumber.

Kormèr frowned, jealous. He might have been tired and bored, but his brain was too unsettled to lapse into sleep. The communication from Berdia had warned of some effect the city had on first-timers as they approached, this being the main reason for the use of Argents rather than piloted craft. The message had shed no further clarity on what the effect might be, and this worry niggled at the back of Kormèr's mind.

As the two-hour mark approached, Kormèr wished more and more he'd been able to use the portal. Night had fallen and left him with nothing to look at but the moons, and even those were difficult to see from his position under the carrier bird. He couldn't see Jeremy anymore in the near dark of dusk, but he heard the man yawn.

Then Jeremy asked, "Wow! We're not there yet? How long was I out?"

"Long enough," Kormèr answered, trying to sound annoyed, but failing since those were the first words he'd said in nearly an hour and a half, and his throat was dry. Why hadn't anyone warned him to bring water? He built up a wad of saliva and swallowed hard, pressing the liquid into his dry throat. It didn't seem to be enough, but it would have to do. "Anyway," he said, trying his voice again, "I think that's it up ahead... those faint lights."

"Ah, yeah! Muuusssst beeee."

Jeremy's words slurred and stretched. Whispers followed. Kormèr strained to hear them, mistaking them for Jeremy mumbling. But the whispers grew louder, coming not from his ears but from inside his own head. Much like the feeling that had overcome him during the raising ceremony, his mind swam with eerie voices, his vision filled with ghostly shapes that beckoned him to release the bindings on his harness and join them forever. He tried not to listen, to block them out of his mind. But they compelled him so... What harm could there be if he simply—

"Ugh!" he heard Jeremy cry out, and the sound broke the spell of the voices.

"Are you okay?" he shouted back.

"Yes...," Jeremy's voice sounded strained in the darkness. "Yeah. That was intense. Not at all what I expected."

When Kormèr craned his neck to focus on the lights of Berdia, he realized just how intense the effect of the voices had been. The lights were closer now, only a kilometer or so ahead, as best he could judge, and they had become distinct pinpoints.

In moments, Kormèr's Argent swooped up, affording him a clear view of a circular platform just ahead. His carrier bird angled down, and Kormèr gritted his teeth as the platform rushed up at him. He cringed, willing himself to press deeper into the protection of the bird's belly. Just when it seemed he'd certainly get crushed into the stone platform, the giant bird angled its body upward and flapped its tremendous wings, instantly arresting their velocity. The bird stretched its legs and touched down gently. Heart pounding, Kormèr barely noticed Jeremy's bird landing.

"Koo. Koo," announced the carrier birds, whether speaking to their passengers, to each other or simply asking anyone within earshot for food and water after the long voyage.

| | Please remain in your harnesses, | | sang a nearby voice. | | You will be disoriented from your voyage, and we would not want you to stumble over the side. | | Craning his neck, Kormèr saw the bottom edge of a brown robe shuffling across the well worn, dark gray stone of the platform. Two other sets of Averian legs strode past the first, one toward Jeremy and the other toward Kormèr. As Kormèr looked up, a young Averian woman wearing a blue cowl motioned with her hand. His Argent squatted low, and when it did, she motioned again, and his

legs came free, just scraping the ground. ||When you are ready,|| she sang, ||press the harness release, here.|| She stood close beside him and pointed at a large metal grip in the center of his harness. Kormèr grasped and pulled the release. He dropped onto his feet, his jellied legs barely supporting him. But the Berdian woman caught him and helped him remain standing. ||Thank you,|| he warbled.

As Kormèr shook the chill from his legs, he watched Jeremy run through the same routine, but with a young, burly male to assist him. Jeremy's assistant also wore a blue cowl. Kormèr then looked at the robed Averian he'd first noticed. Also young and male, this one waited patiently, smiling when he noticed Kormèr looking at him. Beyond him, glowing lanterns ran around the perimeter of the platform and continued across a connecting bridge to the rest of the city.

||Good evening,|| chirped the robed male. ||I am to escort you to the Grand Master.||

||I'm ready,|| twittered Kormèr, taking a few tentative steps away from the young woman.

||Just another minute,|| chattered Jeremy, still stretching his legs. ||Alright,|| he sang after a moment, and tested his legs. ||Lead on, good sir,|| he sang. The cowled Averians remained behind, tending to the Argents while the robed one led the way across the connecting bridge.

Having never been outside the Hovel, Kormèr hadn't actually seen Berdia before. While the glowing lanterns provided some illumination, they were hardly enough for him to gain a good sense of what the city looked like. So as the young Averian lead them toward the Hovel, Kormèr slipped on his nightvision glasses, and the city revealed itself in its magic-imbued lenses. Well-manicured gardens lined both sides of the path. There were fountains with colorful—if rather garish—dancing lights, topiaries, and paved clearings suited for large gatherings.

And there were the ubiquitous pseudo-trees, but not as many as in Birshetland. Instead, directly in their path, in the center of a wide clearing, stood a colossal pseudo-tree that dwarfed all others Kormèr had so far seen. It appeared massive from afar and only became larger the closer they got. Kormèr's eyes traveled up and up the stone trunk, from the arched entryways at the base to the highest branches, in total awe. *I was in there, and I had no idea how massive it was.* He looked at Jeremy to share his reaction, but of course, without nightvision glasses, the man couldn't see the true scale of the tree.

They walked through the archway and into an expansive circular foyer with a polished marble floor and high ceiling. The ceiling contained two concentric rings of light, in the center of which sat a large glowing blue disc. Two floors opened onto balconies that ran around the perimeter of the foyer.

The trio crossed the foyer into a wide corridor with several doors on each side. Their guide opened the door to one and stepped through, and Kormèr and Jeremy followed. On the other side of the doorway was a small room with a single perch and a desk on which sat a glowing lamp. On the perch sat an old Averian wearing a colorful cowl. Kormèr noticed that there were no other seats in the room.

||These are the visitors, Grand Master,|| announced their guide. ||Mister Kormèr Lezàl,|| he indicated Kormèr with a sweep of a wing. Uncertain what to do, Kormèr tipped his head at the Grand Master. ||And Mister Jeremy Tailor.||

||Nice to meet you,|| tweeted Jeremy with a slight bow.

||Thank you,|| chirped the old birdman to the escort, in crisp tones that belied his age. The young Averian exited the room, closing the door behind him.

The elderly sorcerer could only be Grand Master Fitzbew, with whom Kormèr had corresponded, first to request Srrcheel's help in Birshetland, and more recently, to coordinate today's visit. Fitzbew peered curiously at Kormèr, who realized belatedly that he still wore the glasses. He removed them hastily and slipped them into his coat pocket—*Ack! The magic pockets!*—the elder sorcerer watching him the whole time. It was a relief when he finally turned his dark eyes to regard Jeremy.

||Welcome to Berdia,|| Fitzbew sang. ||It's a rare day indeed when a non-sorcerer comes to this city, much less enters this hovel. Rarer still for there to be two in a single day, but a Terran and an Elmarian... Some would say that your being here is a statistical impossibility.||

Fitzbew regarded them for a moment in silence. He hadn't asked a question, so Kormèr didn't know if the Grand Master expected any response. He followed Jeremy's lead and said nothing, and tried not to fidget under the sorcerer's focused stare.

||And yet you're here,|| Fitzbew warbled at last, his voice light. ||How was your voyage?||

The shift in tone caught Kormèr by surprise. But Jeremy had a ready answer. ||It was a unique experience, sir. Thrilling, but long.||

Fitzbew nodded. ||So I've heard. No need to call me 'sir', Mister Taylor. Master Fitzbew is fine.||

The sorcerer focused on Kormèr. ||You're not at all what I expected,|| he sang. ||When you called for Srrcheel's services, I didn't realize you were a boy.||

||That fact does not diminish the importance of the task for which I needed him,|| twittered Kormèr, laying on the diplomatic verbiage heavily, hoping to sound older. ||A task for which I have come here to express my gratitude.||

Fitzbew was still staring at him, which was unnerving Kormèr a little. ||You were here during Srrcheel's raising.||

Kormèr's eyes went wide. *And here I was telling Jeremy that they're not omniscient. Well, no sense in lying.* ||Yes, sir. Srrcheel had warned me not to come. He didn't even invite me.|| He sang this in the hopes of keeping Srrcheel from getting into trouble. ||But I stayed out of sight, to keep him out of trouble.||

Fitzbew made that clucking sound, like a brooding warble, that Kormèr still had no translation for. But Kormèr didn't sense that the Grand Master was angry at him. More like... intrigued. ||How did you meet Srrcheel?||

| | At the jewelry store, the morning after the robbery. He came outside, and we spoke for a few minutes. | |

Fitzbew rocked forward on his perch. | | So you risked coming here, for a boy you hardly knew, just because you were… curious? | |

Kormèr nodded. *And because I could.* | | That's correct, sir… eh, Master Fitzbew. | |

| | Interesting. Not because you wanted to learn something of our ways for yourself? | |

Before Kormèr could answer, Jeremy interjected. | | May I ask how you knew? | |

| | Magic, Mister Taylor, | | sang Fitzbew. | | All I will tell you is that raisings are special occasions, and Mister Lezàl still has that *special* aura about him. | | Kormèr wondered exactly what he meant; was he emitting some kind of odor that could only be smelled by magic? | | I'm rather interested to know how you feel about the ceremony, Mister Lezàl. | |

Kormèr distinctly recalled how horrible he'd felt afterward. | | To be honest, I don't remember a thing. | |

Fitzbew gave him an enigmatic smile. | | As it should be. | | He paused and clasped his hands together on the desktop. | | Gentlemen, I know why you're here, of course, since it was at your request. But it is your reason for coming here, or returning here—as it may be—that has me most intrigued. Please explain. | |

| | Shouldn't we wait for Srrcheel? | | asked Jeremy.

| | Srrcheel will not be coming. We never have our candidates present for these post-outing interviews. Please proceed. | |

Kormèr glanced at Jeremy, who gave him a nod. Kormèr sang, | | We wished to express, in person, our gratitude for Srrcheel's help. | |

| | Come now, Mister Lezàl. You could have done that via digital mediums without having to endure traveling on the Argents or risking my wrath at finding out you've been here before. | |

Kormèr's voice caught in his throat at the last, and he fought to keep from smiling out of nervousness. | | No, | | he managed to twitter. | | That wouldn't have been enough. For all he did for us, and for Averia, he deserves more than that. | |

Fitzbew nodded. | | I've seen this morning's headlines; congratulations to you for solving the jewel heists. | |

Kormèr didn't miss his use of the plural, but he decided not to correct him. Sreel had pulled off both capers, so technically it was true, even if Kormèr had only been working the one store. | | Thank you. But it would have been impossible without Srrcheel's help: he discovered the holographer, which I couldn't have done myself. Considering that the device is highly classified contraband technology, the police department would've never found it either, and the case would've never been solved. | |

Fitzbew's expression was impassive. | | I see. | |

| | And what's in the media is not the entire story. The robberies were just a test… a… | | Kormèr hunted for the right words but eventually settled on, | | …like a proof of concept. The thief had a grander plan to bring chaos down on Averia. | | Kormèr knew that this information hadn't made it beyond the walls of the police precinct until now, primarily because no one had yet ascertained if Sreel was sane. But Kormèr had sensed much more trepidation from Sylvestra and Phatheeo over that revelation than if it had merely been the ranting of a madman. | | I tell you this in confidence, to stress the importance of Srrcheel's involvement. I hope that you'll keep it as secret as you hold your magic. | |

Fitzbew nodded. | | I understand. I will keep it in confidence. | |

| | Your word, Master Fitzbew? | |

| | My word, Mister Lezàl. | |

Kormèr nodded. He had to be satisfied with that, as he had no way to hold the Grand Master sorcerer accountable if he leaked that information. It didn't seem to Kormèr to be all that important, but Phatheeo and Sylvestra had made him attest to the fact that he'd never reveal that to anyone. Kormèr looked at Jeremy. The Terrans had also had to attest to the same, and Jeremy now stared at Kormèr with a raised eyebrow, his look disapproving.

| | And you, Mister Tailor, | | sang Fitzbew. | | What have you to say of Srrcheel? | |

Jeremy cleared his throat. | | Kormèr and Srrcheel came to my ship in Freet-See to research the holographer. While there, my ship was invaded by a… an overzealous competitor. | |

Fitzbew raised a tufted eyebrow at this. | | Yes, I think I recall reading about that as well. | |

| | Well, if not for Srrcheel's quick thinking, I might not be here talking to you today, and my invention would be in my competitor's hands. He kept his cool in the face of immediate danger and saved my crew. | |

| | And my life as well, | | added Kormèr.

Fitzbew rocked back. | | Thank you, gentlemen, for bringing these matters to my attention and providing the details. How young casters handle the situations for which they are called out is a very important part of their training. We rely on the feedback of the callers, and your coming here to deliver yours in-person, will not go unnoticed; it speaks highly of Srrcheel's performance. | | He looked at Kormèr. | | And provides context about his choice of acquaintance. | |

Kormèr tried not to scowl at Fitzbew's ambiguous remark, but Jeremy answered simply: | | It has been our pleasure to make his acquaintance. | |

Fitzbew stepped down from his perch. | | Wonderful. If that's it then, gentlemen, I'm afraid I have another matter to attend to. But I invite you to stay and enjoy some food and drink before your return voyage. | |

| | Ah, thank you, Master Fitzbew, | | sang Jeremy. | | A drink would be much appreciated. But also, I'd like to freshen up before the journey back. | |

| | Of course. Anything either of you need, just ask. | |

The door opened, and Kormèr and Jeremy turned to see their young guide enter. When they turned back, Fitzbew was gone.

Their guide showed them to another room with an empty round table surrounded by ten chairs and invited them to sit wherever they wished. He gestured to the table and explained, ||Focus on what you'd like to eat or drink, one thing at a time. The table will conjure it for you.||

||This I've got to see!|| sang Jeremy, rubbing his palms together. A few seconds later, a tall glass of bubbling yellow liquid appeared. A bowl of steaming broth with vegetables and chunks of pale meat followed, this with a spoon resting on the saucer beneath the bowl. Jeremy drew the items toward him and took a sip from the glass. Then he drank nearly half the glass in one long drink. ||Mmm. I have missed real ginger beer,|| he sang with a pleased smile and closed eyes.

Kormèr ordered up a pitcher of water and one of the appetizer dishes he'd enjoyed from his first lunch with Sylvestra. He didn't remember the ingredients or the name of the dish, but he had only to think of it, and it appeared on the table. He sampled it and marveled at how it tasted exactly as he remembered.

||How much for this table?|| asked Jeremy when they'd finished eating.

The guide smiled. He hadn't eaten with them, but had sat alone by the door, meditating or otherwise lost in his own thoughts. ||I'm sorry, sir. But it isn't for sale.||

Jeremy shook his head. ||That's a missed business opportunity, my friend. You guys could buy half of Averia, just selling tables like this. Or, just open a restaurant with the tables, and let the diners serve themselves.||

The novice smiled mildly. ||While no doubt true, that isn't our way.||

"Your loss," Jeremy shrugged. He looked at Kormèr. "Ready, kid?"

Kormèr nodded. "I'm stuffed. I hope the take-off is easier the second time."

Jeremy gestured at the emptied dishes on the table. "After everything we just ate, I hope those Argents can still bear our weight."

After washing up, they followed the guide back to the stone platform, thankful for the long walk after their over-indulgences. Kormèr left the glasses in his pocket this time and experienced the full nightscape of the Hovel and its surrounding area. *Maybe one day I can see this place in daylight.*

Since Kormèr knew what to expect this time, the Argent's take-off was not as stomach-churning. They had arranged for the carrier birds to take them to Freet-See rather than Birshetland. The trip was shorter, and when the city came into view after only forty minutes, the sight of the illuminated city at night was well worth the trip.

"Why don't you spend the night here, KL?" said Jeremy as they walked the corridors toward Hangar 14. "It's kinda late to be heading back to— Oh! I forgot about the portal."

Kormèr grinned. "I think I'll stay, anyway. Thanks for the offer. I just have to get back in time for a lunch date tomorrow."

Jeremy paused mid-step and raised an eyebrow. "Date?"

"Maybe 'date' isn't quite the right word." Very few people knew that Kormèr and Sylvestra had met for lunch, or that he'd gone to visit her occasionally at the precinct in the few days following, and Kormèr wanted to keep it that way for now. It seemed premature to call their casual acquaintance a relationship, but neither Kormèr nor Sylvestra were in any rush to have their new friendship develop into anything more. "Just lunch."

Jeremy said nothing right away, then smiled at Kormèr's uncharacteristic reticence. "Alright. Well, don't worry. I'll show you around town here in the morning, then we'll ship you off to your... lunch. Freet-See has more to offer than just its spaceport and business district."

"Thanks. I look forward to it."

THE following morning, the *Stardust IV's* boisterous crew woke Kormèr up and hauled him out for an early breakfast. Following that, they took him for a tour of the port city of Freet-See, in all its confused, bustling, eclectic glory. Aside from its architectural mash-up of stone pseudo-trees and industrial, commercial buildings, Freet-See had somehow preserved much of its Averian heritage, as expressed through the local food, music and arts. Jeremy and Morgan took Kormèr to an Averian historical museum, followed by a scaled down re-creation of Berdia, complete with actors who re-enacted what life was like for the initial settlers.

The history and culture of the world absolutely enthralled Kormèr, and the morning went by too quickly.

"There's more," said Jeremy, checking his p-comm. "But it's getting close to noon."

"Yeah. I should go. But I promise I'll be back to see the rest."

Jeremy laughed. "Alright, kid. I know you're good for it."

Morgan ruffled his hair. "Just stay out of trouble, okay?"

Chimes sounded from both Jeremy's and Morgan's comms, and both men checked the message. "It seems we need to get back to the ship ourselves," said Jeremy. "Prepping for another demo."

"Let me not keep you, then," Kormèr nodded. "Thanks for the tour, guys. I'll comm you tomorrow and we'll make plans." They clasped shoulders and said their farewells. Kormèr rushed into a public restroom, made sure it was empty, then opened the portal and stepped through into his hotel room.

Immediately, he noticed the message light blinking on the wall.

||Messages,|| he sang, and the wall lit up with Srrcheel's face.

"Kormèr, please comm me when you get this. You can use this same address." The wall darkened with the words: *No more messages.*

Kormèr looked at his own p-comm and cringed. He had twenty minutes to get ready and meet Sylvestra. But he couldn't wait to hear what Srrcheel had to say, so he sat in a chair and ordered the comm unit to reconnect to the address.

Srrcheel appeared a moment later, the dim background of his room at the Hovel coming into focus. "Hi, Kormèr," he greeted. "I got the news from Fitzbew last evening about your visit. I'm sorry I wasn't there to meet you, but thank you for coming. You really shouldn't... You didn't have to do that."

"Are you kidding? It was the least we could do." Kormèr was relieved that Srrcheel seemed to be relaxed, if not necessarily happy. "And about Syrree: again, I truly am sorry. It was before you and I met, and I—"

Srrcheel waved his hand dismissively. "Kormèr... KL, it's okay. I've spoken with her and... It's over between us, and not just because of you. We'd been drifting apart for a while now, and your affair was just the impetus to end it. Plus, she needs to be with her family, considering her dad's troubles."

"I'm sorry." *For all of it,* he wanted to add, because he'd been responsible for exposing all the things Srrcheel had mentioned. Despite his poise, Srrcheel had to feel something from the ending of the betrothal, and the betrayal that had preceded it. If nothing else, just the loss of the emotional connection to someone he had once loved.

With his feelings for Sylvestra foremost in mind, Kormèr was remembering how it felt to truly care for someone, and to have his happiness linked to someone else's. He had last felt that kind of connection with his father, and he realized how much he'd missed that feeling since his father's death. To know that Srrcheel had lost that now...

"Don't feel sorry for me, KL," Srrcheel said. "You did us a favor, actually. Syrree wants her privacy, especially now, and I can focus on my studies without other distractions."

"Okay." Kormèr wasn't convinced by Srrcheel's breeziness, but if Srrcheel didn't want to dwell on the past, Kormèr wouldn't argue with him about it.

Srrcheel sighed. "Anyway, Grand Master Fitzbew also told me to ask you for the glasses back, the nightvision ones I made for you. I apologize for that, but we're not supposed to give our crafted magical items to outsiders."

"I understand." *But that doesn't mean I'll give them up that easily. They're much too useful. I'll have to find a similar pair and stash these somewhere, where they won't think to look for them.* "I hope you didn't get in trouble over it."

"No," Srrcheel said slowly. "Not much, anyway. It would've been much worse, had it not been for the visit from you and Jeremy yesterday."

"Well, I'm glad our visit did some good."

"Yes." Again, that awkward pause. Kormèr wondered if there was some lag in the transmission, except that the candles in Srrcheel's room flickered the same; it was only Srrcheel who seemed slower and more deliberate. "Well, I've got to go now. When can I meet you to pick the glasses up? I can request a day of-leave, to be in Freet-See tomorrow."

"I could just portal over—"

"No!" Srrcheel laughed quietly. "No offense, but let's keep to the rules for a change."

Kormèr wrinkled his nose, showing his distaste with that idea. "Aww, alright. I can meet you at Jeremy's ship tomorrow morning. How's that?"

Srrcheel nodded. "That's fine. Hangar 14, as I recall? I'll see you then." The link went dead before anymore could be said. Not that Kormèr had expected total reconciliation; how could he expect Srrcheel to forgive him, if he himself still regretted the outcome of the situation?

Kormèr got up and checked himself in the mirror. He had a few hairs out of place, but he'd showered on Jeremy's ship that morning, so he was at least presentable. He rushed out and once again used the service elevator to leave the hotel—the crowds had thinned, but his face still attracted too much attention to use the lobby. He'd done some research yesterday afternoon, and knew just the place to suggest to Sylvestra... to Sylvee, for lunch.

As he cruised across Birshetland in the back of Feestoo's taxi, he allowed himself to relax. Finally, some hope of renewed friendship with Srrcheel, and maybe—just maybe—a glimmer of hope of something more with Sylvestra. Things were finally looking up.

CHAPTER 33

SREEL'S case came to trial only a few weeks after his capture. That had provided the police enough time to find his residence, where they'd discovered all the jewels from the second heist, which he hadn't had time to fence. They'd also found a manifesto that he had recorded for release once his full plan was underway.

The trial took exactly three days, and only because it took that long to present the evidence and forensics reports, and to have the few required subject matter experts to explain the technology to the jury. The jury took only half an hour to convict. Sreel remained silent throughout the proceedings. He had nothing else to say that he hadn't already said.

The magnitude of the crime categorized it as a capital crime. Sreel had expected no less; that the trial had even taken place surprised him somewhat. He'd fully expected the Unseen to intervene and keep their mess out of the public eye. But as he was led from the courtroom, he realized it made sense. His disappearance before the trial would have left no resolution for the public, no sense of safety in their very safe world. And the Unseen needed the public to feel safe; that was their mandate, however flawed they had become.

Sentencing would occur on the fourth day. Averia had no punitive precedent for this kind of crime, so Sreel wondered what they would devise for his sentence. It wouldn't surprise him if they exiled him to the Northern Cluster or perhaps even to the sub-surface, the closest thing to a death penalty he could think of. Having his wings clipped and sealed, to prevent regrowth of his flight feathers, was a certainty.

The morning of the fourth day, he waited patiently to be taken from his cell to have the judge explain his punishment. But the day came and went.

Then the lights went out, plunging his cell into utter darkness. He was not alone in the cell block, so when he heard no complaints from his neighbors, he knew something was wrong.

He jumped to his feet as they appeared in beams of light out of the darkness, harbingers of old secrets, keepers of an ancient command force unknown to the modern world. Complex goggles over their eyes, black feathers from crest to foot, they surrounded him, eight around: a murder. The circumference of them spread wider than the width of his cell, so he knew immediately that he was no longer in the prison.

||At last,|| twittered Sreel.

362

A ninth appeared, walking toward him. ||You are the product of the union of Unseen Twelve and Unseen Sixteen,|| it chirped, its tones modulated so that Sreel could not tell its gender.

||Correct,|| he warbled, needlessly. It hadn't been a question. They already knew.

An immobilization field snapped around Sreel. He could breathe, move his eyes, and other small movements, but nothing more.

The ninth touched a talon to the side of his goggles. ||Update. We have apprehended the last of unregistered brood four. All stolen equipment accounted for and restocked. Return status to monitoring.|| The ninth then hooked a device to Sreel's chest. Sreel had seen a personal teleporter before, long ago. He'd wanted to take it along with the rest of the items he'd stolen, but he hadn't been able to get his hands on one.

One by one, the nine vanished.

Sreel stood alone, in the dark, as the timer on the teleporter ticked down the seconds before it activated. Would it teleport him into a sun, or to a prison cell? He had no way to know. Whatever his end, Sreel resigned himself to it. He'd been expecting this all his life.

The teleporter activated.

MUNCHING a breakfast bar and sipping nutria, Sylvestra rushed out of her apartment. Time had gotten away from her, and now she had to rush to make it to Sreel's sentencing on time.

Her p-comm chimed before she could take three steps.

||Good morning,|| she twittered, seeing Phatheeo's face appear. From the state of his feathers and the flutter of his wings, she knew he was very upset. ||Don't worry. I'm on—||

//We have a problem,// he chittered. //A big problem. Are you on the way to the sentencing?//

||I was.||

//Skip it. I'll meet you in your office.//

Sylvestra took off, knowing that Phatheeo would beat her to the precinct since he lived closer. She wished she'd asked him for some hint as to what to expect, her mind racing through myriad possibilities, despite reasoning that she couldn't possibly guess the right one. After the past several weeks, what could have gone wrong now?

She landed and hastily made her way to her office. Phatheeo sat in front of her desk, head bent over the chessboard displayed on her desktop. ||What is it?|| she asked, as she closed the door and sat at her desk.

||Your move.||

||Theeo!|| She moved a pawn. ||Is this a retirement joke?||

He moved his pawn in response. | |It's not at all a joke. This,| | he indicated the pieces on the game table, | |is the only thing keeping me from tearing my feathers out.| |

| |Well, you're not doing my nerves any good,| | she sang, moving a piece. | |Sing it, mister,| | she ordered.

In low tones he told her, | |Sreel, and much of the evidence against him, are gone.| |

Game forgotten, she merely stared at him. | |What?| |

Phatheeo looked down and moved a piece. Then he looked back at her. | |The sealed evidence case… it's still locked, but empty except for the few pieces of jewelry from each of the stores, the loot sacks he used and the unexploded marker bombs. Even the manifesto is gone.| |

| |I don't…| | She shook her head, incredulous. The case had a biometric lock keyed only to her and Phatheeo. | |But how? What does surveillance show?| |

He activated her wall with a flick of his right hand and caused the active-glass inner wall to opaque. The case file sat open on the wall with the various files and folders arranged around the edges. He selected a file, and Sylvestra watched Sreel sitting in his cell; the date-time stamp at the bottom was from earlier that morning. A moment later, the cell door opened and two guards entered to deliver his sentence: exile to the Northern Cluster. He was to come with them. Sreel stood and walked out, with the guards following.

| |Who are those two?| | asked Sylvestra. | |I can't see their faces. They don't look—| |

| |Watch,| | sang Phatheeo, holding up his hand, palm out.

The surveillance followed the trio to the motor pool, where they climbed into the back of a small prisoner transport. The transport lifted and soared away. Phatheeo switched the recording to one of the other cameras in the motor pool, this one with a clear line of sight through the open door of the transport. He froze the image and zoomed in on a large dark duffel bag on the floor.

| |I'm guessing that's the evidence; it's as if they left it in plain sight so we could see it. There isn't any surveillance to review from the evidence locker… I mean, there is, but there's nothing to see. The aisle with the case… the entire room… no one has even been in the locker since the case was admitted!| | He clucked in frustration.

Sylvestra's eyes strayed from the frozen image on the wall to the chess pieces on the table, but she didn't see them, her mind racing through the repercussions to befall her and her precinct when word got out that their prisoner had escaped. They had to tell the Mayor.

| |We'll have to tell the Mayor,| | Phatheeo warbled, echoing her thoughts.

| |My career is over,| | she warbled.

Phatheeo shook his head. | |No! No. I'll take the blame.| |

| |Nonsense!| |

He waggled a finger at her and overrode her with a higher tone. | | I'm retiring, anyway; there'll be no harm. If he's generous, he'll even let me go with my universal basic-plus-income intact. | |

She had nothing to say that would dissuade him, so she stared at him, her chin quavering, wanting to tell him that she wouldn't allow it, but knowing that he wouldn't let her take the blame no matter what.

She knew he wouldn't want her thanks or her pity, so she focused on business. She asked again: | | So, who are the two officers? | |

| | Not ours, though the uniforms match. | |

Her hands clenched. | | More holographers! He had partners. | |

Phatheeo shrugged. | | Lezàl was wrong, or at least he didn't have the whole picture. | |

She saw a shadow appear through the frosted glass wall by her door, and a knock followed. She waved her hand, and the wall screen blurred. | | Come in, | | she sang.

The door opened, and an officer peeked in. He and another often drove the larger vehicles in the motor pool. | | Oh, there you are, Captain! | | He looked at Sylvestra. | | It's done, Chief. | |

She frowned. | | What's done? | |

| | The prisoner. You messaged me to take him out to the Northern Cluster. | |

She locked her gaze on the officer, though she saw Phatheeo tense and felt his eyes on her. *The Northern Cluster?* The dense grouping of floating rocks sat well west of Freet-See, so the connection to Sreel escaped her. But she couldn't let the officer know this. If he was in on the escape, he could be dangerous—she noted his holstered stunner in the periphery of her vision. But if she played along, she might just get him to reveal whatever plot was afoot. She casually tapped her badge. | | Ah! Yes, of course. Thank you. No problems from the other two. | |

He grinned. | | No, ma'am. It was like they weren't even there, but I guess discreet was the idea. Can't have the public knowing where he's exiled, right? | | The grin left his face, and his youthful inexperience shone through. | | I mean, right, Chief? | |

She could hear the words he was singing, but they weren't registering in her head. The idea that he could truly be involved in the escape didn't let go of her entirely, but it seemed less plausible. | | Right, | | she replied, absently. | | What *did* you see? | |

He frowned. | | Not much, really. I know they were supposed to clip and seal his wings, but it all happened behind the transport, and… well… I'm sorry, Chief. It's not that I felt bad for the guy, but I just didn't want to watch that. | |

She nodded, the sentiment in his tone reaching her at last. | | Of course. Thank you again. | |

The smile returned. | |Anytime, Chief.| | He looked at the back of Phatheeo's head. | |Captain.| | Then he turned and closed the door behind him as he left.

Sylvestra tapped her badge again to stop recording.

She and Phatheeo stared at each other across the chessboard for only a moment before they both hopped onto their feet and rushed to the motor pool.

The transport sat in its spot, charging after the long flight. The doors stood open and the prisoner compartment empty.

Phatheeo climbed into the driver's seat and reviewed the transport's logs. He clucked, frustrated. | |The logs confirm that four individuals flew out to the Northern Cluster,| | he warbled in low tones. | |And only three returned.| |

She stared at the screen, the logs flashing and scrolling as Phatheeo flipped through them, trying to find something abnormal. *As if anything about this morning could be considered normal!*

| |He said I messaged him,| | she recalled aloud. She checked her p-comm's message app and gasped. | |Theeo, look.| | A blinking header at the top of this morning's message list read: 'Prisoner transport request.' She opened it, and the full message text appeared. Short and to the point, it requested that the prisoner be transported, just as the officer had sung. | |I never sent—| |

Phatheeo cheeped loudly, cutting her off. | |Everything checks out,| | he sang, leaving the transport and walking back in the direction they'd come. She followed him back to her office in silence.

When the door had closed again, she sang, | |I never sent that message.| |

| |I know that. Lezàl? Or his Terran friends?| |

She shook her head, then truly considered the idea. Jeremy's crew had leaked the story of Kormèr solving the case to all the media, but accessing the police network required another level of sophistication, and they had no motive for such interference. She shook her head again.

| |No, you're right,| | sang Phatheeo. | |This goes deeper.| | His eyes flicked to her wall. | |You have a message.| |

She looked and found the red message light flashing on her wall. | |Play message,| | she chirped.

The Mayor's face appeared. | |Good morning!| | the Mayor chirped cheerily. | |I just got word that the sentence has been carried out, and I wanted to thank you and Phatheeo personally. But you are either out celebrating over breakfast or busy closing the case. In any case, the city is once again at peace thanks to you and your team. Well done.| |

The image winked out, and the wall darkened once more.

Sylvestra reopened the case file and immediately found the file she wanted, though she knew she hadn't added it to the file not had it come though the add-request queue which allowed her to review data before accepting or rejecting it into the case. The file came from the court, straight from the judge's office. It contained the judge's sentencing statement, which corroborated everything that had occurred.

She looked at Phatheeo while he read the statement. Finally he looked sideways at her, his demeanor the most relaxed she'd seen today. He looked at the chessboard and moved a piece. ||We seem to be the only two aware of anything unusual,|| he warbled, then looked up at her. ||This is a like a gift box, covered in beautiful gems, only there's nothing inside the box.||

She stared through the chessboard again. ||I don't know what has happened here today,|| she sang, then looked up and met Phatheeo's eyes. ||But I think we don't want to mess with that box.||

Still looking at her, Phatheeo tapped a finger on her desktop. She imagined his mind working the angles, much as she herself was doing. ||I think you're right.||

She pushed back the piece he'd moved. ||It's my turn.||

Phatheeo frowned. ||Are you sure?||

||*Now* you're going to start cheating?|| She laughed.

She knew she had some work left to close the case file, but that could wait. For now, she would enjoy what might be her last relaxing game of chess with her captain. The next time she played him, he would be her oldest friend.

CHAPTER 34

IN the dim gray light of early dawn, Kormèr Lezàl stopped in the doorway of Sylvestra's bedroom, hand on the frame, eyes closed and heart screaming for him to turn around. Behind him, the woman of his dreams lay sleeping, the wonderful smell of her still in his hair, on his hands... on his lips.

His resolve cracked, and he turned his head, dared to open his eyes and peer through the near dark at the bed, at *her*, curled under the thin bed sheet. His hand on the frame curled into a fist as his chest tightened with an agony he'd not felt since he lost his father. He forced himself to stay silent, lest he waken her, but he screamed soundlessly in anguish to the gods, to deliver him from this moment, from his misery. To give him the strength to turn away again just one last time. To say goodbye.

Like treading ankle-deep mud, he trudged to the apartment door, opened it and walked out on seven months of bliss. And what a seven months it had been! Given time and patience, his relationship with Sylvestra had grown and blossomed better... stronger than he'd ever thought possible. Every minute spent together had etched itself into the fiber of his being, so that he felt he could recall any moment on demand. He'd learned so much from her, and hoped that he had given her as much in return.

Kormèr had watched Sylvestra grow into her position as Chief, becoming more sure of herself over time, especially after Phatheeo retired. Kormèr had become a regular presence at the precinct, as Sylvestra's trusted friend and confidant, and had been there for her during the highs and the lows. She had been there for him, as well, whenever he'd needed her.

Kormèr checked his pager for Feestoo first, to make sure that the cabbie was awake at that early hour, before he called for a pickup. He stared at the small device as he waited for the taxi to arrive. *Last time I'll be using this, too, I suppose.*

He'd made up his mind two nights ago to leave the planet, and so over the last day, every action, every thing he did or saw had become "lasts". Yesterday, he'd said his last goodbyes to Theeseeo, Almp and the crew of the *Stardust IV*. He had even portaled into the passages behind the walls of the Hovel one last time to say a last goodbye to Srrcheel.

Last night, he had watched his last Averian sunset with Sylvestra from her balcony, and dined with her for the last time. Shortly after that, they had made love for the last time.

Kormèr stirred from his reverie as the shadow of Feestoo's taxi passed overhead. As Kormèr watched the taxi swoop down, he knew this would be his last taxi ride with Feestoo.

||Good morning, KL!|| chirped the birdman cheerily.

As he climbed into the taxi, Kormèr gave Feestoo a smile that felt more like a grimace. Kormèr felt as though he would never have a reason to smile, ever again, but he made the attempt for Feestoo's sake.

||You're up early today. Where to?||

||To the western ridge, please, Feestoo.|| "The ridge" had become their name for that favorite spot Feestoo had shown him months earlier, and the elevation and vantage provided breathtaking views of both sunrises or sunsets, depending on the direction one faced, either through the pseudo-trees or full-on. This morning didn't feel like a "full-on" morning.

Feestoo banked the taxi into a tight turn and zipped off to the west. ||Ah! It's going to be a perfect morning to watch the sunrise.||

A thin chill fog hung between the trees and clung to the taxi's windscreen so that Feestoo had to activate the auto-wick function of the screen. Kormèr sank into his seat as the faint *thrum-thrum* of the auto-wick set his mind wandering through his memories of his time with Sylvestra.

The initial lunch dates and casual drop-ins at the precinct had led to after-work strolls, with even Phatheeo and others at the precinct becoming accustomed to Kormèr's regular presence. Kormèr could see that the transparency of their association meant a great deal to Sylvestra, as well as his respect for her work, whatever his personal inclinations, so he continued to meet her at her office. Gradually, Kormèr and Sylvestra began to socialize on rest days, as well: sometimes to watch a play together, or to see an art exhibit, or to just sit in the park and talk.

At some point, they had held hands. It had begun as an impulse on Sylvestra's part, to catch Kormèr's attention, to look at something, maybe a street performer or a flower; he didn't remember anymore, and had barely noticed even then, as the warmth of her hand had filled his awareness. Displays of affection between Averians and non-Averians still drew attention and gossip, and not all of it benign. So the touches were infrequent in public, but they were more special for it. Loving pecks on the cheek had followed, in greeting or farewell, until the day they both leaned in the same direction one way… then the other… and he'd taken a chance and kissed her. He knew he would never forget that moment, for as long as he lived and perhaps even beyond, as there had to be something about that instant that transcended the universe and time, and maybe even death. It would shine like their private beacon, to draw their spirits together and bind them together, forever.

More had followed to deepen their physical and mental bond, but their first kiss was the pivotal moment for him, when he realized he was past the point of infatuation and was truly, deeply in love. The realization only made their remaining time together more bittersweet, and they had cherished their hours and lived them to the fullest, as though each day could be their last together. It was only a matter of time, and they both knew it. They were each bound to their respective planets: Sylvestra could never leave Averia and be happy; and Kormèr had felt Elmar's call grow stronger with each passing day.

And ultimately, fate had intervened to push them to their final decision point. In recent weeks, as Syrree's father's case came to trial, exposing Kormèr's involvement with it, the renewed public scrutiny into his identity was inevitable. While Sylvestra had been aware of Kormèr's entanglement with Syrree and could easily fend off allegations about his character, she could not honestly answer questions about who he really was: an Elmarian who, by all accounts, had been dead for centuries. Kormèr had watched Sylvestra wrestle with her choice: to lie to protect him, or to tell the truth and be ridiculed—either way, her reputation and career would end up in tatters, for the sake of protecting him.

And he could not allow her to do that. He loved her too much to let her ruin her life over him, so he saw only one option: he had to leave.

When the time came, he had said goodbye to everyone, except Sylvestra. But somehow, she'd known. Their lovemaking on their last night together had been passionate, insatiable, and desperate, because they knew they would never see each other again. It was the one, final "last".

||You're not asleep, are you?|| asked Feestoo. Kormèr forced a smile again, catching the birdman's eyes in the rearview mirror.

||No, just lost in thought.||

Feestoo nodded, but his wings gave a brief flutter. ||You don't seem yourself this morning. Is everything alright?||

||You know me too well, friend,|| warbled Kormèr. ||I'm leaving Averia today, heading back home.||

||Oh! Now you tell me? Calrissa will not be happy that you didn't have dinner with us one last time,|| he sang, referring to his wife.

Kormèr had visited their home several times over the months, and he was going to miss their warm hospitality. ||Tell her that it will be one of my greatest regrets, but it was a last-minute and very difficult decision.||

Feestoo nodded. ||Seeing as you are alone, does that mean this will be a one-way trip?||

Kormèr's throat clenched, and he nodded. He swallowed, composed himself and twittered, ||Yes.||

Feestoo settled the taxi on a flat strip at the top of the ridge, then got out of the taxi and opened the door for Kormèr. When Kormèr stepped out, Feestoo embraced him, then stepped back. Kormèr saw that the man's eyes were watery, and that broke the floodgates that he'd been fighting so hard to keep in place over the past twenty minutes. He smiled at Feestoo through his tears.

||I'm going to miss you, KL. You...|| He stopped, his song breaking up. ||You add color where it is lacking; you bring movement to still air; vibrant sound to silent slumber; and loving happiness from despair.||

| | That's beautiful, Feestoo. Did you make that up? | |

| | No. My mother used to say that to me, and I thought I knew what it meant, but I didn't really until I met you. You truly are something else, KL. I'm sure you already know that, but I think there's even more to you, that you haven't even discovered yourself. | |

Kormèr shrugged, mostly embarrassed but also because he didn't know what to say to that.

| | Averia will miss you. | |

Kormèr nodded, the tears building up again. | | I'll miss you all, Feestoo. | | Kormèr looked to his right at the taxi. | | Even your taxi, | | he sang, patting the roof of the aircar. Before he forgot, he pulled the pager from his pocket and held it out to Feestoo. | | I don't think I'll be needing this anymore. | |

Feestoo looked at the pager but didn't reach for it. | | Keep it, as a memento of your time here. | | He climbed back into his taxi. | | Take care of yourself, Kormèr Lezàl. | |

| | You too, Feestoo. | |

Kormèr stood on the crater's edge of Birshetland as the rising sun shot brilliant rays of light from the East through the metallic leaves of the pseudo-trees. Feestoo's taxi caught a beam briefly, as it banked sharply and vanished into the city. Kormèr sat on the ground watching the city wake up, as he felt the still-cool breezes under the folds of his coat. He wondered if Sylvestra had awakened yet, what she'd think of his abrupt departure. And in time, who would take his place? He couldn't imagine finding anyone that he would love as much as he loved her, but he hoped she was more successful in moving on.

And that she wouldn't think of him too harshly whenever she recalled him. What had he said to her that night by the bath, when he offered her his help? *I can't have someone as beautiful as you thinking vile things of me.*

He lowered his head, and tears flowed like rivulets down his cheeks and over his trembling chin, falling in big salty droplets into his lap. Slowly, he stood and pulled the cube from his pocket. He'd already considered using it to travel back in time and change things, adjust events to create a different outcome from this. But which events? Who would he not meet, or who would get hurt in the process? Could he sacrifice Jeremy and his crew? He'd learned such camaraderie and loyalty from them. Could he give up meeting Srrcheel, and learning that magic could be so much more in the hands of a good friend?

No. After all, what was a jewelry store without jewels? He was the store, and every moment, every person he'd met here a jewel, filling him with their words, their spirit, and the memories of the time he'd spent with them. There was nothing to be gained, and so much lost, from giving any of them up. Trying to undo any part of his past wouldn't change his destiny or give him the lifetime of happiness that he so wanted to have with Sylvestra.

He bit his trembling lower lip and opened the portal. Home beckoned, but he couldn't focus through his anguish, couldn't decide if he really wanted to go home, where he could crawl into his bed and languish for the rest of his days. Or did he want to lose himself in some mindless adventure on another world? Leave all reminders of his life behind and start anew?

Unfocused and heedless of where he would end up, he stepped into the portal as the sun broke over the treetops.

Epilogue

STANDING on the docking platform of Hangar 4, Hassera watched the dock workers going about their business of refueling and inspecting the ships or loading and unloading cargo. She eyed every passerby with suspicion, ready to draw her weapon in defense or flee across the bridge-plate into her ship. Her freedom still felt tenuous, as if the odd events leading to it hadn't been real.

But here she stood, and walking toward her with Cial d'Eliz and Kellan Toure, was the man who had set her—set them *all*—free from prison. Averians were known to be fair-minded and merciful when it came to their judicial system, but not always expeditious, procedure-wise, so while her Suslixan nature had no bearing on her treatment, it also granted her no advantages towards getting a speedy trial.

She had received as fair a trial as she could expect, given the list of charges against her, ranging from vandalism to assault. But even with her employer Harry G in custody—and in pieces—she had very much doubted a favorable outcome for her sentencing, especially as the weeks dragged on, and she heard the sentences handed down to the rest of Harry G's crew. And so she had waited in her cell, week after week, expecting the worst.

Until the day that the guards came to release her. They told her all charges had been dropped. As she'd passed the front desk, a Terran man who had been there speaking with some officers peeled away and introduced himself. She'd acknowledged him and walked out, intending to get to her ship and leave this foul planet far behind. But he'd followed her out to where Cial and Kellan had been waiting.

The Terran, who called himself "Reilly", was apparently already well-acquainted with the two mercenaries. The three of them formed a freelance team, and they needed someone with her skills as their fourth. So the Terran had "pulled some strings" to secure her release. They'd offered little in details, other than to assure her that they did nothing illegal. She had a week to think it over.

Now a week later after her release, Hassera greeted her liberator when the trio got close enough. "Mister Reilly." She tipped her head at Cial and Kellan.

Reilly smiled at her, his short, brush-like blond hair catching glints of lights from the ships and dock machinery. "Hello, Hassera. Have you considered our proposal?"

It hadn't really been much of a proposal, not even a contract or any of the common means of agreement. The terms were simple: she had the right to withdraw from the group at any time and return to her life, exactly as she'd left it; she'd have her own funds, separate from the group's common till for the purposes of food, shelter and medical needs… and for occasionally greasing the right palms to clear inconvenient charges.

"I am definitely intrigued, Mister Reilly," she told him.

"I'm sure you are," he said. "But that's not an answer." He checked his p-comm. "We're leaving in a minute, Hassera. Will you be coming with us tonight?"

She knew the captains of the ships docked here at Hangar 4, and she had researched all the other ships at the port. She had also researched the three members of this group. Much like the boy Lezàl, these three had generated confusing results. "You don't have a ship, nor are you booked on any flights. How exactly are you leaving?"

Reilly nodded. "I see. You need more information to inform your response, of course. I apologize." He shrugged. "But we don't need ships where we're going next." He flipped something from his hand, and it expanded into a tall rectangular window, its borders glowing a soft blue. Only looking through this window revealed something other than the port behind it. It appeared to be another place, sunny and verdant. Hassera's mind flashed back to a memory from weeks or months ago, when she'd seen something eerily similar. That blue was unmistakable.

"Last chance," said Reilly.

Cial stepped up to the window and turned to look at her. "We could use you. Reilly's a bit of a renegade," she half-whispered, then stepped through the window and appeared on that verdant land.

Reilly clicked his tongue with disapproval but reserved comment.

"Hope to see you on the other side," said Kellan, and then he, too, joined Cial through the window.

Reilly stepped up onto the window's border and leaned out. "How does this datum factor into the equation?"

Hassera regarded the Terran with a scowl. "You believe you know me so well."

Reilly shrugged. "Maybe. Maybe not. Does it matter?"

Hassera hissed, but in exasperation rather than anger. But Reilly had been right to reveal the window to her. Whether because she likened it to Lezàl's doorway or because she simply wanted to know more about it and the world she could see through it, the window was an enticing lure that she found hard to resist.

"What about my ship?"

"It'll be right there waiting when you get back."

She looked back at *Ship* and remotely triggered the hatch to seal and lock. Then she strode to the window and glanced up at Reilly.

His eyes matched the blue of his doorway's edges perfectly, or perhaps his irises simply reflected their azure glow. "After you," he said.

"You didn't say what the job was, or what my cut would be."

"No, I didn't." He smiled. "Does it matter?"

Harry G was gone. Royland was gone. *Ship* would wait for her, indefinitely. For once, she had no orders, no plans, no direction. It felt unsettling, but the sunny, green world through the window beckoned and promised a better life… or at least a more interesting one.

"No, I suppose not." Hassera took her last breath of Averian air and stepped through into the unknown.

Interested in learning more about what happens next?
Where does Kormèr end up when he goes through that portal?
Will he ever return to Averia?

All this and more is revealed in the trilogy:
The Trouble With Thieves

Read on for an exciting sneak peek.

by Maurice X. Alvarez & Ande Li
Available from Room 808 Press!

A pinpoint of golden light pierced darkness deeper than a starless night sky. The spot bloomed into a sparkling cascade, then collapsed back in on itself, like a silent pulse of energy waking from a long slumber. The new pinpoint yawned quietly open into a softly glowing blue portal. Not a friendly pale azure, but an intense, electric cobalt that threatened to swallow whole anything that dared enter its depths. It was a living blue contained inside the edges of the portal: slow and sinuous and hypnotic.

Rectangular and roughly two meters tall, the portal looked particularly door-like, but—like others of its type—it could assume any shape and size, as directed by its user. It almost always hovered about twenty centimeters from the ground, as it did now. And an eight-buttoned tab always protruded slightly from its inner top edge.

This particular portal had been to twelve worlds in three galaxies, not counting the present one. On the solid, gray back side of its frame, it bore the nicks and scratches of its travels, including a thin line about halfway up made by a passing obsidian arrowhead, and a little ding from a grain of space debris colliding into it at 150,000 meters per hour. It had not been mauled by a pack of theropods or taken irrevocably apart by an overeager physicist, as had happened to two of its kind. Not yet, anyway.

Its light washed out through the dark, illuminating a section of polished marble floor that ended at two large ornately crafted doors with twin golden handles.

Kormèr Lezàl stepped out from the portal, the leather soles of his calf-length black boots making almost no noise on the marble floor. Peering through the holes in his silk mask, he scanned what he could see of his surroundings and listened for any sound of alarm. Satisfied that he was alone, he reached up with a black-gloved hand and twisted the tab on the portal. The device shut down instantly, pitching the room back into darkness. By some miracle of physics, for which Kormèr had no explanation, he was left holding not the tab but a crystal cube, an inactive miniature form of the portal itself. This he dropped into the pocket of his long black overcoat.

Kormèr took a moment to let his eyes adjust to the darkness, though he knew exactly where he was. Years of using the portal to break into the palatial home of the interim Duke had instilled in him an almost-innate familiarity with the layout of its rooms. Even now, in complete darkness, he could clearly picture the walls of the antechamber in which he stood. But likewise, his years of experience as a thief had also taught Kormèr the value of being well prepared for the unexpected. Kormèr knew that Duke Bederf would be busy for the next few hours, but the Duchess had a penchant for taking lovers. Kormèr wanted to be ready to defend himself against any overzealous—or perhaps overly jealous—competition.

When he felt his eyes had adjusted enough, he moved to the double doors, twisted the handle and eased one open. He gritted his teeth as the hinge squeaked... unexpectedly. Undaunted, he continued pushing the door open and stepped into the royal bedchamber, even as the bed sheets rustled.

<<Zolt?>> inquired the sweet, groggy voice of the young Duchess Menddilal.

Kormèr rolled his eyes at hearing the name of his competition, one of the Duchess's other lovers. <<No, my sweet,>> he said in a near whisper, closing the door behind him. Then, even lower, he muttered, <<Not Zolt.>>

Bathed in the scant moonlight from the window, Menddilal sat up. <<Light, dim,>> she commanded, and enough light filled the room to reveal its opulence. In Kormèr's eyes, the room paled compared to Menddilal, resplendent even in sleep, a siren whose song was that of silken hair, wide chestnut eyes, delicate yet supple lips, a firm, toned physique and very confident demeanor. She took Kormèr's breath away, though he loved her not at all. And he knew the inverse to be true as well. Their relationship was one of convenience; she got to exert her authority over an admirer, while he got another chance to steal the sparkling tiara that lay on her bedside table, the one prize that had eluded him since his first foray into this bedchamber.

<<Eddrin Ciendd!>> She used the false name he had given her long ago. Then she furrowed her brow at him. <<Just where have you been? It's been weeks since you visited last. >>

Kormèr bowed his head. <<I'm sorry, my sweet. Business called me away. It's been torture without your loving caresses.>> This was not untrue. She had been an exciting lover for nearly two and a half Elmarian years.

<<Excuses are mere words, Eddrin. If I wanted to hear words, I'd be with my husband in council.>>

<<Perhaps I should then take my words and this bauble and slink back...>>

<<Bauble?>> Menddilal's eyes lit up.

<<Did I say bauble?>> He feigned surprise.

<<You did, you silly man.>> She rose from her bed, an ivory sculpture of beauty wrapped in the finest silks from the distant province of Yronl. She stood eye to eye with him as he fished in his pocket for something, anything that would

378

be a distraction for a woman who could have anything, and who probably thought she had everything.

He held up a fist-sized chunk of golden ore that caught the light brilliantly. <<A rare metal from a distant land, precious though most likely a trifle to someone who has as much as you. It is called *pyrite*.>>

Her eyes lit up. <<Why, Eddrin! It's beautiful.>>

<<It's yours, my love.>>

<<And I am yours, my dearest lover,>> she said, breathily. She leaned into him, hands on his chest as they kissed.

Tracing his fingers along her neck, Kormèr teased the thin straps of her silk chemise off her shoulders.

But just as the silk slipped from Menddilal's body, the anteroom doors flew open.

<<Duke!>> The Duchess gasped, shoving Kormèr away from her fearfully. <<Get away from me, you swinish cad!>>

Without hesitation, Kormèr backed to the wall and swept his left hand over the light controls, plunging the room into near darkness. As he danced out of the moonlight coming through the window, his other hand pulled the crystal cube from his coat's pocket. He looked down at the cube in his hand but, until his eyes readjusted to the dark, he couldn't see its one black face, the special switch which activated the portal.

<<Help me, husband!>> cried Menddilal.

<<Face me, coward!>> Duke Bederf stood brazenly blocking the inner doorway, his pear-shaped body silhouetted by the dim light from the hallway. <<I've put up with you breaking into my home for long enough!>>

Kormèr's eyes went wide. *He knew?* he thought, surprised. Then his reasoning replaced the surprise. *With her penchant for affairs? Of course he knew... you silly man.*

He grinned at his own joke, as his fingers calmly and methodically pushed each face of the cube.

Footfalls approached from the hall beyond the antechamber, and the anteroom's lights flared on, revealing two guards at the outer doorway, with more behind them. <<There's no escape for you this time,>> he snarled, as the light washed across Kormèr's waist and legs.

Kormèr turned the cube in his hand and pressed on a face with his thumb. He'd lost track of the turns, and didn't know if he was pressing a new face or one he'd already tried. Relief washed over him as the cube began glowing. He tossed it in the path of the advancing Duke as it transformed into the portal.

Duke Bederf stopped and backed away from this unknown obstacle. <<Guards! Guards!>>

Kormèr spared a longing glance at the tiara, but only for a fraction of a second. Pressing his advantage, he jumped into the portal, twisting the tab on his way, and disappeared from his homeworld.

AFTERWORD

Thank you for reading *The Trouble With Love: A Kormèr Lezàl Story*. We hope you enjoyed the novel.

Want to know more about us and keep up with our latest writing projects or extracurricular activities?

* Maurice on Twitter: twitter.com/mauricexalvarez
* Maurice on Amazon: amazon.com/author/maurice-x-alvarez
* Maurice on BookBub: bookbub.com/profile/maurice-x-alvarez
* Maurice on GoodReads: goodreads.com/author/show/4709660.Maurice_Alvarez

* Ande on Twitter: twitter.com/andeliauthor
* Ande on Amazon: amazon.com/author/andeli

* Find us on Facebook: facebook.com/Room808Press/

And if you have a moment, please review *The Trouble With Love: A Kormèr Lezàl Story* on Amazon. It helps us and it helps other scifi-fantasy fans by telling them why you enjoyed reading it.

ABOUT THE AUTHORS

Maurice X. Alvarez is the author of *The Trouble With Thieves* series (available through Amazon.com). Born and raised in Queens, N.Y., he now lives with his wife and co-author, Ande Li, their two children and pets in New Jersey. When he's not writing, Maurice enjoys cycling, science fiction in various media formats, and plotting the next exploits of Kormèr Lezàl and the multiverse.

Ande spent her childhood in Hong Kong, China, and the various boroughs of NYC, and has settled in the NJ suburbs with her husband and co-conspirator Maurice X. Alvarez, their children, their free-range budgie and exquisitely patient mix-breed dog.

OTHER BOOKS FROM THE AUTHORS

by Maurice X. Alvarez
co-written with Ande Li

The Trouble With Thieves Series
Book 1: Return to Averia
Book 2: Trials of Halgarin
Book 3: Elmar of Tranquility

All For Love : A Kormèr Lezàl Story *(this book)*

by Ande Li

The Xonen Archives
Book One: The Healer's Girl
Book Two: The Children of Xon
Book Three: The Second Life of Cyrus Ex
Book Four: The Trickster's Game

The Gideon Files
Book One: Red Lotus
Book Two: White Jade
Book Three: Gold Peony

Movies on DVD and Blu-Ray often have a section dedicated to bloopers, outtakes and/or deleted scenes. This section is the latter. It's not at all relevant to the overall story, so you won't have missed out on anything if you skip it. But if you enjoy watching deleted scenes, you might enjoy the three "clips" that follow, complete with a brief explanation of what they're about and why they were cut.

[THE UNFORTUNATE JUD BAXTER]

[Before Hassera stepped into the story, there had been a crafty but trigger-happy Terran bounty hunter called Jud Baxter. Ultimately, he came off as nothing more than a two-dimensional character who required extra supervision to make sure he stayed in line. When Hassera showed up with her relationship with Royland, I gave Jud the pink slip,]

HARRY G threw down the report. "A lightspace explosion."

"That's right," said Jud Baxter, a very expensive but very thorough hired hand. Out of the group of twenty men and seven ships that had remained behind scanning the wreckage of Jeremy's craft, only Jud had come up with a unique finding. Jud knew he was good, that's why he was so expensive. "Special trick, takes precision timing."

"It takes imagination. I like your theory, Mister Baxter. But tell me, is human precision enough?"

"No. When I discovered that there wasn't enough debris to account for the destruction of the freighter, I scanned for the Y-Tach. It wasn't there either. It too entered lightspace."

"This doesn't answer my question. If Royland's still alive, someone will find him."

"Royland had nothing to do with it." Baxter had been standing for some time now, and he hated lack of courtesy. So he took the liberty of sitting. "Royland wasn't in his ship when it fired on the freighter. One or more of Jeremy's crew was."

"Hmm." Baxter tried to read into that near-grunt, but Harry G's face gave away nothing of what he was thinking. So he plodded on.

"That model freighter came equipped with an AI. It was the only model that did; it was a failed experiment; worked in the factory, not in practice.

"As you said, no human could calc that effect with the needed precision. The AI had to be involved. There was a dumbed-AI patch that the manufacturer distributed, but this one mustn't have gotten it. The two ships arranged it with the freighter's AI to fake the explosions and escape together." G was watching him, quietly. Baxter wasn't easily unsettled by such things. In fact, he'd intercepted a transmission from one of his competitors meant for G. He'd held onto the data, deciding it was important enough to keep for just this moment. "My sources indicate that Jeremy and his crew are, at this moment, on Averia, negotiating a contract."

G's eyes might have twitched at that moment, Jud couldn't be sure in the dim lighting. That last bit about the negotiations he'd actually made up, knowing the effect it would have on G and the credibility it would give his story. But he knew that it probably wasn't far from the truth. After all, what else would Jeremy be doing on such an out of the way planet like Averia. There couldn't be a more inconspicuous place to start a business.

"Good work, Mister Baxter," said G in his rumbling bass voice. "I knew I could count on you."

Jud nodded his thanks. "Mister G, I'd like to get to Averia as soon as possible."

G stood. "And you will, rest assured. Just keep one thing in mind, Mister Baxter, I want that cargo intact. If a contract has been signed, just send word. I'll handle the new players in this little game of ours. You deal with the others."

"Understood." Jud stood, coming nowhere near matching the height of the mysterious Harry G. They did not shake hands. Jud turned and walked out the door.

His ship was ready at the pad. It had been fueled and charged, nothing more. No one touched his ship where they weren't authorized. He slid behind the controls, ran through the pre-flight and, when control cleared him, blasted into space. The Headquarters for Organized Market Evaluation, a government agency set up years before to monitor the new open market, was built into an asteroid. Now under Harry G's direction, it was a front for various illegal activities.

As the ship skipped into lightspace, Jud mused over the G man himself. No one knew much about him, though everyone had feelings about him one way or another. Some liked him, or pretended to out of fear of saying otherwise. Many disliked him, particularly his competitors. He always seemed to be one step ahead of everyone. No one had ever crossed him and survived, business-wise or otherwise. His hand reached far, and his grasp was fatal.

Jud had once run a background check on G and come up with nothing but a tight situation as G's mercs were almost immediately on the scene. Fortunately he hadn't been using a private terminal—he didn't remember ever being that stupid. Jud had been careful to cover any tracks before fleeing. No one had ever caught on that it was him. However, no matter the risk, Jud had decided that, one day, he would find out who Harry G was.

^BAXTER'S a good shot,^ said Harry G to two lanky, smooth-skinned humanoids standing before his desk, ^but he's quick to shoot too. Follow him. If he starts to blow it, stop him. If you get to Tailor first, do what needs to be done. I want no mistakes made on this.^

The beings nodded, then sped out the door and after the human.

Harry G tossed Baxter's report in the disintegrator and arranged the papers on his desk. He then flipped the tip of his right index finger back, like a cap, and depressed the button therein. Immediately, the doorway in the left wall of his office vanished behind wood paneling that slid seamlessly into place.

He clicked on the interoffice channel. "Marge, I'm back from lunch. If Squibbly wants to see me now, he may." He sat back and sighed. *Back to the market-monitoring business.*

ONE light-day out from Averia, Jud Baxter dropped his ship out of lightspace for the fifth time in the last twenty-four hours. He waited while the computer absorbed all stray communication signals that passed its way, then accelerated again and re-entered lightspace. The computer then sorted the frequencies and methodically searched through them for key words/names that Jud had programmed in. He was not doing this as frequently as he should, he knew, passing up opportunities for leads while gaining on arrival time. But the quicker he got there, the better. He worked faster on his feet, anyway.

The computer signaled its finding a match. Jud turned to sift through the message.

Meanwhile, Averia drew nearer.

Not far behind him, safely out of Jud's sensor range, another ship followed. Its landing request was granted, and coordinates were received. Ships were constantly coming and going from Freet-See. This was just another one.

ONE of the smooth-skinned beings spoke into his p-comm while the other kept watch down the corridor they had come up. ~Mister G, we have made contact. Baxter has control of their ship, but they are on their way back to it with weapons drawn.~

~*Stop them before something happens we'll all regret. I'll be there shortly to collect my prize.*~

~We deliver, Mister G.~

~*I'm sure. But I intend to finish their business personally. Just stop them. Out.*~

The two beings rushed back to the pad, weapons drawn and ready to blast Jud Baxter at the first hint of trouble. But when they got there, it was worse than they had imagined.

JUD Baxter's deception had worked smoothly. He'd hired some local contacts to play the part of Freet-See police and lure the crew away from the ship. Then he'd easily broken in, slicing past the ramp security lock with practiced ease. Before he could steal the ship, however, his contacts had warned him that Jeremy and Kit had returned somehow and everyone was now on their way back to him.

He now watched them through a tap into the spaceports security cams as they entered the pad. He waited until the men were too far from the blast-doors to make an escape but just far enough from the ship that they could not run into it before he could pick them off with the cannon. At that precise moment, he opened the gun pod and revealed the twin laser mounts, all business ends aimed at the group of scientists. The computer immediately established target locks on each one.

"Hello, gentlemen," he said into the external comm, his voice resounding in the open space of the pad outside. "I suggest you stay where you are and drop your weapons."

"Who are you?" shouted Jeremy.

"That's not important. I represent a much more important person who's very eager to see you."

"And if we refuse?"

"Ho, hum. What do you expect to gain by keeping your little weapons? Come on guys, let's get real here. Wouldn't you rather be brave and just surrender rather than being smeared all over the pad."

Jeremy hesitated. Jud added, "Let's see here. I have each one of you locked on target; that gives each of you about two microseconds before the cannons pick you off."

[KORMÈR LIES TO SYLVESTRA]

[When Kormèr is first interrogated by Sylvestra, after being picked up by Sergeant Tseeo, he originally told a very different story of his arrival on Averia. He knew it sounded ridiculous when he said it, and I agreed with him during edits, so it ended up in the delete key buffer,]

Using his quick wit, Kormèr sang: | |I escaped from a pirate freighter in an emergency pod. Fortunately, we weren't in interstellar space, but close to Averia. I managed to guide the pod here.| |

She made some quick checks on the flimsy. | |Sky's Eye has no record of unauthorized atmospheric entry.| |

Buomp! I blew it. Sky's Eye must be some kind of planetary surveillance. He remembered the wide rift in the rock/cloud cover and wondered if Sky's Eye was able to keep watch there. It was a chance he had to take. | |I don't know what to say. I remember coming down over an area of heavy updrafts that blew the pod aside and smashed me against a large rock.| |

She stared at him for a few moments before making another note. | |Where'd you get your gems?| |

||I uh… stole them from the pirates.||

||You *are* a thief, then.||

Kormèr's mind screamed. He'd really blown it this time. *Jjled! Kippin jjled! You'll never win her heart now.* ||They were using me!|| he protested suddenly, startling Sylvestra. ||I was taken as a slave when they stopped in my city on Elmar, and held me for one year…uh, one Elmarian year.||

Her eyes went wide. That was a long time.

||I only did what I thought I should do.|| He breathed heavily as if his telling of the story had moved him, but his heart was pounding fiercely, his mind on overdrive. He didn't consciously know what he was saying; instinct had taken over. ||They owed it to me. But yes, I did steal from them. So throw me in jail.||

It took a moment for Sylvestra to react. ||No. That happened out of our jurisdiction.|| She made a few quick notes. ||And since we don't associate with pirates, we won't hand you over to them.||

||Thank you,|| he sighed.

||The contents of your pockets are questionable, Mister Lezàl.||

Kormèr glanced at his coat, which was lying on her desk alongside the objects from his pockets. When his dagger had set off the precinct alarms, they had searched him and taken his coat.

||This dagger, for instance.|| She pointed to the item on her desk.

||It was a treasure from a planet they—the pirates—landed on. I think it was Jordinni. I don't like to leave it lying around; it's very valuable.||

She watched him again. Then, ||Mister Lezàl, I'd like you to stay in the city for the next few days.||

||I'm not going anywhere.|| *Not anymore anyway,* he thought to himself. *I've blown it. Way to go, KL.*

||Where are you staying?|| she asked, and he gave her the hotel name and his room number. Then she handed him back his coat—Kormèr almost hugged it.

||I *am* confiscating the gems, however.||

||But I have no money.||

She thought about that. Then took a small plate from a drawer and filled it out, stamping it in the end with her medallion. ||You can use this as compensation money. It will only allow you to pay for the strictest necessities, including food and shelter. Nothing more. And do not attempt to make any cash advances with it.|| She handed it to him. It was nothing more than a plastic card.

Kormèr stood. ||Thank you for this and for everything else.||

As he opened the door, Sylvestra chirped, ||Mister Lezàl, have you contacted your parents to let them know you're safe?||

Kormèr shook his head. ||I'm an orphan.||

||Is there anyone you can contact?||

||No. Not anymore.|| And he was out the door before she could say any more.

AS soon as the boy was gone, Sylvestra called in Phatheeo. She told him the tale Kormèr had told her. || Send a scout team to the Great Rift. If there's a pod out there, I want it found. Scan for anything and everything. ||

|| You don't really believe we'll find anything, do you? ||

She hesitated. She hated jumping to conclusions, but she'd learned to trust her instinct, and it was telling her to be suspicious. || No, I don't. But I want to be sure. We're lucky he's just a boy and probably doesn't know much about the law. || She looked up at Phatheeo. || What's the word on Reestee? ||

|| Out of town until Cheerretee, on a recovery vacation. ||

|| Wonderful. Alright. Nothing to do then but wait till he gets back so he can id these gems. || She shifted the gem pouch in her palm. She opened it and was taken instantly by the brilliance and variety of the gems within. *My, but they are beautiful.* She quickly closed the pouch and tied it to her medallion, the safest place she could put it.

|| Anything else? || asked Phatheeo, then walked out when Sylvestra shook her head.

Nothing but waiting, she thought. *I hate waiting.*